EX
LIBRIS

Romance Treasury

THE ROMANCE TREASURY ASSOCIATION

NEW YORK · TORONTO · LONDON

These stories were originally published as follows:

STRANGE BEWILDERMENT
Copyright © 1973 by Katrina Britt
First published by Mills & Boon Limited in 1973

CALL AND I'LL COME
Copyright © 1973 by Mary Burchell
First published by Mills & Boon Limited in 1973

DESTINY IS A FLOWER
Copyright © 1970 by Stella Frances Nel
First published by Mills & Boon Limited in 1970

ROMANCE TREASURY is published by
The Romance Treasury Association, Stratford, Ontario, Canada.

Editorial Board: A. W. Boon, Judith Burgess, Ruth Palmour and
Janet Humphreys
Dust Jacket Art by Muriel Hughes
Story Illustrations by Muriel Hughes
Book Design by Charles Kadin
Printed by Kingsport Press Limited, Kingsport, Tennessee

ISBN 0-919860-25-7

Printed in U.S.A.   AO26

CONTENTS

Page 9

STRANGE BEWILDERMENT
Katrina Britt

Page 185

CALL AND I'LL COME
Mary Burchell

Page 397

DESTINY IS A FLOWER
Stella Frances Nel

Strange
Bewilderment
Katrina Britt

Martina was delighted to be in Venice. And she didn't really mind looking after lovable little Marco Vortolini if it would help Eunice and Bruno to straighten out their marriage.

The attractive Dominic Burnett di Ravenelli was the one cloud in Martina's sky. Refusing to mind his own business, he was forever insisting that Marco needed a male tutor.

"You disapproved of me from the beginning," she accused him angrily, "though I can't imagine why. Your life is your own affair. I'd be glad if you would regard mine in the same way!"

But no matter how much she resented Dominic, she certainly couldn't ignore him!

"Love is the strange bewilderment which overtakes one person on account of another."

James Thurber
(By permission of
Hamish Hamilton Ltd.)

CHAPTER ONE

Milan to Venice was a matter of only five hours by coach. One could, if one wished, do the journey more leisurely with brief calls at Gardone, Riviera and so on to Padua. But the perfect approach to Venice was by sea, and one could do no better than take a steamer from Chioggia to the "Queen of the Adriatic."

At least, so Martina had been told by her friend Eunice Vortolini with whom she was to stay. So Martina had traveled by rail to Chioggia, where she boarded a steamer for Venice. Chioggia, remarkable for its bridges, lay between the Venetian lagoon and the sea. Martina arrived on a morning of brilliant sunshine. Fishing boats with colored sails reminiscent of a bygone age crammed the harbor, while overhead, sea gulls circled in the fish-tainted air, their plaintive wail a reminder that Chioggia was the principal fishing port in Italy.

The journey from Chioggia to Venice took almost two hours. But to Martina, seeing everything for the first time, the journey was surprisingly short. There were stops at quaint old places on the way, and soon she was gazing excitedly at the Campanile of San Marco swathed in mist in the distance. Then they were passing the island of San Giorgio Maggiore to sail in between boats and gondolas to the square of San Marco.

By the time Martina had stepped ashore and her luggage was placed beside her, the mist had cleared and she was confronted by a miracle of beauty and color. Her immediate reaction to so much architectural splendor was one of breathless wonder. The magnificent square with its double-tiered palatial arcades was like a fabulous stage setting, a glittering auditorium filled by a promenading audience of people of all nationalities and friendly pigeons.

Martina was so enchanted with her surroundings that

when her name was spoken in familiar dulcet tones, it did not immediately register. Dazedly, she surfaced from past glories to see a tall, elegantly dressed young woman smiling down at her.

"Eunice!" she exclaimed delightedly. "How wonderful to see you again!"

They clasped hands and kissed, with Martina looking fondly at her old school friend. Dear Eunice, the same yet not the same. Time and money had put a perfect finish to the long-legged, sports-minded friend of her youth. In those days, with her fair hair cut short as a schoolboy's, Eunice had been sexless and endearing. Now she was like something from *Vogue*, sophisticated and exquisitely groomed, a woman of the world right to her elegant fingertips. She was wearing a smart turquoise suit with white Italian accessories, handmade and expensive. Her flaxen hair was a gilt frame for the honey-tanned face beneath the chic white hat. Her china blue eyes were as surprising in the skillful makeup as the flashing smile.

"Marty! You don't look a day older than when you wore a gym suit. Did you have a good journey?"

"Super." Martina wrinkled her pretty nose. Of average height, as slender and pliant as a young willow, she was the kind of person that glowed rather than glittered. Her eyes were a clear dark gray in the small, delicately boned face, and the pretty mouth above her firm chin was curved into a smile. "And you, my dear Eunice, are looking very beautiful."

"Against you, my pet, I feel awfully big and clumsy."

"Still sensitive about your height?" Martina teased. "I don't know why. You did what you always said you would, marry a man taller than yourself. At least he looked to be taller in your wedding photograph."

Eunice shrugged. "A couple of inches. Five feet ten to my five foot eight. But I love the man." She chuckled. "Remember how I was always paired with the shortest man on our dates and you always walked off with the tall one?"

Martina chuckled impishly. "Yes, and my brother

Ruan used to get so angry because you were outgrowing him although he was two years older. By the way, he's as tall as your husband now and broad as well."

Eunice said thoughtfully, "Ruan Floyd, dental surgeon. I would have thought he'd have followed your parents' example and gone in for television. Has it occured to you that though we both have attractive brothers neither of us ever became entangled with them?"

"I think we regarded them as part of the furniture because they were always around," Martina laughed.

A sudden movement from behind drew their attention.

"Ah, Ugo!" Eunice addressed the portly Italian in yachting cap and blue uniform who hovered nearby: "Will you take the *signorina*'s cases to the boat, *per favore?*"

"*Si, signora.*"

Two muscular arms swung the heavy cases up effortlessly, and Ugo ambled away leaving them to follow more leisurely.

Happily, Martina pushed her arm beneath her friend's as they crossed the square.

"Are we going by gondola, Eunice?" she asked.

"No, dear, motor launch. We have two gondolas, so you'll be able to enjoy them later."

Martina watched a phalanx of pigeons rising with a flutter of wings from their path and sighed blissfully. "How relaxing not to have to keep your senses alert for cars and other traffic. There are no horse-drawn vehicles either. It's extraordinary."

Ugo was waiting for them at the mooring platform to help them aboard, and soon they were on their way. Martina looked around, entranced. Beneath a vast ceiling of blue sky, the Grand Canal quivered with the rich reflection of palaces, gaily painted mooring poles, barges loaded to the gunwales with market produce, motor launches, gondolas and *vaporetti*. Colors expanded and retracted on the gleaming water; the whole scene was a dancing mirage, exciting the senses and enchanting the eyes. This strange fabulous world of an age rich in culture, courtesy and tradition. Martina sighed at the thought of its crumbling away. The world would be poorer without it.

Eunice acted as guide, pointing out the famous bridges—the Rialto with its double row of shops, the Scalzi and the Accademia. "The Palazzo Cavalli," she said, gesturing toward an ornate palace with a row of bronze horses across the imposing facade. "To a person who appreciates the arts as you do, Marty, Venice will hold a vast appeal."

Martina feasted her eyes on the wrought-iron balconies, the window boxes of cascading flowers and the endless colorful cavalcade of water traffic swirling around them. "I'm going to love it," she murmured ecstatically.

When Eunice turned to speak to Ugo in excellent Italian, Marty studied the new sophisticated edition of her old school friend. She had had doubts when Eunice wrote to say she had married an Italian. What little she had heard of Italians was not commendable. Some of them had the reputation of being unfaithful in marriage. She had heard that while they were very much against divorce they were not averse to small secret affairs to relieve the boredom of marriage.

Bruno Vortolini might be an Italian, but he had fashioned his wife into a sophisticated socialite, giving her poise and a sensuality that would keep him busy warding off her many admirers.

The motor launch was now veering to the left, making for a small landing stage beside a huge oak door. The façade of the palace above it bore a mellow fragility brought into prominence by the sun's rays highlighting the Venetian-Byzantine architecture. They alighted, Ugo reached for Martina's cases and the heavy oak door was swung open.

Eunice addressed the pleasant-looking, uniformed servant who stood on the threshold.

"Here she is, Stefano. My very dear friend, Signorina Martina Floyd from London." Her smile embraced them both. "You'll find Stefano a mine of information if you want to know anything about Venice, Marty."

Stefano's dark eyes twinkled in his leathery brown face. He bent his gray thatched head. "*Como está, signorina?* I trust you will enjoy your visit to Venice."

The hall they entered was impressive with its height and architectural charm. Martina admired the frescoed ceiling, the fine stucco moldings and coves, as they crossed a beautiful mosaic floor and climbed the fine staircase to the first floor.

Eunice explained, "Bruno does most of his business on the first floor—his board meetings, interviews with the press and so on."

The corridor at the head of the staircase took them past pale cream damask walls and an occasional archway containing a piece of sculpture. The thick carpet deadened the sound of their footsteps. Martina felt like whispering amid such grandeur.

"It's fabulous! Your husband must be very rich, Eunice," she murmured on a note of surprise.

"He is, but don't let it scare you. Bruno is a simple man at heart. He's the first of his family to work for a living, and he's made a great success of it. This house has been in his family for generations and his position in the industrial world has enabled him to keep it in excellent repair. The upkeep of these palaces is considerable. Without central heating they can be as cold as tombs in the winter and terribly damp."

Martina believed it. She suppressed a shudder. Maybe that was one reason Italian families tended to cling together—the cost of living was a burden shared when everyone chipped in. It was the poorer Venetians with no families to whom the winter months would prove an ordeal.

"I suppose you have other villas," she said thoughtfully.

"We have several scattered along the Adriatic, on the Greek Islands and in the south of France. We also have an apartment in Paris and one in Rome for Bruno's business trips." Eunice's voice took on a teasing note. "So you see you have plenty of places to choose from for your honeymoon, Bruno and I would be delighted if you stayed in one."

Martina was touched. "How sweet of you, Eunice, and how typical of your generosity. I'm afraid the offer is premature, as there's no man who counts in my life at the moment."

"You surprise me. I'd have thought you would have lots of men to choose from. You were always popular with the boys."

Martina laughed. "I'm waiting until I fall in love. Does that sound naïve?"

"Not a bit. At 23 you've all the time in the world."

Walking beside Eunice up a second flight of stairs, Martina was happy that her friend had been so fortunate in her marriage. At the same time she had the feeling she had lost her to a world of wealth.

The rooms Eunice had prepared for her were a pleasant surprise. She adored the Italian period furniture, the rich furnishings, French tapestry, marble and Venetian glass. Enchanting flower arrangements in stately vases blended with the cream and gold décor. There was a bathroom with a shower, and a room leading off the bedroom that could be used as a small lounge.

Eunice had moved to the tall windows flung open to a balcony and Martina joined her. Enchanted, she gazed out across the Grand Canal, marveling at the clear lines of water and sky. She breathed in the exhilarating air, to find Eunice watching her with a half-cynical smile.

"Your enthusiasm reminds me of my first visit to this house." There was no bitterness in her voice, but Martina's sensitive ear caught an unmistakable irony. A curious sense of awareness came over her at her friend's change of mood. "Come, sit down, Marty. I want to talk to you," Eunice said.

A momentary silence fell as they stepped back into the room. Eunice drew two chairs together and they sat down. Eunice was evidently under some kind of strain, because her long tapering fingers shook slightly as she took cigarettes and a lighter out of her handbag. She lit a cigarette and after she had inhaled, met Martina's gaze with a look that was oddly disconcerting.

"Before I tell you what I have in mind I'd like you to know that I love my husband dearly. I had no idea how wealthy he was until we were married. He never enlightened me. You know we met on a cruise and were married at the end of it?"

Martina nodded, noting the tobacco stains on the beautifully manicured fingers.

Eunice continued, "We've been wonderfully happy but a few months ago Bruno's brother Paolo died very tragically in a fire in his home in Milan. It broke out during the night. Paolo had gotten his wife and small son to safety on the lawn of the villa when the boy ran back inside to rescue his favorite toy. His absence wasn't discovered until the fire was well under way; Paolo insisted on returning to the villa to look for his son. Eventually he appeared at a bedroom window with his son in his arms. He dropped the boy into the arms of waiting firemen but the flames beat him back and he collapsed. He was dead when they brought him out."

Martina's eyes were bright with tears. "How terrible! And the boy?"

"The boy, Marco, was all right. He'd been overcome by the fumes, but he soon recovered. He's staying here with us at the moment." Restlessly, Eunice stood up and leaned back against the dressing table. Folding her arms, she studied the end of the cigarette in her fingers. "Since Marco came, Bruno has changed."

"In what way?"

Eunice took a long pull at her cigarette and blew out a thin line of smoke.

"You know how I feel about having a family of my own. Being the eldest of six children, I vowed I wouldn't have a family when I married."

"Does Bruno know this?"

"Yes, I was honest with him before we married. Mind you, I love him so much that had he insisted I would have agreed to a family and made the best of it. However, he agreed with me, said he wasn't keen on having a family since he travels frequently on business and is never at home for long."

Martina digested this. "You think Marco has made him regret his decision not to have a family of his own?"

Eunice shook her head. "I don't know. He seems to have transferred his affections to the boy. Marco is high-strung. The loss of his father has made a profound impression on him. He has nightmares about the fire and wakes up in the night terrified. Bruno is so concerned about him that he has put up Marco's bed in his bed-cum-dressing room. Our bedroom door is left ajar every night in case Marco wakes up."

"What about the boy's mother? Surely he's her responsibility?"

Eunice gave a shrug. "Mia has turned against Marco. She blames him for Paolo's death. She won't have anything to do with the boy."

Martina stared, appalled. "How tragic! Poor Marco. Surely a governess is the answer?"

"Bruno won't hear of it yet. He says the boy needs his family around to help him over the loss of his father. He's hoping Mia will eventually turn to her son when she recovers from the shock."

"Do you think she will? Turn to Marco, I mean?"

"Mia has been petted and spoiled all her life. Her reaction to tragedy is what one can expect from a person who has never met it before. Don't misunderstand. It isn't that I don't feel sorry for Mia—I do terribly. But with Mia everything is Mia. No one else matters. And Bruno. . . ." Eunice made a gesture of despair. "He's so kind, so considerate, and Paolo's death has been a great blow to him. Naturally, he wants to do what he can for Mia and the boy. I want to help too, but not at the cost of our marriage."

"Neither does Bruno, surely?"

"Something has to be done about it soon. Unfortunately, Bruno has to go to Geneva in a week—something to do with an unexpected meeting of directors. I've always accompanied him on his business trips and we've never been parted since our marriage. Now he suggests going to Geneva alone, leaving me to look after Marco. I'm very much against this. As things stand at the moment, Bruno and I could easily drift apart. He might even want to adopt Marco."

Martina said gently, "My dear Eunice, aren't you torturing yourself unnecessarily? Bruno probably still cares for you as deeply as you care for him. Ask yourself. When the question of you having children arose he was quite willing to go along with your wishes on the subject. Where there's love, there has to be trust."

Eunice turned to push the butt of her cigarette into an ashtray on the dressing table behind her. "You mean I ought to resign myself to the situation as it stands?" She walked slowly to the window, her back straight and elegant. "Have you ever been in love, Marty? Really in love so that nothing else matters?"

"Apart from a few crushes, no."

With her hands clenched by her sides, Eunice turned her pale face toward her friend.

"Then for heaven's sake try to keep a sense of proportion when you do. You become so vulnerable when someone holds your happiness and your reason for living in their hands. You get scared when anything goes wrong, so scared that it's easy to go to pieces."

Martina argued, "Bruno can feel that way too but unlike you, he has his work to fall back on. He's a man and needs to live naturally with a woman. You say you were very happy together until this awful tragedy. Then why worry? If Bruno had transferred his affections to another woman you would have every right to feel as you do. However, he's only showing compassion for a lost little boy."

Her warm, confident smile made Eunice relax a little. Resuming her seat, she leaned forward earnestly. "You are a dear, Marty. You have no idea what a relief it is to talk to someone. I felt so completely alone, a prey to heartache and torturing thoughts. I need your help badly."

Martina waited for Eunice to define her last remark. It seemed she had been in Venice for months instead of hours. Already she knew too much for her own peace of mind.

"Would you mind taking care of Marco next week? If you do I can go to Geneva with Bruno."

Martina lowered her eyes to her hands clasped loosely in her lap. She had expected nothing like this. Not until now did she realize how much she had been looking forward to this visit with her old friend. They had so much to talk about. Hurting her most was the thought that Eunice had invited her there with a purpose. She felt rather than saw Eunice regarding her apprehensively, seeking to read her thoughts. She knew Eunice was upset and scared, and if she was up against a marriage problem because of poor little Marco, Martina simply had to help. But there was some obstacles to be cleared first. With this thought in mind, she looked up and said frankly, "I could do that, with Bruno's consent, if Marco likes me. Suppose he doesn't? And my Italian isn't very good. We might have difficulty in understanding each other. I'm not putting up obstacles, Eunice, merely stating facts."

"I've already talked it over with Bruno and he agrees. As for Marco, he's five years old. He's been taught to speak in English and Italian. I don't have any doubt about him liking you. I've seen that magic you have with children work too often for that. Marco is a very attractive child and you won't be able to resist him."

"Poor kid," Martina said compassionately. Already her sympathy was with the child. He was so young to be robbed of a father. Eunice's unhappiness troubled her, but she was more concerned with a boy who was left to the mercy of a mother who had no love for him. She found herself hoping fiercely that he would never learn the circumstances of his father's death. And because she had to know, she asked, "Where is Marco's mother?"

"She's at a villa of ours in the Greek islands. Bruno thought the change of scenery would take her mind off the tragedy and help her recover."

Wistfully, Martina pictured a small boy suddenly bereft of parents, alone and unwanted when he might have been romping along golden sands on some Greek isle. She could dislike the absent Mia even while she felt sorry for the woman.

Eunice was speaking again. "Would you like to meet Marco before you decide?"

"Yes, I would," Martina agreed, adding hastily, "I'll help you all I can, Eunice, and I do hope everything works out for you and Marco." She smiled warmly in an effort to erase the small worried pleat between the china-blue eyes. "Stop frowning. It'll give you wrinkles."

"Bless you, Marty!" Eunice sounded almost light-hearted as her face cleared. "You won't regret it. We'll have this next week together, you and I. Bruno will be working during the day. There'll be dinners, parties and shows in the evenings and you'll meet all our friends." She straightened and looked at the exquisite jeweled watch on her wrist. "Goodness," she exclaimed. "I had no idea it was so late. I must see about lunch—I've arranged it for one o'clock to give you time to freshen up. The dining room is the last pair of double doors along the corridor at the head of the staircase. See you there when you're ready. And thanks." Bending swiftly, she kissed Martina's smooth young cheek and left the room.

CHAPTER TWO

Alone in the luxurious room, Martina felt in need of air and went out on the balcony. Her conversation with Eunice had proved an unsettling beginning to her visit. The invitation she had received had contained little news; certainly it had not mentioned the trouble between Eunice and Bruno nor Paolo's death. Reading it, Martina had tingled with anticipation. Her parents had added to her pleasure by saying there was a possibility of them doing a television film in Venice quite soon.

The thought of Robin and Jill Floyd brought a curve of pleasure to her lips. Nice people, her parents—her father a broad-shouldered, pipe-smoking producer; her mother, slim as a boy in sweater and pants, working happily beside him. They had met while working for television. Now, 25 years and four children later, they were back in double harness doing the work they loved. Martina's brother Ruan and the teenaged twin boys had christened them Robinson Crusoe and Girl Friday. Jill Floyd laughingly attributed her slim figure to her tyrant of a husband. But the look of bliss on her youthful features showed how she enjoyed being his companion—taking notes, plying him with refreshments between takes on location or at the studios and attending to his needs.

Martina did not expect to be as lucky in marriage as her parents were. She had spoken the truth when she had told Eunice she had never been deeply in love. Maybe she never would be, although the thought of drowning in the typing pool at the television studios was a great incentive toward seeking the right man.

Eunice had been the girl next door. Her father had owned a drugstore in town. Martina's parents had bought the four-bedroom lodge before Eunice and her parents had moved into the big house at the end of the drive. Both the manor house and the lodge had been derelict when the families moved in. Now they were fully restored to their original grandeur, set in immaculate grounds barely ten miles from London.

Stirred by memories, Martina gazed down on to the busy canal where modern crafts look incongruous beside the graceful skimming gondolas. Gradually the magic of the place took possession of her senses. What if Eunice was going away? With a small boy she could see Venice at her leisure. She was smiling when she stepped back into the room to begin her unpacking. *Martina, my girl,* she told herself, *this is going to be the holiday of a lifetime.* She was halfway through her packing when a tap came on her door.

"*Avanti,*" she said, hoping her elementary knowledge of Italian would see her through.

The door opened to admit a maid in a coffee-colored dress and apron. She was short and sturdy with a button nose, square chin and a generous mouth. Her eloquent dark eyes matched the black hair combed back with a satin sheen to a low twist in the nape of her neck. A wisp of lace matching the apron was pinned on her head, which she bobbed forward in a quick curtsy. She spoke a little nervously in accented English.

"*Buon giorno, signorina.* I am Emilia. I am to help you to unpack and to attend to any pressing, mending or laundry you may require!"

Martina, warming immediately to the woman's friendly approach, answered with a smile.

"*Grazie,* Emilia. I will take a shower while you see to the rest of my unpacking."

Emilia had gone when she finally emerged from the bathroom. Everything had been put away neatly and methodically, with her shoes arranged on a rack in her wardrobe and her few cosmetics placed on the glass-topped dressing table.

Her shower had revived her spirits. Martina stood before her dressing table mirror, her dress, white flowered on a blue ground, unadorned. Her hair, a deep russet brown, was brushed around her head in soft abundance and she had used her makeup sparingly.

All was quiet in the corridor when she left her room for

lunch. Opening the gold and cream embossed doors, she entered a long *sala*. The room with its *objets d'art* and satin wall panels was ostentatious but pleasing. To her left a long table had been laid for lunch, resplendent with lace mats, china, silver and superb flower arrangements.

Martina, who had entered noiselessly on the thick buoyant carpet, became aware immediately of the faint aroma of cigars. At the far end of the room near the tall windows she saw two pairs of elegantly trousered legs protruding from a couple of winged chairs. To her dismay two deep voices were discussing her arrival.

"My dear Bruno," drawled a deep attractive English voice, "why leave Marco with an Englishwoman? Why a woman in any case? Surely the boy needs a tutor?"

"Later. Marco needs at least six months to recover from the effects of the fire and his father's loss." The second voice was strangely alien with clipped consonants. "The boy needs plenty of love and understanding to give him back the feeling of security."

"In short, a woman's touch." The voice was openly mocking and Martina stiffened. "But not for long. The boy needs masculine companionship. Women are apt to spoil pretty little boys like Marco. Two women will smother him with kindness."

"Mia won't look at her son since Paolo died."

"There's a good reason for that. Marco is the image of Paolo. In time Mia will love him all the more for that."

"Meanwhile Marco has to be taken care of. He still has nightmares about the fire."

"Which you are convinced this Englishwoman will cure in a matter of weeks." The voice was vibrant with mockery.

Martina bristled. She had not intended to eavesdrop but the conversation made her temporarily speechless. Her face flushed with embarrassment, she opened the door again and closed it with a decisive click.

Instantly, the shorter pair of legs was drawn up and an inquiring pair of eyes peeped around the wing of the chair. A white-cuffed hand reached out to place the cigar butt in an ashtray on a small table and the owner of the legs rose to his feet.

He was a dapper man in a welltailored dark business suit, and he strode forward with a smile. His rather heavy-lidded eyes, moving appraisingly over her slim figure, were shrewd but kind. He glanced at his watch before greeting her cordially.

"*Buon giorno,* Signorina Floyd. Welcome to Venice. I trust you will enjoy your stay with us. I am Bruno, Eunice's husband."

He held out a spatulate hand and Martina placed hers in it.

"Thank you, Signor Vortolini. It is very kind of you to invite me."

He raised a brow with a teasing smile. "Eunice had planned on being here to introduce us. You beat her to it. Which is not to be wondered at with your marvelous English complexion needing so little attention."

Martina liked his crisp approach and spicy dry humor. Like most Italians he spoke with his eyes and was skilled in using them. Her embarrassment at his frank admiration amused him; she found herself liking him unreservedly.

"Ah, Dominic, here we have a peach from one of your English trees." Bruno touched her elbow lightly and piloted her down the long *sala* as he addressed his friend.

Walking beside him, Martina noted his dark hair receding a little from his high, intelligent forehead. She guessed his age at around 35 and he was observant. She could see he never missed a trick, making an excellent businessman but a kind friend. She was sure of that.

The winged chairs were now empty. The owner of the long legs had stood up with his back against the light. Martina had the feeling that he had moved there deliberately so that she had to stand beneath the revealing light.

He was taller than Bruno, hence the long legs. The wide shoulders, as she remembered his English accent, had probably broadened out on English rugger fields.

Martina could imagine the rows of trophies he had won making a tantalizing background for the kind of athletic figure which sent teenage girls hysterical.

Bruno said, "Signorina Floyd, may I present my good friend, Signor Dominic Burnett di Ravenelli. Dominic, Signorina Martina Floyd."

The man bent over her hand. Martina had an impression of a haughty figure in a beautifully tailored beige suit. Thick tobacco-brown hair sprang vibrantly from a straight line across his forehead. His eyes were dark and narrow and his mouth, surprisingly mobile, lifted for a moment endearingly into a crooked, rather aggravating smile which she met with a cool stare. It mollified her a little to see her coolness quicken his detached interest and faint antagonism. How dared he laugh at her after his cynical criticism?

It was fortunate that Eunice chose that moment to enter the *sala*. In a primrose silk pant suit with a bare midriff, she came forward, obviously delighted to greet her male guest.

"Dominic, we thought you were still in Greece!" She gave a small laugh as he bent over her hand.

"I arrived back early this morning," was the cool reply.

"After traveling all night, I presume. Really, you must have the constitution of an ox. You've met Martina?" Martina, meeting Eunice's fond smile, was aware of his dark eyes. Avoiding them, she sat down in the nearest chair, leaving Eunice to take a seat on the sofa with Dominic. Bruno poured drinks from an ornate sideboard and Martina, sitting back in her chair, tried to take stock.

Eunice was talking to Dominic, who had, according to conversation, just returned from the Greek isle where Mia was recuperating from Paolo's death. For the moment Martina's attention like that of Eunice was centered on Dominic. Despite her refusal to be impressed, the man captured her interest—the spare clean-cut line of him, his deep voice, the slow smile which reached his eyes before moving to his lips. He was different from Bruno, who had instantly made her aware of being a woman.

This man could not have cared less. The dark eyes meeting her own had held an icy aloofness that piqued her vanity. She accepted a drink from Bruno, who seated himself beside her and asked about her journey. Presently they were drawn into a discussion about Mia. Bruno was evidently concerned about his sister-in-law, for a worried frown drew his thick dark brows together broodingly.

"I know it is far too soon to say this," he said, "but I am afraid the only answer to Mia's problem is a second marriage."

Dominic digested this while Eunice remained curiously watchful.

It was Dominic who said, "You could be right. Mia is a woman who needs to be taken care of. However, she will have to work out her own future. That is the only way which will make her happy."

He had probably discussed the matter with Bruno earlier, for he tactfully changed the subject to business matters. Bruno's concern for Mia did not hinder him from listening intelligently to his friend.

Dominic's deep deliberate tones held a restful quality which matched the suggestion of hidden strength in his movements. Listening to his quiet voice Martina tried to make up her mind what he was like. The man worked for a living and, if the conversation was anything to go by, did it brilliantly. Bruno obviously respected his opinion and probably found him a valuable ally. Martina was suspicious. He had regarded her without smiling in a slightly superior way, which annoyed her profoundly. She was relieved when he rose to take his leave. He refused charmingly an invitation to stay to lunch, and Eunice saw him to the door.

With the unsettling visitor gone, Martina relaxed with her host. Fortunately her charm made it easy for her to make friends, and Bruno, for all his brilliant business ability, was a simple man at heart. She liked him and could understand Eunice falling in love with him. He was anxious for Martina to enjoy her stay and stressed the importance of asking for anything she wanted.

The small boy had been standing in the doorway at the far end of the *sala* a few moments before they were aware of his presence. Bruno turned his head slowly as if prompted by some second sense and gave a fond smile.

"Ah, Marco," he said tenderly, holding out his hand. "Come, *caro*. Do not be shy."

The boy ran down the *sala* to bury his face in Bruno's lap. A large hand ruffled the dark curls. "*Hai studiato la tua lezione?*" Bruno asked kindly.

"*Si*, Zio Bruno, I have studied my lesson."

Marco lifted his well-shaped curly head to gaze up at his uncle with dark heavily-fringed eyes. In a white silk shirt, black shorts and white shoes and socks, he was a pretty child. His small oval face with its delicate nose and cupid's bow lips was, like the rest of his body, beautifully shaped. Martina was instantly drawn to his fragile loveliness. There were blue shadows beneath his eyes as though he had not been sleeping well. He was pale too, with a blue tracing of veins at his temples. He looked inquiringly at Martina, a quick shy look.

Bruno smiled. "This charming *signorina* is staying with us for a while. Stand up straight and greet Signorina Floyd in English."

Marco straightened slowly and gave Martina a wide-eyed curious stare. Then holding out a small hand, he said gravely, "How do you do, Signorina Floyd." His childish voice had a surprising depth and Martina answered politely with a warm smile. He did not return it, but buried his face again in Bruno's lap.

He met her eyes over the boy's head. "Marco is shy, but he will soon get to know you," he said apologetically.

Martina nodded, thinking what a waste that he had not planned on having a family of his own. He would have made a wonderful parent. Hastily, she brushed the thought aside. It was their own business; he and Eunice could remain close to each other without children to bind them together.

Marco lifted his head and curved his thin young arms around his uncle's waist.

"Stefano says you are going away, Zio Bruno," he said plaintively.

Bruno smiled down on him indulgently. "Only for a little while. Signorina Floyd will look after you while your Zia Eunice and I are away."

The small pretty mouth quivered and the angelic brows puckered mutinously.

"I want to go with you," he insisted in muffled tones as he dropped his head.

Bruno ruffled the black curls and Martina sat silently admiring a man who could find time among his many business engagements to reassure a small boy.

"The time will soon pass, *caro mio*."

But Marco refused to be comforted. "I want to go with you."

"Next time, perhaps."

Immediately Marco lifted his head. "You promise, Zio Bruno?"

"I promise."

Again it occurred to Martina that Marco should be with his mother in the Greek islands. He would have blossomed in the sun and regained his confidence with her. Having lost his father, he was plainly frightened of letting his uncle go in case he too would not return.

Eunice came back at that moment, accompanied by Stefano. Lunch was ready. It consisted of superb fresh seafood and an infinite variety of Italian dishes served by silent footmen beneath magnificent chandeliers of Venetian glass.

During the meal Eunice had occasional flashes of sincerity and humor, but her manner was always a little strained. There was a faint undertone of hardness, a bitterness that reminded Martina that she was going through a difficult phase.

Bruno either was ignorant of the fact or preferred to ignore it. He spoke with a cultured idiom far different from the usual Italian language heard in the square. He did not talk down to Marco, but treated him as intelligently as he would an adult. And Marco had a look on his face far too serious for his age.

It was all wrong, Martina thought. He should have been with boys of his own age, happy, carefree and mischievous. Once when he solemnly met her gaze, she smiled at him and wrinkled her nose. He did not respond. The thick dark lashes came down like shutters. She noticed he ate very little but drank thirstily, and when she helped herself to a peach at the end of the meal she dropped a particularly juicy one onto his plate.

She was rewarded with a surprised stare as he picked it up and sank his small white teeth into the softness of the fruit. Bruno smiled across at her as he witnessed the action. He really was attached to the boy.

Eunice looked on with polite interest but with the manner of one not really listening. Marco might hold no interest for her, but he fascinated Martina. He was a very well-behaved little boy who, so far, had spoken only when addressed. She had noticed he seemed particularly reserved with Eunice. Those great dark eyes of his fixed wonderingly on her face with a blank stare. How different he was with Bruno. There was a glow akin to worship when he gazed on his uncle as though being with him was the acme of pleasure.

Bruno was called away by a long distance call at the end of the meal and he went to his study with an absent pat on Marco's dark curls. Marco watched him go wistfully, and Eunice said rather sharply, "Go ask Stefano to sponge your hands and face, Marco. We're going out this afternoon."

"*Si*, Zia Eunice." Marco slipped obediently from his chair and slowly left the room.

Although he had left the room, Marco's presence seemed to quiver in the air between them.

Eunice was breathing rather quickly. "You saw how it was with Bruno. He had eyes for no one else but Marco. I don't want to be petty, but honestly, I could scream."

"Then it's time you got away," Martina said with conviction. "In the meantime, it might help if you followed Bruno's lead and made a fuss over the boy occasionally. If Bruno senses your antagonism toward

Marco, he will give the boy more attention than he would normally do."

Eunice, however, was in no mood to compromise. She stiffened and her lips thinned. "My dear Martina, if I were to fall all over the boy like Bruno does, he would end up sharing our bed. It's getting so that Bruno is hesitant to make love in case Marco wakes up in the night and needs him."

"Has Marco ever come into your room?"

"Not yet. If he wakes up he calls out and Bruno goes to him like a shot. Sometimes he doesn't return, but spends the rest of the night beside Marco."

Martina watched Eunice take her cigarette case and lighter out of her handbag. She lit a cigarette with shaking fingers, *a sure sign that she is strung up,* thought Martina. She had to help her to get away, and soon. If she didn't, something would have to give, and it could be her marriage. Martina hated to see her so unhappy. She was beginning to see the situation through her friend's eyes and measure it by her apparent suffering.

The situation would not have arisen with herself. Her own delight in children, her ability to enter into their world of fantasy would have removed any threat to her marriage had she been Bruno's wife. Eunice, of course, did not care for children. In her opinion they had ruined her childhood and now threatened her adult life. Martina regarded her with sympathetic concern.

"Don't worry," she said kindly. "This time next week you'll be in Geneva with Bruno on a second honeymoon." She smiled impishly. "I envy you. Bruno is a very charming man. I can understand you being worried about losing him. I could fall for him myself quite easily." Her wide-set gray eyes twinkled affectionately, rallying Eunice.

"I can see I have a rival in you too," she smiled, and rushed on, partly to ease her restlessness and partly in relief at finding a fellow confidant, "You don't know what it means to me to be able to get away for a while." She stubbed out the half finished cigarette as though she had lost the taste for it. Martina, who didn't smoke, hoped the trip might influence Eunice to not smoke so heavily. She was far too nervous.

Eunice was speaking again. Already she was more relaxed. "I have an appointment this afternoon at the hairdressers. Could you manage to amuse yourself for a few hours while I'm away? You could come with me to the square if you like and do a bit of sightseeing. Marco can stay with Stefano."

Marco came in before Martina could answer. His small face was pink and glowing from his recent wash and his curls were freshly combed. He hesitated near the door. There was something so utterly lost and forlorn about the small figure that Martina was touched.

"I'd love to go with you, Eunice. We could take Marco too." She walked across the room to where he stood and smiled down at him. "What do you say to showing me around Venice this afternoon, Marco? I'm a stranger here and it would be fun to have a handsome young man to escort me."

He hesitated, comparing this invitation from a stranger with the alternative of staying indoors. Presently she felt his small hand slide into hers.

"*Si, signorina,*" he said.

Something lurched in her heart when his small fingers curled around her own.

"I'll go and change my shoes," she said, looking across at Eunice who was still seated at the table. "What time shall we have to be back?"

"Marco goes to bed at seven. He has his supper in the kitchen with Ugo and his wife, Maria. Maria is the cook. Besides Stefano and Emilia, there are Pina and Lorenzo who do most of the household chores and look after the garden. It might seem like a large staff by today's standards, but we give them liberal time off and with extra staff there's always someone on duty." Pushing back her chair, Eunice rose to her feet. "I'll drop you off at the square and pick you up around five. All right?"

Her smile was a glimpse of the old Eunice and Martina returned it happily.

"Fine," she answered, and left the room holding Marco's hand.

The first thing she noticed on entering her room was the cheque book, small black suede bag and accompanying note on her dressing table. Tentatively she picked it up. She read: "Dear Martina, I am calling you that because we are friends. Have fun with the cheque book. Taking Marco about will prove expensive, even to satisfy his childish needs. If you are in need of small change at any time Stefano will get it for you from the bank. I trust you enjoy your stay with us, and do make yourself at home. Kind regards, Bruno."

Marco's eyes were fixed curiously upon her as she picked up the small suede bag drawn up at the top with a tasseled cord. How thoughtful and considerate of Bruno to leave the money discreetly instead of offering it to her directly. Her first impulse was to refuse it; then she saw the wisdom of accepting it. Refreshments would cost the earth in Venice and she had a limited amount of cash on hand. She held the bag out to Marco with a smile.

"Would you like to count this, Marco, while I get ready? I don't know much about Italian currency."

Marco's brows knit in a frown. With perfect politeness, he said, "*Io non capisco.*"

"Sorry. Of course, you don't understand. Currency means money. This is Italian currency in this small bag. You will show me how to use it. Yes?"

He nodded eagerly, taking the bag to a chair and tipping the contents onto the tapestry seat. The small black head bent over it and she left him engrossed in his task.

When she returned he had put most of the money back into the bag and she gave him the rest to put into his pocket. His obvious delight set her wondering whether it was the first time he had handled money of his own.

They met Stefano in the hall and almost immediately Eunice came down dressed for outdoors. "Ah, you're ready," she exclaimed, looking much brighter and sparing a smile for Marco. "You must be a good boy with Zia Martina. You understand?"

Marco answered rather subduedly. "*Si*, Zia Eunice. I will take care of the *signorina*."

"See that you do," was the sharp reply. "Ugo is waiting, Stefano?" she asked as the men hovered nearby.

"*Si, signora*." He opened the heavy door and Ugo helped them into the launch.

During the short journey, Marco leaned against Martina, his hands in his pockets jingling the money as though to reassure himself it was still there, giving her a secret little smile which made her want to hug him.

"Don't let Marco bother you, Marty. Make him do what you want," Eunice said when they parted in the square.

They arrived in the Piazza San Marco to find it alive with people and pigeons. Music from an orchestra mingled with laughter and voices as Martina gazed for rapturous moments at the motley crowd. There was a quality of light she could not describe, a kind of bright luminescence as the gold of the sun transformed the whole square into a cave of priceless treasures. Flags hung from bronze poles outside the cathedral, and at the end of the Piazzetta one could see gondolas dancing on the sparkling water. The gondoliers, slimhipped, handsome and picturesque, wore their thin straw hats at a provocative angle, providing an intriguing background for the colorful scene.

Marco went off happily to purchase bread crumbs for the pigeons from one of the trestle stalls. He laughed with glee when a cloud of feathered wings descended upon his head and shoulders. When the crumbs were eaten, Martina bought them both an ice cream with her own money and they sat down to wait for the ceremony of the striking of the hour in a corner of the basilica.

The ceremony began as the bronze Moors, moving realistically from the waist, struck the hour. Marco sat entranced when the small door opened and a trumpeting angel appeared, leading the three Magi. Wide-eyed, Marco watched them bow to the Madonna before circling around her. Then, with the well-worn mechanism whirring like a clock running down, they disappeared inside the small door which closed again behind them.

Later, Marco and Martina hand in hand explored. Occasionally, he rose on tiptoe to look into a shop window, but he never asked for anything. They lingered for a long time at one shop entranced by a toy snake sliding along the floor of a shop window.

Marco, his nose flattened against the pane, was vastly entertained by its realistic movement. He chuckled when Martina flinched at the sight of the barbed tongue shooting out viciously and he laughed up at her roguishly. She bought it for him, of course, smiling when he trotted along hugging the box beneath his arm.

It was tiring walking in the sun, so they found a secluded table at a café in the Piazza and Martina ordered cakes and lemonade. They could have gone to a more moderately priced café in one of the side lanes, but she had chosen a table with a view of the clock so that Marco could again see the striking of the hour. She had not forgotten how his fingers had curled excitedly around her own when the clockwork figures had appeared. He had smiled up at her so angelically at the end that she could have hugged him.

It was easy to nestle in the plush world of wealth and relaxing to think that she didn't have to count every penny. The waiter took a few minutes to bring them their order. When he appeared Marco had slipped from his chair and was winding up the toy snake, which he had named Russo. Then it happened—a sudden ear-splitting shriek from the next table making Martina's blood run cold.

Marco was still crouched by his chair, this time in hiding. Startled, Martina turned slowly around to the next table where an elderly woman in periwinkle blue had leapt up on to her chair and was staring down in horror at the clockwork reptile. Martina did not notice the toy right away because it had disappeared beneath the woman's chair. She did, however, notice that they were the target of all eyes. A small crowd gathered.

The woman glared at Martina. "Well, do something! Don't just sit there!"

Before she could collect her scattered wits, someone moved from the small gathering, a graysuited arm culminating in an immaculate cuff shot out and the offending toy was scooped up in a firm masculine hand. Martina swallowed a gasp of dismay. Dominic Burnett di Ravenelli, of all people! It would have to be him. For a moment he appeared to be taken aback that it was only a toy. Then he was his usual self, cool, arrogant and aloof.

"It's only a toy," he said, holding up the reptile for inspection. Someone in the crowd tittered and people began to move away. Badly scared, the elderly woman stared down at the toy from her precarious position on the creaking chair.

"A toy?" she snorted in disgust, her pale, prominent blue eyes flashing indignantly in the manner of an affronted pekinese. "How dare they play such a cruel trick on an old woman?" She glowered at Dominic, keeping her dignity as much as her quivering form would allow. "I hope you chastise your wife and son very thoroughly for this outrage, *signore*!"

Dominic slid the toy into his pocket with an imperceptible twitch of his lips and said politely, "You may be sure of that, *signora*. I apologize most sincerely, Please allow me." Reaching up, he lifted her gently to the ground. "I trust you are none the worse for this unfortunate incident," he smiled charmingly. "I can assure you there was no intention to scare you. The blame, if any, is with the manufacturers for producing a toy so realistic that I was taken in myself until I picked it up."

"You were?" A change of mood was clearly taking place, for the woman began to regard him with unconcealed admiration. She was beginning to realize that she had been rescued by a tall, handsome stranger who had bravely picked up what he too had thought was a living reptile. "It was indeed brave of you to come so gallantly to my rescue," she said almost coyly. "It might have been a real one, even dangerous."

This amused him. "*Signora*," he said with a twinkle, "there would have been nothing heroic in my picking it up had this been the case. One picks up a dangerous reptile with a certain grip near to the head which renders it harmless. Please allow me to get you a brandy to calm your nerves."

The woman was won over completely. She positively beamed.

"You are very kind, *signore*. I will accept it with pleasure."

The woman had spoken throughout in English and Martina wondered if she was a resident. She evidently did not know Dominic, but Martina conceded that she would never forget him. Dominic ordered and paid for a double brandy from a hovering waiter, and Martina waited in dismay as he strolled over to their table.

Marco had drunk half his lemonade and was now reaching for a cake.

Dominic narrowed his gaze at him, but Marco was quite unperturbed.

"*Per favore*, Zio Dominic, may I have Russo back?" he asked politely.

Dominic's frown took in Martina's flushed cheeks. A dark brow lifted satirically. "Russo? Ah, your toy reptile. I'll think about it."

To her dismay he drew up a chair and sat down at the table to face them. He looked so arrogant regarding them both that Martina disliked him more than ever.

"Well, Marco, aren't you going to apologize to the *signora* for frightening her out of her wits?" he asked dryly, clasping his hands loosely on the table.

Marco flushed and gulped on a piece of cake. "But, Zio Dominic, it was an accident. I did not intend to frighten the *signora*. Russo moved so quickly."

He looked pleadingly at Martina, his wide dark eyes unconsciously seeking her help. Poor pet, was her instant reaction. His good breeding gave the impression of a big boy when he was really only a baby. A wave of emotion swept over her. Her dislike of his tormentor increased. With the sun on his features, he was sitting back entirely at his ease, enjoying the power and languor in his long limbs.

Martina confronted him, sitting stiffly as if tackling an enemy. If her glance was challenging, his was more so. Their eyes collided and locked in battle, culminating in a sharp electric shock which rippled along her nerves like a sudden shaft of lightning.

With her heart beating thickly, she said, "I am sure Marco did not intend to frighten the *signora*. I bought him the toy, so I am as much to blame for what has happened. It was just unfortunate."

Several seconds elapsed during which he favored her with a cool, pitiless stare. She wondered if he had any idea how formidable he looked to a small boy.

His eyes narrowed. "Even so, an apology is called for," he said at last.

Lowering her eyes, Martina bit her lip. His dictatorial attitude annoyed her profoundly. At the same time an innate sense of justice forced her to admit that he was right.

She smiled down at Marco who was regarding her anxiously and patted his hand reassuringly. "You had better go and say you are sorry to the *signora*, my pet. You might get your Russo back if you do," she advised him gently.

Marco hesitated and glanced at Dominic to confirm her words. Slowly, the man drew the toy from his pocket.

"Take Russo with you and explain to the *signora* how it works. She might be interested."

"*Si*, Zio Dominic."

Marco slid from his chair somewhat reluctantly. The waiter was delivering the *signora*'s brandy when Marco reached her. Dominic signaled to the man and ordered wine.

"You will join me in a glass of wine, Miss Floyd," he said as the waiter went to execute his order.

"I have a drink, thanks," she answered, her fingers curling around her glass of lemonade.

Firmly the glass was taken from her and placed next to Marco's half empty one across the table.

His smile held an unmistakable challenge. His eyes mocked. "Marco can drink that along with his. He will be quite thirsty when he has finished demonstrating his toy."

An eyebrow tilted humorously in the direction of the small boy and elderly woman, now completely engrossed in the toy. Marco's gruff little voice, so oddly in keeping with his fragile appearance, brought the usual smile to her lips. Her expression, sweetly compassionate, riveted Dominic's dark eyes to her face.

"Marco appears to have made a friend," he said.

Martina turned and looked at him fully. His eyes were still upon her with a suggestion of satirical humor which she found so annoying. She recalled his cynical remark about Marco being spoiled by too many women.

"I hope so," she said. "He can't have too many friends of either sex."

If he was remembering his remark he accepted the rebuff with unimpaired equanimity. A faint smile lingered in the eyes gazing at her with a curious growing interest.

"You are fond of children, Miss Floyd?"

"Why do you ask?" she wanted to know.

He shrugged. "Merely as a point of interest."

The waiter returned with the wine. Dominic filled two glasses and passed one to her. Raising his own, he gazed at her mockingly over the top.

"To your stay in Venice, Miss Floyd. May it be a happy one."

Martina murmured something, swallowed a little of the palatable wine and felt rather peculiar. It was too soon for the wine to affect her, nor could it be the reaction to the incident of the toy reptile. It was an exciting, pulsating emotion she felt, a sudden overwhelming joy at being alive and in the right place at the right time. The orchestra added to the magic, giving a strange dreamlike quality to the wonderful surroundings.

When raised voices from a party on her left distracted her attention for a few seconds, she turned her head to find Dominic's eyes leveled disturbingly at her. The blood rushed beneath her clear skin and she drank the rest of her wine to hide her embarrassment.

"No—no more, thank you," she said as he reached to refill her glass. "I'm not much of a drinker."

"Neither am I, but this is a special occasion," he said; nonetheless he respected her wish. "Where is Eunice? Is she not with you?" he asked abruptly.

"She had an engagement."

"Did Ugo bring you here?"

The second question was no less abrupt, as though the thought of them being unchaperoned displeased him.

"Yes. He's picking us up again at five."

She spoke hastily in case he suggested taking them home. She had no idea what conveyance he possessed, but she imagined he would not depend upon public transport. Nothing so common would do for Dominic Burnett di Ravenelli! She doubted whether his concern was directed in any way toward herself. Marco was his worry, and probably Mia too.

She wondered why he was staying so long, for she felt as if he would have a reason for everything he did. When he spoke again it was not of Marco.

Unbending a little, he said conversationally, "You are fortunate to be in Venice in the summer, Miss Floyd, when many festivals provide entertainment for visitors. Being young, you will enjoy the crowds of tourists. For me the true beauty of Venice is in the winter when the tourists have gone. Then the snow glistens on the rooftops, the canals are free of traffic congestion and the bite in the air sends people scurrying into cafés for a gossip over hot chocolate. Venetian cooks excel in their excellent dishes of piping hot pizza, fried scampi deliciously crisp, liver and onions cooked in true Venetian style and washed down by delightful wines from neighboring vineyards."

His words moved her strangely, giving her a glimpse into his world. Something very deep within prompted her to say a trifle wistfully, "You make it sound delicious. Few people ever consider taking a holiday in the winter except for winter sports or a hot climate. What a pity other parts of the world haven't been fashioned with the beauty of Venice. It's so sad to think that all the beauty surrounding us will one day be gone."

"Venice is unique because it is built on a 118 small islands connected by hundreds of bridges. It was built by dedicated men."

He went on to talk of everything that had made Venice great in her day. His deep distinctive voice was extremely pleasant to listen to. Martina sat enthralled, forgetting her antagonism as she recognized a quality of calmness which formed a part of his strong resilience. He talked at length of the golden beaches which stretched from Venice to Trieste, and the Alpine foothills protecting the Venetian plains from the north winds. Martina sat until he had finished speaking. Only then did she look up to find him watching her intently. The quick color again flooded her face as she wondered if he had meant to tell her so much. He had asked her nothing about herself, and she resented the fact that he was in no way interested.

When Marco returned to the table, Dominic took his leave. Martina was not sorry to see him go. There were so many conflicting things about him for which she was unprepared. She had met him twice, yet she was far from becoming friends with him. Even so she could not deny that strange excited feelings welled up inside her as she watched him walk away with looselimbed grace and an arrogant tilt of the head.

Marco demolished two more cakes and the rest of the lemonade with ease.

"Did you enjoy it?" she asked with a smile.

He nodded, accepting the paper handkerchief she produced to wipe the stickiness from his hands and face.

"*Si, grazie, signorina.*" The food and the session with the elderly woman had loosened his little tongue. "The *signora* liked Russo. She was not afraid when she saw me wind him up. She thought it was real."

Martina cast a surreptitious glance behind her at the next table to find the woman had gone.

"The poor old soul was scared stiff," she said. "I'm glad you like the toy."

He handled it reverently. "I cannot wait to show it to Zio Bruno."

They sat until the clock struck the hour of five, and when the clockwork figures had disappeared from view they hurried to where Eunice and Hugo waited. Eunice, with a flimsy bronze scarf draped over her freshly coiffured head, greeted them with a smile and asked if they had enjoyed their afternoon. Marco told her they had seen Zio Dominic and proceeded to demonstrate the toy reptile along the floor of the launch. Eunice used the right degree of enthusiasm, agreed that it was very realistic and sent him along to show Hugo at the controls of the launch.

"So you met Dominic," she said, taking cigarettes and a lighter from her handbag. "What do you think about him?"

Martina watched her light up with the ease of long practise. "I haven't got beyond the fact that he's good looking, intelligent, decidedly masculine and charming in a cynical way," she admitted honestly.

Eunice blew out a veil of smoke. The china blue eyes narrowed. "Do I detack a slight note of censure? I call that an evasive answer to an intriguing question. Most women are interested on sight. I adore the man."

"Because he's tall, talented and taboo?" Martina teased.

"Because he's everything a woman could wish for."

"I find him rather overwhelming."

"You're prejudiced because the man is so attractive. It's a pity his kind are in the minority. We could do with more like him to make life more exciting."

Martina puckered her brows. "His name intrigues me—it's so Italian. He looks Latin, but he has a lot of English in him."

"You're right; Dominic is English by birth. He was 12 when his mother, a widow, married the Conte di Ravenelli. Dominic took his stepfather's name, but kept his own father's name of Burnett as well. He was educated in England at his father's old college, and when his education was finished the Conte introduced him into the world of finance. Bruno says Dominic outshone the Conte, who was a wizard at the game. The Conte was delighted, and they became inseparable. Dominic was shattered when the Conte died two years ago of a heart attack."

"And his mother?"

"Dominic's mother died some years after she married the Conte. She never recovered from the car accident in which her first husband died. Her heart had been affected by an internal injury and she died quietly one night in her sleep. The Conte didn't marry again and consequently he and Dominic grew very close. According to Bruno, Dominic is very much like his stepfather in appearance. They were actually taken for father and son."

Martina pictured a tall, immaculate figure, square-shouldered and leanhipped, whose finely chiseled features and arrogant carriage made him appear every inch a Conte. Yes, the title would have been very apt for Dominic Burnett di Ravenelli. The disquieting thought that he was a close friend of Bruno and Eunice meant she would be meeting him frequently. She wondered how long he had known Mia. Eunice unwittingly supplied the answer.

"Bruno is very fond of Dominic and nothing would give him greater pleasure than to have him in the family," she said.

Something tightened in Martina's throat. "You mean Bruno would like Dominic to marry Mia?"

"Yes. They've known each other for years. Her parents, who now live in Milan, were close friends of the late Conte di Ravenelli. Mia, being both beautiful and wealthy, was much sought after before her marriage. Her name was coupled with lots of elegible males, Dominic's included, before she married Bruno's brother. But Dominic only dabbled in affairs. According to Bruno, he spent too much of his time with the Conte racing their magnificent yacht or enjoying winter sports abroad. They were excellent sportsmen."

"He must have missed the Conte a lot when he died."

"He did. When the Conte died suddenly of a heart attack, Dominic went abroad. He was away for a year until a chance meeting with Bruno in Tangier made him decide to return to Venice. Mia would make him an ideal wife. She's an excellent hostess and they're suited in every way. She is also the kind who needs a man behind her. Dominic would pamper her and there would be no fear in his mind of being married for her money, as Mia is a wealthy woman." Eunice tapped an ash from her cigarette over the side of the launch and cast a swift glance at Martina's suit of cinnamon and cream. The gesture was not meant unkindly. Even so Martina felt she was being compared somewhat unfavorably with the absent Mia, who probably selected her wardrobe from the famous fashion houses in Paris and Rome.

She said rather weakly, "Surely it's a little early to talk of Mia marrying again? She must have loved her husband deeply to be so shattered by his death."

Eunice curled a lip. "Most of Mia's grief is for herself. She was an only child of wealthy parents and has been spoiled. To Mia, the world begins and ends with herself. Her marriage to Dominic would delight all her friends. He has known her for years and is no brash boy fresh from university. He's sown his wild oats and is ready to settle down."

Looking at it from Eunice's point of view, the marriage was ideal. Bruno would no longer have the responsibility of Marco and her marriage would be secure. All the same, Martina thought, it was a bit much, arranging other people's lives for them. Yet why should she worry? From what she had seen of Dominic Burnett di Ravenelli, he was quite capable of taking care of himself. As for spoiling a wife, Martina could not see him allowing a woman to have her own way all the time. That determined jaw and those steely hawklike eyes suggested an iron will and an assurance that he would insist upon wearing the pants. Mia was welcome to him.

Marco took Russo to bed with him that evening after proudly displaying the snake's talents to Bruno. He had gone to sleep with a smile on his lips. Martina, looking down at the cherubic face, the long dark lashes against the flushed cheeks and the dimpled hand still clutching Russo, hoped with a wistful tenderness that his nightmares would become a thing of the past. Eunice and Bruno had gone to dine with Dominic. Martina had been invited, but she had excused herself, saying she felt in need of getting to bed early.

Since her arrival in Venice, so much unexpected had happened. Eunice had unsettled her by revealing her real reason for inviting her. The tragedy of Marco had demanded her ready sympathy and the entrance of Dominic Burnett di Ravenelli into her troubled world had made mincemeat of her emotions. This first night of her stay in Venice was filled with apprehension. Maybe she was just overtired. All she needed was a good night's sleep to put everything into perspective. But first a bath.

Normally, she would have taken a shower, but the luxurious bathroom, fabulously soft towels and glass jars of scented bath salts made her want to wallow blissfully in perfumed water. Adding perfumed oil to the water, Martina steeped herself in the delicious fragrance. Allowing the scented softness to caress her limbs, Martina dwelt on the luxuriousness of her surroundings, sparing a thought for the many dark lanes of houses which existed behind the palaces. Many were probably damp and rat-infested. Yet here she was with a fabulous bed waiting to cuddle her with a bedside light, books, magazines and chocolates in an atmosphere of comfort. It was so easy to sink into this morass of wealth, but it was only temporary. Why should she not enjoy it?

Relaxed and utterly refreshed, she stepped into a frothy white negligee with satin ribbons. She had paid more than she could afford for it on a sudden wave of pure joy at Eunice's invitation. She was combing her hair, still damp from her bath, when Emilia brought her dinner on a tray. She had requested it in order to save the staff the unnecessary chore of laying the dining table for one.

She ate leisurely, enjoying her first quiet hour of an eventful day. She thought of Eunice, so different from the tomboy she remembered, and Bruno, kind, gentle and sincere. Martina was sure that it was only a matter of time before he devoted himself again to his wife. The loss of a beloved brother had scarred him. At the moment he needed love and understanding. If only Eunice would play down the hard streak which surfaced toward children!

No doubt Eunice was regarding Marco's presence in a childless establishment as a real threat to her own determination to remain childless. The boy might have roused the paternal instinct in Bruno to the extent of him wanting children of his own. That night Martina went to sleep wishing with all her heart for everything to turn out right for Eunice, her friend.

CHAPTER THREE

Martina never forgot waking up her first morning in Venice. She was up with the sun and went to her window to look down on the barges loaded to the gunwales, on their way to the early market. The morning light spread a golden haze, mellowing the walls of the palaces along the canal awakening them gently into new life. This vision of a beautiful world still sleeping, oblivious to the ugly concrete buildings of modern civilization and comparatively unspoiled by progress, was pure enchantment.

She stood very still, her eyes wide with wonder and delight. Everything to her was as new as the day. Yet were she to gaze on the same scene day after day she would be as moved by it as she was now. "All this and heaven too," she murmured, leaving it reluctantly to wash and dress.

Martina hummed cheerfully in the bathroom and again in the bedroom as she dressed. Her presence in Venice had come about so miraculously as to make the real reason of her visit irrelevant. She was going to enjoy her stay with carefree enthusiasm, spreading an aura of friendliness to warm the lonely heart of the small Marco, thus enabling him to forget the tragedy shadowing his short life.

Emilia brought her breakfast on a tray and was surprised to find her up and dressed.

"*Buon giorno, signorina,*" she said, her dark eyes in her oliveskinned face glowing with friendliness. "Signora Vortolini will be with you when you have breakfasted."

Martina had finished breakfast and was straightening the lovely counterpane on her bed when Eunice came into her room.

"Good morning, Marty. Did you sleep well?"

Eunice glowed this morning with an amiable sociability far removed from her former look of strain.

"Sleep well?" Martina echoed. "More like drugged with the beauty of it all—what with the gorgeous scenery outdoors and all this luxury." She gestured with a slender arm, "I'm going to miss your pampering when I leave."

Eunice laughed. She was wearing one of her well-tailored suits which became her long limbs so elegantly. In a delicate shade of primrose, it toned in well with her flaxen hair and honey-colored tan. Soft beige sandals strapped to her slender feet revealed, pearly, well-manicured toenails.

She smiled indulgently. "You're straightening that bed as though you'd been sharing it with a man!" Eunice adjusted a two-inch band of thin gold bracelets encircling her arm. "Seriously, though," she said, giving Martina her undivided attention, "I'm rather surprised to find you are still single. You were always more sought after than I was by the opposite sex." She eyed the slender form and piquant face curiously. "Sure you don't have a man tucked away somewhere?"

Martina shook her head. "Not guilty. In the permissive society today, one wonders about the ties of marriage."

Eunice strolled to the dressing table to pick up a small bottle of perfume.

"A good marriage is what every woman needs if she's to find fulfilment in life. It's easy to see you've never been in love. Mm, lovely." She had loosened the glass stopper and sniffed appreciatively. "Apple Blossom by Helena Rubinstein."

"Birthday present," Martina said laconically, wondering how it rated with Eunice's expensive brands.

"Sorry, I forgot your birthday," Eunice whispered. "Twenty-three, isn't it? High time you had a man."

"A man or a husband?" Martina queried impishly.

Eunice replied with a twinkle, "You aren't the kind to flourish on casual affairs. You're too softhearted. Mind you, there's ample opportunity to indulge in affairs here. The Italian males are fully aware of their own charms and don't hesitate to use them. They could teach you a lot. A light affair would do you no harm providing you treat it as such."

"Sounds interesting."

"Could be. The average Italian male is so good at the game of love he could convince you easily that you were the only woman in his life instead of the next on his list. Remember that and you can have fun."

Martina chuckled. "Thanks for the advice. I didn't come for a husband or for an affair. There's so much to do and see here I'm sure I'll have no time for either. I'm so grateful to you for asking me here, Eunice, and I want to do something in return. What about Marco coming to sleep in this room adjoining mine? He knows me well enough now to have confidence in me. I'm a light sleeper and if he happens to wake in the night I'll hear him. It will also be one step forward for you and Bruno." She smiled roguishly. "Or should I have said a step nearer each other?"

Eunice was pleased with the suggestion, although her look was tentative.

"Would you mind taking over the responsibility of Marco so soon? Won't it be soon enough for him to move in with you toward the end of the week when we leave for Geneva? I feel awfully guilty about asking you to come to look after him. I didn't mention it in my letter because it's only for a week. But even during that week I want you to feel you're a guest here, not a baby-sitter."

Martina found her friend's concern endearing. "The sooner you and Bruno are on your own the better," she said with conviction. "It's sweet of you to be so concerned about me, but it isn't necessary. I shall enjoy myself while you're away, and I'm sure Marco will too."

Her look of reassurance gave Eunice a twinge of conscience. "You're awfully sweet, Marty. I'll not forget what you're doing for me. I'll get the staff to move Marco's bed and belongings. Tomorrow evening will be soon enough. We're going to the theater tonight and it will be late when we return. What do you want to do today? Tour the islands or visit the places of interest?"

Martina hesitated. "Perhaps Marco would enjoy a tour of the islands better," she suggested.

"Bruno is taking Marco with him today on a business

trip to Murano. So you and I can spend the day together."

They did, touring the art galleries of the Doge's Palace and the Accademia. Martina would have spent all day admiring the works of art, but Eunice called a halt after lunch to take her shopping in Frezerie. They had a drink in one of the smart bars.

Eunice said over her chilled Martini, "I don't know whether you noticed, Marty, but I've seen several Adonises eyeing you hungrily. You'd better watch out."

Martina chuckled, in no way dismayed. "They're probably thinking how naïve I look against your sophisticated self. I'd love to have your poise, Eunice."

She never heard Eunice reply, for a deep voice cut in pleasantly.

"*Buon giorno*, Eunice, Miss Floyd."

Eunice shone up at the tall lithe figure in the sharply-cut pale gray gaberdine suit.

"Dominic! How nice to see you."

He looked down at them, retaining the arrogant tilt of his well-shaped head. In the strong sunlight, his face with its thickly marked brows, dark eyes and firmly set mouth above a strong jaw looked more chiseled than ever. The dark crisp hair sprang back from an intelligent forehead and his mouth curved into a smile of extraordinary charm.

"Mind if I join you?"

"It will be a pleasure," Eunice assured him.

He lowered himself into a chair facing them and Martina met the same measuring look she had encountered on their first meeting. He reminded her of a rock against which the tides of adversity would clash, leaving no impression. Still, ruthlessness and courage constituted a formidable combination. This man appeared to possess more than his quota of both.

"I'm between appointments," he said, observing their drinks. "What are you having? The same again?"

The dark eyes rested briefly on Martina, narrowed as if he sensed her reluctance at accepting a drink from him and looked again at Eunice.

"Yes, please. A cool drink is very welcome when you're hot. Do have one yourself, too. You must be hot, yet you always manage to look so cool, calm and collected. How do you do it?" Eunice asked on a small laugh.

"Force of habit," he replied banteringly.

"Is that what it is?" Eunice raised a brow. "Martina has your gift for being indefatigable. She would have gone on walking all day if I hadn't called a halt. I'm exhausted, and look at her—as fresh as paint."

But Dominic was not looking at Martina. He was busy giving an order to the waiter.

"You know, Dominic," Eunice said when the waiter had gone, "you'll have to slow up a bit when you're married."

He lifted a lazy brow goodhumoredly. "Who said anything about marrying? I didn't."

"No, you haven't. But we live in hopes." Eunice looked across the table to meet his enigmatic gaze. "Now admit it, Dominic. Don't you ever tire of this abiding zest for work?"

His mouth twitched. "You could ask Bruno the same question. Like him, I would have enough energy left over for marriage."

His eyes twinkled devilishly and the laugh which followed at the sight of her flush was deep and uproarious. He threw back his head and roared.

Eunice drew herself up with all the dignity of a shocked matron.

"Dominic!" she exclaimed reprovingly.

He laughed again at her embarrassed flush and was still chuckling when the waiter came. Martina wondered if he had audaciously teased Eunice for presuming too far on their friendship by inquiring into his personal life. She loved his sense of humor. Pity it was a quality which Eunice lacked. It did not take a very discerning eye to see that her friend was very fond of this disturbing man, so naturally she would forgive him practically anything. She smiled at him now.

"I wouldn't put it past you to keep it a secret if you had some woman in mind."

Martina, tense, looked from one to the other. She knew Eunice was probing with Mia in view. Dominic, however, was unperturbed. Pouring out his drink, an iced beer, he said ironically, "If I had I could hardly tell you before telling the woman herself." He held up his glass of sparkling amber liquid. "Cheers." He took a drink and lowered his glass. "You are going to the opera this evening, aren't you?"

Eunice hid her disappointment beneath a polite smile. "Yes. I believe you're taking your house party. Pity— Bruno hoped you would join us."

"At the moment my guests number only five in all. The rest arrive late this evening and are going straight to the opera house. We shall join them after the show, so there will be six in my box including myself. I can't ask you to join us, and neither can we join you, as there wouldn't be room in either box to take us all. I want you to tell Bruno I'm sorry. You will come to my house afterwards for supper?"

"Thanks, we'll be delighted to. Bruno is always saying you two don't see much of each other."

"I agree. We'll have to see what we can do about it when you return from Geneva. You're going for a week?"

Eunice nodded. "Yes, Bruno must have told you about the important business conference he's attending."

Dominic nodded his head, his keen eyes straying to Martina who was sitting slim and quiet.

"So you've been sightseeing, Miss Floyd. What impressed you most?"

"The paintings, works of art unbelievably beautiful and alive. I think one needs at least a year here in order to absorb the intimate detail of each work."

"Really?" He was looking at her as if there was much more to her than the linen suit and withdrawn look.

Martina felt her color rise. Keep cool, she advised herself. The man is aware of his power of attraction. He has that cynical detachment the connoisseur uses as his yardstick. Here was someone who would call the tune every time.

"You like art, then, Miss Floyd?"

Eunice cut in before Martina could answer. "Marty was very good at painting in school. The art master idolized her, said she had the gift to do great things."

Martina moved uneasily in her chair, disliking having attention drawn to herself. She would have preferred to have remained anonymous with Dominic as much as possible. His dark eyes were fixed upon her, alert and critical with that gleam of satirical humor at her sudden deepening color.

He said levelly, "This talent of yours should be encouraged. I say this because I have some pictures that I think would interest you. I've been offered a fabulous amount for them, but I refuse to sell them for sentimental reasons. They were painted by my mother. I would like you to see them."

Eunice sat up abruptly at his words. The china-blue eyes were wide with surprise.

"I knew you had a collection of valuable paintings, Dominic, but I don't remember seeing any of your mother's."

A brow lifted sardonically. "My dear Eunice, you've never spared more than a passing glance for any of my paintings. However, art is not everyone's cup of tea. Some people, like our young friend here, derive endless pleasure from it. Others see paintings merely as wall decoration or as an investment."

Eunice lifted elegant shoulders and Martina found herself rushing to her defence.

"Since we're on the subject of talents," she said, "I wonder if you know how marvelous Eunice was at sports. She was super at swimming and games, far better than I was. Her tennis was first class."

His mouth twitched. "I didn't know. I'll take you on some time, Eunice."

He sat regarding her in lazy amusement. Martina's heart jerked, oddly stirred by his air of distinction and charm.

"It's an idea," Eunice answered gaily. "I'll remind you when we return from Geneva. You might keep an eye on Marty and Marco while we're away."

He frowned. "Why on earth doesn't Bruno have a tutor for the boy and have done with it? The male influence is most important to a fatherless boy. Fortunately he has a mother who won't pamper him."

Martina stared at him in amazement. "I would say Marco is most unfortunate to have a mother of that kind."

He regarded her through narrowed lids. The word ruthless occurred to her and it nettled her enormously.

"Like the rest of your sex, you're inclined to go all sentimental over the boy. A doting mother is a menace to society. She deliberately holds her son back so that he'll need her longer. She pampers him, lavishing everything upon him while robbing him of the most essential thing, the power to paddle his own canoe without her."

Martina clenched her hands. "It seems to me that Marco has lost not one parent but two. Where does he go from there?"

He corrected her imperturbably, "Marco has lost his father. His mother suffers from the loss of her husband. Therefore she can't be expected to interest herself in her son until she recovers."

Martina hesitated. She had made a mistake in discussing the subject with him and she knew it. All her love for Marco was in her answer. She said quietly, "Marco has yet to recover too. Who better than a woman could help him with his nightmares of the fire and his groping in a strange world until he gains confidence?"

Eunice cut in then. It seemed to Martina that they were taking turns standing up for each other against this—this autocrat who was convinced he knew all the answers.

"Bruno is of the same opinion as Marty, Dominic," she said. "Anyway, it's a problem I'll be pleased to shelve for a while."

Dominic's countenance was suddenly inscrutable. "Perhaps you're wise. *Pazienza*. Most things have a way of working out, given time."

"Now what did he mean by that last remark?" Eunice said when Dominic had gone.

Martina had no idea. She couldn't care less. He had the uncomfortable gift of perceiving a woman's weaknesses and the nerve to discuss them. She felt she would be very happy if she never saw him again. As it was improbable she could only try to remain politely indifferent to that formidable, magnetic charm.

Eunice was speaking again. "I wonder if he means to marry Mia." She sighed. "It could be wishful thinking on my part, but what a lovely answer to the problem of Marco. Bruno would have a brother-in-law whom he loves like a brother, and we would all be happy."

Martina sat in heavy silence.

That evening she looked through her wardrobe for a dress suitable for competing with the grand creations she would mingle with at the theater. She didn't own any exclusive models so chose something simple—a white lace, hand-crocheted dress with a scooped neckline and bell sleeves. A friend at the typing pool where she worked was a wizard with a crochet hook; the dress she had made Martina fitted her slender figure perfectly. She was quite pleased with her reflection as she smoothed the skirt over her slim hips. Emilia had dressed her hair becomingly, piling it on top of her head and curling the ends into long ringlets which fell against the youthful contours of her smooth cheeks.

"You look lovely, *signorina*," said Emilia as she helped her put on her short white fur evening jacket.

Martina took a last glance at her reflection in the tall Venetian mirror. Her eyes sparkled and her small face was flushed with excitement. "A trifle homespun," she said, already comparing her unadorned appearance with that of Eunice and her friends. "Thanks for doing my hair, Emilia. You've dressed it beautifully."

"It is a pleasure, *signorina*. Your hair is so beautifully soft and easy to manage. It has a tendency to curl at the slightest encouragement." She tweaked a curl into place and stepped back to admire her handiwork. "What a pity you don't have a diamond necklace to set off the demure neckline of your dress."

"I don't have any jewelry. I'll be discreet and bathe in the reflected glory of Signora Vortolini and her friends." Martina's smile was sweet and without envy. "Thanks again, Emilia."

When she entered the *sala*, Bruno rose from his chair to meet her. He looked distinguished in evening dress.

"*Buona sera*, Martina," he said, his heavylidded eyes appraising her as he drew a long case from his pocket. "I didn't have the slightest idea what to give you to show our gratitude for what you are doing for us. However, it seems my little gift could not be more appropriate. It will give me great pleasure if you will accept this as a small appreciation."

He snapped open the case to reveal a blaze of diamonds. Martina stared speechlessly at the "little gift"—a diamond necklace and earrings which must have cost a small fortune.

"But, Bruno, I—they're real diamonds," she said weakly.

Bruno was smiling at her obvious bewilderment. "And your pretty throat is just the place for them. Allow me," he commented with a twinkle. He fastened the necklace around her neck. "Perhaps you would prefer to clip on the earrings yourself. You have such small ears and I'm afraid I would fumble."

Motionless, Martina stood there looking at him. It was on the tip of her tongue to refuse so costly a gift, a payment out of all proportion to the small favor she was doing in looking after Marco. The cost of it to Bruno was negligible. The important thing was that he was deriving so much pleasure from giving it to her that she was touched.

"They're fabulous, Bruno! I can hardly express my thanks," she said hurriedly to hide her embarrassment. She put on the earrings with trembling fingers. "I'll never be able to wear them without the fear of losing them."

"Of course you will. I have insured them for you, so you can wear them happily."

Bruno led her gently to the ornate mirror on the wall.

Surprised and wide-eyed, she gazed at her dazzling reflection. She was aware of her deepening color and his amused admiring glance. Emilia was right about the diamonds. Their fiery brilliance gave an added sparkle to her eyes and flushed cheeks. She was suddenly transfigured into a vision of feminine loveliness. Martina hardly recognized herself. It was several seconds before she came to earth. When she did so she kissed his cheek.

"Thank you again, Bruno." She gave a soft little laugh of pure enjoyment. "I hardly recognize myself." Her smile at him was very sweet. "You're an awfully nice man, Bruno. Don't spoil me. I'm happy to do any favor, for I can never repay your kindness in having me here."

"Martina," he said with feeling, and there was a note in his voice which made her wonder, "you have no idea of what you are doing for my wife and myself."

He was patting her shoulder paternally when Eunice came in looking brilliantly beautiful in oyster satin. Her necklace and earrings sparkled, her flaxen hair was superbly styled and she smiled radiantly.

"Last but not least," she quipped, looking at Martina. "Well, well! They say diamonds are a girl's best friend, and they're certainly yours, Marty. You look lovely." She turned to her husband. "You couldn't have chosen anything better, darling."

"But, Eunice—diamonds. . . ." Martina began to protest.

Eunice bent to kiss her smooth young cheek. "Enjoy your gift, Marty. With it goes all our love."

Bruno had a box reserved at the opera house. Martina sat in her corner, enthralled at the magnificence of red plush boxes, beautiful frescoes and gilt carvings, and the vast spectacular auditorium filled with a glittering, distinguished audience. By her side Eunice and Bruno graciously acknowledged friends, including a small party entering a nearby box.

Following their gaze, she saw Dominic and his guests. There was an immediate imperceptible quickening of her emotions as his air of easy affluence, his disciplined grace invaded the secret places of her heart. She became aware of him looking her way. Then her own small nod and polite smile was lost in the darkness between them as the lights dimmed. The orchestra suddenly shattered the breathless hush which followed and her seesawing emotions gradually subsided.

The magic moments before the curtain rose remained with Martina throughout the evening. She sat very still through the first act enjoying the performance of brilliant, renowned artists. At the intermission they left their box at the same time as Dominic and his party left theirs. The crowds were so large that they did not meet in the bar. Over drinks there, Martina was introduced to Contes and Contessas by Bruno, who spoke in excellent English, pronouncing strange-sounding names which she was convinced she would never remember.

They returned to their box to see that Dominic's party was already seated—an elderly couple, a slightly younger one and a blonde woman around Martina's own age. The woman's hair was a shining gilt cap, her dress, from which her honey-colored shoulders rose seductively, was a stiff blue taffeta. She looked perfectly poised and worldly, leaning forward to accept a light from her host for the cigarette she held between perfectly enamelled lips. The woman looked capable of handling an affair with even the experienced Dominic.

Martina had never had much time for people who dabbled in affairs. She preferred to stick to her ideals, even though some day, she was convinced, they would be blown sky high. While the amorous glances of Italian males amused her, she had no desire to become involved with any of them. The dates she had kept in the past could hardly be regarded as affairs since a restlessness in her made her cut them short. No man she had met up to now had caught her interest enough for her to think seriously about him. Knowing this, she was amazed that while she sat engrossed in the scenes enacted before her she could still be aware of Dominic's presence in the crowded theater.

When the tumultuous applause had died down at the

end of the performance, Martina surfaced from *La Bohème* to bring herself back to the present. On their way out they met Dominic and his guests and introductions were made. The cool blonde in blue was Kay Younge and the youngest of the two couples with her were her parents, Eldred and Amy Younge from New York. The other couple were a Conte and Contessa Fidelli.

Martina avoided Dominic's gaze and when Bruno paused to speak to an old friend who was passing in the foyer, Martina waited with Eunice. As she watched Dominic move on with his guests to the door of the theater, she was hating the thought of going to his house for supper.

Dominic's house was an imposing pile of mellowed Venetian stone with tall balconied windows. One approached beneath an archway in the imposing façade to a huge door and a landing platform. Dominic was in the nobly proportioned hall to greet them. Martina somehow managed to let Eunice walk up the stairs with him while she followed with Bruno. Their coats were taken by a servant at the door of the *sala* and they entered to join the glittering crowd already assembled.

The number of guests beneath the magnificent Venetian chandeliers was less than two dozen, but the noise with which everyone exchanged greetings and discussed the opera gave the impression of twice that number. They all moved to the supper table where numberous servants seated them, and Martina concluded that it was one of those parties to which no one ever refused an invitation. There were many guests, a fact which in itself contributed to a successful party. From her high-backed chair, she saw enchanting champagne-colored silk-paneled walls hung with superb paintings of old masters. Her eyes wandered to her host at the head of the table, and she wondered about his mother's paintings. *Thank goodness,* she thought, *that I'm way down the table from his eagle eyes*.

"What do you think of Venice, Miss Floyd?" asked the man seated on her right.

She turned her head to look at a brown haired, thin-featured young man about 30 with alert hazel eyes and an easy grace of manner. He was reserved, though friendly.

"Magnificent and breathtaking," she answered promptly, liking what she saw. "With so much hospitality and courtesy one can't help but feel at home." She gave a small enchanting laugh. "Not that home is as luxurious as this, by any means!"

He regarded her with awakening interest, appraising her low controlled laugh and impish smile free of coquetry.

"I should imagine you would be well received anywhere. You evidently like people, Miss Floyd, and there's no surer way of getting them to like you."

Her smile was enchantingly demure. "Are you always so clever at deduction, or is it because we are both English?" She did not wait for an answer. "How long have you been in Venice?"

"Five years. I went through college with Dominic. Two years ago I had a particularly bad accident—I smashed up my car and was pretty messed up. When I left the hospital Dominic invited me here to recuperate. When I recovered he asked me to stay on as his secretary. By that time I had grown attached to the place, so I accepted."

"I suppose, after the leisurely pace in Venice, you would find it hard to leave it."

"Not so leisurely for some of us. I doubt whether Dominic could crowd more into a day than he does already. He works hard and plays hard. I wish I had his energy."

"It will come when you completely recover," she said comfortingly.

He shook his head. "I'll never be as fit as Dominic. We're both 30, but at times I feel more like 60."

Martina's eyes were drawn to Dominic. So there was a brain behind that charming masculine façade, purpose as well as latent strength in those long, athletic limbs. She saw him throw back his head and laugh heartily at some obvious quip from his neighbor. He had a sense of humor and a capacity for being loved by many women. How many had he loved? None wholeheartedly, since he had not married. Thoughtfully, she turned again to her companion.

He had gone on to talk about water-skiing, skiing at St. Moritz, sailing and helping with the harvest on Dominic's farm in the Venetian hills.

"Marco loved it at the farm," he said. "I believe you have charge of him while the Vortolinis go away. Poor little kid!"

Martina sensed an ally in her companion. "Do you know Marco's mother, Mr.—I'm sorry, I didn't catch your name."

He grinned. "Jimmy Ward Baker. Everyone calls me Jimmy. I've met Signora Vortolini, but I don't know her intimately. Few people do in Venice. She only went out on rare occasions when she was staying with her brother-in-law. Oddly enough, she never refused an invitation from Dominic. She has stayed on his farm too. She's in the Greek islands at the moment."

"I can't understand why she didn't take her son with her."

"She'll probably come around to it in time. Family love is second nature to the Italians. Like Dominic, I'm very fond of them and I admire them greatly for their drive, enthusiasm and charm. You have to live among them to appreciate their full worth. Their theatrical gestures and quick tempers are only a veneer covering all the warm-heartedness smoldering beneath. At least she didn't leave Marco behind in Milan with her parents."

Martina was curious about this. "But why? Surely he would have been far happier staying with his grand-parents than coming to Venice where there's no place for him to play?"

His voice was a little dry. "Milan isn't the best of places in which to bring up a child. The weather is appalling—for almost half the year it's covered by fog and rain. When I was there I was surprised at the remarkable good spirits of the inhabitants despite the depressing weather."

He went on to tell her that Dominic had a villa in

Milan. An aunt of his resided there and he used it rarely on business matters. Martina enjoyed listening to him. There was something likeable about him. He might lack the driving force and tireless energy of his employer, but he was far less disturbing.

After supper the guests, satiated with good food and wine, strolled to a *sala* where the windows were flung open to the balconies overlooking the Grand Canal. Martina, escorted by Jimmy Ward Baker, found herself being guided to an open window to breathe in the sweet night air.

It was a warm calm summer evening filled with sweet sounds, the song of a gondolier as he swept by in the scented dusk, the muted sound of an orchestra from a nearby hotel and the subdued voices and laughter of a crowded launch. The launch passed and for several moments there was silence. Jimmy had lit a cigarette and now stood with his hands on the rail gazing up at the sapphire sky.

"What a lot we miss when we sleep through the dark quiet hours of the night," he remarked somewhat sadly. "It's the ideal time to stay awake to unwind from the tenseness of the day and to savor the beauty of a deserted world." The face he turned her way was suddenly boyish and eager. "What do you say to a run along the *autostrada* one night when everyone has gone to bed? I have a sports car. Can you imagine what it would be like?—You and I alone under the stars."

Martina grimaced. "Please," she begged, "I left all that behind me when I came here. My delight would be to ride in a gondola on a night like this. Far more romantic."

He flung her a challenging look. "It would be safer in a car. The driver would have to give all his attention to the road."

Martina, trying to convince herself that he was as harmless as he looked, said curiously, "Do I detect the growl of a wolf beneath that bantering exterior?"

"A has-been. Meeting someone young and sweet like you reminds me what wonderful times I had before my crash." He drew on his cigarette and blew a thoughtful line of smoke into the air. His mouth had a bitter pull.

"I bet the women you discarded don't think so. Why so bitter? Have you run out of affairs, or don't they have the same appeal any more?"

His laugh was short and hard. "Those women have had their revenge, I assure you. All my good times are in the past."

"The accident, you mean? Too bad."

"Jimmy!" the deep voice broke in: Martina tensed and turned to see Dominic framed in the entrance to the balcony. "The Marchese Condiveri would like a word with you before he leaves." He was watching them both shrewdly before he continued with his customary brevity. "It's about that thesis on the Renaissance."

Jimmy, with the air of one bemused by memories of a painful past, smiled faintly at Martina.

"I still prefer the *autostrada*, Miss Floyd. Maybe we can do both. See you later. Thanks, Dominic."

Dominic's expression instantly aroused all her antagonism. Left alone with him, her first impulse was to flee from his vibrant presence, his inner hardness and undeniable charm. But he leaned against the door, blocking her way negligently and effectively. Martina turned to look out over the canal.

"If Jimmy was inviting you to go for a drive in his car, Miss Floyd, I strongly advise you to refuse," he said, his eyes on her tantalizing profile which emphasized the sweet curve of her chin and the youthful line of her neck above the sparkle of diamonds.

"Indeed!" She turned to face him. "Is there some reason why I shouldn't?" she asked frigidly, wishing her heart was not so receptive to certain cadences in his voice.

He eyed her calmly, in no way affected by her hostile manner.

"You'll have to take my word for it. Believe me when I say I'm speaking in your interest entirely."

"I'm afraid you'll have to be more specific. I happen to like him."

"That was what I was afraid of. Women invariably like

Jimmy. He had a whale of a time with the fair sex before his accident. The women continued to flock around him after the accident until they grew tired of his complete absorption in himself. You see, Jimmy is a glutton for sympathy."

She said coldly, "I thought he was a friend of yours?"

"He is, a very close friend. I'm only saying to you what I would have said to his face." His voice became mocking. "You had a dreamy look in your eyes a moment ago. It was dangerously tinged with compassion. It could have been the magic of the Venetian night or Jimmy awakening new emotions in your womanly heart." He lifted a hand as she stiffened for an angry reply. "Please allow me to utter a word of warning. Venice would have you believe she can offer a life that contains sensations one need never weary of. She is an incurable romantic. Take this scene before us." He gestured to a small oasis of light and reflections of a mooring lamp playing upon the water. "Years ago that electric light was an oil lamp. Its tender glow gave life and movement to the old palaces and a sweet mystery to the water which this modern lighting, however skillful and effective, can't produce. The illusion of romantic grandeur had been torn away by the modern glare. So it is with impressions of people. Your untried heart responds to the illusion of the romantic grandeur. Too bad the glare of reality has to tear it away."

Martina thrust out her chin in a gesture of defiance, his mockery acting as a spark to her anger.

"What exactly are you trying to convey? That I'm some kind of romantic idiot who's ready to fall at some man's feet?"

He leaned against the window frame, his gaze humorous and infuriating.

"I'd say you'd already done so, judging by the necklace. I suppose the ring is to follow?"

Martina started. The quiet implication of his tones brought the flags of color to her cheeks.

"What business is it of yours? You can suppose what you like." She looked at him, fully aware of a sudden trembling. "At least I have the good sense not to be interested in you. You're so cold-blooded and cynical, it's pathetic!" To her everlasting shame, she felt near to tears.

His eyes narrowed, giving no sign of displeasure at her words. Instead, he said rather mildly, "Do you know, that's the last thing I'd ever imagined anyone accusing me of being. Nevertheless, I bow to your better judgment. Now, if you'll excuse me, I'll return to my guests."

He made a mocking little bow and was gone.

Alone in the scented dusk of an evening which for her was completely spoiled, Martina gazed down tremulously at her white knuckles gripping the balcony rail. During the next few moments she made herself keep her temper down and determined more than ever to exclude him rigidly from any opportunity of ever being alone with her.

She gave a start as her evening jacket was draped around her shoulders.

"Your wrap, Marty. Dominic sent me with it." Eunice smiled down at her. "He was concerned about you leaving a warm room to stand in the night air. Enjoying the view?"

"I was," Martina replied, a wealth of meaning in her words. "Are we leaving?"

"Yes, dear. Have you enjoyed it?"

Eunice sparkled, leaving no doubt about her enjoying the evening herself.

Martina thrust her arm through her friend's as they left the balcony.

"It's an evening I'll never forget," she answered, wrinkling her nose with a warm smile. It was perfectly true. As for Dominic showing concern about her by sending the wrap, she recognized that for what it was—a gesture to excuse himself for his offending remarks earlier. She resisted the impulse to confide in Eunice. Far better to forget the whole unpleasant incident. Maybe some day she would pay him back—a childish thought, though vaguely comforting.

CHAPTER FOUR

Martina was surprised how easily she fitted in with her surroundings. Marco was moved into the room next to hers; all his clothes were transferred to wardrobes and cupboards there and his small shoes were put outside Martina's door each night for one of the staff to clean. Each morning he was taken to the house next door to stay with the children of Bruno's friends leaving Eunice and Martina free to go out together. Even Bruno was content with the arrangement.

Martina began to enjoy her visit, marveling at the warm hospitality she found wherever she went, chuckling over her determined mastery of the language and delighting in the gay dinners and parties. She discovered a brightness in herself, a talent for picking up sparkling little phrases in Italian which, coupled with the mistakes she made, enchanted and endeared all who heard her. Lunch each day was more relaxed than it had been when Martina had arrived.

Eunice had practically shed her watchful unhappy air and was once again gay and vivacious. To see her friend happy again heartened Martina considerably. Bruno was still as attentive to Marco as before, but her own presence seemed to make it less obvious.

The only cloud on her horizon was the thought of Dominic Burnett di Ravenelli. He was away for a few days on business, according to Eunice. The news had brightened Martina considerably, because she didn't relish unexpected meetings with him. To her dismay, they were invited to dine with him on Thursday, the evening of his return. Martina hoped to the last minute that something would happen to prevent their meeting, but nothing did.

The dress she chose did not require any adornment for it was made of stiff white organza and had an embroidered skirt, collar and cuffs. Ever since Dominic's scathing comments about her necklace, she had felt loath to wear it. She knew she only had to tell him that it was a gift from Bruno to confound his cynicism, yet a stubborn streak kept her silent. Perhaps she was making too much of the fact that they were dining with him that evening. They would not be the only guests, she was certain, she would try to keep away from his irritating expression of censure.

The dress suited her, enhancing her slimness and giving her a look of delicate demureness. Martina surveyed her reflection in the mirror soberly. This was the real Martina Floyd, a woman who dressed simply and smartly without the aid of diamonds, and who was far removed from the world of her friend Eunice.

At a sudden knock on her door she swung around, to see Eunice enter and contemplate her for several moments.

"Why, Marty, what a delightful dress! But then you always had good taste. You look as dainty as a fairy and sweet enough to eat. I'm sure Dominic will never miss Bruno and me," she teased.

Martina was startled. "What—what do you mean, Eunice?" she asked, nervously, with strange foreboding.

"I'm awfully sorry, Marty, but I'm afraid I have to ask you to go on ahead to Dominic's. Bruno hasn't returned from his business conference in Venice. He's phoned to say he'll be delayed. I'm going to wait for him."

Martina tried to hide her dismay and smiled deprecatingly.

"Oh dear," she exclaimed. "Must I go at all? Couldn't you phone to say we can't make it? There are sure to be other guests, and I hardly know the man."

Eunice shrugged. "We're the only guests. Dominic's house party broke up several days ago before he went away. I can't let him down; it's too short notice for him to ask anyone else. I know you aren't thrilled at going alone—though why, I can't imagine. Most girls would give anything for a date with him. And he's an excellent host, as you know," She laughed and patted Martina's smooth cheek. "Cheer up, We'll be over later, I've phoned to tell him you're on the way, Come and have a drink in the *sala* with me before you leave. It will give you Dutch courage." Her smile was suddenly mischievous, "Dominic is sending transport, He'll probably send a gondola now he knows you're coming alone,"

"As long as he isn't in it," Martina said darkly,

Eunice laughed, "Get away with you! I know you're going to enjoy your evening. See you in the *sala* when you're ready."

Half-heartedly, Martina collected her wrap and evening bag. It wouldn't surprise her if Eunice and Bruno never showed up at Dominic's. Not that she blamed Eunice, who she felt should take advantage of having a few hours alone with her husband. She herself was with them most of the time they spent together, And Eunice was fighting to save her marriage. As for herself, she was happy to be able to help her to that end, though she wished she was dining with anyone rather than Dominic Burnett di Ravenelli.

A shadow passed her face as she thought of Marco sleeping in the adjoining room. Poor child, to be the innocent cause of his father's death and now a threat to a happy marriage. Martina walked quietly into his room to see if he was all right before she left. Tenderly she looked down at the cherubic face, the dark silken fringe of lashes incredibly long against the soft contours of his baby cheeks flushed in sleep. His curly hair clung damply to his forehead and one rounded arm was flung out across the pillow. She bent down and gently rearranged the bedclothes, holding her breath as he muttered, "*Papà.*"

With a catch at her heart, Martina realized he must have been dreaming about his father. Poor little guy! She stood for a while until he settled down, then left the room with misty eyes.

Instead of a gondola, Dominic had sent a motor launch to collect her. It was driven by a very handsome Italian in his early twenties with dark eyes which he certainly knew how to use, for they rested boldly upon Martina in open admiration, yet sobered by an imperative courtesy.

"*Buona sera, signorina,*" he said. "Signor Ravenelli said there was but one guest to pick up, your very charming self."

His audacious grin was so blatant that she had to smile. She hesitated before taking his hand and reluctantly allowed his strength to steady her as she stepped on board. They stood poised for a few moments with hands clasped before she disengaged her own. Taking her seat was a cue for him to go, but he was in no hurry.

Martina was amused when she saw the reason. A number of women in a passing launch were eyeing him appraisingly and he lingered in order not to deprive them of their pleasure too soon. He flashed them a charming smile, reminding Martina of the gondoliers she had seen swaggering down the Riva degli Schiavoni each morning with their oars resting lightly on their shoulders and their straw hats set at a provocative angle. This young man was probably one of them.

When he eventually started the engine she avoided his eyes, assuming interest in a distant boat. They sped along the illuminated canal passing boatloads of carefree people until they reached the Palazzo Ravenelli.

Martina was admitted at once by a courteous footman and she stepped into the hall, wishing she was already on her way back.

With butterflies in her stomach she watched Dominic come down the stairs with nonchalant easy grace. The sharp cut of his evening dress accentuated his dark eyes and strong features. His skin had a deep bronze tinge from the sun and he walked with a masculine strength of purpose to bow over her hand in conventional greeting.

"Good evening, Miss Floyd," he murmured politely.

She refused to be impressed by his brilliant smile, borrowing his coolness as she lowered his gaze.

"Eunice begs you to accept her apologies. She'll be along later with Bruno."

He raised an eyebrow humorously. "So I have heard.

Your tone implies that you devoutly hope she does." He cast a narrowed glance at her as they crossed the hall, his fingers barely touching her elbow. "Does the idea of dining alone with me alarm you?"

Martina stiffened at his bantering tone. He was baiting her, of course, delighting in a situation in which he definitely held the advantage.

"We're practically strangers," she pointed out.

"Are we? Then it's time we remedied that." He slanted her an amused smile.

Martina felt her color deepening. "There's no reason to. I won't forget that if it weren't for Eunice and Bruno I wouldn't have been invited."

"But I do entertain women friends on their own from time to time, and as long as I remember I've never invited anyone I didn't care for. I assure you, Miss Floyd, that as much as I like Eunice and Bruno, I would never invite a friend of theirs I didn't care for. May I take your wrap?"

They had entered the *sala* and his cool fingers brushed her neck as he relieved her of her jacket and gave it to a waiting footman. Then he piloted her across the room to a comfortable armchair and moved to the ornate sideboard to mix some drinks. Martina watched his long lean hands handling the glasses and bottles efficiently. There was a relaxed precision about his every move which emphasized his power. When he turned suddenly, two drinks in hand, she knew he had been aware of her scrutiny. She saw again that glint in his eyes which to her seemed openly mocking.

"Actually, I'm enchanted to have you dine with me. I would like to compliment you on your dress. It's perfectly charming." He handed her a glass and touched it with his own. "Cheers, I hope you're as hungry as I am. This will be my first meal since early this morning."

There was a spark of humor in the eyes meeting hers over his glass and she was consumed by a sudden shyness.

She took a sip and lowered her glass. "You did say eight o'clock?"

"I did, and like the perfect guest you arrive with time to spare." He consulted his watch. "We'll give Bruno and Eunice a quarter of an hour."

He did not seat himself but remained standing by the fireplace as he asked how much she had seen of Venice. Something of the thrill she felt about Venice shone in her eyes as she recounted the treasures she had seen; gradually she began to unwind. By the time they sat down to dinner she didn't know if she was glad or sorry that Eunice and Bruno had not arrived.

The meal was not the ordeal she had anticipated. Dominic had set out to be the perfect host. The food was delicious, the footmen silent and swift in their duties, and the wine was excellent. To each topic of conversation Dominic introduced, Martina replied intelligently. She knew he liked his women chic, elegant, adoring and not given to idle chatter and that she qualified for the last, being content to listen to his deep attractive voice. His conversation was spiced with amusing incidents from his early life in Venice. He had an endearing sense of humor and gave Martina the impression that only in his own surroundings, in the place he called home could she learn to know the real man behind the reserved front.

One savory course followed another. The evening had a peculiar quality about it, as if every detail was being stamped indelibly on her memory. Dominic kept the conversation on general topics and she seconded his efforts, aware of being won over gradually by his charm.

When the meal ended Eunice and Bruno still hadn't appeared. Martina felt she had done well without their moral support, so much so that her conscientious temperament made her suddenly feel ashamed of the frigid front she had put up when she arrived that evening. After all, Dominic had gone out of his way to be charming in spite of her rudeness. Politely refusing a cigarette from the box he offered, she wondered how to make the apology that was certainly called for.

It was Dominic himself who paved the way. During the short silence which followed, he reached for a cigar. As he lit it, he glanced at her half-averted face, extinguished the flame and returned the lighter to his pocket. His eyes narrowed perceptively,

"A penny for your thoughts," he said.

Startled, she raised her flushed face. "I was regretting the rudeness with which I greeted you this evening," she admitted frankly. "I'm sorry, I'm not usually like that."

"Why apologize?" he answered with obvious indifference, although his dark eyes studied her high color critically. "You very kindly offered to fill in the gap." Having curtly closed the subject, he said, "Your coming alone gives us time to see the paintings I mentioned when I saw you last."

"Your mother's?"

"Yes, and other ones." He leaned back in his chair as he savored his cigar. "I show my mother's pictures to only a chosen few. I think you'll enjoy them."

Martina remembered Eunice admitting that she had never seen them. It was silly to feel warmly flattered, but she did. She put down her table napkin, suddenly aware of a painting of the Grand Canal on the wall behind his back. He followed her gaze, then slowly turned his head again toward her.

"You like Carapaccio?"

"Yes. I adore his paintings of the gondoliers," she said.

The gondolier on this canvas, a flamboyant young man, wore a provocative cap on his shoulder-length hair and sported a feather over one ear. His tunic had the fashionable slashed sleeves of the period. His gondola, however, like the others in the scene around him, was a tiny painted cockleshell, not at all like the dignified black ones of the present day.

She remarked upon it. Dominic, leaning forward to put out the butt of his cigar, said sagely, "You're very observant, as you must be with everyone you meet. Me, for instance. I have a feeling I don't meet with your approval in some way." He rose to his feet abruptly. "Shall we go see the paintings?"

It had been on the tip of her tongue to say she knew the

dislike was mutual. But she walked silently beside him, reluctant to spoil an evening she was beginning to enjoy. He said no more. The picture gallery was bathed in a rosy glow of light and the walls were elaborately designed to frame the painting which ran the whole length of the room.

Paintings merged with elegant furnishings in a scene of artistic splendor and the next hour was one of pure pleasure for Martina. She moved slowly beside Dominic discussing each work of art, and his interest added to her joy. She lingered over the last one, a picture of children and dogs.

"I imagine it would be a letdown to paint ordinary things after seeing all these masterpieces," she said with a self-conscious little laugh.

The look she slanted up at him was impish and without guile. She was unprepared for the little tingling shock she felt when her eyes met his intent gaze. Swiftly she lowered her lashes. He had drawn her out of her antipathy without her being aware of it.

"I'd say they could be an inspiration to an artist," he commented with a twinkle.

"Did they inspire your mother?"

"Mother was painting long before she came to live in Venice. She studied for two years in Paris on a scholarship she won when she was in her teens. Some of her work of the English countryside has been compared with that of Constable. My stepfather, the Conte di Ravenelli, had the top floor of this house converted into a studio for her."

Slowly they strolled out of the gallery and along a corridor to a charming room where pictures lined delicately tinted paneled walls. Martina drifted along admiring beautifully painted landscapes, still life and portraits.

The man moving silently beside her was forgotten until she came to a portrait of him as a boy. There was no mistaking the arrogant tilt of the well-shaped head, the look of dogged determination on his face as he dug in the sand, apparently for worms to go fishing. Her heart lurched painfully, but she passed on, making no comment.

When she had seen them all she raised clear shining eyes filled with appreciation of work even the critics had raved about.

"Thank you for showing me your mother's paintings," she said sincerely. "I've enjoyed seeing them immensely. I don't think I'm half as talented as she was. I'm sure she must have been a lovely person."

"She was," he replied laconically. They walked back to the *sala* where she sat down while he poured her a drink. "One for the road." He handed her a glass of sparkling red wine with a mocking gleam in his eyes. "I trust you've enjoyed your evening."

"Very much, thanks." She forced herself to meet his gaze, which stirred her like a touch. "I feel drunk with looking at so much beauty!"

"A good way to become inebriated," he said dryly, "providing there are no after-effects."

Martina was too bemused to understand what he meant. Uneasily, she began to realize that his presence was proving too disturbing to her peace of mind. She was feeling not like a guest, but like a woman who was vulnerable to the nearness of a charming man.

Barely sipping her drink, she glanced at her watch. "I really ought to be going. It's getting late."

"Finish your drink. The air is cool on the water at night. The wine will keep you warm." His smile was suddenly teasing. "I promise not to take advantage if it makes you tipsy."

Martina obeyed only because she had to get away. The odd feeling she was experiencing was not the wine affecting her, neither was it a surfeit of paintings. It was something to do with the man looking at her with that gleam of satirical humor she was beginning to hate. He affected her as no other man had ever done in her life. He seemed like the embodied symbol of fate swooping down to capture her unwary heart. Putting down her empty glass, she rose to her feet. She allowed him to help her on with her evening jacket, shrinking inside herself to avoid his touch, and walked with him down to the hall below.

"You have no objection to my seeing you home?" he asked politely before opening the heavy door.

"None at all," she answered, wondering if he intended to run the launch himself.

He swung open the door, and she stepped out into the night. The next moment she gave an exclamation of surprise.

"A gondola!" she cried.

She was relieved to see that the gondolier who was plumping up the cushions was not the bold young man who had brought her in the launch. This gondolier was around thirty and far more sober.

"*Buona sera, signorina, signore,*" he said, courteously.

"*Buona sera,* Roberto."

Dominic steadied her as she boarded and took the seat beside her. Settling in her corner, Martina listened to the liquid sound of the pole stabbing the water as the black boat glided silently away. Suddenly Dominic reached out his long arm and took a rose from a small silver vase.

"For you, Miss Floyd," he said, slipping it into the top buttonhole of her evening jacket.

The masculine fragrance of cigar smoke assailed her nostrils as he leaned across the space between them. His nearness caused an authentic stir to her senses. From their first meeting she had felt his magnetism as something tangible. Now she had to use all her will power to resist the urge to touch the sunburned cheek so dangerously close to her own.

"Thanks," she said, leaning back in her corner and trying to quell the heavy beat of her heart.

Her whole consciousness was steeped in the wonder of his presence, which was awakening the primitive side of her, singling them out as a man and a woman with needs. And Martina, who never would have believed it could happen so quickly, was unashamedly aching to feel his arms around her.

Could it be as he had said, that Venice was a Circe who filled one with romantic yearnings? Dully she looked across the water where an oversized moon was slowly shedding silver splinters on its surface. The spell Venice had cast over her must have gone right over the head of the man who sat beside her for despite their physical closeness their emotional isolation was complete. In the prolonged silence which neither seemed inclined to break Martina's sigh was barely audible. But Dominic heard it.

Leaning forward, he whispered tantalizingly, "What was that sigh for, longing or pleasure? To appreciate a ride in a gondola one has to be young and in love or an incurable romantic."

The mocking inflection in his voice stirred her to answer, "I'm sure you think that I'm all three."

"Undoubtedly. I wouldn't be surprised if Roberto shares my opinion. Any moment now he should burst into song."

Martina clenched her hands, wondering if the moonlight was making her hypersensitive to his taunts. "And why shouldn't he sing? If he does it will prove he's not a hardened cynic like yourself."

She was surprised how light she made her voice sound when she was burning with indignation inside.

Dominic chuckled as Roberto broke softly into song. "Depends on which way you look at it. He might be gallantly covering up our conversation, taking it for granted that I'm making love to you."

Martina turned to meet his mocking gaze, feeling weakly inadequate to deal with his teasing mood. His challenge, if challenge it was, made her seek for words to screen her own feelings.

"What more delightful than that you should point out the romantic places of interest to me while Roberto serenades us?"

He smiled in the gloom with a mocking little bow.

"Your wish is my command. What more appropriate than the place we're now approaching?" Lifting a lazy hand, he gestured toward a palace looming ethereally out of the water to their left. "Here you see the Palazzo

Rezzonico where Robert Browning died while visiting his son."

But Martina was not going to let him have everything his own way. "A romantic figure," she murmured. "I suppose the wicked Byron was more in your line?"

He regarded her unabashedly. "He certainly enjoyed his life, although his girlfriends weren't to my taste." He indicated a palace on his right. "There you see the Palazzo Mocenigo where he resided with a wild, beautiful Venetian named Margarita Gogni, and 14 servants." When Martina turned eagerly to see it, he went on, "It wasn't as romantic as it sounds. Margarita had flashing black eyes and a temper to match. She also had a punch like a prizefighter, which she didn't hesitate to use on her rivals. Byron grew tired of her jealous tirades and told her to leave. She retaliated by attacking him with a table knife before throwing herself off the palace steps into the canal. She was rescued and sent home to her husband."

Martina gazed at the palace, imagining the luckless Margarita flinging herself off the steps into the water rather than leave her lover. A cloud passing over the moon intensified the mysterious shadows along its walls and she shivered at the beauty, harshness and cruelty here.

"Poor Margarita," she said almost to herself. "She must have loved him very much. Was he hurt?"

Dominic raised an amused brow, "You sound concerned. He escaped with a thumb wound. Are you relieved?" He laughed in his easy way. "You accused me just now of preferring the amorous Byron to Browning, yet you show concern for Byron. You never asked how Browning died."

"He died when he was in his seventies as the result of a severe chill. Is it true that he never actually lived here in Venice nor wrote poetry here?"

"Yes. The story goes that he only paid a few weeks' visit to the Palazzo in order to see his son." Casually, he drew a cigarette case from his pocket, flicked it open and offered it to her.

Martina refused politely, watching him light a cigarette and return lighter and case to his pocket. He continued to smoke in silence. It seemed to Martina he had nothing more to say.

Roberto still sang softly, a haunting Italian song which Martina felt she should know. But she was too aware of the man at her side to think about it. How easily he had taken her heart and awakened her to the most passionate emotion. Yet how little she really knew him, withdrawn as he was beneath that cynical air of detachment, that desire to be alone. Womanlike, she asked herself why. She was still thinking about it when they reached Bruno's house.

Roberto swung the gondola against the platform and Dominic got to his feet after discarding the butt of his cigarette. Nervously, Martina moved too quickly and her foot slipped. She would have fallen overboard if Dominic had not caught her in his arms.

"Steady!" he said softly above her ear.

Martina was struck by the irony of the word. She was anything but steady, with her heart beating and her nerves tingling with his nearness as he held her clasped against him. Too shaken to be conscious of anything but the painful pressure of his arms, she leaned for blissful moments against him.

Was he loath to release her or was she clinging to him in an aching need for the haven of his arms? She was in no condition to think clearly. Then she was standing alone on the landing platform with the cool night air striking a chill right into her heart.

"I'm sorry," she said weakly. "I might have caused an accident."

He waved her confusion away. "You slipped. The important thing is that you're not hurt." He gazed down into her flushed face with a frown of concern. "You haven't turned an ankle or anything?"

"No—no, I haven't." Martina gave a wavering smile. He was much too near. "Thanks for a delightful evening."

The charming smile came into play. He offered her his

hand. "Surely I ought to thank you for your company. Good night, Miss Floyd. Sleep well."

There was a palpable silence as his fingers closed strongly over her small hand. She would have given anything if instead he had taken her in his arms.

CHAPTER FIVE

When Martina was preparing for her holiday in Venice she had been too excited to think of any unusual outcome. The visit was every bit as wonderful as she had expected. But she had never expected to fall in love so quickly and so shatteringly. The man's easy arrogance and slight antagonism had captured her senses from their first meeting. She, Martina Floyd, the invulnerable in affairs of the heart, had capitulated without a struggle. The tragedy of it was that Dominic was not aware of what he had done unconsciously. There had been no amorous glances, no velvety words or advances, only a cool aloofness that had piqued her interest.

She only had to close her eyes to conjure up a picture of his magnificent carriage, his sunburned fitness which, schooled by a disciplined grace, set him apart from other men she had known. An inexpressible thrill shot through her when she recalled those brief moments in his arms. Her capacity for deep emotion concerning the opposite sex had lain dormant until that moment. Now it spilled over like an uncovered spring, the great depth of feeling making her suddenly afraid.

That evening Martina lay awake for hours before she went to sleep. The first thing she saw the following morning was the rose Dominic had slipped into the buttonhole of her evening jacket. She had put it in a vase on her dressing table. She gazed at it for a long time, strangely divided by joy and pain. Then gradually common sense asserted itself. What an idiot she was to spare a second thought over a small gift given by a host to his guest as an act of courtesy.

"Miss Floyd! *Signorina?*"

The small voice trembled on an uncertain note, but she heard it and smiled.

"I'm here, Marco," she called reassuringly, "Come in."

He appeared in the doorway, a small pyjama-clad figure hugging a teddy bear.

He hesitated on the threshold. "And Tito?" he asked, holding up the dilapidated toy.

She nodded and her blood ran cold. One of the teddy bear's ears was badly scorched. With a catch at her heart, Martina knew she was staring at the toy that Marco had run back for on the night of the fire, the fire which had caused his father's death. Tears blocked her throat, for it was only in that moment that she began to understand Mia's rejection of her son. Marco, along with the scorched, beloved toy, was a constant reminder of all she had lost.

Dimly, she was aware of Marco climbing on to her bed and snuggling down in the hollow of her arm. She pulled her thoughts together and noticed there was no sign of his toy snake.

She hugged him to her. "Where's Russo? Still asleep?" she teased.

Marco surveyed her solemnly with large dark eyes. "Tito does not like Russo. Bears do not like snakes—Zia Eunice said so. She said that was why Tito ran away and we could not find him. He was afraid."

Gently, she pushed the dark clustering curls back from his forehead.

"When did Zia Eunice say this?"

"The day you bought me Russo. Tito was not there when I went to bed. Zia Eunice said he would never come back because Russo was there and she was sure I would rather have Russo than Tito. But I wanted Tito too." He looked down at his toy tenderly. "I know Tito would not leave me. Would you, Tito? Zio Bruno found him, though." Marco's small face beamed with hero whorship for his beloved uncle.

Smiling down into his dark eyes, Martina realized that Eunice must have hidden the toy which had inadvertently cost Paolo his life. No doubt Marco had been asking for it on the night before he moved into the room adjoining her own, although Russo had taken his mind off it temporarily. As far as she could gather Marco, while she was out, had awakened asking for the toy. Eunice would refuse to give it to him, but Bruno must have insisted upon returning it to the child, who cried himself to sleep clutching the toy; his face was still streaked. Poor Marco! Martina hoped Eunice and Bruno had not quarreled over him.

She bent her head to kiss the tip if his nose. "Some day, Marco," she said gently, "You will find something else to take the place of Tito. When you are a big boy, of course."

"*Io non capisco, signorina.*"

Martina smiled. Marco resorted to his native tongue when he did not understand.

"Forget it," she said, hugging him. "And now we'd better get washed and dressed before Zia Eunice wonders what's happened to us."

But they had finished breakfast before Eunice appeared, to shoo Marco away with Stefano. She refused breakfast, accepted coffee which Martina poured and lit a cigarette.

"Bruno is dressing," she said. "He's taking Marco with him to Torcello this morning. A friend is having a villa built there and he's promised to keep an eye on the project while the owner is away. Sorry about last night. Did you enjoy it?"

"Very much," Martina answered warily, sensing that Eunice was in one of her moods.

"Did Dominic show you his mother's paintings?"

"Yes. They're marvelous. She was a gifted artist."

Eunice gave a shrug of indifference. "You ought to feel highly honored. You've seen something I never have." She drew a rasping breath. "Frankly, the more I see of men, the more I like women!"

"Oh, come now, Eunice, I don't suppose Dominic thought you would be interested or he would have shown the paintings to you. As for Bruno, he's a dear. Don't forget he recently lost a beloved brother. Apart from the shock there must be times when he feels pretty miserable."

"Miserable?" Eunice echoed. "What about me? I was

furious with Bruno last night because he refused to leave Marco to keep our dinner date with Dominic. I've been trying for weeks to get that teddy bear away from Marco. I've hidden it time after time, but he always gets it back. The toy reptile you bought him seemed to have taken his fancy to the point of forgetting his teddy bear. However, he woke up last night after you'd gone and asked for the teddy. I had hidden it and wouldn't have given it back to him if Bruno hadn't arrived to find him in a flood of tears. He can't bear to see Marco cry, so he demanded to know where I'd hidden it." She shrugged exasperatedly. "What could I do? I told him. He gave the toy to Marco and insisted upon staying with him until he went to sleep. By then it was too late to join you and Dominic. We had a fight and I told Bruno he thought more of Marco than he did of me."

"Oh dear!" Martina showed her dismay. "What did he say to that?"

"Denied it, of course."

Martina nodded. "I guessed something like that had happened when I saw Marco with his teddy this morning. It's a very awkward situation for all of you, Mia included."

Eunice gulped down some coffee. "You can say that again! Frankly, Marty, if you hadn't been here, I would have walked out on Bruno last night. I've had as much as I can take regarding Marco!"

Martina was struck by the hardness of her friend's expression. Painfully it occurred to her how often she had seen the same expression when Eunice used to speak of her brothers and sister. The woman had a chip on her shoulder regarding having children thrust upon her. With a lightness she was far from feeling, Martina tried to pour oil on troubled waters.

"My dear Eunice," she said, "your own troubles are nothing compared to Mia's and Marco's. How do you think he's going to feel if he ever finds out how his father died? Naturally the boy has a need for something belonging to him since he's lost the love of both his parents. That's why he clings to Bruno."

Eunice narrowed china-blue eyes through the smoke haze from her cigarette,

"You aren't deserting me for Marco, are you, Marty? I know what you're trying to say, but I can't manufacture any feeling for Marco when he's coming between my husband and myself. At least I'm honest about it."

Martina, sipped her coffee. Sturdily, she said, "You're being a little too honest. Why not play your feelings down a bit? I think you're making too much of a situation which is sure to resolve itself in time. This problem of the teddy bear won't exist when Marco begins to feel secure, As for transferring my affections, I could never do that, You've always been as close as a sister to me." She smiled, a coaxing warm smile which reached out tenderly,

Eunice had to smile back, Despite her mood, Eunice looked very attractive in a white silk pant suit that showed off her honey-tanned throat, well-cared-for complexion and flaxen hair,

"I'm sorry," she said, tacitly excusing herself,

Martina grimaced. "That's the trouble. You're starting to go around looking sorry for yourself, It's not the way to bring Bruno back into the fold."

Eunice shook her head as though at her own shortcomings. "I know Bruno is heartbroken at Paolo's death and I'll do what I can, of course, Only he's so dedicated to Marco's well-being. , , ,"

"Thoughtful is a truer word, and more generous on your part," Martina cut in, "Share Bruno's compassion for a bewildered little boy and you will make an ally of your husband instead of antagonizing him,"

Martina watched her friend's reaction to her words, wondering if she was being wise in interfering. She had no wish to cause a rift between herself and Eunice. She was too fond of her, But Martina possessed a stubborn streak which insisted on making her see both sides of a problem. Her heart ached for Marco, and it worried her profoundly to think that some day he might discover he had been the innocent cause of his father's death. Eunice was her prime concern; it showed in her face as Eunice reached a hand out across the table to cover her own.

"You make me feel like a heel, Marty. I'm afraid I'm not myself these days," she said apologetically. "You're right, I know I should talk to Bruno about the way I feel, but somehow I can't. It's too deep inside me." She gave a small hollow laugh. "It's different talking to you. Confidences come easily between us because we grew up exchanging them. You haven't changed a bit. You're still as sweet and understanding as ever." Eunice crushed out her cigarette. "Here I go loading you with my troubles! Let's forget it. What's your program for today? Anything special in mind?"

"I saw some very pretty sandals when I was looking in the stores the other day. I'd like to get them for Mommy." Suddenly Martina smiled mischievously. "What about us going over to Torcello afterwards to see what Bruno and Marco are up to? Besides, I'd like to see the house being built. Should be interesting."

It was a beautiful morning when they set out for the stores. There had been rain during the night, silken summer rain which had dried quickly in the sun, giving the air that crystal quality which endows a sense of well-being and cheerfulness. Martina bought the sandals for her mother as well as several other presents and they enjoyed a pleasant break over a cup of coffee.

The journey to Torcello, which took a little over half an hour, brought them to some steps leading to a landing stage. Looking around Martina saw flat uninteresting country disfigured with the ruins of churches and houses. Thick undergrowth forced its way through derelict court-yards in a way she felt was depressing, but she enjoyed the novelty of exploring unknown territory.

They took a path along a canal past the ruins of an old monastery. There was no sign of life, until a bend in the road brought them to some stalls at the side of the road where women were displaying their wares to tourists. When Eunice asked directions to the building site, they were shown an unbeaten track and open fields.

The going was rough; tangled vines caught in their clothes and hair. Martina found it fun, but Eunice wasn't amused. Her hairdo was ruined and she almost had hysterics when they found a weed-covered pond directly in their path.

Wryly Martina mused how much she and her friend had grown apart since the old days. They had spent days out roughing it with their brothers, enjoying the tousled freedom, the wind in their hair and the taste of salt from the sea on their lips. Now Eunice had forsaken those joys for more sophisticated ones and had lost part of her sense of humor on the way.

"It's all right for you. You're enjoying it," she grumbled when Martina disentangled her from a tenacious bramble. "Being disheveled suits you, but I look and feel a scarecrow."

"Bruno will adore your tousled look, so stop worrying. You're still the most beautiful blonde on the islands," Martina hastened to reassure her.

So they plunged on. Finally, to protect their faces from the brambles, they had to bend low and fight their way to a clearing. To their left was a road which would have brought them straight to the building site. What they had done, much to Eunice's disgust, was to take a short cut.

They were met by the sounds of hammering and a child's laughter. Straight ahead they saw a villa in the course of construction; workers were moving about industriously. There was no sign of Bruno. Then they saw him with Marco, sitting on an improvised seesaw—a long plank balanced on a stone.

Martina felt guilty about taking them by surprise and trespassing on their enjoyment, but Eunice went forward. Bruno saw them, lowered Marco down on his end of the plank to the ground and came forward to meet them.

"This is indeed a surprise," he said with a frown of amusement at his wife, who was unaware of two twigs sticking out of her hair. "You're sprouting horns, *tesoro*," he chuckled, removing them gently. "Thank heaven they are only twigs!"

Martina, following his gaze, gave a burst of quiet laughter. But Eunice refused to see the humor of it. She stiffened indignantly.

"Bruno!" she cried.

This was too much for Bruno. He threw back his head and roared with laughter. "Do not be angry, *cara mia*," he murmured cajolingly, with a look of possessive pride. "I would love you just the same with horns on your head, *mia bella*."

He threw an arm around her shoulders and they walked across the building site to meet the workers. Marco, disappointed at their intrusion, was mollified by the slab of chocolate which Martina slid into his hand. She thoroughly enjoyed the next half hour touring the half-built villa while Bruno explained the layout of all the rooms.

They lunched at an inn, unpretentious on the outside but pleasing within. A modern bar and sophisticated interior blended with the Byzantine design. Bruno was evidently well known to the proprietor, who greeted him warmly and had his wife take them upstairs to washrooms fitted with hot and cold water. Soon they were sitting down to an excellent meal.

The proprietor and two waiters attended them courteously. A tourist boat plus a few private launches had apparently just arrived, for the place was filling up rapidly. The pleasant aroma of appetizing dishes mingled with the tinkling of glasses and the subdued murmur of voices. Marco's amusingly deep voice sounded staccato when he spoke.

"There is Zio Dominic!" he exclaimed.

Martina turned her head to see Dominic about to sit down with three companions at a table some distance away from their own. On hearing his name, he turned with an amused tilt of his lips and lifted a lazy hand which included them all. Then a few hurried words brought one of the waiters to their table.

"Signor Burnett di Ravenelli will be delighted if you will join him later on the terrace for coffee," he informed them with a polite bow.

For the rest of the meal, Martina's gaze was drawn continually to the back of Dominic's wide shoulders. She had recognized his companions as the Americans she had met at the opera, Eldred and Amy Younge and their daughter, Kay. She caught the clear-cut line of his profile as he turned to talk to the woman at his side. They were evidently good friends, perhaps more than good friends.

Well, his choice was a wide one. There was Mia, who was now free to marry again if she wished, and this gorgeous blonde who wore no ring—not to mention all the daughters of ambitious mothers who attended his parties hopefully.

Knowing this, Martina argued to herself, should be enough for her to put him out of her mind once and for all. At the same moment she could not resist the opportunity she had to watch him unobserved, smitten with the tenderness which comes at the sight of a loved one. Wistfully, her eyes traced the hint of calm strength in the masculine jut of his nose and the air of sternness in the determined jaw. She felt a sense of longing which she dismissed by joining in the conversation at her table.

The restless feeling Dominic's presence never failed to arouse in her was dominant. And it was not until lunch was over and they went out onto the terrace to wait for him and his party that she began to feel more or less composed. Carefully she seated herself at the far end of a curved arrangement of chairs overlooking a garden, with Bruno, Marco and Eunice between her and the expected party.

They arrived with Eldred and Amy Younge taking the two nearest chairs, Kay following with Dominic at the end. The Younges praised the quality of their lunch, which they agreed was equal to any firstclass hotel. Eunice, now fully recovered from the rough journey to the building site, gave an amusing account of their struggles. She praised Martina's fortitude and adventurous spirit, saying she would recommend her friend as a good traveling companion.

Martina became the target of all eyes, flushed hotly and wished Eunice would forget her presence. Dominic, however, with a sceptical gleam in his eyes reached inside his jacket for cigarettes.

"You surprise me," he drawled. "I would have said you were the hardy one, Eunice. Miss Floyd has the delicate air of needing protection. She's admitted she's not the sporty type."

Eunice laughed, leaned forward to take a cigarette from the case he offered and said without malice, "Marty has plenty of courage and the capacity to enjoy life with a healthy contempt for conventions." She gave a wry smile, "I find marriage has inhibited me in that respect."

"What about you, Miss Floyd? Do you expect marriage to tame you?"

Mockingly, Dominic captured her gaze and again Martina was aware of all eyes being focused upon her curiously.

"I've never given it a thought," she admitted honestly, "While I fail to see that marriage would alter me in any way, I certainly wouldn't want to lose my own identity in that of my husband."

"No?" Dominic challenged, his eyes holding her captive until she felt they were the only two present, "Surely it would depend on the success of the marriage? I'd say you're the kind to love wholeheartedly. In which case you would inevitably lose a little of your own identity to someone else."

She had only one answer for him. Unasked she had already given part of herself to him. She could hardly tell him so and hoped with all her heart he would never know, With a dull ache inside her, Martina saw the waiter arrive with coffee and the subject was dropped.

When everyone was served, interest became centered on Marco who, wedged between Bruno's knees, was drinking lemonade through a straw. Kay said he was cute and her parents agreed. They were given an abridged version of the tragedy by Bruno who, conscious of Marco's presence, merely stated that his brother Paolo had perished in the fire at his villa. Then he tactfully steered the conversation to Mia, who he said was staying at his villa in Greece.

The Americans were interested, for Greece was to be their next port of call. Bruno said they were quite welcome to stay at his villa if they wished; Mia would enjoy their company.

Martina wondered if the Americans were on a world tour or if they intended to return to Venice. From their conversation she had gathered that Dominic met them abroad. There was no doubt that they were wealthy people and very much taken with Dominic. Kay Younge was a beautiful woman and Dominic, like most men, was susceptible to beauty. Also he appeared to enjoy her company.

Bruno was the first to stand up and everyone followed suit but not before the Americans had invited them to a farewell party they were giving that evening at their hotel. Martina was not too excited about it. Dominic was going and she would have preferred to keep out of his way. She had nothing against the Younges; Eldred and Amy were charming, friendly people. As for their daughter Kay, Martina had the impression she had been spoiled by her doting parents.

She was also keenly interested in Dominic. Martina noticed it that evening when, with Bruno and Eunice, she attended their farewell dinner. Kay was seated between Dominic and a young American. The latter who had the look of open spaces stamped all over him was bewildered at Kay's attempts to play him off against Dominic. Martina felt sorry for the man. The woman must be blind if she thought Dominic could be caught so easily. He was far too wise to be taken in by such obvious overtures.

If the Younges were anxious for their beloved daughter to make a good match it would have to be with someone more gullible than the handsome, experienced Dominic. Kay's intentions were obvious, but Dominic's were not. While being a man of great courtesy and charm, he never gave way to emotion nor did he show the slightest sign of repressing it. He was charmingly polite to Kay and she played up to him, aware that with her money, background and looks she was as good a catch as any woman in Venice.

From her place down the table with Bruno and Eunice, Martina watched the little drama with a tight feeling around her heart. He was worthy of a better woman than

Kay, who until she had matured wouldn't make anyone a good wife. The petulant, sullen look around her mouth was evidence of that. It was useless to remind herself that Dominic could marry whom he chose; she, Martina, had only the gifts and graces of youth and a capacity for caring deeply for her fellow beings to compete with Kay's heap of worldly goods and social standing.

There was dancing after dinner, which she enjoyed. It seemed she had danced with everyone except Dominic when she finally went to the cloakroom to repair her makeup. She had combed her hair and was flicking imaginary hairs from the shoulders of her dress when a woman walked into the mirrored room. Kay Younge's eyes darted toward her as she began to make up her face. Neither spoke with each waiting for the other to make a move in that direction.

"Miss Floyd, just a moment."

The high-pitched drawl had a note of contained politeness hardly conducive to the sproutings of friendship. Martina turned on her way to the door to gaze into hard blue eyes which were more curious than friendly.

"Yes?" she replied serenely. She had worn the white crochet dress and Bruno's gift. Now she was glad she had decided to wear the diamonds as she intercepted Kay's glance and the more pointed look at her ringless hand.

"Have you known Signor Burnett di Ravenelli long?" Kay wanted to know.

"No," Martina replied laconically.

Kay turned to the mirror and patted her blonde hair. "But you have met Signor Vortolini's sister-in-law Mia, haven't you? I've heard she's very beautiful."

"No, I haven't met the lady," Martina said pleasantly.

Kay, passing a beautifully manicured forefinger over butterfly brows, met her eyes in the mirror. "An awful tragedy, wasn't it—and such a sweet little boy."

"Yes, it was."

In spite of an effort to repress her feelings, Martina felt a growing antagonism for this young woman who was making conversation only to satisfy her curiosity about

Dominic. She did not feel bad about it, for she strongly suspected the antagonism was mutual, a jealous aversion and nothing more.

Kay could have no idea of how she herself felt about Dominic. She would never see Martina as a rival, although she would regard Signora Vortolini as one—hence the probing. Undaunted, Kay inquired further as she replaced her makeup in an expensive gold evening bag which matched her golden slippers: "Don't you think Dominic is the most exciting man in Venice? So excitingly handsome with that marvelous figure and those Latin features! One would never guess he'd been born and educated in England. Of course, his mother was a well-known beauty in her day. I've seen a miniature of her. His father was handsome too, belonged to the peerage or something." The hard blue eyes flicked again over Martina's slim figure, demure despite the added glamor of Bruno's necklace. "Do you have a boyfriend, Miss Floyd?" She gave a small laugh. "How silly of me to ask, when you're not wearing anyone's ring."

"Yes, it is, isn't it?" Martina replied impishly, deciding to keep the woman guessing. She was tempted to giggle at Kay's puzzled look. Instead, she reached for the door, having a sudden distaste for the conversation and wishing the evening was over. Dominic had told her he showed his mother's paintings to few people. Yet he had shown a miniature of his mother to Kay, which could mean one thing—the American girl was more in his confidence than any other woman so far.

A dance was in progress when she returned to the ballroom. Someone tall detached himself from a group of people standing near the door and smiled down at her.

"May I?" Dominic asked, and swung her away.

The next few minutes were filled with a bittersweet joy. As Martina had expected, he was an excellent dancer. She followed his lead, unconsciously responding to his every move with unerring precision and an ecstasy which held her enthralled. His hold was correct, no nearer than courtesy demanded. Neither of them spoke; Martina was afraid to break the spell.

When the music quivered into silence, they were back again near the door. His fingers released her own and she was brought back to earth with the dazed feeling of awakening from a beautiful dream.

"Thank you," she said, lowering her eyes instinctively from his. Her heart was working overtime and she stepped back to catch a glimpse of Kay standing in the doorway.

"Don't you want to dance again?" he asked softly.

Surprisingly, Martina did not. Kay's appearance like an avenging angel had burst the bubble of her enchantment.

"I'd rather not, thank you," she said.

"No?" he questioned with indolent amusement. "Afraid the magic won't work a second time? Perhaps you're right." His hand was suddenly on her arm. His smile was half mocking, half challenging. "Come, I'll show you the Piazza in the moonlight. Venice has many moods and this is one of her most enchanting."

Dominic drew her across the ballroom to tall French windows and they stepped out onto a balcony. The orchestra, beginning the next dance, was muted as he closed the doors behind them and Martina moved forward to breathe in the invigorating air. The scene which met her eyes was one of breathtaking splendor.

San Marco's white domes stood in majestic silence in the moon-washed square. Stars twinkled in a vast ceiling of sapphire blue.

"How peaceful and serene it is!" she breathed. "There's a dreamlike quality about it, a feeling that one has to whisper in order not to disturb it." She leaned over the balcony, her body still tingling from the joy of the dance, and watched a cat move silently out of the shadows across the square. "Do you know what I want to do at this moment?" She turned a bright face to find his eyes dwelling enigmatically upon her.

"No. What would you want to do at this moment?"

"Go dance in the square in the moonlight. What fun it would be to take off from this balcony like Peter Pan!"

He said dryly, "You did very well without wings just

now in the ballroom. In fact I was afraid you would fly away before the dance ended."

"Were you really?" she said, startled by the compliment. "I didn't do anything spectacular. You're such a super dancer."

"I refuse to take all the credit." He paused and she felt his probing as if something tangible. "May I be impertinent and ask if dancing is part of your job?" he inquired at length.

"You may," she conceded. "No, it isn't. I loved dancing as a child, though. Ballet lessons were a must, according to Mother, for growing up with correct posture."

Dominic was leaning against the door frame, a spark of humor in his eyes.

"Is your mother responsible for making you a non-smoker?"

Martina gave a gay infectious laugh, feeling more at ease with his teasing mood.

"Good heavens, no. Mother smokes. I've never wanted to."

He said, smiling faintly, "And your father?"

"My father smokes a pipe," she said, and went on to tell him a little about her parents' occupation. Dominic would hardly be interested in someone he had never met and was not likely to.

"We had a film crew here not long ago," he said when she had finished. "I found it really interesting. It's the kind of work which could become all-absorbing to someone who enjoys it."

"My father loves it; Mother too. They're what you would call a successful team. Father calls Mother his Girl Friday." Martina's smile was tender.

He quirked a brow. "They're happy together?"

"Oh yes!"

"So they've made a good marriage because they share the same interests. Would you say that was a sound basis for marriage, Miss Floyd?"

He joined her by the balcony rail. For that long pulsating moment they were very much alone, miles away from the muted sounds of the ballroom and the world. She felt rapture in his nearness and in the stirring sound of his deep voice, a rapture which rocked her heart, sending out strange warning signals.

"I would say true love is the only sound basis for marriage. Anything less wouldn't stand the strain. It feels good just to see my parents together."

He agreed. "People who are happy usually radiate happiness around them. So you think that true love is the only thing that constitutes a happy marriage?"

"Undoubtedly," she replied. "Marrying for the sake of getting married, for worldly goods or for looks is an act of lunacy."

Dominic looked up sharply when Kay appeared at the other side of the French window. Instantly he strolled across and, holding the door closed, turned to Martina.

"It seems we must postpone this interesting discussion." He smiled charmingly. "Would you care to go with me to the Biennial Festival tomorrow? It's an exhibition of art from all over the world held in the public gardens pavilion. I'm sure you would enjoy it."

Martina's eyes met his with unconcealed delight. She was too happy to be rigidly careful of looks or emotions. Kay, standing on the other side of the door, was forgotten as she shone up at him. To spend a whole morning in his company discussing her favorite subject, to listen to his valued criticism and expert opinion, was something she could not resist.

"I'd love to," she replied eagerly. "Providing Eunice hasn't made any plans for tomorrow."

"I think she could spare you for a few hours," he said.

Kay bore down on them when Dominic opened the door. Her look at Martina was thunderous. She seemed about to stamp her foot in anger. She came between them, looking up at Dominic accusingly.

"Really, it's too awful of you, Dominic, deserting me on my last evening in Venice! And we've missed my favorite waltz!" She thrust her arm through his. "Just for that you can dance with me for the evening!"

"My dear Kay," Dominic drawled, unperturbed,

allowing her to draw him into the dance, "you aren't saying goodbye forever. You're returning to Venice in due course."

Martina missed Kay's answer, for she had seen Eunice beckoning to her.

"Sorry, Marty," she said. "We have to go now. Bruno has some business to attend to before we leave for Geneva on Sunday. If you want to stay, Dominic will bring you back."

But Martina did not mind leaving. She was going to see Dominic on the morrow and that was all that mattered. So they took their leave of Eldred and Amy Younge, who said they expected to be back in Venice after their visit to Greece.

Martina thought of this on the way back to Bruno's house. Were they returning at Kay's request, hoping Kay and Dominic would make a match of it? She recalled him standing with his hand on the lock of the French window as he invited her to go to the biennial exhibition. There was nothing in it as far as she was concerned, but it made her feel absurdly happy all the same.

CHAPTER SIX

Dominic arrived on time the following morning. Eunice had been agreeable to their date because she had last-minute preparations to make for their journey to Geneva. Martina saw that she was looking much brighter. She had danced with her husband most of the previous evening and it looked as if the rift between them was now nonexistent.

The sky was overcast when Dominic helped her into the launch at her door but Martina would have been happy if it had been pouring rain. The somber appearance of the palaces along the canal, all angles and shadows, held a magic which swept her along on a wave of happy anticipation. Dominic had an exciting Latin look about him this morning which made her feel curiously weak. He was wearing a light gray suit which fitted the lazy indolence of his wide-shouldered frame to perfection.

He sat beside her, gazing ahead as if he saw things beyond her vision. His profile, etched against the sullen light, sent an odd quiver along her nerves. Suddenly he turned his head toward her as though aware of her scrutiny. His eyes pierced her own and the color rushed beneath her clear skin.

"Not very bright this morning," he said, "But we'll have the best of the day before the tourists begin to arrive."

The exhibition attracted a large crowd; they were able to move around without being jostled however. All the paintings on view were ultramodern and symbolic of the present violent era. Martina viewed them with a lively interest, tilting her head to one side as she tried to interpret the meaning of some of them. Failing this, she would refer to her catalog for enlightenment before asking Dominic's opinion. With sardonic amusement, he would try to explain. Then her soft fascinating laugh would slip out before she was aware of it and the world would become an enchanted place.

95

But those beautiful tremulous moments were too short and too few. They passed as though they had never happened, and Dominic again assumed that cool, friendly exterior with which she was all too familiar. It was a wonderful morning all the same, and Martina learned much about modern art and the man beside her. She was not merely enamored by his good looks and charm. She loved him for what he was—his strength of character, the humor with which he viewed everything around him, throwing back his head to roar with laughter when he felt like it. His sound common sense, his courtesy and good breeding imprisoned her in a warm cloak of wellbeing. Just being with him gave her life new meaning.

After they'd seen the show, she turned to him, flushed and radiant.

"Thanks for bringing me," she exclaimed. "It's been a wonderful experience, a jolt back to the present from the past. I've enjoyed it immensely."

He smiled down at her and she shifted her gaze from his face, afraid of her own emotions and his too friendly response.

"I trust a surfeit of art hasn't dulled your appetite for lunch," he said equably. "I don't know about you, but I'm ravenous."

"Do you know, I believe I am too." She held out her hand somewhat regretfully. "I'll say goodbye. I mustn't take up any more of your time."

His regard was teasing. "I have to eat too," he jested. "Are you ready?"

Martina was more than ready. To spend another hour or so in his company, whatever the outcome, would be bliss. The clouds were breaking up, revealing blue sky, when they left the pavilion.

In the hotel he chose, Dominic held a chair for her at the table and a waiter attended to them almost immediately. Chilled melon was followed by fresh seafood cooked in the Venetians' way. Loving his quiet assurance, she allowed him to choose the meal. They said little. Martina was content to listen to his deep resonant voice giving every word its true value, his eyes enigmatic in his tanned face. The dining room with its aura of elegance and old-world charm was filled with voices and the quiet expert handling of dishes.

Four people dining at the next table caught Martina's attention—a handsome young couple with their two children, a boy and girl of school age. The children were extremely well behaved. She imagined that Dominic's children would be like them.

A wave of emotion swept over her at the thought of Mia, or Kay on his arm in bridal array. Eunice would describe every detail in the letters she sent. Martina felt feverish, loving him with an ache and a jealousy which shamed her. She would get over it, she knew, although the idea seemed impossible at the moment.

When she returned to London there would be new interests, new shows and new films to discuss with her parents. But no eager anticipation stirred her at the thought. Right now her whole world was Dominic, seated across from her in a first-class hotel in Venice, his dark head held arrogantly, his mouth curved back from perfect teeth, smiling mockingly.

"Thanks for the really lovely time," she said when he helped her into the launch that was to take her back to Bruno's house.

"Glad you enjoyed it," was the crisp reply. "Roberto will see you home. Sorry I have to leave you, but I have a pressing appointment in about ten minutes' time."

Drawing back an immaculate cuff, he swiftly glanced at his watch. She took her leave of him and the launch sped away. Closing her eyes, she imagined him striding out of her life. But not yet, she thought despairingly. Not yet.

Eunice was out when she returned. There was a message to say she would be in around four o'clock. Bruno and Marco were out too and the house was silent. Martina spent the afternoon writing letters home until Emilia came to say that Signora Vortolini had returned and was waiting for her in the *sala*.

Martina found Eunice looking very smart in beige pants and a gay top. Large pearl studs in her ears matched the choker around her throat. She looked *soignée* and sophisticated with her hair newly coiffured. Greeting Martina with a warm indulgent smile, she gestured to a chair near her own. A low table within reach held a tea tray.

"Come, sit down, Marty. Tell me all about the exhibition. Did you enjoy it?"

Martina settled herself in the chair and talked about the morning's outing. Eunice listened attentively while she poured tea and passed Martina a cup.

"I'm pleased you enjoyed it," she said when Martina had finished. "Dominic is a wonderful companion to have on such occasions. Are you liking him any better?"

Liking him? Martina laughed to hide the pain. "Let's say I'm beginning to know him," she replied evasively.

To her relief, Eunice talked of the purchases she had made that day for her trip to Geneva. Eventually she brought up the subject of Marco. They had nibbled minute sandwiches and pastries and were finishing their second cup of tea.

"About Marco," Eunice began, leaning back in her chair to draw contentedly on a cigarette she had lit. "Bruno wants him to continue going next door each morning. The children have a tutor and he shares lessons with them. Besides, it will give you the mornings free. It's the nights Bruno is concerned about; he can go away happily knowing you'll be here if Marco has a nightmare. As times goes on the memory of the fire will fade from his mind. Children are resilient. I know we'll be away only a week, but in case of emergency the doctor's number is on the pad by the phone in the hall, along with the numbers of our friends next door, and of Dominic."

Eunice tapped a long finger of ash from her cigarette into a silver ashtray. "By the way, don't hesitate to call Dominic if you're uncertain about anything. He's so level-headed and sane to have around in a crisis."

Martina said hardily, "I hope I won't need any help. I certainly don't anticipate trouble in the short time you'll be away."

"Don't be too sure," Eunice warned wisely. "There are

always minor ailments when children get together; and don't let Marco become a burden to you. He might look innocent, but he's shrewd enough to latch onto any feeling you have and profit by it if he can. The important thing is to be firm with him from the beginning by making him toe the line." She smiled warmly. "Bruno and I are very grateful to you for looking after him. We'll have another talk before I go in case there's anything you want to know."

There was no opportunity for another talk, however, for friends came to dinner that evening. Others called at intervals the following day and the evening of their departure came too soon. Bruno was in the hall with Eunice, dressed in white, beside him. Stefano and Ugo carried luggage out to the launch and Bruno said, "I've just left Marco, Martina. He's asleep. He knows that when he wakes in the morning we'll be gone. We'll call you from time to time while we're away. And please treat the house as your own. You have full authority to do as you please."

Farewells were brief. Bruno's hands squeezed Martina's shoulders, Eunice bestowed a perfumed kiss on her cheek and they were gone.

Marco was quiet and sulky the next morning at breakfast. While he was being dressed, he had talked unceasingly about Zio Bruno who was going to take him with him next time he went away. His sulkiness increased as the time came for him to go next door.

"I'm not going to do any silly lessons today," he stated in open rebellion. "I want to go to the airport and see a jet like the one Zio Bruno had gone away in."

"Some other time," Martina promised, prepared to be patient. "We'll go to the Lido after lunch. You can build sandcastles and paddle in the sea. You will like that, won't you?"

Marco went pale and trembled slightly. "The sea?" he said in a shocked whisper. He shook his head violently. "Not the sea. Papà said I was not to go near the sea without him. Once I nearly drowned, and Papà made me promise not to go in the sea again." His lip trembled ominously and tears filled his eyes. "Why did Papà have to go away?"

Martina drew him to her, shaken out of her composure.

"Sometimes people have to go and leave us," she said inadequately. "He loves you, wherever he is." Full of compassion, she stooped down and pushed back the tumbled curls from his forehead, surprised at the length of his eyelashes. "Have you ever had goldfish, Marco?" she asked carefully.

He frowned with youthful concentration. "No," he answered, shaking his head.

"Then we must buy a small tank and you can have some and watch them swim around."

He looked at her, in no way excited by the prospect. "Why?" he asked baldly.

Martina smiled. "Because then you would have something of your own to love. You could feed them and give them names and you would not be lonely any more. You will get to know them and they will learn to know you."

He digested this thoughtfully, tilting his head a little to one side with a slight frown.

"Will they get to know you too?"

She nodded. "Yes. Maybe when you see such tiny fish swimming around unafraid of the water you will want to swim too."

"Are you afraid of the sea, *signorina*?" he asked solemnly.

"No. Call me Martina, Marco. It's more friendly—and we are friends, aren't we?" She smiled into his small serious face.

"Zia Eunice calls you Marty," he said.

"Then you can call me Marty, if you like."

He smiled and straightened proudly as if she had done him an honor.

"Can you swim, *sig* . . . Marty?"

"Yes. I would like to teach you to swim."

"Can Zio Bruno swim?"

"I expect so."

"Better than Zia Eunice?"

Martina mentally counted the cups Eunice had won for swimming, chuckled and drew him close. "I expect he can," she answered, although she did not think so at all.

When Marco had gone next door to his friends' house, Martina went to the market with Ugo. A fresh breeze met them as they skimmed over the water. Ugo kept the launch clear of the *vaporetto* which swung to the side of the canal occasionally to pick up passengers from the floating landing-stages.

The palaces on either side of the canal winked sleepily as the rosy glow of early morning sun reflected in their windows. Martina sat enjoying the grandeur and marveling anew at the clear air which had a radiance she had never seen equaled elsewhere. It was like a draught of sparkling wine, and when Ugo began to sing a well-known aria softly, she found herself humming it with him. He had been delighted when she had asked him to help her shop for the fish tank, and had shown a lively interest because it was for Marco, whom he and the rest of the staff adored.

Martina really enjoyed the market with its colorful display of fruit and Adriatic fish being examined critically by thrifty Venetian housewives. She listened, enchanted by their voices rising and falling with soft intonation and reminding her of bees buzzing around a honeypot. It was an easy matter to buy a fish tank and pretty fossils to line it with. With Ugo's help, she selected some beautifully-colored Adriatic fish, and purchased food for them. She asked Ugo to take them home, saying she would follow later on the *vaporetto*.

She spent a pleasant hour shopping for leather goods, old prints and basketwork to take home as presents. Midmorning she sat at a small table in the square for a coffee. The daily tourists were arriving with their cameras ready, while guides, like fussy sheepdogs, rounded people up for sightseeing tours. Sweet music from an orchestra was accompanied by the soft cooing of pigeons circling on high in the golden light.

Martina arrived home to find that Stefano had set the tank of fish on a small table in the main *sala*. The pretty fossils on the bed of the tank and the beautifully-colored fish swimming around were an exciting new world for Marco, who when he came in hurled himself across the room to gaze at it with delight.

"*Essi sono bello,* Marty," he cried excitedly.

"Yes, they are lovely, aren't they?"

Martina gave him a packet of ants' eggs to drop on the water. He kept chuckling to himself as he fed them.

"May I give them names, Marty?" he asked, his eyes glowing.

"Yes. Go right ahead."

He frowned in youthful concentration. "The golden one I shall call Zia Eunice and the browny one swimming around with her I shall call Bruno. The red one in the corner will be Stefano, who goes red when I tease him." He paused dramatically to look at the others. "That long magnificent one swimming around away from the others—is he not a beauty? Is he the Doge, Marty?"

Martina trilled a laugh. "I haven't the faintest idea. What do you know about Doges anyway?"

"I learn about them in my lessons. They were the rulers of Venice. I think he is a Doge, Marty. I shall call him Zio Dominic."

"Indeed!"

They both turned guiltily as Dominic strode across the room.

"So it seems I have a goldfish named after me!" He raised his eyebrows in a mock threatening gesture. "And which one is me?" he demanded, bending his tall frame over the tank.

Solemnly, Marco pointed out the beautifully marked fish swimming around with a lordly air away from the rest.

"There he is, Zio Dominic," he cried. "Is he not magnificent?"

Dominic chuckled. "The handsomest in the tank, I suppose you have names for the others?"

Eagerly, Marco pointed them out. "Yes. There is Zio Bruno and Zia Eunice, Stefano, and I think that bluey green one can be Ugo."

"Hmm." Dominic appeared to be deep in thought. "And which one is Zia Martina?" He cocked a brow at Marco's small face peering intently into the tank. "What about that pretty dainty little thing in the far corner?"

Marco chuckled and looked up at Martina. "Yes," he said, "I think I like that one best of all."

Tongue in cheek, Dominic glanced at Martina's flushed face. Swiftly to hide her blush, she bent down to kiss Marco on his forehead.

"Thank you, Marco. I hope you notice how well they swim and that they're not afraid of the water," she said meaningly.

His eyes went back to the tank. Tenderly, she watched his little hands press against the glass.

But Marco refused to commit himself. "They've eaten all the food I gave them," he said diplomatically.

Her laughing eyes met Dominic's dark ones over Marco's head; his intent regard rocked her heart. It occurred to her that his unexpected visit had been made with a purpose.

He spoke as though reading her thoughts. "I'm on my way to my farm in the Venetian hills. I plan on staying for a couple of days. As Marco enjoys visiting the farm, I wondered if you would care to bring him. It will mean losing two days in Venice. Would you mind that?"

"Mind?" she echoed. She would sacrifice more than that for two days in his company. "How kind of you! I'd love to come. What about you, Marco?" She caught his glance at the tank. "The goldfish will be here when we return. Stefano will look after them," she assured him gently.

He turned eagerly to gaze up at Dominic. "May I ride Lunedi, Zio Dominic?"

Dominic's lips twitched. His eyes mocked Martina as he explained, "Lunedi is a pony Marco rides at the farm. It was born on a Monday, hence the name Lunedi. Do you ride, Miss Floyd?"

Martina shook her head, trying not to feel so idiotically happy. She wondered what payment the gods would demand for two whole days of bliss on Dominic's farm.

"When do we start?" she asked.

"I'll wait for you. Stefano can pack Marco's case. He has done so several times," was the cool reply.

In her room, Martina hastily pulled out the middle size of her three pigskin cases. She included an evening dress just in case. On her way to the bathroom she could hear Marco chatting to Stefano as he packed his case. A splash of cool water left her skin glowing rosily. Hastily she made-up her face, touched a soft pink lipstick to her mouth and tied her hair back loosely with a white ribbon. The tailored, navy and white suit gave her a fresh young look. But she knew the eyes which shone back at her in the mirror were far brighter than they had any business to be.

When Dominic helped her into the launch, she shone up at him, far too happy to cover her joy at being with him. They sped away, him sitting across from her with one long arm draped along the back of his seat.

Marco knelt on the seat beside her, his curls lifting in the breeze. "Are we going along the *autostrada*, Zio Dominic?" he asked as they made for the square.

"No." Dominic turned his head to catch Martina's gaze. "We're taking the old road along the River Brenta. It's little more than a canal, but you will find the journey interesting." He considered her thoughtfully with a half smile. "Your friend Byron once rented a villa along its banks. The story goes that he was out riding in the hills there when he met Margarita Cogni for the first time." He went on to talk of many famous people who had lived in villas along the banks of the Brenta, identifying some of them when, later, they were actually following the curve of the river itself.

Martina looked with interest at villas perched picturesquely in the wooded hills. They were gracious buildings erected centuries ago by wealthy Venetians who, seeking the best of both worlds, owned a house on the Venetian lagoon and a villa in the hills. A mixture of the restored and the neglected, they remained silent witnesses of past glories.

The launch finally drew in at a private landing stage, in good repair like the boathouse next to it. Dominic helped Martina out and lifted Marco while Roberto carried the cases ashore.

"There you see the farm," said Dominic, gesturing with a sunburned hand to a building half hidden by woods. He smiled down at Martina's wide-eyed stare. "It's not as inaccessible as it looks. There are hundreds of acres of cultivated land which you'll see as we approach the farm. The woods start at the river and form a boundary around the actual farmlands."

The sound of a car stopping immediately on a road above them caught his attention. Martina watched a man slide out of the driver's seat and come to meet them. He was swarthy and thick-set, with the blue eyes and high-cheekboned face of the northern Italians.

"*Buon giorno,* Guido," Dominic greeted him cordially in Italian, pausing to talk while Roberto placed the suitcases in the trunk of the car. Martina stood holding Marco's hand while Dominic finished his conversation. "There's a basket of fish for you in the launch, Guido," he told the man, who thanked him profusely as he moved towards the boat, sending a veiled curious look toward Martina and a faint smile of recognition with a courteous salute to Marco.

Martina, with Marco, was put in the front seat of the big car, which smelled faintly of expensive leather. Dominic slid into the driver's seat, turned the key and drove the powerful car forward efficiently. It was warm and sunny as they sped upward along the tree-lined road. Dominic drove with the confidence of someone who knows every inch of the way, anticipating each bump which the superb springs met with a cushioned rise and fall. Blind corners slowed them down; then the car would leap forward again, eating up the kilometers.

They were now passing the farmland Dominic had spoken about—vineyards, orchards and an occasional signpost. Reaching a crossroads they swerved right along a well-paved road and purred gently between massive granite pillars along a drive. For some time they traveled between two rows of trees which cast a lacy reflection on the road as it wound ahead to culminate in a courtyard.

Martina loved the farmhouse at first glance. Wonderfully remote, nestled in a sea of trees, it had been built in the classic architecture of the Byzantine era. She was reminded of a huge iced birthday cake with a tower at one end. Terraces circling the first and second floors were edged in pink marble icing, and the flowers in huge urns around the courtyard presented a scene to delight any artist. It was a gracious dwelling, time-mellowed, and capable of withstanding many more centuries of sturdy life.

The woman who waited to greet them was nearing her late thirties. She wore a full-skirted dark dress, and bore a tranquil air. Her brown skin was glowingly rich.

Dominic said with his charming smile, "*Buon giorno,* Signora Stangeri. May I present Miss Martina Floyd from London?" He looked down at Martina. "The *signora* has a daughter who is at present modeling in London."

Martina greeted the woman with a warm smile, happy to hear her speak English. Then Marco spoke in his gruff voice which so belied his angelic appearance. "*Buon giorno,* Signora Stangeri," he said politely with a quaint little bow before turning eagerly to look up at the tall figure beside him. "*Per favore*, Zio Dominic, may I now see Lunedi?"

"Presently," Dominic answered tolerantly. He slanted a mocking smile at Signora Stangeri. "Think you can put up with him for a couple of days?" He ruffled Marco's curls with a lazy hand.

Signora Stangeri smiled fondly down on Marco. "It will be a pleasure to have a child around the place." Her dark eyes, now slightly troubled, sought Dominic's. "Maurizio is in the stables. Sultan has been off his food since you were here last. He misses you."

Dominic patted her shoulder. His mouth quirked. "Don't worry. Sultan is an intelligent rascal. He has an idea you and Maurizio are concerned about him and plays on your feelings accordingly. I'll go see him. Meanwhile, perhaps Miss Floyd would like to see her rooms."

Martina would have preferred to go with him to see the horse. She watched Marco's small hand seek and find the sunburned one, saw Dominic clasp it and smile down into the eager little face.

"Yes, you can come with me. You are as big a rascal as Sultan," he said. "See you later, Miss Floyd."

Martina was shattered to find herself jealous of a small boy.

Signora Stangeri led her through the open Moorish arches across a sun-drenched patio to the kitchen area. They entered an oak-beamed room with a handsome dresser, long refectory table and sturdy chairs. Old-fashioned benches rested on each side of the huge fire-place and gleaming copper pans with pottery utensils hung from pegs on marble-slabbed walls. In the far corner a beautifully polished staircase led to the upper floor, and Martina walked up this with the Signora.

Her rooms were light and airy, the magnolia walls a pleasing background for the draped fourposter bed wand antique inlaid furniture. A huge copper urn filled with flowers brightened a corner.

"What a delightful room!" Martina exclaimed. "The flowers are lovely, *signora*, and the view is marvelous."

She walked across the room to see through the window a panorama of wooded hills and cultivated fields. Irrigation streams sparkled between windbreaks of poplar and acacia.

The Signora agreed, "Yes, it is a lovely place. A pity Signor Burnett di Ravenelli doesn't marry. It's a family house. However, we live in hopes."

Martina glanced at her, longing for her to say more. Was it Kay or Mia giving fresh hope? To stem the sudden flow of emotion the thought evoked, she said, "You speak very good English, *signora*."

"I am English," Signora Stangeri replied. "My people came from Devon. I came to Venice at the age of eighteen for a holiday with an aunt. Unfortunately, I fell in love with the wrong kind of man while I was here. He was one of those handsome gigolos who roam the Lido looking for affairs. I knew what he was, but it didn't prevent me from loving him desperately. My aunt died suddenly of a heart attack at the same time that I discovered that I was going to have a baby. I couldn't go back home and was pretty desperate when I met Maurizio. I told him my sorry story and we got married."

"I'm glad you met someone else. Is he nice?" Martina asked sympathetically.

"Very." Signora Stangeri shrugged. "A happy childhood gives one a romantic picture of life until a bitter experience like mine distorts it." She sighed. "When that happens life is never the same again. I don't know why I'm telling you this; maybe it's because you look vulnerable. You have stars in your eyes, you aren't wearing a ring and you glow with enthusiasm for ideals which you'll discover can be sadly lacking in many people today."

Martina said quietly, "I know what you mean. Thanks for telling me your experience. I know some men have a hard core of selfishness that's been encouraged by doting mothers. You, *signora*, if I may say so, don't look bitter, despite your disillusionment. You have a sweet look tinged with sadness. Your Maurizio must be a nice man."

The woman smiled and opened one of two doors, showing Martina a luxuriously fitted bathroom in pink and mauve.

"This other door leads to Marco's room," she said, opening it.

Martina liked the pale turquoise walls and deep blue furnishings. The windows opened onto a terrace like those in her own room. When they returned to her own room someone had brought up her case and Marco's.

Signora Stangeri said, "Dinner is at eight. I'll give Marco his supper in the kitchen. While you unpack I'll prepare a tray. I'm sure you must be wanting a drink." Her smile was friendly. "Don't take what I said too much to heart. I hope you enjoy your stay—and don't hesitate to let me know if you need anything."

When Martina opened Marco's small suitcase the first thing she saw was the battered teddy bear. She picked it up and looked at the scorched ear. "You're going to be awfully hard to get rid of, Tito," she said, tweaking the offending ear.

Poor Marco, clinging to the last possession of a world in which he had been so happy. Her eyes were moist when she placed it on his bed.

She was unpacking her own suitcase when Signora Stangeri came with a covered tea tray. Martina drank thirstily, enjoying the fresh farm butter and hot home-made scones. She carried her last cup of tea to the terrace, in time to see Dominic and Marco disappearing indoors below.

That evening when she was tucking a very sleepy Marco in bed, he said, "Will the goldfish have gone to bed, Marty?"

"Yes. They'll be waiting for you to join them in slumber," she teased.

His eyes were large dark pools. "This slumberland. I do not know of it. Tell me about it, Marty."

She made up a story which brought an angelic smile to his face, and gradually the long eyelashes pressed down deeper onto his softly rounded cheeks. His breathing became even and steady. He was asleep. Martina watched him for several minutes. Something, a tender emotion, absurdly blocked her throat.

She took a shower, put on a soft jersey dress in a flattering shade of blue and combed her hair around her head into a chignon. She made up her face lightly with the merest whisper of blue on her eyelids and added a heavy beaten gold bracelet to one slender wrist.

Dominic was standing on the hearth waiting for her when she entered. He was relaxed and smiling, looking heartbreakingly attractive in a dark lounge suit and start-lingly white shirt.

"Sit down, Miss Floyd. I'll pour you a drink." He gestured to a sofa on one side of the fireplace. "Marco go off to sleep all right?"

She murmured, "Yes," and willed steadiness to her fingers to take the drink he offered.

Strange how her need of him was suddenly more

poignant with his nearness. Strange also that she should sense tenderness and passion beneath his cool front. He looked strong and unshakeable, even ruthless, as his eyes, dark and glittering in his tanned face, met hers and held them briefly. She wondered wildly if he could hear the loud beating of her heart. Then he moved away and after taking a sip, set his drink on the mantelpiece. Pushing his hands into his pockets, he looked down at her as she sipped her wine. His well-shaped head and shoulders were reflected in the magnificent Renaissance mirror behind him over the mantel.

"What do you think of the farm?" he asked.

"It's enchanting. I love the solitude."

His keen gaze slid impersonally over her slim figure and lingered on the silken pile of hair, the slender wrist encased in the broad heavy bracelet, the pearl-tipped fingers curled around the stem of her glass.

"Which would bore you after a few days," he scoffed. "Most of my guests become bored with the solitude. The *palazzo* in Venice is usually preferred to the monotony of country life. Do you think you could settle down away from the bright lights of London?"

Martina lowered her glass after taking a drink and said, "I don't see why not. Why do you ask?"

His smile was slightly cynical. "Because many women could never settle in a strange country." He looked up at the high ceiling. "I love this place. I wanted to be a farmer when I was a boy. However, my stepfather, the Conte di Ravenelli, placed the glittering bauble of finance in my hands. It was a challenge I accepted. I learned to work hard and play hard. I've done most things, but so far have drawn the line at marriage. This property has been in the Ravenelli family for generations. I should hate to have it pass into the hands of some tycoon."

So he was going to marry after all. Who better than Mia, who would provide a ready-made heir? He must be planning to follow his stepfather's example—marrying a widow with a son. It would mean a happy ending for Marco; she ought to be pleased at the thought. Martina stared down into her wine glass.

He went on, "Pity you can't ride. You would have enjoyed touring the farm on horseback. After my early morning ride tomorrow I shall take Marco out for a short ride on Lunedì. If you're interested, we can go around the farm by car." He continued to talk about the farm and she listened, wanting to hear every detail of life there.

By the time they were seated at the table conversation was in full swing, with Martina asking questions about cultivation and its problems. Dominic answered them with alacrity and a certain amount of humor. Once or twice he lifted an amused eyebrow. On these occasions she found it so easy to love him, to weave dreams around the two of them which were a menace to her peace of mind.

The table was covered with a white damask cloth and a bowl of violets was in the center. China, silver and glass of the best quality had been handed down through generations of Ravenellis. Silver cider jug, game pie, Parma ham cooked in wine, vegetables in heated silver dishes, homemade bread, peaches, cream, farm butter and cheese had been placed on an ornate sideboard for them to help themselves.

As they ate, Martina felt the sharp curiosity of Dominic's roused interest each time she met his eyes across the table. Her infectious smile, sparkling eyes and warm personality, usually hidden by a certain shyness she felt in his company, entertained him tantalizingly.

Dominic had passed her a helping of each course and they were nearing the end of the meal when conversation flagged. Taking each plate from his hands had created an intimacy which she found to be bittersweet.

"You were reluctant to dine alone with me the last time. How do you feel now?" he asked.

He spoke with obvious indifference, yet he studied her critically. Sitting straight and slender, Martina collected herself. For most of the meal she had kept her eyes lowered from his disturbing gaze and had concentrated on his brown hands and strong wrists, loving the flexible fingers, which now held a cigar. Reluctantly, she raised her eyes to meet his gaze. She even managed a smile, an impish one at that.

"I've always been crazy about farmhouse food, so naturally I'm enjoying it," she answered demurely.

His eyes twinkled devilishly. "Tell me what else you're crazy about," he murmured, leaning back in his chair with narrowed gaze.

Martina would have given anything to have been able to speak out and tell him she was crazy about him. But for the sake of her own pride and to save him embarrassment and amusement at her expense, she maintained a cool front. Keen though they were, those dark eyes shouldn't ever again catch her unawares.

"Why should I tell you my favorite joys?" she answered. "You wouldn't be interested."

"Try me," he said lazily.

But she refused to be drawn. Signora Stangeri came in at that moment to see if they needed anything. When she had gone they lingered for a while while he had finished his cigar. Then he suggested a walk. Relieved to get away from an atmosphere fraught with strange undercurrents, Martina agreed and went upstairs to get her coat and look in on Marco.

He had kicked off the bedclothes and lay sprawling with flushed cheeks and tumbled curls. His head was thrown back and one arm was flung across his teddy bear. Bending over him, Martina drew the covers gently around him, pausing a moment when he stirred. He would be happy having Dominic for his stepfather, and soon there would be other children to keep him company. Patiently, she waited for him to settle down, dismissing thoughts which stabbed like knives. Then, when his even breathing reassured her, she left the room.

She joined Dominic with a smile that hid the tumult of feeling inside her. How many women in his past had felt the same as she did tonight? Martina, afraid of her own weakness, was thankful for his cool aloofness, which gave an illusion of trustfulness. His courteousness was doubly assuring. He politely opened and closed doors so that she could precede him out into the warm night. Nonchalantly, he strolled beside her, lost in thought, his hands thrust into the pockets of his trousers.

The beauty of the night, heightened by his presence, caught at her throat. The moon, brightening in its ascent, silvered the river and streams below and cast an ethereal light over woods and fields. It was left to Martina to break what was for her a poignant silence.

"Why is it that the moon always seems to affect one more abroad than it does at home?"

He tossed her a half smile. "Probably because one expects it to be different, therefore it is. People settle in the place of their dreams and it becomes the most beautiful spot in the world to them. I have a villa overlooking Lake Como with a view of snow-covered peaks which tugs at the heart."

He spoke of places he had seen abroad, unforgettable in their beauty. He talked freely, giving Martina the impression of a lone wolf reveling in his freedom. But she knew his extraordinary charm and good looks had attracted many women to him. He had undoubtedly had his moments.

They had strolled down toward a glen where they stopped and watched the water cascading down onto the rocks below. The moon, now in its zenith, stippled the falls into frothy white mercury and dark purple shadows. The noise of the waterfall seemed to intensify the illusion that they were entirely cut off from civilization and on a planet of their own.

A sudden movement behind Martina startled her and she swung around. Her foot slipped. She would have gone over the edge of the glen had not Dominic's arms whipped out and pulled her against him. Thoroughly unnerved, she clung to him, acutely aware of the pressure of his arms. The sound of her heavy breathing mingled with the knocking of her heart against her ribs as she strove to control her shaken nerves.

"What was it?" she whispered when she had regained her breath.

"Some nocturnal creature in the undergrowth, probably as startled as you are," he replied above her hair.

"Don't worry, there are no wild animals around here. You're in no danger."

No danger! They were the most dangerous moments of her life. Never had she been so near to making a fool of herself over a man who could not have cared less about her. Determinedly, she pulled herself together.

"I was startled," she explained.

She smiled up at him uncertainly. He released her slowly with a frown. She felt crushed and suddenly numb as he stood looking down at her.

"Sure you're all right?" His hands came up to grip her shoulders.

"Perfectly," she answered.

His hands dropped and they retraced their steps in silence. Not until they were well on their way back was normal conversation resumed. Dominic pointed out places they could see in the moonlight as though the incident had never happened. To him the evening had been passed dining and strolling with a guest with no personal involvement even in her rescue.

To Martina it had been shattering. The acute feeling of fulfilment denied left an utter weariness in her body and spirit.

CHAPTER SEVEN

Driving around the farm with Dominic the next day, Martina was once more aware of the beauty of Italy. Beneath brilliant blue skies, she saw fields of grain, melons and tomatoes growing in irrigated rich black earth. All around them, black-eyed people sang as they worked. Some were hoeing, others carrying bundles of hay to be piled around a center pole like a well-baked cake. Dominic stopped to talk and joke with them and the air rang merrily.

Marco was not with them. Dominic had taken him for a ride on Lunedi that morning, so Marco was taking a short rest. They were going for a picnic that afternoon and Dominic did not want to tire the boy before they went.

After lunch Dominic placed a picnic basket in the trunk of his car and, with Martina and Marco beside him, set off. The kilometers ticked away, through villages of Venetian pink and past mellowed stone farmhouses.

Occasionally, Dominic slowed down to allow farm carts drawn by oxen to pass, and once he stopped for several nuns on horseback to cross the road where an avenue of chestnut trees led up a long drive to a convent.

"What a charming scene to paint!" Martina exclaimed when Dominic slid the big car onto a side road along a lake. The water was a blue mirror holding a surface of golden splinters from the sun. It was dotted with small islands, and sailing boats were skimming with butterfly grace against a background of mauve mountains. Villas painted a variety of colors had gardens reaching down to the water. And Marco stood up with lively interest when they passed a gypsy encampment. The lake was enormous and they had been driving for quite a while before Dominic pulled in at a quiet spot near a sandy shore.

Turning in his seat, he regarded Martina speculatively. "Pity you're only in Venice for a short visit. We might have spent a day fishing for trout. Ever had trout cooked over a charcoal fire?"

Martina shook her head.

"It's delicious, isn't it, Marco?" Dominic ruffed the dark curls.

"*Si*, Zio Dominic," he replied. "Are we going fishing today?"

"I'm afraid not. Some other time."

Dominic had rolled down the windows of the car, but it was like an oven without the breeze of traveling.

"Can we see the castle, Zio Dominic?" Marco asked.

"If Miss Floyd doesn't mind the climb." Dominic was smiling at Martina. "The last time we were here Marco was disappointed—his mother objected to the climb. The heat can make you aware of a delicious languor, a feeling of *dolce far niente* which can take away your enthusiasm for exercise."

Some of the brightness of Martina's day faded with the knowledge that he had brought Mia to the same place. Then she forgot all about it when she saw Marco's small face raised appealingly.

"Are you tired, Marty?" he asked.

She smiled at him with affection. Poor kid! There was so little opportunity for him to run around in Venice.

"Of course not. I want to see the castle too," she answered.

It occurred to her then that Dominic had planned the outing for Marco's benefit. Already he loved the boy like a son.

They left the car and walked in a golden haze of heat which drugged like wine. Leisurely they followed a path that increased in steepness through woodland glades and open hillsides until the air took on a welcome coolness. The climb had begun to pull the muscles of her legs, but she was enjoying it despite the moisture on her forehead. For Dominic had taken her elbow in a firm grip and Marco had slipped a hot little hand into hers.

Presently she caught a glimpse of the castle through the trees banked high above her head. Dazzled by the fiery glow as mullioned windows reflected the sun, she saw a fairy tale castle of turrets and pinnacles on a plateau backed by wooded hills. Such was the illusion of distance. When they were actually standing in the shadows of the impenetrable walls, Martina found it rather over-powering and grim.

"What a bloodthirsty lot they were in the old days, to need such protection," she murmured.

"Bloodthirsty, certainly, and cruel," Dominic conceded. "Yet there were wonderful craftsmen among them, with a deep love of beauty to which they gave full rein in the Byzantine era."

Marco bounded up the steps to the battlements where Dominic lifted him up on his shoulders to see the view. And he was the first one down again to enter the castle. Inside, Martina gazed in awe at banquet halls, frescoed ceilings, gold-paneled walls, carved fireplaces and treasures of a bygone age.

"I see what you mean," she remarked, her mind boggling with all the richness. They went out again into the sunshine. "It must have been quite an effort even in those days to keep up with the Joneses."

Dominic chuckled. "It still is if you're inclined that way," he said.

When they returned to the car Dominic got out the picnic basket and they ate by the lake. Dominic stretched out full length, supporting himself on one elbow and gazing across the water. Martina, always conscious of his presence, allowed her head to fill with dreams in which he was her beloved husband and Marco was their son. But dreams are dangerous because they do away with barriers and make all things possible.

The journey back to the farm was swift and unevent-ful, with Marco falling asleep in her lap. When the big car whispered to a halt in the courtyard the barking of dogs awakened him. They left the car and a man strode toward them, two dogs frisking at his heels. The dogs bounded forward on seeing Dominic and flung themselves upon him boisterously. He fondled their ears and Martina knew instinctively that the man was Signora Stangeri's husband, Maurizio.

Dominic introduced them and she felt the strong hand-clasp of the tall, rugged-faced man whose black hair was sprinkled with grey. His deep-set eyes were kind, his smile warm. Signora Stangeri came out and he gave her a fond look which she returned. When the Signora looked at her, Martina smiled with the feeling that they shared a secret; then they all strolled indoors.

That evening after Marco had been put to bed, Martina and Dominic dined together. They were sitting on the terrace after dinner when a phone call came for Dominic. He was away for some time and she thought he looked annoyed when he returned, but he made no comment. Lighting a cigar, he stretched out his long legs and smoked in silence. The silence jarred a little to Martina who could only think of the hours ticking away which were beyond price in his company.

At his suggestion, they were about to take a stroll in the grounds when the phone rang again. Muttering something under his breath, Dominic excused himself and went to answer it. When he returned he had a preoccupied look which didn't invite questions. Martina longed to stand on tiptoe and kiss the frown away.

"I'm awfully sorry, but I have to leave at once. Roberto will take you both back to Venice in the morning. Sleep well."

He held out his hand, and she stared at him with a curious sense of disappointment. Was it ridiculous of her to think that he had guessed her feelings for him and that this was his way of letting her down lightly? The thought summoned her pride as nothing else would have done. She felt his fingers close over her own as she spoke.

"Goodnight," she said quietly. "Thank you for inviting us. We have enjoyed ourselves. I hope it wasn't bad news."

For a brief moment his grip tightened. Then he was himself once more, the polite host.

"It was expected," he replied. No more.

Martina walked from her room onto the terrace. Had he curtailed their evening together for a reason? If so, why invite her in the first place? But she knew the answer to that: it was Marco. She had been invited because of Marco, just as she had been invited to his house because of Eunice and Bruno. With every faculty numbed, she heard the engine of his car spring into life and saw the arc of light as he swerved around and shot away. She stood there for a long time, chilled and unhappy, until pride again gave her courage. When she walked back into her room, she paused outside Marco's open door in case the noise of the departing car had disturbed him. All was quiet.

"This is for you, Signorina Floyd, with the compliments of Signor Burnett di Ravenelli." Martina stared down at the basket of fruit. Signora Stangeri presented to her as they were leaving. The fruit was beautifully arranged on a bed of greenery. A large bow of mauve satin ribbon decorated the handle. There was a smaller one for Marco. With a hollow feeling that she had had since rising that morning, Martina accepted it graciously.

"Thank you, *signora,*" she said with a pale little smile. "It is indeed kind of him. I must send him a note of thanks."

She thanked Signora Stangeri for making them both welcome and had to smile down at Marco, who was already eating a grape from his basket.

They returned to Venice to learn from Stefano that one of Marco's small friends next door was ill with chicken pox, so that Marco's daily visits would be temporarily suspended. He was overjoyed.

Martina lost no time in writing a note of thanks to Dominic for the gift of the fruit. She enclosed a laboriously written note from Marco and addressed the envelope to the Palazzo Ravenelli.

Later that day Bruno phoned to make sure that all was well. She gave him an abridged account of all their activities, but didn't mention the chicken pox next door in case he should worry.

Martina said almost the same thing to Eunice when she got on the phone. She sounded happy and contented. Marco was delighted when Martina let him speak to them. His words tumbled over each other as he told them about the goldfish and his visit to Dominic's farm. She did not know whether it was by accident or design that he failed to mention missing his lessons next door.

He really was an intelligent child. Watching his animated little face fondly, Martina wondered if his mother ever thought about him. He was such a charming little boy and she was already greatly attached to him. If she could help him to get over the tragedy of losing his father, she would be happy. Since Eunice and Bruno had gone, he had slept through each night without awakening. He had had plenty of exercise and fresh air, which left him exhausted by bedtime. She would be happier if he could swim too. In a place like Venice it was essential, and it would also give him confidence.

The next morning, he came into her room eagerly at seven-thirty with his teddy tucked under his arm. With a rush he leaped onto her bed, to snuggle in the hollow of her arm and look up at her with big dark eyes.

"What are we going to do today, Marty? Am I glad I don't have to go for lessons!" he said on a contented sigh.

She smiled down at him. "Everyone has to have lessons, Marco. If we didn't learn we'd never know anything. You wouldn't like it if these small friends of yours knew more than you, would you?"

He shook his head.

"Never mind. We'll treat it like a holiday. What about us going out early on a *vaporetto* instead of waiting for Ugo to take us? We can have breakfast out for once."

Marco wrinkled his nose with delight.

"Where are we going?" he asked conspiratorially.

"Wait and see," she answered darkly.

It was fun getting washed and dressed hurriedly, leaving a note for the staff and creeping from the house. At eight-thirty they were having breakfast—freshly baked rolls, fresh butter and honey—in a café in the square. The coffee was delicious, Marco's milk rich and creamy.

Just before nine o'clock they walked to the end of the Piazza San Marco where a man in peaked cap and overalls was standing with a pail of grain. On the stroke of nine he flung the contents of the pail onto the Piazza with a grand gesture. The waiting pigeons came from all directions, covering him completely in a tarpaulin of gray feathers. Marco gripped Martina's hand, his eyes enormous as he watched the battle for food. When the man finally emerged from the shower of feathers, there was not a piece of grain to be seen.

They lingered to watch the few stragglers strutting around on their raspberry-colored feet looking for leftovers, then made their way to the market. Marco thoroughly enjoyed peeping into cages containing livestock and newborn chicks. He smiled up at Martina blissfully as they made their way between stalls, interested in everything he saw.

The morning went on wings. Marco had ice cream and lemonade before they went to the west door of San Marco to see the beadle, resplendent in his eighteenth-century uniform, guarding the entrance to the basilica. With his buckled shoes planted on the ground and his staff in hand, he was a formidable figure, refusing admission to all who were improperly dressed. It was amusing to see his fat cheeks shudder with revulsion at the sight of uncovered limbs. Marco pushed his small fist in his mouth, convulsed with mirth when the poor man stuttered each time a scantily attired sightseer defied the conventions. Martina, however, was sorry for the beadle, who was sweating profusely in his suffocating cravat and warm uniform.

They arrived back at the house in time for Marco to have a nap before lunch. He lay down willingly, feeling pleasantly tired after his busy morning. Not wishing to distress him, Martina had not mentioned her plan to teach him to swim. She would have to approach it by degrees and win his confidence more fully before she took him into the water. However, with the whole afternoon of a beautiful sunny day ahead of them, she decided to take him to the Lido.

Looking through his clothes, she was disappointed to find no swimming trunks. She decided to buy some on their way to the beach; she put on her own swimsuit beneath a cotton dress and took a beach bag. She might get a chance to swim herself. Seeing that she was not afraid of the water might encourage Marco to paddle. It wouldn't be long then before he was learning to swim.

The Lido with its long stretch of white sand and endless line of huts was very popular with the Venetians. It was fairly crowded when they arrived and Martina sought a place well away from the breakers where Marco could play happily. This quieter part of the beach was inhabited by a few elderly couples in canopied deck chairs. The air was like a furnace.

Stripping Marco, she put on the small swimming trunks she had bought and applied lotion to his skin to counteract the sun. The next hour was spent in building a sandcastle which they decorated with shells, carrying water from the sea for the moat. Marco was delighted. Meeting his smile, Martina was tempted to take him over the hot sand to cool off his little feet in the water. But he was so happy with his castle that she was afraid of spoiling his pleasure. Some other day perhaps. She longed to swim in the blue sparkling water if only for a few moments.

On a sudden impulse, she asked, "Can your *madre* swim, Marco?"

He was absorbed in the task of placing small flags on the battlements of his castle. They had been made with twigs of driftwood thrust through colored scraps of paper.

"*Si*, Marty," he answered without looking up.

Martina longed to ask him more—why he should have a bucket and spade among his playthings and no trunks. The explanation might be perfectly simple. He could have outgrown them. On the other hand, and she shuddered at the thought, they could have been lost in the fire.

She had made a small paper boat and was placing it on the water of the moat when someone touched her shoulder. It was an elderly man who had been sitting close by with his wife.

"*Scusate?*" he said in Italian. "My wife and I will have much pleasure in looking after your small charge while you have a swim if you wish."

Martina hid a smile. The couple evidently thought she was Marco's nanny.

"How kind of you," she said, "I'd love to. I won't be long."

Marco was too interested in his castle to miss her for ten minutes, and she slipped off her dress. Taking the bathing cap from her beach bag, she thanked the man's wife as well.

After the heat of the sun, the blue buoyant water felt blissful. She swam leisurely, lay on her back floating dreamily when she grew tired, then threshed at the water with her legs for the sheer love of it.

Suddenly she was aware of a handsome tanned face and glossy shoulders surfacing beside her. Wet black hair was thrown back from bold black eyes and white teeth flashed in a wet smile.

"You swim well, *signorina*."

The alien voice was Italian, which fitted in with the man's Latin appearance. Quick thinking told her he must be one of the gigolos swarming on the beach like locusts, intent upon any pickings to be had from rich, lonely females who craved masculine company. Startled by his unexpected appearance, Martina studiously avoided him and made for the shore. To her relief, he didn't seem to be following her, until she found him waiting for her with a grin on the beach.

"On vacation?" he asked, unabashed.

He walked beside her, his muscles rippling beneath the polished mahogany of his skin. Martina felt his eyes ravishing her slim shapely form. When she did not answer he persisted, "May I see you again, *signorina*?"

Disconcerted, she shook her head and hurried back to Marco as fast as the soft sand would let her.

He tried again. "What about dinner tonight?"

Martina shook her head, and it was apparent by his frown that he was not accustomed to being refused.

Martina plodded on, silently. The young man stuck like glue to her side.

"Miss Floyd? What are you doing here?"

She was dreaming, of course. The tall disapproving

figure barring her way could not be Dominic. His contemptuous look at her companion made the young man disappear faster than a well aimed blow could have done, to her intense relief.

Feeling ridiculously lighthearted, she whipped off her bathing cap, shining up at him as she did so.

"Thank goodness he's gone! I couldn't get rid of him," she said breathlessly.

Dominic's narrowed gaze slid over the cloud of hair cascading to her shoulders and he frowned at the drops of water trembling on her lashes. Her eyes sparkled with no hint of coquetry, yet his own darkened.

"No?" he said uncompromisingly. "I had the impression you weren't trying very hard."

Martina stiffened. The words were like cold water trickling down her spine. She stared up at the wide shoulders and uncovered dark head outlined against the blue of the sky and the electric shock at his sudden appearance was gone as fast as it had come. She looked at him defiantly.

"Apart from it being no business of yours what I do, you were hardly in a position to judge. I kept my head down, and ignored the young man completely. I never spoke a word, but you wouldn't know that."

There was a perceptible pause, then he said in his detached voice,

"Naturally, the man thought you had come to this beach to attract attention and were playing hard to get. This part of the beach is a well-known rendezvous spot for men of his type. I happened to be in one of the hotels over there when I saw you."

Martina's hands curled over her bathing cap in a grip that hurt. "And you couldn't believe your eyes." She spoke low and vehemently, the bitterness welling up inside her, reaching her voice. "You disapproved of me from the beginning, though why you should when it's no business of yours, I can't imagine. Marco is my responsibility and I'm answerable only to Bruno for anything I do while he's in my care. To me, you're a hardened, cynical bachelor who'd done everything, even to playing fairy godfather to Marco. Your life, however, is your own affair. I'd be obliged if you would regard my life in the same light!"

He surveyed her rather pointedly with a slight hint of mockery. In no way perturbed by her hot and angry speech, he returned her serve with a skill born of much practice.

"Miss Floyd," he said evenly, "you are a stranger here in Venice. I was merely putting you right about certain parts of the Lido. Had I known you were coming here with Marco I could have arranged for you to go to one of the small private beaches belonging to friends of mine. As for disapproving of you, I disapproved of any woman having charge of Marco. I still do." Suddenly his eyes, lingering on her flushed face, twinkled faintly. "It may surprise you to know that I think you're a good substitute for a tutor."

Only half appeased, she said stiffly, "I'd better be going back to him. I left him in the care of an elderly couple."

She gestured over the crowds of people on the beach. The dark arrogant head lifted and his intense gaze seached for the small figure.

"Zio Dominic!"

Marco's voice came from behind them as they strolled up the sand. They turned to see him coming from the direction of the water holding the elderly man's hand. He had obviously been in the water, for his trunks were wet.

"Zio Dominic!" he repeated, breaking away from the man and running to them. "Come and see my sand-castle!" Taking hold of Dominic's hand he pulled him away.

"I hope you don't mind my taking the boy into the water," the elderly man said as they followed Marco and Dominic. "He was covered in sand."

"And he went with you?" Martina asked, amazed.

"Oh yes. In fact he enjoyed it."

"Really? He had made a promise to his father never to go into the water without him. I had an idea he was afraid of it."

"Perhaps it was because I am a man, *signorina*, that he went with me unafraid."

"Whatever it was I am greatly indebted to you, *signore*," Martina said quietly.

"Is it not *magnifico*, Zio Dominic?" Marco was saying proudly when they arrived back at the sandcastle.

"It is indeed. Did you do it all yourself?" Dominic asked teasingly.

Marco shook his head. "Marty helped me."

Martina toweled herself dry, buttoning the dress over her swimsuit while Dominic bent down to examine the castle. Then she dried Marco, dressed him and combed the tangled curls gently.

"We're not going yet, are we, Marty?" he asked.

"Yes, darling, I'm afraid we have to meet Ugo soon," she said with a smile.

She was tempted to kiss the disappointment from his face, but resisted the urge, aware of the immaculate Dominic towering above them. Deftly, she cleaned the loose hair from the comb and returned it to a small leather case. Then hastily she put everything back in the beach bag—swimming suit, used towels, toilet thing and lastly the bucket and spade.

"Allow me."

To Martina's dismay, Dominic bent to pick up the beach bag. So he was going to accompany them to Ugo. She wondered if his business was over for the day and she wished fervently that someone would come and take him away. But he strolled beside them as though they were three people on holiday. The elderly couple had gone.

Martina stalked rather than walked in silence, still smarting from her encounter with him and his rebuff. There was no other word for it. She had taken a ribbon from the pocket of her dress and slipped it on her head to hold back her hair.

"I liked it better loose," Dominic said. His lips twitched in spite of the cool tones. "Actually, I didn't come here to upbraid you. I saw you making your way down to the sea for a swim and I wanted to ask you if you would accompany me to a party this evening."

A spontaneous acceptance was on her tongue. Had he seemed the least enthusiastic about it, she would not have hesitated. As it was, she recognized the invitation as a form of atonement for his recent rebuff.

"I'm sorry," she heard herself saying quietly. "We've had a full day. I need to have an early night. Thanks all the same."

"As you wish," he said coolly.

Achingly she sought to salvage the slightest suggestion of disappointment in his tone. There was none. He had taken her refusal without a murmur! The walk to where Ugo awaited seemed endless. She avoided Dominic's glance when he helped her into the launch and did not turn her head as he strode away. It occurred to her when he had gone that she could have offered him a ride.

Martina returned to the house, glad to be back despite a good day. Being with Marco presented no problems. Venice, with its beautiful ancient buildings, exciting waterways and lovely beaches, offered a diversity of pleasures. Marco was well behaved and easy to please, with childish enthusiasm for simple things. On leaving the beach, he had cast several yearning glances behind him to his sandcastle. Yet he had left it obediently enough, his big dark eyes meeting Martina's in an angelic smile.

They spent some time with his goldfish after supper before she put him to bed, tired but happy. It was only when she was sitting beside him and he was sound asleep that she gave a thought to the lonely evening ahead. Had she been too hasty in refusing Dominic's invitation? She was on vacation and it was up to her to enjoy every minute of it while it lasted. Her love for him was throwing everything out of focus. If she didn't want to be miserable for the rest of her stay, she would have to curb her emotions where he was concerned. Setting her mind to it, Martina gathered up Marco's cast-off clothing, putting his underwear out to be laundered and placing clean clothes in the airing cupboard for morning.

She had chosen a book from a small shelf beside her bed when the phone rang. For seconds she stared at it, thinking it might be Dominic. Then with trembling fingers she picked up the receiver.

The voice she heard was a feminine one speaking in cultured English.

"Hello, Miss Floyd?"

"Yes."

"This is Dawn Agusta, a friend of Eunice. I'm have a few friends to dinner this evening and I would love you to come." She gave a small, pleasant laugh. "I know I'm springing it on you at short notice, but you must blame my husband. He invited a few men friends to dinner this evening to discuss business affairs, and I decided at the last moment to invite the same number of women. I've invited the wives of the married men plus a few single ones. I think it's rather fun, don't you? So will you come, please?"

Why not? She liked the sound of Dawn Agusta's voice and sweet laugh. Impromptu parties were fun and, at the moment, fun was what she needed. Furthermore, she had no qualms about leaving Marco. He was tired with the day's activities and would probably sleep through the night.

"I'd love to," she answered.

"I'm so glad. I'm sure you'll enjoy it. Transport is supplied for you. One of my husband's friends will be passing you door on his way here and will be delighted to pick you up. He'll call at seven-thirty. All right?"

"Yes, thank you."

Martina put down the receiver with a smile of anticipation. Crossing her arms, she hugged herself and waltzed round the room to Marco's open door. A glance assured her that he was still fast asleep and she went downstairs in search of Stefano.

He was crossing the hall as she came down the stairs and waited with a smile.

"I'm awfully sorry to be such a nuisance, Stefano. I shall be going out to dinner this evening after all. Signora Agusta has invited me to her house and a guest is picking me up at seven-thirty. I wondered if one of the staff would mind keeping an eye on Marco in case he wakes. He'll probably sleep through the night, but I'd feel happier if someone looked in on him occasionally."

Stefano nodded, "I will see to it, *signorina*."

At seven-thirty, Martina was at the door when a gondola sliding to a halt.

Someone rose from the cushioned seat, someone tall with wide shoulders. . . . Martina stood very still. Her trembling lips formed his name. Dominic! She might have said it. She wasn't sure. He looked more handsome and disturbing than ever in immaculate evening dress. Beneath the thick dark hair, his face was a chiseled study in mahogany. His deep voice, loaded with sarcasm, sent disconcerting vibrations along her nerves.

"Good evening, Miss Floyd," he drawled insolently. His eyes, glinting like polished steel, flicked over her embarrassed flush. "I trust you're not feeling too tired after your exhausting day."

Her first impulse was to run, for he was the last person she had expected. She realized that ironically this was the party he had asked her to. What must he be thinking? However, it was no time for shrinking. Her face quivered; she controlled it swiftly. Pressing a slim hand to her painfully constricted throat, Martina managed a pale smile.

"Good evening. I feel fine, thanks," she replied, obliged to take the hand he offered to help her on board.

With his fingers closing painfully around her trembling ones, he seated her and took his place by her side. The gondola slid away as she sat with her hands clasped tightly in her lap in an effort to calm her shattered nerves. A swift glance at his firm jaw and unyielding profile did not help.

"I changed my mind." She paused to quell the rush of words. Unfortunately, they were out before she was aware of them. "I had no idea that. . . ." She caught her breath.

"I had been invited?" he suggested with a pitiless stare in her direction.

She had the sensation of walking on a tightrope. Her cheeks flamed. She either had to admit it or lie. She did neither. Instead, she said disarmingly, "Signora Agusta sounds like a charming woman on the phone. I've never met her. I believe she's a friend of Eunice."

To her relief, he accepted the sudden change of topic with the serene coolness that was characteristic of him.

"Luca Agusta has known Bruno since childhood. He and his wife are two of the nicest people I know." He gave her an unnerving glance. Switching the conversation as swiftly as she had done, he went on, "Regarding Marco—aren't you taking your duties too seriously where he's concerned?"

She stiffened. "What do you mean?"

"What I say," he answered curtly. "Bruno would not be pleased to know you're shutting yourself away with him at night when you should be out enjoying yourself."

"I am enjoying myself," she contradicted perversely.

"Spending your evenings with a book? I don't believe it. If that's so, then it's time someone made you aware of what you're missing," he said forcefully.

You have already, Martina wanted to say. "It's only for a week," she said aloud.

"How long are you here for?"

"A month."

He made an impatient gesture with a lean brown hand.

"The second week is half over. Suppose Bruno and Eunice decide to stay on in Geneva?"

She glanced at him swiftly. "They said they would be away a week. If they're delayed, I shall continue to look after Marco until they return."

There was a short silence. Then he said casually, "Pity about the chicken pox. I suppose if Marco decides to have it you'll go all maternal and nurse him yourself."

"How did you know. . . ." she began.

He raised an ironical brow. "About the chicken pox? Bruno's neighbor, the Conte de Savorderi, happens to be a friend of mine. His two children are adorable. The youngest with the chicken pox, Benito, is my favorite."

Painfully jealous of a child she had never seen, Martina said, "You like children?"

His eyes narrowed. "You sound surprised."

She felt her color deepen and sought safer ground. "Does Signora Agusta have any children?"

"Yes. Two boys." He smiled at her with baffling amiability. "Does that make you happy?"

"I suppose they make Signor and Signora Agusta happy," she replied evasively.

He surveyed her with a roused interest, half turning in his seat.

"You've made a hit with Marco. Mia would be jealous if she were here."

"What about his Zio Bruno? Marco worships the man."

"Bruno is very like his brother Paolo both in voice and mannerism. Marco sees his father in him, hence the attachment."

She said bitterly, "If Signora Vortolini was capable of being jealous as far as her son is concerned, surely she would want to have him with her?"

"I've an idea she'll get around to it later, especially if she decides to marry again. Loving another man could help her forget the tragedy, and Marco's part in it, to a certain extent."

Martina smiled wistfully. "Marco is a sweet little boy. Some men resent another man's child when they marry the mother. I'd hate to think of that kind of thing happening to Marco."

"You don't like the idea of Marco's mother marrying again?"

Martina went cold inside. "It's really none of my business, is it?"

"I agree." He eyed her speculatively. "You resent Signora Vortolini's treatment of her son, don't you? You have never been in love. If you had you would understand the depth of emotion involved when one loses the beloved partner. At the moment Marco's mother is still reeling from her loss. She is not a whole person. Part of her is buried with Paolo. Only time can deaden the pain. Happiness with another man can make her whole again, release her from all the pent-up bitterness, including her antagonism against her own son.

"And Marco?" she said huskily.

"Some men, as you say, would resent him. Others will not. I, for one, would love the child as my own son."

Suddenly the passing splendor left Martina cold. She clenched her hands in her lap, recoiling inwardly as from a mortal blow. He could not have told her more plainly of his intention to marry Mia. Somehow, she had known it all along.

CHAPTER EIGHT

The Agusta residence was another beautifully preserved Byzantine palace of similar lines to those owned by Dominic and Bruno. Signor and Signora Agusta greeted them at the door of a *sala* on the first floor.

Signor Agusta was a true Venetian in looks, with a rather long nose, dark deep-set eyes beneath strongly marked brows and thin lips. He seemed to be around the same age as Bruno, and was broad-set and charming.

Signora Agusta, also dark, was petite and animated. She had alert hazel eyes, and lovely expressive hands, and was exquisitely groomed. Her smile reached her eyes, which radiated warmth.

"*Buona sera*, Miss Floyd," she said. "My husband, Luca."

"I've heard so much about you from Eunice," Dawn Agusta went on after introductions had been made. "I would have contacted you sooner, but we've been in Switzerland on a visit to our boys' school. We returned yesterday."

She left Dominic talking to her husband, and with a hand lightly touching Martina's arm, she chatted to her between introductions to her other guests. The atmosphere of pleasantry was conducive to an enjoyable evening. The Agustas were like Martina's own parents, so happy in their marriage that it showed in their spontaneous gaiety and sparkling conversation. Dominic had said they were two of the nicest people he knew. It occurred to her that he would like her parents, too.

"And how is the small Marco?" Dawn Agusta asked when, after dinner, the women retired to another *sala* leaving the men to talk over their business.

"Quite well," Martina replied. "I adore him."

They sat on an exquisite satin-upholstered sofa. Silk-paneled walls were hung with portraits and landscapes. The furniture was elegantly curved and the polished wood mosaic floor was covered with expensive rugs. Some of the women guests were enjoying after-dinner liqueurs. Others, like Martina, preferred coffee.

"Yes, he's a perfect lamb, isn't he, and his father adored him. I'm so glad he has someone like you to look after him. Poor kid!" Signora Agusta finished her drink, then continued in a confidential whisper, "I do think Mia should have the boy with her. There are rumors that she'll soon be marrying again. It's what one could expect, because she's a very beautiful woman." She paused, then added thoughtfully, "I wouldn't be surprised if she and Dominic make a match of it. Mia and Marco have stayed at his farm in the Venetian hills since Paolo died, and I've heard that Marco has gone there several times since his mother went to Greece."

Martina did not enlighten her regarding her own recent visit to the farm with Marco. She was not given to gossip. Neither was Dawn Agusta, if she was any judge; the woman was probably making coversation until the men rejoined them.

When the men returned Dawn rose to greet them and Martina found Luca Agusta smiling down at her.

"What do you think of Venice, *signorina?*" he asked, sitting down beside her.

"I love it," she answered warmly. "And I adore your gondolas."

He smiled. "Yes—a pity they are gradually being driven from the scene by motorboats. We are living in a mechanical age and the rising costs of running a gondola are growing beyond the average man's pocket."

"What a pity!"

"It is indeed. Especially since the increasing number of motorboats are proving a constant threat to the foundations of Venice with their dangerous backwash." He gave a resigned shrug. "Yet what can one do against progress?"

"Nothing, except make Venice immortal on canvas."

"I'm doing my best toward that end," he murmured. "Do you paint, *signorina?*"

"I've dabbled in it. Do you have a studio here?"

"Yes. On the top floor."

"And you're really an artist?"

"Of sorts," he admitted honestly.

"Don't be misled, Miss Floyd. Luca is a clever and talented artist." Dominic had strolled across the room to join them. Thrusting his hands into his pockets, he smiled down at his friend. "He will tell you it's a hobby. What he won't tell you is that it's a very rewarding one." He slanted a mocking glance upon Martina. "Why not take our young friend here to see your studio? I'm sure she'd enjoy it."

"Would you, *signorina?*" Luca asked.

"Yes, I would," she replied, the thought of getting away from Dominic making her more eager.

"Then do you mind, *signorina*, if I ask Dominic to take you? I can't leave my guests yet, having just joined them. I'm sure you will find him an excellent guide. Well, Dominic?"

To her dismay Dominic seemed entirely agreeable to the suggestion. "I'll be delighted. Come, Miss Floyd."

Coolly, he extended a hand. But the strange glint in his eyes which always seemed to mock at her reserve urged her to regain her feet unaided. Then, striving to assume a coolness she was far from feeling, she walked from the room with him.

Wall lights illuminated their way up several flights of stairs to the top of the house. The room they entered was flooded with moonlight. It spilled from a skylight and long windows to reveal a typical artist's studio. Martina saw a miscellany of furniture and props, a working table containing a palette, paints and brushes, and a number of canvases propped around the walls of the room. Dominic did not switch on the light and Martina appreciated the soft moonlight on the paintings. He picked up the canvases one by one—work which, in her opinion, was the kind the critics would rave about. She gazed entranced on scenes of Venice which she recognized immediately. Luca Agusta, she was sure, would one day be a household word in the world of art.

The visit to the quiet upper regions of the house had given their relationship a more personal flavor. But Martina had the constraint of voice and manner which she always felt whenever Dominic drew too near for her peace of mind. The task of filling silences as Dominic put down one picture to pick up another fell mainly on herself so she uttered little platitudes which never strayed from the subject of art.

Dominic was placing the last of the canvases in their order against the wall when Martina walked to the raised dais at the far end of the room and lifted the cover from the painting on the easel. The next moment the cover slid from her fingers unheeded to the floor, for she was gazing on the portrait of one of the most beautiful women she had ever seen.

The woman was wearing a gown of a delicate shade of blue, from which her slender neck and shoulders emerged white as surf from the sea-like illusion. A small diamond tiara was set upon the fair hair which cascaded down to her shoulders in a sunlit cloud. Diamonds and emeralds blazed on her neck and ears.

Her face was intriguing, saucy and coquettish with a delightful nose, small chin, willful mouth and green eyes thickly fringed with lashes darker than her hair. To Martina, her beauty struck a chord of pleasure shadowed by doubt, a tangible doubt. She knew, even while she preferred not to, that those enigmatic green eyes were aware of their power to attract and that their owner would not hesitate to use them to their best advantage.

Then Martina noticed something else, a vague familiarity about the small features, a certain tilt of the head and. . . . A sensation of receiving a cold shower took her breath away in a small gasp. Marco . . . of course, who had obviously inherited his dark Latin coloring from his father.

Without turning, she knew Dominic was behind her,

knew he was gazing at the portrait. Martina had an almost uncontrollable urge to draw her hand over his eyes to shut out the features of the woman who reminded her so poignantly of Marco.

"You recognize the painting?" he murmured, still gazing.

"Yes," she answered, her heart like a coil of lead in her breast. "Signora Mia Vortolini, Marco's mother. If Signor Luca Agusta is not already famous, then this portrait should go a long way toward helping him in that direction."

Her voice sounded flat to her ears. The calmness with which she had disciplined herself, every defence barrier she had deliberately raised against him were swept away by the tumult of emotion raging inside her. She wanted breathing space, somewhere to collect her scattered thoughts, away from Dominic who stood silently as though he had forgotten she was beside him.

Blindly she turned, forgetting she was on the raised dais. The next moment she had pitched headlong flat on her face on the floor. The violent impact vibrated through her slim form like a gong. Then strong arms were lifting her gently to her feet and she felt herself clasped against Dominic's chest.

"That confounded dais!" he exploded. "I blame myself entirely for not turning on a light. That was quite a dive!"

To Martina his voice came from a distance as his hand caressed the back of her head and held it against him. For agonizing moments she fought off the feeling of faintness and deadly nausea which threatened to engulf her. The effort brought beads of perspiration to her temples. She was thankful for his support, but wished it had been anyone but Dominic.

"I'd better sit down," she gasped, feeling her legs giving out. Valiantly she tried to rally. "I'll be better in a moment."

A brown finger lifted her chin and he scanned her ashen face with a frown of concern. Then, with a smothered exclamation, he scooped her up into his arms, strode across the room and lowered her gently onto a divan. Cushions were pushed behind her head.

"Lie still," he commanded, then left the room.

Martina lay back against the cushions gulping in great breaths of air, and gradually she began to feel stronger. The faintness had gone when Dominic returned, full of concern.

"You're not going to like this," he said. "I want you to drink it."

Sitting on the edge of the divan beside her, he lifted her head. His gentleness brought a lump to her throat, until she reminded herself that he was filled with remorse and was blaming himself for her accident. The thought spurred her into taking the medicine into her trembling fingers. Fortunately, there was no risk of spilling the few tablespoons of liquid which she willed herself to drink, for his fingers closed over hers in quiet mastery. It went down with a shudder—Martina had always hated sal volatile. But she would have drunk worse than that to get away from this intolerable situation.

Lying back on her cushions, she watched him leave the room with the empty glass. When he returned he carried something small and white which he bent down to place on her forehead. It was ice-cold and infinitely soothing.

"A paper tissue soaked in cold water," he explained. "Lie still for a while. Want the lights on?"

She moved uneasily beneath his gaze. "No, thanks," she replied, hardening her heart against his own special charm. "I feel better already."

He regarded her with narrowed gaze for a long moment.

"You'll stay put until you feel stronger." Suddenly his charming smile lit up the gloom. "Unless I carry you downstairs. You're certainly not fit enough to make it under your own steam yet." He took her hands lightly but firmly in his own. "Your hands are cold. Are you warm enough?"

She nodded, trying to draw them free without success. His hold was gentle but his fingers were like steel. Gradually, Martina felt his vitality flowing into her. She closed her eyes as though to shut out his nearness, and slept. When she opened them again it took several minutes to realize where she was.

Dominic was standing tall and silent with his wide shoulders outlined against a moonlit window. He was gazing out, and she wondered if he was thinking of the portrait of Mia. The pangs inside her were more of despair than jealousy. One could not hope to compete with the Mia Vortolinis of this world. It was as foolish as dreaming about the Dominic Burnett di Ravenellis.

She still felt very shaken. Her body ached all over, but she was determined to behave as normally as she could. Dominic must have known she was awake, for he came to the divan.

Desperately, she said, "I'm feeling well enough now to go downstairs. If you don't mind."

"I certainly do mind until I've had a look at you."

Striding to the wall switch near the divan, he flooded the room with light. Then he was bending over her and lifted her chin on a lean finger.

"You're a better color. How do you feel? No bones broken?" His keen eyes raked her face before he dropped his hand.

She watched him straighten and push his hands into his pockets, feeling like a butterfly on a pin beneath his intent gaze.

"No. I feel much better. The sudden dive knocked me out a bit." She moved uneasily. "They'll be wondering about us. Have you told them?"

"No. Luca knows we're here. If he misses us he may conclude that we're loitering with intent." His eyes twinkled devilishly. "After all, you're a very attractive young woman. I'm a man and we're both unattached."

She flushed sensitively. "I'm hardly your type," she said painfully.

He raised a brow and smiled faintly. "No? What would you say was my kind of woman?"

"Someone like . . . Signora Mia Vortolini."

He looked surprised. "Why?" he asked, capturing her gaze and holding it.

"Because . . . because she belongs in your world."

"Does she?" He frowned. His look became guarded. "So you're of the opinion that a man should have an affair with someone belonging to the crowd he moves in. How wrong you are. An affair has to be something refreshingly different."

"Someone removed from your own circle who would fade away gracefully, leaving no one the wiser. Too bad I happen to regard affairs as cheap and degrading."

The words were out before Martina was aware of them. How dared he? He would not have dared to suggest anything like that to Mia. She saw the gleam in his eyes, took it for mockery and, furiously, swung her legs over the side of the divan opposite to where he was standing. In spite of her weariness, Martina was aware of an electric tension in the air.

When he spoke his voice was almost a drawl.

"What are you running away from? I have no intention of seducing you, if that's what you're afraid of. Furthermore, you're the last person I would ever consider having an affair with."

Each word he uttered acted like a whiplash across her back. She even detected a hint of laughter in his voice. To him, the mere idea of an affair with her was so absurd as to cause him amusement. Martina was choked with humiliation, but she was not without courage. Ignoring him, she deliberately opened her handbag, found a comb and straightened her hair, after which she powdered her nose, stood up to shake the wrinkles from her clothes and dropped the wet compress he had placed on her head into a waste paper basket.

Suddenly he was barring her way. Against his strength and height, her anger became a puny thing. Its passing left her cold. She felt small and defenceless, clinging to the last remnants of her pride.

"Sure you are all right?" Dominic demanded.

His hands were suddenly gripping her shoulders. His eyes deepened and darkened in the intensity of his gaze. She could have shrieked at the force of his fingers robbing her of all power of movement. But she controlled herself as he looked into her eyes. His mouth thinned when she did not answer and he said somewhat roughly, "What a weary-faced child you look like! For two bits I'd carry you downstairs, even though I know you would hate it."

Still she made no reply. Her heart was leaping at his touch and to her shame she hoped he would do just that. Good heavens, what kind of a weak fool had she become? The man had just insulted her, yet here she was, aching to feel his arms around her. Pride brightened the disgust she felt for herself.

He saw it, frowned and dropped his hands abruptly.

Still shaken by her wild longing, Martina forced herself to speak with quiet composure.

"I'm quite recovered, thanks. Shall we go downstairs?"

He stepped aside instantly and she moved toward the door, giving him no other option than to follow her.

The rest of the evening passed in a blur of pain for Martina. Her knees began to sting and her whole body ached from head to toe. When the time came to go, she tried to ignore the stiffness in her joints and walked naturally with Dominic to his gondola. The short journey to Bruno's house was made swiftly, and taking a hasty leave of Dominic, she hobbled painfully to her room.

Slipping off her evening dress, she found that her knees were discolored and bruised. The thick rug she had landed on when falling from the dais had protected her from serious injury. While her bath was running she went in to check on Marco.

The scented bath water was soothing to her aching limbs, for the fall had jarred her whole being. But the physical pain was nothing to the hurt she felt from Dominic's cruel words. Well, that should cure her of her longing for him! She relaxed in the perfumed warmth, shutting out all disturbing thoughts. Then she toweled herself, put on her pyjamas and crawled into bed.

She slept badly that night. Her knees ached and she was strangely restless, with Dominic's deep voice and intent gaze haunting her dreams.

The next few days were tranquil ones for Martina, apart

from a few temors when Dominic phoned the following morning to ask how she was after her fall. She assured him that she was suffering no ill effects apart from a little stiffness of her joints, and she felt a moment of panic when he suggested sending over a doctor friend of his to make sure she hadn't pulled any muscles. To her sensitive ears, he sounded amused when she vehemently refused his suggestion, and she was annoyed on hanging up the receiver that she was trembling.

Marco became the pivot of her existence. Happily, hand in hand, they explored the narrow water lanes of Venice, peeping into the small shop windows and stopping at cafés for refreshments. Each morning Martina planned their day, allowing Marco to choose what they should do one day and following her own choice on alternate days. The plan worked very well. His tacit obedience and good manners made it a pleasure for her to take him around.

At Marco's request, they spent the first day in the gardens near to the Lido and the next day Martina took him to the Naval Museum which was situated on the site of famous dockyards where, years ago, the Venetians had built some of the finest galley ships in the world. Stone lions guarded the grand entrance to what was now a museum of past glories.

Martina brought her camera and took several pictures of Marco seated on a lion. He was delighted when she showed him how to use the camera and take a picture of herself. The time went by unheeded until Martina, glancing at her watch, discovered they would have to hurry to meet Ugo where he was to pick them up. Marco had lingered entranced at scale models of galleys in the museum, and she had to tear him away.

They were more than half-way to their meeting place when a crowd gathered outside a hotel barred their progress. The place was evidently on fire, for smoke was belching out from upstairs windows.

Martina, remembering Marco's ordeal, determined to get him away as soon as possible. She did not remember letting go of his hand, but, to her dismay, she found he was no longer by her side. Frantically she looked for him in the crowd, questioning people and describing the boy before plunging back the way they had come.

She began to tremble when her search brought no result. To add to her distress, she missed her camera. It had been a gift from her parents and was expensive as well as being of sentimental value. She hated the thought of losing it, though it was of secondary importance to finding Marco.

Her brain began to spin, pinpointing the likely places he could have run to. When it occurred to her that he might be hiding, she retraced her steps to where she had first missed him. Firemen were swarming all over the place, making people keep their distance from the burning building. There was no sign of Marco and Martina disconsolately went to find Ugo with the hope that Marco might be with him.

The sight of Ugo's puzzled frown told her Marco was not there. She explained what had happened.

"There is but one thing to do, *signorina*," Ugo said, helping her into the launch and seating her. "I will go."

"Go where?" she said.

"*Presentarmi al Commissariato.*"

Martina groaned with dismay. "The police?" she echoed. "Oh no! You can't do that, Ugo. It will be in the papers if Marco isn't found, and what's Signor Vortolini going to think when he sees it? He would be dreadfully upset. No, we must think of something. What about Signor Burnett di Ravenelli?" she asked in desperation. "Let's go to him. He'll know what to do."

Ugo gave a very Italian shrug and set the launch off at speed. Martina sat with her hands clasped in her lap, praying that Dominic would be at home when they arrived. They were losing valuable time otherwise. But she had to take the chance before going to the police. Rather than do that she would spend the night searching for Marco herself. How she hated the thought of letting Bruno down by not taking better care of Marco!

On ringing the bell at the Palazzo Ravenelli, she was admitted at once by a manservant who listened impassively when she explained that it was imperative she see Signor Ravenelli at once. Courteously, he bade her wait while he went upstairs. It was a slight consolation to know that Dominic was at home. She paced slowly to the foot of the stairs and ran up them as soon as the servant appeared and beckoned to her.

Leading her along the corridor, he opened a pair of ornate cream and gold doors inward. He had obviously remembered her name from a former visit. "Signorina Floyd to see you, *signore*," he said, showing her in.

Dominic came across the room with his long economical stride. His charming smile shook her heart. He was wearing a black velvet smoking jacket over light slacks. A dull gold cravet tucked in at the firm brown throat gave a glow to his bronze skin. The dark hair, immaculately trimmed, gave him an alien look. The well-cut lips lost their curve when he saw her look of concern.

He frowned. "Miss Floyd!" he exclaimed on a deep note of surprise. "Is anything wrong?"

Martina nodded. The relief of sharing her trouble with someone she felt she could trust help her lower her guard. She caught his arm to gaze up at him appealingly.

"It's Marco. He . . . he's gone! Disappeared."

His eyes narrowed down at her, noting her distress.

"You'd better sit down and tell me all about it," he ordered, and led her to a comfortable chair.

Martina gave an abridged account of the day's activities, leading up to the fire at the hotel and Marco's mysterious disappearance. Dominic had leaned back against a table facing her while he listened. When she had finished, he looked her over speculatively, still frowning at her bright eyes and eloquently appealing look.

"And now relax,' he said, his eyes on the small hands gripping the handbag on her knee. "There's no need for you to become so upset. Venice is fairly safe for children. We'll take it slowly." He gave a faint smile when she relaxed her grip on the bag and sat back in her chair. "You say you took pictures of the lions outside the museum? Where's your camera?" he asked curiously.

Color flooded her paleness. "You'll think I'm an idiot. I lost that too."

"Where?"

Martina floundered beneath his intent gaze. "I . . . I have no idea. I missed it about the time Marco disappeared." She lifted trembling fingers to her temples, which were beginning to throb with anxiety, and tried to concentrate. "Marco was carrying it when we entered the museum. I'd shown him how to use it and he was thrilled when I let him take a picture of me. I might have had it later—I don't remember."

"Don't distress yourself. It didn't occur to you that Marco might have left it behind in the museum and, suddenly remembering it, ran back for it?"

Martina was startled. "Then you don't think he ran away because he was scared of the fire?"

"Hardly. Marco very bravely returned to a burning villa to rescue a toy. He's not likely to run away from a fire."

"But his nightmares of the fire at the villa—" she began.

"Were the result of losing a beloved father." He straightened as though coming to a decision. "I'm going to pour you a glass of wine to bring a little color to those pale cheeks. I want you to drink it while I make a few inquiries. I presume Ugo is waiting for you at the door?"

She nodded.

"Don't worry too much about Marco. Children are apt to get lost in spite of constant surveillance. He's in no immediate danger."

Dominic strode across the room to a cabinet and poured out a glass of wine which he brought back to her. Martina took it in trembling hands, trying to find comfort in his words as he left the room. She had no desire for the wine. Her throat felt too constricted for her to swallow. But she had asked his help and the least she could do was to go along with him.

He was absent for about ten minutes, during which time she glanced around the room which comprised a study and a library. She saw book-lined walls, a beautiful glass cabinet crammed with silver trophies, a writing desk, comfortable furniture and a collection of objets d'art. A painting hanging over the fireplace caught and held her attention. It could be none other than the tall stately figure of Dominic's stepfather, the late Conte de Ravenelli.

They were very much alike, both dark-haired and dark-eyed with aristocratic features, except that the Conte wore a small van Dyck beard. He was a haughty figurte in the long robes indicative of some honor being bestowed upon him.

Seated in a room which had known them both set up vibrations inside her. Strange that even in the midst of her distress she could still be moved by thoughts of Dominic. When he returned, she scanned his face anxiously.

"Don't look so stricken," he said curtly, his eagle eye taking in the untouched glass of wine. "I don't intend to tell you anything until you've drunk the wine."

Martina picked up the glass and drank obediently while he walked over to the window. Presently, he turned to watch her set down the empty glass.

"Marco is quite safe," he said. "He was never lost."

She stared up at him bewildered. "I don't understand," she said huskily.

"It seems Marco had been carrying your camera," he explained, watching her gravely. "He left it behind in the museum and remembered it when you were on your way to meet Ugo. With childlike impetuosity, he ran back for it while you were watching the fire at the hotel."

Martina's eyes widened incredulously. "But how on earth did he find his way back to the museum? We'd taken endless short cuts. I'm sure he could never find them."

He said dryly, "Apparently he did in the end; the museum was closing. Someone had found the camera on a seat in the museum and had turned it in to one of the staff, who remembered seeing Marco with it earlier. Fortunately the *custode* of the museum knows Bruno well and has to pass his door on his way home. So he took Marco with him."

The color had risen to her cheeks. She was immensely moved and excited. Her eyes shone and her red lips curved enchantingly over her small pearly teeth. Martina's smile was one of her charms, half sad, half gay, as she laughed up at him. She rose to her feet clasping her hands in a sigh of relief.

"As simple as that," she whispered as though she still could not believe it. "I must go at once. Thank you so much for your help. I'm very grateful."

"Why the hurry?" He retained the formidable look he had brought into the room. "I've phoned to verify the fact that Marco had arrived home and Stefano assures me that Marco is there with the camera."

"Oh yes, the camera. I would have hated to lose it, although it was of secondary importance to Marco's safety. It's of sentimental value, apart from being expensive."

He gave her a brooding look. "The giver means a lot to you?"

"Both of them," she corrected him. "My parents." She bent down to pick up her handbag which she had placed on the floor. "I feel I must apologize for taking up so much of your time. I'm more than grateful for your help." She gripped the bag, aware of him watching her rather pointedly. "I hated the idea of going to the police with the possibility of Bruno reading about it in the newspapers. It would have been awful to let him down."

He had come across the room to her and she had the impression that he was barring her way.

"So you came to me. I'm glad you did, although it was for the wrong reason. However, it gives me the opportunity to make a suggestion I have had in mind these last few days. You'd better sit down while we discuss it."

He waved a peremptory hand to her chair, which she immediately resented.

"I'm sorry," she said steadily. "I'm sure you'll understand that my main concern now is to return as soon as possible to Marco. I fail to see what we have to discuss."

She saw his jaw come into sudden prominence. "Sit down," he commanded with a sternness which made her obey. "You're not leaving yet. For one thing it wouldn't be good for you."

She restrained herself with an effort. "Not good for me? What do you mean?"

He said evenly, "You were emotionally upset when you arrived here not long ago. Marco's escapade has taken more out of you than you realize. A short spell away from him will do you no harm. He'll be looked after by Stefano, who will put him to bed. Forgive my impertinence, but is your visit to Venice in lieu of a holiday?"

"What business is. . . ." Martina pulled herself up sharply. After all, the man had helped her out of an embarrassing situation. No need for her to be so touchy. "In a way," she supplemented.

Dominic had pushed his hands into his pockets and was regarding her in his usual enigmatic fashion. "Then are you not disappointed?"

"Disappointed?" she echoed, prepared for argument.

"Yes. Having charge of a small boy when you could be having a good time."

"But I *am* enjoying it. Besides, I'm only taking charge of Marco for a week," she reminded him sharply.

He made an impatient gesture with a lean hand. "A temporary expedient that might last for the duration of your visit. Have you thought of that?"

Martina gazed at him with a puzzled frown. Drat the man! If he knew something why didn't he come right out with it?

"I don't know what you mean," she said stiffly.

"Then I suggest you have dinner with me and we can discuss it more fully."

Her chin rose stubbornly. "I've taken up enough of your time already. I can assure you I'm quite happy the way things are."

Dominic didn't answer. Instead, he strode coolly toward a bell to summon a servant. Martina, assuming he was ringing for a conveyance to take her home, strolled toward the door.

"Ah, Guido," Dominic greeted the manservant who had appeared promptly. "Will you escort the Signorina to a guest room?" He slanted a mocking smile at her startled expression. "When I phoned Stefano just now I took the liberty of informing him that you were dining here this evening. No doubt you'll want to freshen up."

Martina teetered. There was nothing else for it. Guido stood waiting at the door and she could hardly refuse and create a scene in front of him. Neither could she stalk from the house without a conveyance. With a look which was meant to be one of withering contempt but which only served to deepen Dominic's mocking smile, she stalked from the room.

She refused to take the slightest interest in the luxuriously furnished bedroom and adjoining bathroom which Guido conducted her to. She plunged her face, burning with indignation, into cold water, and her hands were trembling when she thrust a comb through her hair. The upset was doing no good to her nerves and gradually she began to take deep breaths in an effort to calm herself.

She refused to allow her thoughts to dwell upon Dominic or his reasons for forcing her to stay for dinner. When she was ready, she lingered, but not for long. In his present mood he would be capable of sending up a servant if she did not appear promptly. The man was probably even now lurking in the corridor waiting to escort her.

He was. Courteously, he came forward when she appeared in the doorway. Dominic was waiting for her in the dining room. He wore a dark lounge suit which suited his dark good looks and excellent carriage.

"Still angry with me?" he murmured as he led her to a table set for two.

"What do you expect?" Martina asked when he had seated her. "Do you usually force your women guests to dine with you?"

He walked around to take a seat facing her and picked up his table napkin.

"No," he replied whimsically. "Usually my women

friends are only too eager to dine with me. Incidentally, I'm only trying to help."

She lifted eyes dark with bitterness and some anger. "Unlike Marco, I'm not in need of a fairy godfather."

His eyebrows shot upwards sardonically. "I was not aware that you were," he said coolly.

There was no chance for further conversation, for a servant came in with the first course and the meal progressed. Dominic became the considerate charming host. Whatever it was he wanted to discuss was shelved for the time being, and Martina hoped he was not going to mention it. She said little during the meal until he began to talk about London.

Martina never could resist talking about her own beloved city. Softened by his flashes of sincerity and humor, she told him about her job in the typing pool at the television studios, and they fell to discussing her parents' work of producing documentary films. She was surprised at his knowledge of the subject and wondered if there was anything he was ignorant about. He had the gift of understanding and appreciating anything that came his way, the clever perception of a man whose brain was always on the alert.

While they talked Martina felt that he had tremendous reserves of feeling and passion which he would only let himself go so far with. He appeared to be radiantly in keeping with his life in Venice—British in a humorous, arrogant way and Italian in his innate courtesy, experience and charm.

The conversation passed over books, pictures and finally cameras. Dominic spoke of one he had bought while skiing in Austria and mentioned her own which he said he would be interested in seeing some time.

Martina murmured something, aware that the subject was leading up to Marco. It did. Dominic came straight to the point with the utmost serenity.

"What do you say to Marco spending a few days at my farm with Signora Stangeri, who would be delighted to have him?"

"Why?" Martina asked, using her table napkin daintily.

"To give you the opportunity to enjoy yourself. You don't imagine you're deceiving anyone about having a good time as you are, do you?"

Her face grew hot beneath his scrutiny. She might have expected something of the kind. He was clearly of the opinion that she was not doing a very good job of looking after the boy. Well, let him have his say. Bruno had placed Marco in her care and she was not going to relinquish her charge of him, least of all to this man who sat looking at her so searchingly.

"What an odd question," she said. "As if anyone could help enjoying a stay in Venice!"

He raised an unbelieving brow. "I wouldn't say you were enjoying it today when you came here to tell me about Marco."

"It was an isolated incident for which there was a perfectly simple explanation!" she exclaimed indignantly.

"Meanwhile it put you through purgatory."

Martina controlled shaking limbs. "What has that to do with it?"

He said quietly, "Everything. You ought to be going to parties, dancing until the small hours of the morning, dining on the roof of a hotel in the moonlight, even enjoying a few stolen kisses." He leaned forward tatalizingly, his dark eyes glinting devilishly. "Don't tell me you've never dreamed of these delights?"

She felt her heart hammering against her ribs. "I've thought of nothing apart from looking after Marco."

"And if you knew Marco was content and happy staying on the farm and enjoying his rides on Lunedi, would you not then be happy to be free and enjoy yourself with no ties or responsibility?"

It took all her courage to meet the eyes regarding her so relentlessly. But she did so, resenting their probing as bitterly as she resented his unwarranted interference.

"Did you ask me. . . ?" She broke off and said

deliberately, "I beg your pardon. Did you force me to dine with you in order to quarrel with me?"

He smiled faintly. "I asked you because a few days away from Marco will help you to relax and enjoy your visit. You were very upset this afternoon, and returning home to sit and watch over Marco wouldn't have done you any good. He'll be quite happy on the farm and well looked after. Originally, you were only meant to have charge of him from lunch time until he went to bed. Since this chicken pox affair, you've made him your whole concern, to the extent of refusing invitations."

"I enjoy looking after Marco."

In an effort to convince him, Martina forced herself to meet his gaze. The expression in his eyes mocked her words. He leaned forward tantalizingly.

"What fun have you had since arriving in Venice? And I can assure you there's a surfeit of fun to be had. Have you cut across the lagoon at high speed against a head-wind bringing the color to your cheeks and the stars to your eyes, scorched along on a surfboard, swum from a yacht like mine anchored out there in the lagoon, seen the sunset from a *campanile* or danced a night away, ending with a run along the *autostrada* to enjoy breakfast at a mountain inn? It would give me pleasure to show you all these delights."

While he talked, Martina pictured herself beside him, laughing up at him in the spray with the taste of salt on her lips. Her heart missed a beat at the thought of drifting around a ballroom floor in his arms. Her senses swam. He was offering her days and nights in heaven. She had only to say the word. Then he remembered why Eunice had invited her to Venice—her fear for her marriage. She had come at Eunice's suggestion, so if anything happened to Marco while they were away, Bruno would blame his wife and their marriage could be wrecked.

She collected herself with an effort. She was sorely tempted, for it would be something to remember in the dark days when she returned to London knowing she would never see Dominic again. But loyalty to her friend came first.

"I appreciate your offer," she said firmly. "It's very kind of you, although I don't imagine for a moment you expect me to accept. I gave my word to Eunice and Bruno that I would look after Marco until they returned, and I intend to keep it."

There was a short silence during which Martina could hear the slow beating of her heart coming in dull heavy strokes. He would never know what it cost her to refuse him. He sat for several moments not moving a muscle or giving the slightest indication of what he was thinking.

"You are the most exasperating young woman," he said at length. "Do you enjoy being a martyr, or is it my company you object to?"

Martina lowered her eyes and wished she did not care so much. It was all she could do to keep her composure.

"I'm sorry," she said huskily. "I'd rather not discuss it any more."

"In that case we'd better adjourn to the *sala* for coffee."

Dominic stood up and Martina followed suit. Miserably, she walked with him, shaken by a jumble of confused emotions, hating fate, which for once had given her a choice between duty and a few days in heaven. The rest of the evening passed a bittersweet blur of pain.

In the *sala* Dominic seated her in a comfortable chair, put on records and made polite conversation. He lit a cigar and was unconcerned when she voiced her desire to leave early. He was walking her to the door of the *sala* to take her back when the phone rang. He lifted up the receiver and she saw his grim look gradually relax. A familiar highpitched voice came through.

Dominic said with surprise, "Why, Kay! When did you arrive? On your own? . . . I see. . . . How are you? . . . And your parents when you left them? You enjoyed your trip to Greece, then? You saw Mia? . . . No . . . I see." He laughed, a deep hearty laugh, his teeth a blur of whiteness in his tanned face, and looked at his wrist watch. "I can be with you in about half an hour."

Martina had watched the well-shaped head and wide shoulders outlined against the silk-paneled wall. The deep quiet tones which were characteristic of him reacted painfully on her heart and made it ache for him. Tonight, the thought of him going to see Kay was almost unbearable. He put down the phone, not troubling to hide the fact that the call had given him pleasure.

"Sorry for that delay," he said sarcastically, and his look told her he had expected her to abscond at the first opportunity.

The short journey to Bruno's house was made swiftly. Martina took a hasty leave of Dominic as Stefano admitted her at her door. Marco was in bed, he informed her. She thanked him and went upstairs to Marco's room to find him lying awake waiting for her.

The big dark eyes looked up at her rather sheepishly and a small hot hand slipped into hers.

"You are not angry with me because I forgot your camera and went back for it, are you, Marty? I was an awful long time finding the museum again and when I got back, you had gone. So the *custode* brought me home."

She smiled, squeezing his hand, and bent to kiss his forehead. "No, darling, I'm not cross with you. Only next time you run away tell me first where you're going, will you?"

"*Si*, Marty."

Marco sighed, content to know she wasn't angry with him. Gently she turned him on his side, pulled the sheet around him and placed his teddy bear nearby.

"Now go to sleep and dream about where we shall go tomorrow. It's your choice, you know."

"I would like very much to take a picture of Lunedi on Zio Dominic's farm," he said.

Martina winced and sat down on the bed. Had she been wrong to refuse Dominic's offer to have Marco on the farm? He was evidently very attached to the pony and his nightmares had not occurred since Eunice and Bruno had gone.

She recalled, with a fierce stab of pain inside her, Dominic's smile, his deep laughter and obvious pleasure at hearing from Kay again. And it was all her own fault. She had curtailed her evening with him and had thrust him into another woman's company.

Marco was looking at her hopefully. Already, she was thinking with dismay, he thought she could work miracles.

Martina smiled with little gaiety. "We'll see tomorrow. We shall have to wait until Zio Dominic invites us again. Now go to sleep." She drew her hand gently over his eyes. "I'm now going to tell you a story of a very shy litle pony who didn't like being photographed."

Little by little, she told an amusing story of a pony who hid himself away in all kinds of places because he did not like being photographed. Marco chuckled at intervals before going off to sleep with an angelic smile on his face.

In order that Marco would not be too disappointed about not being able to photograph his beloved Lunedi, Martina asked Ugo to take them along the river Brenta in the hope of seeing a horse in the fields. To her joy they saw one and Marco was able to take a photograph. It was not Lunedi, but he was very excited and happy about it.

The rest of the week went by on wings, brightened by an invitation from Dawn Agusta to an art exhibition Luca was giving in the hall of the public gardens. It was to be followed by a dinner party at their residence in the evening.

Martina accepted, hoping yet dreading to see Dominic again. Knowing Marco would be bored by the opening ceremony of the exhibition, she arrived just afterward, to be greeted warmly by Dawn. Among the distinguished gathering, Martina spotted Kay Younge with the American man Martina had already met. They were talking animatedly to a group of young people at the far end of the room.

She turned away blindly, half expecting to see Dominic's tall figure, and bumped into his secretary, Jimmy Ward Baker. She thought he looked ill and haggard, but his smile was gay enough.

"Miss Floyd!" He greeted her with obvious pleasure. "I was thinking of you only this morning. As a matter of fact, I've been thinking of you more often than I care to admit. How are you?"

He took her hand and held on to it until she gently withdrew it. Hiding her surprise at his drawn look, Martina answered lightly, "Very well, thanks. And you?"

He shrugged his well-tailored shoulders. "So-so. You look delicious with your peach tan. The air of Venice suits you. You're blooming like a rose."

His eyes slid appraisingly over her bright face and clear eyes, and she hastened to change the subject.

"You've already met Signor Marco Vortolini, I believe," she said impishly, looking down at Marco.

"*Buon giorno,* Zio Jimmy," Marco said politely.

Jimmy made a playful feint with a closed fist at the small pointed chin.

"*Buon giorno,* Marco. How does it feel to have a gorgeous *signorina* to hold your hand and take you around?" He slanted a sly look at Martina. "I don't know why he should have all the luck. What about going out with me one evening?"

She felt the urge to put him off at least until Eunice and Bruno returned. At the moment, Martina was in no mood to have another male tell her she was spending too much time with Marco. But there was something rather forlorn about him that touched her.

"Why not?" she said with a smile.

He grinned. "Are you going to the party tonight at the Agustas'?"

"I am."

"What about tomorrow evening? I have tickets for an orchestra concert at the Doge's Palace."

"I'd be delighted," she told him.

That evening, when Marco had gone to bed, Martina dressed for the Agustas' party. Her dress was in polyester cotton, printed with a profusion of summer flowers on a white ground. Romantically flowing sleeves had a velvet bow at each elbow. The neckline was demurely scooped out and a narrow velvet ribbon set off her small waist. She pulled her hair back into a ponytail, which delighted Jimmy when he collected her in Dominic's launch.

"You look about 16," he murmured as he helped her in.

It proved to be a very enjoyable evening for Martina. The exhibition had been a great success, with every picture sold and others commissioned. After a dinner a room was cleared for dancing and a tuneful quartet coaxed everyone to his feet. Even the presence of Kay Younge didn't detract from Martina's enjoyment.

The only discordant note came at a break in the dancing. She had gone with Jimmy to the buffet for refreshments and found Kay and her American boy-friend beside them. Kay looked very attractive in a back-less white evening gown. Sleeveless with a halter neckline, it showed off her deep tan to perfection. Diamonds glittered at her neck and ears.

"I do love your dress, Miss Floyd," she said in her high-pitched, little-girl voice. "Isn't this a swell party?"

Martina agreed. "Did you enjoy your stay in Greece?"

"Did we? Ask Rod. He thought it was terrific."

Rod passed her a drink and smiled on Martina, his face as brown as mahogany. He looked amazingly fit and far more confident than when she had last seen him.

He said, "I had a whale of a time. Talk about pretty girls! I'd recommend it any time for a holiday—not to mention a honeymoon. But Kay doesn't agree." He passed Martina and Jimmy a drink. Martina liked his smile. There was nothing affected about him, which was more than she could say for Kay.

"I refuse to be rushed into anything so binding, especially when I'm having such a good time," said that young woman with a pout. "What do you say, Miss Floyd?"

"I would say it depends whether a certain man means more to you than the rest," Martina answered quietly.

"I'm not telling," Kay replied. Then she turned to Jimmy, who stood by Martina. "Where's Dominic this evening? I expected him to be here. I wanted his opinion on several of the paintings I saw this morning. Our host isn't very well known yet, is he?"

Jimmy regarded her with narrowed gaze. "Dominic is

out of town. If you wanted advice about the quality of Luca Agusta's work, I can assure you that anything you buy with his signature on it is a sound investment. Some day he's going to be known as one of the most gifted artists of the century."

Kay gave a small affected laugh. "Strange you should say that, because I overheard the same remark several times at the exhibition this morning."

When dancing was resumed, Martina was swept away in the arms of Rod Manvers. She smiled with the feeling that he was playing Kay at her own game. He was wide awake enough to know Kay had more than a little interest in Dominic.

As for Kay, it was clear that she would seize any excuse to demand Dominic's attention. But then he might have given her reason to. He had been happy to hear her voice when she had phoned him the other evening. Calling herself an idiot for caring so much, she was especially nice to Rod because, like herself, he was suffering the pangs of unrequited love. Later, when Jimmy dropped her at her door, she promised to see him the next evening.

On Saturday morning Martina took Marco to the Piazza San Marco, where she used up the last film in her camera. Much to Marco's delight, they took a picture of the beadle outside San Marco before going up into the gallery to photograph the four bronze horses. In the afternoon they went to the wading pool in the public gardens. She had bought Marco a toy yacht and sat watching him sail it. It wouldn't be long before she could give him his first swimming lesson.

When she put him to bed that evening, she was pleased to see how healthy and brown he was. He seemed to have grown taller and he looked much brighter. The unhappy, bewildered look had left his face. She would playfully pinch his cheek when, on occasion, she had found him gazing wistfully at some small boy walking happily with his father. Then he would smile up at her angelically and she would hug him tightly.

She wore the flowered dress for her date with Jimmy

that evening. He was in good spirits when she met him and she thought he looked better than he had the previous night.

"My favorite dress on my favorite girl," he said with his winning smile.

Martina wondered how many women he had said the same words to in the past.

She knew his rakish look had held a fatal attraction for the opposite sex. Like Dominic, he had enjoyed affairs. Unlike Dominic, however, his look of dissipation betrayed the fact that drink had played an important part in his life and still did.

The concert in the Doge's Palace was well attended by a distinguished gathering, and Martina was glad she had worn her diamond necklace and earrings. Jimmy was in evening dress and heads turned their way when they took their seats. She enjoyed the music, which included her favorite piano concerto. It was Dominic's as well.

The rippling melody brought him back into her heart which had been vainly trying to shut him out. She wondered if he had gone to see Mia. Martina, who believed in minding her own business, found herself longing to ask Jimmy where he had gone. The fantastic splendor of her surroundings, the haunting tones of the full symphony orchestra, only served to make her thoughts of him more poignant.

When the concert ended, she strolled with Jimmy to a nearby restaurant for supper. Martina loved the old-world atmosphere, the waiters standing at attention, the sea of immaculate tables covered with snowwhite cloths, the silver vases full of flowers. While Jimmy ordered, she watched the place filling rapidly with concert-goers. They were a distinguished clientele, vibrant and colorful as they talked in low, well-bred voices. She listened, never tiring of their soft pronunciation, entranced by their expressions—the raised eyebrows, the puckered mouths and the practised gestures of the hands. Wistfully, she envied them the calm unruffled existence unspoiled until now by progress.

The meal was so delicious that Martina couldn't help doing justice to it. She realized that the bill would be enormous.

When Jimmy was leaving her at her door, he asked when he could see her again.

Martina smiled and said teasingly, "Sure you can afford it?"

He looked startled. "I'm not exactly poor. I have an income from the family estate in Sussex. I don't have to depend on my salary from Dominic, which is a good one." He grinned. "I wouldn't say this to any woman in case they were interested in my financial status."

She said impishly, "What if I am?"

"You're not the kind." He looked seriously down into her glowing face. "I don't think I'd mind if you were. I'm in your lovely little hands completely."

He raised the hands he was holding to his lips and she released them gently, knowing she could never care for him that way.

"You're very sweet, Jimmy, and I want to thank you for a lovely evening. I've enjoyed it immensely."

"So have I," he answered. "The sooner we meet again, the better. Tomorrow evening?"

Martina gave a breathless little laugh. "Eunice and Bruno are returning tomorrow evening from Geneva. I want to be home when they arrive."

"Monday, then?"

She shook her head. "I can't. Eunice might have planned something for me."

He was disappointed and begged her to let him know as soon as she had a free evening. She promised, and Jimmy left, saying he would phone her. Perhaps a little of his disappointment touched her loneliness. He was charming company and she had the feeling that he needed companionship badly. At the moment there was nothing she could do. Already her visit was half over and the thought of leaving Venice and Dominic in two weeks again filled her with despair.

CHAPTER NINE

Sunday began with a heavy mist that lifted before breakfast. Martina's spirits lifted with it when she saw blue skies and brilliant sunshine. After breakfast, she went in search of Ugo with the result that by ten o'clock they were skimming across the lagoon in the launch.

Marco was beside her. The staff had filled a picnic basket, including a cold storage box of ice cream. Martina also had her beach bag well filled. Their destination was a small island with a secluded bay. As they neared the semicircle of white sand, Martina felt elated. Not a soul was in sight and Ugo assured her that there was nothing on the island apart from a derelict monastery and some trees.

He left them on the sandy beach after carrying their paraphernalia ashore, promising to come for them at five that afternoon. They found an ideal spot and Martina put Marco into his swimming trunks. Then, covering him with suntan lotion, she left him to building a sandcastle while she went for a swim.

Blissful leisurely movement in the warm caressing waves left her glowing and refreshed when she returned to the beach towel she had laid out near Marco. Taking off her bathing cap, she leaned back on her hands and lifted her face to the sun. The day passed too swiftly. She used up the film in her camera, helped by a happy Marco, and they had a picnic, with lemonade and ice cream at intervals between games on the beach. Marco had his first swimming lesson and he enjoyed it so much that he was still in the water when Ugo arrived to take them home.

That evening, when Marco was in bed, Martina took a shower to wash the salt from her skin and wondered what time Eunice and Bruno would return. She hoped with all her heart that they had made up their differences. Deciding to write a few letters home, she put on a pretty tailored wrap. There would be time enough to put on a dress when she was told of their return. She had hardly picked up a pen when Emilia knocked on her door.

"*Scusa, signorian*," she said courteously. "Signora Vortolini is in the *sala*. She wants to see you."

"Thanks, Emilia."

"But, *signorina*—"

Emilia's voice struck empty air, for Matina, impatient to hear how Eunice had fared, was already moving along the corridor as though she had wings on her feet. Down the stairs she ran, with the thick carpet deadening the sound of her footsteps until she reached the *sala*. Flinging open the double doors she burst in, hair flying, eyes sparkling, with all the beauty of a day outdoors.

"Eunice!" she cried eagerly. "Did you—"

The next moment she stopped dead in her tracks to stare like a half-awakened sleepwalker at a tall, beautiful young woman in blue who rose from a chair near a window. Martina, whose heart was beating a tattoo against her ribs from her swift flight, was conscious of everything at once—her own casual appearance certainly not in keeping with welcoming visitors, the beautiful stranger whom she felt she should know, and most of all the tall silent figure with his back against the window. She stood quite still, the heightened color slowly ebbing from her face.

Dominic was the first to speak. Did she imagine the gleam of something like humor in his eyes?

"Good evening, Miss Floyd," he said smoothly, complete master of a situation that was sending prickles down her spine. "May I present Signora Mia Vortolini." He smiled down at the woman in blue. "Miss Floyd is doing a wonderful job looking after Marco." His smile at Martina was wholly apologetic. "Please accept our apologies for arriving so unexpectedly and taking you by surprise." Those keen eyes took in her scrubbed look and lingered on the pretty wrap belted around her small waist, outlining the soft contours of her bust.

By now Martina was herself again. Her smile, when it came, bore the unmistakable stamp of welcome. She held out her hand.

"*Como está*, Signora Vortolini. Please excuse my wrap and my somewhat precipitate entrance," she said quietly and with dignity. "When Emilia informed me that Signora Vortolini had arrived, I naturally thought she meant Eunice."

The figure in blue arose, condescendingly polite. "*Como está, signorina*," she said without expression.

Her hand was as cool as her greeting, her voice perfunctory, her eyes twin green stones void of feeling. They slid over the slender figure with the impression intended—one of cold indifference. Her skin was perfectly tanned, she was immaculately groomed. And Martina experienced the same uncomfortable reaction as she had standing before Luca Agusta's portrait.

But her dignity equalled the Signora's. "Won't you sit down again, Signora Vortolini?" she said, taking a seat herself a little distance away and wishing it was not in Dominic's direct line of vision.

Mia sat down again gracefully. Her expensive skin handbag with long elegant matching gloves laid on top was on the carpet beside her chair. Martina, watching the beautiful haughty face, felt relegated to a paid servant—a feeling, she was sure, that Mia Vortolini instilled in most of the people she met.

"Signora Vortolini is paying a visit to my farm. We are on our way there."

Dominic's cool deep tones struck her like a mortal blow. They could only mean one thing. It would not be long before their engagement was announced. She said without looking at him, "Marco is asleep—I'm afraid he's out like a light." She smiled, forgetting her own pain in reminiscing. "We've been out for the day."

Mia's butterfly brows arched a fraction higher. "I have not called to see my son."

"No?" Martina's indrawn breath and swiftly mounting color came from the depths of her own feelings for Marco. It was on the tip of her tongue to tell this beautiful iceberg how her small son was longing to take a picture of Lunedi at the farm, and that the presence of his mother would surely add to his delight.

The Signora was speaking again. "I called to collect a few of my clothes to wear at the farm, my riding habit and so on." Signora Vortolini's smile was coldly polite. "Emilia is packing them for me. You are here on a visit, *signorina?*"

"Yes," Martina replied laconically.

"And you don't mind having charge of Marco while you are here?" The eyebrows shot up as though she found this incomprehensible. "Are you experienced in looking after children?"

"No, I am not. My work is far different. I have found looking after Marco very rewarding." Martina borrowed the Signora's cool smile. "Marco was a lonely, bewildered little boy when I arrived. Now I would say he is almost happy."

"Almost?" The green eyes flashed like twin daggers.

"As happy as a small boy can be who is suddenly bereft of loving parents and a favorite uncle."

"Ah, my brother-in-law, Signor Vortolini." The faint emphasis on the "Signor" set Martina's teeth on edge. "Marco was always fond of his Zio Bruno. He is quite happy here. Frankly, I fail to see the need for him to have someone to look after him while my brother-in-law is away. I understand he is only paying a short visit to Geneva, during which Marco could have stayed with the children of the Conte di Savorderi next door."

Dominic, who was standing silently, hands thrust in pockets, intervened with those dangerously deep tones. "Benito has chicken pox, which developed while Marco was staying at my farm with Miss Floyd."

Color swept up to the Signora's lovely face. She gave a small exclamation of surprise and turned her head to look up at Dominic.

"You didn't tell me, Dominic. I had no idea Marco had been to your farm recently."

Her smile was openly disarming. She was tacitly excusing her former manner, relegating it to his not informing her of the visit.

"It's not important. Benito is improving." He chaffed her with a quizzical look. "What is important is that

Marco did not catch it. He would certainly have done so
had Miss Floyd not been here to take him to the farm.
Incidentally, Marco is looking decidedly better since she
came. You ought to appreciate what she has done for
him, Mia."

Slowly Mia turned her head to look again at Martina,
this time with a quickened interest—and something more:
an awareness that Dominic was reproving her for her
treatment of this friend of her sister-in-law's, who, she
decided, was quite attractive.

"If that is so, then I am more than grateful, Miss
Floyd," she conceded graciously. "It would have been a
pleasure to meet Signor Vortolini when he comes, but I
am a little fatigued with my journey. I shall not be far
away, however." Her sudden frown was one of
impatience as she consulted the exquisite gold watch on
her slender wrist. "Emilia is awfully slow collecting my
clothes. I had better go see what she is doing. *Scusate*. I
shall not be long, Dominic. Sorry to keep you waiting."

She swept from the room on a wave of expensive
perfume. The scent remained on her handbag and gloves
she had left by her chair, almost tangible reminders of her
presence.

Martina sat silent. Her heart was beating furiously. In
the soft light of evening the room had a kind of listening
quality about it. She did not look up at Dominic, but she
was aware of him looking at her. He was still standing
with his back to the window as he had stood on that first
day they had met. With dry throat and burning eyes,
Martina realized that they were no closer now than they
had been then. They were not even friends.

"Why didn't you go out tonight?" he asked suddenly.
"Was it necessary for you to stay home because you
expected Bruno to return?"

Startled, Martina lifted her eyes to meet the strength
and vitality gleaming in his own. Instantly it put her on
edge.

"I was tired after spending the day outdoors with
Marco."

"Yet you looked bright enough when you burst in here

a short while ago. It was quite a welcome for Eunice." An eyebrow lifted. "Do you always welcome your friends so enthusiastically when they've been away?"

Her chin tilted. "Eunice is a very close friend," she answered.

"I appreciate that. Nevertheless, you set far too much store by your friends. You will inevitably get hurt if you persist in doing so, human nature being what it is."

Martina felt a sudden chill in the warm air. "What do you mean?" she asked.

"Simply that you're far too intense where personal relations are concerned. I've watched you go to bat on Marco's behalf, ready to defend him at the slightest provocation. You do exactly the same where Eunice is concerned."

"I happen to care deeply for both of them," she said defiantly. "I know you resent me taking care of Marco while she's away, but I—"

Martina broke off abruptly after almost saying too much. His eagle eye and sharp wits were adept at deduction.

"Did it for a reason," he finished for her. "Eunice's relations with Bruno are a little strained because of Marco. Are they not? Don't look so surprised. Bruno was evidently discovering what he was missing with no family of his own. And Eunice doesn't want the responsibility of children."

Martina flared, "Why should she have children if she doesn't want them? Bruno knew this when they married. Eunice made it clear beforehand."

"So I believe. Their marriage is no marriage. A perfect union between a man and a woman means children, with all the cares and joys they bring." His eyes narrowed mercilessly. "You'll never persuade an Italian to think any differently. A family to them is the whole pivot of their existence. You defend her so vehemently that I must conclude that your views on the subject coincide with hers."

Her response came from her unguarded tongue. "Indeed they do not—" She pulled herself up abruptly.

"You can conclude what you want to, You don't know the circumstances, in any case, Eunice was the eldest of six children whom she had to take care of." Incensed by his judgment of her friend, Martina, her eyes sparkling, her hands clenched by her side, had leaped to her defence.

He veiled a sudden gleam in his eyes. "Eunice indeed has a champion in you," he said, in no way affected by her outburst. He made a gesture of distaste with a lean hand and cynical slant of his mouth. "This capacity you have of caring deeply for other people. I trust you will be more prudent when you fall in love. You could so easily mistake a passing fancy for the real thing."

"I'm not likely to do that."

He shrugged. "Women who are young and inexperienced about men are apt to do so. I'd say you were both."

Her resentment flared. "I'm learning," she answered bitterly, "I know I don't meet with your approval in many ways. I should imagine there are few women who do."

"You surprise me. What gives you that idea?" he chaffed.

"Because you haven't married, You are probably searching for the kind of woman who does not exist."

"When a man reaches a certain age without having married, it doesn't mean he isn't the marrying kind. He's in all probability waiting for the right woman to come along. Up to now I've never met a woman who could make marriage an attractive enough proposition for me. Perhaps I've been unlucky. If I have, I'm glad of it. So far I've enjoyed every moment of my life with no time to spare on any particular woman. Personally, I'm of the opinion that no man should take on the responsibility of marriage until he has matured sufficiently to appreciate its worth." He raised that tantalizing brow. "That's why so many marriages fail."

"And yours won't, of course?"

She clenched her hands again unconsciously, Why was he so maddeningly cold-blooded? He was making her as cynical as himself.

His smile mocked. "I'm sure it won't. I'm confident that it will be wildly and absurdly happy."

Martina felt a sick pain inside her, urging her to turn and run away—anywhere, away from the tall mocking figure whose cruel words were sword thrusts to her heart. Did he sense her unhappiness? Was he being deliberately cruel? It appeared so to her bewildered mind. He suddenly strode across the room to confront her coolly.

"I'm sure that's enough about me," he said with finality. "There's something I have to say to you before Mia arrives back. It's about Jimmy Ward Baker. You've been going out with him recently. I want you to make me a promise."

"What kind of a promise? If it's not to see him again I—"

"You can see him as much as you wish." He paused, looking grim and adding pointedly, "In Venice. Should he ask you to leave Venice for a ride along the *autostrada* in his car, I want you to refuse to go. Will you give me your promise that you'll do that?"

"What a strange request." Martina gave him a wide-eyed stare. "Why?"

"Because I asked you to."

"And that's sufficient reason? I'm sorry—I like Jimmy, and unless you can be more specific I won't promise anything regarding him."

Dominic's mouth set and she could sense his anger. He gripped her arms and for a moment she was sure he was going to shake her. Then Mia appeared. Instantly his hands dropped and he was turning to greet her as though Martina was not there.

"Everything settled, Mia?" he asked smoothly.

She came across the room to pick up her bag and gloves. "Yes," she replied. "Emilia has taken my case downstairs. I'm ready when you are." The smile she gave him was singularly sweet. She held out a hand to Martina. "See you again, Miss Floyd. Thanks for looking after Marco."

Surprised at the hint of friendliness in her tone, Martina took the proffered hand. Then Mia withdrew it to link Dominic's arm as they strolled out of the room, for all the world as though they were already married. No charming smile accompanied Dominic's departure. His look was cold and impersonal.

They were two of a kind, Martina concluded bitterly. As she went back to her room she wished with all her heart that she had never met Dominic Burnett di Ravenelli.

Eunice and Bruno had not arrived when she went to bed at midnight. Martina had written her letters, undressed and climbed wearily into bed. She was bitterly disappointed that Eunice hadn't arrived when she had promised—although it could be a mixed blessing. Her continued absence meant that Martina could choose where to go in the evenings, and this meant she could avoid Dominic's company whenever possible.

Right now he would be at his farm with a house party including Kay Younge. Maybe he would get a kick out of seeing the women fight over him. She wondered what reason he had for not wanting her to go out in Jimmy's car. In any case she could not see herself staying another two weeks, so there would be little opportunity for her to go out with Jimmy. But there was ample time for Dominic to announce his engagement to Mia.

Wildly and absurdly happy, he had said about his marriage. Well, she wished him luck. He would need it with the beautiful, cold Mia. Slowly, Martina turned her face into her pillow and quietly wept.

CHAPTER TEN

Two letters came for Martina on Monday. They were delivered while she and Marco were at breakfast. One was from her parents, saying they expected to be in Venice toward the end of the month. Her brother Ruan was arriving with them and could she arrange to stay on an extra week or so for them to have a holiday together? *Very funny,* Martina thought, *when I'm seriously considering cutting my visit short!*

The second letter was from Eunice, saying they would be staying in Geneva for a few more days so that Bruno could tie up a few loose ends of his business there. She said they were very happy after having had a heart-to-heart talk and that she would tell Martina all about it when they returned. She would also like her to prolong her holiday to make up for looking after Marco.

Relieved though she was at hearing the good news concerning Eunice, Martina felt vaguely depressed. Looking up from the letter, she found Marco watching her with big dark eyes, waiting politely until she could give him her attention.

"Yes, Marco?" she asked.

"Where are we going today, Marty?"

He was halfway through his breakfast and paused, spoon in hand, his small face alight with anticipation.

"Where would you like to go?"

She had put the letters back into their envelopes, deciding to forget about them for the time being.

"I suppose we couldn't go swimming," he said hopefully.

She smiled. "Eat your breakfast and we'll see what the weather is like."

The sky had been overcast when Martina looked through her window on awakening that morning. By the time they had finished breakfast it was raining hard.

"No swimming this morning, dear," she told Marco. "Unless it clears later. Have you phoned your friend next door to ask how he's progressing?"

Martina had shown him how to use the phone and he had called each morning to ask how the small Benito was faring. It had given him confidence and she watched him dial the number and pick up the receiver very seriously. Then he caught her smile and smiled back in the angelic way which always gave her the urge to hug him.

"Zio Giorgio, this is Marco. How is Benito this morning, *per favore?*"

Always it was the same answer. "Benito is a little better today, *grazie*, Marco." This morning, however, Benito came on the line and Marco was delighted when they spoke together.

Martina decided that Zio Giorgio, the Conte di Savorderi to her, must be a very nice man. She wondered what he was like, not knowing that later in the day she was to see him.

They spent the next hour or so doing a jigsaw puzzle on the floor of the *sala*, and when Marco had a little nap before lunch, she cleared away the puzzle and leafed through one of the glossy magazines Eunice subscribed to.

Idly, she turned over pages containing news and photographs of engagements of Venetian socialites, to find herself staring down at a photograph of Mia in riding habit walking with her horse. Beneath it she read, "Signora Mia Vortolini, the beautiful Milan socialite who lost her husband so tragically in a fire at their villa last December, is again contemplating marriage with a well-known sportsman of wealth and social standing in Venice. Nothing has been announced, but the Signora did not deny it. She also admitted that she had known him for years before her marriage."

Martina stared down at the beautiful face, so calm and serene. Her heart was a heavy stone in her chest. The magazine had been delivered that morning. The next one, a month hence, would contain pictures of their engagement party or wedding, if Dominic decided to get it over quickly. So he had unconsciously followed in his late stepfather's footsteps after all—marrying a widow who had a son.

Martina did not blame him. He had probably loved

Mia all along. That was what he had meant when he said he had been waiting for the right one. Yet, for all her unhappiness at the news, she would not have missed knowing him. She would always remember meeting him as the most climatic moment in her life, recalling in her loneliest moments his virile good looks, extraordinary charm, and, above all, his intense, disturbing masculinity.

She must have sat there for a long time making plans to curtail her stay, until the shrill ring of the phone drew her to it. It was Jimmy asking her to go out with him that evening. With visions of a long night during which she would be alone with her unhappy thoughts, Martina agreed that he call for her at half past seven.

That afternoon she took Marco to a cinema to see a Walt Disney show. They went in the launch and sat in the little cabin listening to the rain pattering on the roof. Marco was enchanted with the show and chatted about it on the way back to the house. The rain had stopped and the world was drying quickly in the golden haze of the sun which pushed the last of the rain clouds across the lagoon. They were well on their way back when a gondola passed them going in the opposite direction and the lone occupant lifted a hand.

"That is Zio Giorgio," Marco exclaimed, waving back.

At this, Martina also lifted a hand in greeting to a man who was definitely Venetian, not more than 30 and good-looking with a small moustache.

So that was the Conte di Savorderi. She tried to imagine what his wife would be like. Another Mia, she decided, and gave up the thought.

"He looks nice," she said, warmed by his friendly smile.

"*Si*, Marty. I like him, and Benito too."

"Benito with the chicken pox?"

"*Si*. He is nice." Marco gave a grown-up shrug. "Felicia is not so nice. She always wants to be the Doge when we are playing, and she is only four. I am five."

Martina laughed. "Your Zio Giorgio has two children?"

"*Si*. I would not mind being his little boy because he is always so kind and makes me laugh. If I were his little boy I would be the Doge every time instead of Felicia."

"Don't you think you ought to take turns?" she suggested.

He gave her the full benefit of his black eyes. "But, Marty, Doges were men!"

To which she had no reply. He was a monkey, but a lovable one. That evening she was both surprised and dismayed when Marco did not eat his supper. She had taken some chocolate to the cinema that afternoon, but he had not eaten enough to ruin his appetite. When she put him to bed he seemed hot and restless, and on an impulse she found the doctor's phone number on the pad in the hall and phoned him. Then she phoned Jimmy to say she couldn't see him that evening because Marco was unwell.

When the doctor arrived he diagnosed a chill and was pleased she had sent for him. A day in bed, he said, could prevent the chill from developing into something more serious. He gave Marco a pill and left several more for her to give him, one every four hours. He left saying he would call again the next day.

Marco seemed much better the following morning, but the doctor insisted upon him staying in bed for the day. Martina followed his instructions and kept Marco amused all day, feeding him hot soup and giving him the pills. Marco enjoyed all the extra attention he received from the staff and Martina, but she was exhausted by the time she put him to bed.

Only the thought that Eunice and Bruno might return at any time roused her into taking a shower and changing into the flowered dress she had intended to wear for her date with Jimmy. Poor Jimmy! He had sounded dreadfully disappointed, but it couldn't be helped. Taking a book, she went to sit on the balcony and breathed in the fresh air she had missed all day.

At ten o'clock, Marco awoke for a drink of water and soon fell asleep again. At eleven, when Martina looked in on him, he seemed settled for the night. Leaving his door ajar, she was startled by an imperative rap on her door.

Closing Marco's door quietly, she turned, amazed to see someone burst in. And Dominic was standing there looking perfect in evening dress, immaculate as ever in his male way but decidedly wild-eyed. There was something rather strange about him, as though he had been charged with something vibrant, something positively dangerous.

Her startled eyes met his across the room and a slim hand went to her throat. One moment he had the look of a man about to do desperate things, the next he had relaxed visibly and he gave her a smile so beautiful that her heart somersaulted queerly.

He crossed the room in a couple of strides holding out his hands as if . . . as if he was meeting his beloved after a long absence. Her skin was moist and cold as he took her hands in his. He appeared so exuberant that she thought he was going to kiss her there and then. But he took his time, looking her up and down with that brilliant, delighted smile, taking in the pretty dress, the soft rose color flooding her pale cheeks, her clear eyes, wide and incredulous, and above all, her mouth. His gaze lingered there while he drew her into his arms.

His embrace was enchanting, his face cool from the air outdoors, his firm lips warm urgent as they fastened on her mouth. His kiss lingered until she was out of breath before he lifted his head to regard her smoulderingly.

"I still can't believe I'm holding you," he murmured. "When I think—"

He broke off abruptly to shower more kisses on her face, sending Martina into an orbit of esctasy such as she had never dreamed of. She found herself equaling his passion and permitting herself the luxury of reveling in it. For a long time she was only conscious of his firm demanding mouth and her own surrender.

When at last Dominic slackened his hold, she put her face against the fine texture of his dinner jacket, breathing in the sensuous masculine fragrance. So they remained, standing close and silent until she felt him shake with laughter.

"Stefano will think I'm either mad or drunk," he said above her ear. "I asked if you were at home, couldn't believe it, and took the stairs three at a time with Stefano calling what room you were in after me."

"I don't blame him," Martina said dazedly, with a

wildly beating heart. "I'm inclined to think that myself!"

His arms tightened painfully. "Thank heaven I asked you to refuse to go along the *autostrada* with Jimmy!"

"But I didn't refuse him for that reason. Marco wasn't very well and I decided not to leave him. He's better now—he had a chill."

Dominic looked startled and she was sure he paled beneath his tan.

"You would have gone if Marco had been well?"

"Yes."

"It seems I owe Marco more than I can ever repay," he said slowly and grimly. "He was the reason you and I met in the first place. He has also saved you from a nasty accident, preventing a tragedy which would have blighted my whole life. Come, let's go down to the *sala*. If I know Stefano he'll now be brewing a cup of delicious coffee for us there."

Praying that she would not wake up and find it all a dream, Martina walked downstairs with his arm around her waist. Sure enough, even as they entered, Stefano appeared behind them with a covered tray sending out a delicious aroma of freshly made coffee.

"*Grazie*, Stefano. You're a treasure," Dominic greeted him with a smile. "I'll take the tray."

He carried it to a table and set it down.

"I wish you would tell me what this is all about," Martina said shakily as he straightened. "I can believe anything after . . . after . . ." She broke off beneath his mocking smile.

"After my kisses?" he suggested. "They were only an introduction for all those that are to follow. Come, we're going out on to the balcony where I shan't look at you while I explain. Your wide-eyed fragile loveliness distracts me."

On the balcony, he drew her back against him, put his arms around her and dovetailed his fingers beneath her bust. They gazed across the canal.

"I can tell you now why I asked you not to go with Jimmy along the *autostrada*. That bad car accident he had resulted in him taking a lot of drugs. To begin with they were part of the treatment. He was badly injured

internally and the need for drugs lasted well over a year.
In the end he couldn't do without them. His brother, a
surgeon who saved his life, contacted me when Jimmy left
hospital to ask my help. Jimmy and I had gone through
college together and I had a great deal of influence over
him which his brother thought might help in his fight
against the drugs. My stepfather was only too pleased to
help too, so we invited Jimmy to Venice.

"Between us we managed to wean him off drugs. He
was completely cured and I offered him the post as secretary because I thought he needed more time here before
going back. He seemed happy enough and accepted at
once."

Martina felt his deep sigh. "Twelve months ago I found
he was taking the drug again. I could tell right away by
his appearance. I confronted him about it and he gave me
his solemn promise not to touch it again. I threatened
that I would send him back home to his brother if I
caught him not keeping his word. He didn't. That second
night you were at my farm, the phone call I received was
from a trusted member of my staff who had found Jimmy
in his room at the Palazzo Ravenelli. He was unconscious from an overdose of drugs, and my man was
ringing for the doctor, a friend of mine and also in my
confidence. The second phone call was from the doctor
himself, asking me to go at once."

Martina put her hands over his, filled with remorse at
misjudging him as she had done that night. His fingers
curled around her own.

"How I hated leaving you that night! When I arrived
the doctor said it had been touch and go to save him and
advised me to send him to a London clinic before it was
too late. Unfortunately, Jimmy's brother was away in the
States at a conference and was expected back this week. I
left word at his residence for him to get in touch with me
as soon as he returned. In the meantime I had to make
sure that Jimmy had no access to my cars. In his
precarious state of health he could easily have smashed
himself and the car to pieces. I always had an idea he
would seek to end it all that way, for he was forever

saying they ought to have let him die when he smashed himself up."

She shuddered, and his arms tightened around her.

"This evening I had a phone call from the police. Jimmy had crashed on the *autostrada* in one of my fast cars—and he had a woman with him."

There was a sudden silence during which Martina's mouth and throat went dry. Her dream was fading rapidly.

"So you came here to see if I was that woman, because if I had been, you would never have ceased to blame yourself for not telling me the truth in the first place. Your relief was so great that you went a little berserk and kissed me."

She turned in his arms. In the twinkling of an eye Dominic had gripped her shoulders. His eyes deepened and darkened in their intensity. Something about him made her stare up in wild palpitation.

"So," he said ominously, holding her in a vice. "You thought it was reaction to the accident of a dear friend?" He stared down at her broodingly. "If I remember rightly you also stated that I was either mad or drunk. As it happens, you're right on both counts. I am mad—mad about you, your gestures, your walk, your smile, the soft light in your eyes that up to now was only for Marco. I love your soft voice and quiet seductive laughter and I'm drunk with your kisses. And I intend to get drunk on them for the rest of my life."

He proceeded to demonstrate then what he meant. Martina's head began to whirl and she was more than drunk herself when he finally let her go.

She began as she gasped for breath, "But . . . Mia. . . ?"

"What about her?"

She swallowed hard. "I saw a report of her intended marriage to a well-known sportsman whom she had known before her marriage. I thought—" Remembering the pain, she could not go on.

"That I was her intended?"

"Aren't you?"

"The Conte di Savorderi would be inclined to challenge me to a duel if I was! Mia and he were engaged, but broke it off after a quarrel and she married Paolo, Bruno's brother. Her friends will tell you that she married Paolo to spite Giorgio, who was very bitter about it. A year later he married her friend Celia, who died after giving birth to Benito. They were to have married this weekend. That was the reason Mia came to stay at my farm, to keep it quiet. Benito caused the postponement. The Conte decided to wait until he was better." He looked down at her with all the intensity and passion of a lover. "I hope that look of rapture is for me."

"Oh, Dominic, can't you see?" Martina cried, all heaven in her eyes. "Marco is going to have a father who adores him and one he adores too. He told me only yesterday how happy he would be if he was the Conte's little boy. He'll be the eldest of the three and won't be bullied by older brothers." She laughed with sheer joy at the thought of it. "I'm afraid Felicia isn't going to be overjoyed at first." She went on to tell him about the little girl and the game of Doges.

He laughed heartily, then sobered. "Enough of Marco," he said with all the old arrogance which now she loved. He moved his lips down her cheek. "I want your parents' address to tell them I'm going to marry their tiresome daughter, who has to be taught that husbands are far more important than small boys."

Martina's laugh was one of pure happiness. "My parents are coming at the end of the month, along with my brother Ruan, to spend a week with me."

"Good. They'll be just in time for our wedding," he said with some satisfaction.

"Dominic!" she cried. "So soon?"

He glowered down at her. "What do you mean, so soon? One can acquire a special licence in three days. I'm only waiting until the end of the month because I know you'll want your parents to be there."

She had to kiss his frown away, suddenly remembering the coffee and the fact that he had probably gone without a meal that evening. It was many minutes before she could speak.

"The coffee . . . will be . . . cold," she managed at last.

But it was not the coffee that finally broke them

apart. It was Emilia, smiling at the sight of Dominic persistingly holding Martina around her waist as they came from the balcony into the room.

"*Scusa, signorina*," she said. "Signor and Signora Vortolini have just arrived. They have gone to their rooms, but will be down soon."

"Which means," said Dominic masterfully, when Emilia had gone, "I can take you out for the day tomorrow to a small island which I believe you know quite well and where we won't be disturbed."

Martina couldn't imagine herself remaining undisturbed by Dominic. No matter how many years she knew him he would always fill her with a delicious glow whenever she saw him. But she had not forgotten Marco in her happiness.

"What about Marco?"

"Mia is coming for him soon. Her grief over Paolo was mostly over the way she had treated him. He knew she had never loved him like Giorgio and she was full of remorse because she thought Paolo had given her the freedom she wanted."

"Poor Paolo," Martina sighed.

"Don't pity him. He wanted Mia on any terms and he got her."

"When did you first decide you like me?" she asked.

"Loved you," Dominic corrected immediately. He paused and considered seriously.

"From the moment you walked into Bruno's *sala* with little daggers in your eyes. I knew you'd overheard what I said concerning a tutor for Marco, but I meant it even more when I saw you. I hated the thought of you spending time with Marco that could have been spent with me." He drew her close and set his firm cool cheek against her warm one. "I was going to take you out and sweep you off your feet, wine and dine you and make love to you in a gondola under the moon."

"What about Kay Younge?" Martina asked. "You were very happy to see her that night she rang you up at the farm."

He chuckled. "I played on that for all I was worth because I wasn't sure of your feelings for me. Several times I was going to tell you how I felt about you, but you appeared to dislike me so much."

"Purely self-defence on my part. I must have loved you from the start, because right away you had the most peculiar effect on me. I was awfully jealous at the way you devoured Mia's portrait in Luca Agusta's studio."

He lifted his head and looked startled. "Devoured it?" he echoed in disgust. "I was admiring a clever painting which bore out the impression I had of Mia when I first knew her years ago—that of a spoiled child who would always demand more than she was willing to give. Giorgio di Savorderi appears to be the only man who's capable of bringing out the best in her. He's more than welcome to her."

Martina sighed with relief. "I was so afraid you loved her. She's so beautiful, and I'm sure Bruno is going to be disappointed when he knows you're not going to be his brother-in-law."

"Are you, my sweet? Bruno will be delighted, because he knows I fell in love with you from the start. As for Mia and Kay Younge, both are selfish little creatures who'll have men much too good for them."

"What about you?" she asked impishly.

"I'm not half good enough for you, but you've got to have me. And heaven help any man who tries to take you away! I haven't forgotten how I felt when you admitted you liked Jimmy. Which reminds me," he consulted his watch, "I must go to the hospital tonight to see him and the woman—someone to whom he probably gave a lift."

"Poor Jimmy," Martina said with tears in her eyes.

He gripped her arms and glowered down into her face. "And poor Dominic, who has to leave you so soon after declaring his love."

She reached up to put her arms around his neck, loving his fierce possessiveness. "But not for long," she said. "We have tomorrow."

"And all the tomorrows," he whispered softly against her mouth.

And Martina, clinging to him in heavenly bliss, heard the words echoing in her heart.

CALL AND I'LL COME

CALL AND
I'LL COME

Mary Burchell

Their meeting was unusual, their marriage hasty . . . but based on love.

Strange then, for two people with such a strong bond between them to make such a mess of their marriage.

The trouble was that Anna was a person who needed to give and yet felt she had nothing to offer. And Tony . . . well, Tony had everything.

"You see," she explained to him desperately, "I can't possibly live your kind of life. Our marriage was just a mistake. And the only way to deal with mistakes is to attempt to undo them."

They almost lost each other for good before they realized the real mistake was in trying to deny their love!

CHAPTER ONE

Hamilton Roone stopped his car and cast an unusually discontented glance over the gloomy landscape. The early March twilight was already fading, and an unfriendly wind whistled over the hill, rattling the windshield of the car and snatching spitefully at the ends of his scarf.

He had not thought it possible to become so completely lost in England, even on the Yorkshire moors; but it was his own fault, of course. He should have had more sense than to leave his map at the little country hotel where he had stopped for a late lunch.

As it was, he had gone 30 miles farther on his way before he realized the map was missing, and by then it had been too late to do anything about it. At the time, it hadn't seemed so vastly important, for the friend at whose house he was to spend the week had given fairly explicit directions, and it should not be too difficult to find Coryton Manor

But it had become extraordinarily difficult after all, and for the past hour, Roone had to admit to himself, he had been hopelessly lost.

He tossed away the end of his cigarette and pulled on his driving gloves again. Sitting in a windy hollow, with darkness creeping across the gray and purple moorland, was not a cheerful occupation; and, with an anxious glance at his fuel gauge, he pressed the self-starter and the car purred into life again.

Something would turn up sooner or later. It always did, he reflected, with a quick return to his usual philosophical good nature. And, cold though he was, and just a little annoyed, Roone still wore that indefinable air of easy confidence that is seen only in those who have never had any reason to dread the future.

For 30 years life had treated Roone remarkably well, and he was quite sure it would go on doing the same thing for another 30 years.

As he gazed ahead, his eyes narrowed a little against the gathering darkness and the first few snowflakes, that something about him, which made women call him "boyish" long after his actual age warranted the term, was apparent.

It was partly the smile that always lurked at the back of his clear gray eyes, partly the extremely sweet-tempered curve of his well-cut mouth. The contrast between that and his strong chin was oddly intriguing. There was a suggestion that, though he was probably slow to anger, he would make a very bad enemy when roused. And there was quite enough lazy strength in his big, well-built figure to support that notion.

"Doesn't anyone live in this godforsaken place?" he muttered to himself; then he drew up sharply, for, set so far back from the road that he had almost missed it, was a silent, little house surrounded by a tangle of neglected trees and bushes.

He looked a little distastefully at the dilapidated gate and then, glancing up, suddenly began to laugh. For, creaking in a melancholy way as it swung in the icy wind, was a sign that read, "Teas and Light Refreshments."

"The best bit of unfounded optimism I've seen in years," Roone said aloud, as he climbed a little stiffly out of the driver's seat. The sign must have hung there since the summer, and probably many summers before, but, even in the summertime, he thought, there must be few travelers anxious to avail themselves of the dispirited offer in this remote spot.

As he went up the ill-kept path, his big, well-groomed figure looked oddly out of character in this tumbledown place.

He knocked on the door with his knuckles, as there seemed no other way of attracting attention, and almost immediately it was opened by a thin little woman, who looked timidly out at him.

Instinctively dropping his voice a tone or two, he said: "I wonder if you could oblige me with a meal of some sort? I've lost my way and I'm very hungry."

She looked so surprised at being asked to provide a

meal that Roone felt she must long ago have forgotten there had ever been a notice offering to do so.

"Oh . . . yes," she said doubtfully, in a pretty voice that was as timid as her looks. "That is, if you don't want anything too elaborate."

"No. Bread and cheese, or something like that, will do quite well," he assured her; and she stood aside silently for him to pass.

"I hope she's not as sparing with the food as she is with her words," Roone thought, half-amused and half annoyed as she silently directed him into a room at the back of the house.

When she had stirred up the fire and lit a big, round, yellow lamp, he tried the effect of his friendly smile on her. The response was remarkable. She came quite close to him, and he was irresistibly reminded of a small brown bird that had decided to accept some crumbs after all.

"If you'll sit down by the fire and make yourself comfortable," she said, in a little eager rush of words, "I'll get you a meal at once. You'd like something hot, I expect. Some ham and eggs and coffee . . . and there's some new bread I made this morning."

"That sounds very good to me," Roone told her kindly. "Yes, I would like something hot. It was very cold driving."

"Cold?" she repeated, in an odd little voice that seemed to come from a long distance across frozen wastes. "Yes, it's very cold. There'll be terribly heavy snow tonight." And she left the room, leaving Roone with the uncomfortable impression that she had inside information about the weather.

An indescribable silence settled down on the place, so that the crackling of the fire sounded aggressively loud in the stillness.

"I would go crazy if I had to live in this dead-and-alive hole," Roone muttered. "No wonder that timid little thing looks frightened of everything." She couldn't live here all alone, of course, but there was no sound of any other living soul.

He tossed off his coat and went to the window, but it

was too dark to see much, and the flakes of snow drifting across the panes confused the outlines of anything that lay beyond. A mournful gust of wind rattled the window frame and sent Roone thankfully back to the fire, which was blazing cheerfully by now.

He sat down in a shabby but comfortable chair and, reaching for a newspaper, was not especially surprised to find that it was three weeks old. It seemed in character with the rest of the place, somehow.

Presently the woman returned with an excellently cooked meal. She drew up a small table so that he need not move from the fire and seemed pathetically gratified when he said, "Why, this *is* nice. Thanks very much."

He supposed she seldom saw people and was probably quite glad of an opportunity to talk. Anyway, rather to his amusement, she stayed and poured out his coffee for him.

"Do you know if I'm anywhere near Coryton Manor?" he asked. "I'm supposed to be there some time tonight."

She shook her head. "Oh no, you're on the wrong side of the moor, I'm afraid. I think it's miles away."

Roone gave a vexed exclamation. To his astonishment and slight dismay, the woman started nervously and said in a placatory voice, "I'll go and ask my daughter. She'll probably know."

She hurried away out of the room; he heard her call "Anna" in a soft voice; then a door closed and everything was silent again.

"Confound it!" he said aloud because he was growing sick of the silence. "Did she think I was blaming her for the distance to Coryton? I never saw such an odd place or such an odd woman."

Still, at least the food was excellent and after a moment he continued his meal.

He couldn't possibly have said why, but suddenly he became acutely aware of the fact that he was being watched; turning sharply, he saw a girl standing in the doorway. Or rather she was leaning one thin shoulder negligently against the side of the door as though she had been there quite a while studying him.

Roone gasped slightly, half annoyance at being watched and half admiration at her strange attraction.

"Good evening," he said, faintly uncomfortable under her unwavering scrutiny.

"Good evening." Her voice was low-pitched and slightly husky. She didn't move and Roone thought he had never seen anything so graceful and boneless as her thin figure in its cheap frock of indeterminate color.

This must be Anna, he decided.

"Er ... won't you come in?" he said after a second.

She came forward at once, and he realized with a sense of quite extraordinary shock that her feet were bare. It seemed somehow the final peculiarity in an already fantastic situation. Certainly they were the prettiest feet he had ever seen, but that didn't seem to make much difference.

"Please do sit down," he said rather helplessly, indicating a chair.

She obeyed him immediately, but she chose the rug at his feet.

He looked down at her as she sat there gravely in the firelight, and his slight sense of irritation softened suddenly into something much more indulgent and appreciative. She was so curiously lovely, he thought. Like someone—suddenly he had the word—like someone enchanted. She looked as though she might be under a spell, or perhaps, even more, as though she could weave spells. . . .

Roone emitted a vexed little laugh, and at that she looked up, fixing her eyes on him in a faintly sulky interest.

They were slightly long eyes, genuinely hazel in color and with beautiful thick dark lashes. Her face was thin, but the bone structure perfect, and her hair, like heavy strands of smoky brown silk, was perfectly straight and drawn back from a center parting to twist in a knot on her neck.

But what attracted and irresistibly held Roone's attention was the pale, warm gold of her skin, as though the tan of long-past summer months still lingered. As for her soft red mouth, he couldn't decide whether it was wise enough to look innocent or innocent enough to look wise.

"Well, why do you look at me like that?"

He hadn't really spent more than a few seconds in his scrutiny, but she looked a little suspicious and resentful, like some wild, shy creature that already regretted the confidence it had given.

"I was trying to decide what it is you remind me of," he was rather surprised to hear himself say.

"Oh!" her eyes widened a little with interest. "And what do I remind you of?"

He smiled suddenly. "King Cophetua's beggarmaid, I think," he said slowly.

She looked startled and then sulkily dropped her eyes. "I'm not a beggar," she muttered resentfully, and quickly drew her bare feet under the hem of her shabby dress.

"I didn't mean that." He saw at once that he had offended her and was very anxious to undo the hurt. "I mean you're like the Burne-Jones's picture, you know."

"I don't know," was all she said, which made Roone very uncomfortable.

"It's the way you do your hair," he explained earnestly, "and your honey-gold skin, and your little thin wrists, and— Really, I beg your pardon!" He broke off, shocked to find he had said so much and had been going to say more.

"It's all right," the girl said, as though this were the usual way to talk after five minutes' acquaintance.

Roone cleared his throat and began to pour himself some more coffee. "I think your mother said you would be able to tell me how far I am from Coryton Manor." He made that sound as matter-of-fact as he could.

"It's a long way. You're on the wrong side of the moor," she told him.

"Well, can't I cross the moor by some road or other?" he asked a little impatiently.

"You'd get lost," was all the girl said in what seemed to him an unnecessarily solemn tone.

"What do you suggest I do, then?" he inquired, pushing away his empty plate and regarding her with a good deal of pleasure.

"I?" She looked startled. "I wasn't going to suggest anything."

"Weren't you? Well, I wish you would," Roone said cheerfully. "Do you mind if I smoke?"

"No, I don't mind," she answered gravely. She watched him take a cigarette from his case; then she leaned forward and lit a twist of paper from the fire. She knelt beside him to light his cigarette.

Something in the kneeling attitude and the gravity of her thin young face profoundly touched Roone; he felt a growing curiosity about this half-shy, half-sulky girl with her elfin charm. No. Elfin implied something happy, he told himself, and he was piqued to realize that he hadn't seen her smile even once. He came back to the word "enchanted" and smiled a little to himself.

"Is that real gold?" He saw she was touching his cigarette case with an awed forefinger. He felt amused and, again, a little touched.

"Yes. Do you like it?"

"It's beautiful," she said gravely. "Your coat is beautiful too, isn't it?" She leaned forward and ran her hand over his big coat lying tossed over a chair.

Roone looked extremely astonished, and then he grinned engagingly. "Well, as a matter of fact," he admitted, "I do rather fancy myself in that."

For a moment she seemed to find that amusing too, because he saw a fleeting smile quiver on her red mouth. But she quickly turned her head away as though she must not let him see her laugh.

He was suddenly immensely intrigued by that hint of amusement and leaning forward to look at her he said, "Don't you find it extraordinarily quiet living away on the moor like this?"

"Yes, it's quiet."

"Do you just help your mother to keep house?" He hoped he didn't sound inquisitive, but he very badly wanted to know more.

"Yes."

"And I suppose your father farms or something?"

She shook her head. "My father is dead," she said.

"And so you just live here with your mother?" Roone's voice was quite grave now and rather kindly.

"There's my stepfather, too," she volunteered in her abrupt way.

"Oh, your mother married again?"

The girl nodded.

"And what does your stepfather do?"

"He drinks."

The uncompromising tone of her reply stirred Roone's sense of humor more than he felt was proper.

He stroked his chin thoughtfully in order to have a hand to hide his smile. "Well, that's scarcely a full-time job, is it?"

She didn't answer, but looked straight at him and said, "You find most things funny, don't you?"

Roone flushed quickly. "I'm sorry. Do I seem rather inane to you?"

"Oh, no."

He was annoyed that she didn't elaborate on that and wondered what to say next. Then she said thoughtfully, "It must be nice to be so sure of things that you can find most of them funny."

Wondering uneasily if she were reproving him, he said awkwardly, "I suppose it was an idiotic sight—my sitting here laughing."

"No," she said. "It was like watching the sun rise."

He was silent from utter astonishment, and the next moment her mother came into the room.

"It's snowing very hard," she said worriedly as though someone might blame her for it.

"Is it?" Roone got up quickly. "Then I must be going. If I follow this road straight ahead, where will it take me? I'd better find somewhere to stay for the night and head for Coryton tomorrow."

"It's about three miles to the village," began the girl, when Roone's exclamation as he looked out at the storm cut her short.

"Lord, what a night! It will be dreadful driving in this.

I suppose," he turned suddenly to the little woman and said with a boyish diffidence that was singularly attractive, "I suppose you couldn't put me up here for the night?"

The girl said "No" just a split second before the woman said, "Yes, I think so."

"Mother, you know it's impossible," the girl muttered.

"Oh, Anna," her mother began in a troubled voice.

Feeling embarrassed but amused, Roone turned away a little, while a whispered discussion went on between the two.

Apparently the mother's arguments prevailed, because presently she said, "I can let you have a room if you like, and there's a shed where you can put your car."

"Thank you very much. That is—" he smiled in the girl's direction "—if Miss Anna doesn't object."

Anna gave him what Roone described to himself as "a smoky look" and went out of the room without a word.

Her mother looked worried, but Roone gave her a reassuring little grin and, flinging on his coat, went out into the whirling snow. It was already sufficiently thick and bewildering to make him glad he did not have to drive farther that night. Besides, he reflected, half-vexed, half-intrigued, he wanted to know a bit more about that girl.

She wasn't like anyone he had ever seen before, either among his own or his sister's many friends. In fact he laughed a little as he thought of Katherine in connection with that girl. She would undoubtedly have looked down her exceedingly well-shaped nose, murmured, "Sulky, ill-mannered peasant" and dismissed her as completely uninteresting.

Well, whatever else she might be, the girl was not uninteresting.

He drove his car slowly down the narrow path until the doors of the shed loomed ahead. She was there already, struggling with the stiff, snow-covered bolts, and he realized in a second's glance that she still had no shoes on. Her slim bare feet were braced on the snowy pathway as she pushed her weight against the door.

"Here!" He was out of the car in a moment, moved by

a quite unusual spurt of anger. "What do you think you're doing?"

She turned her startled face to him, and a second later he had picked her up off the ground as though she were a child.

"Do you want to catch pneumonia?" He shook her slightly as he held her because he felt so angry.

"I was . . . only . . . opening the door for you," she stammered, and he was suddenly conscious of an overwhelming quality of pathos in her thinness, as he held her rather tightly against him.

"You silly little thing," he said more gently, as he freed one hand to pull his heavy coat around her. He strode with her across the yard to an open doorway. "Don't you have enough sense to put on a pair of shoes first?"

She didn't say anything, and glancing down at her he thought she looked sulky.

"Well?" He was smiling a little now.

"It doesn't matter."

"Oh yes it does, young woman," he said firmly, as he set her down gently just inside the doorway. "I'm not going to have your death on my conscience."

She didn't say anything, just stood in the doorway watching him. Presently, having stowed away the car, he came back.

"May I come in this way?"

She stood aside for him at once, and he saw that one door led into a stone-flagged kitchen and a short passage ended in the room where he had had his meal.

"Well—" he paused for a moment "—shouldn't you dry your feet and put on some shoes and stockings?"

"I don't have any." It was just a whisper.

"You haven't— What on earth do you mean?"

"Just that."

"But you must." He felt he had never heard of anything so ridiculous.

"Can't you mind your own business even a little?" It came like a blow, although the tone was soft.

"I . . . I beg your pardon." Roone felt terribly put out. He looked at the girl as she stood there, her eyes cast down. He thought then that even her motionless eyelids looked sullen, but as he turned away with a shrug, the idea struck him that they might have been heavy with unshed tears.

Still, he plainly could not say any more about it. And so he went back to the room with the cosy fire and sat there for the rest of the evening, smoking and reading a book that he had with him.

About half-past ten he decided to go to bed. There was not much else to do and in any case he was genuinely tired. But it was the little woman, not Anna, who took him upstairs to his clean, bare bedroom under the pointed eaves. She seemed very anxious that he should not notice the various shortcomings of the place; but to Roone it was more amusing than anything else that he should have to go to bed by candlelight.

Presently he heard the girl come up to bed in the room next to his. The partition between the two rooms was so thin that after a minute or two he could identify the soft, monotonous "swish-swish" as the sound of her brushing her hair.

He fell to wondering what she looked like with the smoky cloud of hair framing her serious face and falling over her shoulders. It was ridiculous that she should exercise such a hold over his imagination, and yet, the whole place was so curious that he felt it would always be stamped on his memory. . . . This isolated house on the moors with the wind sighing around it and the snow whispering at the windows; the little frightened woman, who had nothing apparently to be afraid of; and then the girl with her odd abrupt answers and her eyes that hid so much.

He didn't know how long he had slept—not very long, he thought—when he started awake so violently that he was sitting up in bed with his heart thumping before he knew what had happened.

Heavy, uneven sounds like stumbling footsteps were coming from downstairs, and then the woman was saying in a quiet, urgent voice at the door of the room next to his, "Anna, Anna, he's come home after all."

"All right, Mother. It's all right. I'll put on some clothes and come down." The girl, too, spoke in the same quiet tone with that tense note of urgency running through it.

Roone lay down again and pulled the blankets around him. It was no business of his, and he had been well snubbed already this evening for interfering. All the same, he listened drowsily while the girl joined her mother, and the two quietly descended the creaking stairs.

Almost immediately the sound of voices in some sort of dispute reached his ears. There was a man's voice—much louder than the other two—and then the concerted murmur of the woman's voice and the girl's.

Suddenly something jerked him quiveringly awake. Something tore the last vestige of sleep from him. The sound of a woman's scream, high and ragged in the quiet of the night. Roone sat up, his heart beating unpleasantly high in his throat.

Confound it! Should he go down and interfere? The voices had dropped once more, and there was an odd, regularly repeated sound that he couldn't quite identify. Then again, on a note of extreme terror, came the scream. And in that moment of horrible revelation he knew what the sound was—the lash of a whip.

In a second he was out of bed, dragging on his dressing gown, cursing as he fumbled for slippers in the pale gleam from the window.

He took the stairs three at a time, realizing as he did so that the sounds were coming from beyond the closed kitchen door.

White with a rising tide of fury he tore open the door . . . and was suddenly the center of the most melodramatic scene his well-ordered life had ever known.

In the garish, unshaded light of the kitchen stood a huge crimson-faced man. One hand, twisted in her silky hair, held the girl almost still; the other rose and fell in that sickening measured rhythm as he flogged her with a heavy leather belt.

Every bit of Roone's considerable strength was behind

the uppercut he loosed to the man's jaw, and with a surge of sheer primitive joy he felt the bone almost crack under his knuckles.

The falling belt caught him across his other wrist, but he was quite unconscious of the pain. All he realized was the fact that, as the man went down, he dragged Anna with him by the hair he was still holding.

In a moment, Roone was kneeling beside her, gently disentangling her hair, lifting her tenderly so that she was supported against him. Afterward he was surprised to remember that all the time he was murmuring, "Oh, my child, my child, there's blood on you."

"It's all right." She spoke at last in a hoarse little whisper. "But Mother . . . she was so frightened . . . the shock is so bad for her. . . ."

"It was your mother who screamed, then? I thought it was you."

"I wouldn't scream," she said, and for a moment he saw her bitten lips curve disdainfully. He suddenly found he wanted to kiss her thin face, cuddle her like a child against him and murmur the sympathy she refused to ask for.

But sanity was beginning to return, and he looked up quickly. The man was lying there breathing heavily and muttering. Drink and the well-directed blow would keep him quiet for a little while. And the woman. . . .

He looked around and saw that she was slumped very quietly in a chair, her head fallen a little to one side. Fainted, poor little devil, he thought quickly. But even as he formed the idea another unaccountable suspicion set his heart knocking against his ribs.

Instinctively he gathered Anna up so that she could not see her mother, and got to his feet still holding her.

"I'm going to take you into the other room," he said.

"Mother . . ." she began.

"I'll come back and see to your mother as soon as I've settled you comfortably." He spoke gently, but with unmistakable authority, and when she found her slight movement of protest was nothing against the quiet strength of his arms, she gave in.

He carried her into the next room and laid her gently on the wide, old-fashioned sofa, which he pulled up near the fire. A few coals were still glowing there, and he quickly raked them together and added some more.

She watched him silently, then whispered impatiently, "Now Mother."

"Yes." He bent over her kindly for a moment. "You'll be all right?"

She nodded, and turning away with an oddly sinking heart, he went back to the kitchen.

As he entered, he saw that the man was on his feet again. He stood in the open doorway leading to the yard swaying a little and holding on to the jamb of the door. He measured Roone for a moment with a sullen eye, but he was in no mood to fight anyone who could hit so hard.

"I'll have the police on you," he told Roone thickly. "Assaulting a man in his own house. It's a police job."

"Yes, you're right, it's a police job," agreed Roone grimly. "But it's you they'll want to talk to, not me."

He made a quick move across the kitchen, but the man, for all his unsteadiness, was quicker. He banged the door shut, and almost before Roone had wrenched it open again, there was a sound of a horse and cart crunching along the snowy path and out into the road beyond.

Roone's first impulse was to run after the fellow, but the next moment he realized the absurdity of that. Even if he had been dressed for a chase through the snow he would have been outdistanced in a few seconds.

Closing the door, he turned to the silent figure in the chair, and even before he touched her he knew that his first faint suspicion was a horrible certainty. There would never be anything else for her to be afraid of again.

As he bent over her, trying uselessly, as he knew, to find the faintest spark of life the girl called softly from the next room.

"All right, I'm coming." He managed somehow to keep his agitation out of his voice. He hoped he didn't look too grim and pale when he went back to reassure her.

She seemed less faint and dazed now, and her eyes searched his face anxiously as he crossed the room.

"Where is the nearest doctor?" he asked abruptly.

"For my mother?" she countered sharply.

"For both of you." His voice was cool and determinedly matter-of-fact, but he was thinking, "Poor child, how am I going to tell her?"

"I don't need a doctor." She was sulky again.

"Don't be silly," he said gently. "Is there one anywhere near here?"

"Three miles away. Is she still fainting? I must go to her."

"No, you can't do anything." He caught her gently as she tried to struggle off the sofa and firmly put her back.

"What do you mean, I can't do anything?" Her eyes were suddenly wide with frightened suspicion.

"Just that." He made his tone very cool and impersonal. "There's nothing useful you could do if you went."

"Why not?" Resentment and hostility showed in every line of her.

"Well, I can do anything that's necessary, and you—" he cleared his throat "—you must be still like a good girl."

"She'd want me to go. She'll need me."

"No, she doesn't need you."

There was a long moment of silence, while he watched the resentment die out of her eyes. Then, with an odd little movement he would never forget, she put up her thin hands and stroked them nervously up and down his arms.

"I'm sorry," she said very quietly. "I'm making it terribly hard for you to tell me."

"What . . . . do you mean?" He stammered a little, feeling desperately inadequate.

"She's dead, isn't she?" Her voice again held that resigned, almost laconic note that Roone found far more pathetic than tears.

He dropped his eyes before her unwavering glance and was terribly moved to feel her pat his arm absently as though it were he who needed comforting.

Quite naturally he put his arms gently around her. "I wish I could have told you less clumsily," he said. But she shook her head.

"That part doesn't matter. It's scarcely a surprise, really. I knew she couldn't stand any strain like that . . . that scene."

"Is there anyone near whom I can send for a doctor?" Roone looked very troubled. He couldn't leave her here alone with the possibility of that brute coming back; yet to take her out in an open car in this snowstorm would be dangerous after the shock she had suffered.

She shook her head again. "A boy comes with milk about half past six. You can send a message with him."

Roone nodded. With a little air of timid appeal, she looked at him and he drew her gently close and said, "What is it, my dear?"

"You're quite sure about . . . about. . . ."

He felt his heart ache. "I wish I could say anything else, but I'm absolutely certain."

"Please," she said with terrible urgency, "I must know for myself. Oh, do understand."

Without a word he gathered her up and carried her back into the kitchen.

Afterward, he thought the saddest thing he had ever had to do was to convince that tragic, tearless child that her mother was really dead. But at the time it seemed a natural part of that incredible night.

Presently he carried Anna back to the other room and fetched warm water to bathe her hurt shoulders. And as she sat there drooping slightly, her hair swept forward over one shoulder, he thought she was the loveliest thing he had ever seen.

He touched her with the clumsy tenderness of the totally inexperienced and was strangely thrilled by the feel of her warm, golden skin. He had never had to do anything so intimate for any woman before. If his sister had—quite inconceivably—been hurt, there inevitably would have been some person who would do the correct thing, or have the correct thing done, in the middle of the Sahara Desert.

But this suspicious waif—helpless now but still, he knew, on the defensive—knew nothing and was not concerned about whatever the correct thing might be.

He felt his heart warm to her for her very difference from anything in his conventional, well-ordered life. In the language of his own womenfolk, she was entirely impossible, but she moved and intrigued him like no one else he had ever known.

"Is that better?" He had completed some awkward bandaging.

"Yes, thank you."

"Would you like me to carry you up to your bedroom?"

"Oh no . . . please." Her voice was pleading. "Let me stay here."

He gave in at once and made her as comfortable as he could on the sofa.

"Y-you're not going to leave me?" She stammered a little, then started up nervously as he turned to go upstairs for blankets.

"No, no, I'm just going to get something to keep you warm." He realized suddenly that her unnatural calm hid acute fear as well as grief.

When he came down she was looking into the fire so gravely and sadly that after he had tucked the blankets around her, he said ridiculously, "Would you like to hold my hand?"

But she had retreated again into the deep recesses of her own reserve. She shook her head, looking so surprised that he felt it had been thoroughly foolish to make the offer.

He stoked the fire and sat down in an armchair to pass the rest of the night as best he could. If she insisted on wrapping herself away in that impenetrable reserve there was little he could do for her; he would only make her suspicious and shy again if he tried.

Then he looked at her and saw that, though her eyes were closed, big tears were creeping under her lashes to trickle unheeded down her thin cheeks.

"Anna," he said softly, using her name quite naturally.

As she opened her eyes he thought she resembled some stricken little animal that was afraid to die alone, but was even more afraid to ask for help.

With an exclamation of pity he leaned forward suddenly and gathered her up in his arms, blanket and all. He lifted her onto his lap and cuddled her like a child. And as she lay there quietly sobbing, he put his cheek against her silky dark hair and knew somehow that, though no word was spoken, she was comforted.

Presently the sobbing stopped, and he saw that she was gazing thoughtfully into the fire again as though trying to see a little way ahead in her troubled life. But her face looked more tranquil, and glancing down at her bare feet, he saw she was curling her toes childishly in the warmth from the fire.

"Feet feel a bit warmer now?" he asked kindly.

"Yes, thank you."

"They're such pretty feet. You ought to treat them a bit more kindly," he told her. "Not run around barefoot."

She was silent for a moment, and then she said in a whisper, "He took my shoes away, you know."

"What do you mean?" Roone bent his head to catch her words.

"He took them so that I couldn't run away. He was furious with me about something this morning and said he'd punish me tonight. He took all my shoes so that I couldn't run away."

Roone muttered something and felt again the rush of primitive rage he had experienced when he knocked that scoundrel down.

"You poor child! I wish I'd broken his jaw instead of just bruising it."

"I'm not a child, you know," she said seriously. "I'm 20."

"Are you?" Roone smiled. "That's a great old age."

She looked at him doubtfully, and he saw that faint hint of a smile again.

"Well, you're younger than my sister," he told her,

feeling that Katherine was a suitable topic to bring into this extraordinary scene.

"Am I? How old is she?"

"Twenty-seven." He wondered a little if Katherine would have minded his saying that. "And her name's Katherine."

"Is she pretty?"

"Yes, very. At least, I think so."

"Are you very fond of her?"

Roone felt amused at this solemn catechism.

"Of course," he said. "There are just the two of us, you see, and we've always been together a good deal."

"Haven't you any mother or father?"

"Oh yes, there's my father. My mother died before I can remember much, and my aunt has always run the house for us."

She was silent for a while, then said unexpectedly, "Are you very rich?"

Roone was enjoyably scandalized. He knew Katherine would have branded her once and for all as an outsider for asking such a question, but somehow it was quite inoffensive the way Anna said it.

He laughed a little. "Well . . . yes, I suppose we are. My father is the head of Roone & Salusbury, the big iron people, you know."

She shook her head. "I don't know," she said gravely.

"Oh well, it doesn't matter. Perhaps we're not as important as we sometimes think we are," he admitted with an easy grin that would, he knew, have intensely annoyed his family. "Anyway, he's a Member of Parliament and all that sort of thing, too. He's the man who made all that fuss about the copper shares scandal last December. He's terribly upright and decent himself, you know, and just the right man to show up any shady practice like that. I expect you will remember. It made quite a stir at the time."

"No," she said, "I don't know about it."

"Don't know much about anything, do you?" he smiled teasingly.

"No, I'm really rather ignorant," she said humbly.

"Oh, my dear girl," he exclaimed, in distress, "I didn't mean that literally. I was just teasing you." He anxiously gathered up one slack, cold little hand in his. "Still a bit cold, aren't you?" and he slipped her hand inside his dressing gown, chafing it gently, and feeling more ridiculously protective than he had ever felt about anyone.

She seemed to like his doing that, and presently she asked interestedly, "Are you an M.P. too?"

"Oh no! Do I look like one?"

"I don't know," she began again, then checked herself. "I've never seen one," she added, as though speaking of museum pieces.

He laughed. "I'm what's called 'something in the city,' " he told her. "My father wanted me to go into the business, of course, but I didn't see the fun of going into something ready-made. It's the only time we had a real argument. Anyway, I had my own way in the end, and now you see me—a fairly successful stockbroker. Do I look right for that part?"

She considered him very gravely and said, "I think you look like a prince."

"What!" He flushed boyishly and emitted an exceedingly gratified little laugh. "You silly little thing," he said tenderly. "I'm not in the least like a prince. But you are rather like a princess in a fairytale. Like a princess under a spell."

"I'm not under a spell," she said solemnly.

"Well then, perhaps you work spells instead." He smiled down into her serious face. "Like the princess who used to touch the hearts of men, and then, ever afterward, she had only to close her hand in order to make their hearts ache for her, because once she had put her hand against a man's heart he was hers till the end of time. Is that it?"

She shook her head slightly and was silent.

But in that moment, to his incredulous astonishment, he felt the thin hand inside his dressing gown slide slowly downward until it rested lightly and gently against his heart.

And, as though in helpless response, his heart leaped into frantic life under the touch of her fingers. He became acutely aware of her slim figure so close against him, of the warm honey-gold of her skin, the soft scarlet sweetness of her mouth. Reluctantly his eyes traveled up to meet those long, secret hazel eyes of hers; and then his breath, which had been held pent up with excitement, was freed in a little gasp of astonishment, for those eyes were closing in irresistible, childlike weariness, and even as he watched her he knew she was asleep.

Roone found that he was trembling; his heart had settled down into slow, heavy thuds. In all his life he had never been so moved. Twelve hours ago he hadn't known that this waif existed. Now she was lying close to him, with her hand on his agitated heart.

Was that extraordinary little movement a gesture of girlish bravado? An insinuation that she could put her hand on his heart and he would be hers? Or had it just been that, as she fell asleep, her hand quite naturally slid downward?

He realized suddenly that it had become of tremendous importance to him that he should know. Was she as innocent as she seemed, or was she a little village intriguer, deliberately exploiting her amazing physical attraction?

He knew that if her eyes had not closed so finally he would have been kissing her by now, regardless of any circumstances. He had spoken about enchantment, and as he realized that his forehead was slightly damp he told himself that the right word had been used.

And then he remembered those big, quiet tears creeping down her cheeks and with a little sigh he drew her close, and lay there watching her sleeping face in the firelight until his own heavy eyelids closed.

CHAPTER TWO

It was still dark when Roone awoke, but the clanking of a can on the path outside told him that "the boy with the milk" had come, and therefore it must be about six o'clock.

Gently transferring the still-sleeping Anna to the sofa, he stood up stiffly and went to the door. A loutish-looking boy outside stared at him in complete and disconcerting silence. Even while Roone explained that there had been an accident the previous night and that a doctor was needed, not a word was uttered by his stolid audience.

"Well," Roone finished impatiently, "will you take a message?"

"I've got me round," was all the proposed Mercury said.

"But don't you understand this is urgent?" Roone felt and looked profoundly irritated.

"Is Mrs. Rainer ill?" asked the boy, scuffling his foot backward and forward in the snow.

"She's dead," said Roone curtly, aware that only something drastic would move the fellow.

A certain gleam lit his eyes now. "Did *he* kill her?" The boy looked almost amiable in his curiosity.

"No. He's not here." Roone controlled his temper with difficulty. "She had a heart attack."

"And what about the girl?"

"Look here," exclaimed Roone angrily, "never mind about Miss . . . Miss Rainer." (Hang it, of course that wouldn't be her name; but, in any case, he was not going to discuss Anna with what appeared to be the village idiot.) "All I want you to do is fetch a doctor," he exclaimed again impatiently.

"I've got me round," was the stolid reply, as they got back to the salient point.

"Well, damn your round! How long does it take you?" snapped Roone.

"I'll be at the doctor's about nine," the boy said with unexpected alacrity. "I'll send him up."

"All right." Roone was rather annoyed to find he had let himself get so angered.

For a moment the boy didn't move, and as he stood there, his eyes slid slowly down over Roone, taking in the details of his pajamas and dressing gown. Then, with a grin of sly stupidity, he turned away, leaving Roone feeling quite astonishingly uncomfortable.

He went back into the house wondering if the message would really be delivered.

Apparently it was, because about half-past nine, just as a few rays of pale sunshine were breaking through the heavy clouds and sparkling on the snow, up drove a rather ancient two-seater car.

By this time Roone was shaved and dressed and had managed to concoct some sort of breakfast for Anna and himself. She was almost wordless again this morning and had submitted in complete silence when he had insisted she have something to eat. It made him half wonder if he had dreamed that strange, intimate little scene last night.

The doctor proved to be a busy, pleasant, hard-headed man. He expressed no surprise about the dead woman, and Roone gathered that he had attended her before and had almost expected something like this to happen eventually.

After he had done what he could for Anna he came into the kitchen, where Roone was standing, hands thrust into his pockets, staring rather moodily out of the window.

"Do you mind telling me just what happened?" the doctor said, sitting down and beginning to write something.

Roone explained as briefly as possible.

The doctor tapped his pen thoughtfully on the table. "Um, I see. Oh well, I suppose Tom Beal made up the rest." And he went on writing.

"Eh?" Roone flushed in annoyance. "What do you mean? And who is Tom Beal? That nitwit this morning?"

The doctor nodded.

"Look here, Dr. . . . ."

"Irwin," supplied the doctor, without looking up.

"Dr. Irwin. What did the fool say?"

"Not much. He's very economical with words," said the doctor dryly. "But I gathered Mrs. Rainer had interrupted some guilty scene between you and the girl and that there'd been an argument that resulted in a fatal heart attack for her."

"Damn it all—" began Roone furiously.

"That's all right," interrupted Dr. Irwin calmly. "I see he was wrong. I wouldn't get upset if I were you."

"But I suppose he's busy spreading this tale all over the village by now?" demanded Roone.

"Yes, yes, I dare say." The doctor didn't seem especially perturbed. "You mustn't begrudge them their village gossip, you know. It's the only entertainment they have, except for television."

"It's all very well for you!" Roone felt quite unable to be calm. "But I don't want to figure as chief actor in their confounded stories."

The doctor shrugged. "You'll go away from here and never see the place again. Why worry? And as for Anna, I think they've already decided that she's a bad lot, so I don't suppose one story more or less will matter."

Roone was arrested by that sentence, and for a second he remembered the feel of a thin hand resting lightly against his heart.

"What do you mean?" he asked slowly. "You don't think she's . . . that sort?"

The doctor shook his head. "I really have no idea. I've never thought about it."

Roone was conscious of extreme indignation. "I would have thought it was the business of the few intelligent people like yourself to put a stop to this sort of scandalmongering!"

The doctor leaned back in his chair and looked at Roone with some amusement. "My dear fellow," he said with a laugh, "if I were to make it my business to defend all the tarnished reputations in the district I would have no time to look after my large and very scattered practice. I have my work cut out to look after their bodies. They must scrape along themselves as far as their morals and reputations are concerned."

Reluctantly Roone supposed that there was something in this, but he was still put out by the doctor's impersonal view of the matter.

"In any case, there'll have to be an inquest," the doctor pointed out, "and then you will be more or less cleared, even in the eyes of the village."

"I wasn't thinking about myself," Roone said in a troubled voice, and the doctor suddenly decided he liked him very much.

"Well, it's a rotten business all around," he admitted. "I don't know very much about these people myself. They've been here about a year, I think, and the man has been the scandal of every pub for miles around, which naturally prejudices people. The woman seemed inoffensive enough, a poor little soul, and the girl's always been quite civil to me in a sulky way."

For a second Roone almost smiled at the familiar picture of Anna.

"I think she tried going to one or two of the village dances when they first came here," the doctor went on. "But there was trouble over some of the other girls' beaux. I don't know if Anna really vamped the young men, but anyway, that, combined with Rainer's drinking, made things very unpleasant. I think the other girls froze her out."

Roone felt he could see the scene very well: Anna lovely and sullen, the other girls flushed and indignant and furiously jealous.

"I'm afraid there probably *was* some vamping on Miss Anna's part," said the doctor reflectively, "because she isn't exactly attractive in the ordinary way, is she? I mean, she's not particularly pretty."

"Not pretty!" exclaimed Roone. "Why, she's the loveliest thing I've ever seen." And then he slowly turned crimson under the doctor's amused stare.

Taking pity on the other's confusion, the doctor changed the subject and said, "Well, the point is that all this makes it very difficult to find anyone to put the girl up while she's getting over this. I suppose she'll have to go to the Y.M.C.A."

"The what? She'll do nothing of the sort," exclaimed Roone.

"Well," the doctor shrugged, "what else do you suggest? I don't think you'll find anyone around here to take her in. They're mostly poor people and, as I've said, they neither like nor approve of her."

"She must have people of her own," said Roone, who had a large supply of relatives himself—all of them approving.

"No. She tells me she has no one," answered the doctor.

For a wild moment Roone thought of calling off his visit to Coryton and taking her to his own home. But one second's thought of trying to explain to Katherine and his aunt settled that suggestion.

"Well—" Roone was beginning to feel desperate "—what about the clergyman of the parish? Isn't he supposed to take an interest in cases like this?"

The doctor looked thoughtful. "As a matter of fact, the vicar is an awfully nice fellow, and his wife is a good sort too."

"Well then," began Roone.

"On the other hand," pursued the doctor, "they're anything but rich people and have countless demands already on their time and purse. I hardly feel it's fair to ask them to shoulder the burden of this girl's convalescence for six or eight weeks. For that's what it will mean. She's in a very poor state of health."

"Oh, but if it's only a case of money . . ," began Roone, suddenly overwhelmingly glad that he was rich. He had never thought about it before—the money had always just been there—but now he was actively thankful for it. "Can't I arrange something with them? I feel terribly responsible about this girl, somehow."

"Well," the doctor said as he stood up, "I'll see Mr. Orpington myself right away, and find out if anything can be done. Meanwhile, can you stay here an hour or two longer? I really don't see what else we can do."

"I suppose so. Perhaps you wouldn't mind sending a wire for me? I have friends who have been expecting me since yesterday evening."

The doctor nodded, and Roone hastily scribbled:

"Unavoidably delayed. Hope to arrive today. Roone."

Unavoidably delayed. He smiled rather grimly as he went back into the house after seeing off the doctor. In a way that did describe the situation, he supposed.

He went into the room where Anna was. The doctor had given her a sedative and she was lying deeply asleep. For several minutes Roone hung over her, anxious but intensely interested.

So they thought her "a bad lot" in the village, did they? He wondered how much there was in that besides local spite.

Roone had innumerable casual friends among the girls and women in his family's large social circle. He had even supposed sometimes lately that it was time he became thoroughly romantic about one of them and eventually married and settled down.

But not one had ever affected him the same way as this inexplicable witch of a girl. He found that he liked just to watch the gentle rise and fall of her breathing; that he wanted to touch her thin cheek and the soft curve of her neck. Not at all familiarly—in fact, he felt a little awed—but just to touch her and discover afresh how warm and silky soft her skin was.

The very fact that he couldn't possibly have explained the sensation to anyone made it all the more strangely sweet and exciting.

He was still watching her when the Orpingtons arrived.

Roone liked them at once. They were kindly, practical people, who accepted the situation as he described it, without question. They agreed, with a mixture of dignity and common sense that profoundly relieved him, to allow Roone to take full financial responsibility.

He was so impressed with them himself that he was astonished and distressed to find that Anna didn't apparently share his feelings. She only shrank back among the cushions and murmured, "I don't want to go away from here."

Finding that all her reasoning failed, Mrs. Orpington said with some distress to Roone, "Perhaps you can persuade her."

Roone, feeling oddly flattered at the implication, came over at once and took her thin, resisting figure in his arms.

"Anna," he said gently, "I want you to listen to me for a moment."

The stiffness and resentment relaxed slightly. She didn't look at him. She stared sulkily at a button on his coat, which she began to twist nervously backward and forward.

"I know you must feel sad and frightened at having to leave your home, but it's the only thing we can possibly do for you right now." Roone hoped he didn't sound too smug and pompous. "Mr. and Mrs. Orpington want only to be kind to you, and they're going to look after you until you are well again. Then we'll have to see what . . . well, what will be best for you."

"Do you want me to go?" was all she said, still without looking at him.

"Why, yes, Anna," he said. "I'm really very worried about you, and I would feel much less anxious if I knew you were being well looked after."

He looked down at her small hand and had a great desire to take it and kiss it.

"Here, you know, you'll have that button off," he said, smiling as he covered her hand with his.

There was a second's silence, and then she said briefly, "I'll go."

"Good girl," said Roone. "If you will tell Mrs. Orpington just what you want to take, I'm sure she will be kind enough to collect things for you."

"Of course." Mrs. Orpington was all kindly efficiency, and Roone felt it was really tiresome of Anna to look so hostile. Katherine would have said exactly the few graceful necessary words at once.

Anna just muttered quietly, "I haven't got much." And Roone, who knew nothing whatever about the sensitiveness of the poor went out to get his car, quite uncomprehending.

But all the same, it was he who tenderly tucked blankets around her and carried her out to his car, while the vicar and his wife climbed into their workmanlike little sedan.

As they drove away over the snowy crest of the hill, Roone glanced back with the profound hope that he would never see the place again. But Anna stared ahead with bleak eyes that seemed to see an empty world.

From the moment they entered the pleasant, shabby vicarage, it seemed to Roone that life took on the glow of sanity once more. Mrs. Orpington, now completely in charge of the situation, swept Anna off to bed on a wave of kindly firmness. It took only ten minutes of discussion with the vicar to make the simple arrangements for the girl's immediate future.

By the time Mrs. Orpington came down again, Roone was ready to start for Coryton.

"I shall be there for about a week," he explained, "and I'll come over, of course, for the inquest." He paused, and then turned a little diffidently to Mrs. Orpington. "Shall I—may I—go up and say goodbye to her?"

"I don't think I would disturb her now; she looked very much like going to sleep again," was the practical reply. And because there didn't seem much to argue against that, Roone found himself agreeing to leave his next meeting until he returned to the village for the inquest.

As he drove on to Coryton, the memory of the strange, attractive girl beside him was clear; but, once he had reached his journey's end and was with his friends in his own world again, she faded to extraordinary indistinctness.

It was partly that he had nothing with which to connect her in his everyday life, so that she seemed like a sweet and disturbing dream; partly that he instinctively said little about her to his friends. He couldn't possibly have described her. Why try?

Not until he was alone in his bedroom at night did she take full possession of his thoughts again. And then it was with an intensity that almost hurt. He lay in bed thinking of her with a strange, almost frightening mixture of pleasure and pain.

"She's closing her hand . . . and my heart is inside it," was his last half-laughing thought as he fell asleep.

In the end, his visit to the inquest was brief in the extreme. Business recalled him to London much sooner than he had expected, and Dr. Irwin managed to have things so arranged that Roone merely called in at the village on his way home.

The evidence of Dr. Irwin and of Roone himself was practically all that was needed. Anna was still laid up in bed, and Mr. Orpington presented a short, formal statement on her behalf, which the country coroner accepted unhesitatingly.

The proceedings were purely formal. The deceased, it seemed, had been in a precarious state of health and had, intermittently, been under the care of Dr. Irwin. A family dispute had precipitated a fatal heart attack, and the husband—a man of very irregular life—had immediately left the neighborhood. Fortunately for Anna, a casual visitor had been in the house, and had done all that was possible in the circumstances.

The absent husband was censured (which did him no harm). A verdict was entered of "death from natural causes" (which seemed singularly inappropriate to Roone). And the proceedings were over.

Roone was returning to London by train in order to save time; he was having his car sent later. Until the moment of coming from the bare, stuffy room where the inquest had been held, he had fully intended to go to the vicarage to visit Anna. But he suddenly discovered that, since the proceedings had been so short, he could, if he wasted no time at all, catch a much earlier train.

He made some quick calculations, stifling the strange ache of disappointment at the back of his consciousness.

After all, he argued, she was in excellent hands, and he would be coming back quite soon to settle something about her future. And it was really tremendously important that he should get home as soon as possible.

He explained to Mr. Orpington, who promised to give his greetings to Anna and tell her why he could not see her this time; and ten minutes later he was in the local train on his way to the nearest junction to pick up his connection to London.

And then—and only then—he asked himself in slight bewilderment why he had arranged things this way. Again, with that strange mixture of pleasure and pain, the memory of Anna's thin, lovely face rose before him. And, instead of being almost a stranger who had touched the fringe of his life, she became suddenly the most important thing in the world.

He stared out of the window, biting his lip and trying to combat the hot little waves of feeling that kept surging over him. Then, by and by, common sense returned, and he was able to remember that he had been with her less than 24 hours, and that she was just some unknown village girl.

"But there's something about her, of course," he told himself very calmly, as he lit a cigarette with hands that trembled slightly. "A quality that women in legends must have had. I can imagine she would only have to call, and some men would come to her from the ends of the earth. She doesn't know she has it, of course."

Or *did* she know?

Suddenly, for some inexplicable reason, he was overwhelmingly glad that he was going home to the people and things he knew and understood.

The moment he arrived home he began to see his strange experience in its right proportion.

He had always been pleasurably aware of his position as the adored only son, and, having sufficient sense of humor, was able to enjoy it without taking it too seriously. Indeed, Roone was used to taking most things in life with comfortable lightness. He supposed, if he ever thought about it at all, that his family would have been intensely uncomfortable if anything deeply emotional had come their way.

He had no idea that therein lay the fundamental difference between himself and his family. Actually, he would have been surprised and distressed to know that there *was* any fundamental difference, for to run true to type was one of the cornerstones of the Roones' social creed.

All he knew was that it was indescribably good to be back again in the pleasant, conventional richness of his home, to have his father rolling out agreeable platitudes from the head of the table, to listen while his aunt inquired with detailed interest about his doings, and to watch the beautifully correct and controlled movements of his very pretty sister.

"Miss me, Kate?" he inquired affectionately, as his sister's clear gray eyes met his across the dinner table.

"Of course," said Katherine pleasantly, without any sign of having done so. But Roone was completely satisfied because it would never have entered his head to expect any signs of genuine emotion from his sister.

"What was this business about an inquest?" his father wanted to know. "Katherine tells me you said something about it in your letter."

"Yes, Tony," exclaimed his aunt—this was how the family affectionately shortened his name. "What a terrible experience for you."

"Oh, I don't know that it was so terrible for *me*," Roone said slowly. "It was terrible for the girl."

"What girl?" asked his father.

"I told you, Father," said Katherine patiently. "Hamilton was snowbound and had to put up for the night with some dreadful people. The man was drunk and beat the woman or something, and she died of heart failure, and Hamilton was left with some common girl to look after."

"Kate! That's not right at all," exclaimed her brother, unaccountably distressed. "The girl wasn't . . . wasn't common in the least."

"I thought you said they lived in a cottage," said Katherine, as though that settled the matter.

"Well . . ." began Hamilton. "Kate, she was a most unusual girl. Frightfully pretty and . . . and gentle and intelligent."

"You have only to add that she was clean and honest, Tony, and you've given her an excellent reference as a cleaning woman," said his sister with a slight laugh as they left the table.

Hamilton was conscious of acute resentment. Of course it was quite impossible to make them understand Anna. He didn't really understand her himself, if it came to that. But it hurt unaccountably to have Katherine dismiss her like that.

He wanted to reopen the subject. He felt somehow that he was being disloyal to Anna not to make his family see her differently. But their polite and complete indifference rose like a concrete wall and barred any possible attempt.

The matter had to be dropped for the time being, but he decided to tell Katherine all about it later. He had an entirely mistaken belief that there was a strong bond of sympathy between his sister and himself, and that anything that interested him must interest her as well.

But it was a week or two before the opportunity arose, and during that time the picture of Anna was inevitably faded. Then, one evening he came in to find Katherine alone. His father was at the House of Parliament and his aunt out at a bridge party.

Katherine was doing some tapestry work, and Hamilton lounged in an armchair for a few minutes watching her capable, beautiful hands as they worked. Usually her calmness pleased him, but for an incomprehensible moment or two he rather resented her perfect poise.

She sat there with the light full on her unusual coronet of thick fair hair. Her skin was that perfect pink and white that connotes constant attention since babyhood, and her movements were those of someone whose education had included "deportment" so early that calm grace now came perfectly naturally. No one could have mistaken her for anything but the valued daughter of wealthy, indulgent parents, and the firm set of her mouth suggested that she would know what to do if that indulgence faltered.

It was very perverse of him, of course, but Hamilton suddenly found himself longing for a few signs of unreasonableness, for waywardness and unaccountable resentment, for long hazel eyes instead of wide gray ones, and for hair of smoky brown instead of thick pale gold.

"Katherine," he began suddenly, "I never told you any more about that girl."

"What girl?" Katherine didn't even look up.

"Anna. The girl in that house on the moor."

"Was there anything else to tell?" Katherine's voice held only the mildest curiosity.

"Well . . . yes." Her brother ruffled his hair rather anxiously. "I more or less made myself responsible for her, you know."

His sister did look up at that, faintly startled. But "How very silly of you" was all she said.

"Oh no, it wasn't. If you'd been there you would have understood. She was so ill and . . . pathetic and . . . thin," he finished lamely.

"Really, Tony! That class can always exploit their wretchedness for anyone as gullable as you," Katherine told him coolly.

"Don't say 'that class' in that perfectly disgusting way," exclaimed her brother angrily. "She's . . . she's just like us in most ways."

His sister put down her work and looked across at him. "What do you mean exactly about 'making yourself responsible for her'?"

He explained eagerly about the Orpingtons then and was glad it all sounded suitable and ordinary.

"I see." Katherine tapped her thimble thoughtfully against her excellent front teeth.

"There was no choice between that and letting her fend for herself," her brother explained earnestly. "And I couldn't do that, of course."

"No? Well, I don't know why not. But still, it's too late

now. Surely this Mr. Orpington can find her a job or something?"

And suddenly Hamilton knew it was worse than useless to discuss the question with Katherine.

"I don't know," he said quickly. "I'll see about it. I will be going up there in a week or two and I'll talk the whole thing over with Mr. Orpington."

But when he did decide to go, there was a little trouble with Katherine.

"You can't go this week, Tony. I have Marilyn Slater coming to stay and I want you to meet her."

"I'll meet her some other time," her brother promised carelessly.

"Oh, no. I want it to be this week," said Katherine obstinately, and his aunt added, "We do want you to meet her, Tony dear. She's such an exceptional young woman."

"What sort of a young woman?" he asked absently, conscious of a strange desire to escape.

"Well, our sort, of course," said Katherine impatiently. "What else?"

"Oh lord!" said her brother.

"What do you mean?" Katherine spoke sharply. "I don't know how else to describe her."

"I do," broke in his aunt. "She's the sort of woman we would like to see you marry, Tony dear."

Hamilton gave a short, annoyed laugh.

"Oh, that's it, is it? Well, Aunt Charlotte, you must put off your matchmaking a little longer. Kate doesn't want to lose me just yet, do you, Kitten?" And he affectionately pulled the little ends of hair at the nape of Katherine's neck.

"Don't call me such ridiculous names," said his sister coldly. "And it wouldn't be losing you to have you marry someone like Marilyn. It's only when a man becomes tangled up with somebody quite unsuitable that his family loses him."

Hamilton didn't say anything to that, but, very much

to his sister's surprise, he clung obstinately to his determination to go north that weekend.

He would never have believed, he told himself, that eight weeks could have made so much difference in any landscape, but after a hard winter, spring had come early that year, and the first weeks of May were as warm as midsummer. Even the moors looked gracious instead of bleak, and when Hamilton turned down the lane leading to the vicarage, he thought he had never seen anything more beautiful than the warm green of the grass and the white and pink of the fruit blossom on the trees.

The vicar and his wife welcomed him most cordially. After a minute or two, Mrs. Orpington said, "Anna is out in the garden. I like her to be out of doors as much as possible. Perhaps you would prefer to go out and find her yourself."

With a murmured thanks, Hamilton pushed open the French windows and went out into the vicarage garden. He was surprised and a little ashamed to find that he was trembling slightly as he went along the uneven, moss-grown paths, looking for her at every turn.

It was a very large garden with unexpected paths and corners—the sort of place, he told himself, where you would expect to find something or someone a little mysterious.

And then suddenly he saw her. She was sitting on the grass near the gate that led into an attractively untidy orchard. There was an open book in her hand, but she was not reading. She was looking away across the orchard with her characteristic grave expression.

He came quite close to her, his footfall deadened by the grass, and spoke her name quietly.

"Anna."

She turned her head, and her book fell from her hand.

"Oh," she said slowly, and he thought her voice was like the warm wind blowing through the apple blossom. "You've come back."

She smiled as she sat there looking up at him, and suddenly Hamilton knew why she had haunted his thoughts, drifting in and out of them like a strange, sweet ghost. He had never seen her smile before, and in his heart he must have known that he could not rest until he had seen it.

He was conscious of a desire to fling himself down on the grass beside her, to put his head in her lap, to press his face against her and feel her thin fingers on his cheek. His heart was beating so high he felt it would choke him.

She ventured timidly, "Won't you sit down?"

He dropped to the grass beside her, somehow summoning a conventional, kindly smile to his lips.

"You sounded as though—" he began, and then broke off. "Didn't you think I would come back?"

"No."

"But I said I would."

"But you didn't come. You didn't even say goodbye." And he found himself wishing desperately that he had taken more care not to hurt her.

"Oh, Anna, were you hurt that I didn't come?"

"No," she said, and her lashes came down in that sullen sweep he remembered so well.

"Look at me, Anna."

"No."

"Please." But she was perfectly still, and he gave up trying to persuade her. "What were you reading?" He put out his hand to turn over her book. But she snatched it away and held it against her.

"*No!*"

He looked amused and said teasingly, "Come on, let me see."

But she sprang up suddenly and ran into the orchard. At the gate she glanced back for a second over her shoulder. At that look Hamilton was on his feet and after her like the wind.

He was laughing a little, but it was not amusement that sent him speeding after her. He had never known anything like the tide of feeling that swamped him when she looked back as she ran from him. He knew that, if ever he was to know peace again, he must catch her and hold her now.

His hand shot out to grasp her by her shoulder, and she was snatched back into his arms. She stood there panting a little and staring up at him, while he could feel the warmth of her body through her thin frock, and the wild beating of her heart against his.

"Let me go," she whispered. "Let me go."

And suddenly the world he had known all his life broke around him in a million fragments. And every one of them shone dazzlingly in a strange and frightening radiance he had never known before.

"I'll never let you go," he said slowly. "Never, never, never. You've called me, and I've come, you witch, with your warm red mouth and your honey-gold skin." And he kissed her and kissed her, all over her startled face and her smoky hair and the warm gold of her neck.

And as his lips touched her throat her hand fell slackly to her side, and her book slipped unheeded to the ground, to lie there in the long grass of the orchard. A little old-fashioned, forgotten book from the back of Mr. Orpington's bookshelves. The title was *A Gentlewoman's Guide to Good Manners and Etiquette in English Society*.

CHAPTER THREE

Hamilton looked down at the woman who was so still in his arms.

"Anna, have I frightened you?"

"No." It was scarcely more than a whisper.

He touched her cheek with fingers that trembled a little. "When I caught you, you struggled as though you were afraid."

"Yes, I know. I didn't understand then."

"What didn't you understand, my dearest?"

She looked away across the orchard. "I didn't understand that I belonged to you."

He kissed her again at that, but much more gently. "And now you do? And there is no need to discuss your future with Mr. Orpington because it's settled. You are mine—always."

"Always is a long time," she said, with an odd touch of sadness. "But I'm yours, for as long as you want me."

"Anna—" he was distressed at her way of putting it "—why do you say such things? Don't you understand that I want you for my wife?"

She turned her head and looked full at him. "Are you sure that it is as your wife you want me?"

He flushed a slow, deep red at that. "Well, my God, what other suggestion did you suppose I was making?"

"I didn't know," she said quietly. "You said you loved me and that I was yours; that was all."

He felt indescribably shocked at the calm way she said that. "But, Anna," his voice was troubled, "what sort of cad do you think I am?"

She looked surprised, and suddenly began to stroke his arm with a little placatory gesture that he found unbearably touching. "I never thought you any sort of cad. It was only. . . ."

"Well?" he prodded gently, while he tried not to remember what the village had said of her.

"It was only . . . I was thinking . . . it's so much more important that you should love me than that you should marry me, isn't it?"

He cast a troubled glance at her dark head. "Is it?" he asked slowly. "I don't really know." And for a moment he wondered again whether to trust the innocence of her mouth or fear the wisdom of her eyes.

Then he deliberately shook off his misgivings and said smilingly, "Not that the relative values of love and marriage need worry us, because we're going to have both."

"You do know, don't you," she said slowly, "that I shall be quite unsuitable as your wife?"

"I know that no other woman will ever seem more suitable to me," he retorted with a laugh.

But she didn't laugh. She looked indescribably grave, and he was conscious of a great desire to hold her and reassure her. But it seemed suddenly that there was very little to say in reassurance, because what he proposed to do was utterly crazy, and quite impossible to explain to nice, conventional people—like his sister and his father, for instance.

Presently they walked slowly toward the house, and he knew she shrank a little as they approached the French windows. He thought the slight pressure of his arm would be sufficient to reassure her, but he didn't notice that the thin line of her jaw tightened as though she were clenching her teeth.

Both the vicar and his wife looked up as the pair entered, and Hamilton realized that the first of difficult explanations was upon him.

He was secretly annoyed that his voice had a touch of nervousness as he said, "We won't need to discuss Anna's future after all, Mr. Orpington, because she and I have just settled it."

Mr. Orpington took off his spectacles and said, "Oh?" with a touch of something like apprehension; while an expression of extreme astonishment spread over his wife's face.

"Anna and I are going to be married," Hamilton

explained coolly, and then, for the life of him, could think of nothing to add to that bald statement.

"Going to be married?" Mrs. Orpington repeated, in a tone of stupefaction; then, recovering herself, she added hastily, "But what a very sudden engagement."

"My dear Roone . . ." began the vicar rather helplessly. "Well, Anna, this is a very wonderful end to your troubles."

But he didn't look as though he thought it at all wonderful, and to Hamilton—who was used to approval greeting most things he did—it was odd and a little embarrassing to realize how appalled the Orpingtons actually were.

"Suppose we sit down and talk this over," said Mr. Orpington.

"There isn't really much to talk about." Hamilton's pleasant mouth set firmly, and his usually smiling gray eyes looked cool and very determined. "All we want is to have you marry us by special licence just as soon as it can be managed."

"You don't think it would be wiser to wait a little?" began the vicar.

"No." Hamilton's tone was final. "I see no point in waiting. Anna and I know what we want." He turned his head and smiled at Anna. She tightened her hand nervously on his arm, but she didn't smile.

"There's nothing to stop us—Anna is of age. You told me you were 20, didn't you?"

"I'm 21 now," Anna said, speaking for the first time.

"And when were you 21, Anna?" For some reason Mr. Orpington sounded a little stern.

"Today," said Anna shyly, and colored.

"Oh, darling!" Hamilton's arm was around her again. "Darling, you never told any of us it was your twenty-first birthday!"

"It didn't seem very important," whispered Anna.

Quite suddenly Hamilton remembered Katherine's twenty-first birthday, with the innumerable presents and good wishes, the dance at a famous hotel, the pearls from her father and the superbly simple white dress. And the little ache that Anna seemed to bring to his heart so easily was there again.

"You'll have to tell me what you want most in the world, and you will have it for your present," he promised her eagerly.

"I have had what I want most in the world for my present today," she told him gently, and she looked at him with a tenderness that somehow made him feel years younger than she.

"Well, that settles the question of age," said Mr. Orpington, bringing them back to the matter in hand. "Your own people, Mr. Roone, of course will—"

"Will hear any necessary information from me," Hamilton finished, with a slight touch of hauteur. And that settled the thorny subject of his family.

But of course it was not quite as simple as that. Hamilton had to face facts. Until today his family had always been very much the pleasant background of his life. Now the family loomed as something almost formidable in the path of his intentions. With a pang of anxiety he realized how little he liked the idea of his own people being opposed to him. Finally, as explanations seemed so difficult, he determined not to argue things out before his marriage. Once Anna was his wife, he reflected rather mistakenly, there was not much his family could say.

From the little inn where he was staying for the few days necessary to complete the wedding arrangements, he wrote explaining that he was going to marry Anna. But he did not add that the wedding would be within the next few days.

Back came a telegram from his father on the day before his wedding:

> Please reconsider ridiculous proposal. Am coming north at weekend. Will discuss it then.

With an anger entirely foreign to him, Hamilton crumpled the telegram in his hand. His mouth was set grimly

as he went down to the little village post office and tele-
graphed back with almost brutal curtness:

> Anna and I are being married tomorrow and will be
> home in the evening.

Then he determinedly thrust the matter into the back
of his mind and went picnicking in the sunlit woods with
Anna, where it was easy to forget that things such as
family explanations existed.

It was a hot, still afternoon, but under the trees the
faintest breeze was stirring; presently they sat down on
the grass and ate their tea and threw crumbs to an
adventurous squirrel, who came near and peeped at them
with bright beady eyes.

And Anna was so charming and her hazel eyes so wide
and serene that he was surprised to remember he had
sometimes thought them secretive.

"Happy?" he wanted to know, as he flung himself
down contentedly and put his head in her lap.

She looked down at him with her grave smile.

"Very happy."

"I used to think you such a sad little thing," he said
slowly.

"Well, I am sad sometimes," she admitted.

"You mean you *were* sad sometimes," he retorted
quickly.

She said, "Very well," but she gave a funny little smile
as though she were indulging a child. Oddly disconcerted, Hamilton felt that he really knew very little about
her.

He looked at her thoughtfully and said, "Were you
very unhappy as a child, Anna?"

She looked surprised. "No, not at all. My father—my
real father—was an artist, and we traveled all over the
continent. Why?"

"Oh, I just thought . . . it must have been an unsettled
life, surely, roaming around like that."

"I suppose so. But I didn't feel it much. My mother and father were very fond of me. And besides, it was an exciting, friendly life, you know.

"Anyway, I was only 13 when my father was killed, and we came back to England," Anna's voice went on calmly.

"Yes? And then?"

"Then we lived for some years in a town in the Midlands. My mother had a small amount of money and we lived in a house that belonged to a little old French music teacher. I think he had been in quite a good French orchestra at one time, but his health had failed, and when we knew him he taught singing and the violin for ten shillings a lesson."

"My God!" murmured Hamilton.

"Oh, we were not at all unhappy," Anna said tranquilly. "He taught me French and a little Italian, and he taught me how to sing. I went to school too, of course, much more regularly than I had before. I hadn't really learned very much by then, I suppose, except from my mother."

Hamilton looked smilingly interested in this picture of an Anna he had never known.

"And do you sing very sweetly, my darling?" he wanted to know.

"He used to say mine would be a great voice one day," she said, and then she smiled in the curiously gentle way she did sometimes. "But when people grow old, and the great days of their youth are only memories, I think they often create something out of their imagination just to comfort themselves for what is gone."

"You strange, wise little thing," said Hamilton slowly, "I believe you know a lot about human nature."

"Don't you too?" she asked gravely.

He frowned a little and shook his head. "No. I sometimes think I'm really rather stupid about people. In fact, at times, I wonder if I even know my own people very well."

She was silent for a moment and then said, "They will be very angry about me, won't they?"

"They won't be pleased at first, Anna," he admitted. "But they can't help loving you as soon as they really know you."

Anna said nothing in answer to that, and after a moment he said impulsively, "Sing to me, Anna, in the voice that would have been great one day if you hadn't married me instead."

She smiled a little. "What shall I sing?"

"Whatever you like. I don't know any more about singing than I do about human nature." He grinned up at her.

"Very well," she said, and after a moment she began to sing.

At first he could think of nothing but the beauty of her voice and the astonishing purity of her French. And then suddenly he realized what she was singing.

"Plaisir d'amour ne dure qu'un moment. . . .
Chagrin d'amour dure tout la vie."

He lay quite still against her until she had finished, and then he sat up abruptly.

"Why did you choose that song of all things?" he demanded roughly.

She shrank a little. "I don't know. You said you didn't mind what I chose. Why shouldn't I sing that?"

"Oh, my heaven, can't you see these things?" he exclaimed, careless, in his anger, of whether he hurt her or not. "We're going to be married tomorrow. . . . I'm lying here against you in a sunlit wood with all the romance of the world around us. . . . I ask you to sing to me, and you choose some damned song about the joy of love lasting only for a moment, and the pain of love enduring for a lifetime. Do you expect me to be pleased?"

"I'm sorry," she whispered, and his anger left him as quickly as it had come. He was astonished and ashamed to find that such a small thing had provoked it.

"No, my dear, my dear, it's I who should be sorry." He caught her in his arms and covered her face with kisses. "It was ridiculous of me to mind. Of course you didn't mean anything, and your voice is adorable."

"It's all right," she said, but she didn't smile.

"Are you sure?" he begged eagerly. "You have forgiven me, haven't you?"

"Yes, of course." She spoke gently, but he thought her downcast lashes looked a little sulky.

It was not until much later, when he had left her at the vicarage with a tender last good night, that the thought came to him, as it had once before—perhaps those downcast lashes had meant unshed tears and not sullenness at all.

"Oh, I will be good to her," he told himself passionately. "There won't be any more tears because of me—shed or unshed."

When he reached the inn a letter from Katherine was waiting for him, sent even earlier than his father's telegram. It was fairly short but very much to the point.

> "*I'm sure you will agree, Hamilton, that only a perfect fool would rush into a marriage of this sort, and Aunt Charlotte and I suggest that it would be a good idea for you to bring this girl home to stay for a while. Then you could see her in surroundings you are used to.*
>
> "*Some girls might adapt themselves successfully, of course, but others could only make you—and themselves—perfectly miserable. There isn't anything like a little practical experience to clear the situation, is there?*
>
> "*In any case, there is nothing whatever to be gained by rushing into things, and everything to be said for considering them coolly and dispassionately. I need hardly say how anxious and upset we are about the whole thing. We beg you to do nothing rash.*
>
> *Affectionately, Katherine.*"

"Oh, lord! Kate's going to be sticky," was Hamilton's muttered comment.

And his peace of mind was not increased when, a moment later, the door of the inn parlor opened and he heard Mrs. Bates, the innkeeper's wife, come out in earnest conversation with her friend, the postmistress.

"You can see from the telegram," Mrs. Bates was saying with gusto, "that his father's terrible mad."

"Still, what can *he* do?" The postmistress's tone expressed limitless contempt for parents in general. "Probably the young man has to marry her—or thinks he does."

"Got her into trouble, you mean?" Mrs. Bate's voice was full of pleasurable shock.

"Him or another," amended the postmistress succinctly.

Hamilton wished furiously that they were men, so that he could have gone and knocked their heads together. Then he asked himself angrily where his sense of humor had gone. There was surely something amusing in a suggestion so ridiculously wide of the mark. But somehow he failed to find it.

He had expected to lie awake that night, but instead he fell almost immediately into a sleep that was tranquil at first, but gradually broken by disturbing dreams.

He became aware that he was deadly afraid, though he didn't quite know why—something to do with Anna. Everything was to do with Anna nowadays.

And then he knew what it was. Katherine was somehow forcing her to enter a cage full of lions. There didn't seem to be anything preposterous about it in the dream; only a terrible fear because he was unable to reach her, and when he called out to her she didn't seem to hear him.

Hamilton awoke with a choked cry, and found himself grasping the bars at the head of the old-fashioned iron bedstead. But the horror of the dream was still so clearly on him that he called, "Anna!" like a frightened child; and then again, "Anna!"

With a little groan of relief, he rolled over and buried his damp face in the pillow.

Somewhere a long way off a clock struck four, and he knew it was his wedding morning. Soon the light would be growing stronger, the birds would twitter sleepily outside the window, and by and by he would go down to the little gray stone church and Anna would come to him there. . . . Anna, with her innocent red mouth and her large hazel eyes that held so many secrets.

The sun was pouring in at his window when he awoke again. In a second his spirits were soaring, and the misgivings of the previous evening had vanished. As for the strange and horrible dream, it was wiped so completely from his mind that, not until he saw her, two hours later, coming down the little Norman aisle to meet him, did it touch the fringe of his consciousness again.

And then it was only because, as she raised her head and smiled at him, he remembered the smile in his dream.

Nothing could have been simpler than the short ceremony. There were no visitors, no relatives, no curious onlookers, for it was very early in the morning. Only the Orpingtons, a church warden to act as second witness, and Dr. Irwin, who had offered to begin his busy day by giving Anna away.

They walked across to the vicarage afterward, past a few stragglers who hung about the old lych-gate, to stare at the pair in unnatural and disconcerting silence.

Mrs. Orpington, with unfailing kindness, had insisted on giving them something in the nature of a simple wedding breakfast. And then there was nothing left to do but to say goodbye, with what thanks they could put into words, and to set out on their journey in Hamilton's long, black racing car.

For a little while they drove in silence, and then Hamilton glanced at her. She had taken off her hat, and the wind stirred the smoothness of her silky brown hair and put a little color into her serious face.

The ivory linen suit which Mrs. Orpington had bought her emphasized the warm golden tone of her skin, and the girlish collar was turned well down, to reveal the slender column of her neck.

She seemed to sense his scrutiny, because although she looked straight ahead she began to smile. And at that he drew the car to a standstill and put his arm around her.

"I wish it could always be like this," she said, as she leaned her head against him.

"Why, dearest, what do you mean? It always will be like this."

"No," she said. "No. I mean, just the two of us alone."

He laughed and drew her close. "But what do other people matter, anyway?"

"Other people always matter," she said somberly. "Even when they say nothing, they can spoil everything. Today, there was nothing but beauty inside the church. And then, when we went out, those people staring and staring, as though they hoped I'd be unhappy."

"Anna!" He was shocked at the intensity of feeling in her voice. "But why should you think they wished you ill? It was probably just curiosity."

She gave him a funny little look; then she said, almost pityingly, "Of course they wished me ill. They were some of the village girls, and they hate me."

Her mouth looked unhappy and fairly sullen, and he realized with dismay that she was trembling.

"But why should they hate you?" he asked gently.

"Don't you know?" She looked straight at him.

He smiled and shook his head. "How could I guess any reason for hating you?"

But no smile touched her mouth as she said deliberately, "It's because I had only to raise my hand and any of their men would have left them . . . and they knew it."

Hamilton had the confused impression that someone had struck him. He was wordless, and for a moment the silence was so intense that the purring of the running motor seemed shattering.

Then he caught her by the arms and jerked her around to face him. "What are you saying?" he demanded roughly. "How dare you fling that in my face only an hour after I've married you?"

It was he who was trembling now, as he looked down at her with something like terror in his heart. Then he saw that her eyes were as they had been in his dream, with that look of indescribable mournfulness.

"Anna," he stammered. "Anna . . . Anna! Don't look like that, beloved!" And on an incredible impulse he covered her eyes with his hand, and kissed her red mouth over and over again, "Forgive me. I must have been crazy to say such a thing. Only I don't understand you, and sometimes I think I'm almost afraid of the strangeness that is my love for you."

He was softly smoothing her hair with both his hands now, and suddenly she flung out her arms and clung to him.

"It's something that I can't help, you know," she said, in a little quick whisper. "Even if I am shy and have no words, it makes no difference. They still look at me and . . . follow me. Do you understand?"

As though recalling something in a dream, he remembered his own overpowering desire to know more about her, to touch her, to make her smile at him.

"Yes," he said slowly, "I think I do understand. I remember distinctly now that even that first evening, when you fell asleep in my arms with your hand against my heart, I thought, "If she called, I would come to her across the world."

"Oh, Tony, did you?" She smiled faintly, though the corners of her mouth quivered.

Suddenly very earnest, he leaned forward. "Listen. I want you to remember that always. Because it's true. You have only to call and I will come."

She returned his grave look.

"I'll remember," she said. "And, Tony. . . ."

"Yes?"

"No, it doesn't matter."

"What were you going to say?"

But she only shook her head. "Perhaps I'll have the courage to say it to you one day, but not today."

"But—"

"Please, Tony," she put her hand nervously on his arm. "Let's just drive on."

And after a half-puzzled little glance at her he did so.

It was ten o'clock by the time they arrived at the house in Eaton Square. Hamilton knew it was not only weariness that had deepened Anna's pallor, but he was secretly glad that she looked so calm.

As they entered the house the housekeeper hurried

forward to greet them. Mrs. Bentley had known Hamilton since he was a little boy, and he realized it was the first time in all the years he had known her that she had displayed a hint of nervousness.

"Hello, Mrs. Bentley." He smiled at her. "Are you going to be the first to welcome my wife?"

Mrs. Bentley murmured something almost unintelligible and shook hands with Anna.

"Where is my father? In his study?" Hamilton inquired a shade abruptly.

"No, Mr. Hamilton," she said, using a form of address that was unusual with her. "He is in the drawing room. And so are Miss Katherine and Miss Roone."

Hamilton laughed a little crossly at the way she spoke. But Mrs. Bentley didn't laugh. She put her hand on his arm for a moment and looked at him in a way that reminded him of the few times he had been in disgrace as a boy.

"It's all very sudden, you know, Mr. Hamilton," she said. "You must remember it's natural for people to be upset when things happen a little too suddenly."

Hamilton's eyebrows shot up, half in vexation and half in amusement.

"All right, I'll remember," he said.

Then, with an instinctively defensive little movement, he put his arm around Anna and together they went toward the room where his family were waiting.

As they crossed the threshold of the long, beautiful drawing room Hamilton felt he could not begin to guess all the thoughts lying behind Anna's impassive young face.

For a moment the three figures in the room seemed indistinguishable to her frightened eyes.

Then Hamilton was saying, "Father, this is Anna," and her hand was taken by a tall, elderly man while a deep, slightly pompous voice uttered some formal words of welcome.

She looked up into his face and had an odd impulse

to say, "Why, you're a little bit like Tony. I could love you . . . if you wouldn't look so stern and . . . blank."

But of course, one couldn't say that, and so she said nothing. She only smiled timidly and was immediately aware that her silence had disconcerted the others—even Tony. For no doubt she should make some charmingly worded reply that would have eased the tension.

Too late now, however; for Tony was presenting her to his aunt—another blank face, another closed door. The elder Miss Roone said quite pleasantly, "How do you do? We are naturally very much interested to meet Tony's wife."

But Anna guessed what she really meant was, "We thought the poor boy must have made a frightful mistake. Now we know."

With rising terror she turned almost blindly to Katherine.

Tony's sister. . . . He had said that he loved Katherine, that a strong bond existed between them, that she always liked what he liked in the end.

"Kate," Hamilton's voice held a hint of boyish appeal, "I've promised Anna that you'll love her."

"How exactly like a man, isn't it?" Katherine's indulgent smile was perfect. "To promise something he can't possibly control."

Smiling mouth, quiet voice, but eyes that were cold, cold, cold. . . . Chilly as the gray mist that rose from the moor, and just as baffling.

Anna recovered herself sufficiently to smile and remark, "Tony says you always like the same things he does in the end. I expect he was just hoping I wouldn't be an exception."

"Oh, Tony dear, how horribly docile you make me sound." Katherine's carefully modulated voice was quite blank of either amusement or annoyance.

It was unspeakably bewildering. Every person in the room must be seething with one emotion or another. Then why this almost menacing calm that nothing was allowed to ruffle?

Anna had the confused impression that if she suddenly stood up in the middle of the room and screamed, "Why don't you say what's on your minds?" they would all remain perfectly calm. They would pretend she had been merely clearing her throat or something equally preposterous.

But Tony's aunt was speaking now, and Anna knew she must keep her mind on the conversation because it was difficult enough to do and say what they wanted even if she kept her wits about her.

"You must have had a very long drive today. You must be tired."

"Yes . . . a little." Was she supposed to say she was tired, and go to bed so that they could discuss her, or was she expected to go on keeping up appearances?

Now Tony's father was asking if they would like something to eat. But they had had dinner on the way there, and in any case Anna felt food would have choked her.

"Well, at least have something to drink," begged Katherine, with polite indifference. And Anna, suddenly knowing what it was she really wanted, replied, with a little relieved smile, "I would simply love a cup of tea."

"Of course," said Hamilton at once, but that didn't cover the astonished silence from Katherine and his aunt.

"How brave of you," drawled Katherine, "to drink tea at this time of night. Aren't you afraid of being kept awake?"

"N-no," Anna said timidly, realizing that Katherine meant something like, "I suppose you're one of those dreadful people who drink tea at all hours of the day and night."

But the tea was brought, and Tony seemed an angel as he said smilingly, "That's a good idea of yours, Anna. I think I'll have some, too." Anna didn't miss the astonishment on Mr. Roone's face, however, as the older man helped himself to a solitary whiskey and soda.

It was Tony, too, who dared to fling the first word about their marriage into the conversation. With a frankness that Anna guessed would sorely try his family, he said, "I suppose we owe you people an apology for having married in such a hurry. It was too bad that you couldn't be at the wedding, Kate, because I know you revel in that sort of thing."

"I don't imagine I would have *revel*, as you put it, in your wedding, Hamilton," retorted Katherine dryly.

"Oh, I don't know." Hamilton grinned at her teasingly. "It was rather a nice wedding, wasn't it, Anna?"

"It was beautiful," Anna said gently, and she felt suddenly soothed by the memory of that quiet scene.

"A register office wedding, I suppose?" That was the older Miss Roone, trying, at least, to appear politely interested.

"Oh no, Mr. Orpington married us in his church," Anna explained. Perhaps that would mollify them.

"Oh, you poor things!" exclaimed Katherine. "I always think hurried weddings in an empty church must be so depressing."

Anna felt herself flush, and she knew her eyes had gone sullen, the way they always did when she didn't know whether she were more hurt or angry. "It wasn't in the least depressing . . . for us," she said coldly and rudely.

"No?" Katherine was invincibly polite. "Well, I suppose it's just prejudice on my part. Somehow I always associate that sort of wedding with an undignified scuttle to put things right after."

"Kate!" Her brother's angry voice interrupted her. "How dare you say such a thing?"

"I'm sorry, Tony." Katherine looked extremely surprised. "I was only speaking quite generally, of course."

Suddenly something snapped in Anna's aching brain; everything went quite red for a moment, and, to her horror, she heard herself say in a rapid, choking voice, "You weren't doing anything of the sort. You were trying to insinuate that Tony couldn't possibly marry someone who wasn't chosen by his smug family unless he'd *had* to marry her!"

"Anna!" She felt Tony's arm go around her. "Be quiet, dearest. You're exciting yourself terribly for nothing."

For a moment, in her anger, she resisted the pressure of Tony's arm; then suddenly she hid her face against him in a rush of horrified despair.

The curtain had fallen on the first and disastrous appearance of Tony's wife before the select audience of Tony's family.

CHAPTER FOUR

In the end, it was the elder Miss Roone who picked up the shattered pieces of that first encounter with the family and gallently put them together again.

"I think Anna is very tired and just a little hysterical," she said firmly. "I am sure she is longing to go to bed, and I am going to take her there at once."

She obviously meant, "Before any more damage is done," but Anna immediately detached herself from Tony's clasp. She wanted nothing but to be alone at this moment, and afterward Tony would come, she would be happy with him again, and perhaps this nightmare of terror and bewilderment would be over.

She said good night to her father-in-law, who added nothing to his "Good night, Anna" but a look of puzzlement slightly tinged with distaste. To Katherine she could manage only the barest civility. She knew that the hate that had blazed up between them would not be put out by a sentence.

Hamilton came with her to the door, and put his arm around her again. "All right? Or shall I come up with you?"

"No, I'm all right, thanks," she said, wishing her sudden emotion would not make that sound so curt.

On the way up the wide, shallow stairs she scarcely heard Miss Roone's pleasant platitudes. The house was furnished with a richness that seemed very frightening to her, though she realized it was everywhere disciplined by good taste.

Then, through an open doorway, she saw Tony's rather worn suitcase; there was something so dearly familiar about it in all this alarming strangeness that she went toward it quite instinctively.

"This is Tony's room," Miss Roone explained. "It has always been his room since he was a child."

"Oh!" A smile touched Anna's soft, quivering mouth. "Did Tony really sleep here when he was a little boy?"

The quick tenderness in her voice touched Miss Roone a little. "Yes."

"And it looked just like this?"

"Very much the same, I think. I don't remember any drastic changes—except, of course, it is a little tidier these days."

"Oh, I'm . . . so . . . glad," Anna said slowly, thinking with a great rush of relief, "I won't be frightened here. This room has known Tony as a little boy. It must *know* I love him."

"We have put you in what we call the rose room, at the end here," went on Miss Roone's voice smoothly.

Sudden indescribable panic assailed Anna. It was as though a newfound refuge were being snatched away, and she was being pushed back to drown in an icy flood.

She didn't stop to choose her words. She stammered like a frightened child: "Oh, but can't I be here? I don't want to sleep alone. I mean—"

The expression on Miss Roone's face suddenly pierced the mist of her distress.

"My dear Anna," she said, "I am merely going to show you the room we have alloted to you, and will you please not indulge in such coarse talk? I am afraid it is going to be very difficult for us all if you are in the habit of dragging such topics into ordinary conversation."

In bitter humiliation Anna allowed herself to be led along the paneled passage to a beautiful, softly lighted bedroom. She didn't attempt to answer Miss Roone's perfunctory remarks about the room. Only when she said, "Good night. I hope you have everything you want," Anna felt herself start into life again.

"Miss Roone," she flung out her arms in a gesture of appeal, "I didn't mean—"

"*Please*, Anna." Miss Roone was very firm. "I think quite enough has been said. I suggest you go to bed and have a good night's rest."

And she closed the door with a firmness that told Anna that the verdict had been passed.

Anna sat down slowly on the side of the beautiful bed. She felt sick and cold and deadly afraid.

"Oh, Tony!" she whispered desperately. "Surely my love for you isn't coarse!"

She quickly caught back a sob. If once she let herself weep she would never stop, and then Tony would have to know—for surely he would at least come in and say good night?

Even that didn't seem quite certain in this hateful new world of uncertainty and bewilderment.

She undressed slowly and crawled into bed, feeling more bruised and hurt than when she had been beaten by her stepfather. But then it had been Tony who had comforted her and looked after her. She remembered now the clumsy tenderness of his fingers on her bruised shoulders. Perhaps this time he would not know how to soothe the pain of her bruises. Perhaps he wouldn't even try.

And then she heard his step.

She put her hand to her throat to ease the terrible ache there. She must not cry. She *must* not.

"May I come in, Anna?"

"Yes."

She rolled over so that her face was away from the light.

"Dearest!" He was bending over her now. "You're terribly tired, aren't you?"

"Yes."

"Poor little thing. You mustn't worry. You'll feel quite different in the morning."

"Yes."

Her unsteady lips seemed unable to frame any other word.

He put his arm about her, but she stiffened. She couldn't help it if he thought she was sulky and resentful. If she gave way an inch now she would be clinging to his neck and sobbing that he take her with him to the one room in the house where she was not afraid. But it was coarse to say things like that. Coarse, coarse, coarse! The hateful word repeated itself in her mind like something striking a bruise.

"Good night, my darling."

"Good night."

"Aren't you going to kiss me?"

She obediently kissed him at once. He held her for a moment so that her cheek was against his. But she made no response, and presently, with a slight sigh, he laid her down.

He tucked her in as though she were a child—that nearly broke her composure, but she dug her nails into the palms of her hands and made one last effort to keep calm.

"Shall I turn off your light?"

"Yes, please."

He flicked the switch and the room was in darkness—blessed, blessed darkness. He shut the door . . . and she was alone. It was relief and sickening misery in one.

She said his name over and over again between little gasping, broken sobs. She could cry now. No one would see her or ask questions. The tears poured in an overwhelming flood down her cheeks to seep between her fingers pressed hard against her face.

"I don't understand," she sobbed. "I don't really know what they want me to do. Oh, I will try, but it's so difficult when they know everything and I know nothing. I can only love him one way . . . and they seem to think that's wrong. Oh, Tony, Tony—"

And then she thrust the sheet against her mouth, because her door had opened quietly.

"Anna."

"Yes."

"I was worried about you, dearest. Are you all right?"

"Why . . . did you think . . . I wasn't?" She didn't know how pitifully her little quick gasps broke up that sentence.

"I don't quite know. Except that I had the strange feeling you were calling me. And . . . don't you remember? I promised I would always come."

"Oh, Tony, I was calling you, really." She held out her

arms to him in the darkness. "Don't put on the light, but come here to me. Please, beloved, please, please!"

She heard him quickly cross the room to her. And then she was snatched up in his arms, so that her final "please" was sobbed against him.

"Little Anna! What is it? What is it?" He was holding her tightly and kissing her. "Oh, sweetheart! Your dear, wet little face and your beautiful hair all tumbled . . . and you're so hot and trembling. What's wrong, dearest?"

"I don't . . . like my room," she stammered.

"Don't like your room?" he repeated, a little bewildered.

"I wanted . . . to be . . . in your room. . . . The room where you were as a little boy. I didn't think it was wrong to want to be there. I feel safe there. I wanted your arms around me—I thought that was what being loved meant. I didn't know it was . . . coarse to feel like that."

She couldn't help it if he heard the angry pain in her quivering voice.

"My darling, there isn't anything coarse about it." He was holding her against him and speaking very gently. "It's sweet and natural and adorable of you."

"But you only kissed me good night and left me alone here. I . . . I thought you were ashamed of me after . . . after this evening." Her voice still trembled, but she was not sobbing now. The way he held her hot hands in his gave such unutterable comfort.

"Listen, my dear. I thought you were desperately tired and wanted to be left alone. I'm sorry. I was terribly stupid, I'm afraid, and I didn't understand."

"No, no," she interrupted eagerly, "it was I who was stupid and didn't understand."

He stopped her by putting his mouth gently against hers. "Hush. You mustn't think you're the only one with things to learn. I have a lot to learn, too."

She gave him a long, sweet, grateful kiss at that, and then she felt him put out his free hand across the bed.

"What do you want?" she asked.

"Something to wrap around you."

"Oh, Tony, why?"

"Because I'm taking you back to my room now."

He found an eiderdown and, wrapping it around her, lifted her tenderly in his arms.

She lay perfectly still against him now. Nothing mattered. Nothing in the world. Not Katherine's hatred, nor his aunt's scorn, nor anything in this new bewildering life. Tony was not ashamed of her in spite of the awful things she had done this evening. He loved her and wanted her.

And that was all Anna asked.

At the breakfast table next morning the family met with every sign of polite cordiality. And Anna, to her surprise, found herself doing her best to join in the peculiar social conspiracy to pretend that nothing out of the ordinary had happened.

If this was what Tony's family wanted, then this was what she must try to do. It was little enough to do for a lover such as Tony.

"Katherine was going to have a small party tonight, Tony," Miss Roone said, "so we carried on with the arrangements because it seemed a good way of introducing Anna to some of our friends."

"Yes, of course." Tony narrowed his eyes for a second, but the expression was gone again almost before Anna could register it. "Who is coming?"

"Mostly my crowd," Katherine explained carelessly. "The Forsythes and the Durhams, and Jeremy Deane . . . oh, and Marilyn Slater—you haven't met her." For a second the eyes of brother and sister met.

"No, I haven't met her," agreed Tony coolly. "Who else?"

"About half a dozen others," replied Katherine equally coolly. "Jennifer Forsythe phoned yesterday evening to ask if she could bring along Mario Frayne. I couldn't definitely say 'no,' of course, so I had to agree. I don't know why the Forsythes are so friendly with the man."

"Oh yes, you do, Kate," smiled her brother. "For the same reason that you agreed to let him come here. It's nice to have the most famous actor-manager in London on your guest list . . . even if his morals are a bit rocky."

Katherine shrugged, and Anna said, "Surely he isn't entirely English, with a name like that?" It really cost her an effort to join in the conversation at all, but she was determined to do her best.

"Oh no," said Katherine. "The Frayne part is English, of course. He was the son of Mortimer Frayne, the artist— But surely you must know of him! I thought everyone did. His name is a household word."

"I . . . I don't know very much about the theater," Anna stammered a little and gripped her hands together nervously under the table.

"Well, it isn't of any great importance," Hamilton said carelessly. "Frayne really is a superb actor and very well known on the London stage. He's about 40 now, I imagine, and manages his own theater. As Kate says, his father was Mortimer Frayne, the artist, and, since no one makes any secret of the fact, I suppose there's no harm in adding that his mother was an Italian model whom his father didn't bother to marry."

"Well, scarcely," interjected Katherine. "She wasn't exactly the kind of woman a man would marry. It would have meant social ruin."

Anna felt her color rising, but Hamilton merely said, with determined good temper, "You're getting ethics and social values a little mixed up, Kate, I think. But anyway, it doesn't matter now. Frayne inherited remarkable good looks from both parents and more than his share of what is generally called sex appeal. I'm afraid he is a sort of Don Juan of the London stage."

"Is he as good-looking as you?" was all Anna asked.

Hamilton laughed and flushed, while Katherine and her aunt exchanged glances.

"Why, Anna dear, I imagine Frayne's admirers would consider me very much an 'also ran,' " he said, good-humoredly. "But I'm vain enough to hope you won't be too much dazzled by him tonight to notice that I look passable in a dinner jacket."

"Oh," Anna was suddenly reminded of something, and however desirable it might be to suppress unpleasant truths, this at least had to come out. "Tony, I . . . I haven't anything to wear at a party."

"I expect there's something in your trousseau that will do." Katherine permitted herself that enjoyable little bit of malice.

"I . . . I didn't have a trousseau," stammered Anna.

"No trousseau?" repeated Katherine. Her tone was only mildly protesting, but it somehow gauged the appalling social depths of anyone who married without a trousseau.

"Well, there's plenty of time to buy something today," Hamilton pointed out equably. "I have to go to town myself this morning. Suppose you take Anna with you, Kate, and make a start on the trousseau-buying now."

"Very well." No one could have told from Katherine's manner whether she was pleased or annoyed.

And so, with more money than she had ever had in all her life, Anna spent her first morning in London with her sister-in-law, buying clothes.

"We'll start with your dress for this evening," Katherine told her, "and then we can buy everything to go with it. I'll take you to Fanchette. She's wonderful with rather unformed types."

Anna did her best to look pleased at being treated like a mild mental defective, but she felt very nervous as she entered the softly carpeted gray and silver *salon* with Katherine.

"Fanchette" was a slim, dark-eyed Frenchwoman, so admirably preserved that no one would have been so silly as to try to guess her age.

"This is my new sister-in-law, Fanchette," Katherine explained carelessly. "We want something for a small dinner party tonight."

"It is Madame's first party since her marriage?" the Frenchwoman asked, with a kind glance at Anna.

"Yes," Anna smiled at her.

"Then it must be something especially lovely."

"Nothing that requires any style in the wearing, Fanchette," said Katherine in French. "As you see, my sister-in-law has not yet acquired style."

"Nevertheless, Madame has an exquisite figure," replied Fanchette dryly, in the same language, "and I notice that she walks like a dancer. She shall see what we have."

Somehow, Anna managed to keep her color down during this conversation. She was helped by what she feared was an ignoble pleasure in the discovery that Katherine's French was inferior to her own.

She watched with grave eyes while several dresses of an elaborately simple style were paraded for her benefit. Then she turned to Fanchette.

"My sister-in-law is quite right, you know," she said gently, in French. "I really have none of what she means by 'style.' Have you anything that is more picturesque than stylish?"

And this time it was Katherine who had difficulty in controlling her color.

Possessed of an excellent sense of humor, Fanchette wanted to laugh, but, having an equally excellent sense of salesmanship, she contented herself with a smile.

"I know what you mean," she nodded. "I think I have what you want. A moment. I will bring it to you myself, because I do not want you to see it on anyone but yourself. I think it is your own personality that will make it."

She went away and, for the minute or two they were alone, Anna and Katherine did not exchange a word.

Then Fanchette returned, and on her arm was a mass of green and gold. She spread it out for Anna to see—wide, Arabian Nights trousers and long-sleeved blouse in glittering silk, with a tiny brown-and-gold brocade bolero.

Anna stood up without a word, and followed the smiling Fanchette to one of the fitting rooms.

"Madame's beauty is of a rare kind. She should always wear exotic styles in the evening," Fanchette said, as she laced the little bolero and hung huge bell earrings from Anna's ears.

Still wordless, Anna gazed at herself in the glass. The faintest flush had crept up under her honey-gold skin, and her hazel eyes looked almost green. The Frenchwoman fastened a wide, glittering gold necklace around her neck, and stood back to admire the whole effect.

"Madame's husband will be very proud of her in that," she said firmly.

And at that Anna did a quite extraordinary thing. She turned and put her arms around Fanchette and kissed her.

The Frenchwoman's rather metallic composure broke for a moment.

"My child, you are very sweet," she said. "Shall we go and show Miss Roone what a beautiful sister-in-law she has?"

Anna nodded, and they went out together.

"But it's such a fancy dress," objected Katherine when she saw it.

"It is like the Arabian Nights come to life," retorted Fanchette. Katherine shrugged and said, very well, if Anna liked it, she supposed she had better have it.

The rest of the shopping expedition was unimportant to Anna. She lived for the moment that Tony would see her in the outfit.

As soon as she was dressed that evening she ran to Hamilton's room.

"Tony, may I come in?"

"Of course."

He was still in his shirtsleeves and murmuring mild blasphemies about his studs, but he turned around with a smile to greet her. The smile faded slowly from his face and an almost awed look took its place.

He came toward her. "Anna, how beautiful you are," he said slowly. And he took her face very gently in his hands and kissed her mouth softly.

"Are you . . . are you proud of me?" stammered Anna, remembering what the Frenchwoman had said.

And at that Hamilton laughed, and lifted her right off the ground. "I'm bursting with pride about you, you little goose. Now run on down and cover the fact that your husband is disgustingly late. Besides, I want my father to see you in that as soon as possible."

Anna hung back for a moment. She didn't want to go

down alone; but if Hamilton wished her to go that was sufficient. And after all, he was proud of her, so why should she be afraid?

She walked quickly along the passage, and then paused suddenly. Katherine's door stood half-open and Katherine was speaking to someone. "My dear Marilyn, you simply can't imagine. . . . She's just a common, little working girl. Of course, we're simply shattered."

The color was whipped out of Anna's face. She stood there for a moment, her fists clenched, her breath coming in little gasps. Then she fled, blindly, furiously, down the stairs.

She was only three steps from the bottom when she realized someone was in the hall below—someone who came forward and stared up at her where she had halted, breathless and startled.

"Why, you little ghost of old Baghdad," he said slowly, "what are you doing on a London staircase? You ought to be leaning from a wrought-iron balcony, breathing vows of love to a desert sky."

It seemed rather tame to say "I'm Mrs. Roone," after that, but it was the literal truth and so Anna said it. Whereupon the man laughed, showing the most beautiful teeth she had ever seen.

"Oh no, you're not," he said, calmly putting his hands around her slender waist and lifting her lightly down the last three steps. "You're Scheherazade."

Anna didn't know whether to laugh or to be annoyed; and the next second she realized that Katherine and another young woman were halfway down the stairs and could scarcely have failed to see the peculiar little scene.

However, Katherine coolly descended the rest of the stairs and said, "Good evening. It's Mr. Frayne, isn't it?"

And Anna watched the so-called Don Juan of the London stage bow over Katherine's hand and apologize smilingly for having arrived before his friends.

After that, other people arrived, Tony joined them, and everything was a confusion of introductions. Gradually the melée resolved itself into the ordered formality of a dinner table, set as Anna had never seen a table set before.

She prayed frantically that she would make no mistakes. She knew that, as Tony's unexpected new wife, she had someone's eyes on her at all times. And she knew equally well that Katherine was hoping she *would* make mistakes, that half her intention in asking these smiling, pitiless people was that she should make a humiliating fool of herself in front of them. Then Tony would see her as she was—a common, little working girl.

For a moment a choking sense of panic assailed her again. Under her long lashes she cast a hunted glance around the table. And then she saw that Mario Frayne was looking at her. He gave her a lazy little smile of reassurance, and suddenly Anna's nerve steadied again.

She remembered what Fanchette had said. Her husband would be proud of her; and something in Frayne's laughing dark eyes told her the same thing. Unconsciously, she drew deeper breaths of confidence. Tony should be proud of her. This was her big chance not to let him down.

She was still too shy to take much part in the conversation, but with Tony at her one side she felt fairly safe; the man on her other side took singularly little interest in her. So she occupied some of the time in watching Mario Frayne.

What had been said about him was perfectly true. Frayne was almost as handsome as it was possible to be. Tall and powerfully built, he had, nevertheless, a grace that was typically Latin. His thick dark hair was a little inclined to stand up, as though the radiant vitality in him permeated even that; his eyes, which were being used now with considerable effect on Katherine, were brilliant and laughing; his skin was warmly brown; his mouth was unexpectedly firm, and his teeth quite superb.

But it was his complete unselfconsciousness that made him so interesting. He cared nothing for the effect he created, and all the time his flame of almost insolent vitality made him impossible to ignore.

No doubt, thought Anna, he did and said a thousand things that Katherine and her friends would call "impossible" in anyone else, but because he was so incredibly sure of himself, so insolently good-looking, he got away with it.

Anna had never heard the expression "animal magnetism," and so she didn't know that was what he possessed in an almost terrifying degree. But she did know quite instinctively that here was someone who probably made most men do what he wanted—and certainly most women.

And then Miss Roone was getting up from the table, and Anna realized with horror that she was going to be alone with Katherine and the terrifying young women who were her friends. Tony wouldn't be there to help her, and—ridiculously enough, she thought—nor would Mario Frayne.

She forgot that she was beautiful, that her dress was designed to make Tony proud of her. She only knew that this was the most terrifying thing that had happened yet, as she moved stiffly into the other room, among incredibly smart and self-possessed young women, who talked in what seemed to her almost a foreign language.

"Wasn't it too exciting, you and Tony marrying so unexpectedly?" drawled Jennifer Forsythe beside her, in a tone from which every trace of excitement was successfully banished.

Anna privately thought it was much more beautiful than exciting, but she said timidly, "Yes, I suppose it was."

"Did you do it to annoy your people or something?"

"Oh, no."

"Just to be original, I suppose? Well, really, I do admire you. I think a big society wedding is such a frightful bore. I know after mine all I wanted was a nursing home. And then, of course, one had to go tearing off instead on one's honeymoon."

Anna couldn't imagine what to say in answer to this, and just then someone else broke in with, "I hear you come from Yorkshire. Did you get much hunting in your part of the country last season?"

"I don't know," said Anna blankly.

"Which pack do you hunt with?"

"I don't hunt at all," Anna said curtly. "I think it's cruel and stupid, anyway."

This created a mild sensation, and a good deal of hostile amusement.

And then, incredibly, Mario Frayne was beside her, looking down into her frightened eyes.

"Come and talk to me," he commanded smilingly. "I've only heard you say about four sentences as yet, and each time it's been like a few bars of music. Why aren't you standing up making speeches to us while everyone else is silent in admiration?"

Anna laughed, and suddenly the awful tension relaxed. Everything was not lost after all. Katherine had tried so cruelly to make her fail, but the most important man in the room had thrown the careless mantle of his protection around her. She had another chance. Perhaps even yet Tony might be proud of her. She didn't want it for herself—only for Tony—because he had been so wonderful to her. They mustn't be able to sneer at him because he had chosen her.

And now here was Tony himself smiling at her, telling her with his eyes that she was the loveliest thing in the room . . . or in the world, for that matter.

"I was just complimenting your wife on her beautiful speaking voice, Roone," said Frayne candidly.

Hamilton smiled. "Yes, it is lovely, isn't it?"

"Do you sing at all?" Frayne asked her abruptly. He wasn't making fancy speeches now. He was looking at her with intense interest.

"Yes, I sing." Anna smiled back at him with none of the nervousness she felt with the others.

"Come and sing now," he said.

"Oh, but I think it would be rather nerve-racking for her just now," protested Hamilton.

"No, Tony, I don't mind." Anna was, all at once,

completely confident. She *could* sing. She could do that supremely well, and a curious sort of exaltation entered her at that moment, so that she was not in the least afraid.

"But the party. . . ." began Hamilton, looking a little doubtfully at Katherine who was managing her party exactly as she wanted it.

"Oh, that is of no consequence." Frayne swept aside everything carelessly to make way for his whim of the moment. "Come!" And he led a faintly apprehensive Anna to the piano.

"Miss Roone." Katherine turned at once in the direction of his voice, "your sister-in-law is going to sing for us. I want to hear her voice."

"Oh, but I don't think she—" began Katherine.

"Oh yes, she does," he interrupted her firmly. "Now!" He ran his hands over the keyboard and turned to Anna, who stood smiling beside him. "In what language are you most at home? English? German?"

"French," said Anna.

"Good. This?" He began to play the opening of Mignon's song, "*Connais-tu le pays?*"

Anna nodded, and with her hands pressed rather childishly against her breast she began to sing. And, as she sang, the people who bewildered and frightened her were nothing more than figures in a dream. She was the wandering Mignon, asking with touching reiteration of every passerby, did they know the country from which she came, the land where the orange-trees lay warm in the sunshine?

There were no actual tears in her voice, only that inarticulate sadness that knows no expression in words—the longing for home that every wanderer in every corner of the earth must know.

She finished amid dead silence, and then a little babel of congratulation broke out. But Frayne's voice broke across it immediately, "Ah! I thought I was not mistaken. Now tell me, do you sing any Italian?"

"A little."

"Do you know that old and most beautiful of all love songs 'Star vicino'?"

"I can't remember all the words."

He repeated them to her, his dark eyes on her face, and slowly she repeated them. But her eyes were not on him, they were on Tony. And when she began to sing again it was Tony to whom she sang, in simple, old Italian—that humblest plea of any lover just to be allowed to stay near the beloved.

She didn't know that Hamilton wanted to get up and go to her, to take her in his arms in front of them all. But she did know that he smiled full at her, and that in his smile there was all his love for her . . . and his pride.

Frayne was saying, "That is really superb. I must get Conrad Schreiner to hear you. He's in London just now." And people were murmuring: "Schreiner, you know. Frayne must think well of her." And, "Yes, but I don't wonder. Isn't she lovely?"

But to Anna there was only one thing that mattered. "Madame's husband will be proud of her," Fanchette had said, and Fanchette had been right.

She didn't even hear the slight disturbance in the hall. She didn't notice the subdued little scuffle at the door. Her soul was on a mountaintop, and she knew nothing but peace and great happiness.

And then, like a thunderbolt in the sunlit scene of her happiness, a raucous, angry voice struck on her ears. "Let me alone, I say. Anna's a good girl. She wouldn't be ashamed of her stepdad just because she's married to a swell. She'll be pleased to see me."

And, incredibly, like a figure from a nightmare, her stepfather—flushed, quarrelsome, obviously tipsy—advanced a little unsteadily across the room.

CHAPTER FIVE

In wordless horror Anna watched her stepfather's unsteady progress across the room, while, on every hand, people fell back, curious and amused, to see what would happen next.

It was quite incredible that Katherine should have arranged this as a sort of joke, of course. They knew she didn't do things that way. Besides, there was no hint of a joke in young Mrs. Roone's face. Her eyes were wide with disbelief, her cheeks ashen with dismay.

The creature had called himself her stepfather, and it looked as though that were the truth. Hamilton Roone's father-in-law, in a way. It was appalling and amusing at the same time.

And there was Hamilton, too, looking as though he had been frozen into stone, while in the background a couple of servants dithered helplessly.

The man had reached Anna's side now, and was looking down at her, swaying a little as he grumbled:

"I've come all the way from Yorkshire, and you won't even say you're pleased to see me. I'm ashamed of you, Anna."

At that moment Frayne rose and took him by the arm.

"Look here, old man," he said affably, "what you want is a drink. Nobody welcomed you, eh? Well, that's too bad. But then you didn't give us any warning, you know."

He was propelling the slightly protesting man back toward the door.

"Come along and let's see if we can find something worthy of the occasion."

Mutterings of, "I meant it as a surprise. She's an ungrateful girl," died away along the passage, and because the real center of interest was now removed they all turned their eyes to Anna.

Hamilton had come over to her and was talking to her gently, standing so that he sheltered her partly from the other people in the room.

256

But nothing he said did much to relax the rigid misery of her taut figure or clear the sullen despair and bewilderment from her eyes.

She knew these people had forgotten all about her singing, forgotten that she was beautiful, that Mario Frayne had said she was superb, worthy to be heard by Conrad Schreiner—whoever he might be. All they remembered now was that she was a common girl whose stepfather turned up in a horrible checked suit, drunk, in a London drawing room.

She made a weary little gesture to silence Tony. It was impossible to explain, but she couldn't bear even the sound of his voice at the moment.

"I'd better go to him," she said quietly at last. "There's no reason why Mr. Frayne should have the task of managing him."

"Nonsense, my dear." Tony's voice was gentle but quite final. "It isn't a matter for a woman. I'll go."

"Then let me come too. I can't stay here. Don't you *see?*"

He let her come at once, but he made her wait in the library at the end of the big square hall, while he himself went in search of Frayne and his unwelcome charge.

"You mustn't worry, dearest," he had told Anna, though his own gray eyes were intensely worried. "It won't be difficult to make him understand that it's no good his turning up here if he wants to keep on the right side of the police."

She mustn't worry! Anna smiled bitterly as she walked up and down the big library, her hands clasping and unclasping with the intensity of her despair.

It might be quite easy to get rid of him. She didn't know. But in any case, what did it matter now? Her whole world was in ruins. There was not much point in promising her that there would be no second earthquake.

At last there was the sound of a step in the hall, and she went to the door. But it was not Tony. It was Mario Frayne, and he was putting on his coat. She stood quite still, watching him, her eyes dark with apprehension.

Perhaps she made the faintest sound, because he turned

suddenly and came toward her, wrapping his white scarf around his throat as he came.

She supposed he meant to say something comforting about the horrible incident, and braced herself so as not to wince. But he didn't mention that. He just said, "Now don't forget what I told you about your voice. It's quite out of the ordinary, if my judgment means anything. And I would like Schreiner to hear you."

"Who is Schreiner?" she said almost in a whisper.

Frayne laughed delightedly at that, as though no such thing as the shattering tragedy of half an hour ago had happened.

"I wish Schreiner could hear that. It would do him good. He's one of the greatest operatic conductors and directors in Europe."

"But I don't suppose he would think anything of me." The faintest interest lightened the shadow in Anna's eyes in spite of her wretchedness.

"Possibly not, but possibly yes. Anyway it will be interesting to hear what he has to say about you. Will you call me one day this week? Any time before 11—and we'll arrange something."

He gave her a card, and she stood there, turning it over slowly in her hands.

"I'll have to ask Tony," she said at last.

He laughed. "My God, what wifely docility! All right, ask Tony. And now I must go. Good night, Mrs. Roone."

He kissed both her hands and turned away. It was not until he had reached the hall door that she realized she had not thanked him for his quite extraordinary kindness in dealing with her stepfather, nor for the brief, sweet moment of triumph he had given her.

"Mr. Frayne!"

He turned at once, and as she ran to him across the hall, with her hands outstretched, the sudden smile that leaped into his eyes made her remember, a second too late, what Tony had said about his reputation.

"Well?"

He looked down at her, and in that moment she felt the

full impact of his brilliant, laughing eyes and his fine, flaring nostrils.

"It's only," she stammered a little, "thank you . . . thank you for everything."

He took both her hands and smiled.

"Sweet child. It was nothing." He calmly bent his head and kissed her lightly on her startled mouth. And as his lips touched hers she knew quite well that, whatever his reputation, that kiss had been given in sheer kindness, and nothing else.

She turned away, faintly shocked but oddly comforted too; and as she did so Katherine stood in the drawing room doorway.

It was all over in a second; and then the hall was full of people talking and taking leave. But Anna knew that Katherine had seen the kiss and had read every beastly shade of meaning she could into it.

There would be some sort of reckoning, she supposed wearily, but for the moment it scarcely seemed to matter.

She thrust Frayne's card down the front of her blouse, and somehow the feel of the little stiff square against her gave her courage to join in the goodbyes to the guests.

It was over at last. Everyone had gone. Anna went slowly back into the brightly lighted room that had seen her moment of triumph and her complete and utter humiliation.

Her father-in-law was there, fidgeting about and clearing his throat unnecessarily loudly. He gave her a glance of puzzled distaste and began to light a cigar.

Katherine and her aunt entered the room then, and, a moment later, Tony, looking tired and grim, joined them.

"Well?" said his father.

"What?"

"Did you get rid of the fellow?"

"Oh, yes." Hamilton went to the bar and poured himself a whiskey, which he drank at a gulp.

"The point is—what guarantee have we that this won't happen again?" His father was smoking furiously.

"There's no guarantee," said Hamilton dryly. "But

I've made it quite clear to him that it will be worth his while to keep away, and things will probably be unpleasant for him if he comes here again."

"Do you mean you're paying him?"

Hamilton shrugged.

"Tony!" That was Anna, from the depths of her misery.

"Be quiet, my dear." Hamilton spoke curtly and wearily. "You must let me settle this."

"But it's blackmail," fumed his father.

Hamilton made an impatient little gesture.

"I suppose Tony means that if he takes on in-laws who include drunkards he must expect this sort of trouble," observed Katherine calmly.

"Oh, for God's sake, Kate—" Her brother threw her a furious look.

"Oh, Tony, we knew all along that something awful would happen," his aunt exclaimed plaintively. For even she had given up all attempts at keeping up appearances.

And as Anna watched in impotent despair, it seemed to her that they took the delicate fabric of her love story and tore it to pieces.

"This sort of thing is always a terrible mistake." Old Mr. Roone was walking up and down by now.

Hamilton stiffened angrily. "Will you be quiet, all of you, please! It's beastly that this should have happened, of course, but it's worse for Anna than for us. I will not have you talking as though it's her fault. The man's no relation of hers—and if he were, I still can't see that any blame attaches to her."

"We're not talking of blame, Tony," protested his aunt. "It's just the horrible disgrace. Think of your father's position. You can't wonder he is upset. Think of your own position. This sort of thing is bound to be damaging. And we were looking forward so much to your marriage. There were a dozen nice women for you to choose from—women you could have been proud to have as your wife."

Anna uttered a small, wordless sound at that, and Hamilton flung an angry, protective arm around her.

"Aunt, you will not say such a thing. I chose Anna because I love her and because I *am* proud of her—frantically proud!"

"It would be interesting to know *why* you feel this touching pride in her," observed Katherine dryly.

"Kate, will you stop being so disgusting! If you must know, it's because Anna's sweet and good; she's beautiful and she's accomplished, and she has an exquisite sense of the fitness of things."

Anna turned her face to him and kissed him with passionate, trembling gratitude.

"I think if you'd seen what I saw this evening," said Katherine slowly, "you wouldn't have been quite so confident of that 'exquisite sense of the fitness of things.' "

Anna stiffened.

"Kate, I don't want to hear anything more. You're just being abominably spiteful." Hamilton's voice was sharp with impatience.

"My dear Tony, you've hidden your head in the sand long enough," retorted his sister contemptuously. "Whether you want to know or not, while you were busy getting rid of her tipsy relations, Anna, with her 'exquisite sense of fitness,' was flirting with Mario Frayne in the hall. I came upon them myself."

Hamilton went white, and his eyes were suddenly bleak,

"You're lying, Kate."

"I have never lied to you in all my life," returned Katherine contemptuously. "I have no need to lie about my actions."

"It's not true, Anna, is it?" His nervous fingers were gripping her arms so that he hurt her.

"No. Not as Katherine puts it." She was shaking, and he knew it.

"What do you mean, 'not as Katherine puts it'?" he repeated harshly.

She was silent, and in his dismay he shook her slightly.

"Did Frayne kiss you?"

"Yes."

"God in heaven! And you let him?"

"Yes. I . . . I had been thanking him for . . . for what he had done—"

"Do you kiss every man you say thank you to?" he asked bitterly. Wordless and wretched, she shrank from him.

"He didn't mean it like that," she whispered at last.

Hamilton gave a little exclamation of disgust and turned away. And at that moment Anna saw that Katherine was smiling very, very slightly.

Some flame in her that had never been there before was lit. Such burning hate and fury took hold that she shook with the fever of it, and every vestige of self-control went up in a white blaze of passion.

That Katherine—Katherine who had trampled her heart and soul in the mud—should be smiling at her lost dreams, the tattered banner of her love!

She was blind to everything but that hint of a smile, and in a fury beyond any control, she raised her hand and struck Katherine full across her pink and white face.

"Anna!" Hamilton was the only one who found his voice. "Are you mad? How do you suppose anything so vulgar can help a situation that's vile enough already?"

She was silent, a little dazed now by the evidence of her own feelings. It *was* vulgar, of course, horribly vulgar to slap anyone's face. No use trying to explain that quarts of blue blood would have made no difference to that furious impulse.

She had played straight into Katherine's hands. Hamilton could see her now just as Katherine had meant him to see her—a common little nobody before his friends, his family, himself.

With an anguished little sob she ran out of the room and up the stairs to the beautiful bedroom that she hated. And that night no Tony came to comfort her.

For hours Anna lay awake staring into darkness that was no blacker than her thoughts. And every minute her despair and apprehension, not for herself but for Tony, grew deeper. With extraordinary clearness she seemed to see the past three months now through Tony's dismayed, astounded eyes.

Three short months ago he had not even known that she existed. And then, by an utterly unexpected chance, she had been there beside him, weaving herself into the very fabric of his life, dazzling him with her peculiar charm, befogging his judgment because there was something about her that entirely fascinated him.

And because of his wild infatuation for her—Anna's mind stumbled a little over that word—he had turned his back on reason, on all that his own world meant.

He had imagined, just as she had, that together they could make a world of their own—out of their love for each other. But now they were both discovering that there was no such thing as making a world of your own. There was only one world, and love, however deep, was only a part of it.

"Whither thou goest I will go. . . . Thy people shall be my people. . . ." But that only held good in the Old Testament, where an all-seeing Providence was forever leaning out of heaven to put things right. It was true she could go wherever Tony went, insisting that he noticed her, that he looked at her, even that he loved her. But, "Thy people shall be my people"—that was something quite different.

To "his people" she would always be the impossible outsider, the interloper who had thrust her way into Tony's life, putting it out of gear, so that it could never again run smoothly. . . . Never, that was, as long as she remained as the obstruction.

And Tony—Tony, who saw life in such kindly, simple, undemanding terms—would always be the center of a problem that had no solution, the cause of a struggle that bruised and wearied and eventually embittered him.

She could give him nothing that he did not have already. She saw now how pitiably foolish her feverish hopes of doing something to make him proud of her, something to justify his preposterous choice of her, had been. She could do nothing but tarnish his bright prospects with her sordid connections. And in a crisis, what had she done? Behaved, it seemed, in a way everyone considered utterly unpardonable.

For a terrible moment she wondered if she actually

were nothing but the common little outsider Katherine thought her.

"But Tony wouldn't have loved me if I'd been just that," she pleaded in a whisper, as though Katherine were there, accusing her. "He *couldn't* have loved me, could he? Could he?"

And Tony did love her. She knew that was true. He himself had said to her that she had only to call and he would come. That, in a sense, was still true, too. Even this evening's deadly scene, even the fact that Katherine had made him see her as a cheap little flirt, would never be enough to keep him away if she really pleaded.

He would come—bewildered, powerless to resist—but he would come, to have a little more of his peace of mind destroyed . . . *if she called.*

The choice was hers. She could call him to her—to his ruin—or she could let him go.

"Oh, God, must I give him up?" she whispered. "I can't do that, I can't, I can't! Isn't there some other way? He's all I have. I haven't had much. Oh, I'm not complaining—please don't think I'm complaining—but he is all I have."

She tried to think of something else to say, but there was nothing else, and she just went on repeating over and over again, "He is all I have."

The light was growing quite strong when at last, utterly chilled and fatigued, she lay down and slept exhaustedly.

When she awoke it was broad daylight, and Tony was standing beside her bed, fully dressed.

"I'm sorry to have to wake you, Anna," he began.

"It doesn't matter," she said hastily, and sat up with a little feeling of guilt. "It . . . it's rather late anyway, isn't it?"

"Yes, after ten."

"After ten!" Anna was horrified. "I'm terribly sorry."

"There's no need to be." Tony's voice was kind, but curiously formal, and, for the first time in all their acquaintance, she noticed that he had some difficulty in meeting her eyes.

"But it's long past breakfast-time."

He smiled faintly. "Well, suppose you have breakfast in bed this morning. I only woke you because I had a letter this morning that calls for me to go out of town on business today."

"Yes?" Sudden eagerness clutched at her heart. Perhaps she might go with him, and explanations would be so much easier when no one else was with them. She shrank for a moment from her feverish resolution of the night before.

But his next words brought it back very clearly.

"I won't be back until tomorrow morning, I expect, and then only in time to go straight to the office. Will you be ... all right here?"

If she said, "Oh, *please* take me, too," he undoubtedly would. If she didn't. . . .

She heard herself say clearly and steadily, "I shall be quite all right, Tony. I doubt I would enjoy a business trip."

"No." He gave her a troubled little look. "I only thought—" He hesitated. Then suddenly he flung his arms boyishly around her and was holding her close. "Oh, Anna, it's such a beastly muddle, and none of us meant half the things we did and said last night. Did we?" he added eagerly, as she made no answer.

"I suppose not." She was quite unresponsive in his arms, and her lashes were cast down in that peculiar baffling sullenness.

"Anna."

"Yes?"

"Look at me, darling."

She looked at him. She knew she had banished all expression from her eyes, but she didn't know that their blankness was almost frightening.

"You're sure you wouldn't like ... to come with me?" The almost artless little note of appeal in his voice shook her resolution badly. But she reminded herself fiercely that she must not make any more false steps. She had made enough of them ... and dragged him after her.

Only he was inexpressibly dear. It was cruel that she

couldn't draw his head down and kiss him. She must not call . . . because he must not come.

She said: "But it's only a day and a half, Tony. And what would I do in a strange place while you were busy?"

"Yes, of course. You're quite right." He kissed her quickly. "And, Anna. . . ."

"Yes?"

"Don't worry, will you? We . . . we can work out explanations afterward, or perhaps forget about them altogether."

"Yes, Tony."

She kissed him gravely and watched him go.

Dear, foolish, generous Tony—trying so hard to put the rope around his neck again.

Anna lay back and suddenly pressed her cheek into the hollow which his elbow had made when he'd leaned against her pillow. The despairing fever of last night was almost past. She thought of him now with great tenderness . . . and the first touch of a peculiar resignation.

She closed her eyes again for a moment. When she opened them once more it was nearly lunchtime. Feeling rather ashamed, she got up and dressed quickly and went downstairs.

To her relief, only the elder Miss Roone was in for lunch, and with her almost superhuman talent for pretending that everything was all right when it was really all wrong, she contrived to make the meal at least bearable.

Afterward, Anna decided to go out, for it was a close, heavy afternoon, and there seemed to be little air in the big, silent house. She went upstairs and put on the little ivory suit she had been married in. It looked cool, and she had a silly feeling it might bring her luck. As she took her handbag out of a drawer she noticed Mario Frayne's card lying there where she had thrust it last night when she undressed.

She picked it up slowly and read the address. "Seven Killigrew Mansions, St. James's."

She sighed a little, and was about to tear the card in two. Then, apparently changing her mind, she dropped it into the bag, next to the thick roll of pound notes still left from yesterday's shopping, and went downstairs.

As she closed the big front door behind her she had the curious feeling that she didn't really belong anywhere. As though no one would notice or comment if she went away and never came back.

It was silly to feel like that, of course, because she *must* belong to a certain extent wherever Tony was.

Or was that all just a false situation that fell to pieces when it came into contact with reality? She shivered suddenly in the sunshine, and turned quickly to go into the park, where it looked quiet and shady.

As she did so, a very fat little boy stumbled against her and clutched her knees. Anna put out a hand to steady him, and he lifted a round, beaming face to hers.

"Why, what are you doing?" she said, touching his soft brown cheek with her fingers.

"Wunning away," he said engagingly. And she laughed with a sudden lightening of her heart, because she had nearly been doing the same thing herself. And she saw now how absurd it was.

"Are you?" She bent down and gathered up the naughty little figure in her arms. He felt all warm, fat curves as she hugged him.

A smiling nanny came up just then and said, "Thank you very much, madam. I'm afraid he's being very naughty this afternoon. Come along, Alistair."

Anna looked wistfully at fat Alistair and wished she could have kept him to play with. But, with a nonchalant wave in her direction, he staggered off in the wake of his captor.

Still smiling a little, Anna strolled into the park and sat down under the trees. Other children were there, running about, playing and quarreling with the intense concentration of the very young. Anna looked at them and thought, "It must be beautiful to have children who love you and want to be loved."

Children were so blessedly uncritical. They accepted you without question, and you didn't have to pretend with them. And then if you had children of your own they *began* by loving you. You didn't have to struggle wearily for their love and approval, worrying all the time if you were on quite the wrong lines.

Suppose she completely ignored that terrible idea at the back of her mind about leaving Tony, determined to start again, persuaded herself that she might not be hopelessly bad for him, after all?

Then they could begin to make something of life together. And by and by they, too, would have children, and that would give some permanent foundation to their world. And because her children would love her, not critize her, she would gather confidence again; she wouldn't keep on doing the wrong things out of sheer fear and bewilderment.

She would feel that she had given Tony something really worthwhile.

That terrible, heavy weight seemed to be rolling away from her heart. It had been silly to feel so lost and despairing because there hadn't appeared to be any roots to this new life of hers. Of course not. She must grow them for herself. It might hurt a bit at first, but then most worthwhile things did hurt.

She suddenly decided to go home. Perhaps Miss Roone would know where she could telephone Tony. He must be feeling very worried after the chilly way she had behaved this morning. But she would put that right now. She would make him understand.

She was almost running by the time she reached the house, and she let herself in quietly with the key that Tony had given her. Miss Roone was almost sure to be in the library, because it was nearly time for tea; Tony had said she liked tea served in there.

But, as Anna reached the half-open door, it was Katherine's voice she heard. That gave her a disagreeable pause for a moment, and then she gathered all her resolution. After all, even if Katherine had been unkind last night, she herself had been abominably rude. There *was* an apology owing and, on a quick impulse, Anna decided to make it.

It would be horribly difficult, of course, but that didn't matter if it were the beginning of better things.

And then there was a most peculiar sound—a quite incredible sound, really, in that household. Someone was crying; and the next moment Katherine's voice said, "Really, Aunt, it isn't any good distressing yourself like this!"

Miss Roone crying! Anna stood there petrified. She couldn't possibly have imagined such a thing happening, and she felt sure that the last thing they would want would be for her to know about it. She was turning away when Miss Roone herself spoke, in a voice not easily recognizable because of her tears.

"But Tony is like my own son," she exclaimed. "It's so awful that this should have happened."

Anna suddenly felt terribly sick. She leaned against the wall, wondering numbly if her face had gone as white as it felt.

"I know, I know." Katherine sounded impatient. "But he isn't the first man to make a fool of himself over a girl, and there's usually a way out. At least he realizes now what he's taken on. I never saw anything so illuminating as his face last night when that tipsy creature stumbled in."

"Oh, Kate, don't remind me of that scene again!" Her aunt's voice rose plaintively. "Suppose he routs out Tony at his office when there's an important client there? It's perfectly possible. And then the girl herself! Quarreling with your friends, making herself cheap with Mario Frayne and then slapping your face—actually slapping your face, in our own drawing room."

"All right, Aunt Charlotte." Kate's tone was grim. "In a sense, it was worth it for the way it opened Tony's eyes."

"Do you think she would take money to go quietly, and let Tony divorce her?" The momentary hope in Miss Roone's voice was like acid on Anna's shrinking soul.

"Later on she might." Katherine answered her aunt's question. She was cool and positive in her estimate of her brother's wife. "The danger is that it might be too late."

"What do you mean?" Apprehension trembled in Miss Roone's voice again.

"Well, so often in these cases, before the man has time and sense to struggle free, there's a child."

"*Katherine!*" Miss Roone's exclamation drowned the terrible little sound that Anna made. "When I think how much I'd hoped from darling Tony's marriage. After all, he's the only boy, and even nowadays there is some sort of a duty to one's family," Miss Roone sounded as though she was going to weep again. "And now here he is married to this common little good-for-nothing, and the best we can hope is that she won't saddle him with a lot of common babies too!"

It was that which moved Anna at last.

She went slowly back toward the front door, walking as though she were carrying a heavy load. Very quietly she let herself out again, shutting the door behind her as softly as possible. And then she walked up the road, with no idea at all of where she was going.

It was strange, she thought painfully, that she felt so utterly bruised and insulted not only for herself, but for children who had never existed . . . and now never would.

So that was what they really thought of her marriage to Tony. It hadn't been said for effect. It hadn't been said with any special intention of hurting her. It was their honest opinion—that she could bring nothing but disgrace and unhappiness to Tony.

And, after all, they should know. Tony was theirs. He had lived their life and seen things with their eyes for 30 years, and now he had done something so silly and disastrous that Miss Roone had wept for him.

It was no good pretending any longer. *They knew*—and Katherine had spoken of Tony's disillusionment last night—had even thought it was worth the indignity of being struck if it meant that Tony saw something at last of his danger.

She walked and walked without knowing or caring where she went. All she knew was that she could never go back to that house. One could not just walk out and disappear, of course. She wasn't so crazy to think that.

But some time tomorrow when Tony came back, she must see him and convince him it was all a mistake; make him believe that *she* had no wish to go on; that she had no use for him. Though for a while he might wish to come, she would never call.

"Call and I'll come!"

She heard a funny little high laugh and was shocked the next moment to realize that it was she herself who had made the sound.

It was stupid of her. There was no need to be hysterical. She just needed something to pull herself together—a cup of strong coffee, perhaps. There was some strange refuge in having even such a small thing to occupy her mind. She must find somewhere where she could get a cup of coffee.

There was a large crowded teashop on the corner of the next street. That would do. It was almost a relief to be among so many people, even though not one of them cared an atom about her.

She ordered her coffee and drank it eagerly when it came. It made her feel a little less ghastly, and she opened her bag to take out her mirror and see if she looked all right now. Subconsciously she noticed the big roll of notes, and thought "At least I have money."

It hurt to remember it was Tony's money, but that couldn't be helped. She would have to have something for her immediate wants—a night at a hotel and so on.

At that moment a big man sitting beside her stood up abruptly, just as a waitress was passing with a fully laden tray. There was a crash of sliding crockery as his shoulder caught the tray and a hysterical shriek from the harassed waitress. The next moment a large glass of hot milk was emptied in a stream on the table, most of it pouring down onto Anna's skirt before she could spring to her feet.

"Oh dear, now, look at that. I'm terribly sorry, but it wasn't my fault. Oh dear, let me wipe you down with a cloth." The girl had set down her tray and was scrubbing Anna's skirt with a hastily snatched cloth.

A supervisor hurried over, and Anna unwillingly found herself a center of interest.

"It wasn't my fault . . . really it wasn't," the girl kept

on saying. "It was that gentleman—gone now, he's made all this trouble, I suppose. But I couldn't help it."

"It really was an accident. It doesn't matter," Anna said to the supervisor.

"I'm extremely sorry, madam. If you'll leave your name and address, we'll arrange to have your suit cleaned."

"Oh no, no, really. It scarcely shows," stammered Anna.

Leave her name and address! She would rather have had everything she possessed ruined.

"It's perfectly simple, madam. No one will be at any loss." The supervisor glared acidly at the waitress. "We have insurance that covers accidents of this sort."

Anna felt a sudden impulse to say, "The suit isn't of any importance. It was only my wedding suit." But instead she said gently: "I won't bother, thank you. The mark is almost gone and it isn't a new suit anyway."

She stooped to retrieve her dropped bag and gloves.

The gloves were there, but the bag was not.

Quickly she glanced at the chair where she had been sitting. It was not there either. She pulled out the next chair. Nothing.

She sat down again quickly, trying to think out this horrible development quietly, staring unseeingly at the marble-topped table.

Of course! The man who had upset the milk—it hadn't been an accident at all. He had seen the notes in her bag and acted in a second.

Now what was she to do? What on earth could she do? Call back the supervisor?

"If you will leave your name and address, madam—"

Insist on sending for a policeman?

"If you will leave your name and address, madam—"

Endless questions, and no money, of course. She groped in her pocket and found a few coins. That at least would pay for her coffee. And then?

There was not a soul in London to whom she could turn. Or was there? She hastily reviewed her few days there, and suddenly, with immense and ridiculous relief, she remembered Fanchette.

There had been a peculiar kindness in the way the Frenchwoman had treated her. Surely she would not refuse to lend Anna enough for a night's lodging? It was awful, of course, to borrow like that. But what else could she do? And, somehow, she didn't think she would have to explain a great deal to Fanchette.

Anna glanced up at the big white face of the clock opposite. Ten minutes to six. She would have to hurry, for of course the shop would close at six, and it was quite a long walk.

She paid for her coffee, which left her only two shillings. A shilling of this she spent on taking a bus to save time. Even then, she had to run along the quiet little street to Fanchette's gray and silver shop.

A pretty, calm-faced girl was just about to draw a blind over the window of the door as Anna breathlessly pushed her way in.

"I must see Madame Fanchette, *please!*"

Anna had no idea of the urgency in her voice, or of the weariness and fear in her eyes.

"I am sorry, madam, but Madame Fanchette is not here. Could I do anything for you? Is it an urgent order?"

"Oh no, no." Anna bit her lip to keep it from trembling. "I *must* see her. Could you . . . would you give me her private address? It's . . . it's quite a private matter."

The girl looked faintly curious, but still perfectly polite. "I'm very sorry, but Madame Fanchette went to Paris by the afternoon plane. We don't expect her back this week."

"Paris," repeated Anna stupidly, as though she had never heard of the place. "Paris."

"Yes. Perhaps there *is* something I could do for madam?"

"No. No, thank you. It doesn't matter."

Anna turned slowly away, without another word, and, looking curiously after her for a moment, the girl drew down the blind.

And again Anna walked the streets. Walked and walked and walked.

Presently it began to rain, and she stood for what seemed hours in a shop doorway. Two or three men spoke to her while she stood there, but it was not until one tried to take her by the arm that she fled from her shelter.

She ran through the rain, stumbling a little, her breath coming in little short gasps that were very nearly sobs. Her thin shoes were soaked and her linen suit clung damply.

It was getting dark now, and as the light faded so Anna's terror grew. Only one fact stood out clearly in her mind. She could not—she *would* not—go back to Eaton Square.

She wondered where she was at the moment, and glanced up at the name written over the doorway.

"Killigrew Mansions," she read, in the fading light.

For a second she could not remember where she had seen that odd name before.

And then she remembered. Seven, Killigrew Mansions. Mario Frayne's smiling face seemed to dance before her eyes.

Slowly she entered the thickly carpeted hall and found the elevator. There was no attendant, just simple instructions printed in the elevator for passengers to work it themselves.

Her breath was coming fast now. She was not quite sure if it was with fear or relief. But as she stood outside number seven, her finger on the bell, she wondered if she would ever find words to explain her presence.

An almost alarmingly discreet-looking Italian man-servant opened the door.

"Mr. Frayne, can I see him, please?" Anna's mouth was dry, and her voice scarcely more than a whisper.

"He is not in, madam. I do not expect him until half-past ten or perhaps 11."

"Could I . . . wait? I'm very tired," Anna said childishly and very hopelessly.

The man hesitated. She was by no means the first unusual woman visitor to his master's flat, but none of them had looked so exhausted and piteous as this.

Then, because he could not resist a pretty woman, and one in such obvious despair, he stood aside and let her pass into the luxurious sitting room beyond.

"Thank you." Anna sat down wearily.

"May I bring you anything, Madam?"

"Oh no, thank you," she said shyly. And after a moment he went away into another room.

It was very, very quiet in the apartment; very sheltered and rich and comfortable. Strangely different from the turbulent, rainswept hours through which she had just passed.

She leaned back with a little sigh and closed her eyes.

When the manservant looked in half an hour later she was asleep.

He shrugged. It was no business of his, but he wondered a little what that gentle, startled-looking girl had to do with his employer.

He was still wondering when Frayne came in about 11. The servant didn't sleep at the flat, and he already had on his coat, in readiness to leave if his employer required nothing further than the light supper that was waiting for him.

"There is a lady to see you, sir," he told Frayne.

"A lady, eh? Who?" Frayne paused inquiringly.

"I do not know her, sir. You were not expecting her?"

"Not unless my memory is failing me, Umberto." And Frayne gave the other a brilliant smile.

He went quietly to the door of his sitting room and looked in.

Anna was still lying there asleep. She had roused herself sufficiently to take off her hat, and it hung now slackly from her hand. Her soft, dark hair was a little tumbled around her thin, weary face, and her crumpled linen suit had dried on her.

Frayne gave a long, quiet whistle as he stood there

motionless, his hands in his pockets. Then he glanced back at his servant, who was looking curiously over his shoulder.

"All right, Umberto," he said slowly. "I shall not need you any more tonight."

CHAPTER SIX

Slowly Anna opened her eyes and looked around.

She had never seen this room before; at least, there was something vaguely familiar about it. . . . And then she remembered. She was in Mario Frayne's apartment.

She turned her head sharply, and there he was standing behind her chair, leaning his arms on the back of it and looking down calmly at her.

"Oh," she began, rather frightenedly. "I'm sorry . . . I—"

"No, don't be sorry," he said, smiling. "*I* am not in the least sorry to find anyone so charming waiting for me in my home."

"But I must explain—"

"Why should you?" he said carelessly, straightening up now. "The best things of this life need no explaining."

"Oh, but really—"

"At least let us have supper first," he begged amusedly. "Explanations are always twice as disagreeable when one is hungry."

She was silent then, watching him as he moved a small table near to her chair, and stooped to pick up her hat, which had fallen to the floor.

"I've left Tony," she fired at him desperately.

"Yes?" He looked unimpressed. "Believe me, it's quite usual for ladies to leave their husbands behind when they come to visit me at this time of night."

"*Oh!*" Her eyes looked wide and horrified. "You think I—"

"I'm not really thinking about things at all," he assured her pleasantly. "I haven't the English passion for explaining. I just take everything as it comes. Tonight I find a charming woman in my apartment . . . and supper ready laid. You must admit that the most reasonable thing is for us to eat supper together. Come now, drink

this, and see if the world doesn't seem a different place."
He held out a small glass to her.

"I don't want it," she began.

"Drink it," he said peremptorily.

She took the glass and drank what was in it obediently.
"Feel better?"

She nodded. "I . . . I don't feel so cold," she said, but
she shivered a little.

"Cold!" He looked surprised. "It's very warm in
here." Then he glanced at her crumpled suit. "Were you
out in all that rain?" he asked abruptly.

"Yes."

He frowned. "Well, eat up your supper quickly. The
sooner you're in bed the better."

She had no idea at all what to make of that, so she
slowly tried to eat what he put before her.

"Did you have any dinner?"

She shook her head.

"Then what *have* you been doing all evening?"

"W-wandering about," she said, in a whisper.

He was silent for a moment, studying her. Then he said
calmly, "So it took you two days to find out that those
Roones are impossible?"

She laid down her fork with a little clatter.

"Well, I think you showed great tenacity," he went on.
"Two hours would have been enough for me."

Still she said nothing.

"You see," he was smiling again, "you don't have to
make the explanations to me after all. I can tell you all
about them myself. You thought you might manage
Roone's ghastly family—make them love you, or some
such idea. But, when you arrived, you found the father a
fool, the sister a cat, and Roone himself so stiff with
convention that he talks like a Government blue-book,
and, I suppose, makes love in terms of stocks and
shares."

All the Latin in Frayne went into his indulgent
contempt for Hamilton's love-making.

"No." Anna got that out somehow.

"No?" Frayne smiled. "Well, it's near enough. And

then, when you found it was all quite hopeless, like a sensible girl you cut your losses and came to see the only person who had shown a fairly intelligent interest in your . . . remarkable self."

"It isn't really like that," Anna began, in a husky little voice, so faint that he leaned forward, with his arms on the table, to hear what she was saying. "I know you must think it terrible of me to come to you like this."

"On the contrary, I think it charming," he assured her.

She gave a wordless little exclamation at that, and stumbled to her feet.

He got up quickly too.

"Where are you going?"

"I don't know." She looked bewildered.

"Not back to Tony?"

"No. Oh, no," she said. "I mustn't go to Tony. And I mustn't let him come to me. He said I had only to call and he would come. But I mustn't call, you see; I mustn't call." And suddenly she began to weep.

She made no attempt to cover her face. Just stood there while the tears ran slowly down her cheeks, and the sobs rose in her throat in little sounds of despair.

Frayne stared at her a moment, his eyes a little narrowed. Then, as her sobs choked her, she began to cough breathlessly. And at that he sprang forward and put his arms around her.

"Heavens, don't do that!" he exclaimed, with a little flash of alarm in his eyes. "Be quiet, child; be quiet. I didn't understand. Here." He picked her up off the ground and carried her back to the armchair.

He laid her in it, but he kept his arm around her and held her still until her sobs presently died away, and she leaned against him, exhausted.

"Can you tell me about it now?" he asked at last. This time his tone held no hint of mockery.

"Yes, I think so," she whispered. "It's just that . . . I didn't realize until today how terribly I had injured Tony by marrying him."

"And what has driven you to that painful conclusion now?" Frayne's voice was strangely gentle.

Anna moved slightly, as though something hurt her, but she said steadily, "It wasn't only the miserable business last night. It was something Katherine and her aunt said that finally showed me."

"Oh," Frayne made a gesture of contempt, "you mustn't listen to what they say. They would have hated anyone they hadn't chosen themselves."

"Yes, I know that. And I think I hated them too at first. But I don't now."

"Why not?" He looked down at her white face curiously, and thought how terribly she had grown up from the girl who had sung Mignon's song.

"Because I know now that it was their love for Tony that made them resent me. Oh yes—" as Frayne exclaimed impatiently "—they do love him very dearly in their way. And they are honestly sure that he could never be anything but wretched with me."

"But perhaps they don't know?"

"They've known and loved Tony for 30 years," Anna said slowly. "I've known him and loved him for less than three months. Which of us is likely to understand him better?"

Frayne didn't answer that. Instead he said, "But many men have to find a new viewpoint when they marry, I suppose."

Anna gently touched Frayne's hand. "You are being very kind. You want so much to reassure me, don't you?" Frayne nodded. "But it isn't only what *they* said, you see. It's Tony, too. He tries so hard not to see me with their eyes, but I've seen him look at me already with bewilderment and—I'm nearly sure—a touch of disillusionment."

"But, good heavens, a man must make some effort to adapt himself," Frayne said.

"Oh, but he would, he would!" Anna cried. "It isn't that at all. He would try his hardest never to let me know that he changed. I think he would die if he knew how much I've been . . . hurt . . . already." Her head drooped for a moment.

"I still don't see why," began Frayne.

Anna broke in with sudden fierce pain: "Do you know that his aunt wept—*wept*—this afternoon because he had sunk so low as to marry me!" She bit her lip.

Frayne gave her a troubled glance. "Perhaps that was specially for your benefit," he suggested.

"Oh no." She shook her head wearily. "She didn't even know I heard her. She and Katherine were talking about it, and, oh, I can't!" She broke off and gripped her hands together.

"All right, my dear." Frayne put his hand warmly over her clasped ones, and the feel of that steadied her.

"They were discussing whether or not they could . . . buy me off," she said, in a low, unsteady voice, "before I had time to saddle Tony with a common baby."

"Oh, damnation!" exclaimed Frayne.

"You see, I'd been silly enough to suppose that if, later on, Tony and I had children— Oh, what's the good?" She stopped suddenly, unable to bear the memory of her pitifully foolish plans that afternoon. Then she said slowly, "Our marrying was just a mistake. And the only thing you can do about mistakes is to try to undo them."

"But Tony does love you," Frayne pointed out earnestly.

"Yes." Anna looked straight at him. "But then, in a way, I suppose your father loved your mother."

Frayne's eyebrows shot up. "I suppose so. Why?"

"Well, he didn't marry her."

"No, but he should have," was the rather dry retort. "I've always had a good deal of respect for my mother and a good deal of contempt for my father, if you want to know."

"Perhaps so," said Anna slowly. "But that isn't really the point, is it? A marriage between them would have been an absolute failure, wouldn't it?"

There was a short silence. Then he said reluctantly, "Yes, I suppose it would."

"You see," she said, and again there was silence for a minute or two.

When at last he spoke again he made no further attempt to argue with her. "Why," he asked curiously, "did you come to me? Was I the only person in London you could think of?"

"No, it wasn't that. I hadn't really come here intentionally." And then she told him a little of how she had lost all her money, and gone vainly to Fanchette, then wandered about in the rain until, in her weariness, she had felt that the only thing in the world that mattered was to be able to sink down somewhere.

He frowned then, and his handsome eyes were graver than she had ever seen them.

"Well, you will stay here tonight," he said crisply. "Oh, yes, you will," at her movement of protest. Then he smiled dryly. "It's all right. I have friends here in the same block of flats. Conrad Schreiner and Manora, his, er, wife have one of these apartments while they are staying in London. I'll phone them and get her to come over and stay with you. And I can stay with Schreiner."

Anna bit her lip to stop its trembling. It seemed silly that kindness hurt almost as much as anything else just now. "But . . . I can't turn you out like that," she protested. "And what will your friends think?"

"Oh, they aren't the kind of people to ask questions," Frayne assured her with a smile. "And Manora will be very kind to you."

"But—"

"It isn't any good," Frayne interrupted firmly. "You can't possibly go to a hotel at this time of night with no luggage and looking the way you do. Besides, you are not fit to go anywhere alone just now."

Anna protested no further. She lay back in her chair and a strange sort of laziness crept over her. She felt incapable of any more argument or struggle, and there was something infinitely soothing about letting Mario Frayne direct her troubled life for an hour or two.

"Won't your friends be in bed at this time of night?" was all she said now, but it was a very half-hearted protest, and when he replied, "No. They keep unearthly hours," she was quite satisfied.

While he telephoned, she watched him idly and found a

good deal of comfort in the strong, firm lines of his determined mouth.

He was talking now, explaining in rapid Italian, which her mind was too tired to follow, and from the other end of the wire she could hear a woman's voice. Then Frayne laughed at something that was said, and a moment later the voice changed, and it was a man who was speaking. Anna could hear the deep, abrupt tone.

Frayne said in English, rather slowly as though to a foreigner: "Manora will explain to you. She understands and she does not mind." Then he hung up.

"Was that Conrad Schreiner?" Anna asked, with faint interest.

Frayne nodded.

"Did he mind much?"

"Oh no. He never minds anything that Manora wants. Except, of course, where her singing is concerned. I think he is a tyrant there."

"Is Manora a singer, then?"

"Yes."

"Is she . . . is she kind?" Anna asked timidly.

"Very," Frayne said soothingly.

"And what is she? I mean, does she speak English?"

"Oh yes, very well indeed," Frayne assured her. "I don't really know what nationality she is—I don't think anyone does. Some sort of Balkan, I imagine. Anyway, she talks every language I've ever come across."

"Oh." Anna closed her eyes wearily.

She had no idea how much her pallor worried Frayne, but she heard the anxiety in his voice as he said gently, "Would you like me to carry you into the bedroom?"

"Oh no, thank you," she began. But he had already picked her up and, carrying her into the next room, he laid her on the bed.

She murmured a word of thanks, and the next moment the doorbell sounded.

Frayne left her and, weary though she was, Anna forced her eyes open. She felt very nervous again and wondered what this unknown woman would be like.

Frayne had said she was kind—but she remembered, wincing a little, Tony had somehow implied that Katherine was kind. It took a woman to find out the cruelty of another woman.

Suppose this Manora were curious and critical? A little impatient, as well she might be, at being called out at this time of night? Oh, she wouldn't say so to Frayne, of course, because women always did what he wanted.

She could hear Manora speaking now—a low-pitched voice, very full, with a curious impression of changing color in it. A siren's voice, thought Anna; and, in sudden panic, she closed her eyes and refused to open them again, even though she knew that the other two were in the room by now.

"I think perhaps she has fallen asleep," Frayne said worriedly.

"Poor baby," the other voice said, and Anna knew Manora was leaning over her. "But I think she is not asleep. She is just a little afraid . . . of me."

Anna's eyes flew open at that, and she stared straight up into the bluest eyes she had ever seen.

"Well, my child, are you afraid of me?" Manora smiled, but she did not attempt to touch Anna. She sat down at the end of the bed and looked at her.

At that moment Anna could not have said whether Manora was plain or beautiful. All she saw was that smile and the warm blue of her eyes.

Without a word, she began to crawl rather feebly across the wide bed toward her. It was quite instinctive, like the movement of a wounded animal making for home, and with a little cry of pity, Manora leaned forward and gathered Anna against her.

"I'm so glad you've come. I'm so glad you've come," muttered Anna, leaning her forehead against Manora, with an extraordinary feeling of having found a refuge.

"She will be all right now." Manora's eyes met Frayne's over Anna's smooth dark head. "You can go, Mario. And give Conrad my love."

"Give Conrad your love!" mocked Frayne. "You only left him five minutes ago."

"I know. But he will like to know I still love him, all the same," replied Manora calmly.

"Very well. Good night, Anna," Frayne said gently.

"Good night and *thank* you!" Anna put out her hand without looking up, and she felt Frayne kiss it lightly.

"*Buona notte,* Manora."

"*Buona notte.*"

A moment later the front door closed behind him.

Anna looked up then. "It's very, very kind of you to come and look after me like this," she said earnestly.

"No. Is for me a pleasure," was the smiling reply. Although Manora's actual pronunciation was excellent, she often put her words in a peculiar order, and she practically never used the word "it."

"Will you go to bed now?" she asked gently. "Shall I help you undress?"

"Oh, I . . . I can manage for myself, thank you," Anna said, but in the end she was glad of Manora's help, for she felt strangely feeble.

"Would you like that I sleep here or in the other room?" Manora asked, when Anna was in bed.

"Would you mind . . . sleeping here with me?" Anna said diffidently.

"No. I will sleep here," agreed Manora without question.

Anna watched her idly, and thought how pretty she was. At least, pretty was hardly the word, she supposed. Something much stronger and more vital than that.

She must be somewhere between 35 and 40, Anna decided, and she would not have been surprised if that thick fair hair, with its beautiful deep wave, had the faintest touch of gray in it. Not on account of her age, but because of experience. For there was a good deal of varied experience behind Manora's smile.

As Anna studied her, she decided that she liked the unusual shape of her face, with its wide cheekbones, sloping to a rather pointed chin, and the odd attractive way the corners of her mouth lifted when she smiled. Above all, there was the slightest hint of the adventuress about her, which Anna found intriguing.

"Well?" Manora came over to the bed. "You feel better, eh?"

"Yes, thank you," Anna smiled.

"You like that I leave on the light for a while?"

"Do you mind?"

"Oh no. Conrad and I keep very late hours."

"Conrad is your husband?" Anna asked shyly.

There was a short pause; then Manora replied, "Yes."

Anna didn't pursue the subject. She said instead, "Did . . . did Mr. Frayne explain about me?"

"A little. He said you were not happy about your husband and that perhaps you leave him."

"Oh! Yes, that's true. At least, there's no 'perhaps.' I am going to leave him," Anna said doggedly.

"Because you do not love him or because you do?" was the unexpected question.

"Because I do," said Anna, in a low voice.

"You are generous. Most women hold on, without regard for the man's happiness." Manora's voice had a touch of bitterness that Anna could not help guessing had been put there by personal feeling.

"Well, I want Tony to be happy more than anything else in the world," she replied slowly. "More than anything else in the world," she repeated drowsily. And suddenly she was asleep, with her cheek against Manora's warm, bare arm.

When she awoke she seemed to have slept dreamlessly for hours, and she felt extraordinarily refreshed. She realized that her head was still against Manora's arm, and she started up with a little apologetic murmur.

Manora was lying there with her eyes wide open, exactly as though she had not been asleep at all.

"I'm terribly sorry, I must have cramped your arm, I'm afraid," Anna said.

"No." Manora shook her head. "I am used to it. Conrad nearly always sleeps like that, and he is much heavier than you."

"Oh," said Anna, a little nonplussed by such frankness. Then she smiled. "I think anyone would feel rested just to have your arm around them," she said shyly, and she was surprised and touched to see that Manora flushed deeply.

"Thank you. Is a very nice compliment," she said with a pleased little laugh. "And now, do we get up for breakfast or—?"

"Oh yes, please." Anna sat up quickly, with all the fear and bewilderment of yesterday clutching at her heart. "You see I must see my husband this morning and explain that . . . I mean, make him believe that—" She stopped helplessly.

"I see," said Manora calmly. "Then I telephone Mario and tell him to come to breakfast. Conrad, he will not be up yet. Besides, you do not want to meet anyone new just now."

It was a strange breakfast, really, with both these unusual but kindly people so concerned about her. Somehow, it was much easier to explain things to them than to anyone else she had ever met. Few things surprised them and nothing at all appeared to shock them. It was curiously soothing after the atmosphere of the Eaton Square house.

"I suppose what you really need more than anything else at the moment is a job," Frayne said thoughtfully.

"I suppose it is," Anna agreed, her anxious eyes on him.

"Well, if you have some idea of dancing. . . . Have you?"

"Oh, yes."

"And with your exceptional voice, I can always get you into the chorus of one of the musical shows—"

"Would you?" Anna interrupted eagerly.

Frayne laughed a trifle uncomfortably. "Well, of course . . . if you want that. But I don't know how the life would suit you. And I'm afraid, if you were a protégée of mine, that implies, well, something you probably wouldn't like."

"Do you mind? I mean on your own account?" Anna asked.

"*I*? Good heavens, no, child. I haven't so very much reputation to lose," Frayne said dryly.

"Then I don't care either," said Anna defiantly.

Frayne gave her a troubled look. "There might be nothing at all said, of course, but on the other hand. . . . Well, it could be very unpleasant. Anyone like your charming sister-in-law would make a nice story of it."

Anna's face went quite blank and hard.

"Katherine has nothing whatever to do with my future," she said almost coldly. At which Frayne shrugged and said no more.

When Anna was ready to go, in the linen suit, from which the invaluable Umberto had miraculously removed all the crumples and most of the stain, she found, to her surprise, that Manora was coming too.

"But, really you don't have to," she stammered. "I can manage very well alone."

"I wait for you outside," said Manora calmly. "I have my car here." And Anna, feeling oddly relieved, didn't protest any more.

Just as they were going, Frayne drew her back a little and let Manora go on ahead.

"Anna," he said, using her Christian name quite naturally, "are you quite determined to break with Tony?"

"Yes," Anna said steadily, without looking at him. "I know it's the only decent thing to do."

"Very well. Then the more finally you do it, of course, the better. I just wanted to say that, if you want to use the fact that you spent last night in my apartment, you can do so, without any further explanation."

Anna stared at him. "But—"

"There, run along with you." He laughed, and gave her a gentle little push. "Look after her, Manora!" he called, then returned to the apartment.

Manora, who, rather surprisingly, drove the big Mercedes herself, had the tact not to talk to Anna on the way to Hamilton's office.

Anna knew the address, but had no idea how to get there. However, Manora appeared to know London well, and she drove unhesitatingly, while Anna sat wordless beside her, hands gripped desperately together in an effort to keep herself from trembling.

"Is the place, I think," Manora said at last, pulling the car up to the curb. Anna felt her heart give a sickening lurch, and, for a moment, she thought, "It's quite impossible. I cannot, *cannot* go on with this awful thing."

Then she remembered Tony's aunt weeping because his life was ruined, and she remembered Tony's disgust and bewilderment over that scene with Katherine, and she remembered Katherine saying how awful it was when a man was saddled with a common baby as well as a common wife.

She climbed slowly out of the car, wishing her legs didn't feel so dreadfully hollow.

"I wait here half an hour," Manora said, as though it were an appointment with a dressmaker.

Anna thought, "She's rather insensitive really. She doesn't understand, after all." Then, because she immediately felt remorseful, she smiled faintly at Manora and said, "Thank you very much. But perhaps I shall be longer."

Manora leaned forward at that, and put her hand on Anna's. "These scenes hurt less if you shorten them," was all she said.

And Anna went into the big building wondering at the back of her aching mind where and how Manora had obtained all her experience.

The moment Anna told the polite junior clerk that she was Mrs. Roone he showed her at once into Tony's private office.

"Anna!" Tony sprang to his feet and came forward eagerly. "Don't let anyone in, Bentham, until I call. I shall be busy."

"Yes, sir." Bentham withdrew.

"My dear, what on earth has happened?" Tony looked white and anxious as he led her to a chair. "They've just telephoned up to say you didn't come home all night."

"No, that's right—I went away." Anna thought how stupid it sounded as she said it.

"You went away? I don't understand. Why did you go away?"

Now was the moment.

Anna drew a deep breath and stared straight in front of her.

"I went away because I couldn't possibly stand it any more. It's all a dreadful mistake. I ought never to have married you. I can't possibly live your life. It's—it's all wrong for me to try."

"But, my darling!" She didn't know how to bear the tenderness in his voice. "You've just got this idea because of that beastly business with your stepfather—and then Kate being horrid afterward—haven't you?"

"No." It was extraordinary, she thought, how far that had faded into the background. It had seemed so hideously important 24 hours ago. Now it was only one ugly fact among many.

"But, Anna dearest," he put his arms around her in spite of her slight resistance, "we haven't given things much of a trial, have we? It will all be so different when we're in our own home away from Eaton Square."

She hadn't thought of that, and for a moment she was silent. Then she was frightened to realize how her resolution bent and crumpled before the gentleness in his voice.

"*No*," she said almost violently. "Won't you understand I just can't go on? I want to do something else instead."

"You *what?*" He looked thunderstruck. "What do you want to do instead?"

"I want to go on stage." She wished her voice wouldn't go so ridiculously faint. "It's—it's dull just being your wife and having to do and say all the things I dislike."

"Dull!" His hands gripped her nervously. "What do you mean, dull? Was it dull when you lay in my arms the other night? Is it dull when I hold you and kiss you like this?" He kissed her so fiercely that he almost hurt her.

"Don't!" Anna gasped, struggling frantically, because

every vestige of her strength and resolution seemed to be slipping from her.

"Look at me."

"No."

"*Look* at me!"

In sullen despair she raised her eyes to his. She felt as though a heavy hand were closing around her heart and crushing it.

"I only want to ask you one question," he said slowly, unaware that he was hurting her arms. "Do you love me, or don't you? Nothing else matters at all."

If she gave way now, she could lie in Tony's arms while he kissed her and soothed her and made her forget all the horror that had passed.

But what would that do to Tony? They would be just where they had been before. No use denying it. It would be Tony who would have to pay for their mistaken marriage. Pay with deepening misery and disillusionment. Both of them had made that mistake, but only one need pay for it.

Only one need pay.

From a long distance she heard herself say quite steadily, "That's just it. I don't love you. I can't go on with it."

"But, my little love, won't you give our life together a chance?" He was pleading now in a way she had never expected, and it hurt so that she thought she must scream aloud. "I know I've been to blame. I must have hurt you dreadfully over that cursed business with Frayne. It was that, wasn't it? Oh, when I think of your going away all alone! Dearest, where did you go? Where were you all last night?"

And at that Anna picked up her last weapon.

"I was at Mario Frayne's, if you must know. And you had every right to be jealous about what happened before. And it's Frayne who's going to get me on the stage. . . ."

Oh, if only Tony would say something—not just stand there slowly going gray, as though she had wounded him and the blood was draining out of him.

"God in heaven," said Tony at last, in a hoarse little whisper. "Then it was true all the time, even before I met you, what they said about you in the village."

Anna was silent, in a sort of leaden despair.

"No wonder that postmistress sniggered, and Irwin looked wise, and Orpington tried to delay things. And *you!* You stuffed me up with that foolery about not liking men to touch you, that it was something you couldn't help, that it was different with me. And all the time you were nothing but a little—"

"Oh, don't!" Anna found her voice at last.

With a fearful effort Tony controlled himself, though she saw he was trembling. He sat down rather heavily at his desk, fingering the papers nervously as a much older man might have done.

"Can I go now?" she said at last.

"Go?" He looked up stupidly. "Yes, yes, go where you like—with Frayne, or anyone else you fancy. Go to the ends of the earth if you want to. I don't care."

She got up slowly. She wished achingly that he hadn't used that expression. He had said once—a long, long time ago, or was it just a few days? —that he would come to her from the ends of the earth . . . if she called.

She paused beside his chair for a moment, but he didn't even look up.

And so she went slowly out of the room and through the outer office, where Bentham looked curiously at her because she didn't appear to notice that he held open the door and said "Good morning" to her. Down two flights of marble steps, because she didn't see the elevator door standing open, waiting for her. Out into the sunshine, where Manora waited in the car.

"Why, you're still waiting," she said vaguely.

"Yes, I said I would wait half an hour," Manora reminded her.

"Half an hour," Anna repeated wonderingly. "Have I only been half an hour?"

"Less than that. Just twenty minutes."

Twenty minutes!

Twenty minutes to smash her world to atoms.

CHAPTER SEVEN

Manora drove rather slowly, without attempting to speak.

Then at last Anna asked, "Where are we going?"

"Well, home, unless you want to go anywhere else?"

"Oh no, there's nowhere I want to go, thank you. Nowhere at all." And then Anna had to bite her lip to keep herself from weeping because Tony had told her she could go anywhere she wanted. Right to the ends of the earth if she liked. He didn't care.

When they reached the block of apartments in St. James's, Manora said, "You come up and see my apartment now."

And because it didn't seem to matter what she did or where she went, Anna came without protest.

The place was bigger than Frayne's, and everywhere there was the scent of extremely expensive cigars.

"This is the studio," Manora explained, leading Anna into a long, pleasant room. "For this we choose the apartment."

Except for a grand piano and some comfortable chairs, there was very little furniture in the room. But everywhere were piles of music—on chairs, on the piano, and even on the floor.

At one end of the modernistic black marble mantelpiece stood a large, three-quarter-length photograph of Manora. She was wearing a velvet evening coat over a light dress, but something in the way she was laughing, and the unexpected pose with her hand on her hip, suggested a Balkan peasant girl, working havoc among the men of her village.

At the other end was the photograph of a man. Just the head and shoulders. He was extraordinarily handsome in a slightly flamboyant way, and was gazing away to some far horizon with great, melancholy dark eyes. But the arrogant determination of his mouth rather contradicted the melancholy, and somehow suggested that he could look after himself very well.

"Schreiner," explained Manora, touching the photograph with an odd little mixture of awe and condescension.

Anna thought it strange for Manora to speak of him by his surname like that, but perhaps one did that with a very great person.

Manora tossed off her hat and made Anna remove hers.

"Here I do my practising," she told Anna.

"Oh yes, Mr. Frayne said you were a singer." Anna suddenly remembered that Frayne had mentioned the fact.

"But of course." Manora's blue eyes opened wide. "You had not heard of me before?"

Anna smiled faintly. "I don't know your other name, you know," she said.

"Vanescu. I am Manora Vanescu. Now you know? *No?*" Manora gave a little shriek of laughter. "You have not heard of me? Oh, how wonderful!"

"I'm sorry," Anna stammered a little. "You see, I—"

"No, no," Manora interrupted her, still laughing. "You must not mind. Is so *amusing*. But there," she added tolerantly, "in England all things are possible."

Anna laughed a little at that, and Manora immediately seized on the break in her unhappiness.

"You must sing for me," she said. "Yes, Mario Frayne has said to me that you are good, and I want to hear you."

Anna shook her head. But Manora took no notice; merely began to run through a pile of music scores.

"Mario says you are good in French opera. What will you have? Whatever you please—*Carmen, Manon, Thaïs, Faust, Hoffmann?*"

"It doesn't matter. Please, not anything," Anna said.

"Yes, you must." There was no arguing with Manora's smiling determination. "*Hoffmann*, then, since you will not choose. See, I will play for you, though very badly."

She flicked over the pages.

"Here," she announced triumphantly, "You sing this? Antonia's air?"

Anna stood rather obstinately silent in the curve of the piano, while Manora played the opening bars. Then, since there was no resisting her smile, Anna began to sing.

She had sung the air a hundred times for the old Frenchman who had thought her voice so beautiful. But today there was something specially poignant in the song of the dying Antonia who snatched pathetically at a happiness that she knew, in her heart, had already vanished.

Oh, why did everything seem to remind her of the aching bruise on her own heart?

There was faint hope still struggling with resignation in Antonia's song, and Anna's voice reflected it more pitifully than she knew. By the time she reached the end she was very near tears, and she stood there waiting, only half-interested, for Manora's verdict.

But the verdict came from the other end of the room:

"Sehr schön!"

Anna swung around to face a very tall man, who was standing there with one hand holding a cigar and the other thrust into the pocket of his magnificent purple dressing gown.

She recognized him at once. There was no mistaking him. Conrad Schreiner—even handsomer than his photograph, and even more awe-inspiring than his reputation.

Anna looked at him shyly, fascinated by a face of such contrasts—the unexpectedly gray hair against his tanned skin, the kindly expression of his soft brown eyes contradicting the arrogance of his mouth.

He came forward slowly and, towering over her, addressed her in German in a deep, abrupt voice.

"She speaks no German. She is English," Manora said, apparently quite unmoved by this apparition.

"And I," said Schreiner, speaking with a very shocking accent, "speak nearly no English. Except—" and suddenly he flashed a quite wonderful smile at Anna "—when I am in France. Then I speak English to the French, and they say my accent is good."

Anna smiled and felt less nervous.

"You don't know French, then?" she said timidly.

"I? No. Three words perhaps. No more." Schreiner seemed to have great contempt for any language he knew only a little. "But not matter. You understand me. And now you must sing again."

Anna made a quick movement of protest, for, since the last song had brought her so near tears, she felt she could bear no more. But Schreiner brushed that aside.

"The trio near the end of the act. You know that?"

"Yes, but—"

"We will have that."

Anna had no wish to sing, but she was powerless against the force of Schreiner's commanding vitality. She was swept into the musical whirlpool in her turn—singing as Antonia was supposed to sing, desperately, under protest, because she was being forced to do so by the power of someone else's personality.

It seemed to Anna that she and the character of Antonia were one. That she shared Antonia's terror in knowing that if she sang she must die . . . and yet she could do nothing but sing. It merged into the tragedy of her own impotent struggle against the inevitable.

She could hear the steady stream of Manora's heavenly voice, the sweet, pleading despair of her own singing, and the occasional sinister bass cackle from Schreiner.

After a while she knew she was crying, that the tears were running down her cheeks; but even that could do nothing to stop the inevitable forward sweep of the music, driven on by Schreiner's almost demoniac power.

And then, suddenly, it was over. And she was standing there drained of all emotion, shivering a little and sobbing.

She heard Schreiner say calmly, "There is no reason to cry. You are nearly a great singer. Give to her a handkerchief, Manora."

And Manora's arms were around her, and she was drying her tears and comforting her, "for all the world," thought Anna, "as though I'd had a tooth out."

"You must not mind," Manora soothed her. "Very often he makes me cry too, but he is not really angry."

"Sometimes I am angry," came a warning from Schreiner, who was pencilling something on a score. "Come here."

Manora gave Anna a friendly little push, and she went slowly over to where the great man still sat at the piano.

"You cry no longer, eh?" he said, looking up at her.

Anna shook her head and smiled faintly.

"I am sorry," she began.

"It is of no consequence," said Schreiner. "Now, sing these scales."

Anna sang, and was suddenly rather intrigued to see the nod exchanged between Schreiner and Manora.

"You . . . you do really like my voice?" she asked Schreiner timidly.

"Do you think I sit here and listen to you all this time if I find your voice horrible?" was the reply. "Tell me, do you have any stage experience?"

"No." Anna shook her head.

"That we should have to give her," Manora observed. "Mario too will be helpful. He is a good friend of hers."

"Eh?" Schreiner looked at her with eyebrows slightly raised in inquiry.

"No, no, not like that." Manora frowned quickly and shook her head. "But I mean he will like to help her. I will telephone him."

And before Anna could protest she had seized the phone and called Frayne with the request that he would come across to their apartment.

Five minutes later Frayne joined them.

As he came in he gave Anna a queerly concerned glance, but she managed to smile a little at him in return.

Schreiner nodded curtly to Frayne and merely stated, "She is good. I take her. You explain."

"Is that really so?" Frayne turned to Manora.

"I think so," Manora said, smiling.

"Yes, yes, yes," affirmed Schreiner impatiently. "You explain to her."

Anna had the odd impression that it could not really be herself in whom these voluble and apparently famous people were so much interested. She felt more as though she were just a spectator while they discussed someone quite different from the Anna whose life had ceased to mean anything important two hours ago, when she had left Tony's office.

Then Frayne began to explain to her, gently, almost soothingly, as though she had been ill and hadn't quite recovered.

"Schreiner thinks your voice even more beautiful than I expected, and he says you have been very well trained."

Anna smiled at that, and none of them knew that the hint of tenderness that made her mouth quiver was for the little old Frenchman who had believed so passionately in her voice, and had not been wrong after all.

"And what does he want to do about it?" she asked, still waiting rather nervously for the exact interpretation of Schreiner's abrupt, "I take her."

Frayne laughed a little.

"He wants to complete your training, Anna—your stage training, I mean—and, if you turn out as well as we expect, he wants to launch you in opera as his find. It's a tremendous opportunity for you. No one will train you better than Schreiner."

Anna glanced across at Schreiner, who was pencilling his score again, and once more she felt the tears very near the surface.

"But why should you all be so kind?" she said a little unsteadily.

"It is not kindness," put in Schreiner without looking up. "It is business."

"We wish to be kind, too," amended Manora earnestly.

Schreiner got up suddenly and came over to Anna. He took her by the shoulders and turned her so that she had to look up into his face.

"Listen to me," he said slowly, in his bad English. "I can make of you, I think, a great singer. There will be very hard work and probably more tears before I finish—but the material is there. For you in the end there will be fame and money, if you want it. For me it will be enough if I have found and made another great voice."

Anna stared back, fascinated, into Schreiner's intent face. She felt as though she were drifting rapidly away from the shores of any life she had ever known, and she was powerless to resist the current that carried her along.

"Well?" Schreiner suddenly gave her his wonderful smile.

"Yes. I will do whatever you tell me," she said slowly.

"Ha!" Schreiner laughed shortly. "Then you will be unique."

Manora smiled at Schreiner and said, "Is not good for you if we always say, 'Yes, yes.' "

He looked at Manora then, and Anna was staggered at the amused tenderness in his glance. As if Schreiner had said it aloud, she knew in that second that Manora was all his world. That he needed her just exactly as he needed air and food and light; and that everything that made him Conrad Schreiner would die if he lost her.

"Oh!" she thought passionately. "To be loved like that! To know that you are necessary. To *give* instead of always gratefully receiving!"

For a moment her longing and envy almost choked her.

Reserved and inarticulate herself, Anna was astounded and more than a little embarrassed by such a display. But Frayne merely grinned; he seemed to be quite used to this.

Frayne said with a matter-of-fact air, "Well, we seem to have settled the broad lines of Anna's future. Now, what about the details?"

"I settle that," Manora announced firmly. "I think, my child, is necessary we find a home for you." Her blue eyes were very kind as they rested on Anna's troubled face.

"I'm afraid it's terribly difficult. You see . . . you see—" Anna broke off.

"I know." Manora came over to her quickly and took her hand. "Is not possible that you ask your husband for anything—"

"She has a *husband?*" exclaimed Schreiner, his face going dark with annoyance. "In a career that is not good."

Perhaps Manora saw the way Anna's teeth caught at her trembling lower lip, because she said quickly, "This you leave to me. We have a room here in the apartment and for now you stay with us."

Anna's head was bent a little, so that she did not see the warning look Manora threw Schreiner.

"I can't. I really can't," Anna said, in a low voice, "You've been much too kind to me already."

"No, no, you need friends just now." Manora stroked her dark, bent head, in a way that was oddly comforting. "And we are glad that we can help you. Schreiner agrees with me."

"Most certainly. When did Schreiner do anything else?" murmured that gentleman. But he too smiled kindly at Anna, and added, "It seems that either I am stupid, or Manora knows more than I. But if in our house you will be happy, then, please, I hope that you will stay." And he took her hand and kissed it with a ceremonious little air she found touching and faintly amusing.

And so Anna stayed.

Sometimes during the next few weeks she had the peculiar feeling that she stood upon some fantastic stage, and that, instead of being a real person, with feelings and impulses of her own, she just waited for strings to be pulled, and then automatically responded.

She tried very hard to fit into this new life satisfactorily. The part of her mind and heart that had been Tony's was almost numb. Just a dull, heavy ache remained which she tried desperately—and not very successfully—to ignore.

She was touched and a little dismayed at the extent of Manora's generosity. Nothing would do but that she must supply Anna with money when she found she had none at all.

"But suppose I'm not a success?" Anna protested, very troubled. "Suppose I never make enough money to pay all this back?"

Manora shrugged. "Why think of that? You will be a success. Schreiner has said so."

"Does Mr. Schreiner never make a mistake?" Anna could not help asking.

"Very seldom. And he does not like to be reminded of those he does make," added Manora, with a little laugh.

That was all very well, of course, but it hardly settled her problem, thought Anna.

Schreiner guardedly expressed himself as pleased with her. She was docile, she was hard-working, and her technique was good. But one morning he sprang up unexpectedly from the piano seat and walked up and down the studio, his hands thrust into the pockets of his smoking jacket, the inevitable cigar in the corner of his mouth.

"Something is missing," he said, frowning. "You sing like someone in a dream. Technically good. But *you are not really here!*"

He stopped abruptly in front of her and stared at her through a cloud of smoke.

Anna stared back with wide, troubled eyes. "I'm sorry—" she began.

"No, no," he interrupted, and she was relieved to see that he looked at her not unkindly. "You need not be sorry. It is not that you do not work. It is something in you. When first you sang here for me you were not like this. When you cry, you sing with all your heart and feeling. But I cannot make you cry each time. That would be too inconvenient."

"I was very unhappy that morning," Anna explained.

"Yes?" Schreiner looked at her very thoughtfully. Then he said abruptly: "Tell me, do you love Mario Frayne?"

"No!" Anna looked horrified.

"Very well." He brushed aside her indignation. "It would not be surprising. Many women do. But if you do not love him then he may be useful."

He didn't elaborate on the subject, and Anna, who was

still very much in awe of the man, felt that she dared not inquire further,

But that afternoon when Frayne looked in to see them, as he always did at least once in the day, Schreiner said: "Frayne, I want that you have Anna study a rôle with you."

Frayne looked up with a smile. "Dramatically, you mean?"

"Of course."

"It would give me great pleasure—if she would like it." He glanced inquiringly at Anna, but Schreiner seemed to think it a foolish formality to consult her wishes in the matter,

"What rôle do you want us to take as a start?" Frayne asked.

"Antonia in *Hoffmann*." Schreiner was quite positive, "Musically she knows it well, and there is something in the character that is like her. I do not know the English way to say it."

"I do." Frayne smiled. "Like Antonia, she is a little bit bewitched—under a spell."

"Oh, *no*!" Anna was surprised herself at the pain and sharpness in her voice. But, as Frayne spoke, it had seemed to her that she was lying again in Tony's arms by the fire in that room at home, and she heard him say, with that teasing smile of his: "You are like a princess in a fairytale. A princess who is under a spell."

Both men looked surprised,

"Don't you want me to teach you?" Frayne's voice was gentle,

"Oh yes, yes. I didn't mean that at all." She was very eager not to hurt him, or to seem ungrateful. "It's very, very kind of you. Only please don't talk about my being under a spell."

"I do not understand," said Schreiner.

"It's not necessary that you should," said Frayne curtly, with one of his quick flashes of insight. Then, turning to Anna, he said, "We'll study Antonia together. Come to my place tomorrow afternoon, Anna, and we'll make a beginning."

saw her. She came to the town where I lived, to give a short season of ballet. I was a stagehand at the theater there."

"You were. . . ." Anna looked astonished, and he smiled a little.

"Didn't you know that I, too, came from nothing?" he said with a simple frankness that somehow took away all the sting of that.

She shook her head. "I always imagined that because of your father—"

"Oh no," Frayne laughed. "The Frayne part of me was not remembered until long after, when I had made myself famous. *Then* the people who think they matter were only too pleased to accept me . . . as they will accept you, Anna, when Schreiner has finished with you."

She smiled a little unbelievingly and urged him to go on.

"My mother had taken me back to Italy when I was a child, and there I stayed. The first time I saw the dancer, she was coming from the stage after a rehearsal, and I was in her way—nailing something together, I think, on the ground. She was in a temper. She often was," he added, with a little reminiscent smile, "because she lived on her nerves and was never very happy. I did not move from her path quickly enough, and she said something sharply to me and stamped her little foot down on my hand."

"Oh!" Anna looked horrified. "How mean of her!"

"Oh no." That funny, indulgent smile still lingered round Frayne's mouth. "I think perhaps she had just been hurt and had to hurt someone else in her turn. Anyway, I scarcely felt what she had done to my hand. I thought I had never seen anything so lovely, and I think I just knelt there gaping at her."

"But didn't she say she was sorry?" Anna thought it an odd way to begin a love affair.

"No. But two days later she asked me abruptly how my hand was. I showed her the mark she had made and told her she had made a deeper mark on my heart." Frayne grinned up at Anna suddenly. "In England you do not do these things, but in Italy any man may tell a woman she has bruised his heart."

Anna laughed a little and though she could visualize the 18-year-old Frayne smilingly using all his physical charm on the spoiled little dancer.

"After that, she always noticed me. If things had gone badly she would just nod, but if things had gone well she would smile and perhaps ask how my hand and heart were."

"And that was all?"

"Yes, that was all. Except that I would stand in the wings every night and watch her dance. At the end of the season I asked her to marry me."

"You—" Anna gave an incredulous little laugh.

"Yes. She laughed too, of course. She had such a pretty laugh, even when she laughed a little spitefully at me. She told me that she never meant to marry until her career was over, and then only someone who could keep her in luxury to the end of her days."

"And so?"

"And so, Anna, I determined to make money. To make her take me seriously one day. I had always had a great flair for the theater, only I'm by nature extremely lazy. But she was something to slave for, and when one loves the almost unattainable, one must work hard and be very patient."

Anna suddenly put out her hand and gripped his shoulder. "Say that again," she exclaimed, with a curious intentness.

He smiled and just put his hand over hers for a moment. "When one loves the almost unattainable, one must work hard and be very patient," he repeated.

"I hadn't thought of it like that, Mario," she said slowly. And at her first use of his Christian name he bent his head quickly and pressed his cheek against the hand that lay on his shoulder.

Anna drew her hand away almost immediately, but her voice was very gentle as she said, "And so you began to work?"

"*Work!*" He laughed. "Work was hardly the word,

Anna. I slaved. I took any job and every job that brought me near a stage. I did crowd work, small-part work, then crowd work again. I was understudy to people who never had an evening's illness, and I traveled up and down Italy the whole of one sun-baked summer in a tenth-rate touring company."

"From time to time I heard of her in other parts of Italy—usually the important places, where I couldn't hope to go—Rome, Milan, Genoa, and so on. For about two years I didn't see her at all. Meanwhile my luck had turned, and I began to make money, and I saved it. Then I met her again, and she told me she had leukemia.

"Her doctor said she had only about three months to live. I remembered then what she had said years ago—that she would never marry anyone until her career was over, and then only someone who could keep her in luxury to the end of her days.

"Well, her career was over, and even if I was not yet rich, I could at least keep her in luxury to the end of her short days. So I married her."

"You married her? I never heard anyone mention that you had been married."

"No. No one has ever heard this story before," Frayne explained quietly. "We took a villa among the hills outside Florence. It had always been the height of my peasant ambition to live in such a place, and she had a fancy to go there because she had lived in Florence as a little girl."

Anna gently took Frayne's hand in both of hers. "And she died there?"

"Yes. She lived just three months, as the doctor had said, but they were three months of absolutely perfect happiness. I spent every penny I had on her, so that she could live in luxury to the end of her days. And she died one evening when the sun was setting across the Arno, and the water was looking like liquid gold. She didn't really know anything about it. She had been talking of when she would be well enough to go back to the stage. And then she was gone, just like a light being blown out."

There was a long silence. And then Anna said soberly, "I never associated you with anything like that."

He smiled. "You mean, I'm not the faithful type."

"Yes, I suppose I did mean that," she agreed diffidently. "Particularly—" She stopped, and then went on, "Mario, I know it isn't my business, but are the stories about you true?"

"Most of them," he admitted.

She looked troubled, and he patted her hand kindly. "I know. You can't reconcile the two things, can you? But in a man of my type they haven't really much connection, you know."

"No?" She looked at him very seriously, and all the while she was thinking, "But if I never see Tony again, I couldn't, I *couldn't* let any other man make love to me."

Presently she said, "Did you mean, all along, to tell me that story?"

"Yes," he smiled.

"Why?"

"For two reasons, I think." He looked thoughtful. "One was to show that one *can* make the effort to get over the frozen despair after one's world has crashed."

"Oh, Mario!" Light suddenly broke on her. "How very sweet you are to me." Her voice shook a little. "You mean that you understand what is the matter when Schreiner says I sing like someone in a dream?"

"Yes."

"And you want to show me that it lies with *me* to get over it, that it can be done?"

He nodded, his smiling eyes on her face.

She shyly tightened her fingers on his, a little surprised to find she was still holding his hand. "You have helped me. I don't feel so lost and . . . and frozen when you take me into your confidence and make me feel I'm not isolated because of my unhappiness."

"I'm glad, Anna dear." Frayne let his hand lie slackly in hers, making no movement that might scare her.

"Your saying that about having to work hard and be patient seemed to give me something to hold on to again," she said slowly.

"You feel more like working now? *Wanting* to work, I mean?"

"Oh, *yes!*"

"Then let's begin at once."

And after that they talked no more of personal affairs, but worked. And to Anna it was more absorbingly interesting than she could ever have believed possible.

It was not until she was going that she suddenly remembered something.

"Mario!"

"Yes?"

"You said there were two reasons why you told me about . . . about *her*. What was the second one?"

"Oh," Frayne laughed a little and colored—a very rare thing with him. "I'll tell you that the night you make your first great success."

"But—"

"No. Run along now." And bending his handsome head he lightly kissed first one hand and then the other, as he had that evening in the hall at Eaton Square.

And slowly Anna went back across the wide landing to Manora's apartment.

CHAPTER EIGHT

After that oddly revealing talk with Frayne, Anna found that, for some reason, life seemed to flow much more smoothly.

It was not that the thought of Tony hurt any less or that, even now, she could remember the disastrous two days at Eaton Square without wincing. But some purpose was slowly creeping back into the weary business of living.

No wonder she loved her lessons with Frayne, she told herself. He was a brilliant teacher, endlessly patient but above all, he was kind, kind, kind.

It was not that he paid her the smiling, almost exaggerated attentions he paid most women. It was something much deeper, warmer and more sincere.

The thought did just enter her mind once or twice that perhaps the very fact that he did *not* make love to her held a warning significance. But she dismissed the thought almost before it was formed.

In the first days after that terrible scene in Tony's office she had supposed she would hear something from him. Surely he would write to her, make some attempt to see her. Surely it couldn't all just end like that, as though a path had broken off at the edge of a cliff.

She was a little surprised to find how quickly the days passed, now that she was concentrating heart and soul on learning to be the success Schreiner vowed he would make her. And it was with something curiously like alarm that she heard Manora say, "One week, two weeks more, and then we leave for Paris." She and Schreiner were to do an opera season there, and Anna was going with them.

"Are you sorry?" Anna asked, with a funny little feeling of regret.

"Me? No, no," Manora laughed. "At first I am so pleased that I have a holiday, but now I am impatient to

310

go back. Like a horse stamping in his stable and waiting to be let out so that he can run."

"Do you love the life so much?" Anna smiled a little wistfully.

"In some ways, yes. But at times I hate it, and I long and long to be free. And then Conrad is very wise, and if he possibly can he says to me, 'Go away then and be free. Take your holiday.' "

"And do you go?" Anna asked, amused and curious.

Manora shrugged. "Once or twice I have, but almost immediately I come running back. There is a fascination that one cannot resist, you know. I think," she said slowly, "that is why so few of us will not or cannot listen when time says, 'Stop now if you would be remembered at your greatest.' "

Anna wondered if Manora meant that she herself would be an exception and listen to the warning. Presently she said gently, "And what will you do, Manora? Be wiser than all the others?"

"I?" Manora smiled and shrugged again, letting her hands fall rather heavily to her sides. "How do I know, my child?" She only called Anna that in moments of real seriousness. "I never look into the future," she added, with sudden passionate intensity. "Never, never, never."

And Anna was silent, thinking how odd and sad it was that Mario looked back to the past for his greatest happiness; Manora looked neither backward nor forward, but caught at the present with both hands; while she herself. . . ? She could look only to the future, hoping against hope that some day, some day. . . .

It was silly, of course, to feel so reluctant to leave London. The gulf between herself and Tony was so immensely wide that no question of physical distance could affect it.

She could go to the ends of the earth, Tony had said. It made no difference at all.

And yet, with that lack of logic that is pitiful or ridiculous according to whether you have known despair or not, she began to feel again that her heart would not ache quite so much if she could see him just once before she went.

But the days were slipping away fast now. The frail links of connection were snapping.

And then, on the day before they left, she met him. She was walking up Bond Street in the afternoon sunlight, intent upon some last-minute shopping, and there he was, almost at her side.

"Tony!" The word was out before she could stop it.

He swung around at once and caught her hand.

"Anna!" That seemed all he was able to say. For he just stood there, looking down at her with a hungry expression that made her heart ache.

Presently he became aware that they were being jostled by passersby, and he said with a sort of weary impatience, "I can't talk to you here. Come and have tea with me, will you?"

She knew she ought to refuse. She would only hurt both and complicate things by allowing herself this precious indulgence. But when Tony looked at her with that pleading, anxious air of expectancy she knew she could do nothing but agree.

"I haven't very long," she made herself say coolly. Then she felt sick with pain, because he said humbly, "I won't keep you long."

They crossed the road, and for a moment she felt his hand lightly around her arm, as he held her back to allow a car to pass.

She didn't know what to say to him. There wasn't anything to say, she told herself. And by the time she was sitting opposite him in the almost deserted tea-shop, her heart was beating in heavy, panic-stricken thuds.

He ordered tea, and then glanced at his watch and asked politely, "How long can you spare?"

It was all so sad and ridiculous, she thought, when she really had the whole afternoon. However, she must say something, and so she answered quite calmly: "Not more than half an hour."

"Oh, well. . . ." He didn't finish what he was going to say. "How beautiful you are, Anna."

It was so entirely unexpected that for a moment Anna's heart rose in her throat, and her treacherous reason began to whisper, "You see, you were wrong about him. He's wretched without you. It's silly to go away to Paris, chasing this mirage of fame. All he really wants is you. He doesn't mind your being a nobody."

But she knew how hollow all that really was when you put it to the test of reality. And after all, one must expect him to take more than these few months to get over his love for her.

So she just smiled with the new baffling coolness she had learned and said, "Am I? It's always nice to be told that when one has on a new dress, isn't it?"

It wasn't really very well done, but he didn't seem to notice that. He looked a little bewildered and glanced down with a touch of embarrassment that hurt. Tony—Tony who had always been so lightheartedly sure of himself and his surroundings—to look nonplussed at some silly thing she had said!

After a moment he said rather huskily, "What have you been doing with yourself since . . . since. . . ."

"Since I left you?"

He looked sulky at that and answered, "Yes."

"I'm on the way to becoming a singer, Tony," she told him calmly.

"Helped by Frayne, I suppose?" he said, with sudden violence.

"Mario has been a great help to me," she agreed coolly. "But not in the way you mean. As a matter of fact, Conrad Schreiner and his wife are very much interested in my voice."

"His *what*?" Tony made that sound coldly disgusted because he wanted to hurt her a little too.

"His wife. Manora Vanescu." Anna spoke firmly.

"She's not his wife," Tony said brutally. "She's his mistress."

"Please don't." Anna's voice was very cold. "You don't help by abusing my friends."

"But it's true." Tony spoke like a truculent schoolboy. "He has a wife somewhere in Budapest. Everyone knows. She won't divorce him."

"Oh. . . ." Anna suddenly remembered that when she

had asked Manora if Schreiner were her husband there had been a funny little pause before Manora had said "Yes." She wished passionately now that she hadn't driven Manora to that pitiful little lie.

She looked up with sudden gentleness in her face.

"Well, never mind, Tony," she said much more softly. "I suppose it isn't really our business."

With an almost touching eagerness he responded at once to her softer mood. "Very well. Only I just thought. . . ."

"What, Tony?"

He was silent for a moment, and then burst out with passionate misery, "Are you living with them, or with . . . with. . . ."

"I'm living with them," she said firmly.

"Anna—" he caught her hand "—God knows I can't have much pride to be saying this, but I don't care about Frayne. You don't have to make excuses for that night or explain it or anything—"

"Don't," she interrupted faintly, and something in her voice stemmed the tide of his stumbling eloquence.

"I'm sorry, my dear," he said much more quietly. "It's frightful of me, I know, to go on pestering you when you haven't any more use for me. Forget what I said."

"I . . . I won't forget it," she said slowly, "And it's not frightful of you at all. It's unbelievably generous. Only it isn't any good."

"Very well." His voice was not absolutely steady. "Let's talk about your singing, then. That's what you're really thrilled about, isn't it?"

So Anna told him something of Schreiner's plans for her; and, as she did so, it seemed to her that the way stretched in front of her gray, arid, and stony.

"I see," Tony said slowly. "But there's just one thing I want to say. May I?"

"I suppose so." But her eyes were a little apprehensive.

"Please, darling—" He stopped, and looked startled. The endearment had just slipped out. After a second, he went on, "Won't you let me give you an allowance? I hate to think of your being dependent on that raffish couple for everything."

"Oh no, Tony, please. I couldn't." Her voice was sharp with distress.

"But surely I have more right—" began Tony.

"No. You see, they'll let me pay it back when I begin earning, and you would never let me do that, would you?"

"No, my God! I wouldn't," he agreed rather violently. "But— Oh, hang it, Anna! In any type of . . . of separation the husband expects to pay an allowance."

"You weren't really my husband—"

"How *dare* you say that!" She could see he was white with pain as well as anger.

"I'm sorry," she said quickly. "I didn't quite mean that. I mean that as it was all wrong really, from the very beginning, the best thing we can do is to wash it all out. There would be something indecent about taking an allowance for making a mess of your life."

"But—"

"*Please*, Tony. There isn't anything more to say . . . and I must go now."

He paid the bill in silence, and they left the shop.

Outside there was a man standing with a tray of violets, and on a sudden impulse, Tony said, "Well, at least may I buy you some violets? I could do that for anyone, even if she didn't matter in the least to me."

"Oh, Tony. . . ." She laughed a little, with a sudden sound of tears in her voice.

She didn't add either "yes" or "no"; but as she raised her hand to summon a taxi, with a sureness that the old Anna would never have known, he turned to buy handfuls of dark, sweet-smelling violets.

He brought them to her as she stood by the open door of the taxi.

"Please take them," he said, clasping her hands around their stems.

"Oh, Tony, they're lovely," she said gently. And for a moment she put them against her cheek.

He stared at her with those unhappy, puzzled eyes for a moment.

"God bless you, sweetheart," he said, with sudden roughness in his voice, and he bent his head to the violets for a second. She wasn't quite sure whether it was a little movement of embarrassment, or whether he kissed the flowers just where her cheek had rested.

Then she climbed into the waiting taxi. As it pulled away she did not look back.

Life in Paris proved to be rather different from life in London. For one thing, they lived at a hotel, and Anna missed the easy informality of the apartment in St. James's. She thought Manora found the change irksome also, and she was certain that Schreiner did.

He was greatly sought-after, and although, in a way, Anna knew, he enjoyed playing "the great man," there were times when she thought he watched Manora as though the very sight of her rested him . . . and he needed that rest.

Manora never made the slightest demonstration of affection toward him in public. But often, when they were alone in the sitting room of their suite, which was also used as a practice room, she would show by some word or look that nothing that Schreiner said or did was lost upon her.

To Anna there was something very touching in their attitude toward each other, and, at the same time, something that excited her envy, too. If she could have given Tony what Manora gave Schreiner she felt she could have asked no more of life.

She went to most of the rehearsals of Manora's performances because Schreiner said there was a great deal to be learned that way, and it was useful to get to know the "feel" of a theater. It was here that Anna first realized to the full the extraordinary genius of Schreiner.

If he was exciting in a studio, urging one shy student to sing, in charge of a full orchestra he was dynamic. He was wonderfully skillful with his singers, too, and showed a sort of ruthless patience that invariably achieved what he wanted in the end.

Even Manora could have cried herself sick in opposition to something he had laid down as necessary. It would have made no difference whatever. When he said a thing must be done it was done, and usually, to tell the truth, willingly done.

Once, when a rehearsal was over, he made Anna come on to the stage and sing into the empty theater. She was petrified with horror at first but, like the others, she felt it impossible to question Schreiner's decision.

It was Manora who whispered to her, "Don't be frightened, and don't think of the size of the theater. Keep the quality of your voice pure, and remember to float it."

Anna found herself in the middle of an empty stage, with the yawning gulf of the empty auditorium in front of her. For a moment she thought that her throat was going to close and that she could not sing. Then she caught sight of Schreiner. The light from the conductor's desk was on his face, and he was smiling up at her in that peculiarly kind way he occasionally bestowed.

There was something absolutely compelling about that smile, and Anna felt her fearful tension relax. She was not quite sure when she became aware of the fact that the orchestra was playing, nor when she herself made her entry. But she supposed she must have instinctively done what was right, because the next thing she knew was a feeling of immense exhilaration and wonder.

It was her voice—*hers*—that was soaring in those heavenly cadences.

She felt she was really as surprised as anyone else at the amazing effect, and when she had finished she just went on standing there, looking slightly bewildered, while the orchestra and several people in the wings applauded.

She thought suddenly that it seemed ungracious not to make any acknowledgment. So she bowed shyly toward the orchestra. Schreiner laughed. But it was a pleased laugh, she knew.

Then Manora came and kissed her, and one or two of the other singers spoke kindly to her. Even the very famous and superior soprano who had been engaged to do several of the leading French rôles observed, "One day, *mon enfant*, you will be great."

Schreiner said nothing until they were in the car on the way back to their hotel, when she ventured to say, "Were you pleased with me?"

"Very pleased," said Schreiner, patting her shoulder.

"The others were kind, too," Anna said, with a happy smile. "They are so . . . friendly."

Manora laughed and Schreiner said, "What does she say they are?"

"Friendly," repeated Manora dryly, whereat Schreiner let out a contemptuous bark of laughter.

"So are tigers, Anna. Very friendly . . . until they wish for the same piece of meat."

Anna found the comment a little disturbing.

As the days slipped past, it seemed impossible after all for Frayne to fly over to hear Manora. But there were plenty of others to be interested and admiring. For Manora, Anna discovered, was very popular with both critics and public.

Not that this fact appeared to make any difference to her invariable attack of nerves on the day of a performance. Anna was appalled the first time she witnessed the miserable hours that preceded a performance.

Manora awoke in the morning with the announcement that she had a terrible headache, and obviously the beginnings of a cold; that, indeed, she doubted if it would be possible for her to sing that evening.

Schreiner took this very calmly, merely telling her to gargle and spray her throat. Anna, terribly worried, could only admire his composure.

During the morning Manora wandered restlessly about the apartment, unable to settle to anything but refusing to go out because of her throat. At lunchtime she said that she felt too sick to eat; but, on Schreiner's advice, she managed a remarkably good meal.

"I will lie down after lunch," she told Anna sadly, "and see if I can sleep. I did not sleep at all last night."

Anna, worried and sympathetic, went to see her comfortably settled. She gently tucked a wrap around Manora and hung over her affectionately, thinking how very dear she had become.

"I hope you will sleep, darling, and feel much better by the evening," she said anxiously, noticing with relief that Manora's blue eyes looked rather sleepy.

But Manora shook her head and said she was afraid that was unlikely.

During the afternoon Anna went out and strolled about aimlessly, feeling very unhappy. She sat in the gardens of the Tuileries for a little while in the wintry sunshine, but it was too cold to sit there long, and she was back again by the time Manora rang for a cup of tea at five o'clock.

Anna came into her room and asked how she had slept.

"Not at all," Manora replied. "And my throat feels terrible." Then she relapsed into gloomy silence.

Anna went out and asked Schreiner if he didn't think it better to substitute another singer.

Schreiner looked amused and said, "There *is* no substitute for Manora."

It was touching that he should be so proud of her, of course, but a little callous that he should take no more notice of her illness.

When they went off to the theater together Manora was completely wordless, and her usually animated and lovely face was almost blank of expression. Anna herself was going later. She hugged Manora warmly, and felt it was almost an insult to wish her luck.

However, she did so, and was rewarded with a faint smile, one more suggestive of an operation patient than a successful singer.

All the while she was getting ready and on her way to the theater, Anna felt sick with anxiety about Manora. She had received strict injunctions not to go backstage before the performance, and so she just sat there waiting wretchedly for the opera to begin.

She wanted to turn to the laughing, uncaring people around her and explain, "If she doesn't sing very well tonight, it's because she is ill. She has a terrible headache and a sore throat. But really she's utterly marvelous."

However, of course, she couldn't do that, and it would not have been much use if she had.

By the time Schreiner came to the conductor's desk,

Anna felt cold all over. He, on the contrary, appeared miraculously calm and undisturbed. He was a callous beast, Anna thought suddenly, with quite unusual vehemence.

She scarcely heard a note until Manora was on the stage, and then she sat there with her head bent and her hands gripped together. And then Manora began to sing.

It was a few minutes before Anna raised astonished eyes to the stage once more—to see Manora using her wonderful smile, with its inevitable effect, in her part of an engaging, warm-hearted Victorian coquette.

That she was singing like an angel seemed quite a detail of her performance. And, with a relief that almost hurt, Anna realized that Manora was singing as beautifully as she had ever heard her.

Trembling a little, in the first intermission she hurried backstage and into Manora's dressing room.

"Manora, you're *wonderful*!" she exclaimed. "There isn't a trace of your sore throat in your singing."

Manora turned round from her dressing table. "No?" she said, holding Anna's hand and smiling up at her. "My throat feels better. I think perhaps the gargling did good. Maybe I shall not have a cold after all."

"And the headache?" Anna was still anxious.

"A little better." Manora put her hand to her head. "You enjoy the performance, eh?" She glanced indulgently at Anna.

"Oh yes!" Anna overlooked her misery of anxiety earlier in the evening.

"Very well. Run along now," Manora said, as though Anna were a child. "But come and see me in the next intermission," she called cheerfully after her.

Immeasurably relieved, Anna thoroughly enjoyed the second act. As she made her way slowly through the crowd, she heard two people speaking near to her. "Do you see that lovely girl there—the one with the smooth, dark hair and honey-colored skin? She's wearing an ivory-colored dress."

"They mean me!" thought Anna, astounded, as she

glanced cautiously around to see that there was no one else in an ivory-colored dress.

"Yes. What about her?" said the second voice.

"She's a find of Schreiner's. I've been told she has a glorious voice. We're going to hear a lot about her when he does finally launch her."

With the oddest little thrills running up and down her spine Anna slipped through the door that led backstage.

Was that really true? Were people going to "hear a lot about her" in just the exciting and impressive way the man's voice had suggested?

"Tony!" she said suddenly to the empty corridor. And then, with a happy laugh, she caught up her long skirt and ran childishly along the passage and up the stairs to Manora's room.

Manora glanced at her absently and asked, "Did you want something?"

"N-no." Anna felt slightly embarrassed. "Only to tell you how beautifully the performance is going."

"So?" Manora scarcely appeared to be listening. "I am glad you enjoy it."

"Manora dear, there's only one more act," Anna pointed out anxiously. "You'll be all right now, won't you?"

"The third act is the most difficult of all," Manora said gloomily. "I do not know *how* I shall get through it."

"Is your headache worse?"

Manora nodded, and Anna, all her anxiety returning and full of remorse that she had been rushing about so happily herself, went in search of smelling salts and eau de cologne.

That seemed to cheer Manora a little, and she squeezed Anna's hand when she went, and said, "Do not worry."

But of course Anna did worry—right through the third act, until the curtain fell, on thunders of applause. Manora had given a truly great performance.

She felt almost hysterical with relief as she stood there clapping. It was incredible that Manora could have risen above so much misfortune and sung so magnificently.

Anna half expected to find her in a state of collapse

afterward. But nothing was further from the case. She was flushed, bright-eyed and radiant when Anna came in.

"Hello!" she cried, as though she had not seen Anna for months. "Was good, the performance?"

"It was heavenly." Anna came over and kissed her warm cheek very tenderly. "I can't imagine how you did it, feeling as you did."

"Oh," Manora shrugged, "the throat is all right, after all."

"But I expect you want to get home to bed," Anna said understandingly.

"No, no." Manora dismissed that suggestion at once. "Conrad will take us out to supper somewhere."

"But your headache?" Anna looked surprised.

"Headache?" Manora paused in the act of removing her makeup and looked equally surprised. "I have no headache now," she explained briskly, beginning to smear cold cream over her face. "I am ravenous with hunger; that is all."

"Then be quick, for I too am ravenous," said Schreiner's voice from the door.

"*Ich komme, ich komme!*" exclaimed Manora, who always seemed a trifle nervous of keeping the great man waiting.

And as soon as she was ready Schreiner swept them both off to the Café de Paris, where a table had been reserved, and where they held court until the early hours, among the dozens of friends and acquaintances who came up to congratulate them.

When at last they went home Anna said, with a smile to Schreiner, "It is good that Manora has completely recovered, isn't it?"

Schreiner and Manora both laughed.

"You must not notice that," Manora told her gaily. "I am always like that. Is only nerves."

"*Always* like it?" Anna looked appalled, but Manora nodded indifferently.

"You will be the same. Won't she?" she added to Schreiner.

Schreiner smiled and said, "When her turn comes,

yes." Which somehow brought back with redoubled effect Anna's earlier excitement.

"When my turn comes," she repeated, and her lips curved in a singularly lovely smile.

And her turn came very much sooner than she expected.

Two days later Schreiner came in, tossed down his hat on the table and announced, "Next Friday you sing Antonia."

"Sing Antonia? Where?" Anna stammered.

"Where? At the theater, of course."

"In *public?*"

"Certainly in public. Why would I wish you to sing it to yourself?"

"Oh, but I couldn't." Anna was quite positive in her terror.

Schreiner was unmoved. "It is a great chance," he said carelessly. "You wish I give to someone else?"

Anna was silent.

"Come here, my child."

Anna went slowly over to the great director, and he took both her hands. His own hands were strong and beautiful, and she knew he was inordinately proud of them, but there was great kindness now in the strength and warmth of his clasp.

"Have you any confidence in me as a director and conductor?" he asked her.

"Oh, *yes*," Anna said eagerly.

"And if I say to you, 'Such-and-such a singer is good, even great,' you believe me?"

"Why, of course."

"Then why doubt it when I say to you, 'You are a good singer, perhaps a great singer'?"

Anna hung her head. "It isn't that I doubt your judgment. It's just . . . I'm so afraid."

"That is inevitable. All artists are afraid. Even I am afraid sometimes," Schreiner added, with his ingenuous vanity that was so entirely inoffensive.

"Are you?"

"Certainly."

"Oh." Anna considered that. After a pause, she said, "How did you arrange that I should sing?"

Schreiner smiled at the implication that he had won his point.

"That is too much for my English to explain," he said. "I will call Manora."

He summoned Manora and talked to her for a few minutes in rapid German. Then she flung her arms impulsively around Anna.

"Is too exciting!" she declared. "You do indeed sing next Friday. The Antonia is ill and cannot sing."

"But there must be a dozen singers in Paris who could do Antonia at a few days' notice," Anna pointed out timidly.

"Yes, yes. But this is a special occasion. There are to be very important English visitors there. Conrad thinks they are diplomats or something," said Manora with engaging vagueness. "And you see, is a pleasant compliment to them that an English girl should make a great success that night."

"Mr. Schreiner is sure that I shall be a great success?" asked Anna doubtfully.

"Perfectly sure," said Mr. Schreiner between puffs at his cigar.

"Then I will do it," Anna promised suddenly.

"Good girl!" they both said.

The next few days were a nightmare. There were continual rehearsals, during which Anna was subjected in her turn to the iron discipline of Schreiner. There were minutes when she was sure she would be a success and hours when she knew quite positively that she would not.

A thousand times she regretted her decision to play the part. And then she would remember that, on the other hand, she could not possibly have gone on imposing on the generosity of Manora.

At the dress rehearsal everything that could go wrong did, or so it seemed to her. But never once did Schreiner's inexorable patience break down. By the end she was almost in tears, and her nerves were stretched to breaking-point.

She went slowly and dejectedly to her dressing room; on the way she met the tenor of the production, humming cheerfully. For a moment she quite hated him for being able to remain so calm.

He stopped her and said, "You are really quite well, I hope?"

Anna looked surprised. "Yes, thank you. Why? Did I sing so badly?"

"No, no. Your singing is most beautiful. But you play the consumptive girl so convincingly that at times I'm quite nervous," he told her half-seriously.

"Oh, how absurd!" Anna laughed. "But how nice of you," she added.

And she went on, considerably cheered. It was thanks to Mario, of course, she thought, with a warm rush of gratitude, that her playing of the part was so convincing. Thanks to Mario and the long-dead Italian dancer, on whom he had modeled his idea of the consumptive girl.

Suddenly she thought very tenderly of Mario, and wished frantically that he could have been there tomorrow. It would have made a difference to have known that such a good friend was in the house.

When she reached the hotel a letter from Mario awaited; it said that, if he could possibly arrange to get away the next day, he would fly over to hear her "triumph."

It raised Anna's spirits miraculously, and when Schreiner assured her that the rehearsal had been much better than she imagined, she felt almost cheerful again.

But the next day her terror returned with redoubled force, and she wandered about, unable to rest or to do any of the sensible things that Manora suggested.

"I must go out," she said desperately in the afternoon. "I can't stay boxed up here."

"Well, we will go for a short walk," Manora agreed. "Although it is not good in this damp weather."

As they came out of the hotel, into the Place de la Concorde, Anna caught herself wondering if the victims of the French Revolution had felt very much as she did now when they were brought here on their last journey to the guillotine.

But at least the walk filled in a little time and made her feel less sick. And she was thrilled as well as frightened when Manora pointed out her own name on the playbill for the evening, pasted up on the Colonnes Morris pillars.

Sometimes it seemed to her afterward that those were the last clear impressions in her mind, until she was sitting in her dressing room, with Manora putting the finishing touches to her makeup. The waiting had been almost unendurably long because she did not come in until the last act.

When the call came for her Manora said quickly, "All the waiting is over now; it is always the worst part."

As she moved into the wings, Anna didn't believe it. Her face felt stiff with makeup and her limbs felt stiff with terror. Above all, she had a terrible desire to yawn. It was ridiculous, but almost irresistable.

She never knew how she found herself on the stage staring at the blank curtain. She could hear the storm of clapping greeting Schreiner's entrance. The strains of the orchestra, muffled, reached her ears. And then, in a moment of unspeakable horror, she realized that the curtain was rising.

In a sort of dream she saw Schreiner's keen, handsome face in the light from his desk, the dimly lit, bustling activity of the orchestra, and beyond that a great cloudy space. She could hear someone singing very beautifully—a voice that seemed to float on the air, resting lightly from time to time on the supporting notes of the orchestra.

And then suddenly she realized that the voice was her own.

She was distinctly conscious of thinking, "How beautifully I am singing." And that was the last time she thought about herself as a person at all. For the rest of the act she was Antonia.

So much so that, when the curtain finally fell, she was faintly surprised to find she was not really dead.

The part she had just played seemed far more real to

her than the scenes that followed. The curtain calls, the applause, the congratulations, Manora kissing her—and Schreiner, too, for that matter. And then the elegantly turned speech of the manager to the audience about this young English "find" who had so gallantly come to the rescue at the last minute.

And everyone forgot that, as Anna herself had said, there were probably a dozen adequate Antonias to be found in Paris. And they all clapped again, and she had to take a call alone, feeling perilously near tears.

"Now hurry to your room and change," Schreiner ordered her. "You come to a celebration supper. All is arranged."

Wild with excitement and happiness, Anna ran to her room, where her dresser was eagerly waiting to point out all her flowers to her and help her to make ready for the celebration supper.

Every few seconds there was a knock at the door, and someone would put in their head to call out good wishes and congratulations. Anna thought she would never be ready in time.

But at last all her makeup was off, and she had changed into the slim ivory frock that showed off her honey-gold skin beautifully. She stood up and slipped on the little sable cape Manora had lent her for the great occasion. She was standing there, pinning on a spray of orchids that Schreiner had sent her, when yet another knock came.

"See who it is, please," she said to the dresser. "But I can't wait more than a minute."

The dresser went to the door and spoke to someone. Then she came back and said, "It is a gentleman, madam, who says he has come all the way from England to hear you."

Mario! Darling Mario had managed to come after all. It was the crowning touch.

"Oh, come in!" she called eagerly. "Come *in*, Mario dear!" She went toward the door, and then stopped dead.

The gentleman who had come all the way from England to hear her was Tony.

CHAPTER NINE

"*Tony!*" The word broke from her in a mixture of joy and astonishment and something like dismay. Then she stood there staring at him, unable to think of anything else to say. That she should have flung at him a rapturous greeting intended for another man was beyond her powers of explanation.

He came forward into the room. His face, she saw, was rather pale and set, but his voice was perfectly calm as he said, "I—just wanted to come and congratulate you, Anna. You were wonderful."

"Oh, thank you. How . . . how nice of you, Tony." She wished her voice didn't sound so nervous. She held out her hand to him, though it seemed a silly way to greet him, and when he took it and gravely kissed it she felt almost shocked. It was all very well for Schreiner, or even Frayne, to greet her like that. But for Tony it seemed almost frightening in its incongruity.

She made a little sign of dismissal to the dresser. But even when they were alone the only foolish sentence she could summon to her lips was, "It seems odd for you to kiss my hand."

"Why?" He smiled faintly, but not as though he were genuinely amused. "Am I not to be allowed to add my homage at the shrine of the new prima donna?"

"I'm not a prima donna," she said hastily.

"Oh, yes, Anna. See, you have only to look in the glass." He spoke gently and, she thought, oddly, his voice sounded almost sad.

She turned quickly to the dressing table and stared wonderingly at her own reflection.

She had the strange sensation that she didn't really recognize herself in the lovely, radiant creature who looked back at her. She thought perhaps it had something to do with Manora's sables and Schreiner's orchids.

But it was not that at all, of course. It was just that the shining crown of success was resting lightly on her smooth dark head.

"The . . . cape isn't mine at all—I borrowed it from Manora," she stammered childishly. "And Schreiner sent me the orchids, more . . . more for fun than anything, I suppose. Just to pretend I was a prima donna."

"Don't, Anna dear." Tony's voice was suddenly very tender. "Why should you try to explain away your triumph? Do you think I begrudge you it? Tonight perhaps your sables are borrowed, and your orchids sent half in fun, but there will be sables of your own in future and orchids sent in admiration and all seriousness. And I'm very glad it should be so."

She stood with her lashes downcast to hid the threatening tears.

"Thank you," she said in a whisper. "Thank you, Tony; it's sweet of you to want me to be a success."

"But of course I want it." Tony was smiling now, "I want you to have whatever will make you happy."

Anna gripped her hands together nervously. This wasn't, of course, the moment to tell him what would really make her happy. To explain that all this excitement and triumph meant nothing in itself, that it was simply a means to an end. One brief triumph didn't entitle her to speak. One must be patient, Mario had said.

But oh, she *had* been patient—so desperately, achingly patient. . . .

"What is it, Anna?" Tony gently took her hands and unlaced them. Something in his voice reminded her irresistibly of that very first evening when he had been so dear and kind to her. She thought for a moment that she could yield to the bitter longing to tell him everything.

But the next moment she shrank from the idea, frightened that she had come so near to spoiling everything.

"Oh, it's nothing." She laughed nervously, then said, "I was just wondering how you knew about my singing here tonight."

"I happened to see a line or two in the gossip columns

of a lunchtime paper today. Something about Schreiner's English find making her debut tonight. I knew it must be you."

"But wasn't it terribly difficult for you to get away at such short notice?"

He pressed the palms of her hands together, and now it was he who seemed nervous.

"Yes," he said abruptly, "it was difficult, but I was determined to come."

He set his mouth in an obstinate line, and Anna wondered suddenly if it were her imagination that he looked much older, and that there was a strained expression around his eyes.

"I can't tell you how glad I am that you did come," she said slowly. "But tell me, why was it so important to you?" She held her breath as she awaited his answer; her heart seemed to stop beating.

"I know it sounds silly now, after you've been such a glorious success, but—" he looked down in sudden, boyish confusion "—I was afraid you might *not* be a success, and then these people might have been nasty to you."

"Oh, Tony," her voice was unsteady, and as she looked at his bent head she felt an overwhelming sense of tenderness for him, an odd sort of protectiveness. She leaned forward and very softly kissed his cheek, just where the faint flush of embarrassment showed. "You dear, funny boy," she said.

He dropped her hands abruptly and said, "No, don't do that. It . . . isn't any good."

Anna flickered her lashes quickly as though he had slapped her.

"What . . . do you mean?" she asked slowly.

He made a little movement of impatience. "You know what I mean," he said roughly. "It's no good our letting ourselves get, er, sentimental. You said it yourself very clearly that last time in England. I didn't want to believe you then, but you were right, of course. Our paths don't lie anywhere near each other. I'd forgotten for a moment, but I won't forget again. Why, even when I came in, it was Frayne you were expecting, wasn't it?"

"Yes. But Tony, Tony—" she was powerless to stop the words now "—only because I dared not even hope for you."

He took a step forward, catching her hands in his again: but this time he was not gentle, hurting her fingers with the strength of his grip.

"Anna, what are you saying?"

And at that moment the door was flung open by an impatient hand, and Schreiner's deep voice sounded imperiously:

"Anna, my child, must we starve all night, waiting for you?"

"Oh, I'm coming." Anna turned desperately, to see not only Schreiner and Manora, but several other people waiting for her "Only a minute, one minute."

Schreiner came forward, toweringly impressive in his heavy overcoat. He looked inquiringly from her to Tony.

"This is . . . this is . . . my husband," Anna said helplessly.

Tony and Schreiner looked blankly at each other with completely unconcealed dislike. Then Schreiner bowed, just a trifle too deeply, and said, "Then perhaps Mr. Roone will join our supper party."

"Oh, Tony, do." Anna snatched eagerly at this chance.

"I'm extremely sorry." Tony's voice was coldly formal. "I have to catch the night plane back in one hour."

"But, Tony," Anna didn't know that she clung feverishly to his arm, "surely you could wait a few hours?"

"You could take the first plane in the morning, Mr. Roone," Schreiner pointed out. "The time would be much the same."

"I'm sorry," Tony said again. "It's quite impossible."

"Tony!" It was a desperate whisper. She had forgotten now about waiting until she had made so great a name that she could be worthy of him. "Tony, I *want* you to stay." Her teeth caught at her trembling lower lip.

"I can't."

"Do you mean you won't?"

"Very well, then, I won't."

Her hands fell to her sides, and her long lashes came down in a sullen curtain.

"I see. I didn't understand."

He didn't say anything to that, and after a moment she said in a toneless little voice, "Well then, goodbye."

He kissed her hand again in that ridiculously formal manner. "Goodbye, Anna. I wish you every possible success." Then with the faintest inclination of his head to Schreiner he left the room.

Anna stood where she was, aimlessly fiddling with some things on the dressing table. Her mouth was trembling a little and she seemed quite unaware now that anyone was waiting for her.

"Come," Schreiner said, his voice unexpectedly gentle.

"I can't," whispered Anna, looking up despairingly at the big director as he stood between her and the laughing, chattering group beyond the doorway.

"Yes," said Schreiner firmly, "you can, and you must. Remember, it is not only on the stage that one must sometimes play a part."

There was a second's pause. Then Anna drew her borrowed sables around her and tilted up her chin with a desperate little flicker of pride. "I'm ready," she said and, taking Schreiner's arm, went out into the corridor with him.

She tried to remember that, as he had said, she was playing a part. So long as she kept that in mind it should not be so difficult. She was able to smile and talk to the people on the way downstairs, to smile again at the crowd near the stage door, to smile as Schreiner handed her into the big car. She wondered if the smile were painted permanently on her face.

Somebody pressed forward to the door of the car and begged her for an autograph. She looked staggered for a moment. It wasn't possible that her name, just her name written down on a piece of paper, should have any importance.

She looked inquiringly at Schreiner.

He shrugged and smiled. "As you wish," he said. "It is as well to be gracious. It is by our audience that we live."

She slowly wrote her name, the name she had had before that meaningless, almost nonexistent marriage to Tony: Anna Lemwell.

She gave back the book and was oddly touched by the thanks.

Several people called out good wishes to her as the car drove away. It was all quite fantastic and very like a dream.

As they entered the crowded restaurant people turned their heads to look at her, because, miraculously, the word had already gone around that she was "news." That made the unreal atmosphere of a play seem more believable, and she smiled again dutifully, just to show how happy she was.

And then, with a rush of indescribable relief, she saw the familiar figure of Frayne coming toward her.

"Oh, *Mario!*" She caught his hands. "I'm so glad...." And then she couldn't say any more.

But he seemed to understand, for he held her hands tightly and said, "Darling Anna, I'm so glad, too. A million congratulations. I arrived as the curtain went up on your act, and I shall never be sufficiently thankful that I was just in time to see this new star rise."

Everyone laughed and murmured agreement, while Manora said anxiously:

"Is a nice surprise, Anna? You did not expect that Mario was here? We sent him on to see that all was ready for the supper and so that he could welcome you."

"It was a lovely idea," said Anna gently. "I'm very happy."

Everyone declared afterward that the party was an immense success. The new soprano was so charming and unspoiled, with an engaging touch of shyness about her, although she was almost brilliantly vivacious.

Schreiner was obviously more than satisfied, and the handsome actor who had come all the way from England was obviously more than admiring. As for the young star herself—well, it was amusingly significant that it was in Frayne's taxi that she finally departed for her hotel.

The distance to the hotel was very short, but Anna heard Frayne order the taxidriver to go a longer way.

"Why did you do that, Mario?" she asked gently, as he sat back beside her.

"Because there's something I want to say to you, Anna dear, and it will take longer than the two minutes we would have had."

"Something to say to me?" Anna looked up quickly and saw that Mario's usually laughing eyes were deadly serious.

He nodded abruptly.

"Do you remember I once told you a story about myself, that afternoon in my apartment?"

"Yes, I remember."

"You asked me why I told you. I gave you one reason, Anna, and I promised I would give you the other one on the night you made you first great triumph."

And then Anna knew perfectly well what was coming. She saw, too, that he had generously waited until success could give her an absolute freedom of choice. He wouldn't tell her before how he felt, because he knew that in her bewilderment and gratitude for his immediate help she might have said things she would bitterly regret.

It was just like Mario to do that, she thought.

But she couldn't let the words be said, now or any other time, she *couldn't*. It would be a betrayal of everything she felt. Even if Tony let her go—wanted to let her go, and had no more use for her—it still made no difference.

She turned and put her hands gently on Frayne's shoulders.

"Mario, please don't put it into words. You see, it isn't any good, and it's better to leave it unsaid."

He covered her hands lightly with his and smiled into her eyes.

"Are you so sure? You know I told you that story

because I wanted to show you that I could love—really love faithfully, I mean."

"Yes, I know."

"Anna, is it that you feel I'm offering you only second-best, because there was once someone else?"

"No." She shook her head. "That wouldn't matter because, you see, I could never offer you anything but second-best in return. It's because. . . ."

"Yes?" Frayne looked at her bent head very tenderly.

"Mario," she tightened her hands suddenly, "Tony came to see me tonight."

"Tony!"

She nodded.

"Do you mean he made overtures to you?"

Anna gave a dreary little laugh. "No, Mario, he didn't make overtures. He just told me as plainly as any man can tell a woman that he didn't want me."

Mario frowned and muttered something.

"I know, I know," she said wearily. "I can't have any pride to feel as I do, and I don't think I could put it into words to anyone but you. But I've learned a lot of things tonight, Mario, that I shall never forget. One of them is that I would rather wait years for one kind word from Tony than be adored by anyone else in the world."

"I see. Poor little Anna." Frayne's voice was very gentle, and he didn't attempt to argue the point.

There was a long pause, and then she said timidly, "There's really nothing else to say, is there?"

"No, my dear," Mario said. "There's really nothing else to say." He turned his head and looked out of the window. "And our driver seems to have judged his distance admirably, for here we are."

As he helped her out she gripped his hand anxiously. "Mario, I'm terribly sorry."

"Darling, I'm not. I can't be sorry about anything that still leaves me your sweet friendship. Don't lose any sleep about this because you'll want to be very wide awake to read the papers in the morning. Good night and bless you." He kissed her affectionately and quite unembarrassingly.

With the first sensation of comfort since Tony had left her that evening, Anna earnestly returned the kiss. Then she turned and went into the hotel.

She knew he stood looking after her, but she didn't look back. What was the good of looking back . . . ever?

And yet, perversely enough, even as the door swung to behind her, she felt the first stirring of doubt in her heart.

She went straight to her room and, just as she had got into bed, Manora tapped on the door and came in.

As she leaned her arms on the end of the bed, she smiled at Anna but her eyes were anxious.

"You wish that I do not disturb you so late?" she said. "Or shall I come and talk?"

"Come and talk, Manora," Anna said, a faint smile just touching her own serious mouth. I won't sleep for a while yet."

"With excitement, you mean?" But Manora's glance suggested that she knew it was something else.

Anna shook her head slowly.

"No, not excitement, Manora. It's odd how almost unimportant all that success seems now."

"You must not let Schreiner hear you say that," Manora said with a little laugh. But she came and sat on the side of the bed and put her arm around Anna.

Anna leaned her head against Manora, and for a little while neither of them spoke. Then Manora said calmly, "So you decide not to take Mario?"

Anna started.

"How did you know? Did he tell you he was going to . . . going to. . . ."

Manora shook her head.

"No, no. Some things one does not need to be told. When I saw him this evening I knew that he would ask you. Now I see you, I know you have said 'no.' "

Anna moved slightly and gave an impatient little sigh.

"I suppose you think I'm a fool?" she said, almost resentfully.

"I, my dear?" Manora's eyes widened. "I cannot tell you whether you have been foolish or not." She stroked

Anna's hair gently. "Your heart can tell you much better than I."

"Oh, Manora!" Anna clung to her suddenly, weeping. "My heart's so bruised and aching that I don't think it knows what to say."

"Listen to me," Manora drew her close. But for a moment Anna could listen to nothing, and Manora had to hold her and soothe her with those murmured little words of endearment in her own language that were so oddly comforting. At last Anna lay quiet, her face strangely childish in its pallor and wistfulness.

"I'm sorry to have made a scene," she whispered, though the slight pressure of Manora's arm bade her say no more about that. "I think it's partly . . . oh, I so *hate* hurting Mario. He's always been so dear and kind to me, kinder than anyone else in the world, except you, Manora."

Manora smiled and presently Anna went on. "All he asks is to be allowed to smooth things for me. He'd always be a barrier between me and things that hurt. There'd never be any loneliness. . . . Nothing is ever a problem with him. . . . It's as though—" She stopped suddenly, at the sight of Manora's little smile. "Why do you look like that?"

Manora laughed quietly. "Which of us are you trying to convince? Me . . . or you?"

Anna dropped her eyes almost sulkily. "Everything I'm saying is true," she said, in a low voice. "You know it is."

"Everything you say is true," agreed Manora. "Only we talk of nothing that really matters." Anna looked up quickly, and the tenderness in Manora's face startled her. "My child, there is only one question. Do you love Mario?"

"Oh, Manora, it's not so simple as that—"

"You little fool, it *is!*"

"Well then, I don't know," Anna cried passionately.

"You don't *know!*" Manora caught her suddenly by her arms, and jerked her around, with the only touch of harshness Anna had ever seen in her. "Well then, I'll tell you. Do you feel when he comes in that the world grows brighter, and when he goes, that he takes the sunlight with him? Do the days seem meaningless if you cannot talk with him, and the nights unbearable if you cannot sleep with him?"

Anna shrank before the blue flame in Manora's eyes and wordlessly shook her head.

"If he beat you would you crawl back to him? And if you found him with another woman would you choke her . . . and yet forgive him? Is *that* how you feel?"

"No . . . no!" Anna was shaking now. She tried to twist herself away from Manora's grasp, because she knew what was coming next.

"Is there anyone who makes you feel like that?"

"Manora—"

"Is there?"

"Yes!"

"Who?"

Anna suddenly went slack in Manora's hands. "Oh, Tony, Tony, Tony," she sobbed despairingly.

Manora dropped her back against the pillows.

"You have your answer," she said quietly.

The next moment, full of remorse and affection, she was hanging over Anna.

"Darling, I have been too brutal with you. But one had to say this thing to you. You torture yourself with uncertainty. Always you would have wondered if you had been wrong to say 'no' to Mario."

"I shall never wonder now," whispered Anna.

"No, no." Manora kissed her and held her close.

"Manora."

"Yes."

"Do you think many people feel as you said when they love someone?"

"I think not. For me, I could not go with a man for less," Manora said simply. "And I think with you is the same."

Anna nodded slowly.

"I suppose that's the way you love Schreiner?" she said diffidently.

"Oh yes." Manora spoke again with that rather touching simplicity.

"Only with you it's different, because . . . he loves you in just the same way." Anna sounded very wistful again.

"Yes. I am very fortunate," Manora said gently.

Anna sighed a little. "Sometimes I feel that loving Tony has brought me nothing but pain."

"Would you rather you had never met him?" asked Manora quietly.

Anna was silent. She thought back over those disastrous months since Tony had come out of that snow-storm into her life. Scene after scene of mounting bewilderment and misunderstanding and misery.

Yet there were other scenes too. Tony smiling at her with pride because she looked beautiful and had sung divinely that first evening Frayne came; Tony carrying her from the room where she had cried because she was alone, Tony as her lover in the dear, untidy room that had known him as a little boy; Tony making love to her in the orchard; Tony holding her in his arms as he sat with her by the fire that first evening; Tony laughing with boyish pleasure and embarrassment when she said he looked like a prince.

And suddenly, that brought her back with a quick, sweet pain to the present. . . . Tony that very evening, boyishly embarrassed once more as he tried to explain his impulse to come to Paris in case she should be a failure and alone.

"No," she said slowly. "Whatever the cost, I wouldn't have missed knowing and loving Tony."

Manora laughed softly.

"Is always the way. We wince at the price, but always we would pay again."

Anna smiled faintly. "I suppose that's true." And then, "Manora, did you have to pay heavily for loving Schreiner?"

"I do pay—still," Manora said quietly. "I pay every

time I hear someone say, "There goes Vanescu. She is Conrad Schreiner's mistress, you know." And, God knows, they say it often enough. To most people our love is just a common intrigue. A little amusing, a little shocking, and they wonder how long it will last."

"Manora dear," Anna clasped her arms around Manora, "do you want so much to be Schreiner's wife, then? I didn't think, somehow, that you felt like that."

"I would give my voice to be able to marry him," Manora said simply.

"Oh!" Anna was profoundly shaken and moved. "*He* wouldn't have you do that."

Manora smiled slightly and shook her head. "Oh no. He would not have me make any sacrifice. But he said once that he would give his right hand—and he meant his conducting—to be able to marry me."

"But, my dear, my dear," Anna stroked her arm gently, "you couldn't possibly love each other more if you were married ten times over."

"No, of course not."

"Then does it matter so very much what people say or think?"

"Not of itself, Anna. Only for what it implies."

"I don't see—" Anna began, but Manora interrupted her.

"Would you like that your love for Tony should be belittled and laughed at? That people should speak of it with a shrug, as something wrong and slightly disgusting? So many *little* things are sweet and significant when you are in love, Anna, but so easily they are crushed and spoiled."

Anna nodded understandingly. She knew all about that. She bit her lip with sympathy as Manora continued.

"Have you not noticed that he never kisses me in front of people? Is not natural to him not to, you know. He always did at first, until they hurt him enough to make him remember not to. If he had kissed me as my husband everyone would have said, 'Is so nice that Schreiner is always so devoted to his wife,' and thought no more about it. But, as things are, they smile and say behind their hands, 'Is funny how that *affaire* lasts. He has been keeping Vanescu for years, and look he is still so infatuated that he hasn't the decency to wait until they are alone before he starts kissing her.' "

"Oh, Manora," exclaimed Anna eagerly, "don't think of the people who say that sort of thing. They don't understand. They don't understand. What do they matter?"

"Not very much, I know," Manora said gently. "But always, always, they remind you that you only have what you hold in your hand today. You can build nothing much for the future together because you have no foundation on which to build."

"Do you really think that?" Anna said doubtfully.

"Why, of course. Marriage is the foundation on which two people start to build together. Sometimes they build terrible things," Manora admitted with a smile. "But, if so, is their own fault. For anything permanent and enduring you must start with marriage for your ground."

"Darling Manora," Anna spoke very affectionately, "did you and Schreiner want to build something permanent and enduring out of your beautiful love for each other?"

Manora nodded. She was silent for a moment, and then she said, "Have you ever seen Conrad with children?"

Anna shook her head.

"He is passionately fond of them, you know, and they always adore him," Manora said, without much expression on her face.

"Do they?" Anna was surprised in the first second; and then she thought it not at all surprising, after all. There was something in the great director's magnificent, imperious yet kindly personality that *would* appeal to children. "he never . . . had any of his own?" she asked hesitatingly.

"By his wife?" Manora laughed shortly. "Oh no. She was not that sort of a woman at all."

Anna tried to imagine Schreiner with any woman but Manora and failed completely.

"What sort was she, then?" she asked, with involuntary interest.

"Um?" Manora looked at Anna absently for a moment. "Oh, spoiled, possessive, utterly selfish. Small and very, very lovely. A typical Viennese to look at. She loved to play the director's wife in public and shirk playing the director's wife in private."

"You knew her? Or did Schreiner tell you this?" Anna asked.

Manora looked surprised. "*Conrad* tell me?" she exclaimed. "You cannot suppose that Conrad would say anything against a woman he had married."

"Oh, Manora—" She stopped.

"What?"

Anna smiled. "There's something so terribly nice about Schreiner. He's very . . . simple, really, isn't he?"

"Yes." Manora laughed a little. "I know how you mean. He is so magnificent and loves to play 'the great man,' and yet he is very like a child himself at times. Was for this he was so much at *her* mercy," she added somberly.

"Was she very unkind?"

"She was so ungenerous, Anna. He would give and give and give, and always she asked for more, and never once said thank you. He loves to be generous, but like a good child, he also loves to be thanked."

"I know." Anna smiled at this picture of the great Schreiner.

"I have seen him a hundred times wait so eagerly for just one word, and then at last go away very quiet and disappointed. He never learned. And he never saw how was, to her, the way of showing her power."

"Manora, how disgusting of her! And is that why she won't divorce him?"

Manora nodded. "Is very good to her that she can still say 'no' to such a great man as Conrad Schreiner; and she does not mean that I should ever give him what she would not give him."

"Oh, Manora dear! If you could have married Schreiner, you would willingly have risked your voice to have his children?"

"My voice?" Manora laughed rather sadly. "If you had to choose between a voice and a child who would look at you with the eyes of the man you love, what would you do?"

Anna thought of the applause that evening, and she thought of Tony. She turned suddenly and clung to Manora.

"I'd say, 'Take my voice, and leave me dumb if you like. Only let me keep my eyes, to see the two people I love so dearly.'"

"Poor child." Manora kissed her gently. "Perhaps one day things will be right for you."

"And for you too, my dear," Anna exclaimed.

Manora shrugged slightly. "For me, there is not so much time." She made a little face, as though she disliked very much what she was saying. "I am not so young now, Anna."

Anna flung her arms around Manora's neck and kissed her. "Don't say such things. I never saw anyone who was so ageless. You're like . . . like Helen, and people like that."

Manora laughed, but she returned Anna's kiss very earnestly.

Somewhere a clock struck three.

"Is so late?" Manora looked up, startled. "My child, you must sleep. Is very bad that you stay awake like this after a performance."

Anna lay down slowly.

"I couldn't have slept before. But I think I can now," she said.

Manora touched her hair gently. "Sleep well and dream of your Tony."

Anna smiled. "Manora, you are odd. Anyone else would tell me to forget him."

"But dreams hurt no one," Manora said.

"Not even when you wake?"

"One can always dream again the next night," Manora pointed out, with smiling philosophy.

Anna gave a sleepy little laugh like a comforted child.

"No wonder Schreiner loves you," she said, too sleepy to hear Manora's little exclamation, half pleasure, half pain.

And then she fell asleep and dreamed she was back in the orchard with Tony, and it was springtime again.

CHAPTER TEN

It was very late the next morning when Anna awoke. Manora and Schreiner were knocking on her door.

"Come in," Anna said sleepily, leaning up on her elbow.

They both promptly entered. Manora was dressed, but Schreiner was wearing his purple dressing gown, which always struck Anna as being amusingly imperial.

"What is it?" she asked.

"What is it?" repeated Schreiner. "The newspapers, of course."

"Oh yes, yes, of course." She sat right up. "Are the notices good? Let me see." She caught eagerly at the papers in Schreiner's hands, while Manora put a wrap around her, saying something about her being "a real singer now, and so she must not catch cold."

It gave Anna the oddest feeling to read lines of print that were actually about herself. It seemed as though it *must* be some other girl. But no. There was her name, over and over again. Not in large-type headings, certainly, but mentioned in every notice as a worthwhile artist—possibly a great star in the making—at any rate, someone to be reckoned with in the future.

She slowly put down the last of the newspapers. The notices had varied between cautious prophecy and fulsome praise. But the sum total was that she had "arrived."

"Well?" Manora smiled indulgently. "Is good, eh?"

"Yes," said Anna gravely. "It is good."

She was wondering a little if there was anything in the English newspapers, and, if so, whether Tony had seen it.

Schreiner took his cigar out of his mouth and regarded the tip contentedly.

"Sometimes even the critics are right," he observed, and, with a satisfied little nod to Anna, he went out of the room. Manora and Anna exchanged an amused little smile of appreciation before Manora followed him out.

Anna was up when, an hour later, Frayne came to say goodbye before leaving for England once more.

He came into their private sitting room where all three were discussing the criticisms once more. To all appearances he was as excited as they, as carefree and congratulatory.

No one, thought Anna, could possibly have known that, for him, this visit to Paris had been a bitter disappointment. He was just as kind and carelessly affectionate to her, just as teasing to Manora, just as matter-of-fact to Schreiner.

And she knew, gratefully, that it was all done intentionally. She was not to feel that things had changed or that the friendship they had both grown to value so much was in any danger.

Only, when he actually said goodbye, he did not kiss her. It was not specially noticeable . . . and yet she missed it. He and Manora exchanged their usual half-laughing, entirely unimportant kiss, but perhaps he could not quite bring himself to do the same with Anna, and so he had to leave it out altogether.

Instead he held her hand very warmly between both of his and said, "I shall always remember with happiness that I was able to come to Paris and hear you make you debut."

She smiled a little nervously. "I hope it was worth the journey, Mario."

"It was worth everything," he told her, with his smiling eyes on her face. "Please never think anything else."

And she felt most strangely comforted.

She remembered the overwhelming sensation she had had the evening before—that it would never be any good looking backward in her life. It was only in the future that perhaps one day she would find comfort.

And so, during all that strange and brilliant winter, Anna forced herself to look forward, ever forward.

She gave several more performances in Paris under Schreiner's direction, and each time she sang, the criticisms were a little more complimentary. In each one she seemed to take on added stature and significance as an artist.

And then, after Christmas had come and gone in an unbroken wave of work and excitement, she went with Schreiner and Manora to Vienna and then on to Italy.

It was a strange life, Anna thought. Always traveling, never calling any special place "home," and all the time there was work to fill every moment of the day. Her natural shyness lessened, and she gained an odd little popularity of her own among the people they met. But she knew she would never have Manora's easy manner with people. She instinctively withdrew a little from the eager courting of a star, which was beginning to be part of her daily life.

Schreiner said once that her "inscrutable pose" was excellent publicity, but Manora hushed him at once. She knew too well that Anna's calm hid a good deal of pain and bewilderment still, and above all, a restless longing that was never entirely absent.

Ironically, all this gave pathos and poignancy to her singing and acting. "So good for her art," thought Manora, with a sigh. "So bad for her."

And she did not fail to notice that never once in all that time did Anna so much as glance at an English newspaper.

She scarcely even spoke her own language much, because, as Schreiner said, other languages were likely to serve her better in her career. In any case, she seemed curiously anxious to sever every connection with her old life.

It was a little difficult for her to judge for herself the full extent of her success. She did what Schreiner told her, accepting or rejecting engagements on his advice; she read the critiques of her performances with an odd feeling of pleased detachment, and she knew that, for the first time in her life, she was making a very great deal of money.

"Does it please you to find that you were quite right about your prophecies for my future?" she once asked Schreiner.

He looked a little surprised and answered, "Yes, it pleases me, of course. But, in any case, I knew that I was right."

Whereat Anna laughed.

She was strangely moved when she found that their engagements took them to Florence in the late spring. She could not forget that it was here that one of the strangest chapters of Mario's life had been written. And, illogically, she had the feeling that something important in her own life, too, might happen here.

The flicker of the sunlight on the pink and white houses; the deep, indescribably sweet notes of the bells in the Campanile, the rushing round of the Arno as it swept under the arches of the Ponte Vecchio—all seemed to have some message for her. She could never quite catch what it was. Only she knew that it excited her and gave her an odd little feeling of hope.

Not that she looked for anything concrete, like letters from England. Indeed, since those terrible days when she had waited and waited in such an agonizing alternation of hope and disappointment, she never appeared to take much interest in letters at all. Nor did she expect to see Tony suddenly present himself before her as he had on that incredible occasion in Paris.

It was just that the warm, smiling carelessness of life under blue Italian skies seemed to suggest a loosening of every bond—even those around her heart.

Sometimes Tony felt oddly near—not in actual face, but in spirit. As though, if she could have talked to him then, they would have understood each other and been happy.

She used to pretend that he was probably thinking of her at these times. But the days slipped past, and Anna began to tell herself that, after all, these were all just silly fancies of hers. What *could* happen here in Florence—or anywhere else in the world—beyond the usual success that seemed to follow her so easily now and yet mean so little to her?

On their last morning, she stood at the window of her room, looking out across the Arno, trying to make herself believe yet again that, if one *had* to forget, one could manage to do so, somehow.

All the principal luggage was packed once more for the next stage in this never-ending move from place to place. Tonight they were to leave Florence for a short holiday in the Dolomites before fresh engagements claimed them.

Anna would really rather have stayed here, but there was no reasonable excuse for doing so; so, tonight she too would leave this heavenly spot where she had foolishly supposed something important might happen.

She turned away from the window at the slight knock at the door. Manora's golden head was thrust round it.

"You come with me for a last drive out to the Piazza Michelangelo?" Manora said. "Conrad is busy and cannot come. Besides, he says it is too hot."

"Yes, I'd like to come."

Anna reached for a big, shady hat. She never minded the heat of the sun.

As they came out of the room Schreiner called Manora from across the landing.

"Wait for me in the lounge," Manora said, "I will be only five minutes."

It was cool and rather dim in the lounge, for the blinds had already been partially drawn against the hot morning sunlight.

Anna stood by a table, idly fingering the newspapers that lay there. And then, on a sudden impulse, she picked up the only English paper. It was really rather ridiculous of her, she thought, refusing to take any interest in her own country simply because of what had happened. Like shutting up a room in a house because someone dear had died there.

Her eyes skimmed the headlines, without taking in very much. Extraordinary how soon one lost touch. It made her feel ashamed of the way she had shut herself away. After all, it was not as though—

Suddenly her attention was riveted. The one name in the world that really mattered stood out from the print as though in scarlet letters—Hamilton Roone!

Anna groped for a chair, her knees strangely weak and

insecure all at once, her eyes unable to leave the printed lines that said such ridiculous and incredible things.

". . . trial of Hamilton Roone . . . partner in the firm of Roone & Montagu . . . son of Mr. Everard Roone, M.P. . . . next Thursday . . . charge of embezzlement . . . delay in bringing the case before the court owing to the considerable investigations that had to be made. . . ."

Anna was taking in only about one word in six, but it was sufficient. And then, the final paragraph. "It will be remembered that it was the suicide of Montagu, the senior partner, that drew attention to the serious irregularities in the firm's financial dealings. The prosecution is expected to attach some considerable importance to the fact that on December 4, immediately after being informed of his partner's suicide, Mr. Roone flew to Paris. . . ."

Mr. Roone flew to Paris.

"Ready? I am sorry to have been so long." It was Manora speaking from the doorway.

Anna raised her head. She looked a little dazed and as though she didn't see Manora very clearly.

"Do you remember," she said a little huskily, "the date of the night I first sang in Paris?"

"The date?" Manora wrinkled her forehead. "No, I have forgotten."

"Well, think, Manora, think! We *must* remember!" Anna stood up, crushing the newspaper together in her hands.

"What is it, my dear?" Manora came forward in quick concern.

"Nothing." Anna brushed her hand across her eyes. "Only, do remember. I don't seem able to think at all."

"Wait. I can tell you exactly." Manora was triumphant. "Was just five days before Conrad's birthday."

"Was it?" Anna still looked a little bewildered. "Whatever made you remember that?"

"Because he was 45 and he say to me that it is a nice present to find a new singer just before his fortieth birthday," Manora smiled indulgently. "And I think, 'He takes off one year for each day.' " She was perfectly serious now as she counted rapidly on her fingers; and Anna watched her with wide, anxious eyes.

"The fourth," announced Manora. "Was the night of the fourth of December. Why?"

"Oh!" Anna gave a funny little cry and ran to the door.

"Bring me a timetable quickly," she called to a passing servant. "I'm leaving for London today."

"Anna!" Manora stared at her in bewilderment. "Are you crazy?"

"No." Anna caught both Manora's hands. "Listen. It's about my husband." It seemed so natural suddenly to be calling him that. So dear and natural. "He's in terrible trouble. They think he has stolen money or something. Of course he hasn't, but I must go to him. You see, don't you, that I must go?"

"But, Anna—"

"It isn't any good," Anna broke in fiercely. "There aren't any arguments that matter, Manora. I love him and he just may need me a little. I *must* go. If Schreiner were in trouble and you were on the other side of the world even, you would go to him, wouldn't you? *Wouldn't* you?"

Manora nodded.

"Well, this is the same. Nothing on earth would keep me here. He came to me in Paris that time because he thought I might need him. He thought I might be a failure—" She stopped, biting her lip, as she remembered Tony, awkward, boyishly embarrassed, trying to explain his impulse. Such an utterly crazy impulse.

"I will speak to Conrad. I think perhaps I make him understand."

Darling Manora, who always understood!

"Yes, make him understand. Please, Manora." Anna gripped her hands together in nervous agitation. "He won't mind if you tell him. He'll do anything in the world for you."

"Most things," amended Manora mechanically. "But when will you come back? They expect that you sing in Monte Carlo, remember, in two weeks."

"Yes." Anna was only half-listening, for the servant had brought the timetable, and she was quickly flicking over the pages. "Monte Carlo? Yes, I will if I can. Otherwise they must find another singer."

Manora looked as though she were going to say something else. But suddenly changing her mind, she turned and went out of the room, only pausing at the door to say, "I explain to Conrad. You do not need to worry."

Anna never knew quite what arguments Manora used, but they must have had an effect, for by the time she had looked up planes and packed the last of her baggage, Schreiner had somehow been persuaded to view her immediate departure quite calmly.

"The husband, I hope, will not need you for long," he remarked as his only form of protest.

"Don't say that." Anna's eyes were suddenly bright with tears. "I wish he could need me for always."

Schreiner didn't answer that, but he, as well as Manora, came to the airport to see her off.

For a moment Anna clung to Manora, keenly aware of how dear she had grown. She wished she could have framed some sort of thanks to them for all they had done, but the words couldn't get past the lump in her throat.

All at once, it came to her that there was something they had always longed to have put into words—something that a scornful, smiling, curious world would never say.

She stretched out one hand to Schreiner and still held tightly to Manora with the other.

"I can't say the things I ought to say," she told them, "because I shall weep if I try. But I want you to know this: you have rebuilt everything for me, you two—my confidence and my faith and the power to go on living. It isn't only that you have been so kind. It's the wonderful experience of living near anything so touchingly beautiful and so *good* as your love for each other. It's the kind of simple revelation that makes one believe in God."

It was the longest speech she had ever made to them, and neither of them replied. Then she kissed them both, as they stood there wordless, and walked to the plane.

Four hours later Anna reached London. As she rode in the taxi from Heathrow Airport, she thought a little wonderingly of that first time she had come into London, and how much she had changed since then.

The Anna of a year ago seemed like another person—timid, unsure and shrinkingly resentful. Well, she was still timid, still desperately unsure of herself at times, but she knew now how to hide all that. In the careless, uncritical company of Schreiner and Manora she had learned, quite painlessly, not how to suppress her feelings, but how to shelter them from critical, unfriendly eyes.

And in that knowledge lay a certain measure of defense. Never again would she have to face the world unarmed, unknowing, at the mercy of people like Katherine. She felt overwhelmingly sorry for the poor, silly little creature who had been herself; now she could even think of Katherine without those familiar tremors of fear . . . or nearly so.

She went straight to Eaton Square, because that seemed to be the only place where she would be likely to get definite news. Tony's office was probably closed. She had only the vaguest idea of what happened in these cases. For all she knew, he might be in prison, although Manora—who always seemed to know at least a little about everything—had said that he was almost sure to have been allowed bail.

Anna shuddered a little. Used in connection with the Tony she knew, the expression was so terribly sordid and incongruous.

She paid off the taxi, and went up the short flight of well-remembered steps. It didn't seem so long now since she had been here, and her breath was beginning to come uncomfortably fast.

An unfamiliar servant opened the door for her. Somehow that made things easier.

"Can I see Mr. Roone, please?" she said. "Mr. Hamilton Roone, I mean."

She thought the servant looked very slightly put out. But perhaps that was just her imagination. In any case, the look was gone in a moment.

"I'm sorry, madam," he said quite civilly. "Mr. Roone is not here."

"You mean he's not in?"

Another almost imperceptible pause.

"He is not living here just now, madam. Would you like to speak to Miss Roone, Miss Katherine Roone? She is in."

Katherine! She had thought she was no longer afraid of Katherine. She knew now, from the sickening lurch of her heart, that she was. But this was her only way of finding Tony.

She hesitated only a second. "Yes, please, I would like to see Miss Roone."

She entered the big paneled hall—the hall where Mario had kissed her that memorable night. It helped a little to think about Mario just now.

"Who shall I say it is, madam?"

"Tell her it's Mrs. Roone," Anna said quietly. "Mrs. Hamilton Roone."

The servant went away into the library, but returned almost immediately with the request that she come in.

When Anna entered the room, Katherine was standing by the fire, calm, unsmiling and completely unwelcoming.

"Well, Anna," she said, without even suggesting that they sit down, "what do you want?"

"I want to see Tony." Anna was surprised that her newly acquired poise crumpled at once, and that she sounded truculent and scared.

"I'm afraid I can't help you," Katherine said coldly.

"But where *is* he? The servant said he wasn't here. You don't mean he is in . . , prison?"

"No." Katherine's mouth grew a little thinner. "I believe he was allowed bail."

"You believe he was? What do you mean? Don't you know where he is?"

"No."

"But. . . ." Anna's voice failed for a moment in her

dismay. Then she found it again. "Won't you please explain? I'm sorry to seem so stupid, but I don't understand."

Katherine turned away with a little gesture of impatience.

"I suppose you heard how he'd been embezzling, using his clients' money."

And then all Anna's nervousness went up in a blaze of anger. She leaned forward, catching Katherine by the arm and whirling her around.

"Do you mean—you *can't* mean—that you believe he did it!"

Angrily Katherine tried to shake her arm free.

"Unfortunately the evidence is overwhelming," she said shortly. "The shock and the disgrace made my father ill. There really wasn't anything for Hamilton to do but leave the house. It was bad enough having the newspapers drag our name through the mud, without having him here as a perpetual reminder."

Pale and aghast, Anna fell away from her.

"You contemptible beast!" she said slowly. And she thought quite dispassionately, "I'm glad I slapped her face that time. I know it was vulgar. I only wish I'd hit harder."

Katherine colored very faintly. "I don't think you help matters by that sort of abuse."

It was true, of course. Anna made a great effort to control herself again.

"But you're condemning him even before the court does!"

"What has that to do with it?" Katherine's voice was sharp with impatience. "The court proceedings are only a formality. We *know*. He's just a common swindler. Do you think I like having to say that about my own brother?"

Anna stared at her and said quietly, "You do know, don't you, that Tony would have stood by you even if you'd committed murder?"

Katherine shrugged. "But I'm never likely to need such championship," she pointed out dryly.

"Katherine, don't you love Tony?" Anna was speaking quite gently, and neither of them realized the curious fact that it was now she who pitied Katherine for her ignorance.

"Of course I love him . . . or I did. He's my brother." Katherine spoke as though she didn't want to answer, but could not quite help it. "But when something like this happens it spoils everything that has gone before. You can't realize, I expect, how proud we were of Tony." The words came out with difficulty. "And now he is nothing but a disgrace to us. He just isn't what we always thought him. He's someone else. But I don't expect you understand."

"Yes, I think I do," Anna said slowly. And, as she listened to the quiet bitterness of Katherine's short sentences, she did understand.

Tony had not been a real person to his family at all—someone to be loved or hated or ignored. He had just been a wonderful asset. Something that counted when they reckoned up what a marvelous family they were. His looks and his charm and his popularity had always added to their pleasant sense of superiority. Now, his need, his unhappiness and his possible disgrace weighed down the other side of the balance.

All Katherine's little bright world of pride and pretensions was broken up and, because appearances were all that had ever mattered to her, she had nothing left. For appearances you were miserably dependent on other people, and if they failed you that was the end.

"I'm sorry, Katherine," Anna said. In a way, it was true. "I'm sorry you should feel so wretched and bitter about things. You're quite right—I can't feel that way myself. It doesn't really matter to me whether Tony is a swindler or a murderer, or a coward or a hero. He's simply the man I love. And I must go to him, just in case he needs me."

Katherine was quite herself again by now. She said contemptuously, "I would scarcely think he would need you to complicate things for him. But if you insist on going, that is your own affair. His solicitors can tell you where to find him. They are Bury & Winterton, and you'll find their address in the telephone book."

"Thank you," Anna said. "And goodbye, Katherine."

She went out of the room and out of the house, closing the heavy front door quietly behind her as she had that other time. And as she did so she thought, "And it was because I thought these people loved and understood Tony that I deliberately broke my heart into little pieces."

CHAPTER ELEVEN

The solicitors' office was not difficult to find. An incredibly quiet place in an incredibly quiet square. The sound of a typewriter from an open window opposite seemed like the crackle of distant musketry in the overwhelming stillness—a fitting background to the slow, measured "booming" of Mr. Bury's bass baritone in the room itself.

She explained that all she wanted was Tony's address. She had no intention of actually discussing the case at the moment.

Mr. Bury's eyebrows rose, and she gathered that neither had he any such intention—certainly not before she had furnished something like documentary evidence of her identity. He accepted her statement that she was Tony's wife with courtesy but as though he reserved final judgment until he had received additional proof.

However, apparently the evidence was slightly in her favor, because he eventually gave her the address of the little private hotel in Kensington where Tony was living.

Outside in the taxi once more, driving westward, she leaned forward to stare out of the window; she did not see much of the passing streets.

She knew she was sitting unnecessarily still and rigid, but she had an idea that if she relaxed at all she would find herself trembling violently.

Not that she was afraid. Even the odd fluttering of her heart was not fear. It was just that she was going to Tony at last. Going to him, not because she needed him or had any plea to make, but because *he* was in need, and she could possibly help him.

Fifteen minutes more. Ten minutes. Five minutes more and she would be with him. . . .

Suddenly her breath caught in her throat. The outlines of the passing people wavered and became blurred. She closed her eyes tightly to keep back a quick rush of tears.

She mustn't cry now, for she was going to see Tony.

He was in, it appeared, when she inquired for him. She was Mrs. Roone? Would she go straight up? It was the door directly in front of her on the first floor.

She went up.

Tony said "Come in" the moment she knocked, but she hesitated a moment in a sort of panic, so that he called again, impatiently, "Come in."

She turned the handle and went in, closing the door behind her.

"Yes?" Tony said absently, without looking up from the desk by the window.

She didn't know what to say; at the silence, he turned sharply to look at her.

"Anna!"

She was beside him in a second, even before he could rise from his chair. She saw then how changed he was. The smile was gone from his gray eyes, and his mouth was grim instead of boyish.

"Why, Tony dear," she said, and very gently she put her hands around his face.

"Don't do that." He quickly put up his own hands and took hers away, but he kissed first one palm and then the other before he let her go.

"Don't you like me to touch you?"

He gave an odd little laugh at that. "Yes. But it's just—" He broke off, then said sharply, "Why have you come, Anna . . . now?" She didn't know that the bitterness in his voice meant, "Now that I can't be of any use to anyone."

"I couldn't come before, because I didn't know. I only saw about it in a paper yesterday in Florence. I came at once," she said earnestly.

He gave her a curious look. "You came from Florence? Why?"

"Well, I thought . . . I thought . . . ."

"Don't you realize that I have to appear before the

court tomorrow on a charge of swindling?" His voice was harsh.

"Y-yes."

"Well?"

"Well what?"

"You don't ask me if I'm guilty," he said dryly.

"But . . . but I don't imagine for a moment that you are," Anna said. "Anyway, it doesn't matter."

"It . . . doesn't *matter!*" Tony's voice was slightly hoarse. And then suddenly he was clinging to her like a little boy, his face hidden against her. "Oh, you darling little fool! You silly little angel!" She could just hear the smothered words.

"Tony dear. Tony dear." She was stroking his thick, rather tumbled hair and trying quite unsuccessfully to make him look up at her. Then she said ridiculously, "It's all right, I'm here."

He laughed a little unsteadily at that and sat up, pushing back his hair. "I'm sorry to make such a fool of myself, only. . . ."

"Yes, I know," Anna said. "Please, Tony, don't try to explain it away. It's very precious."

He glanced at her curiously, but didn't make any comment. Finally he asked, "Don't you really mind whether I did it or not?"

Anna smiled. "It isn't as important as lots of other things—at least, not so far as I am concerned."

"Isn't it?" He smiled too. "Well, I didn't do it."

"Then I'm glad," Anna said simply.

He pressed the back of her hand against his cheek. "I wish I could tell you what it's like to have you say these dear, unreasonable things, when even my own people—" He broke off and bit his lip.

"Yes, I know about them."

"You *know?* How did you know?"

"I've just seen Katherine," Anna said quietly.

"Oh, but, my dear—" he looked startled "—you must have hated that."

"Yes, I did." Anna looked thoughtful. "But it was the only way of finding out about you."

"And was that so terribly important?"

She nodded. "Just as important as the time you came to Paris to see me even though you knew everyone would think you were running away from the police."

"Oh!" Tony looked embarrassed. "Do you know everything, Anna? There doesn't seem to be much left to hide."

"Nearly everything," Anna said, with a little smile. "I suppose the reason you had to go back that night—the reason you wouldn't come on to the supper-party with us—was that you simply dared not stay away from England any longer."

"Partly that, Anna. Partly. . . ."

"Yes?"

He smiled slightly in his turn. "If you could realize how you looked that night—so lovely and radiant and triumphant. And I was on the edge of disgrace and ruin. The two didn't go well together, you know," he added grimly.

"And if you could realize how I *felt* that night," began Anna impulsively. Then she stopped and said, "Well, never mind. It doesn't matter now. But I want you to come with me to your lawyer or counsel or whoever it is."

"Why?" Tony's voice was suddenly sharp.

"They may need my evidence to prove why you were out of England that night."

"Oh no, my dear." Tony was suddenly on his feet, very firm, very determined. "I will not have you mixed up in this wretched business."

"But I am in it, Tony. I'm your wife. And that evidence may be important. Please come with me. I'm a little afraid of going alone."

Tony stopped in front of her. "Do you think I'm going to let you be dragged into this as a witness?"

"I don't think you have much choice," she said. Her lashes lowered in that determined finality he had so often misread as sullenness. "I would rather you came with me. But if you won't, then I shall go alone."

So he came without further protest—silent, puzzled, almost a little resentful.

She was surprised that neither Mr. Bury nor Tony's counsel, Sir Derek Venables, appeared to attach overwhelming importance to her explanation of Tony's actions on that unfortunate day.

She gathered that they both thought Tony ridiculous not to have explained long ago, instead of firmly insisting that it had been a business trip. She also noticed that they entirely ignored his growing restiveness at the idea of her appearing as a witness.

"Is it absolutely necessary for my wife to be dragged into this?" he asked impatiently.

Sir Derek looked surprised and said, "My dear Roone, it may be of vital importance or of no importance at all. It depends on how much significance the prosecution choose to attach to your sudden departure to Paris. They will, of course, press the line that you lost your nerve and fled abroad, but that on reflection you considered it best to face things out. In any case, it would be absurd to ignore Mrs. Roone's evidence."

"I don't mind in the least, Tony," she said earnestly. "I'm used to appearing in public now, you know."

But he refused to answer her smile.

Afterward he went with her to collect her baggage from the airways terminus where she had left it.

He didn't talk much, and it seemed very odd to have Tony sitting beside her so unsmiling and silent.

She made one or two rather timid attempts to start a conversation, but he didn't help her much. Presently she too lapsed into silence.

Then suddenly he appeared to collect himself, and with something of an effort, he said, "By the way, where are you staying while you're in London? I suppose your operatic crowd are still abroad?"

"Your operatic crowd" didn't sound particularly friendly, and Anna began to feel nervous and chilled.

"I thought perhaps—" she hesitated, then went on "—perhaps I might stay at the place where you are?"

"I don't think we could manage that," Tony said very blankly, "There isn't a vacant room there."

She was silent. And then, because she must find courage to make the first advances, she gripped her hands together and said desperately, "Couldn't I stay with—"

"No, you couldn't," he interrupted so brutally that she winced. And he didn't even attempt to apologize, although he must have seen how much he had hurt her.

It wasn't going to be easy, she saw. She mustn't suppose that, because his need had suddenly given her a place in his life again, all her difficulties were at an end. Indeed, it might have a very different result.

For a moment she felt terribly afraid.

Until now she had thought of Tony's danger only as something that must inevitably draw them together. Now she realized that, in his hurt pride, his bewildered humiliation at what had befallen him, he was more likely to shrink farther away from anyone who had known him only in the days when he had been successful and happy.

Her courage almost failed her in the face of this fresh difficulty. She remembered what Mario had said all those months ago, "When one loves the almost unattainable, one must work hard and be very patient."

She picked up the broken bits of her determination and hope once more. She managed to look as though Tony's rebuff had not shaken her at all, and said quite steadily that perhaps it was better that she stayed at one of the big hotels, so that she could be right in town.

Tony nodded indifferently, and when her luggage had been collected he drove her to the kind of place that would have terrified the old Anna, but where the new Anna was entirely at home.

Keeping her voice as steady as she could, she asked him to stay and have dinner with her, but he said that he was sorry, he had to go back and see Mr. Bury.

"Perhaps you could come back here again afterward?" she said with difficulty. "I could easily wait. I'm not at all hungry."

"I might be quite late," he began. "There are several things—"

"It doesn't matter," Anna spoke eagerly. "I'd rather wait if you could come. It's lonely by myself."

"Very well," Tony said, but she couldn't tell from his expression as he left her whether he was pleased or irritated.

It was nearly half-past eight before the telephone message came through that he was waiting for her downstairs again, and she had had time to form a dozen new fears. But she resolutely dismissed them all from her mind. Tony needed someone with courage and calmness just now, not someone who was a prey to doubts.

She saw him the moment she came into the lounge. He was standing beside a table, half-turned away from her, idly fingering the pages of a newspaper. He looked quiet and grave and just a little careworn. She longed to go to him in front of everyone and put her arms around him.

Just then he saw her; at the sudden smile of relief and pleasure that came over his face Anna felt her heart turn over.

He greeted her much more naturally, much more like his old self. And quite unselfconsciously he said, "I think you're more beautiful than ever, Anna."

She laughed and said, "Thank you, Tony. How nice of you. But I think that perhaps food would be even better than compliments just now. I'm starving. Aren't you?"

She wasn't really hungry, but she had an idea that he hadn't taken much interest in his meals lately, and perhaps if she pretended to be very hungry he might contrive to eat a good dinner.

Anyway, he smiled and said, rather as though he hadn't realized it before, "Yes, I think perhaps I am."

He was very earnest about selecting just what she wanted and ended by ordering an excellent dinner himself.

They were very leisurely about their meal, and sat late over their coffee. He made her do most of the talking and seemed eagerly interested in all that she had been doing.

Once she mentioned Mario Frayne; staring at the tablecloth, he said, "I'm sorry for the things I thought about you and Frayne. They weren't true, were they?"

"No, they weren't true. But how did you know? I meant you to think they were."

"Yes, I know that, too," he said curtly. "Did you know it was Frayne who put up bail for me so that I wouldn't go to prison?"

"Mario!" Anna's eyes were suddenly bright. "How like him."

"Yes," Tony said slowly, "I suppose it is like him. I'm beginning to find that out. Of course, I told him to go to hell when he first offered because I thought—"

"Yes, I know what you thought."

"But he *made* me listen. Made me understand just how things had been, and that there was no reason why I should refuse to let him stand by me as a . . . friend." The word came out slowly, but it was spoken sincerely.

"I'm glad it was like that," Anna said.

Tony smiled a little grimly. "It's strange that it takes a disaster like this to show you who your real friends are and who the shams are. You know, Anna, I'd have thought I could put my finger on half a dozen fellows who would have stood by me, apart from my family." For a moment his face clouded over. "But I was wrong about all of them. Do you remember I told you once that I didn't know much about human nature? Well, it looks as though I was right."

"Tony, did your father refuse to—"

"Yes. Don't let's talk about it," Tony said abruptly. "I'm past blaming them now. They're honestly convinced that I'm guilty. And for them, that's the end."

She was silent for a moment, and then a thought struck her. "Tony, did Mario know almost from the beginning about this? He *must* have."

"Yes, of course. As soon as he returned from Paris. It was in all the papers."

"Then why didn't he write and tell me?" She flushed with unusual anger. "He must have known that I would want to be told."

"I wouldn't let him, of course." Tony's voice was curt.

"Oh, Tony, why?" she said in dismay at his lack of understanding.

"What? With you at the beginning of a dazzling career and me on the threshold of prison? You must think I'm a cad."

"Oh, won't you understand?" she cried in desperation.

But he stopped her almost peremptorily. "Yes, my dear, I do. I understand a lot better than you, I see. Don't let's say anything more. You might say some things you'll regret afterward. Anyway," he stood up abruptly, "I must go now. You'd better go to bed early. You've had a tiring day, and tomorrow may be a bit of a strain."

"Very well," she said obediently. It was no good trying to make him see reason just now. She must wait until the anxiety that was wearing his nerves thin had been removed.

"I won't come here to fetch you tomorrow," he said, not meeting her eyes. "You had better go straight to Bury's office; he will look after you."

"Why?"

"Well, it's not very nice coming with me." He stammered a little. "Sometimes there are people from the press—cameras and that sort of thing. And, with your career to think about, I dare say it's better not to be seen with me, in case . . . in case things don't go well."

"I want to be seen with you, Tony," she said quietly. "The only thing that would make me ashamed would be for you to be seen without me when you were in such trouble."

He didn't say anything. He only looked at her, then dropped his eyes and stared at the ground, profoundly moved.

"All right," he said unsteadily at last.

She took his hand and patted it—kindly, calmly, as a much older person might have done.

"Try not to worry, Tony. I *know* it's going to be all right tomorrow. You'll go straight home to bed now, won't you? And, sleep well."

"I can't sleep," he said, in a very low voice. "I haven't been able to sleep much for weeks. That's why I'm so vile-tempered and jumpy."

"Oh, you poor boy!" Her eyes darkened with dismay.

"How awful. Do you mean you have just been lying awake night after night, worrying?"

He frowned.

"Something like that. At least, I don't *lie* awake. I usually take the car and go driving. It seems easier to get away from things if I can just drive like mad." Unexpectedly he smiled at her—a faint suggestion of his old, boyish grin. "I believe I told you once that I was a bit of a speed fiend at heart. Well, it's true. There's something almost soothing in it for me."

Sudden fear clutched at Anna's heart. The thought of Tony speeding in his black racer had always had the power to rouse her almost superstitious terror. Now, the idea of him driving alone through the night—rash and uncaring in his misery—seemed to be fraught with nameless terror.

"Tony! You aren't going to do that tonight, are you?"

He didn't meet her eyes. "I might."

"Please. Promise me you won't. Just this once."

He made an impatient little movement. "Anna, you don't understand."

That wasn't true, she thought. She did understand, only she was afraid for him.

"You mean you can't face going home alone and doing nothing?"

He nodded abruptly.

"Then I'll come with you."

It came out almost defiantly. The next second she longed to recall it.

His eyebrows shot up. He took her lightly by her chin and turned her face toward him, not very gently.

"You'll come with me?" he said slowly and deliberately. "Where? In the car?"

That wasn't what she had meant, of course, and he knew it wasn't. He was refusing her impulsive advances again. Not quite so brutally, perhaps, but quite as firmly. Giving her a chance to withdraw with some remnants of pride left.

"Y-yes," she stammered. "In the car, of course."

"It wouldn't do, Anna." He laughed slightly, but without much amusement. "You'd be terrified. You always hated it when I went fast."

"I wouldn't mind. I wouldn't really." She spoke with almost breathless eagerness, but she had to shut her eyes for a second to keep back the tears.

The next moment she felt his hand close on hers in a grip that made her fingers crack.

"Would you really come?" His voice was very low and a little rough.

"Of course, if you want me to." She pressed her lips together to keep them from trembling.

"And you won't be frightened?"

"I expect I will be," she said honestly. "But I'd be much more afraid if you went alone."

He didn't answer that. He just said, "I'll wait here then while you get a warm coat."

When she returned, a mink coat flung on over her brown dress, he gave her an odd little look.

In that second she remembered him saying, "If you could realize how you looked that night—so lovely and radiant and triumphant."

She wished frantically then that she had put on anything else—the plainest thing she had—rather than again give him the impression that success had carried her so far away from him.

She couldn't possibly explain that she had flung on the mink coat quite unthinkingly, just because it was the warmest thing she had with her. It was the very fact that it meant so little to her that had made her put it on without a second thought.

As she went out with him to the car she longed to say, "Tony, don't think about this wretched coat. I like it, of course, and I was thrilled when I was able to buy it, but darling, I'd give it away now, this very minute, if only you'd smile instead of looking so remote and serious."

But of course, she couldn't say that, and if she had he would probably have pretended to be surprised, and have said he hadn't thought twice about the thing, anyway.

And so she had to let him go on looking remote and

serious. And because that made her feel terribly serious too, she just sat quietly beside him in the car.

She had half hoped that he would go fairly slowly after all, even though she had assured him that she wouldn't mind. But one or two surreptitious glances of terror at the speedometer assured her that her presence was not making much difference.

For an hour they drove in almost complete silence. Then he said abruptly, "Feeling frightened?"

"No. Oh no." Anna swallowed slightly, but the lie came out gallantly.

Tony drew the car up at the side of the road.

"I'm sorry, Anna," he said, with a contrite, unhappy little laugh. "You're horribly scared, I know."

She didn't say anything.

"And anyway, you didn't mean to let yourself in for this, did you?"

"I said I was quite willing to come," she began.

"Yes. But you didn't mean this. You meant you were willing to come home and sleep with me."

Anna was dumb before the crude truth of that. Then she nodded slowly without looking at him.

"You know you're being a little fool, don't you?" he said quietly. "And that I'm a perfect cad to even let us discuss it."

"No." Anna looked away from him still. "It's simply that you're wretched and afraid to be alone tonight, just as I was afraid to be alone that first night in Eaton Square. I do understand. You just want someone *there*. It's the sort of feeling that makes men go off the rails. Only I happen to be your wife, so it's all right."

"Good God!" said Tony.

Then without another word, he backed the car, turned it, and drove back to London.

But this time he drove more slowly, so that even Anna could not be afraid.

CHAPTER TWELVE

She sat very still beside him, wondering from time to time if she ought to speak.

But what was there to say? She couldn't tell what he had meant by that one exclamation, and she couldn't imagine what he intended to do . . . if anything.

At last, as they were driving through the quiet streets of the inner suburbs once more, he said, "Shall I drive to your place, or mine?"

She hesitated only a second, then said very gently and firmly, "To your place, please, Tony."

So they drove to the street in Kensington where Tony had been living. He put the car away in a garage at the end of the quiet road, and as they walked the few yards to the house, his hand was gripped tightly around her arm.

The sort of angry excitement that had possessed him before seemed to have gone; he looked terribly weary and dispirited as they came into his room.

She stood there for a moment, just inside the doorway, looking around and feeling strangely out of place.

Frowning, Tony glanced at her.

"Well?" he said. "It's rather a ridiculous situation, isn't it?"

"Oh no," she replied quite calmly. "I don't think it's a ridiculous situation at all. But you're terribly tired, and to tell the truth, so am I. We'd better go straight to bed, don't you think?"

He looked as though he were going to say "Good God!" again. But he didn't, after all. "I suppose you'll have to borrow a pair of my pajamas, though they'll be miles too big for you."

"I'll sleep in my slip," she said seriously. And somehow she looked so like a good, earnest child trying to make a helpful suggestion that he laughed.

She smiled too, then, and the tension immediately relaxed.

"All right," he said. "Here you are." He went over and collected some things together. "Here are towels and some soap. And you'd better borrow my sponge. You'll find one of the bathrooms at the end of the passage there."

"Thank you, Tony."

She knew he watched her curiously, particularly when she took off her mink coat and hung it carelessly over the back of a chair.

He didn't say anything as she left the room, but later, when she returned, ready for bed, her coat had been put carefully on a hanger, which now hung from a peg on the back of the door.

She smiled a little, very tenderly.

Tony wasn't there, and as she stood combing her hair, she looked around the room. It was a dreary place really, and she thought, "I'm glad I didn't let him spend tonight here all alone. He wouldn't have slept—not with the thought of tomorrow in front of him."

He came back just as she had got into bed. For a moment he leaned against the door, looking at her as she sat up, her long, dark hair plaited back, and the slender straps of her petticoat showing white against the golden tan of her shoulders.

Then he tossed off his dressing gown and sat on the side of the bed.

"Well, Tony?" She smiled at him.

"I don't understand you at all," he said. "But then I never have." And he climbed into bed.

She laughed a little. "Shall I put out the light?"

"If you like."

She put out the light. "Come here, and let me put my arm around you."

He came without a word.

"I'm beat," he muttered after a moment.

"Yes, I know," she said gently. "But you'll sleep quite soon."

"No, I can't sleep," he murmured protestingly. And then she felt him turn his head and sleepily kiss her bare arm.

She lay perfectly still, while he moved restlessly once or twice.

"How . . . comforting . . . you are," he said slowly at last. And a moment later she knew, by the sudden relaxing of his big figure against her, that he was asleep.

She smiled a little into the darkness, and gently drew the blankets more closely around him. She thought, "Even if there is never any more than this, it was worth the journey from Italy—and even all the waiting too."

Afterward she realized that she must have slept quite a long while herself, because when she opened her eyes the early morning light was already strong.

She looked at Tony, who seemed scarcely to have stirred; then she softly drew her arm away and crept out of bed. He groaned slightly, but settled down again when she patted him as gently as though he were a baby.

She dressed as quickly and quietly as possible. Then, when she was ready, she found a piece of paper and hastily scribbled:

"I'll be ready, if you'll call for me at the hotel at 9:30.
—Anna."

She didn't even kiss him, for fear of interrupting the sleep he so badly needed. Then she slipped silently out of the room and out of the house.

She had to walk quite a distance before she was able to pick up a slowly cruising taxi. She knew the man looked at her rather curiously.

That didn't worry her, however. Nor did the equally curious glance of the sleepy night porter at her hotel, who was just preparing to go off duty. Anna had never cared greatly for appearances, and she cared even less now.

She gave orders to be called in an hour, and during that hour she slept heavily and dreamlessly.

When she was wakened she had a leisurely bath and dressed very carefully. She examined her face in the mirror, and removed any traces of weariness with a subtle touch of makeup. Finally, she forced herself to eat a good breakfast.

"Always look well and eat well before a crisis," Schreiner had once told her. She found it excellent advice.

The Anna who went downstairs to greet Tony looked wonderfully composed and tranquil.

He was pale and looked a little strained, but the air of deadly weariness had gone; and when she came toward him he smiled brilliantly.

"Did you sleep well, Tony?" was all she said.

"You know I did, bless you," Tony answered, in a low, moved voice.

And after that they didn't say much as they drove through the streets in a taxi. Evidently Tony had not felt quite like driving that morning.

Actually, the trial turned out to be much more like a stage performance than anything Anna had ever imagined. There was the same long, long wait first behind the scenes, while you watched other performers—or witnesses—take their places on the stage. There was the familiar overwhelming sickness of stage fright, when your head seemed on fire and your feet felt like ice.

Then the horrible moment when you took the center of the stage. There was Sir Derek acting as conductor—only his calm, dry air was very different from Schreiner's smiling, picturesque arrogance—and then there was the deliberate, clear-thinking effort to play your part convincingly.

She scarcely looked at Tony. She had a idea that it might unnerve her and this time, of all times in her life, her nerve must not fail.

It was quite easy answering Sir Derek's questions. She had been coached in her rôle here, and knew how to play it. But it was a little disconcerting when the prosecuting counsel rose to put a few suave questions. She had been prepared for this, of course, only it was terribly like having to make up your part as you went along.

"Mrs. Roone, were you surprised when your husband presented himself before you in Paris?"

"I did not know he was coming."

"So that it gave you some surprise to see him?"

"Yes."

She wondered where this was leading. And then, before she could decide, that trail of questions broke off and another began.

"I think you will agree that for a man to fly to Paris for the sole purpose of hearing his wife sing might be interpreted as a sign of great regard and devotion?"

Anna hesitated. "It was a very special occasion. It was my debut."

"Oh, certainly, Mrs. Roone. But even so, that does not minimize the fact that it was something that might please and gratify any woman?"

"Oh yes, of course." She remembered her surprise and joy very keenly.

"That it was, in fact, a mark of regard and devotion?"

"Y-yes."

"Particularly in view of the fact that a very serious construction could be put upon such an action?"

"Yes."

"Now, Mrs. Roone, I want to have one or two dates quite clear. The date of the performance—the one your husband attended in Paris—was the fourth of last December?"

"Yes."

"What was the date of your return to England to appear as a witness in his defense?"

"Yesterday."

"Yesterday. That is to say, something like five and a half months after your husband was first charged?"

"Yes."

"This is a very serious matter your husband has been charged with, Mrs. Roone. Why did you delay until the very last minute to come to his assistance?"

"I didn't know until the day before yesterday that he had been charged. I saw something about it in an English newspaper in Florence, and I came at once."

"I see." Something just underneath the silkiness of the tone made Anna sense danger, and she narrowed her eyes in sudden nervousness.

"So that the situation between you and your husband was such that for five and a half months you knew nothing whatsoever of his life except something gleaned casually from a newspaper? Yet you ask the court to believe that on one certain day, by a curious coincidence, the very day on which his partner committed suicide, he was suddenly overwhelmed by such devotion to you that he flew to Paris for the sole purpose of hearing you sing?"

With a slight, deprecating smile the prosecuting counsel prepared to sit down. A second, half a second, and the chance would be gone. But one thing, above all, Anna had learned under Schreiner: act quickly and calmly in an emergency.

"No," she said gently, "I don't ask the court to believe anything of the sort."

Up went prosecuting counsel's eyebrows.

"But, Mrs. Roone, everything you have said in answer to my questions goes to prove just that."

"No." Anna still spoke quite gently. "What I ask the court to believe is not that my husband was overwhelmed by sudden devotion for me on the fourth of December, but that he had always been devoted to me. So devoted to me that even when I wanted to live my own life as a singer, he was willing to let me do so, if that would make me happy. So devoted that when I came to the testing-point of my debut he risked his good name and his liberty to be there with me in case I failed and thus need him again. So devoted that when he saw for himself that I had succeeded he deliberately engineered a break between us, so that his possible disgrace would not tarnish my success. How convincingly he did that, you can judge by the fact that I severed all connection with him for five and a half months. How artifical that break really was you can judge by the fact that, the moment I heard of his danger, I returned to his side. That's all."

The deprecating smile froze slightly on the prosecuting counsel's face.

"That is one interpretation of the facts, no doubt, Mrs. Roone, but I would suggest to the jury that it is hardly the *only,* or even the most probable, one. That is all, thank you."

And her part was over.

It was terribly difficult to know whether her evidence had been important or useless. It was terribly difficult to make any sort of guess at the progress of the case at all.

There was more endless waiting, more sensation of burning head and frozen feet. A growing, leaden despair, a certainty that Tony was lost, that nothing anyone could say or do could help him. Wave upon wave of hopelessness, a dark, choking sea of misery....

And then suddenly, blessed land under one's feet again. The sun was shining, the misery was rolling away....

". . . Case against the accused dismissed . . . entirely innocent of any complicity in his partner's frauds . . . leaves this court without a stain on his character...."

And Tony was there beside her, holding both her hands very tightly. He looked terribly white and exhausted and a little dazed.

And Sir Derek was congratulating and being congratulated, and—once more as though he were conductor of a stage performance—insisting on a celebration dinner afterward.

So there was a little celebration dinner with Sir Derek and Mr. Bury and Tony and herself.

And she tried very hard to be cheerful and talkative, as Sir Derek seemed to expect. But, all the while, she was frightenedly aware of Tony sitting there, growing quieter and grimmer every moment—looking as though he had lost the case, not won it.

Surely everything was all right now? She could see no reason at all why it should not. But every time she looked at Tony her heart knocked against her ribs. He seemed almost like a stranger—a chilly, distant stranger, at that.

He took her back to her hotel afterward, and in the taxi he said abruptly, "When do you leave for Europe again?"

She was utterly still, feeling as though someone had put a cold hand around her throat.

"I . . . I hadn't thought about it," she said at last.

"No?" He wasn't looking at her. He was staring grimly out of the window. "Well, anyway, I expect I shall see you again before you go."

Another awful silence, and then, "I expect so."

They were drawing up outside her hotel now. She looked at his weary face, and for a moment everything was forgotten in her pity for him. Words forced themselves to her lips, spoken tenderly, protectively.

"It shouldn't be difficult for you to sleep well tonight, Tony, and there are a good many things for us to talk about in the morning."

He shook his head impatiently.

"There's not very much to discuss, Anna. And . . . I don't feel sleepy," he added irrelevantly.

She felt suddenly frightened again, just as she had last night.

"Are you going out driving again tonight?" she asked quickly.

"Yes."

"Then I'm coming too."

He laughed slightly. "No, Anna. You were scared enough last night. It's ridiculous for you to come and terrify yourself deliberately like that for nothing."

"I won't mind. However fast you go, I won't mind. Tony, please. If you send me away tomorrow, at least let me come tonight."

He stared at her gloomily for a moment. And then suddenly he gave in.

She *was* frightened, of course—just as she always had been. But that didn't really matter any more, because this was her one chance of making him listen to her.

Her one chance!

Hatless, quite silent, she sat beside him in the low-slung black racer while they threaded their way out of London.

It wasn't too bad until they were clear of the suburbs because he was forced to go fairly slowly. But once they were out in the open country the purr of the engine rose to a whine; she could feel the wind beat on her face until it almost brought tears to her eyes.

Once she glanced at him, but there was nothing reassuring about his face. It was strange and frightening to see Tony—her once kind and understanding Tony—so hard and uncaring.

She knew it was unhappiness that had built this wall

around his naturally sweet nature. The betrayal by his family; the crashing of his hopes; his bewilderment and misery; perhaps, above all, his fixed belief that he had failed her. . . . It was all there in the grim line of his jaw and the unsmiling eyes.

"Where are we going?" she said at last.

"I don't know. Anywhere."

"Can I talk to you," she asked timidly, "or do you have to direct all your attention to your driving?"

"No. You can talk if you feel there's anything to say."

That wasn't very encouraging, but she had to go on somehow.

"Tony, there *is* something to say."

"Well?"

"Tony, now that everything is all right, what are you going to do?"

"Everything isn't all right. I'm cleared, of course, personally, but the business is finished completely. There's nothing left. But that doesn't really matter much. I can start near the bottom again."

"I see." She gripped her hands together. "And . . . what about me?" The wind seemed to snatch the words away from her as she spoke them.

"You?" He smiled without looking at her. "Why, you'll start near the top again and go right up there, of course. Unhampered by me. Do you understand?" His voice was almost harsh.

"Tony—" she was desperate now "—that isn't what I want. I—"

"And this isn't what *I* want" he cut in fiercely. "I don't want your pity, just because I've failed you completely. Great heavens, you'll be offering me money to make a fresh start in a minute! Oh, I know I'm a hound to talk to you like this after what you did for me in court today, but it's only brutal frankness that can serve us now. And, to be brutally frank, you're far better off without me. Don't let's confuse the issue with sentiment."

"But last night—" she began.

"For God's sake, forget about last night, Anna!" he exclaimed impatiently. "I had no earthly right to let you do such a thing. I think I'm more ashamed about that than anything."

She sat very still, struggling wearily to frame some sort of appeal that would reach past this strange, bitter Tony to the Tony she knew.

"Do you remember," she said huskily at last, "the last time we were driving together? Oh, not yesterday. I mean all those months ago."

He refused to answer, but she could see that he remembered.

"It was our wedding day, Tony."

"Do you have to say these things?"

"And you told me something then that I was always to remember. You said I had only to call and you would come to me—from the ends of the earth."

His hands on the wheel seemed to blur before her eyes, and she felt the cold, slow tears on her cheeks.

"I wanted to say something to you then, too, but I hadn't the courage. Do you remember?"

"Yes, I remember. I've often wondered what it was," he said reluctantly.

She suddenly put her cheek down against the rough sleeve of his coat and felt him go rigid.

"I wanted to tell you that *you* had only to call and *I* would come. But I was ashamed—it was so silly—I had nothing to offer and you had everything. That was the awful part. You always had to give and give, and I always had to take and take. I've only been allowed to do something for you three times in all the time I've known you."

"Don't, Anna." His voice was rough with agitation. And then, as though he couldn't help it, he asked, "What were those three times, child?"

"When I stood by you in court today." She was speaking almost in a whisper. "When I . . . held you in my arms last night, and managed to make you sleep." For a moment her voice failed entirely.

"And the third time, Anna?" He, too, spoke gently now, like the Tony she knew.

"You let me . . . light your . . . cigarette, the very first time I saw you. . . ." And then she was crying, desperately, helplessly, with her hands pressed childishly against her face.

"Anna!"

At the sound in his voice she raised her head again. For a moment his eyes were off the road. He was staring at her, so that it was she who saw what was going to happen, she who saw the black hulk of the stationary truck as it reared up in front of them.

A second before the shattering impact she flung herself across him. She felt the back wheels of the car leave the road as the whole thing stood on end.

And then the world seemed to fall apart in crashes of rolling thunder. Anna sank through endless, lightning-shot clouds . . . into nothing.

CHAPTER THIRTEEN

Slowly Tony opened his eyes, and tried to think what had happened. It was dark except for a streak of light from a car lamp, which seemed to be at a preposterous angle.

A rough voice was asking him again and again if he were all right.

And there was something lying, soft and inert, against him.

Anna!

He struggled frantically into a sitting position, lifting her in his arms as he did so.

"Anna! Anna! Anna!"

For a moment he wondered who kept on repeating her name. Then he realized that it was himself.

Somebody was holding a flask to his lips, and he took a gulp of raw-tasting spirit that scorched his throat but made him able to think much more clearly.

He saw that there were a couple of men, scared and anxious, standing beside him.

"I'm all right," he said thickly.

"But the girl ain't," one of the men said. "Better get her across to that cottage there. There's a light in the window now. They must have heard the crash. Here, let me take her."

"No!" Tony looked almost murderous as he clutched Anna against him and staggered to his feet.

Little, limp, sagging figure that hung so pitifully still in his arms. She seemed to weigh on his very heart. But he couldn't let anyone else hold her, he couldn't let anyone else hold her. She was his—alive or dead.

He lurched up the path to the open cottage door, where a scared-looking woman with a gray pigtail down her back, and a dressing gown thrown over her night clothes stood, exclaiming, "Oh, for the Lord's sake, what a terrible business! Is she dead? There. Bring her in and put her on the sofa. And one of you men go for the doctor. He's straight down that road, almost half a mile on the left."

Tony had put her on the sofa now, and stopped to wipe the sweat out of his eyes. Only it wasn't sweat—it was blood, he saw, when his fingers came away crimson.

He submitted to having a bandage bound quickly around his head, but all the while he never took his eyes off Anna. And when the woman went out to the kitchen to heat water in readiness for the doctor, he hung over her, looking at her as though to compel her to open her eyes by the sheer force of his own pleading gaze.

And then, as he watched her, memory slowly rolled back the curtain. . . . Nighttime in a cottage room. . . . Anna lying hurt upon a sofa by a dying fire . . . he himself gazing at her with his soul in his eyes.

"Oh, my little love," he exclaimed softly, and he came and knelt beside her, so that he could put his cheek against her cold, quiet hand.

The year between didn't seem to count any more. All those strange, disturbing scenes held no significance. Anny trying to understand his family. Anna in his office saying that she had stayed the night with Frayne. Anna as a successful singer, with that fool of a foreign conductor looming in the background. Anna defending him in court.

They had all narrowed down suddenly to the little Anna that was his. The enchanted girl who had put her hand against his heart and made him hers for always. The Anna who had knelt beside him in the firelight, happy because he had let her light his cigarette.

All she had asked was to be allowed to give, poor child, and she had held so pitifully little between those thin hands of hers that she had been ashamed even to offer it.

Instead she had had to receive and receive. To be grateful, to be humiliated by the bounty of the man she wanted to serve.

He'd meant so well. He'd meant so well. But oh, why had he been such a blind fool?

Her fingers stirred slightly against his cheek, and he started up.

Her eyes were open now. Wide, smoke-fringed, hazel eyes, dark in her white face.

"Tony." Her voice was very quiet.

"What, my darling?"

"Are you there?"

"Yes, yes." He pressed her hand feverishly against his cheek again.

"Was there an accident?"

"Yes, Anna. But I don't think you ought to talk much," he said a little agitatedly.

"Why?" The question came very coolly and quietly. "Am I badly hurt?"

"I don't know. No, my dear. I hope not."

"You sound frightened." She looked at him with those large, shadowy eyes; then she smiled very faintly. "Poor boy. You look like you did when you had to tell me Mother was dead."

How odd, he thought; she was thinking of that time, too.

"Why do you look like that?" she said gently. "Are you frightened to tell me that *I* am going to die?"

"Anna, don't!" Tony spoke almost violently. He was desperately afraid. He didn't know much about illness, but it seemed to him that there was something terribly serious in those deepening shadows around her eyes, and the way the smooth golden tan stood out on her thin cheeks.

"But what does it matter?" she said impatiently and very wearily. "You can't mind really—not after things you've said. And I—" to his inexpressible terror her voice began to fade "—should be almost glad."

"Oh, darling, my little darling. Don't say such things!" he implored.

That she should suppose he didn't mind if she died!

But surely now she could hear the pain and terror in his voice. But she didn't seem to be hearing anything. Her lashes were lying heavily on her cheeks again, and it was as though she were drifting farther and farther away from him.

Just once she opened her eyes and said very sadly, "I

wish Manora would come. She's always so kind." But she didn't sound as though she expected anything to happen as she wanted it, and she closed her eyes again almost at once.

It hurt badly that she should ask so pathetically for anyone but himself; but he, too, wished in that moment that Manora would come—wished it passionately, if that were what Anna wanted. He'd never liked the sound of the woman much, but evidently to Anna she represented some refuge of kindliness and strength. And, in an odd, humble way, he suddenly felt grateful to her.

The sound of the garden gate swinging brought him stumbling to his feet. He went out eagerly into the little hallway, as the woman of the cottage came from the kitchen.

But it wasn't the doctor. It was just one of the men who had gone to fetch him.

"Doctor was out," he reported laconically.

"Oh no!" Tony scarcely recognized the hoarse, despairing exclamation as his own.

The man looked pityingly at him and added quickly, "But Bob's got out his motorbike and gone for Dr. Channing. He can't be very long."

A painful gratitude to the unknown Bob pierced Tony's wretchedness and impatience.

"It's very good of him," he muttered. "Only time's so important . . . so terribly important."

"Don't you worry, sir. Dr. Channing's the cleverest doctor in the district," the man began, while the woman patted him kindly on the shoulder.

But Tony turned away and went back into the room where Anna was. He shut the door behind him and leaned against it. They meant well, but they couldn't comfort him. Only Anna could do that, and she was lying there so quietly with her eyes shut.

He wanted her as he had never wanted anything since the occasional bewilderment of childhood. It was something like that feeling—the same unreasoning desire to be held close and reassured.

It was ridiculous, of course, because it was he who ought to hold her close and reassure her, tell her that her terrible idea of his not caring was all wrong.

He couldn't face the fact that he might never be able to explain that to her now. . . . How he had loved her so desperately all the time, only he had thought he had known what was best for her.

That anxiety struggled painfully in the back of his mind, but even that was partially blotted out by the overwhelming desire just to be held in her arms, just to be told with such sweet, illogical comfort that "it was all right."

He came over slowly and sat in a chair near her sofa. He stared at her with boyish, scared eyes, quite helpless to do anything, hope slipping away bit by bit.

It wasn't any good. He didn't deserve that she should open her eyes. He'd been so stupid, so lacking in understanding, holding her roughly and carelessly instead of warmly and tenderly.

Even Frayne, even those raffish foreigners whom he had always despised, had understood her better. She'd asked so pitifully for Manora because "she's always so kind."

Poor little Anna. There hadn't been much kindness for her. And she asked for so little, really—so very little.

Burying his face in his hands, he sat very still. Everything was so quiet in the cottage. He wondered vaguely if anything would ever break the silence again. And then. . . .

"I thought you would come," Anna's voice said slowly.

He started violently and looked up. Her darling, wonderful eyes were open, and she was smiling her faint, shy smile.

"I've been calling you," she said. "Did you know?"

Sudden, ridiculous tears stung his eyelids.

"Yes, I . . . I knew," he stammered, coming to kneel beside her again.

She looked at him very wistfully and said, "I tried not to say your name, but I was frightened and wanted you so much."

And then he saw suddenly that this was his moment.

"I was terribly frightened too," he whispered. "Did you hear *me* calling *you*, my dear?"

"What did you say? Did you want me?"

There was a look in her eyes that drove all eloquence from his lips. He suddenly hid his face against her in helpless abandon. It was selfish of him. It was probably bad for her. But he couldn't help it.

"Oh, Anna, Anna, Anna. There's nothing to say but your darling name. I've been calling to you desperately in my heart ever since you left me. Won't you listen to me? It's I who need you, my beloved?"

"Tony—" she moved feebly, put her arm close around him "—what are you saying?" And then, as he moved convulsively, she said, "All right, don't try to explain, my dear."

She lightly kissed his rough, tumbled hair, just where it showed above the bandage.

"Does your poor head ache badly?" she asked him tenderly.

He nodded. But he leaned his aching head against her and knew the most perfect peace. He could feel the quiet, measured beat of her heart, and he knew that if that stopped so would his world.

The minutes slipped away, and then he whispered almost childishly, "May I explain now?"

"Yes, Tony dear, if there's anything to explain." Her voice was tranquil and infinitely tender.

"Oh yes," he uttered eagerly, "there's so much to explain. So much."

"Well, you tell me, then." With loving fingers she gently ruffled his hair.

He searched for words. "It's just that I need you and want you so terribly," he began desperately. "Oh no, I've told you all that before. That wasn't what I meant to tell you. It's about that ridiculous thing I said . . . that you'd only to call and I'd come."

"Wasn't that true, Tony?" she asked, putting her cheek down against his hair.

"Oh yes, of course it was true. Every word of it. Only,

don't you see? It implied that you would be the only one who would be in need."

She laughed softly and said, "Do you remember almost the first thing you told me was that I looked like a beggarmaid?"

"Oh, Anna! And one of the first things you told me was that I looked like a prince. I don't know which was the sillier remark, dearest. We neither of us said anything about *my* desperate need for *you*."

"Well, we didn't know anything about it, did we?" she said gently.

"I've known for a long time," he whispered pleadingly.

"Poor boy! My poor Tony. And yet you wouldn't tell me."

"It wasn't until I lost you that I knew so clearly." He turned his fingers nervously in her thin ones. "And then, almost immediately, the world was growing so bright for you."

"Bright?" Anna laughed a little and shuddered.

"Well, I mean, fame coming to you and all that sort of thing," he explained awkwardly.

"Do you know *why* I tried so hard to be famous?" she said.

"I think I can guess." It was he who spoke very tenderly now. "But, my little love, why did you suppose you could be any dearer to me because you were a celebrity?"

"It wasn't that. I thought. . . ."

"What did you think?"

"Well, that if you could be proud of me in that way, it wouldn't matter so much about your having to be ashamed of me in other ways." She spoke very low.

He stared at her, a little flush of indignant astonishment putting color into his pale face.

"But I was *never* ashamed of you, not for one minute in all my life. How could you think such a thing?" he demanded. "Did I ever say the least thing to make you think so?"

"No. No, not you yourself."

"Who, then?" He had forgotten it was not good for her to talk—certainly not good for her to be questioned so determinedly.

"Oh, Tony, never mind now?"

"But you must tell me. It's only right."

"Well, it was something Katherine said—"

"*Katherine!*"

She winced a little, and immediately he was all contrition.

"I'm sorry, my sweet. I didn't mean to be so violent," he said much more gently. "But please tell me what Katherine said."

She was talking to your aunt—they didn't even know that I heard, so you mustn't blame them. Your aunt was crying because . . . because you'd married me."

Tony pressed his lips together angrily. "Go on."

Anna's fingers tightened on his.

"She said how awful it was when a man spoiled his whole life by marrying a common little outsider. And she said he usually didn't manage to struggle free before—"

"Before what?" Tony asked grimly.

"Before there was a common baby, too." Her voice sank to a whisper and she looked away from him.

There was a long silence. Then he put his fingers against her thin cheek and gently turned her face toward him, so that he could look into her dark, hurt eyes.

"Anna, did you really suppose I would have found your darling babies common?" he said quietly.

Her eyes slowly filled with tears.

"I didn't know," she began.

He leaned forward and kissed her roughly on her mouth.

"Now do you know?"

"Yes," she said rather humbly.

At last there was the sound of the gate again; a slight bustle in the hall told him that the doctor had arrived.

Tony's mind was jerked back to the fact that Anna was injured—probably dangerously so. Somehow the sharp edge of his terror about that had been blunted while her arm was around him.

But now, as he rose unsteadily to his feet, panic flooded over him again. He felt very sick and giddy, and his head throbbed unbearably; but that was all nothing compared to the chill at his heart.

The doctor cast one look at Anna and then glanced at Tony with a sort of surprised disapproval.

"I hope you've had the sense to keep her very quiet," he said.

Tony was dumb, weighed down now by a sense of guilt as well as fear. It was Anna who said gently and untruthfully, "Oh yes, Doctor."

"Glad to hear it," said the doctor dryly, as though he didn't attach much value to her assurance.

Then Tony was sent out of the room. He paced nervously about the kitchen just as he had all that time ago, when Dr. Irwin had been looking after Anna.

The woman of the cottage was sympathetic but pessimistic, and, while Tony gratefully drank the strong tea she made him, he wished irritatedly that she wouldn't talk. It reminded him of the terrifying way Anna had hung in his arms when he had carried her in. Like someone dying.

But it couldn't be like that now. Not when he'd just found her, and some of the awful misunderstanding was removed at last. It couldn't, couldn't. He found himself repeating the word in his aching brain in time to the measured beat of the old-fashioned kitchen clock.

Presently he sank his weary head in his hands and sat very still for what seemed an eternity.

But at last the door of the other room opened. Tony was out in the passage immediately.

"How is she?" He shot out the words somehow.

The doctor patted his arm. "She'll be fine. It's going to mean some weeks in bed. . . ." The floor sank away from Tony for a moment. The next thing he knew was that the doctor had him firmly by the arm and was leading him to a chair.

"She'll be fine. She'll be fine." Tony kept repeating the words to himself while the doctor attended to him. "Little darling Anna. She'll be fine. Oh, my God, it's a second chance!"

Finally they let him go back to her, to wait until the ambulance arrived.

She smiled at him when he entered the room and held out one arm to him. He came at once and knelt beside her again, so that he could put his head against her, just as he had before the doctor had interrupted them.

They were silent for a moment; then she said timidly, "You won't force me to go back and be a singer now, will you?"

"Force you, Anna!" he exclaimed, horrified. "My dear, I wouldn't force you to do anything."

She nodded her head slowly and smiled gravely like a wise child.

"Oh yes, you would. You'd think you knew what was best for me. That's why I've been lying here hoping and hoping I was badly hurt, so that you couldn't send me away for a long while, not until I'd had a chance to plead with you."

He held her close.

"I have been a fool, haven't I?" he said a little bitterly.

"Yes," Anna told him. "But so have I. We've both made some terribly silly mistakes, considering that people in love are supposed to understand each other."

Tony touched her cheek with gentle, anxious fingers.

"You do realize how much you're giving up if you stay with me, don't you?" he said.

"Giving up?" She looked surprised.

"I shall be quite a poor man, for a while at any rate," he pointed out.

"I don't mind," Anna said. "I never really got used to being rich. Being poor comes much more naturally to me."

He laughed with genuine amusement.

"And what about your career, your voice? Darling, don't think I'm jealous of your heavenly voice. I'm wildly proud of it. When I listened to you that time in Paris, the beauty of it brought a lump into my throat, even while it frightened me too."

"Why should it frighten you?"

"Because. . . . Oh, it's caddish of me to influence you like this—" he pressed his head boyishly against her "—only every note seemed to take you farther away. And every round of applause seemed to show more clearly that there was no place for me in your life. If I'd been really decent, I wouldn't even have come to see you afterward. I would have just gone back to England quietly without saying anything."

"And why didn't you?" She was smiling now.

"Couldn't," he said, dropping his eyes. "I just *had* to see you for a minute. I thought it would give me courage to go back and face the business over here. I was a bit scared about it, you know."

"Oh, I wish I'd known," she said impulsively.

"Would you have given it all up even then?" he said very tenderly. "Even in all the first excitement and triumph?"

"Of course."

"There really isn't any 'of course' about it, my darling. Not many women would see it that way."

"Oh yes, they would. Why—" She stopped.

"What, Anna?"

"I was thinking of something Manora said once," she said slowly.

"And what was that?" He smiled a little. He didn't think he would be interested in anything Vanescu had said, but evidently Anna had agreed with her.

"She said that no woman worth the name would value her voice above a child who would look at her with the eyes of the man she loved."

"Anna!" He wasn't smiling now. He was quite still and quiet. At last he said very humbly, "I think perhaps I have an awful lot to learn about you, Anna. But I will try, darling. I will try, if you'll find the patience to teach me."

"Oh, Tony, how sweet you are when you say that," she said. It was she who smiled at him now.

He remembered wonderingly that once he had been a little scared when she had smiled like that, as though she were years older than he. Now it was the sweetest and most reassuring thing in the world.

"Why do you smile at me as though I'm a little boy?" he said, pressing his cheek against her.

"Because to every woman there are always moments when the man she loves seems to be her little boy, too," she told him.

"Darling, how ridiculous and wonderful!"

"But you like it?"

"I adore it."

"And it reassures you, doesn't it?"

"Yes," he said slowly, "that's just what it does. I don't quite know why."

"Don't you? Then I'll tell you." She gently tilted up his face, so that he looked into her eyes, which he had once thought held so many secrets. Now they were radiantly clear and held nothing but tenderness for him. "It's the smile that mothers give their children when they mean 'Don't be frightened. I'm here. You have only to call . . . and I'll come.' "

DESTINY IS A FLOWER

DESTINY
IS A FLOWER
Stella Frances Nel

Theresa Stanton's broken engagement and Scott Milward's recent divorce gave them something in common. Both were quite convinced they were immune to falling in love again.

However, there were several practical reasons why they should marry—for instance, Scott's small daughter, Melinda—but love was not one of them.

Theresa was well aware of Scott's feeling on the matter. "I've been bitten once too often to fall into that trap again," he'd said with bitter cynicism. "Let's shelve our past heartaches and live just for the moment."

It was foolish to expect such a marriage to succeed. Especially after Theresa unexpectedly, but unquestionably, discovered she loved Scott.

CHAPTER ONE

Theresa Stanton watched the train disappear into a curve of tall, thorny scrub. She was quite sure the tail end of the last coach flipped cockily at her as it, too, was swallowed by the prickly jaws of waiting greenery. She forced down rising hysteria—the heat was causing strange hallucinations—and brought her gaze back to the dusty wayside station. She seemed to be the only person within miles at the moment. With sudden apprehension she drew a letter out of her bag and scanned the contents again.

A sigh of relief escaped curving lips. She was in the right place, at the correct time and on the appointed day according to this letter. So where were Dan and Mary? Theresa hoped sincerely that the delay in meeting her was not caused by a car breakdown. She studied the letter for the umpteenth time.

"My dearest Terry," wrote Mary Rourke, "Dan and I are very pleased that you have accepted our invitation. It's high time anyway—we haven't seen you for ages and your constant promises never seem to materialize. So at last, with your resignation (why?) we'll have the pleasure of your company. What does the haughty Doctor Derek think of your leaving his precious nursing home? Do I hear the distant sound of wedding bells? Don't mind me, I'm dying with the disease that killed the cat, but I guess I can hold out if I take a deep breath and wait for you. You'll love our poppet (Glynis Theresa Rourke)—she's rather superior for the wise old age of four months. When I tell her Auntie Terry is coming at last she gazes superciliously in the distance and gives a wet, knowing grunt! Well, all can wait until I see you in person. Dan is still a pain in the neck, and I'm looking forward to a demolishment of his flirtatious manner with one look from your cold blue eyes. 'Nuff said! We'll meet you, providence willing our mechanical contraption doesn't have its periodical inner tantrum at Guntha siding on Friday morning at ten-thirty. That's the time the train should arrive but never does. Don't do your block, honey, we'll be there even if I have to call the faithful wheelbarrow into action. Dan pushing, of course. . . ." Further details followed, and Theresa smiled in genuine amusement at her friend's quaint ramblings.

Her expressive face sobered as she thought of the explanations she would have to give on the subject of her broken engagement. Slim fingers ran through honey-blond hair distractedly and blue eyes darkened as bitter thoughts clouded her tired brain. A grizzled old man suddenly appeared from the direction of a tiny shack on the opposite side of the track and ambled toward her. So, she was not alone in this desolate speck of nowhere after all! Theresa walked eagerly to meet him. Old Truscott studied her intently for some moments, then his gnarled fingers took the chewed-up match from his mouth.

"Could be you're the lady for Windimount. A bit young for the job, I'd say. Miss Melinda be a handful for the likes of ye. What's come over that Master Scott?"

Before she could answer his enigmatic query, he turned away to watch as a low-slung gray car came to a smooth stop at the siding.

A perplexed young woman and an inquisitive, expectant old man watched as the dark-haired man at the wheel opened the door and climbed out with a quick, lithe movement. Smoky gray eyes met Theresa's gaze, and he stopped with a startled exclamation. Swift, circling scrutiny took in her cinnamon brown summer suit with the tailored yellow blouse showing at the pale column of her throat. His gaze dropped to high slim-heeled sandals and a matching bag. Hot sunlight sparkled on shoulder-length hair accentuating, in startling contrast, eyes the deep blue of hyacinths.

In turn, Theresa stared into the arrogant, suntanned face of the man before her. For some reason he seemed to be angry. His eyes had darkened, and she had the wayward thought that never had she seen such absurdly long eyelashes on a man. High cheekbones planed down to a square jaw, but this chin was redeemed by a vulnerable-looking cleft. He had a well-defined mouth, which could well be humorous but at this moment was drawn into a grim line. Dark hair was relentlessly brushed back. He was tall and slim-hipped, his resilient grace apparent as he slipped his thumbs into the waistband of tan whipcord slacks and surveyed her, almost contemptuously.

"What the devil . . . ? That woman must be out of her mind! I distinctly wrote her to send someone older and qualified!" His voice was deep and matched the quality of his arrogance.

"I don't qualify? How utterly devastating! For what, may I ask?" Theresa had found her voice and the words were out before she could bite them back. A tiny pulse started in her throat as her sarcasm matched his.

"Good grief, ignorant of the necessary qualifications as well! This is the end!" He turned to the old man. "All right, Mike, party's over. You can draw up your chin."

Taking a firm grip on Theresa's bags, the tall stranger slung them through the back door of his car and onto the seat. "You must be tired after that long trip, Miss . . . er . . . so come along. We'll discuss what's to be done at home when you're rested. The front seat, please. . . . I'll think of your name in a moment." He held the door politely.

"Theresa Stanton. How do you do Mr. . . , er . . . ?" She remained where she was and lifted her own chin a fraction higher.

"That's not the name of the applicant—" He swung around and smoky eyes studied her again. "Stanton? That's the girl Dan was expecting—the bluestocking. I beg your pardon. Thank goodness you're not the one for Melinda. What could have happened to the silly woman?" He gazed around as if expecting someone to materialize out of the thorny scrub, then collected his wits. "Forgive me, Miss Stanton. Scott Milward's the name. Dan seems to be somewhat delayed. May I take you to your destination? It's not far out of my way." He waited, an enigmatic look on his face as he watched her.

Theresa was fuming with indignation, but she took

pride in her outward coolness. She heard another car approaching and knew it must be Dan or Mary.

"Thank you, Mr. Milward, it won't be necessary for you to go out of your way at all. My friends have come. May I have my bags? And I second that very expressive remark of yours."

"Expressive remark?" Puzzlement clouded his face.

" 'Thank goodness you're not the one for Melinda,' whatever that may imply. Hello, Dan darling. The train was on time for once."

Theresa almost hurled herself into Dan Rourke's arms as he joined them. With a great shout of laughter the stocky new arrival gathered her into his arms, swept her up and planted a whacking kiss on her lips.

"It's me own darling, come to lighten up me dark days. Begorra, girl, 'tis good to see you. And lovelier than I remembered!"

"My word!" Mike Truscott's grizzled chin hung down as far as it could go.

"Yes, Mike, ain't she gorgeous? No tales to Mary now, you old reprobate. Hi there, Scott! Didn't your woman turn up? Mine did, and she sure ain't dowdy, hmm? Mary couldn't come, dear; Poppet has a slight hangover from an earache—nothing to worry about. Have you met Scott, honey? Our local candidate for the mommas' and lassies' caps."

"We've met, Dan." The ice in Theresa's voice cooled Dan's exuberant spirits somewhat. His bright eyes swiveled from her to Scott's uncompromising face as he climbed into his car.

"Yes, we have met. There was a slight case of mis-understanding, mistaken identity for which I apolo-gize—" a mere hesitation as the man eased himself into the seat "—if an apology is called for. . . ." A wave of a hand and he was gone.

"Well, of all the. . . ." Theresa turned and spoke in fury to a bewildered Dan. "Who and what is this woman that was supposed to be on this train, Dan?"

"Scott was expecting a governess for his daughter, Melinda—" Dan began.

"If an apology is called for? Not if I look like an ordinary, dowdy governess. Do I look like one, Dan?"

"Of course not, honey, you look every inch a princess." Dan eyed Mary's friend, drawn to her full height, a haughty tilt to the delectable chin. Trouble in store for someone!

"So I rate an apology, then, right? And he deliberately said '*If* an apology is called for.' I'll call for one if it's the last thing I do, *and* expire in the attempt!"

"Ha, Mister Dan, she's sure a spirited filly, begging your pardon, miss. You'll need it to stand up to that Mr. Scott, that's for sure." Mike showed his glee by demolishing another match between surprisingly strong white teeth.

"Did you not enlighten him as to who you were?"

"I had no chance, Dan. He simply stood there and tried to mow me down with sarcastic remarks on my youth and capabilities. When I eventually introduced myself he called me a . . . bluestocking!"

Theresa suddenly fixed a suspicious eye on Dan. He hastily turned to her bags and deposited them with great care on the back seat of the vintage station wagon. "Shall we go now, sweetie? Mary's likely to start walking to meet us. She's that excited about your visit."

Theresa climbed in beside him, her fury subsiding. Blow Scott Milward. She was going to see her very dearest friend again and the baby she had heard so much about.

Mary had met and married her Rhodesian farmer after a whirlwind courtship, leaving almost immediately to settle in this forsaken-looking place where Dan evidently cultivated tobacco. She waved her hand to Mike and the old man saluted courteously.

"Sorry I was late, Terry. This old wagon played up again and, for truth, it's time she was pensioned off. This month I intend to go to Salisbury and come back in a spick 'n' span what-have-you with luverly shining trimmings, so help me! How was the journey up? I guess I needn't ask—long and tiring. How much illegal goods confiscated at the border? Surely not the case of whisky you so stealthily slipped under your miniskirt?"

Theresa laughed in delight at Dan's anxious expression. "Oh, Dan dear, I had the bottles strapped around my waist under said mini, but the customs chap said I looked too suspiciously like Annie Oakley. So I had to haul them out, and one by one we solemnly drank the contents. Not a toothful left for Danny Rourke." She looked suitably ashamed and regretful.

"They come and go, mostly go." Dan sighed, looking darkly at her. "I might just spare a toothful of my own precious stuff for you, but not if it's a hollow tooth. Not that much!"

"Thank you, kind sir." Her eager eyes watched the road. "How far do we have to go?"

"It's only an hour's drive from the siding. This is where my land starts."

"And all those weeds . . . aren't they tall?" Theresa spoke mischievously.

"Weeds indeed! I'll have you know those are not weeds, it's tobacco—" He caught her sidelong glance. "Away with you, you ignorant city miss!"

Mary Rourke was waiting on the steps of the wide porch as they drew up. She flew down to envelop Theresa with loving arms. "My Theresa, come at last, and more beautiful than ever! Let me look at you—just stepped out of a fashion page and not a dusty train, I do declare!" She stepped back. "A bit on the thin side?"

Sudden tears threatened and Theresa's eyes sparkled as she greeted her friend. "Mary darling, it's good to see you again. Now don't give with the mother act, I can see it surging to the fore. I'm not thin and my health is good. I still have my own teeth, no hollows unfortunately." A quick, naughty glance at Dan.

Dan grinned, "All right, girls, stop drooling. Step smartly, I hear tea things. How's Poppet, Mary?" He led the way into the large, cool living room.

"She's sleeping. I think her troubles are over now. We'll have tea, and then Terry can meet the head of the house." Mary made bustling sounds at the tea trolley that a smiling maid had wheeled into the room.

Theresa sank into an easy chair and kicked off her sandals with a sigh of contentment.

Mary smiled at this familiar gesture that she remembered from the days when they had shared an apartment in Pretoria. Theresa might have contradicted her remark that she was thin, but Mary could see the difference. Also something . . . sad, perhaps, that lurked in the blue eyes usually so gay with a love of life. What had saddened them so?

The sitting room was furnished to induce contentment. Soft green broadloom, beige curtains across wide windows and easy chairs ranging in colors of dark brown to light tan. One deep rocking chair with a high back looked startlingly lovely, covered in a material of deep bronze with a slight tracery of green. The walls and ceilings were white, and Dan's bar fitted into the lower curve of the L-shaped room where the natural redwood used for the counter and fittings gleamed richly.

Dan had his tea and headed for the door, muttering that "Man's work was never done." He turned at the doorway. "Scott's gal didn't turn up, Mary. If you stop delving into your lurid past Terry will tell you all about it. She has firsthand knowledge, having met the lord of Windimount at the siding. . . ." His voice trailed off as he hastily made his exit.

"So you met Scott. Isn't he just the most?" Mary asked eagerly.

"The most? The least as far as I'm concerned," Theresa retorted. "He has the manners of a savage!" She went on to relate the incident that led to the introduction of Scott Milward.

Mary laughed unexpectedly. "Oh, that sounds just like our Scott. He's nothing if not straightforward, and you must forgive him. He must have received a shock when he saw you, not the staid lady he expected to see! The woman in charge of Melinda is leaving soon to be married, and he was counting on this other one to get into the routine before that time."

"Where is his wife, and how old is Melinda?" Theresa was suddenly curious about the Rourkes' tall, outspoken neighbor.

"Melinda is four and a sweet, precocious little handful. Scott adores her. Elaine, his wife—" Mary hesitated, "—left him almost two years ago. I believe she's in Pretoria. Scott is very bitter."

"Why did she leave him?" Theresa asked bluntly, shocked that a woman could simply walk out leaving a small child. Could there possibly be such extenuating circumstances as to warrant such an act of desertion?

Mary remained silent for moments. "Well, Terry, it's hard to explain. Elaine is a city girl, she's American and very glamorous. Scott is very closemouthed about the whole affair. He met and married her in New York, and she wasn't very happy here in the wilds, as she called it—" A sudden wail reached them and Mary jumped up. "I'll tell you more about it later. Come and meet Madam. That's her imperious call you've just heard."

"She's lovely, absolutely adorable!" Theresa cuddled Mary's tiny daughter on her lap.

"Glynis Theresa Rourke likes you too, love."

The eyes of the two friends met above a cooing roly-poly baby in the younger girl's arms. Mary noticed a wistful darkening of blue eyes.

"Something is troubling you, Terry. Would you care to tell me about it?" she asked quietly.

"I don't know how, Mary, I can't bear it. I. . . ." Theresa's usually clear voice came to a stammering stop. There was a frightful choking in her throat as she looked into Mary's kind, inquiring eyes.

Mary Rourke lifted her baby from the other's arms. "All right, honey, give Poppet to me. You go have a shower and climb into something more comfortable. Jeans are quite in order—that's my national dress these days. Lunch will be ready soon, and then we can gossip some more. You need only confide as much as you think fit and we've all the time in the world. Come, I'll show you to your room."

Briskness hid her sudden uprush of love for this quiet, unsure girl. Something awfully upsetting must have happened, for normally Terry was vibrant and full of joyous laughter and vitality. And she had not mentioned her fiancé, not once. In her third year of nursing and a glowing future before her, engaged to one of the smartest doctors in the Transvaal, Dr. Derek Mann, Terry was devoted to her profession, so why had she suddenly resigned? Mary had a strong suspicion that it had to do with Derek. What had the superior (*she* was not too taken with him) medico done to her Theresa?

Theresa gratefully accepted the offer of a shower and changed into white jeans and a soft yellow shirt. She brushed her hair and slipped on a white band to keep the mass off her face.

A delicious lunch of cold ham and salads made her realize how hungry she had been. Disillusionment with her love life by no means deterred a young, healthy appetite!

When Dan left, Mary practically ordered Theresa to rest for a while during the hottest time of day. Later the two friends sat in grass-woven chairs on the cool side of the porch. Baby Glynis was dumped on a blanket and they watched her antics in amused silence. Intent on the embroidery work in her hands, Mary started to talk about mutual friends they had known when they had roomed together in Pretoria.

The conversation came to an end eventually and a long silence ensued. Theresa looked up from the book on her lap and watched her friend's busy hands while "poppet" gurgled at her feet.

She spoke then. "Mary, I must tell you what happened. You're my friend and, as such, an explanation is due to you." A restless hand went to her hair.

Mary put down her work. "Fire away, lassie."

"I can't think how it all started, believe me. I'd loved nursing, as you know, and Derek and I were the proverbial happily engaged couple—at least I thought we were. Oh, Mary, why couldn't he trust me? I never thought that word 'trust' would ever be needed!" Theresa was quiet for a moment, lost in bitter memories. She drew a ragged breath. "I guess it did look rather compromising to other people. Do you remember the real estate agent who found our apartment for us?"

"Mitch Saunders, yes. He was rather sweet on you and pestered us for quite a while before you managed to drum home your engaged and unavailable status. You can be an iceberg at times, honey, I'll never forget that Don Juan's face when you showed him the door! Go on."

"Saunders also had a sister, Sylvia. Widowed and rich." Theresa clenched her slender fists.

"So?" Mary ventured to break the silence.

"So she fancied my fiancé. In a big way. You see, he had everything she wanted—a good position in society, rich in his own right, a lovely home in the right snob center. . . . Mary, I'm almost certain she engineered the whole—this difficult position I'm in at present. And I would not fight back because there was no trust in Derek. We met her quite often, at parties, and things. She was always underfoot making a big play for Derek's attention. The flattery that man can swallow amazes me, and my handsome doctor swallowed elephantine gulps and loved it. Don't get me wrong, he was just as attentive and loving to me as ever, but the way was being paved for him, poor man. I can even pity him now."

Theresa looked out at the sunlight playing on the leaves of a tipuana tree. "What I can't forget or forgive is his lack of trust and pompous disinclination to believe my true version of what followed. 'His own eyes could not deceive him, not only once but twice' was his verdict, so that was that."

"What was what?"

"I can only go on if I know you're going to believe me."

Mary studied her intently without a word. Theresa met her eyes and sighed with sure conviction.

"Thank you, Mary. Forgive my doubting mind. I should have known, but my ideals have been somewhat shaken. You can't imagine what two silly episodes can do to one's morale—not the episodes themselves but the misconstrued conception as they appeared to others, to Derek mostly. I'm dithering and can't seem to get to the point. . . ."

"Dither along, darling, if it helps. I'm not going to vanish." Mary's quiet, compassionate voice soothed the other's taut nerves.

"Well, Mitch Sanders phoned one day and seemed so upset he could hardly speak coherently. It was about his sister. He desperately wanted my advice because I had knowledge of medical procedures. I told him I was only a third-year nurse, and why didn't he call the right authorities, meaning a doctor. He interrupted, insisting that he would like to talk to me first, and I could then advise him what to do. I asked him what was wrong with his sister as she looked in splendid health to me. He was quiet for so long that I thought he had hung up, and then his voice came over rather ashamedly admitting that he had pried among Sylvia's private papers and had made a startling discovery about her health that upset him very much. It was quite evident that she wasn't doing anything about said health. He was fond of her, and so on. I've since found out that she was very generous with her money, so he would be fond of her!" The sarcasm slipped out and Theresa shook her head as if to clear it of cobwebs. Tonelessly she continued, "I ventured that he should insist on medical attention, and he replied that Sylvia wasn't the kind anyone could force, least of all her brother! Please would I meet him somewhere to discuss the matter, and if I thought it proper maybe I could confide in Dr. Mann and he, in turn, could speak to Sylvia? He promised to disclose the full story about her health, having confidence in my integrity (what a word!).

"I told him to come to my apartment, but he refused, saying he wouldn't like to jeopardize Dr. Mann's fiancée in any way. Well, to be brief, I agreed to meet him at a certain restaurant on Church Street. The moment I hung up the phone rang again. Derek informed me that he was free for the evening, and would I like to go out? I was in a quandary and after some hesitation (which, incidentally, was pointed out later) told him I'd rather have an early night. Having given my promise to Mitch the matter was confidential at this stage, or so I thought. Mitch's story was plausible and I was a gullible fool."

"His story was very good so far. What then, Terry?" Mary leaned forward, following Theresa's narrative with thoughtful interest.

"I found Mitch sitting in his car at the curb in front of the stipulated restaurant. He was very jittery and said the place was full. He'd recognized acquaintances who might gossip. The fleeting thought did cross my mind that he was suddenly very careful of my reputation, but he looked so worried that I agreed to drive with him to another place. No one was more surprised than I when he turned into the circular drive of the Union Buildings. Before I could protest he had reached the top and parked the car facing the lights of the city.

"I waited, thinking he was trying to formulate a way of telling me bad news. He asked rather hesitantly after my health, not having seen me for some time. I assured him that I was quite well and would he come to the point; why this devious, unethical way of discussing things? I realized afterward that he was watching the curve of the road rather closely. Another car was coming up slowly and Mitch moved closer to me as if to avoid the glare of its headlights."

Theresa unconsciously rubbed her ringless fingers as she gazed at her friend.

"The car came to a standstill and Derek stepped out! Dramatics? Oh no. He opened the door on my side, asked politely if he could drive me back now that I had received the required fresh air. Mary, it was . . . funny—so funny that I nearly burst out laughing!"

"Pompous fool!" The epithet was involuntary.

"Oh no, darling, he was every inch the gentleman. No scenes—they could wait. I turned to Mitch expecting him to explain, but he moved behind the wheel, muttering that he would get in touch. The wretch! Dear Derek couldn't help a slight descent from dignity, for he retorted, 'good-night Saunders.' "

Theresa relived the time, later, when they were back in her apartment.

Derek Mann was tall and fair-haired. His light blue eyes stared down at her accusingly, making her feel small, definitely giving her a feeling of guilt. She stood facing him proudly, her hand resting lightly on the chair beside her.

"Well?" Derek teetered casually on his feet, but his hands were tightly clenched. "Did I interrupt your 'early night'!?"

"I still intend to have that early night, Derek. This was a confidential matter that came up—"

"Very confidential, I noticed. He was sitting very, er, confidingly close." Sarcasm dripped.

Theresa kept her tone even. "Mitch called and wanted to see me on a private matter that he promised I could discuss with you later." Something was trying to get through to her and she had a moment of puzzlement.

"So private that you had to leave the privacy of your flat and drive to that very public place, where couples are notorious for their confidential secrets—"

"Don't be silly, Derek, it wasn't like that at all. It was a medical matter, if you must know." Theresa was suddenly impatient with his lack of understanding.

He looked at her contemplatively. "If I must know? A medical matter? What's the implication? Is Mitch in trouble with some woman and seeking your assistance?"

"Not as far as I know. He has a problem concerning a woman, but not the way you mean." Theresa was suddenly furious with him for daring to think she would help anyone in the way he was insinuating. "How dare you suggest that I would meddle—" and then it hit her. "How did you know where to find me?"

"I received a phone call. Anonymous." His cold manner warmed slightly as indignation made her more vitally alive and beautiful.

"Anonymous!" Blue eyes flew to his in amazement. "This is a set-up, Derek. There's nothing wrong with Sylvia, and Mitch is in this up to his traitorous eyes!" she stated flatly.

"Sylvia? Should there be something wrong with her? You'd better explain, my dear." Derek was clearly puzzled at this enigmatic statement.

"Mitch phoned and wanted a private talk about some illness of Sylvia's. He sounded extremely agitated, that's why I was with him."

"And why should someone phone me and say that it wasn't the first time they had seen you in that particular spot?"

"Good heavens, Derek, you can't believe that of me. You trust me, surely?" Theresa sank into the chair in complete bewilderment.

Derek said slowly, "Sylvia did come to see me today at my consulting room. I've started treatment of a slight . . . indisposition. Nothing serious enough to warrant your version of Mitch's agitation."

"My version? That sounds as though you don't believe me! Oh, forget it. Sylvia's coming to see you is proof of my explanation anyway. But the phone call, that's deliberately malicious. Have you no idea who it was, a woman or a man?"

"I can't say. A muffled voice that could have been of either sex."

"Why didn't you tell them to go to blazes and slam the phone down? Or did your curiosity overcome your trusting nature?" The scorn in her voice was in startling contrast to the bland innocence of her face.

"Well, after all, Terry, I have my good name to watch, and if any of our friends had seen you there they would have jumped at the chance of misconstruing the whole episode. That's reasonable, isn't it? I had to satisfy myself, and I can tell you it was quite a shock when I found you there. Anyway, you seem to have explained the whole episode, so I'll forget it. Just don't get yourself involved again, sweet. Send would-be patients to me, I'm the doctor."

After he had left, Theresa looked at the door contemplatively. Had Mitch deliberately tried to compromise her? Who else had known they would be there? Why did he drive to that particular spot? She had an instinctive feeling that his sister was the mainspring of the plot to discredit her in Derek's eyes. The phone call? To top it all . . . Derek's insinuation that she, a nurse, would possibly dabble in illegal abortion!

Oh, to the devil with it! Theresa stripped, showered and scrubbed as though trying to cleanse herself of some taint. . . .

"That was the first time, Mary. Two weeks later came the anticlimax. I always thought of love as a 'many-splendored thing' and I sure crashed on that mythical rock. Love would see to the core of things, see through pretense— Oh no, love is a delusion!"

"Hey, pet, hold your horses! Your view is a bit cloudy at present, and I don't blame you. Carry on while I dry Poppet's tail. So Madam Sylvia didn't stop there?"

"I'll make it short and—should I say—sweet. The whole thing leaves a bitter taste in my mouth. I was doing my bit of district duty—it does land me in some queer places—and a call came from an apartment in the better part of town. I didn't question it, so you can imagine my fury when Sylvia opened the door. I was prepared to blast her when she suddenly staggered and clutched at me, spilling a small glass of tomato juice down the front of my uniform; it was in her hand when she'd opened the door. She looked about to collapse, so I helped her to the bed-room and did the usual things a nurse does for a fainting person. She recovered mighty quickly. Thanking me, she explained that the apartment belonged to a friend whom she expected any minute. I asked why she hadn't sent for Derek, and she said she had tried but he wasn't available. Very upset about the mess on my uniform, she insisted that I remove it and sponge it as best I could. I slipped into the large paisley dressing gown hanging behind the door and took my uniform to the bathroom. I was busy cleaning it when I heard the front door open and close and wondered if her friend was a male. Going back to the bedroom, I discovered Sylvia was gone!

"There was a knock on the front door, and I was still standing in stunned surprise when it opened and Derek confronted me. To make it short, the apartment belonged to Mitch, I had on his dressing gown, another anonymous call to the good doctor and there you have it! His accusations were flung at me before I could pull myself together. They were so brutal and demeaning that, without bothering to explain, I handed back his ring. My pride was up in arms, Mary. If a man didn't have enough trust to wait for explanations, I wanted no part of him. I resigned the next day."

"And Sylvia?"

"I never saw her again."

"So you ran away?"

"You can call it that, which probably made the situation look worse than ever, but I didn't care. Derek tried to get in touch again, but I refused to see him or speak to him except to inform him that Sylvia could supply the details. Matron was upset and difficult, but ended up giving me a good reference." Theresa hesitated, her face pale and withdrawn. "I've thought of going to Salisbury or some other hospital where I could carry on nursing. Money from Dad's estate is still in the bank, but it's not going to last forever—" She lowered suddenly moist eyes and bit her lip.

Mary knew that Theresa was thinking of her parents and that tragic air disaster that had left her an orphan at 17—more than three years ago, but the heartbreak was still there. She had turned to nursing, a profession she had yearned after since childhood.

"Well, I do think you acted impetuously honey, although I probably would have done the same thing. However, thanks for telling me. I can read between the lines and realize that you haven't revealed how much you must have suffered because of that obnoxious couple. There should be a law against types like that. As for the high-handed Derek, I confess that I never liked him anyway. You're well rid of him. You're very welcome to stay here as long as I can manage to keep you, and that's as long as I have breath in my body!"

Theresa swallowed back the lump in her throat and spoke quietly. "I'm blessed to have friends like you and

Dan. Thank you. Please let me help in any way possible. I'm not afraid of work."

Mary smiled. "Go on with you! Everything is run on oiled wheels. There's not even enough for me to do except care for Dan and that young miss. I know of your propensity for work; you'll find something to do if it kills you! You're here to have a good rest; so relax and forget the past. We have some top saddle horses, so you can ride and explore to your heart's content. Our village club provides tennis, dancing and golf—believe me, there are scads of eligible males who would jump to partner you and take your mind off other problems." The smile turned into an irrepressible chuckle. "I'm sorry, Terry, but I've suddenly had a clear picture of you standing in a man's apartment and a disapproving doctor looking at you with deep suspicion. Picturing Theresa Stanton drawing up her haughty five-foot-what-have-you, in a man's dressing gown, and imperiously handing him the ring!"

Theresa smiled too and a heaviness lifted from her heart. Mary was right, it did sound corny. The way to view it was lightheartedly. Somehow, Derek's suspicions and distrust would be seen in the right perspective and she would be wary of so-called love in future. The shock of disillusionment had been painful; the ideal of eligible men in the neighborhood left her cold. She did not voice this feeling to Mary, but decided to be more circumspect in her dealings with the opposite sex in future.

Humor came to her rescue and lit her eyes as she wondered how Dr. Derek Mann had explained his sudden loss of a fiancée to his society friends. Her name must be well coated with mud by this time! Well, Sylvia had the field now. Was it possible to fake a faint as well as she had? Theresa came to the conclusion that she was not such a good nurse after all, not to distinguish a fake from the real thing.

CHAPTER TWO

Standing on the porch, breathing deeply in the fresh morning air, Theresa looked at the distant hills and reflected that her first impression of the country had been wrong. It was not desolate or forsaken at all. Across the tobacco lands, umbrella trees dotted the landscape and the veld was lushly green—ideal for cattle farming as Dan had informed her. Beyond the deep green line of trees that grew along the riverbank and delineated his land from Milward's vast cattle ranch she could see softly rolling hills, the early morning haze giving them a wavering, unreal appearance. Later, the harsh, hot sun would reveal outcrops of huge rocks with thickly fleshed aloes and other strange plants growing in crevices and gullies.

Land of the Flame Lily! A curious thrill of excitement coursed through her body as she stood looking into the distance. It seemed to beckon to her with impelling, expectant arms—as if willing her to "come and discover what mysteries we hold for you, come and explore nature in all its beauty."

"It's a lovely view, don't you agree, Terry?" Mary joined her and sat on the encircling wall. "Although that same view can turn out excruciatingly hot if you happen to be out there later in the day. Don't ever go out riding or walking without a hat; it's fatal."

Theresa turned an eager face. "Oh, Mary, could I take a horse out after breakfast? My riding has gone rusty, but I'll be very careful and promise to glue my hat on. I'm so intrigued to see what's down there among that line of green trees. I can almost hear them calling me."

Mary looked into her friend's face, noting that the blue eyes held a sparkle that had not been there the previous day. That lost look was not in evidence and she hoped sincerely it would be banished entirely during Terry's stay at Oaklands.

" 'The Call of the Wild,' It's getting you already, pet.

414

Either you remain immune or its velvet claws hold you in a passionate embrace from which there's no escape. One or the other, there's no in-between."

Mary spoke dryly, but the look in her own eyes belied the even tones. This land had already claimed her.

"That sounds wonderfully romantic and you've got it bad, that's for sure, friend." The misty outlines drew Theresa's eyes again and she added contemplatively, "Yes, I guess it could enthrall one very easily if one were so inclined."

"Even against one's inclination, my dear. If you answer that call just once then you're sunk, for good."

"Scott Milward's wife—were her ears deaf?" Theresa's question, coming up suddenly from the depths of un-conscious thinking, surprised even herself.

Mary considered. "Elaine was simply not cut out for this kind of life. Scott indulged her recklessly. She's spoiled and very lovely, but . . ." she hesitated.

"Did he . . . does he love her very much?"

"He worshipped her," Mary stated flatly.

A dull ache of pain at her own lost love was suddenly affiliated to that of Milward's awry marriage. Theresa shook the bitter mood, as if it were a heavy black cloak, off her shoulders. She spoke with enforced brightness. "Well, I hope the claws are sheathed this morning; I only want to explore a teeny bit and won't heed any clarion calls. Do you think Dan will let me have a horse?"

"Of course. But you must promise to be careful and not go too far. The men are busy in the fields and I haven't anyone here to go with you. I can't get away on account of Poppet. If you promise . . . ."

"Cross my heart and hope—" Theresa chuckled at Mary's earnest expression and gave her a quick hug. "Let's eat, I'm famished. I'll have to watch my figure at this rate!"

"Ha! From what I remember you could eat oodles of everything without any noticeable difference to your vital statistics. I was the one who gained a pound everytime I looked at a cream-puff!"

Dan came around the corner of the porch. "Do I get

breakfast or are you two going to stand in mutual admiration all morning? I'm a working man, alas, otherwise it would give me great pleasure to spend my days gazing at the view."

His twinkling eyes traveled slowly over the slender figure of the woman at his wife's side. Theresa stepped back in mock alarm.

Mary put a fist under Dan's chin. "Stop leering, Casanova. Come and eat, and take that hungry look off your silly face."

"Jealous spoilsport!" Dan grinned wickedly and slung long arms around their shoulders as he led them inside.

Theresa dismounted and tethered the horse to a stout branch, then made her way to the water's edge. The river was rippling cheerfully over shallow rocks to settle into deep pools fringed with grasses and reeds. Wild bauhinia and spathodeas were struggling to reach the sunshine amidst tall gums. Masses of swordfern grew in damp crevices on the banks and she followed the course with fascination, stepping over fallen branches and undergrowth.

A slight rustle in the reeds startled her and her heart started to beat heavily. Heavens, she had forgotten that Dan had mentioned many types of snakes to be found hereabouts! Theresa stood perfectly still, her eyes glued to the spot the noise had come from. Not even a stout stick in her hands for protection; there were plenty lying around, but she didn't dare move for fear of attracting attention.

The silence lengthened, and just as she decided to move the sound came again. She was staring straight into the large velvety eyes of a small furry animal. Hypnotized blue held equally mesmerized brown for seconds on end, and then Theresa expelled her breath with a gasp. A startled squeak at the unexpected guest and the furry ball backed out of sight!

Theresa moved out of the brush and found a large boulder jutting into the water, its smooth top already warming in the sun. She sat down on it, her legs suddenly weak, and fumbled for a cigarette. If a small animal could frighten her like that, what would happen if she met up with crocodile or hyena or . . . were there lions in this vicinity? Her hands shook as she inhaled deeply and stared across the river.

"Coward!" she castigated herself sternly. "The rustle of a small creature and you nearly die of fright. Shame on you, Theresa Stanton!" Her eyes roved and rested on an outcrop of rocks limned with a brush of golden sunlight. A brilliant flash of scarlet flowers bloomed in a pocket of ground among the rocks. Their regal beauty drew her delighted gaze. In no time she had found a crossing of flat rocks; all thoughts of fearful animals were forgotten as Theresa climbed the outcrop and peered into the crevice at this blaze of color and beauty.

Could it be the St. John Lily, she wondered. It would be sacrilege to pick them—they looked so right in that setting. She would leave them just so, her own private treasure trove to come and gloat over again and again. With a sigh of pleasure the girl backed down and walked around the rocks seeing more beauty.

A deep, blowing grunt close to her unsuspecting back spun her around and again she was staring into large velvety eyes! But these were large gleaming eyes of the biggest domestic beast she had ever seen. One involuntary leap and she was up on the rocks again.

Looking down with her heart in her mouth she observed that it was not a cow but a very red, large-humped, ferocious-looking bull. The beast grunted again and Theresa drew her feet up in agitation; could that hulk of an animal climb rocks? His eyes were also red in close-up; probably a stud bull with the usual bad temper accorded to the breed. . . . Theresa sat perfectly still, her mind desperately seeking a way out of her predicament, while the animal stood below with swishing tail. Perhaps getting ready to charge?

With relief she spied a horse and rider topping the rise several hundred yards away. She was afraid to move in case the animal became excited. But the rider, unaware of impending tragedy, turned away. In desperation a piercing whistle left her lips and the horse reared in fright.

Calming his horse, the man turned to take in the situation at a glance: a golden nymph huddled on a large boulder while her red-eyed captor emitted deep noises from a well-developed neck and throat. To Theresa's ears came the heart-relieving words as Scott Milward rode nearer.

"Sit very still. I'm going to rush him, frighten him away. Be ready to jump on my horse when I stop. Here I come!"

A shrill, cowboy yelp rent the air and hooves thundered as he dashed forward and the startled beast below her turned tail and fled. With a flourish the rider drew up. In an instant he had scooped the nymph into the saddle and they were away!

Flying across the veld at this speed brought more terror to Theresa. She had been rescued from one hazard only to be flung into another—a broken neck to say the least. "Stop, oh, stop, please!" She screamed into the passing wind. Scott slowed down and she stammered in a choked voice, "You're going in the wrong direction. M-my horse is . . . is over that way."

He veered around and slackened speed as they approached the river, finally stopping at the crossing where Theresa had left her horse. Scott loosened his firm grip on her waist, dismounted with a lithe movement and lifted the trembling girl down. Theresa's legs were wobbly and Scott held her with strong arms while she steadied herself.

Breathlessly, she looked up at him while endeavoring to stand firmly on her own stupid feet. Gray eyes gazing down into hers suddenly made her feel more limp than ever, as if she was being hypnotized. For the third time in one morning and, inexplicably, she was most afraid of the eyes now holding hers. If she wasn't careful she would surely drown in the depths of those smoky-gray pools!

Slowly Scott dropped his arms and stepped back; Theresa experienced almost a physical wrench when his eyes left hers for a casual look at the river. "You'll be all right now, Miss Stanton. I guess your fiery beast is over the horizon by now."

She stammered, "I don't know how to thank you, Mr. Milward. I was terrified . . . it was very good . . . I mean courageous of you to rescue me in that reckless fashion—"

" 'Twas a pleasure, ma'am, think nothing of it." He touched his hat.

Did Theresa detect slight sarcasm in his manner—the way a sudden dimple played at the corner of his mouth? The humble touch of hand to hat somehow did not accord with the autocratic bearing of the rest of that sun-browned body and compelling face.

"Well, I'm grateful," she repeated. "I wonder who that beast belongs to, and if he's as fierce as he looks? I'd hate to meet up with him again. But he certainly got a fright when you descended on him with that heathen yell!"

"I agree, a yell like that would frighten the devil out of his lair. Forgive the spectacular rescue, my dear. Boys will be boys even at my age. You'll find your way home from here?"

The hooded eyes and change of manner bewildered her, and the cold dismissal in his question was so evident that she felt a chill around her heart.

Theresa collected herself, her voice equally cool and casual. "Thank you, yes. Again, many thanks for your help and the trouble I caused you."

She turned on her heel and very carefully stepped onto the stones crossing the river. Only when she'd reached the opposite side did she hear the sound of his departure. She watched as horse and rider vanished from sight. What a strange man, and how moody could one get? Why in heaven's name did he apologize for rescuing her, and that crack about boys being boys? Scott Milward was certainly a contradiction of sardonic inflections and quick, warm actions. Theresa still felt breathless when she remembered his incredibly swift movements as he swept her off the rock onto the horse and the sureness of his arms in that mad gallop.

Absorbed in her thoughts, she scarcely noticed the time or distance, surfacing only when her horse ambled through the home-gates. Dan was climbing out of the jeep and they met on the front steps.

"Have you been out all this time, doll? That was real naughty of you."

"Oh, Dan, is it really midday? I hope Mary isn't angry with me." Theresa removed her hat and felt anxious as Mary, appearing in the passage, stopped to survey her, arms akimbo.

"I'll cancel that call I put through to the local policehounds," she remarked evenly. At Theresa's shocked face she continued chidingly, "Anyway, I was going to put a call out for you, but I didn't, so now I don't have to cancel it, do I? Lucky for you, my girl, because if I had I would—"

"You're getting slightly tangled in the tongue, Mary *mia*. Give the girl a chance to explain her tardy appearance." Dan slapped his wife's bottom affectionately.

She glared at him indignantly. "Don't get fresh with me, Daniel Rourke. I'll have you know I'm a respectable married woman. Come on in, Theresa. Now sit down and explain."

Grinning at her friend's stern countenance, Theresa sank into a deep armchair. "You'll never guess what I went through this day. I met up with three wild creatures! The first one ran in fright (so did I), the second cornered me on a rock and the third—the third, on a horse, rescued me from the second one, so there!"

The Rourkes stared at her, and the looks of amazement on their faces were so similar that she burst into delighted laughter. Mary gave Dan a meaningful look. He started loosening his belt in a threatening manner.

Theresa stopped abruptly. "All right, Dan, don't spank me! I'll be more explicit for your dense benefit, although my condensed effort was rather fabulous, don't you think?" Dan threatened again and she continued hurriedly. When she came to the end of her story Mary's face was a study of blankness and Dan was equally poker faced. She looked from one to the other in puzzlement.

"Neither of you seem to be enthralled at my tale of gallant rescue—"

"I think it's absolutely astonishing—" Mary came alive, but her husband forestalled her, drowning further words in a loud voice.

"Yes, yes, my colleen, it was a good thing Scott was in the offing, wasn't it, otherwise you never know what might have happened." He strode hurriedly to the door and turned. "You did say it was a ferocious beast that confronted you?"

"Yes, that's what I said." Uncertainty clouded Theresa's voice, for a humiliating suspicion was taking form.

Dan remained deadpan. "Mm, that's what I thought you said. Excuse me, please, I must wash my hands." He disappeared.

"Mary . . .?"

"Darling, it must have been thrilling, especially that terrifying ride—I'll speak to that Milward! Oh, heavens, I smell something burning!" The young matron smartly exited, blowing vigorously into her handkerchief.

Theresa lay back and darkly nursed indignation. "So!" she snorted aloud, "it was a big frame-up. And my two very good friends have realized that. How tactful of them to disappear so conveniently. Not a ferocious beast at all, only wanting to be friends, *and* belonging to that odious man, I presume. Boys will be boys, eh? That's why he did have the decency to ask forgiveness for the spectacular rescue. How big of him, Mr. wonderful Milward!" She stopped, her fury choking her. But her thoughts were savage, precipitating hot color to her cheeks as she dwelt on the person responsible for her present humiliation.

When Dan came back Theresa was cool and composed. "Is lunch ready, Dan dear?" Her smile was transparently ingenuous. "What's wrong, dear man? Is my face dirty? You're looking so hard at me. I shall wash immediately, sir!" Theresa blew a fluttering kiss and ambled out, swaying slim hips in an exaggerated motion.

At lunch she rubbed it in good and hard. "Mary dear, I am so sorry I caused you worry by staying away so long.

Surely now that you've heard of my terrific experience wouldn't you say it was worth it?" Clasping her hands together, looking dreamy, she continued, "And that fabulous, brave man, his heart must have stopped when he saw my danger. . . ."

Her friend looked worried. "Really, Terry, I think I would . . . I think, I mean . . . you should really know that—"

"Please, Mary, you should try not to repeat yourself so often, try not to stutter, it will be a bad influence on Glynis Theresa."

"Would it?" Mary caught herself. "Oh, Terry, I don't always stutter! It's that I . . . I should tell—"

"There you go again. Dan, you should look into this." Concern was in Theresa's voice, and then she brightened. "But of course, how silly of me. You're worried, hence the stutter. Well, honey, I know what you're trying to say and, forgive me, I know my manners. I'll thank the obnox— the gallant Mr. Milward very sweetly when next I see him. Oh, be very sure of that!"

Theresa smiled radiantly at her hosts and changed the subject. How was Poppet's earache? She was glad she was better. Could she take her for a walk later? How were the men doing on the land, and at what stage was the fertility of the dear little tobacco plants? Theresa jabbered on until it was time for Dan to leave.

Her dismay showed for an instant, when he stopped at the door to remind his wife that Scott was coming to dinner. When Mary turned back she was brushing bread crumbs into a neat pile on her side-plate.

"I feel sorry for Mr. Milward. Know what, Mary?"

"Yes, dear?" Mary's voice quavered.

"I have a good mind to offer my services to him—for Melinda. After all, he saved my life, and with nursing experience I should qualify, shouldn't I? She's too young for schooling, so a nurse would be more suitable, I would think."

"No! I don't think you should—"

"Thinking again! You were certainly more sure of yourself in the old days. Darling, I'm only teasing—don't look so upset, You mean I'm too young, as Scott remarked when he mistook me for a governess?"

"No, not really, but . . . well. . . .," Mary tried again.

Theresa decided she had gone far enough. She stood and stretched her arms. "I'll put it to Mr. M. when I see the old dear tonight. Time for the universal siesta. Boy, do I need it! See you later, dear friend, Mary," She sang loudly as she walked down the passage to her room, twisting the placement of words in an old song, "A friend is just a stranger you'll never know!"

CHAPTER THREE

Theresa gave a last glance at her reflection in the mirror. Hair piled in a neat swirl on top of her head, slim body enchantingly sheathed in creamy, embossed linen with a high front neckline that dipped daringly low down her back. Light makeup accentuated her thickly fringed blue eyes. Amethyst earrings and gold sandals completed her dress.

Full battle dress—to meet Mr. Joker Milward!

Mary raised an admiring eyebrow and Dan raised his glass when Theresa joined them at the bar. Drinks were enjoyed while they waited for the dinner guest. It came as a slight shock to the girl when she suddenly realized that Derek had not touched her thoughts for a full day. That did not mean she had forgotten. At the moment she was only concerned with would-be jokers. Scott Milward evidently regarded her as a silly girl who needed thrills to disperse boredom. A thought struck her and she looked long and hard at Dan and Mary.

"By the way, why was I called a bluestocking by your neighbor at the station?"

Dan opened his mouth guiltily but his wife forestalled him.

"My fault entirely, Terry. When we mentioned your visit I rather harped on your classical background. Having known the Professor, your dad, so well, I often spoke of his brilliance and personality when Scott was present. I guess that gave him the impression you were a bluestocking. It's not an insult, dear, for you to have a cultural background. Your dad was the finest man I ever knew, and his love of the classics has rubbed off on you as well: I recall quite clearly that you always preferred the opera and would rather browse in his library than lead a gay life of dancing, parties, etcetera."

"Oh, I see." Theresa accepted the explanation and did not pursue the subject. Mary must have told Scott that she was also a nurse, but he had probably ignored it and thought she was merely after the glamor of the profession and not seen it as a serious occupation.

The sound of a car outside put an end to her thoughts. She stiffened slightly as Scott walked into the room; she studied him as he greeted Mary and Dan in a courteously familiar way. He really was incredibly handsome and looked cool and suave in a light tropical suit. Dark-lashed gray eyes turned now to her and a smoky flame flickered in their depths as they swiftly appraised her gleaming hair, circled her face and came to rest on the full curve of soft lips.

"Good evening, Miss Stanton. How are you?" Scott held out his hand to enclose hers in a warm clasp.

"Very well, thank you, Mr. Milward. And you?" A queer tingle ran up her arm and she was very conscious of his long brown fingers.

"I'm fit, thanks." He dropped her hand suddenly.

"The usual, Scott? I'm sure Terry and you need not be so formal. Theresa, meet Scott." Dan handed him a glass.

Scott Milward's sudden smile transformed his imperious face into lines of boyishness. "Hello, Theresa." Her name had a caressing quality on his lips.

"Hello, Scott." An inner tremor softened her voice and Theresa gave herself an invisible, angry shake. "Don't get soft now, simpleton. This is the man who took you for a ride in more ways than one, and don't you forget it just because he has a dimple in that brown cheek and his mouth looks generous and vulnerable. A double-crossing face!" Theresa silently admonished herself while she smiled sweetly and accepted the glass handed to her. To Dan she said mildly, "I shouldn't really have so much to drink, Dan dear. You know how silly it makes me."

That worthy raised surprised brows at this blatant lie, but she had turned back to Scott. "Mary told me about your daughter. How is she?"

"Melinda is fine, thank you. A little put out because she couldn't come with me." A light gleamed in his eyes at the mention of his daughter.

"Have you solved the mystery of the missing . . . governess?" Sweet venom showed for an instant.

Scott studied Theresa intently for a moment and then answered, noncommittally, "Yes. A phone call, late this afternoon. Of all things, the unfortunate woman developed mumps and there's no available substitute at present. I mean no one who is suitably qualified."

"A qualified nurse? Staid and not too young?"

Mary interposed hastily, "I'm sure they'll find someone for you before Vera leaves." She flashed a warning glance at her friend.

But Theresa smiled enigmatically. "Dear Mary is so worried about you and Melinda, Scott. I have a proposition to discuss, later, if you care to listen. . . ."

The maid announced dinner and Mary quickly led the way, giving Theresa's arm a pinch in passing. But her friend merely cast her a surprised, innocent look of reproach. However, she did not reopen the subject until dinner was over and they sat sipping coffee.

The conversation covered recent movies and shows, and Theresa took the cue from there. "I like good shows, but you'd never guess what my favorite books and movies are." She looked dreamy, then opened her eyes wide as Scott raised an inquiring eyebrow. "Westerns! Oh, those cowboys!"

Three pairs of incredulous eyes met her wide blue gaze.

"Do you know, Scott, I have a sneaking feeling that my friends think I'm slightly highbrow, but they're so wrong. And that's why I want to thank you again for our thrilling ride this morning—it put me right into my favorite picture. Handsome hero rescues desperate maiden! Of course," she added deprecatingly, "you didn't realize that the poor little beast was only being friendly and there wasn't any danger really. I'm glad, though, because it was exciting, and you do ride superbly. Please forgive me for not putting you wise to the real facts, but I couldn't resist the Western melodrama of it all. My piercing whistle was most realistic, wasn't it? And you responded so gallantly. Am I forgiven?" bland innocence entreated.

Scott Milward looked at her steadily. "Touché," he murmured softly. "You're forgiven, Theresa. I'm pleased to have given you the thrill of living up to your favorite—Westerns."

"Thank you kindly, sir." Theresa turned her attention to the silent, dumbstruck Rourkes. "I did put it over you as well, and I'm sorry, but it was such fun watching your faces. Deadpan Dan and Muttering Mary listening to the escapades of Titillating Theresa! Well, now that we're all friends again, my proposition—"

"Theresa!" Mary found her voice.

"Yes, dear? Oh, I know you're going to warn me that Mr. Milward—Scott—will turn down my proposal, but I'm going to put it to him, regardless." Theresa looked serene, but her insides began to wobble as she met Scott's disconcerting gaze. She was quite certain he would not accept her offer, yet something was driving her; she wanted to see that look of acidulous contempt appear and then inform him blithely that she was only joking.

"I'm a third-year nurse, which includes extensive training in the children's wards. If I can be of assistance in caring for your Melinda, at least until such a time as you find another—governess or nurse, I herewith file application for said vacancy."

A long silence ensued. She asked timidly, "Or am I too young and flighty, perhaps?"

Acidulous contempt was not forthcoming. Scott considered her with unreadable eyes, his expression inscrutable. "May we adjourn to the lounge, Mary, while I consider Theresa's generous offer?"

"Certainly. I'll, er, follow as soon as I've pacified Poppet; I can hear her grumbling."

Dan also found a farm matter to settle, so Theresa and Scott walked in silence to the sitting room. She seated herself as he wandered over to the window, standing with his back to her. An uncompromising back, straight, autocratic.... A peculiar feeling feathered over her scalp as she waited for him to speak. All of a sudden Theresa did not want contempt or any other form of sarcasm from this man and was bitterly sorry that she had deliberately invited it.

At last, he turned to face her. "Would your doctor-fiancé approve of a position for you as nursemaid to a divorced man's daughter?"

The question came so casually that it took a moment for Theresa to assimilate its content; then she was shaken at the pain that gripped her heart. She looked down at her hands, fighting for control. Did that pain stem from her own broken heart or was it pain for his casual admittance of the final wrench from the woman he adored? She still did not know, and when she raised her proud head, she stated simply, "Derek and I are no longer engaged. I've also resigned my position at the hospital."

"I see." He rubbed his chin reflectively. "Well, I'll take you up on that offer, Theresa. You may want a day or two to visit with Mary. Let's see, it's Sunday tomorrow; I'll call for you on Wednesday. Suit you?" The question was shot at her in a brusque, husky voice.

Theresa stood up suddenly, walked away from him and leaned her elbows on the bar. The shock of his acceptance of her impulsive offer was like a blow between the shoulder blades, coming on the heels of her swift pain. She felt his presence beside her, and his elbow brushed against her arm as he idly fingered an ornamental opener.

Scott spoke sardonically. "It evidently doesn't suit you. Well, I don't blame you; you're entitled to have your holiday and good times. I'm afraid my predicament is rather urgent as Miss Smith is leaving quite soon. Getting married, poor woman."

The bitter sarcasm brought a quick retort. "There are happy marriages too, Scott. I've lost a fiancé and you've lost a wife, so we don't see life through rose-colored glasses at present. Dan and Mary, for instance; who could be happier than they?"

"You're still young, my dear Theresa. Quite possibly there will be a reconciliation with your doctor, or you may find so-called love elsewhere. So don't couple my troubles with yours."

"But you're not an old man, Scott. Pain recedes after a

while. Soon one finds new horizons and other compensations follow. You have your daughter to love. To me, love is an illusion—"

Scott cut across her words with grim finality. "Spare me the details. We seem to have deviated somewhat."

Dan had an affectionate arm across his wife's shoulders as they came in and joined the couple at the bar. "Serious discussion?" he asked jocularly.

"Ah, very serious. Theresa's love life has gone awry; so has mine. We've been commiserating. Also, because of that I'm about to lose a would-be applicant, if my guess is right." The mocking eyebrow was high, and grim amusement glinted in imperious eyes.

Theresa was seething with fury at his curt dismissal of her attempt to comfort him. Their eyes met for a timeless moment while wills clashed, one arrogantly confident, the other indomitable, spirited. Theresa turned away from the magnetic personality of the man and slipped her arm through Mary's. "Scott, or should I say Mr. Milward as he's my future employer, has accepted my application. I'm to start on Wednesday. Not having met Melinda I can't conceive what my duties will be, but if she's as kind and gracious as her old dad, I have no need to worry. Don't look so surprised, Mary, I'm sure to have a day off occasionally to visit you and enjoy other exciting times such as my extreme youth yearns for. Whew, that calls for a drink! What do you say, gang?"

Scott spoke imperturbably. "It certainly does, especially for you, after that noble speech. Of course you may call me Scott; I won't consider it an impertinence. Dan, don't be mean with your hooch. Fill 'em up and drink to this charming young lady's and my grateful alliance." He added, almost as an afterthought, keeping his voice deliberately casual, "I've told Theresa, and I want you to know as well, my . . . separation . . . is finalized."

Mary spoke quietly. "Scott, I don't quite know what to say. To be honest, I think it's better this way." Her eyes were shining with compassion as she placed a comforting hand on his arm.

Dan looked wordlessly at his friend, a world of feeling in his warm eyes.

"Cheers, folks. Here's to your freedom, Scott Milward, and to my slavery!" Theresa challenged him to break the pall of bitterness that threatened.

"Thank you, Theresa. You're good for the morale," Scott smiled, and lifted his glass in an arrogant salute.

The party suddenly became happier and Dan took over and channeled everybody into a brighter mood. His spirited Irish humor and Mary's dry repartee kept them vastly amused. Scott was not lagging and Theresa was amazed at his easy, descriptive knowledge of people and countries he had visited. She noticed that he did not talk of the United States, even though he had met and married Elaine in that country. His ex-wife now, the woman he adored, so Mary had told her. Was that adoration a thing of the past or was it still in his heart?

When Scott announced that it was time to depart he turned to Dan. "Bring the women over for tea tomorrow afternoon. Melinda worries because she hasn't seen Mary and Glynis for some time, and it will give her and Theresa a chance to become acquainted."

"Sure thing, chum," Dan acquiesced, and Mary seconded the invitation.

"Good. Thanks for the dinner." A salutory wave and Scott strode out.

"Well now, my girl, explain your wily ways. I could have cheerfully conked you one at the dinner table. What have you let yourself in for?" Mary demanded.

Theresa giggled deliciously. "Oh, dear, my tale of rescue—"

"I gathered that you'd cottoned on and you turned the tables very neatly; you had us all tongue-tied. So much for that. Now what about this job business?"

Theresa sobered. "Yes, Mary, it started as a joke and boomeranged with a vengeance. I never dreamt Scott would accept my offer. My pride wouldn't let me back down after he remarked that, being fond of my pleasures, I probably wouldn't like the idea of starting immediately. That's my case in a nutshell."

Mary considered thoughtfully. Dan came over and squatted on his heels. "As master of the house, may I say something? I think it's a good thing. Theresa will be near us instead of miles away as she'd be if she goes back to nursing again. Scott is a good man, and he'll look after her interests. She'll soon show him she's not too young to take the responsibility of caring for his daughter. He really needs a nurse and companion, not a governess. That word is extinct anyway, and being companion-nurse is not demeaning in any way. It's a responsible and worthy vocation, and Scott will be generous with salary. Have you discussed the financial side with him, Terry?"

"I never gave it a thought!" she exclaimed.

"If you're set on taking on the job, I wouldn't worry. Scott isn't mean, especially where his daughter is concerned."

"I'm taking it because I've given my word and to show him I can do it! After all, I have you two at my back if he should become—obstreperous." A defiant tilt of chin testified that heaven help the one who dared become difficult with her.

Dan laughed. "Obstreperous . . . Scott? Never that, dear girl. Elaine cured him of any yen or leanings that way. I wonder how he really feels about his *decree nisi*. He's always been a dark horse. . . ." Dan stopped smiling as he reflected on the inner feelings of Scott Milward.

The family passed a leisurely Sunday morning. Theresa washed her hair and dried it in the warm sun on the lawn while baby Glynis sprawled on a blanket at her feet. The little imp was trying her utmost to reach the green grass so aggravatingly out of reach.

Mary called her in to lunch and she had difficulty in wading through the heavy meal of roast beef, Yorkshire pudding and vegetables with a baked honey dessert to follow. The heat was unnerving.

Back in her room Theresa took off her dress and sandals and flopped on the bed. A questing breeze blew through the open window, cooling her hot brow slightly. She dozed off for a while and was amazed to find it nearly three o'clock when she awoke. A slow surge of excitement welled up at the thought of afternoon tea with Scott Milward. Of course, it was only curiosity to see his daughter and their home. He had been cynical about his lost married status last night, but Theresa was sure it was merely an outer cover for feelings that ran deep. She sensed unplumbed depths in him, a passionate savagery that was curbed with supreme mastery under a show of nonchalance.

After an invigorating shower she slipped on a light, square-necked cotton dress and brushed her hair into a smooth cap that flipped out at the ends. Dainty white sandals completed her attire. She looked cool and fresh as she waited with Mary and Glynis for Dan to bring the car.

A symphony of green and white met Theresa's gaze as they drove up the long avenue leading to Scott's home. The stark white of the house stood dappled in golden sunlight amid the green of tall trees. A swathe of smooth green lawn sloped from the front entrance down to a circular driveway. A woman was seated in one of the chairs under a cool shade tree, and her little companion jumped eagerly off her chair as the car stopped in the drive.

Theresa had her first look at Melinda Milward. The child threw herself into Dan's waiting arms with a cry of glee and then wriggled down to hold up her face for Mary's kiss. The most important thing came now as she was very carefully allowed to carry Glynis—Mary's hands held in protective readiness—across the lawn.

Theresa followed slowly, her eyes on the little girl, a startling miniature of her father—dark hair, cut short in gamin style, gray eyes thickly fringed with dark lashes and the same proud, easy grace. Barefoot, she wore only a scanty white top with red shorts.

Dan spread the blanket on the grass. Melinda bent down slowly and, with infinite care, deposited her treasure on it. She turned to silently scrutinize Theresa with those amazing eyes.

Theresa gasped audibly as she lifted her own eyes to

find an identical pair studying her with the same intensity. Scott had appeared suddenly and was standing a few yards away. He wore tight-hipped brown slacks with an open-neck shirt that showed off the tan of his neck and arms. With quick, easy strides he closed the gap and put his hand on his daughter's head. Turning to the woman who was standing now, he spoke. "Miss Smith, meet Miss Stanton." They acknowledged the introduction and Scott looked down at his daughter. "Miss Melinda, this is Miss Theresa Stanton."

Theresa smiled and held out her hand to her future charge. Melinda put a small, suntanned hand into hers and announced gravely, "Your hair is like sunbeams and your eyes is like . . . what, Daddy? I know, like the sky. Tresa's very pretty, isn't she, Daddy?"

Theresa thought her voice had the same caressing quality her father's did when he said her name.

"I like you too, Melinda," she answered quietly.

The strange spell was broken as Scott turned to speak to his other guests and Melinda sat down next to the baby.

"I'll organize the tea." Vera Smith moved away, but Scott called her back.

"Everything is organized, Vera. Don't run away, get acquainted with Theresa (that inflection again!). I'm hoping she hasn't changed her mind and will be relieving you very shortly."

He held a chair for Theresa and lifted a quizzical eyebrow. "My daughter waxes rather lyrical at times. She has her father's love of nature . . . and beauty. You and she should get on well, I hope." The last came out with sardonic inflection and she shot him a hostile glance before answering.

"I don't doubt that we will get on very well. What I am beginning to doubt is whether I would like the constant proximity of her father!"

Scott sat down on the chair next to hers and leaned forward. "Does my charming presence disturb you so much, or is that merely an excuse to vacillate?" he asked softly.

The aura of his presence was magnetic and Theresa drew back slightly to fight a sudden pounding in her ears.

"I am not the vacillating kind. I'll keep my word; I don't make a habit of thinking up excuses." With an effort she turned to Vera. "I believe you're to be married, Miss Smith? Please accept my congratulations and wishes for a happy future."

Vera Smith had brown hair with bright birdlike eyes of the same colour, and Theresa guessed her age somewhat near the thirties. Her very ordinary features now lighted up into a lovely smile.

"Thank you, Miss Stanton. I'm quite sure Dick and I are going to be very happy. He owns a small garage in Salisbury and he's worked hard to buy a home for us. We've waited a long time and now at last we can afford it. I'm so glad you're coming to help Mr. Milward, although you are a bit young . . . I mean. . . ." She stammered, and glanced at the small girl who was chattering animatedly to Mary. "Melinda is a darling but quite a handful . . . a bit spoiled and. . . ." Her face went scarlet as she caught Scott's amused glance.

Theresa came to her rescue. "I'm twenty-one, have a nurse's qualifications and am quite able to face responsibility, Miss Smith, whatever it may be." Defiant blue eyes challenged the man sitting next to her. He looked so amused and vital that she could, quite easily, kick him hard! If she were not a poised twenty-one-year-old. "So I'm not as young as you think. I hope Mr. Milward doesn't share your views."

"Not at all, dear *old* thing, I'm sure you'll cope with Melinda's tantrums." The wicked gleam left his eyes. "We'll discuss the proposition later, in my study." Abruptly he dismissed the subject and drew Mary and Dan into conversation.

"I'd like you to see the horse I bought from Colonel Strang's stables, Dan."

"I believe that stallion's quite something to look at. Bit on the wild side so the colonel's yardman told me. He'll take some taming."

"He's a gorgeous hunk of horse. He'll ride tough and

he's got a hard mouth. I'll tame him." Scott stated this fact with a simplicity that was the negation of boastfulness. Theresa thought he looked like a man who would tame anything by simple, arrogant domination if nothing else. His decision would be law.

"If anybody can, you will be the one," Mary exclaimed. "You have yet to see Scott Milward on a horse, Terry. It makes my blood run cold if I happen to be in the vicinity when he's busy taming a wild horse!"

"I've seen him on one," Theresa dryly recollected.

"So you have, but not on a half wild one. By all the laws of nature his neck should have been broken by now."

Scott grinned. "Necks don't break so easily, my blood-thirsty one. Not as easily as—" He stopped abruptly.

"As hearts, you were going to say?" Theresa laughed, to cover her confusion. "But, then, necks are literally broken while hearts break figuratively only and can be mended, with time."

"Yeah, when your neck is broken you're good and dead; you've had it, as they say in the classics. Thank goodness, horses don't break their hearts, Theresa. That's a privilege of the human race—the superior, heart-breaking human race. Ah, here comes the tea. Vera, you may do the honors."

"Come 'n' see my baby, Tresa. She's sleeping now, so we must be ver' quiet." A small, commanding hand tugged at her arm.

"Theresa will have her tea first, Mel." Scott was firm.

"But, Daddy, I want Tresa to see her now 'cos she closes her eyes just like Glynis does." Petal lips pouted in appeal.

Scott hesitated and glanced from her to Theresa.

"When daddies speak to their little girls they must always listen." Theresa added earnestly, "And you must teach your baby to listen when you talk to her, Melinda. Then she'll be a good girl too, just like you."

Melinda stopped pouting to consider this statement. "She's very naughty, I spec' 'cos she's small, but I'll learn her." A confident elbow dug into Theresa's knee.

"Teach her," Vera corrected automatically.

Melinda looked her scorn, turned back to her new friend. "Is your tea very hot? I'll give you a cookie. This's my fav'rit. You can have it." Magnanimously, the plate was offered.

"That's very kind of you—I also like the gooey ones—thanks." An inward shudder as she took the proffered creamy concoction.

Melinda promptly relieved her of the empty cup when she finished her tea. "Now may she come, Daddy?"

"If Miss Theresa wishes," Scott smiled at his daughter.

Theresa was led on to the wide porch into a roomy lounge. Her quick eyes took in the furnishings. Large windows were heavily curtained in maroon velvet which made the room dark and close, not counteracting the hot, humid climate at all. "Furnishings should be light and airy, to give an illusion of coolness," she thought. The passage to the bedrooms was carpeted in dark green. Melinda's room was big and airy, the juvenile bed and cupboards painted a dull, drab brown.

Theresa duly looked and admired the quite exquisite baby doll lying in its own little cot. Roughly clothed, the frayed squares of covering were tenderly straightened. (Miss Smith was certainly not imaginative or needle-minded.) Theresa made a mental note to do some sewing for Melinda and wondered if the household sported a sewing-machine. She asked the child to show her the bathroom and was amused when asked, "Does Tresa want to use the jazz?"

"Yes, dear, but I call it toilet."

"Vera does too, but Daddy and me say jazz."

So whatever Daddy says or does must be right! Theresa pondered while she washed her hands. She could foresee a few clashing of wills if Daddy was the fond, spoiling kind. Oh well, she would cross the bridges as they came.

Her heart wept for the motherless child and, unwittingly, the wifeless man as well. If he loved Elaine so much it must hurt unbearably at times. And Melinda barely four years old! What had been the cause of her desertion; surely something deeper than dislike of environment? The house looked strongly built, the rooms she had seen were large, but no effort had been made to make use of wide windows or lighter, brighter furnishings. There was not a touch of wifely pride in the home. Elaine might not have had an eye for decor—or was it that she did not care?

Theresa itched to pull down those dark curtains and toss out the stuffy furniture of the lounge! Light, sun-filter curtains and furnishings in green and autumn shades . . . she stopped her wandering thoughts as Mary called from the door.

"Have you gone down the drain, honey? We're waiting for you. Come and see the fabulous horse."

"Coming, Mary!" She opened the door and they walked back to the lounge. Mary stopped and wrinkled her forehead. "I do wish Scott would do something about this room. . . ."

Theresa laughed. "It's quite hideous. I've just been going quite mad in the bathroom, thinking of what I would do to it if I had the chance."

"Oh, you have?" Mary studied her thoughtfully. "Well, perhaps you can do something. It doesn't seem to bother Scott unduly, but maybe if you play it right things can be—"

Theresa interrupted swiftly, "It's Scott's house and I'll be an employee, don't forget." She ran her fingers through her hair and continued, "One thing I am going to do: fix Melinda's room and paint or replace that drab furniture if I have to do it myself. Do you know if this establishment possesses a sewing-machine?"

"Not that I know of, but you could borrow mine."

"What needs to be borrowed?" Scott inquired from the doorway.

"Terry wants a sewing-machine and I said she could borrow mine," Mary explained.

"What for?"

"For the normal use, to sew and mend." Theresa showed amused sarcasm for the density of males while she hoped uneasily that he had not heard her remarks on the hideousness of the lounge.

His eyes held hers; tiger-yellow lights flickered in their

smoky depths when he spoke. "I see. Are you two coming to the paddock? Dan wants to look at the horses." He turned on his heel and the two hastily followed his long-legged stride.

Theresa leaned her arms on the rail next to the others while Scott vaulted it with lithe grace. Three of the horses cantered up confidently, the fourth one watched them warily from a distance. He was a magnificent animal with a glistening sherry-brown coat and silky blond mane. The two men watched admiringly, waxing enthusiastic on his finer points. The dappled horse at the rail came up to Theresa and nuzzled her arm sharply. At her sudden exclamation Scott turned and extracted a sugar lump from his pocket.

"Frost has taken a liking to you. Give him this—he has a sweet tooth. You may regard him as yours while you're here. He's a reliable old nag if you treat him nice. He recognizes you!" Another wicked grin brought out the dimple at the side of his mouth.

Scarlet flags of colour unfurled on the girl's cheeks as she realized it was the horse of her dramatic ride with Scott. She held out the sugar lump in a tentative hand. Frost took it delicately between strong teeth, lifting his lips in a wicked grin that matched his master's!

Melinda climbed onto the rails and Theresa put a protective arm around her, not only for the purpose of safeguarding the child but to hide and overcome an alarming, feathery feeling that coursed down her spine as Scott kept his gaze on her. His look darkened as it moved to the child and then back to the girl with the shining honey hair. He turned back, almost as if it were an effort, to answer Dan's questions on his next cattle drive. They discussed this important matter while Mary, Theresa and Melinda started walking back to the house.

Vera Smith was crooning to a very discontented baby and sighed in relief when they appeared. The houseboy wanted to know if the visitors would have coffee, but Mary vetoed the suggestion. It was time to leave as the baby's bath time was due and she was becoming fretful.

Scott held the car door for Theresa. "We haven't had

our talk. You don't need to come until next Sunday; that will give you a few more days with Mary and Dan. Vera will be leaving a week from tomorrow. I'll be over during the week to discuss finances and anything else you would like to know. Are you still agreeable?"

"Yes, Scott, and thank you for the respite. I like Melinda," Theresa said quietly.

"Good, that's half the battle won and your feeling is evidently reciprocated by—my girl."

"But not by you, Mr. Milward," she thought as they drove off. "Judging by the dark depths in those gray eyes, I've been weighed and found wanting!" Well, he had a week in which to change his mind about employing her, but if he decided to stick to the arrangement, she would show him her capabilities or die in the attempt! Not all women should be judged by the irresponsibility of a few.

Theresa watched the miles of orange orchards pass by and the sweet smell of their blossoms hit her nostrils and senses like a physical blow, intensifying a sudden pain in the region of her heart.

CHAPTER FOUR

Hair and linen hat damp with perspiration, Theresa looked up from her hot, absorbing task in the garden, as a shadow fell across the flower bed and the next moment Scott Milward was down on his heels helping to pull out the tough weeds. Stubborn with her, they slipped out of the ground at his first tug, roots and all.

"Hello, Theresa. Hard at it, I see. Weeds are always sturdier than flowers or vegetables. People wouldn't use the term 'a weed of a man' to denote weakness if they could work among our resistant vegetation for one day only!" His khaki sleeves were rolled up and a tanned arm inadvertently brushed against her bare elbow.

The sudden vibrating shock of contact coupled with his equally sudden appearance brought swift color to cheeks already flushed from sun and exertion. Theresa was inarticulate for moments and Scott finally turned from his chore to look at her with sharp eyes.

"No talkie today, ma'am? Velly solly, missee, humble self will letleat—"

"Of course I can talk . . . if I want to. And don't speak in such a silly way!" She spoke in irritation, more with herself than at the teasing, singsong intonation. Standing up from her cramped position, she took off her hat and brushed the earth off her brown jeans. The darned man must be wired for electricity.

"Well, kindly 'want to,' if you please. I came over especially to talk terms regarding our arrangement." His voice was curt and abrupt, but softened as he also stood up and scrutinized her face.

"Don't you know better than to work outside in this heat? Your face is very flushed . . . and dirty. Go and have a quick wash, I'll wait and have tea with you. Go on, Theresa, you're not hypnotized, or has the sun got to you?"

"I thought you were in a hurry—" she began indignantly.

"I am, but will contain my haste long enough to cure your hypnosis—" he stepped closer and brought his face down. The startled girl took a step backwards. "—with a cup of tea, if you'll play hostess. Run along," Scott finished, and shot out his hand to flip strands of her hair across her face.

He watched her walk away, her slender shoulders stiff with inner fury, and called out clearly yet softly, "Don't hate me so actively, honey, it gives a most provoking swing to your . . . er . . . posterior!"

Provoking indeed! And the nerve to call her honey, who did he think he was, king of all he surveys? And telling her to wash her face, like . . . a child!

This was all hissed at her reflection in the bathroom mirror. The dust-smeared girl hissed back at her. Suddenly Theresa saw the funny side of it and started an hysterical giggle. Her reflection giggled back and she turned away in disgust to rinse her face and hands in the cool water. She ran a comb through her hair hastily. She must not keep the arrogant man waiting; he was quite capable of opening the door and demanding explanations.

Dan and family were away on a shopping trip to the village, so she would have to be the polite hostess to Scott. Theresa had declined to go with them, intending to have a quiet rest. She had been out riding the day before and her posterior, as Scott called it, was still smarting from unfamiliar exertions. Becoming restless later, she had wandered out to the garden and, spying the weeds, decided she would work a little for her keep. So Scott had found her.

He was sprawled out in a low deck chair when Theresa returned, his dark head resting back and his eyes closed. She came close over the grass and studied the thick smudge of eyelashes fanned over dark, tanned cheeks, the reposed, well-cut mouth.

"Handsome guy, hmm, Theresa?" He spoke without opening his eyes.

She turned away and busied herself with the tea things. "Handsome is as handsome does," she quoted satirically.

"Hmm, so they say." Scott opened his eyes. "What

does that mean, exactly? I don't mean your satire but the words of that silly quotation. If handsome does, is handsome is? You said it, so elucidate, please."

"Quite candidly, I don't know." Theresa considered gravely. "I guess it means if you think you're handsome then you are, and if you think what you do is handsome, then it is, even though others don't think so. Skin-deep vanity, in fact," she stated with aforesaid (handsome) sagacity.

"Wisely and shrewdly put, dear nymph, sweet Theresa."

He had never foreshortened her Christian name and it rolled on his tongue smoothly, almost caressingly. Prickles tingled her scalp every time he said it, and yet she would not have it any other way. It sounded so right—especially with the endearment attached. She caught herself and asked primly, "Sugar, Scott?"

"Two, thanks." He sat up and took the proffered cup. "We have Cleo, Melinda's nanny, to give you a hand when necessary, so if you want time off to visit she's quite capable of taking over until you return, but only while I or my manager are in the offing. I've never left Melinda in sole charge of servants. That's very important: definite arrangements must be made if you go out."

"Of course, I understand, and will make arrangements accordingly," she answered.

"They are fairly reliable, but . . . call it a whim . . . fairly reliable is not good enough for me, not with my daughter's welfare at stake." Scott lifted his cup and drained the contents. "Now, about your salary. May I know what you were paid at the hospital?"

Theresa told him and he exclaimed in astonishment, "A mere pittance! How could you live on it?"

She shrugged her shoulders. "We get by. After all, our uniforms are free and if one lives in it's not too bad. Living out is only possible if you share an apartment and expenses."

"You still have an income from your father's estate?"

"Most of that has gone for my training, but there's still enough to last a year or so, depending on how I handle it," she stated candidly. "It's a good thing there aren't any movie theatres close by showing dashing Westerns. My pocket money will be saved!"

Scott laughed suddenly, delightedly. "Thank goodness for a sense of humor, otherwise I would be in the doghouse right now! Forgive me, but that situation was irresistible. It happened to be one of my tamest bulls and they're all most amiable. You certainly turned the escapade neatly. I was shamed to the depths." His laughter was infectious and Theresa joined him.

He then named a salary, which she protestingly declared too generous. Scott insisted that she accept it. "It's worth that to me if Melinda is kept happy and healthy."

"Well, if I find that my services and the work entailed don't demand so high a salary, I shall refuse to accept it," Theresa said flatly.

Scott stood up and smiled. "We'll fight about that another day. Did Mary tell you about a dance and barbecue in the village, on Saturday evening?"

"Yes, she did. We're going. I believe a room is cleared at the club for the children and infants and one or two women offer free services as baby-sitters, while everybody else chokes outside in smelly smoke, downs great drafts of beer and dances into the early hours of the morning."

Scott hitched his trousers in a decisive gesture. "I'll have the pleasure of escorting you and Melinda to said bingo."

"Oh, will you? It's the first I've heard. Do Mary and Dan know of this . . . decision?"

"No. But they'll be informed very shortly."

Theresa felt exasperation rise. "The correct procedure is to, firstly, request the pleasure from the lady of your choice. Secondly—"

Scott looked over her head. "Will you come with Melinda and me?"

"—Secondly, it's not proper for an employer to escort his child's nurse to bing—dances and other entertainments," she finished determinedly.

Scott's gaze fastened on her face. "To hell with

seemliness, will you come with me? On Saturday I'm still not your damned employer."

Ungrammatical but reasonable. Theresa forced calm on a wild impulse to go with this man and his daughter. Well, why not . . . ?

"I accept your very polite invitation, Mr. Milward—perhaps only because somebody will have to stopper Melinda's young ears against profane language."

A long silence ensued while they studied each other, he with a sardonically lifted eyebrow and she with candid blue eyes.

Scott broke it at last. "I seem to spend my life apologizing to you. Till Saturday, about six o'clock, then? Au revoir, mademoiselle, my fondest to the Rourkes." He tipped his hat at a dangerous angle and strode off.

Theresa waited until she heard the clatter of hooves and then walked slowly towards the house.

At supper, Theresa told Mary and Dan of Scott's visit and the subsequent invitation. "He didn't even discuss it, simply informed me that he would be taking me."

"Just like him to do that. Scott seldom discusses, he makes statements. I'm surprised at him, though; he rarely attends the local functions. He likes polo. We have quite a good polo field, and he turns up for that fairly regularly. Must have taken a shine to you, my girl."

"Shine my foot!" Theresa exclaimed. "He has some ulterior motive, I'll bet."

"You're a very attractive woman, why shouldn't he get cracking before the other men monopolize you? I think that's a superior, not an ulterior motive," Mary put in.

"Vera Smith's fiancé is coming on Saturday. He'll spend the weekend at Scott's place and take his bride-to-be back on Monday," Dan told them.

Theresa looked darkly at her companions. "Ah, the solution comes! He wants my presence in case Melinda becomes unmanageable or catches her finger in the door."

Dan laughed. "Well, be that as it may, Scott Milward

is actually coming to our do. That does show he's getting over carrying a torch for Elaine."

"Why did she leave, Dan? It can't have been only her dislike of the surroundings. You have a social club, other entertainments and Salisbury is barely a day's drive away. Is she very beautiful?" Theresa asked tentatively, a strange constriction in her chest as she waited for his answer.

"Yes, she was . . . is rather lovely, in a slightly flamboyant way. Gorgeous, dark red hair, green eyes and a figure that stops the traffic. Scott doesn't talk about it, but I think something happened in Salisbury—" Dan stopped.

Mary leaned her arms on the table. "Scott went away for a week to Umtali on business and came back sooner than expected. In his absence, Elaine took herself and Melinda off to Salisbury and he followed them. He came back with only Melinda. What transpired is anybody's guess, but Elaine never came back. Scott clammed up and not one of us could get a word out of him on that subject."

"That was nearly two years ago," Dan remarked. "He has occasionally taken other girls out, but spends most of his time on the ranch. Lately he's been going to Salisbury fairly often—whether it's *amour* or business I can't say."

"You'll enjoy the dance on Saturday, Terry. Our friends are all agog to see and meet you, so put on your best bib and tucker, and wow them."

"With Scott Milward looking on superciliously, I presume?" Theresa retorted, and pushed her chair back.

"Envy, I predict," Dan chuckled as they walked to the verandah.

The next morning Theresa strolled down to the gate that led to the main highway. The mail bus was due today, and she had offered to meet it. The gate was a good quarter of a mile from the homestead and the overhang of tall trees made her walk cool and pleasant. She opened the large metal box attached to a post and looked inside. No mail yet, so she settled down on a log to wait for the bus.

Five minutes had passed when she heard the drumming of hooves. A rider appeared in a cloud of dust. The girl on the horse stopped with superb horsemanship as she spied Theresa and swung out of her saddle to face her.

Her dark, windblown hair was held back with a rubber band in a rough ponytail and she wore faded blue jeans, a grubby denim shirt and worn tennis shoes. "Are you the nurse?" she asked without any formality. At Theresa's nod of assent she continued abruptly, "Will you come with me? My sister is in a bad way."

Equally abrupt, Theresa demanded, "Explain as quickly as you can. Where do you live, and what's wrong with your sister?"

"About three miles from here. Her husband, Sam de Wet, works for Mr. Milward. I'm Georgia Masters. Lily's baby was due in two weeks, but I think it's coming now."

"Isn't there a doctor in the village—?" Theresa began.

Georgie Masters cut in angrily, her voice staccato with anxiety. "I've been up to the big house to phone, but the doctor is away on a call. I left a message at his surgery . . . he may be too late. Are you coming?"

"I'll climb up behind you on your horse. Have you a medical cupboard at home, cotton wool, disinfectant, etcetera?" Theresa asked tersely as she prepared to mount behind the other girl, who was already back in the saddle.

"Yes, let's go!"

She hung onto Georgie's slender waist as the horse was turned and put to a reckless gallop.

Legs shaky from the mad ride, Theresa entered the cottage that nestled in a grove of orange trees. A deep crimson bougainvillea almost obscured the front porch. Georgie pushed past her to lead the way to her sister's bedroom. A swift look at the woman on the bed and her training told her that the birth was imminent.

Theresa smiled with steady eyes at Lily de Wet as she started rolling her sleeves. "I'm Theresa Stanton and I'm going to help you. Have you a clean smock for me?"

Georgie ran to the wardrobe and snatched a light blue

smock off a hanger, Theresa thanked her. "Go to the kitchen, find your largest saucepans and kettles and get the water boiling. I'll find the bathroom." She slipped into the large, sleeveless garment and tied it tightly at the waist. In the bathroom she scanned the medicine cabinet and sorted out what would be needed. Thank heaven it was well-stocked!

"I'm Sam de Wet, nurse, and very grateful that you're here." The tall, gangling man stood in the doorway twisting his hat nervously. "I was in the fields when Mr. Milward's girl brought the message from Georgie. Lily . . . will she . . . is she . . . ?"

"She is, Mr. de Wet, and don't worry. Everything is going to be all right," Theresa smiled confidently, hiding her own anxiety beneath a cheerful manner. She dumped the cotton wool and bottles into his arms. "Put these things in the bedroom while I scrub. Tell Georgie you'll see to the hot water, so she can put on something clean and scrub her hands, in case I need her."

On examination, she found no signs of any complications and breathed a silent sigh of relief. Slipping a rubber sheet onto the bed, she turned the woman on her side and rubbed her back with comforting hands. "Your baby is in a hurry, that's all, Lily. Don't worry, first babies are often that way." A measure of peace came to the frightened woman when she felt the sure hands and confident words.

The next hour flew by, with a dazed but dutiful Georgia Masters following the nurse's orders. A car stopped outside, but a negative shake of her head answered Theresa's inquiring eyebrow. "Not the doctor."

In the kitchen, Sam started as he heard the angry wail of his newborn son.

"Sit down, old chap. They'll call you when you're wanted," Scott grinned as he put a hand on the nervous father's shoulder. "Congratulations. It can only be a boy, with that lusty gruff voice. Sounds just like you when you're yelling at the stockmen."

"*Magtig*, man, I am that glad the slip of a *meisie* turned up so promptly. I hope Lily is all right." Sam started as Georgie appeared in the doorway.

"Sam, he's lovely. Lily's fine, but Nurse sent me to tell you to be patient a while longer, some more things to do," she said importantly. A look of awe came into her face. "She's absolutely wonderful, she knew just what to do and let me help her too! Oh, Mr. Milward, her hands were so quick and gentle, and—" Georgie turned smartly as a voice called from the bedroom. "Excuse me, I'm wanted." Some time later she stuck her head around the doorway. "You can come in now, Sam."

In his hurry the poor man tripped over a chair. Scott leaned against the windowsill and rubbed his chin reflectively. Had he acted that way, almost four years ago? He remembered the miracle of joy when a tiny bundle was placed into his eager arms, and shared for a brief instant the awe and wonder with Sam de Wet.

Theresa wiped perspiration off her face with a wet towel in the bathroom and took off the stained smock. She left her hair tied up in a topknot and walked into the kitchen.

The tall, rangy figure framed in the window straightened up as she entered. "Everything according to the books, Nurse Stanton?"

"Yes, Scott—heavens, you startled me! When did you get here? One time I almost had a heart attack, when Lily disobeyed certain instructions. Whew, am I thirsty!"

A quick, firm movement of hands under her armpits and Scott had her sitting on the well-scrubbed table with her feet resting on a chair. "Sit down, honey, sustenance coming up in a jiffy." He turned to the stove and lifted the coffeepot. Seconds later Theresa accepted the large cup of coffee with a huge dollop of cream floating on top.

"This looks good. Georgia, take a cup for your sister, she needs it more than I do." This to the girl standing hesitantly in the doorway. Georgie complied with alacrity.

Theresa sipped the coffee and glanced at the man standing so close to her. He was studying her topknot of hair.

"What's the matter, Scott?"

"You look like a prim little schoolteacher." He lifted a

hand and, before she could stop him, pulled the ribbon loose. Her hair cascaded onto her shoulders. "That's better." Scott ran his fingers through it and said wonderingly, "It's so silky. Melinda's right, your hair is like sunbeams."

"Rather damp sunbeams at the moment. I haven't done midwifery for ages and this one surprised me." She laughed and buried her face in the large cup to cover her confusion at this unexpected action. A nerve tingled in her neck where his fingertips had brushed.

Doctor Lessing stopped his car and came bustling in. "Hello, Scott. How's Lily and what's she up to, is it a false alarm? At least another 14 days. . . ." He put his bag on the table and looked long and hard at the girl seated in it. A whistle of appreciation formed on his mouth. "I . . . er . . . I. . . ." Scott made no move to introduce him. "Well, what's going on here, anyway? The call was urgent." With great difficulty Dr. Lessing removed his eyes from the girl and noticed the kettles on the stove. "Good, I see somebody has prepared—"

Theresa lifted her feet off the chair and stood hurriedly to attention, professional etiquette coming to the fore. "Good morning, Doctor. I'm Theresa Stanton. May I take you to the patient? This way, please." She led the way with subdued formality, ignoring Scott's amused eyes, to the bedroom and stood aside as she had been taught .

With a puzzled glance at her, Dr. Lessing walked in and surveyed the contented mother, happy father, and then, his eyes flew to the small cot.

Theresa spoke politely. "An emergency case, doctor. I'm a nurse and did what I could. I trust everything is in order." She motioned to Sam to leave the room.

Hugh Lessing stepped over to the cot and uncovered the new baby. A sharp scrutiny of eyes, ears, nose, mouth and umbilical cord assured him that all was well. He examined Lily while Theresa studied him unobtrusively—a man in his early thirties, brown hair and eyes, mouth widely generous, build slightly stocky and incredibly long, blunt-edged fingers. She liked what she saw. He replaced the quilt over the smiling woman and sat down at the foot of the bed, turning his attention to the silently dutiful girl.

"All's well, and a very good job you made of it. No complications?"

"None, doctor."

"Hmm , , , Theresa Stanton? Yes, I recollect someone talking about the Rourkes' expected visitor. Are you on vacation?"

"No, doctor. I've resigned."

"Why? In the course of duty or for personal reasons?" Hugh Lessing's scrutiny was sharp.

"Personal, sir. I'm still on the Nursing Register." She quite understood the probing questions.

"Do you intend carrying on with your profession here in Rhodesia?"

"Maybe later. From Sunday on I'll be employed by Mr. Milward, as nurse and companion to his daughter."

Hugh blew a long breath. "I see. Well, Lily, everything is fine. You were very fortunate to have Nurse Stanton within calling distance. I'll be out tomorrow, so take it easy. Maybe I can get Georgie to follow instructions as regards the baby, but she's such a tomboy, I'd better talk to Sam." He congratulated Lily on her fine son, gave medical advice and then walked into the passage. Theresa followed and put her hand on his arm as they reached the kitchen doorway. Scott, Sam and Georgia were still there. The doctor stopped and waited.

"Doctor, Georgia is a very capable girl, and I was very grateful for her help. I thought it worth mentioning." Theresa looked at the girl and was startled to see a deep flush spreading across her face.

"Any simpleton could have done what I did, so don't bother with kudos!" Georgie tilted her head angrily. Dark eyes flashed for an instant at Hugh Lessing, and then she stalked to the back door, flung it open and banged it shut as she went out.

"My, my, tantrums! When is she going to grow up?" Hugh shrugged his shoulders.

Scott spoke from his lazy pose against the window ledge. "She's 19, Hugh, and getting prettier by the day."

"Is she?" Hugh looked puzzled for a moment. "I'll take your word for it. Sam, I wish you all the best, he's a fine boy. Thank you, Miss Stanton, for helping out in a sticky spot. Are you sure you won't reconsider about nursing? We desperately need nurses out here, and with your qualifications—"

Theresa broke in, suddenly very conscious of the tall man at the window. "Thank you, doctor, but at present I'm perfectly content. If you wish, I'll attend Mrs. de Wet every morning until Saturday."

The medical man looked so long and hard at her that she felt a warmth creeping into her cheeks. "The name is Hugh—Hugh Lessing. Yes, I'd be glad if you would—one worry off my shoulders. I'll be around tomorrow; better push off now. 'Bye, Nurse—'bye, chaps." He turned at the door and looked at Scott. "You lucky dog, you!" and he was gone.

For the second time Theresa was startled to see a flush on someone's cheeks as, his gray eyes smoldering, Scott muttered, "Silly quack!"

They walked toward the front door and Theresa popped in to say goodbye to Lily, telling her she would be in to see her tomorrow. She walked out to the front garden. Scott was leaning against his car, talking to Sam. Georgia was not with them and Theresa started to walk around the house but was stopped by Scott's voice.

"Where is your horse, Theresa? Sam can bring him later, I'm taking you back in the car."

"Well, I didn't come on my horse."

Scott straightened abruptly. "How the devil did you get here? You surely didn't walk all this way, in such a short time?"

"I think I was . . . hijacked." Her answer was demure.

"Hijacked!" Both men spoke in unison.

"I'm beginning to think so. You see—" a chuckle rose in her throat at their expressions "—I was sitting at the gate, waiting for the mail bus and minding my own business, when—" she snapped her fingers "—just like that I was whisked onto a horse and woke up holding a baby in my arms!"

"Georgie?" Sam exclaimed. "She didn't even give you time to let Mary know? *Magtig!* Mary must be having hysterics by this time, not knowing what's happened to you."

"And a good thing too, otherwise you would have been in a nice pickle, Mister Sam. I left my hat on the only wayside rock, so Mary will come to either of two conclusions—I've absconded with the bus driver, or a lion has enjoyed a tasty breakfast."

Scott laughed. "The sooner I hijack you back, the better for that lady's peace of mind. Come on." He held the door open for her.

While Sam thanked her again, Scott climbed in and started the car, revved the engine, and they shot headlong down the dusty road.

"I'm not in that much of a hurry, Scott, or is this breakneck speed normal procedure?" Theresa asked dryly.

"Sorry. There I go again, apologizing." His glance appraised her swiftly, then his eyes went back to the road. She leaned her head back, smiled secretively and closed her eyes. "It's no crime to apologize, dear man, it's a sign of good manners."

Scott did not reply and Theresa suddenly felt happy, in a contented way. He had his finer points and she felt fulfilled, somehow, by the work she had done this lovely morning. No word passed between them, she merely reminded him to stop at the gate for her hat and the mail. The silence lasted and she closed her eyes again, oblivious to the searching glances of her companion, to come abruptly from her dreaming as he stopped the car with a jerk in the driveway. Before Theresa had completely collected herself, Scott was out and had the door open for her.

"Will you come in, Scott—" she began, and was stopped by that same dark flame smoldering in his eyes.

He closed the door and walked around to his side. "No,

thanks. I'll see you." He slid into the seat and whirled away in a cloud of dust.

Amazed, Theresa thought, what now? Is he angry because he had to bring me back? Whatever was wrong with the man? So much for finer points and contented clouds! "Oh, what the hell!" Theresa spoke aloud and walked quickly up the porch steps.

Fortunately for her peace of mind, Mary knew of the morning call to Lily's bedside. A passing stockman had witnessed her flight with Georgia, and Mary had phoned through to Scott's household. Vera Smith had been in such a dither when asked to help that Georgia had tempestuously flung back on her horse and was on her way to Mary, only to accost Theresa at the gate.

Theresa briefed Mary on the latest news, then walked to her room and flopped across the bed. For no reason, she felt completely miserable and only pulled herself together when Mary tapped on the door to say lunch was ready. She did not feel hungry but forced herself to eat and converse normally with Dan and Mary.

The day passed somehow and, long after the lights were out, Theresa Stanton lay awake, battling with unfamiliar emotions brought on by a man's curt departure.

Theresa tucked in the soft blanket neatly and placed the hungry baby into his mother's arms. This was the third morning she had come over to attend Lily; mother and baby were doing fine and Sam was as proud as a peacock.

She was puzzled about Georgia Masters. The girl was exceptionally gauche for her age and acted either brashly abrupt or like a startled fawn whenever Theresa approached her. A long talk was indicated, even if she had to lasso Georgia in order to do so. Her deep flush and defiant look at Hugh Lessing, on that first morning, raised certain suspicions in Theresa's mind. At Hugh's consequent visits Georgia had made herself scarce and only yesterday, as he drove away, Theresa had noticed the girl leaning against a tree in the background, her attitude and face yearning as she watched the receding car.

Georgia could be a very attractive girl if she took

herself in hand—did something with her lovely hair and discarded the tattered jeans and shirts for neater, prettier clothes. Lily said she had tried to interest Georgia in fripperies, to coax her to go out more; but her sister obstinately refused and seemed quite happy to roam around the countryside on her beloved horse, alone. She had been home with them for six months, having had her education at a college in Salisbury. At first eager to go back, being a qualified shorthand-typist, she had suddenly changed her mind and decided to stay on with her sister and Sam. Now Georgie seemed to have become a loner and didn't care what she looked like!

Theresa walked out of the house, through rows of lush orange trees and eventually found Georgia, who was busily grooming her horse. She sauntered up to the girl. Georgia looked up for a moment, gave a slight smile of recognition, then went on with her chore. Theresa found a currycomb and casually drew it through the silky hair on the horse's tail. The two girls worked in silence, the sun hot on their backs.

Georgia stopped to push tangled hair, damp with perspiration, off her face. She fumbled in her pocket, pulled out a short length of ribbon and proceeded to tie the dark mass in a rough topknot.

Theresa also stopped and watched her critically, and then such a dreamy gaze came into her eyes that Georgia had to speak. "What gives? Why are you looking at me like that? My hair—"

"You know, Georgia. I have a magazine at home and there's a picture of a girl in it. She resembles you, the same shaped face—it's a 'before and after' article."

A flush suffused the girl's cheeks. "Before and after? What exactly does that mean?"

"Well, this girl had just such lovely hair as yours. She looked very nice, but her hair was quite unmanageable, so she had it cut short and styled. The 'after' picture of her was most attractive, and the article tells how to shape the hair. I'm picturing you with a similar style."

Georgia stood quite still while Theresa casually brushed her own chin with a silky tail-end. "Georgia, I wonder if you could help me? I brought a couple of dress lengths of the most gorgeous materials with me and I'm dying to make them up. Mary has a super machine, but I'm so dumb about sewing." Crossing her fingers at this blatant lie, "Do you know anything about patterns, cutting, and so on?" Theresa turned large, appealing blue eyes to her companion.

Brown eyes looked directly back at her. "You can afford to be dumb about certain things, if you're clever about others—like nursing—the way you helped Lily. Who wants to sew if you can do all that? I did take a course on basic needlework at college—"

"Oh, good, just the girl for me. I'm going to kidnap you tomorrow, for the whole day! And don't refuse, because you owe it to me, in return for my services to your sister. Stop stiffening that pretty neck—" she hurried on before Georgia could protest, "I'm going to have a go at that mop of hair. I'm not quite ignorant about haircuts; I did a fair amount of it in the hospital on the patients. We'll follow the book instructions carefully—what say, Georgia M.?"

That young lady looked at the eager, vital face of her tormentor and a slight gleam of interest showed for an instant in her dark eyes before she dropped them, answering with feigned indifference. "You can give me a Yul Brynner for all I care, it's cooler anyway and nobody would notice."

"Are you referring to a particular nobody or just generalizing?" Theresa deliberately teased her.

"Of course n-not." The sudden stammer and flush belied the quick retort.

"Well, a little bird tells me that one particular somebody in the medical world would certainly notice any change, if confronted—" Theresa was afraid she had jumped the gun, for Georgia suddenly threw the brush on the ground and interrupted her.

"Don't be absurd! As far as he's concerned, I'm still in rompers!" She stalked off, calling over her shoulder, "I'll help you with the sewing tomorrow!"

Theresa watched her and heaved a sigh. At least

Georgia knew who she was talking about when she spoke of a medical somebody. She was going to make Scott take the girl with them to the barbecue, whether he liked it or not. If a certain doctor attended, he would be induced to join their party. She hoped to overcome Georgia's stubborn pride, to coax her to accept one of the dress lengths for a party dress. Walking back to the jeep she pondered ways and means. Mary must be roped in to help. . . .

Mary was quite willing to help. The matchmaking urge bubbled in her motherly breast when Theresa told of Georgia's yearning look while she watch Hugh Lessing drive away from Sam's house.

The next day when Theresa had finished with Lily, she found Georgia waiting for her at the jeep, dressed neatly in jeans and spotless clean shirt and hair tied in an awkward roll. She scowled self-consciously and climbed into the jeep with a muttered greeting. Theresa smiled back delightedly and started a gay, whistling tune as they bowled down the gravel road. After a few sidelong glances of shy amusement Georgia suddenly joined in. Mary Rourke was startled out of her usual calm when she heard a squeal of brakes accompanied by 'Oh, what a beautiful morning' piercingly whistled in deafening crescendo!

Later, Mary watched in amazement as Theresa, a very good seamstress, deliberately fumbled with the pinning of patterns. Only when Georgia took over with frustrated eagerness did she catch on. Theresa gave an exaggerated sigh of thanks and stepped out of the way, the solemnity of her face belied by twinkling blue eyes as she sent Mary a quick, warning glance.

Leaving the younger woman to her task, she slipped out of the room, to reappear shortly with a swath of pure Thai silk, burnt-orange in color, folded over her arm.

Georgia finished the last cutting line with the remark that the latest sheath dress fashions were so much simpler to make than full skirts and intricate tops. She caught sight of the material on Theresa's arms and a gasp of admiration escaped her lips. Her gentle fingers touched the silk reverently.

"Come to the mirror, Georgie." Theresa propelled the fascinated girl and held the fabric under her chin. Three pairs of eyes studied the reflection and Mary and Theresa nodded simultaneously. Georgia glanced up, a deep flush spreading across her face.

"Oh no, you don't—" she began, but Theresa put a cool gentle hand on her arm.

"Please, honey, it will give me great pleasure if you would accept it—as a birthday present. Oh, it does things for you that could never happen to me...!"

Georgia's eyes returned to her stunned reflection, and she stammered, "Why, it could do things to any girl . . . the plainest, ugliest girl could achieve beauty . . . with this." She turned suddenly. "You don't even know when my birthday is . . . no, I can't accept it. You're only doing this to—"

"Because I would love to have you accept it in the spirit it's given, with pleasure and because it's you—" Theresa stopped as Scott's voice drawled lazily from the doorway:

"Flaming stars, Georgia, you're going to look smashing in that stuff! What is it, anyway? Hopsack? Calico?"

Three feminine heads turned in indignation at this utter blasphemy! Theresa found her voice as sudden inspiration struck. "Oh, Scott, I'm so glad; you've come just at the right time. We're all wearing new frocks to the barbecue and dance and Georgia won't have time to shop before Saturday. Now she's being silly about using this material, and who cares if it's not her birthday. After all, every day is another day nearer to one's birthday." She stopped for breath and rooted him to the spot with large, hypnotic eyes. "You did ask her to join us, as planned?" Whirling round to an astonished Georgia, "Has he asked you, because if he hasn't I'll . . . I shall be . . . I was praying you would join us because I don't know . . . Melinda . . . very well and . . . well, have you or have you not, Scott Milward?" Flashing eyes turned back to the man.

That man straightened abruptly from his leaning position. A look of understanding crossed his face. He put a hand to his heart.

"You wound me to the heart, dear atom, with your suspicions. I've been chasing Georgie M. all over the countryside, but she's been too elusive for me to extend our invitation. I extend it now, before your threat to do whatsoever is carried out." Scott smiled mockingly. "What is it, anyway?"

Theresa drew a silent breath of relief. He had played it well, thank goodness. She sent him a brilliant, condescending smile. "Really, you men! It would have been simpler to send a note with Sam, instead of tiring your horse. As for my threat . . . well, you'll never know now, will you?"

Under his steady scrutiny she started to breathe hard to steady a sudden, suffocating turmoil in her breast. Scott's eyes left hers, and dropped to a deliberate, study of the soft femininity of her silk blouse. The smoky look sent color flying to her face and a strange, hot tingling engulfed her. With an effort she turned back to Georgia, who still clutched the material in trembling hands.

"All right, let's get cracking, there isn't much time. Georgia, you cut. I'll help you and Mary can start sewing when we've finished, while I tackle your hair. Close your mouth, honey, you look like a fish on a hook! Where's that pattern you liked so much, just the thing for this gorgeous silk."

Georgia Masters still looked mesmerized and then a slow beatific smile spread across her face. Beauty was indeed achieved; even Scott appeared to be enchanted, gazing in wonderment.

"Fish on a hook! The understatement of the year! We were all neatly hooked with great cunning. Mary dear, you'd better close your mouth as well, there's a fly dangerously near to it. I actually dropped in for a cup of tea, but I'll forgo that pleasure. Hand me needle and thread, I'll tack the split seams!"

Gales of laughter greeted this helpful offer as Scott lowered himself limply into an armchair. The laughter helped Theresa cover her inexplicable confusion. She was grateful for Scott's quick understanding when she had shot her query at him. He could quite simply have denied knowledge of any invitation for Georgia to join them. Her eyes thanked him over her teacup and he acknowledged it with a mocking threat of his own.

Mary and Georgia became immersed in their work and Theresa walked with Scott as he took his leave.

He looked at her quizzically and there was a sardonic inflection in his voice. "So you don't know Melinda very well? Hmm, could it be her father you're afraid of, hence Georgie's presence, for protection?"

"You know quite well that was trumped up on the spur of the moment. I'm not afraid of handling Melinda, or her father for that matter, but I do want Georgia to mix with other people. She's too young to become introspective, antisocial. Do you think Hugh Lessing will come on Saturday?"

"Aha, now your quixotic impulses become clear. Matchmaking female!" He rubbed his chin reflectively. "The unsuspecting doctor is the target, and I'll be cajoled into asking him to join us. Or does your own interest lie that way, with Georgie the sop to my ego? Not a bad idea at that. I've often wondered what makes her tick—maybe this is my chance to find out."

"You've had ample time to do that, right here, and I strongly advise you not to cradle-snatch while she's in my care. Anyway, I think she likes Hugh, but he treats her like a child." Theresa did not deign to contradict his version of her own interest in the doctor.

"To Hugh she's not a child, but where I'm concerned it's cradle-snatching? How ancient you make me feel!" A slight bitterness tinged his next words. "Well, we're well matched, you and I. Our torn hearts know very well that love explodes or fizzles out quicker than a wet firecracker."

A hot protest rose in her throat, but she willed it back and her reply came quick and light. "Firecrackers are manmade, Mr. Milward, but the stars and sun will last an eternity. Maybe true love is not a flashing thing but an everyday occurrence that we know as friendship, companionship . . . and trust." Theresa felt a sudden prickling behind her eyelids. "I'm going to tackle Georgia's hair now, and I'm willing to bet that on Saturday not even an old man like you will be able to resist her. That woman's got possibilities. Thanks for playing along and inviting her, you're a dear." She dashed up the steps before he could reply, turned to salute him palm upwards.

The sun was setting when at last Theresa stood back and surveyed her handiwork. Mary putting the finishing touches to the silk dress, also looked critically, then approvingly at Georgia's hair. "I didn't realize we had such a beauty in our midst."

"I feel so light-headed . . . but I like it. It makes me look older, which is just fine." Georgia spoke shyly.

"Heaven forbid any young woman wanting to look older than her years, precious years that pass so quickly!" mourned still young Theresa Stanton. "Georgia Masters, you're going to wow the gentry tomorrow, make no mistake."

"I really don't think—" the other began, but Theresa interrupted with distinct, definite emphasis on each word and syllable. "You're not supposed to think from now on. You're to go home and not, I repeat *not*, clean the stables or any such unclean work. Here's the nail polish, bubble bath and gold sandals; where can I find a box for that ravishing dress? Thanks, Mary." She changed her voice back to normal and impulsively hugged the strangely docile Georgia. "You look delicious, honey. Between the three of us we'll wake up that little old town, that's for sure!"

Georgia chuckled at her sparkling vitality and wondered briefly about the story of a broken engagement. . . . It did not seem to have touched Theresa too deeply. For then surely she would be pining away in a darkened room, mournfully refusing to eat any food offered to her. That was what she, Georgia, would be doing if . . . someone . . . she loved did not love her back. . . . She suddenly felt very hungry indeed!

Theresa waited on the porch and watched the approaching car lights. Surely it would be Scott and Georgia at last! Mary, Dan and baby Glynis had long since departed, because Dan was on the committee and had to put in an early appearance. Scott was exceptionally late and she hoped he had not had trouble with Georgia. The car came to a standstill and the man at the wheel extricated long legs from the driver's seat.

The light on the porch made a nimbus of the waiting girl's honey-blond hair. Her slim dress of creamy linen outlined a silhouette of soft curves. Scott greeted her rather curtly and she, in turn, felt illogically disappointed when he made no comment on her appearance. . . . As if that mattered! After all, he was probably sated, used to glamor, having possessed such beauty as his wife had . . . still had.

Theresa's greeting was equally stiff as he took her arm and led her to the car.

Georgia emerged from the front seat and Theresa scrutinized swiftly. An involuntary sigh of pleasure escaped her; at least *she* could be generous and open in admiration. "You look absolutely divine, Georgia—doesn't she, Scott?"

"Absolutely, fantastically, unbelievably so," Scott answered gravely, but his smoky glance was on herself.

Georgia dived ungracefully into the back seat while Scott's eyes commanded Theresa to take the front. A small voice piped from the back, "Tresa, are you going to dance with my daddy?"

Melinda's gamin face pushed forward to gaze earnestly at her.

"Hello, Melinda, what a lovely dress you have! Yes, I shall dance with your daddy if he asks me very politely."

They shot off down the driveway. Melinda addressed her father. "You will ask Tresa pitely, Daddy, will you, Daddy?"

"I shall, poppet, I shall." Daddy spoke rather gruffly.

"Have you got a cold, Daddy? 'Cause if you have, Tresa is a nurse and she'll kiss it better."

"In that case, even if I haven't, I'll get one as fast as Timothy can blink an eye."

"Timothy is my cat, Tresa, and he prob'ly blinks a lot." Melinda passed on this information, her small hands hovering over Theresa's hair.

A mildly electric pause followed, broken by a sudden chuckle from the man behind the wheel. "Apropos of this interesting conversation, Theresa, sorry I kept you waiting. One prize cow suddenly decided to drop her calf and your nursing experience will tell you that these things happen at awkward times. Normally we leave them be, but this one had some difficulty and needed help."

"Oh. Is the calf . . . is everything all right?"

"Fine, thanks." Scott gave her a quizzical glance and smiled as Melinda ran her fingers through the shining hair. "Don't do that, baggage. I know you're trying to catch moonbeams . . . leave it for another time."

"Yes, Daddy. Tresa, have you smelt Georgie? She smells gorjus, can I smell you too?" The "baggage" sniffed hard over the front seat. Georgia tickled her; she turned with a whoop; and a general scramble ensued.

Scott spoke softly. "I hope you will teach my daughter more ladylike manners and discretion."

"She probably misses feminine company and is slightly overcome by the sudden influx—" Theresa bit her lip.

"No need for embarrassment, young one, I have a heart of steel, and you're quite right. Vera Smith is hardly what I would call feminine—she scorns perfumes and all that alluring jazz. Miss Melinda is going to appreciate the change. Be forewarned, though, keep that hank of hair out of her reach . . . and mine," he added *sotto voce*, but she heard and glanced sharply at him. His face was bland and his gray eyes were concentrated on the road, so she let it pass.

The lighted fires of the barbecue were now discernible and Melinda exclaimed delightedly at the festoons of colored lights lacing the trees and buildings.

They alighted and Georgia hung back, clutching Melinda's small hand. Scott lifted the child and tucked a hand of each girl firmly under strong arms. "Forward march; no retreat in this 'ere army!"

In no time they were in the midst of cheerful company. While Scott kept a watchful eye on Georgia, who looked ready to retreat ignominiously, Dan took Theresa's arm and gravely did the round of introductions. His smile was smug and proprietorial as admiring looks were cast at the attractive girl at his side.

Scott Milward's arm was resting casually round Georgia's shoulders when Dan and Theresa again joined them. Two good-looking youths were in earnest conversation with him, although Theresa noticed with satisfaction that their eyes were on Georgia in the circle of his protective arm. That young woman's eyes showed a sparkle of excitement. Was it caused by the two lads' interest or the tanned arm resting on her shoulders?

Theresa shivered suddenly as a thought brushed her mind: that arm looked so strong, gentle. . . . She pushed it ruthlessly from her mind as she saw Hugh Lessing approach.

"Watch it, man, you're walking to your fate!" she silently warned the unsuspecting doctor. The stupid man walked right past his fate and took her own hand in a warm clasp, nodding to Scott and Georgia briefly.

"Miss Stanton, how nice to see you. I was hoping for miracles . . . lo and behold they came to pass! Hello, Scott, did you bring her?" Hugh's smiling glance rested on Georgia. "Hi there, muggins; who lassoed you into coming? Some brave soul with little value for life, I'll bet!"

Theresa could have hit him then and there, with calculated pleasure. Not even a flicker of admiration or recognition of the change in the girl—some men were just too dense, even when their future was thrust right under their questing noses!

"It's my pleasure to escort three glamorous wenches tonight." Scott's eyebrow tilted wickedly as Hugh continued to hold on to Theresa's hand. She jerked it free impulsively.

Melinda caused a diversion by calling for attention from her beloved doctor. Hugh swung her up and complimented extravagantly on her lovely party dress. Georgia bit her lip and tried to back away, but Scott's hand was firm on her shoulders.

"I hope you're not going to be greedy and hang on to all three. Even you, Casanova, will not manage that, and seeing you've already laid claim to the morsel at your side, I shall deem it a pleasure and honor to feed Miss Stanton . . . Theresa . . . may I?" Hugh bowed and offered his arm.

Theresa's eyes flew to Scott in appeal, but he merely quirked a challenged eyebrow. The flickering firelight danced across his face, highlighting strong cheekbones, but leaving his expression utterly incomprehensible.

For the second time within minutes she could easily have hit a man! He was spoiling the whole show by keeping his arm so possessively around Georgia's shoulders. Maybe that was the way he wanted it? A slight lurch in the region of her heart was severely quelled as she allowed herself to be led away. She vowed that before the evening was through she would get even with that spoilsport. Hugh handed her a glass. She smiled at him and started her crusade.

"Georgia is a stunning girl, Hugh. She looks quite lovely tonight, don't you think?"

"Yes, not bad at all, quite a surprise. You're a knockout yourself, honey."

Theresa pointedly ignored the latter part. "Well, why didn't you tell her so?"

Hugh raised surprised eyebrows. "Should I have?"

"A girl likes a bit of flattery, and you did Melinda and me the honor."

"That's the girl, showing up my manners, or lack of them! Anyway, Scott seemed to be fulfilling all her needs. . . ." A frown puckered his forehead. "Do you think there might be a slight romance starting? He's a bit old to. . . ."

"Don't be silly, Scott could have started a romance

long ago, if he were so-minded. He sees her often enough at the ranch. Georgia is a little like a scared fawn tonight and he's being protective." Theresa found herself rather short of breath in her swift defense of Scott's intentions.

"Hmm. Maybe that's why Georgie disappears into the blue so often on her horse—"

Theresa interrupted furiously, "That's a rotten thing to say, Hugh Lessing! Scott has . . . had a wife, if you remember. He doesn't strike me as that kind—"

"Whoa! Theresa, I apologize. I merely said that to get a rise out of you. Your eyes are as dark as a velvety night when you're angry and, at the moment, I'm very interested in the woman attached to those eyes. So why are we getting so wound up about Scott and his Georgie? Let's talk about ourselves, then we'll have some food and I'll dance with you all night." Hugh Lessing looked charmed at the thought.

Theresa sighed in exasperation and immediately became very conscious that someone was standing directly behind her. A certain, sure instinct came that it was Scott Milward.

"Mary sends greetings and will we all kindly join her at yonder table, loaded with goodies for our delectation." While delivering this request he drew his forefinger down her bare back to where the low neckline started.

A shocking vibration through her body made Theresa gasp in surprise and she turned as though drawn by an irresistible magnetic quality. Scott was standing very close, a vibrant, smoldering anger in his eyes at variance with the half-smile on his lips.

With calculated coolness he continued, "You are invited to join us, Hugh. Take my arm, Theresa, the ground is slightly uneven. Although if you fractured a limb, I'm sure the doctor would be only too delighted to aid you in the course of duty."

Hugh laughed delightedly as he fell into step beside them. "You should have taken up my profession, old boy, you can be quite pompous at times and it has its compensations. Relax, Scott, I won't devour this tasty morsel, much as I would like to. After all, she did me a good turn with Lily and I may need her help again in the future."

The "tasty morsel" was hardly conscious of his prattle, for she was trying very hard not to be so aware of the warm grip on her arm and wondering at the inexplicable anger in smoky eyes. , , ,

Mary hailed them and, with gracious dexterity, led Hugh to the seat beside Georgia. Scott seated Theresa and swung long legs over the bench next to Melinda. Plates of sizzling lamb chops, sausages, T-bone steaks with salads, bread, rolls and barbecue sauces were handed out in a spirit of general merriment. Brimming beer mugs made the rounds.

Scott and the Rourkes were evidently popular with the community, and their table drew considerable attention, besides having the added attraction of two pretty, eligible girls. Scott personally attended to Theresa's wants, but with a formal politeness at variance with his warmth to others. A barnlike hall had been gaily decorated, and now the band could be heard tuning up amid much hilarity.

Theresa walked with Mary to the rest rooms where three elderly ladies were preparing to babysit. Glynis went happily to sleep and Melinda was soon busily engaged with crayons and coloring books. The dancing was in full swing when they returned.

She noted with satisfaction that Hugh was dancing with Georgia and an earnest conversation was in progress that seemed to hold the girl enthralled, judging from her expression.

Dan and Scott were still at the table, deep in shoptalk with three other men. At their approach the men stood up and Dan claimed Mary for a dance. Scott turned on the seat and leaned his elbows on the table as Theresa sat down next to him. The three men murmured apologies and wandered into the hall. Scott offered cigarettes and her hand shook slightly as he leaned forward, lighter in hand. The small flames reflected a tiger-yellow echo in smoky eyes that held hers for a mesmerized eternity.

Highly annoyed with herself at this show of emotion, she forced her gaze away from hypnotic depths and followed his example of leaning her elbows on the table. They watched the dancing in silence until Scott suddenly stubbed his cigarette and stood up. "I guess we should join the merrymakers. Are you ready?"

Theresa straightened up and he gripped her elbow in a hard hand, his face very close. "Remember this, Miss Stanton, when I invite a female out, I don't expect her to disappear with some other man the moment we arrive. Is that clear?"

Her reply was sharp and quick. "I can't remember you inviting me; I can only recall you stating rather flatly that I was to accompany you! Your familiarity with Georgia probably led Hugh to think I was not your particular property. Which I'm not, anyway." She tried to shrug his hand off her elbow, but the grip became firmer.

"For tonight you are, spitfire, make no mistake, and stop splitting hairs about my invitation. Your devious ways with Georgia and Hugh might boomerang right back to your own pretty shoulders. He seems to be smitten with the wrong girl. When you throw that limpid gaze at a man he immediately forgets the world around him—"

"Do you feel that way too?" The question was out before she could stop.

Scott paused in his stride, turned her toward him as the kindling anger faded to a deep, calculated scrutiny.

"I've been bitten once too often to fall into that trap again, so rest assured, I shan't let the world fade for the sake of a pair of alluring eyes. Eyes that could be untrustworthy, as your ex-fiancé probably found, to his cost. As I did too. . . ."

The implication of his words hit her like a blow in the solar plexus. The pain in her voice spilled into darkened blue eyes as she looked directly at him. "Are you merely judging the majority by your own experience with the minority, Mr. Milward, or have you official knowledge of my affairs?"

The hand on her arm became suddenly gentle and contrite. His mouth softened amazingly. "By heavens, forgive me, Theresa. My own bitterness clouds my judgment sometimes. As I know nothing whatsoever about your affair, that was a vindictive remark, and I beg to apologize for my very bad manners."

"Your apology is accepted, Scott. Just . . . just don't jump to hasty conclusions without a hearing from your victims."

Scott looked at her gravely. "I'm sorry. Maybe one day you might want to confide in me. Very often, to share your feelings is to lighten them considerably."

Theresa spoke softly, hesitantly. "You speak words of wisdom but don't follow them yourself. Perhaps if you did so, the bitterness in your own heart would be washed away. . . ?"

She sensed his body go taut for a moment, before he relaxed again and they started walking slowly. He did not speak until they entered the hall and he led her into a slow foxtrot.

"Shall we shelve both our past heartaches, and live just for the moment? I have a lovely girl in my arms, the night is beautiful, the music is hot and I want you to forget the past. Play along with me . . . please, Theresa?" Scott's voice was urgent and husky.

"Right you are, sir." They merged into the happy crowd of dancers. A Paul Jones came next, but Scott held on to his partner throughout and smiled at the cries of "spoilsport!"

His body, lithe and firm, sent strange vibrations through her. They seemed to emanate from the gentle caress of a suntanned hand on her bare back. Scott was a good dancer and the fluidity of movement made Theresa relax after a while, to enjoy the pleasure of being guided by him.

Georgia Masters was not allowed a moment of rest as the party shifted into high gear, and Hugh Lessing cut in often, dividing his dancing mostly between the two girls. Scott did not participate every time, but kept a careful eye on Theresa while standing to one side, smoking and chatting to various men and women.

Theresa enjoyed herself as she swung from one pair of arms to another, but she was very conscious of the aura of

Scott's presence in the background and sensed his approach, to claim a dance, before she heard his voice. It troubled her inner consciousness until she noticed that he was equally popular with either sex, so she put it down to a certain stimulating power that he obviously possessed. His charm was dangerously disarming!

Hugh had partnered her and he acquiesced with alacrity when the music stopped and Scott stepped up to announce, "Time for a spot of fresh air. Join us outside, Hugh, there's a smog in here." They relaxed in cushioned chairs and a waiter took Scott's order for three frosty drinks.

Hugh spoke. "You know, Terry, that youngster Georgie is a strange girl. I had my time cut out to make her say a few words, most exhausting. . . ."

"She's rather shy, Hugh, and covers up with a veneer of stiff disinterest—and she's a young lady, so stop calling her youngster. You're only about five years older than Georgia, you old sophisticate!"

Hugh looked thoughtful, then surprised. "Good grief, that's so. . . . Anyway, that stiff disinterest, as you call it, melted with astonishing swiftness when I, in desperation, reverted to 'shoptalk' namely doctoring and nursing. She's mighty keen on nursing, but I don't think. . . ."

"Well, don't. Georgia can think for herself. Let me tell you she was most capable with her help when I got stuck with Lily. Her tomboy exterior hides a very sensible and sensitive nature—"

"Crusader!" came softly from Scott.

Theresa shot him an indignant stare and continued defiantly, "—And I was going to ask you if something can be done about her, but I'll find out elsewhere if you're going to be superior and stupid about her youth!"

Scott grinned as Hugh looked flabbergasted. "I warn you, doctor, this female's sweet exterior hides a snaky tongue. Be warned by one who knows."

Sweet venom dripped while hot color played in her cheeks. "Certain people are so obtuse that sledge-hammers are sometimes necessary. Does Georgia look like a tomboy tonight? Does she, now, Hugh Lessing?

Look at her closely. There she is, surrounded by personable young men who surely consider her the epitome of beauty—of womanhood." Theresa dropped a pointing finger in exaggerated despair. "But of course, you're too old to appreciate extreme youth. . . ."

"I'm not too old to—by George!" Hugh's mesmerized eyes tore away from the 'epitome of beauty' and settled on the 'crusader' who looked slightly breathless. "Say, Scott, do you think she's taking the mickey out of me?"

"No doubt, old chap, no doubt." Scott's voice was a lazy drawl of amusement.

"So are you going to ask her very nicely, in a decent adult way, to help you in your consulting rooms and also pay her well and not treat her like a—an office boy—but like a girl worthy of her occupation? Are you going to do that, Doctor Lessing?" Theresa ignored a mocking chuckle from Scott Milward and kept her eyes on the stunned man.

Dr. Lessing swallowed hard and answered in a meek, subdued whisper, "If you think it proper, Nurse Stanton—if you think it in order—"

"I do." The singular beauty of her smile caused two distinct intakes of breath. "I thank you, Hugh. It will not be regretted," Theresa finished simply.

The boy delivered the drinks and they sipped in quiet enjoyment. Still dazed, Hugh stood up and started to walk away, muttering, "Pay her well . . . office boy . . . occupational hazards. . . ."

Theresa's voice stopped him. "Did you come alone, Hugh?" He nodded apprehensively. "Then I'm sure you won't mind taking Miss Masters home? Melinda will have to lie on the back seat, not much room, and Scott will be so grateful. . . ?"

A slight hesitation, and Scott recovered. "Oh yes, Hugh, I . . . er . . . would be."

The other man's chin drew up belligerently, then sagged hopelessly. "A pleasure, I assure you. Although," a brief gleam of mischief showed in his brown eyes, "seeing as Georgie lives nearer to you, Scott, you could take her and I'll take—No! I might be further victimized by. . . . I go now to my fate!" He squared his shoulders and walked away.

"Fate's the keyword to that jumble," Theresa chuckled hysterically, and Scott smiled at her animated face.

"Do you often play this dangerous game of juggling other people's lives, *chérie?*"

The endearment gave her a sudden warm feeling deep inside. "First time ever, Scott."

"Aren't you rather rushing things? Hugh could easily shy off, for good."

"Strike while the iron is hot. Give Georgia time to cool down and she'll retreat into her lonely shell again. Hugh can stop that now by asking her to fill the vacancy in his office. All businesslike and aboveboard; she won't suspect that romance might be included."

"If you think so." Scott spoke noncommittally. "Would you like to go in again, or shall we make a move homeward? By the way, I didn't realize my car was so small."

"That was what one calls strategy!" Theresa stretched her arms above her head. "I'm ready to go and have had a heavenly time, Scott. Thank you."

"It was a pleasure, ma'am." He raised a servile finger to his forehead.

They rode swiftly through the velvety night, in a mood of silent empathy, and Theresa breathed deeply of the cool air coming through her window. Scott stopped on the front driveway. Melinda was sound asleep on the back seat.

"Would you care to come in for a cup of coffee?" Theresa invited him.

"Thank you, no. I want to have a look at that cow before I go to bed."

Theresa put her hand on the doorknob, but he leaned over suddenly, imprisoning her hand under his. Scott's face was very close to hers and she had an instinctive feeling that he was fighting some deep emotion. His glance clung with a hot, embracing quality that brought a flush to her cheeks. Was he about to kiss her? She closed her eyes involuntarily and braced herself. . . .

Moments passed while her heart beat against a hard shoulder. And then she opened her eyes to meet woodsmoke ones, dancing mockingly close. His breath was warm on her cheek as he spoke in satirical amusement.

"Something tells me that could have been easy and delightful. . . . But we will forgo the pleasure; another time perhaps? I merely wanted to know if you're still coming tomorrow?"

"You flatter yourself, Scott Milward, as you may have found if your so-called intuition had led you further. You have a distorted sense of your charms!" Theresa lashed words at him, to cover her own complex sense of frustration and fury. She had a brief moment of insight: this man had an insidious, physical attraction for her.

He straightened up, opened his door and strode round the car to hold the door for her. She found a strange weakness in her legs as they faced each other. He broke the silence, to say woodenly, "Do I come for you tomorrow?"

Theresa's back stiffened proudly. "You may, after lunch, if it suits you."

"Thanks, it does." A brief good night, then she watched the tail lights of his car rapidly disappear down the drive.

Such a lovely evening, and he had to spoil it all with his arrogant, cynical remarks! Theresa's heart quailed as she thought of having to live in the same house as he. She was strong and would combat this fatal attraction, avoiding him as much as possible. . . . Her chin jutted determinedly as she climbed into bed. Within minutes she was asleep.

CHAPTER FIVE

It was with some trepidation that Theresa awaited the arrival of Scott Milward, the following day. Would he be in a friendly mood, or the hard, sarcastic one of the night before? She was puzzled by the many facets of his nature—tenacious, volatile, arrogant and at other times gentle, and whimsical. It seemed that any adjective would suit him at any given time, according to his mood.

She felt a slight sympathy for the absent Elaine. To live with Scott must be very exhausting! He could, quite possibly, soar you to heaven or push you down into dungeons of despair. Why she should sense this, goodness knew, and Theresa mocked herself ruefully, now that she was walking right into the lion's den. Well, she was not married to him at least!

The Rourke family were sitting with her, under the cool of the trees, when they heard the deep purr of an approaching car. Sudden panic struck and Theresa wished she could fly into the surrounding thicket and hide, like a small animal, until the man had gone. She took pride in her serenity of face, while under her sky-blue shift-dress beat a floundering uncertainty.

The car door opened and a small volcano erupted, followed more slowly by its owner. Melinda was full of prattle about the lovely party and the fact that "Tresa was coming to our house." Scott lowered into the deck chair and extended his long legs. "She's been sitting in the car since after lunch. Vera has had the devil's own time with the minx."

Long, frosted orange drinks were served and later, after many admonishments from Mary and Dan to visit often, Scott swung the car down the driveway. Theresa waved goodbye, and felt small and lonely.

Scott had been very ordinary and noncommittal, for which she was grateful. It had stilled her own unrest.

Georgia waved frantically from the de Wets' gate and

473

Scott trod hard on the brakes. She ran to Theresa's window and thrust in an eager face. Her hair was wind-blown, untidy, but, being shorter, did not look as scruffy as usual.

"Thanks for stopping, Mr. Milward. Nothing is wrong; everybody's fine. Terry, I just want to wish you luck, and here are some flowers for you, St. John Lilies." She thrust three beautiful specimens onto the girl's lap. "Also to tell you that Hugh—Dr. Lessing—has asked me to help in his office. I don't know what to do . . . Lily says it's wonderful . . . but I simply must talk to you. Can I come and see you tomorrow?"

"But of course, Georgia. I'm sure Scott won't mind. . . ." Theresa looked at him hesitantly, suddenly realizing that he was now her employer.

He looked across to her, to Georgia, with warmth in his smile. "Please do that, Georgie. Come as often as you wish. No need to ask me." His glance switched to the girl at his side. "The more feminine company for Melinda the better, isn't that so, Theresa?"

"Thanks. See you then, Terry. 'Bye, Melinda." Georgia stood back and waved as they moved off.

A short silence prevailed. Theresa's eyes were on the lean hands manipulating the wheel with relaxed power in the blunt-edged long fingers.

Scott spoke quietly. "Theresa, please don't contemplate asking my permission every time you have visitors. You have it, and also consider my house as yours, while you're there. By looking after Poppet you're doing me a great favor. I don't want you to think of me as your employer, rather as—a friend, and grateful father of your charge."

"Thank you, Scott, I'll do that, and be circumspect in the amount and choice of friends who will visit."

The smile turned to her illumined face, bringing a sparkling glint to his imperious gray eyes. She turned quickly and became absorbed in the passing scenery, clutching the flowers in her hand harder than they deserved. The sudden thought of her own precious cache in an outcrop of rock made her hope fervently that

Georgia had not raided that particular spot. It brought back memories of a hard body and strong arms holding her in a wild ride. . . .

Melinda showed her to her room while Scott busied himself with her luggage. The room was austerely furnished, but Theresa was delighted with the large windows. He walked in with her bags. A rueful expression crossed his face as he put the cases down and studied the room.

"Heavens, I didn't realize what a dreary room this is. I'm seeing it now, through your eyes—"

"Oh, what a lovely window; just look at the view!"

Theresa drew back the heavy curtains as far as they would go, but, being heavy and thick, they obscured most of the light and view. Scott looked at them distastefully.

"Pull them down if you don't like them, and make a note of any alterations to suit your taste. I'll see to it." He showed her an inner door. "Through here is Mel's room. The bathroom is two doors down the passage. When you're ready, we'll have tea on the terrace. Vera and her fiancé must have taken a walk. The poor dope can't wait to carry off his bride-to-be." Scott gave her a malicious grin as he walked out.

Melinda washed her own face and hands, imitating the older girl's every movement. When the little girl's hair was brushed Theresa ran a comb through her own silken mass. She dithered slightly about unpacking, then decided that tea would be kept waiting, so took Melinda's hand and walked to the terrace. Scott was chatting to Vera and Dick.

Vera Smith stepped forward. "Good afternoon, Miss Stanton. So sorry I wasn't here to show you to your room. Dick and I walked farther than we intended." Her voice dropped to a lower note. "Mr. Milward has been kind enough to let me leave right away, instead of tomorrow as planned. Dick likes to be at the garage early on Mondays, so if we push off as soon as possible we should be in Salisbury before midnight. Could you manage on your own? I mean Melinda's bath . . . her clothes . . . supper. . . ." Her voice trailed anxiously.

"I'm a nurse, remember?" Theresa answered brightly.

Vera tittered nervously. "Of course, dear, nurses do have a knack of finding their way. . . . I've prepared a rice pudding for Melinda's supper."

"Oh, do you prepare all her meals?"

"No, I just tell the cook or nanny what's needed, but I love making rice puddings."

"And I hate them, Tresa!" Melinda piped up forcefully.

"So do I," thought Theresa as she assured Vera that she would cope quite well. She would find out about Melinda's likes and dislikes herself.

An hour later the couple left, with Theresa and Scott's good wishes for a happy marriage. Vera thanked the tall man again for his generous wedding check.

"Melinda, will you help me unpack? Pardon us, Scott, I want to get my bearings. Melinda can show me where everything is."

Scott stood up politely and Melinda said in surprise, "You needn't 'pologize to Daddy, Tresa. He lives here too."

"It's polite to do so, honey, even though your daddy and you live together."

" 'Scuse us, then, Daddy, we have so much to do." The gamin face took on an air of gravity. Scott and Theresa exchanged quick, amused glances before the girl took a little hand in a tender clasp and led her away.

Scott watched them, an unreadable look deep in his gray eyes. His firm, generous mouth softened into sudden tenderness.

Much later, after her cases had been unpacked, Theresa wandered through the house with Melinda. The sun had set behind a rosy glow of clouds on the horizon. They looked for Scott because she wanted to find out about the child's bedtime procedure. He was not to be found, so she decided to bath and feed her charge, in case he wanted to be with his daughter before she went to bed.

Scott did not put in an appearance until she was about to leave Melinda's room. The night lamp was a soft glow as he walked past her and gazed down, touching the sleeping child's forehead with light fingertips. They left the room and he beckoned Theresa into the lounge.

"I usually have a bedtime chat with her; she doesn't normally go to bed so early," he remarked as he busied himself with glasses and ice.

"This is normal bedtime for little girls and Melinda was really tired. She worked hard at examining everything I unpacked, and then decided that every stick of furniture had to be dusted." Theresa smiled thinking of the busy little bee.

Scott handed her a glass. "Try this, it should give you a lift. Melinda's nanny had the day off today, I completely forgot. So you had your hands full on your very first day here—I hope it won't frighten you off?"

"Don't be silly. . . ." she began indignantly, and stopped as she realized that was not the way to address one's boss.

The 'boss' chuckled suddenly. "That's right, have respect for the master of the house! Seriously though, Theresa, don't take too much on your shoulders. Nanny—that's Cleo—does all the groundwork: bathing Melinda, washing and ironing clothes and making her meals. You will only supervise the jobs and concentrate more on Madam's health, soul and manners. That alone is a full-time job, believe me. Now polish off that sherry. Daniel has set a cold supper on the patio, so let's tuck in!"

Over a surprisingly delicious arrangement of cold meats and salads Theresa informed Scott that she would take her evening meals with Melinda in future.

"You'll do no such thing," he returned sharply. "Only if I'm not here may you share hers. Otherwise I expect you to dine with me. No arguments, please."

She looked at the frown on his tanned forehead and thought he could be pretty grim and masterful when he chose.

"If you wish it, sir," she remarked primly, though a dimple lurked on her cool cheek.

"I do." Scott looked suspiciously at the softly rounded cheek. "I also want you to make a list of things you may need: curtaining for your room, and Melinda's needs . . .

er , , . clothing, etc. I'll leave it to you, I would also regard it as a favor if you'll help Daniel compile a list of food-stuffs needed. He's always running out of something or other and then sulks if he can't make certain dishes for lack of ingredients."

"I'll do that, Scott. Where do you do your shopping?" He did not know it, but she was going to put white paint on top of the list, for Melinda's room. She hoped the store he patronized would have paint, and curtaining for her and the child's rooms, and some pretty murals—nursery ones? She would write it all down and hope for the best!

"I'm going to Umtali tomorrow afternoon and will be away for a day or two, depending on business matters. They have good shops there, and please don't worry about the expense. My bank balance is fairly healthy. Sorry to leave you alone so soon after your arrival, but I have to go and I'm confident you'll cope on your own. Maybe you would like Georgie to stay with you?"

"I'll manage perfectly well, thank you, and would rather be on my own. I'll have the list ready for you tomorrow." Theresa rose and hesitated. "May I say good night now? It's late, and I'll take a bet Miss Melinda is an early riser."

"For heaven's sake, you don't have to ask my permission to go to bed, or for every little thing you want to do. Any major problems and I'm yours to command, but you're as free as the air otherwise." The slender young woman standing in front of him suddenly irritated him beyond measure. She looked so young, vulnerable and, illogically, he did not want her to leave him just yet.

Her cheeks flushed slightly at his evident irritation and she spoke stiffly. "Politeness wouldn't be amiss all around, Scott. Thank you for a very nice supper. Good night."

The slender back was uncompromisingly straight as she walked indoors. She was going to have difficulty, trying to understand this baffling, moody man!

In the early morning Theresa met Cleopatra—buxom,

dark skinned, a gay red bandanna knotted cheekily on the top of her dusky head.

"Ah done come from de banks of dat river Nile, so call me Cleo, eve'ybody does, ma'am," she announced learnedly and gaily. "That there Cleopatra must have bin some gal. Mister Scott done tol' me eve'ything. Fancy nursing *nyoka* dem snakes to youse bosom. . . . That pore reptile sure get lost in this Cleo's bosom . . . ha. . . !" Cleo stood, arms akimbo, and shook her generous front voluptuously, every white tooth on show with laughter. "Come to brekfis, ma'am; Miss Melinda is waiting. Master Scott left with the horses, ver' early."

Theresa battled manfully with the great breakfast spread before her on the table. "Daniel, please, not so much for me! I'll have only toast, marmalade and tea in future."

Cleo and Melinda helped to measure the windows for the shopping list. They studied the little girl's clothes, noting down what was needed. Theresa took a rough guess and ordered two gallons of white emulsion and one of gloss paint. Next to the nursery tiles she wrote, "Leaving choice to Mr. Milward or assistant." Daniel was consulted and by the time the last item was listed it looked quite formidable! Theresa hoped Mr. M. would not think her extravagant as well as flighty. She would get in touch with Mary as regards the loan of her sewing machine.

The rest of the morning was passed on the patio, sorting out Melinda's books, of which there was a large and varied amount. While reading from *The Wild Swans* she became aware of thudding hooves and lifted her head to watch Scott cross the paddock. He rode easily; there was perfect communion between horse and rider.

Theresa admired the lithe movement of limbs as he dismounted. Slim hips moved with supple grace and corduroy-clad legs paced with long, deceptively lazy strides toward them. Unaccountably, the girl's heart beat a little faster as Scott pushed the large-brimmed hat to the back of his head and his penetrating gray eyes surveyed the scene on his patio. Melinda flew to bear-hug his knees and he lifted her high.

"How's my girl? Has she been good, Theresa?"

"Good morning, Scott." The smile on Theresa's lips was reflected in them when she answered him. "Melinda is a good girl and I'm proud of her. She helped to draw up this list for you. . . ."

Scott fingered the fat envelope thoughtfully. Theresa felt the traitorous flush rise in her cheeks. "Please don't let him open it now, and query the contents," she prayed silently. She spoke hastily. "If you open it at the store and decide that some items are unnecessary, please delete them, Scott."

He quirked a knowing eyebrow. "Right you are, ma'am, I'll use my discretion." He tucked the sealed note into his pocket. "I'm going for a bath and shave . . . be a dear and help Daniel pack a grip for me. Enough for two days—don't forget my dinner suit."

"But . . . but I've never. . . ." she watched his receding back and finished, *sotto voce*, "—I've never packed a bag for a man in my life! Is this part of my duties, dear master?" There was no one to answer, so she shrugged her shoulders resignedly and went in search of Daniel.

They were putting the finishing touches to his bag when Scott walked in, whistling, in Bermuda shorts with a towel slung over one shoulder. Damp, dark hair hung over one eye, making him look piratical, gay and sinister all at the same time. A sharp smell of sandalwood after-shave lotion emanated and Theresa's eyes were glued to the broad expanse of tanned chest. A strange feeling leaped across her scalp. She dropped her eyes with some difficulty to the open bag on the bed.

"I hope we've packed all your needs. I . . . er . . . I'm not used to . . . er. . . ."

"Packing for a business gent like me? Well, are my socks in? Last time Daniel forgot and I had to rush round madly looking for an open store—most embarrassing, I assure you!"

"Yes, they're packed." Theresa started to back out

while Scott unbuttoned the white shirt Daniel had put out for him.

"Okay. Scram, will you—not that I mind if you stay," he stated wickedly, "but I'm afraid of maidenly blushes. We can have lunch, then I'll push off."

Theresa "scrammed," color high in her cheeks.

Long after he had gone, a persistent picture of ludicrous floral shorts on long brown legs haunted her. Ludicrous, and yet so virile—manly.

Fortunately, Georgia turned up with her problems, pushing thoughts that were both besotted and silly back into unconscious regions.

They spent a pleasant afternoon discussing Georgia's future. An elderly cousin was reached by phone, and was only too pleased to have the girl come and stay with her, for she was alone and her home was near to the consulting rooms. Georgia became too excited and shy to talk when Hugh Lessing was next contacted. She looked at the mouthpiece as if it would bite when she heard his voice, and shoved it into Theresa's hands. "Hello, hello, who's calling?"

"Theresa Stanton here, Hugh."

"Hello there, love, nice to hear your dulcet tones. What gives?"

"No one ill, Hugh, we're all in the best of health. I'm speaking on behalf of Georgia. She was called away when this call came through. When do you want her to start? She's ready, able and willing."

"Oh, she is, is she? Then why is she standing right beside you, breathing so heavily?" He laughed at the dumbstruck silence that ensued. "All right, put her on. I won't bite. How's Scott?"

"He's gone to Umtali."

"Good. Maybe I'll take a run out there this evening. Without his charm to distract you, my own charms may be appreciated."

Theresa spoke hastily. "We'd love to see you again, but not tonight, please. You know, my first day on the job, I'm having an early night. Thanks all the same; go spread your charm elsewhere. Goodbye now, here's Georgia."

She thrust the phone back at the trembling girl, walked hastily out of the room and stood in the passage where she could hear without being seen.

"Hello, Dr. Lessing." Silence. "Hello then, Hugh. . . . Yes, I have . . . yes, my cousin's house. . . . So soon? No, but . . . very well, Doctor . . . Hugh. No, Sam will . . . very well . . . er, thanks. Goodbye."

Theresa came back and pried the receiver from still fingers, set it back in its cradle and gave the ring-off twist to the handle. "So?" she inquired.

"He says I need only call him 'Doctor' in the consulting room. He says to call him Hugh, as I've always done in the past. He says. . . ." Georgia stopped.

"All right, he says all that. But what does he say about the job? When do you start, what is he paying you?"

A dazed look was cloudily focused. "He said I was to start on Monday. Pay me? I forgot to ask, and he . . . forgot to say. He's coming for me on Sunday afternoon."

"Oh, really, Georgia Masters, you'll have to pull up your socks if you're to work in a doctor's office. Vagueness won't get you anywhere," Theresa said sternly.

Georgia recovered partly. "Of course I'll pull up my doctor—I mean my socks, Terry. It's just that. . . ."

Theresa dissolved into laughter. "Oh, Georgie, you're priceless! Perhaps you're dithering because you're a little in love with your doctor?"

"Don't be absurd, Theresa Stanton. Now you're the one that's talking rubbish. Why, I wouldn't be in love with that man. You're talking through your hat. . . . I'm not in love with anyone." An indignant flush was fast dispelling the dazed look in Georgia's eyes.

"Methinks the lady doth protest too much!" Theresa grinned at the girl and took both her hands. "Come on, I was only teasing. Let's have tea. You look as if you could do with sustenance."

Over tea they discussed pros and cons and Theresa offered Georgia three white nylon, nurse's overalls she had brought with her. "I have stacks of them, so won't run short myself. In any case I don't often wear them now."

Georgia left, with fervent thanks for her help, promising to see her again before she started her new job.

After supper Theresa read to Melinda until her bedtime. The house was very quiet; outside, the night was velvety purple. She stood on the lawn, fascinated by a crescent moon rising in a sky studded with winking stars. The night seemed to tug at her heart and she knew a nameless longing, stirring deep inside her breast, for what she knew not.

The telephone aroused her and her steps were quick and light. Surely it would be Scott, to let her know he had arrived safely, to inquire in his deep voice if all was well at home.

A throb in the pulse of her throat subsided as Mary's voice inquired if all was well.

"Yes, thank you, Mary." Theresa stammered slightly as she pushed down a wayward disappointment. After all, Scott could look after himself and he knew that all would be well at his house. So why should she expect a call from him?

"And Dan will be helping with Scott's cattle roundup next week, so I shall spend a whole day with you. It's usual for the wives to help with the cooking at drive time; the men are so hungry when they get back—are you there, Terry?"

"Yes . . . yes, Mary, I'm listening. That will be perfectly marvelous and sounds exciting. No, I haven't had time to arrange a day off yet. Not while Scott is away . . . no, I feel quite safe and happy. Melinda is a darling, so don't worry. How is Glynis?" She listened to a long rhapsody on baby's charms, and then her friend rang off with a warm good night.

There was a soft, sighing wind outside her open window. For a long time sleep eluded Theresa and the whispering wind seemed to coax her heart out of her body with a deep, velvety call. She punched her pillows and turned her back to the inviting night. "You're getting soft, pal," she chided herself scornfully, settling down at last.

Melinda was fretful and restless the next morning,

quite obviously missing her father, for she kept asking when would he be back. Theresa concentrated on keeping her entertained and occupied, and after a mid-morning sleep the child awoke refreshed and in a better mood.

Lunch over, Theresa scratched through her own belongings and found a length of sprigged voile that was intended for a blouse. She now proceeded to cut and sew it into tiny clothes for Melinda's lovely doll. The child was delighted and fascinated when she, too, was provided with threaded needle and a small square of material to hem, for a scarf.

Tenderness welled up as Theresa sewed and watched tiny clumsy hands work with laborious care, while a little rosy tongue was constantly in evidence. What an amazing feminine replica of her father! She felt an urgent need to take Melinda Milward in aching arms, to cuddle and comfort her with soft words of love and kiss away the sweet frown of concentration on her puckered forehead. This feeling was replaced by sudden fierce hatred for a mother who could forsake her child so ruthlessly and bring such bitterness to a man's woodsmoke eyes. Her hands were still shaking when they started to dress the doll.

"Oh, Tresa!" Melinda's eyes were rapt as she held her "baby." She looked at it in long silence and then, with glistening lashes, climbed onto the older girl's lap and put chubby arms around her neck. "Tresa, I do love you so much, I love you forever 'n' ever. Don't go away, please!" Then she promptly burst into tears.

Gently Theresa cuddled her, murmuring words of love, as she had yearned to do only moments ago, soothing and comforting the little girl, promising never to leave. "Heart's promise?"

"Heart's promise, darling." Tears were magically dispersed; now Cleo and Daniel must be called to exclaim over the wonder of "my boot'ful child."

Later, Theresa sat on the patio and watched a solemn gardener and little boy raise their hands in awed delight at the transformation of their beloved "Nonny's" baby.

Timothy, the cat, was honored next and the watching girl smiled as a small imperious finger pointed to admonish him for lack of manners in yawning in a lady's face! "'Scuse him, Tresa, my daddy says he's just a tom-foolish cat."

Sam dropped in to check if all was well after Melinda had gone to bed, her doll looking very snappy in new shortie pajamas, and when he left Theresa settled under the reading lamp in the lounge to cut strips of white cardboard into one-inch widths by various lengths. She then printed simple everyday words on them. Starting tomorrow, she was going to teach Melinda to sight-read, having heard about the new method of teaching the very young. Her thoughts wandered to Scott. . . . What would he be doing, right now? Out with cronies, or maybe some attractive girl, seeing a show, nightclubbing. She envisaged him, sleekly dark in black trousers and the snowy jacket Daniel had so reverently packed.

Suddenly restless, she lit a cigarette and walked out to the darkening patio. The stars were so bright they looked unreal. Maybe he was looking at them too, this very moment, an arm around his companion. Mutinously she forced her thoughts further south of the continent, to Derek. Would his suave, sophisticated arm possibly be resting on Sylvia's elegant shoulders? Theresa miraculously realized, after a moment of thought, that this picture which should have instantly raised her blood pressure left her strangely empty and cold. A maliciously insidious voice hoped that the gay widow had hooked her doctor—talk about just deserts! "How mean can you get, Theresa Stanton?" her good spirit prevailed reproachfully, and the nurse-cum-ex-fiancée moodily pitched a half-smoked cigarette into the night, turned her back on the bright stars and walked indoors.

She was standing under a stinging shower when the sound of their telephone shrilled through. Turning the tap off, she listened as Cleo answered, but the conversation was indistinct and of a short duration. Cleo entered the bedroom soon after with a glass of hot chocolate. "Master Scott phoned; I tol' him the missy's in the shower and he say to give'm regards, he'll be back tomorrow. I brought this drink 'cos Master Scott he say to look well after you 'n little nonna. Everyt'hing is good and locked, so I'll wish you God bless'n good night."

"Thank you, Cleo. Sleep well."

So while she was having malicious thoughts Scott Milward was patiently waiting for his call to go through! Even though, when it did, he did not demand to speak to her personally. . . . Well, why should he? It was not imperative.

The next morning passed pleasantly. Melinda was an eager pupil and quick in absorbing the printed words. Her favorites were "Daddy, Theresa, Melinda and Timothy" because they were the best "shapes." "Daddy 'cause it reminds me of his long legs; Tresa looks like a soft bed and the other two 'cause them are me 'n my cat!" Soft bed indeed? Theresa studied her own name long and hard.

CHAPTER SIX

The hot sun had reached its zenith and moved with inexorable heat to its allotted place to the west. Theresa found her eyes straying often to the ribbon of dusty road. No puffs of dust heralded an oncoming vehicle. Eventually she dropped the book she was trying to read. Irritation at her lack of concentration made her sneer scornfully at herself. "Stop it, you idiot! Why are you so anxious for his return. . . . Do you expect a smile and a hug, like Melinda? What you'll get, old girl, is an arrogant turn of the head and a haughty inquiry after duties well done, and he'll ask what in hell did I mean by giving him such a ridiculous list. Did I think I owned the place, by any queer misconception?

Her thoughts brought forth a nervous giggle, and she decided to take Melinda for a walk before bath time. The sun was much lower now, so it was not too hot, and, the light remained long after sunset. So it happened that the two of them were some way from the house watching a gush of water flowing into the reservoir and listening to the slow regular beat of the pump when Melinda suddenly shouted, "Daddy's home!" and tugged Theresa's hand frantically.

Reaching the house somewhat breathless, Melinda hurled herself at the tall man who was standing at the steps and directing unloading operations. He greeted his daughter with matching enthusiasm and turned a tired but smiling face to the quietly waiting girl. A fleeting, wondering expression sobered his smile for a moment and then it was back again as two warm brown hands enclosed hers. The strong, sensitive hands sent a sudden flare through her pulses and her eyes dilated.

"Hello, Theresa."

"Hello, Scott." Her reply came husky, soft.

Cleo broke the spell. "Sure, Boss, but dem's a helluva. . . . I mean dat's a lot of parcels. Dat long box, likely a new radio?" Her black face beamed expectantly.

487

"Who knows, inquisitive woman. Patience is good for the soul. A lot of parcels, you say? Well, whose fault is it?" He wiped his forehead with a handkerchief. "It takes a woman to think up a list like the one I was handed. Snakes alive! I never want to go through that again." His groaning chuckle was reproachful and resigned.

Theresa gave a slow sigh of relief. He was not going to storm and rant as she expected—not now anyway. "Let me get you a long cool drink, Scott. I'm sure you must be parched." She ran up the steps. "I'll bring it out to the patio; would you like that?"

"Sure. I'll wash the grime off my face and hands. Come, Melinda, don't gawk so, I haven't forgotten your request. Daniel, that box can stay on the verandah, and that one, and that. . . ." He ticked off the boxes for the kitchen, then went his way.

Ten minutes later, sitting with satisfied ease, Scott allowed Melinda to open her parcel and she squealed with delight at the miniature sewing machine, complete with needles and thread, that actually worked, as a sample under the foot showed. A neat chain-stitch appeared when the handle on the wheel was turned.

Theresa almost followed suit with her cry of joy when lengths of curtaining were opened for her inspection—sun-filter in dove gray for her room, cinnamon and yellow for Melinda's, complete with cottons, rufflette and rings, and exquisite nylon net falls. Another box revealed a soft rose bedspread for her and a blue one for Melinda, with matching scatter cushions.

She held a cushion against her breast and looked at Scott, wordlessly. Not so Melinda. Chubby arms hugged him, kisses rained on his face. Through this he managed to splutter, "I've brought the paint and brushes as well. I'm certainly going to absent myself for the next few days. Something is going to be whitewashed and it's not, I repeat, not going to be me!"

"Scott, you're an angel already; you don't need to be whitewashed . . . I mean. . . ." Color flooded Theresa's cheeks as a sudden, quizzical gaze held hers. "Thank you so much. The colors are wonderful. I didn't think you had such a taste for . . . I mean, they're beautiful. . . ."

"I get the message, ma'am. Now, before you collapse completely, let's open that large one." He stood up and in a businesslike way snapped the packing wire with pliers, then stood back. "Open up!"

Theresa stared in awe at the lovely table-model sewing machine, complete with handle and motor. Her conversation with Mary had been heard and noted! Dazedly she looked at him, trying to speak, but her tongue would not cooperate.

"Tresa, kiss Daddy thank you." Melinda added excitedly. "The cat's got her tongue, the cat's got her tongue, Daddy!"

"It sure has, pet. Shall I help her find it?" He came closer. The nymph's open mouth and the way she clutched that cushion as if it were a lifebelt made him burst into delighted laughter. He took her face between his hands and kissed her full on the mouth. The friendly caress became prolonged and she found herself incapable of drawing back while her heart reached top gear and raced madly.

Scott dropped his hands and drew back. His voice was brusque. "Sorry, honey, but the invitation was irresistable. Have I annoyed you?"

"Not at all, Mr. Milward. I didn't find it annoying at all. I liked it, thank you."

"Well then, let's be rational from now on. Here's the book with instructions for using all these gadgets. During the day you can use the handle and if you want to sew in the evening our plant has the standard volts and amps, so we'll fix a plug wherever you want it."

"You're very good to us, thanks. I can't wait to try it out. Come on, Melinda, a quick bath and supper; then you can talk to Daddy again till bedtime." Theresa wanted to get out of reach of his magnetic gaze as quickly as possible; otherwise she would start dithering like a silly schoolgirl with a crush.

It took her some time to calm the excited little girl, but eventually sleep claimed her and Theresa joined Scott for dinner. While they ate he was silent and answered in absentminded manner when she spoke to him. She was rather relieved, for it gave her time to compose herself.

They moved to the patio with coffee and cigarettes. She persevered with small talk and had the satisfaction of drawing him out on a subject which interested him greatly—local lore, fauna and flora.

Scott was certainly knowledgeable and spoke at length, holding her intense interest. She was surprised to learn that he was born in Australia and had come to Rhodesia with his father, as a young lad. The older Milward had worked hard to establish Windimount. Meanwhile Scott had attended university, qualifying as a surveyor engineer. The death of his father was a terrible blow and he had finally come back to the ranch which was now his property. Scott omitted to mention the tale of his conference trip to America, where he met and married Elaine. Theresa felt this was deliberate and temerity forbade her to question him on a subject which was evidently still too raw and painful for this moody man to relate.

Finally he stood up and stretched long arms. "Bed for me. I've had a hectic day. There's another parcel of underclothes, etc., for Melinda. Thanks for giving sizes; it was a big help. If anything isn't right put it aside to be sent back for exchange." He studied Theresa as she too arose. "Are you settled, Theresa—more important still—are you happy here with Melinda?"

"I have no complaints sir. Melinda is a good child and responds like a kitten to affection. She's bright and has a quick brain, although she's slightly blasphemous at times."

Scott caught her clear, direct gaze and smiled back sweetly, albeit a slight flush was noticeable across his forehead. "O.K., ma'am, I'll watch my tongue in future. You'll have us all ladylike very soon, with those violet eyes looking so sad and reproachful." Playfully Scott grabbed her shoulders. "Be still, you're in my power, woman. Dr. Jekyll was a healthy cousin of mine. I can be a worm, but I can also be cruel and savage and drink every drop of your heart's blood! That is, if you have a heart. A nip in the jugular vein is the usual procedure, I believe. . . ."

Theresa stood petrified, not in fear, but in the mesmerizing aura of his close, vital presence. Scott looked at her for a moment, then loosened his hold on her shoulders. A brown hand flicked her hair and cheek carelessly as he stepped back, an impish glint flickering in his smoky eyes.

"My word, you scare easily. I'll have to curb any—savage impulses—otherwise I'll find my golden nymph has flown the nest."

"I'm not scared, Scott Milward," she retorted, and retreated hurriedly to the door. "I didn't realize my boss was demented, that's all!" Before he could speak she made her escape.

The following day was a busy day indeed! Theresa did not see Scott as he had breakfasted early and departed to the tobacco lands. She thanked her lucky stars for that, being somewhat dubious of his reactions to her parting speech of the night before. Her sewing machine was proudly installed on a large table in a spare, sunny room which was duly dubbed as "The Workhouse." Melinda's tiny machine was screwed on at the opposite end of the table.

Georgia came visiting and was promptly roped in to pin curtain hems. The morning passed in a swirl of sewing and happy chatter. Scott did not appear for lunch and again Theresa felt a sense of reprieve. She could not pin down her feelings as regards her boss. At certain times she hated him for his proud arrogance, then melted at his generosity. And now take last night. . . . He was not above playing silly games! Then he would look at her in a certain way or come too close and she would instantly become aware of his physical attractions. Then again, coldly contemptuous, superior and distant. . . . How on earth was she going to keep track of this complex man in order to meet his moods on equal ground? And above all, why couldn't she forget or disregard it all and enjoy her job? She loved her surroundings, was vastly intrigued with the ways of the Africans, and a mutually satisfying affection had developed between Melinda and herself. She must forget about the man of the house whose moods probably stemmed from bitterness and disillusionment at his ex-wife's behavior.

Theresa stopped and watched Melinda. That absorbed young lady was working on her tiny machine, sewing along the lines of penciled flowers drawn on a square of linen. Not quite on yet, but she was getting the hang of it and her manipulations were dextrous, clever for her years.

"Let's stretch our legs and get some fresh air, girls. My back's aching like the devil."

They walked round to the cooler side of the house where a slight breeze cooled them. Georgia pointed in astonishment. "Whatever is Scott doing at the swimming pool? It's been dry and neglected ever since Elai—for a long time." The three girls hurried over and watched three Africans diligently scrubbing the walls and floor of the tiled pool.

Scott tipped his hat back. "Hello, girls, feel like pitching in to help, seeing as you're all loafing?"

"Daddy! We working very hard all day. Tresa and Georgie have done the curtains and my baby's quilt is almost done." Melinda could look very indignant.

"Pardon me; such diligence, I do declare!"

"Goodness, Terry, you've made a difference here but fast. Mr. Scott is waking up to feminine needs. Er . . . may I come over for a swim . . . when it's full? Did you choose all that lovely curtaining and bedspreads all by yourself, Scott? They're gorgeous!"

"You may swim, and I'm fully aware of female needs *and* I chose everything myself. That's the second time someone has queried my good taste. I am a sophisticated man of the world and have acquired discrimination by my contacts with many distinguished, beautiful dolls. Furthermore—"

"And what does all that mean, Daddy?" interrupted a small voice from the vicinity of his knees.

"It means that Daddy has seen the light," ventured Georgia.

"What exactly are you insinuating by that dubious remark, Miss Masters?" His tone was haughty and Theresa rushed to the rescue.

"It simply means that we're going to have gorgeous swims and . . . er . . . gorgeous curtains and . . . er, lovely beds."

"Very well put, Theresa; your perspicacity is fantastic. Such intuition or prescience is rare in golden nymphs. The species are fast becoming obsolete—"

"Come off it do, Professor, please! Your men can't work when they can't follow the conversation. Look at them gawping. Come on, ladies, back to the workhouse; we've had all the rarified air we can take." Theresa marched off and the other two followed rather reluctantly.

After dinner she politely excused herself and climbed into bed, very pleasantly tired and with hopes of tackling the painting on the morrow.

Stepping back to survey her handiwork, Theresa wiped her hands on a paraffin cloth. What a change glossy, white paint made to Melinda's bed, dresser and stool! Gone was that drab uninteresting brown. The dressing table had quaint white enamel knobs with hand-painted forget-me-nots, and now they added an elegant touch to the finished effect.

The ceiling was white and clean so all that was needed was a coat of soft, eggshell blue on the walls, which were a nauseous green at present. With the sun-filter curtains hung, it would be a dream room fit for a princess. The floor could be sanded and scrubbed to remove the dark polish revealing the natural golden wood.

Her own room had a similar floor; the suite was light oak, so she would leave it and paint the walls white. Theresa curbed her desire to pull the dark curtains down and hang the dove gray ones which were hemmed and ready. Scott had glanced in while she was painting the furniture and she stifled his protest that it was not a job for girls by requesting help in scraping the walls prior to painting them.

Her request was met and a young boy was even now busy in Melinda's room. Watching him, she thought it should be ready to paint the following day. A bed had been moved to her room to accommodate Melinda until this room was complete. That lass, supplied with a small tin of yellow paint and brush, was carefully painting her doll's cot. The floor of the side veranda was covered with newspapers to prevent any mess and the newly painted furniture glistened in the strong light.

Later that night the reading lamp cast a soft halo on Theresa's hair as she sat reading in the lounge. Scott was seated at the writing-desk across the room, writing in his ledgers. The desk lamp brought into relief his strong, brown hands and cast emphasis on his high cheekbones. A now-familiar gesture of running his hands through his hair had ruffled it, and an unruly lock hung over his forehead. Theresa, glancing at him, had a sudden urge to smooth it back with her hands. Scott raised his eyes and intercepted her gaze.

Confusion brought color to her cheeks. She lowered her head and fumbled with the book on her lap. There was a long silence while she was very conscious of his appraisal of her.

"You look very cosy in that chair, Theresa, with the lamplight shining on your hair. Almost as though you . . . you belonged." His deep voice quietened.

"I am comfortable . . . it's so peaceful here," she stammered. "Just listen to that nightbird calling outside."

Scott turned his head towards the window. "Rather a plaintive call, don't you think? When he eventually finds his mate (she plays hard to get) the call becomes more joyous, masterful, and nature comes into its own."

Theresa considered this. "Nature is cruel but wonderful. One seems to be more aware of it here than in the cities."

"Oh, definitely. In densely populated areas there's so much of the rat-race that nature is obscured by greed, lust and money. Don't you feel a slight longing for the bright lights sometimes, Theresa?"

Laughter bubbled up. "Shades of lust and greed! Honestly, Scott, I haven't had time nor the inclination up to the present. Stop worrying about my gay spirit wanting that sort of outlet. When you see me climbing the walls, then you can start panicking. I'm going to do that tomorrow, but only to paint 'em."

"You'll do no such thing. The young boy I sent to help you knows what to do. He only needs supervision; he's apt to get lazy on his own. Like the great Sherlock Holmes I shall examine the wall through my spyglass every night, and if I discover dainty footmarks, then I shall know the time has come to send you back to civilization—especially if they're on the ceiling!" Scott smiled wickedly at some unseen vista.

Theresa closed her book with a snap and stood up. "Do you get like this every night? Anyway, until that time comes, we'll say no more. 'Night, boss."

"Just a moment, please, Theresa." She stopped at the doorway and faced him inquiringly. "I'm going to Salisbury at the end of this month. I want you and Melinda to accompany me. Tobacco and cattle sales—we'll be there approximately four days. During the day you and Poppet can explore the town and surroundings and in the evenings we can visit night spots. They sport a very good theater and the lights are satisfyingly bright as well."

"Oh, Scott, you don't have to worry. We'll be quite content to stay here. There's no need to drag us—"

He retorted sharply, "I don't intend to drag you. I'm merely stating that it's my wish that you come with me. I have good friends in Salisbury where I usually dump Melinda and Cleo, while I go about my business. Cleo can come with us as chaperon, if you're feeling prim and jittery. Dave and Val would feel most annoyed if I didn't put up at their house as I usually do. You'll like them, they're good company."

Theresa answered mildly enough although, unaccountably, her heart started hammering in her throat. "As you wish, Scott. I would like the trip very much, thank you."

"My pleasure, ma'am. Good night, and pleasant dreams."

Excitement boiled strangely, with a queer foreboding in her breast, as she prepared for bed. Excitement at the forthcoming trip, that she could understand; but the other feeling was beyond comprehension and troubled her greatly.

Rain fell softly throughout the night and dawn came, sparkling fresh and bright, giving no warning of the upheaval which was to come later and cause Theresa's world to streak beyond heaven's delight and then to the very depths of despair, alternately and ruthlessly.

A boxed parcel arrived on the mail bus, containing four nursery mural tiles. Theresa and Melinda were delighted; they were just what the little girl's room needed for the finishing touch. Theresa had presumed that item on her list had been ignored, but now it was evident that the shops did not stock them, so Scott had ordered the tiles to be sent by mail.

A serious discussion started between Cleo, Daniel, Melinda and herself as to where the murals must hang. It was Nonna's room, so she had first choice. Unerring taste in so small a being showed in her final selection. "These three must hang on that wall opposite my bed so that I can see them when I wake up, 'n this one—" pointing to a picture of two big-eyed kittens watching a fluffy yellow chicken, "must hang over my doll's cot, 'cos then she won't feel lonely when she wakes up." Against the newly painted wall the three pictures were duly hung.

Melinda and Theresa lunched alone and after the child had her afternoon nap they settled under a shade tree with picture books. An hour later Cleo called Theresa to the telephone. It was Mary, to inform her that they would be over that evening in order to discuss the coming cattle roundup.

"How are you, dear? I hear you've been busy with the rooms. Have you tackled the lounge?" Mary chuckled knowingly.

"Good heavens, no! I'm dead scared to ask Scott for anything more after that last lot, although he didn't blast me. I'll give him time to recover and then insinuate—" she broke off as Cleo suddenly appeared in the passage. Her dark skin was a queer gray color and she was extremely agitated. "What's wrong, Cleo?"

English was forgotten; two terse words choked out. "*Nyoka!—Nonna!*"

As the dreaded word left her lips, the receiver was slammed down. The girl streaked past her and ran down the front steps. Daniel stopped her head-long rush and pointed. Her blood ran cold, she beheld Melinda, absorbed in her book, quite unconscious of the ugly head reared within four yards of her small, vulnerable back!

With cold calculation Theresa took the spade from Daniel's nerveless fingers, praying silently, devoutly, that the child would not look up or move. She approached the evil reptile from the rear and, as it sensed her presence, some inner spring uncoiled in her to a forward leap that buried the spade edge cleanly in the writhing neck and ground.

Simultaneously, Scott stopped the jeep with a squeal of brakes, was beside her in seconds.

"Good girl!" He moved to take the spade, but she clung to it with hands that were white-knuckled, stiffly paralyzed.

"*Bulala yena!*" Daniel recovered his wits, sprang to beat the shining flat head to a pulp with a rock he had found. Melinda jumped up, alarmed and white faced. A jittering Cleo scooped her to an ample bosom and carried her to the house with babbling endearments pouring from her thick, shaking lips.

"You can let go now, darling. . . . That was very brave of you. . . . God, that was a close shave!" Scott stood behind the rigid girl, his arms encircling her waist, brown hands gently massaging white fingers that would not, could not open. "It's all right now, love; it's quite dead."

Theresa let the spade drop from sudden lax fingers and found her vocal chords. "Melinda . . . it was going to strike her, it . . . dear God. . . ." A white fist clenched against her lips and the man turned her round and held her close.

"Relax, my dear. It hasn't struck her, thanks to your quick action. . . . Thank heaven she didn't move. I've never seen a human being uncoil and leap the way you did! Stop trembling, honey. . . . It's reaction. Daniel, fetch a glass of water with three teaspoons of sugar, chop chop!" Scott stroked damp hair and her stiff back with sensitive fingers.

Quite suddenly, Theresa was no longer trembling with fear. Another terror . . . mixed with delight . . . had taken hold of her senses. Nothing mattered in the world but the feel of this strong body against hers, those wonderfully gentle hands and the beautiful words of endearment that pierced her shock-clouded brain. "Darling, love, honey"—surely they were the most beautiful words in the world? The heavenly feeling deepened as his hands cupped her face and he kissed her gently on her mouth.

Scott let her go rather suddenly and she had the strange sensation of bones becoming fluid, melting. She closed her eyes in a supreme effort to still the wild fluttering of her heart. His hands moved to her shoulders.

"Sit down, Theresa. Daniel has brought a chair. Drink this . . . you certainly are numb with shock . . . a delayed reaction." She was firmly pressed down and a glass held to her lips.

Theresa sipped the water, her thoughts in hysterical confusion; of course that was her name—Theresa. Not darling or love or honey. Just Theresa, the girl who had killed a snake that was dangerously near his child (Had there been danger? Why had the spade stuck to her hands?). She must see Melinda. . . . Oh yes, Theresa was the girl who needed soft words to calm her shock. Anodyne for hysteria. And with that came the quite hopeless realization that she, Theresa Stanton, had fallen utterly, desperately in love with Scott Milward, her boss. Who was still in love with his ex-wife.

Warm hands were chafing her cold ones and she opened her eyes, to meet his darkened, smoky ones, very close as he bent in front of her, speaking softly. Her eyes were drawn to his mouth and longing filled her so that she scarcely heard the words, but watched his lips in fascination.

"Good, you're looking better now, there's more color in your cheeks and lips. For a moment I thought you were going to faint. Do you know, I feel like kissing you again, I'm very grateful for your quick action, Theresa."

Her smile was watery. Grateful kisses, that's all, dear Theresa. Remember that.

Scott did not kiss her but looked at her, long and searchingly, drew a deep breath and straightened up as Melinda came running across the lawn. He held her closely in his arms as she chattered excitedly about the

" 'orrible weptile" while the girl in the chair wished achingly that she could also creep into that warm, loving embrace. She stood up and found that her legs could hold her after all. The stiffening aid of her pride helped her to toss back her unruly hair and to speak with quiet composure.

"That 'orrible reptile has had it, for sure. If that spade had gone any deeper it would probably have frightened the life out of some poor wombat down under. If I'd had a revolver and could shoot, then I needn't have come so close to the . . . to the. . . ." Words failed as she met his penetrating eyes again and she turned quickly, almost stumbling, to walk away, calling over her shoulder, "Tea, that's what we need!"

The man lowered his daughter into the chair, but his gaze lingered on the slender, retreating figure. Tenderness gleamed for an instant, then was blotted out by lowering lids.

During the course of the day and evening, Theresa hugged her newfound, dangerous knowledge close to her heart and fed it on small things, like the quirk of an eyebrow above dark lashes, the turn of a high cheekbone, a lithe movement as Scott poured drinks for Mary and Dan. Sweet torment, listening to his husky, compelling voice. They played Canasta, Dan partnering her. Normally a good player, she now needed superb concentration to keep her mind on the cards, to stop it from veering away at the sound of that soft arrogant and always slightly mocking tone.

Theresa took pride in her deceptive outer calm; no one guessed at the tormenting emotions surging beneath her cool exterior. Scott remarked at one time on her prolonged contemplation of the cards in her hand. "You're concentrating with such devout severity, dear Theresa. Like those women who read your future in the cards. What do you hold, a fifty-joker or an ace of hearts? Be careful you're not caught with it, points against you, love."

Sudden poignant resentment at his easy use of endearment made her voice sharp as she retorted, "That's for my partner to groan about, if it happens. And it's not going to happen, partner; may I play out?" To Dan's nod of delight, she played out, catching Mary and Scott with full hands.

"Proper witch, she is! Painting, sewing, slaughtering dragons, cheating at cards, and maybe turning the world topsy-turvy next and that's a fact!" Scott grimaced ruefully.

Amid laughter, Theresa stacked the cards while her heart repeated, "You've turned my world topsy-turvy, Scott Milward. That is an irrefutable fact, beloved."

She stood with him in the velvety night, watching the receding lights of Dan's car. He put a friendly arm across her shoulders. Tension shot through her arms and she shrugged irritably, almost physically sick with the violence of recent emotions.

He stepped back immediately, sardonic mockery in his voice. "So sorry, ma'am. Shall we adjourn to the lounge? You in your small corner, I in mine? I have no grim intentions, so don't snap and snarl. Were you going to do that?"

"Of course not. . . . I guess I'm tired."

"You've been through a lot today, Theresa."

"The understatement of the year, if you only knew," she thought.

"And if you'll creep into bed, I'll whip up a glass of hot milk. I have very good pills—tranquillizers—and I'll bring you one. No arguments now; I'll give you ten minutes to retire and look proper." Scott moved down the passage.

Theresa looked desperately into the night for guidance, but none was forthcoming. She turned away and walked to her room. The bedside lamp glimmered softly; Melinda slept peacefully in her small bed in the far corner. Scarcely had she time to compose herself under the bedclothes when Scott whistled a warning and walked in. He placed the glass of milk in her hand, fumbled in his shirt pocket and handed her a pill. Silently he watched as she swallowed it and drank the milk.

"Good night, Theresa, sleep well." At the doorway he turned, looked at his daughter and then again at the older girl. The door closed softly.

Theresa was grateful for the ensuing busy time which started on the following morning and lasted for three very hectic days. Mary, Lily, Georgia and another neighbor, Mrs. Henning, came over with their menfolk. Horses were saddled and the male party set off to comb the nearby gullies and scrub, for stray calves and steers. The next day they would ride farther afield.

Great activity prevailed in the kitchen as the women baked joints of meat, bread and large saucepans of sweet 'n sour beans. "*Sous-boontjies*," Aletta Henning informed them. Hungry riders would be back for the midday meal and supper. The following days would be spent in the open as the roundup took them farther into the hills and valleys, so enough food had to be cooked and packed into saddlebags to satisfy vast appetites away from home base.

No time at all to brood on the sudden awakening of her love for Scott Milward. Georgia took charge of the small fry while she helped in the kitchen. At noon the men returned and clattered onto the verandah where a long trestle table, loaded with food, awaited them. Healthy badinage was exchanged among them as Scott joined them, flinging his hat on a chair. All were dusty, from hat sweatbands down into the open necks of their khaki shirts. Having washed dirty hands at the tub outside, there was not time enough for further niceties before mealtimes.

Theresa inadvertently brushed Scott's arm as she replaced his plate and he raised shocked eyebrows as she stepped back hastily.

"Scared of a bit of honest dust, lass? Hmm, may I tell you, there's a luverly smudge of flour across your pert nose? Sam, remind me to buy some face powder for the desperate girl. No wonder there's a mighty depletion of it in the larder!"

Indignation colored her cheeks, and then she joined the laughter that followed as her natural sense of humor was restored.

The ladies sat down to a leisurely lunch after the men had left. Lily's baby was admired and Melinda was in her element, having two babies to croon over. Aletta

Henning, pregnant with her first baby, hoped fervently that Theresa would be around in case of an emergency! Lily was full of praise at the expert handling of her own case.

Melinda's room, ready for occupation, came in for inspection. Lily helped Theresa to hang the curtains while Mary smoothed the bedspread. She stood back to admire the effect. "I can't believe it; the transformation is terrific. How far are you with your room, Terry?"

"The boy is scraping the walls."

"Well, tomorrow won't be quite so hectic. Aletta can watch the children and we'll help you paint while the men are away."

"That will be great. I love the teamwork that goes on here. Do you . . . er . . . all sleep here?" Theresa asked tentatively while visions of sheets, pillows and rooms swam before her.

Mary laughed. "Of course not, dear. We can all drive a car."

They trooped to the lounge. Lily looked around thoughtfully and her gaze finally rested on the fair-haired girl. Intercepting her thoughts, Mary and Theresa burst into convulsive laugher. "Oh, so already there's a conspiracy in the air! Yes, it certainly needs a woman's touch." Four pairs of eyes swiveled in accord, and Theresa became the focus of attention!

She blushed furiously. "I simply can't go around changing Scott Milward's house as if . . . as if I owned it!"

Aletta studied her intently. "As if you owned it. . . . You've got something there, *meisie*. Maybe you could. . . ."

"What are you getting at?" Theresa became speechless.

"Well, he's good-looking and . . . er . . . eligible, and no one else had got this far about altering the house. Elaine did damn all while she was here. Melinda is fond of you, and you're a very attractive girl. Any man with sense. . . ." Aletta's voice trailed off as she met the full glare of Mary Rourke's angry eyes.

For Theresa's friend had glimpsed, and read rightly,

the sudden deep pain and love that showed in her eyes, moments before she dropped a curtain of dark lashes. "Oh, my God!" she thought amazedly. "She's gone and fallen for Scott. And his heart is buried beneath an avalanche of disillusioned love for Elaine. What now?" Her glare took in everybody. "Stop acting like a lot of matchmaking biddies. Terry will find her own way without the desperate means of . . . marrying . . . the wretched man, just to get her way in his house. Come on, you bloody lot of conspirators, we've still got that batch of scones to bake." She softened her harsh words with a smile. "Bet you mine'll be lightest and bestest!"

Standing aside, she waited while they trooped out; only Theresa was still standing, petrified, at the window. "Fetch Glynis's bottle, please, Terry dear. I left it in the bathroom." On this blatant lie Mary turned and followed the others.

In the bathroom, Theresa gazed around unseeingly. What was she looking for . . . oh yes . . . the bottle. What a funny place for Mary to leave it anyway. Dawning realization came when she failed to find it. Mary could always read her like a book. She had sent her here to recover. Dear heaven, was it so obvious; had anyone else noticed? Dan? Or Scott himself? Oh no, no, that couldn't happen! Then she would have to leave, very soon. . . . No, this place had become so dear to her. What of her promise to Melinda never to leave her? Could she possibly stay, with an aching love that would never be reciprocated, while Scott's heart belonged to Elaine. And could she keep it hidden? Already Mary knew, and Scott was quick, perceptive. Her emotions could slip. The scorn in his eyes, the thoughts in his mind: "Fickle, hardly out of sight of the old love and on with the new!"

The feeling she had had for Derek Mann paled into insignificance beside this love, physical and spiritual, that had awakened within her. Could she stifle her feelings, knowing the poignant joy of being near to him, or would it be far better to leave, soon, before making a bigger fool of herself?

Theresa dashed cold water on her face and emerged from the bathroom looking cool and placid. She smiled at

Mary's quick, anxious gaze. "Bottle's not there, Mary," and had that woman wondering if she had misread the signs. Or was her friend only a superb actress?

With a sense of satisfied weariness, the families took their leave at dusk. The hot bath Theresa wallowed in produced a sort of protective, languid feeling. No one was more surprised than she when sleep claimed her the moment her head touched the pillow.

Two more days passed in bustling activity. The men returned, tired and dusty but triumphant. There was a great bawling and lowing behind the cattle rails when, on the last day, dipping and tallying was done. Theresa was amazed at the great number of cattle Scott possessed. There seemed to be miles of white faces milling around the men as they shouted in the dust-laden air.

Meantime, her room was completed and she reveled in its beauty and freshness. Yet sweeter was the torment as, with aching heart, she watched a tall rangy man slap on his big-brimmed hat and stride away, brimful of vitality.

CHAPTER SEVEN

"Something wrong, Theresa?" Scott noted the white face and queer attitude of the girl as she stood at the window, a letter clenched in her hand. She turned dazedly and sank into a deep armchair.

"Well, what is it?" the commanding voice repeated.

Theresa looked at the letter in her hand. "A letter from . . . from Derek." She swallowed painfully.

"Derek . . . your fiancé?"

"Yes, ex-fiancé. He's in Salisbury and wants to come here, to apologize for his behavior . . . wants to know if my friends could put him up for a day or two."

"So?" Scott's question was curt.

"So Sylvia finally overplayed her hand, and the great man wants to apologize . . . and carry on where we left off. Just like that."

Scott regarded her in silence for a few moments, then voiced mockingly, "So that's why you're so pale! Excited at the thought of seeing him again. . . ."

"No!" she exploded. "I don't even hate his guts for being so gullible, but I'm revolted at his certainty that I would fall into his arms so readily. 'All is forgiven, dear heart. I shall die without you. . . .' Bother him and his man's conceit!"

"And all is forgiven?" The query fell softly.

"Forgiven?" Candid blue eyes were raised to his. "Why, I've even forgot, now that. . . ." She stopped abruptly.

"Now that. . . ?"

"I mean . . . he means nothing to me. I couldn't have really loved him, after all. My pride was hurt and his distrust was hard to take. I don't want to see him ever again."

"Well, what are you panicking about? Write to him and tell him just that."

"He's not the sort to take note of a letter. Derek believes his presence is more convincing and . . . his charms will make one capitulate instantly. He can be most charming."

"Would you capitulate?"

Theresa answered with grave finality, "No. For reasons of my own, I could never go back to Derek. Aside from his weak loyalty I simply have no feeling left . . . for him."

"I'm not in full cognizance of your affairs, but why not prove it by inviting your doctor here?"

"He'll probably come, with complete disregard of my letter. What should I do, Scott, if he won't take no for an answer?" Her reliance and trust in his wisdom was sweetly naïve.

Scott drew out a letter from his own pocket and said slowly, "I have a proposition to make, Theresa."

"Yes, Scott?"

"I have here a letter from Elaine. No, don't say anything, hear me out. She's coming here to pick up some personal things which she has suddenly discovered she needs. She's in Salisbury. Could be the thin wedge of the wedge if she wants to come back. . . ."

Theresa could only stare at him, shock curling down her back. His jaw was steel as he continued, "I don't want her back here. Aside from anything I may still feel for her, she can't come back here. So, until we both know exactly what we want, I suggest we protect each other."

"How do we do that?" The rigid shiver up her spine frightened her.

"By becoming engaged . . . to each other."

"Are you joking?" Theresa stared at him, appalled.

"I was never more serious in my life."

She stood up in agitation, "I couldn't possibly agree to such a . . . cold-blooded arrangement!"

"My dear, it's merely a protective arrangement."

"But l-love is part of an engagement. . . ."

"As I've mentioned before," the sarcasm was back "love explodes and fizzles out. You should know that. Where's the love you thought you had for Derek?"

"That wasn't true love."

"What is true love, then? Describe it!" he taunted

Theresa was silent, while she yearned to shout, "What I feel for you, my beloved."

The unconscious "beloved" asked cynically, "You'll recognize it, I suppose? The all-powerful and everlasting Love, spelled with a capital L. . . ."

"Scott! Don't let your own experience make you cynical and disbelieving. There is such a thing."

"I'll take your word for it. Now, Miss Stanton, will you kindly become engaged to me? For mutual protection only, I assure you. Advantages will not be taken. Also, it will be broken at such a time when either of us feel there's no longer need for protection."

Her chin tilted defiantly. "I'm sure you'll not take advantage, and I'm not in such dire need of your protection. On the other hand, being engaged to someone else would be the surest way to impress Derek that all was over, finally. As for you, if you're so weak that you need my help while making up your own mind, well then, I accept your proposal!"

Flame flashed deep in his eyes as he returned her gaze. With calculated candor, he spoke at last.

"Thank you, my dear. I may look strong, but where my emotions are concerned, I'm . . . awfully weak. Shall we break the seal on a bottle and celebrate?"

"Yes, let's," Theresa said.

Trying hard to examine the situation dispassionately while Scott was out of the room, her mind was so chaotic, the only solid thought to be pinned down was of Melinda. What had Scott told the child about her mother's absence? How would she react if Elaine suddenly turned up here? Theresa stifled her own feelings relentlessly. She must not think about that aspect and how it would affect herself. Had Scott really meant that he did not want his wife back? According to Mary and Dan she was very beautiful and had the advantage of being Melinda's mother. All that, plus her proximity, would surely make Scott change his mind. He would forgive her for whatever she had done and welcome her back.

Elaine would see through the engagement right away, if she was determined to stay. Unless Theresa and Scott played it to the hilt, pretending to be very much in love. It would be no pretense on her part. Could Scott play sincerely in front of the woman he had loved, or still loved deeply?

Scott came in with bottle, ice and glasses. While he busied himself at the sideboard she walked over and watched him in silence. She accepted the frosted glass and asked tentatively, "Scott, what about Melinda?"

He leaned back against the sideboard, studying his glass. "Melinda? Hmm, that's my biggest problem. She has only a vague memory of her mother. To her question on the lack of a "mommy" I simply said she had gone away. It satisfied her then. Now she's older; if Elaine comes here. . . ." A world of pained experience shadowed his eyes and his fist thudded against the top of the table, "I will not allow her to come here and upset my daughter! No. I'll ring her in Salisbury, take a list of what she wants and send it to her."

"You'll not want to see her yourself?" Theresa's heart wept at the sudden clouding of his gray eyes.

"Perhaps it would be best, more polite anyway. We'll take her things on our trip to Salisbury and confront her with you, my fiancée. That will convince her that I have no wish to take her back . . . if she had those intentions." A clenched fist showed white at the knuckles.

"And Melinda?" The question came inexorably.

"My child will be kept out of the way. Her mother forfeited any right to see her, long ago."

"She's the child's mother, Scott. Maybe she did something dreadfully wrong, but surely there's still some mother love. . . ." Theresa could not stop flagellating herself . . . and him.

Scott's face became grim. "Not knowing the circumstances of our last meeting, would you kindly stop this . . . , persecution . . . and take my word. Elaine is not fit to be a mother to any child nor a faithful wife to any man."

Restrained contempt hardened his voice to such an extent that the girl was perplexed, almost afraid. How very much he must have loved her, and how terrible to be so disillusioned, to let this awful, implacable scorn replace the feeling he once had for this woman. Theresa walked to the window and stared out into the clear, star-studded night. Soon she felt his presence near and then he cupped her elbow lightly.

"This should be a happy celebration, my dear. Let's smile and wish each other luck. May our hearts' desires come true. Look at me, Theresa."

She turned her head and the fathomless look was back in her eyes. The man's heart missed a beat as he tried, unsuccessfully, to pierce the obscuring mist. He raised his glass. "To our future, honey, and may it be a lovely engagement."

"While it lasts!"

She smiled sweetly and the misty allure enthralled and enchanted him, making him ask huskily, "Can we seal it with a kiss?"

"We can and we will." Theresa lifted her lips.

The kiss was fatherly, gentle. He lifted his head and the slow smile set her pulses on fire. With an effort she restrained herself from leaning forward to beg for more.

Scott turned abruptly and drained his glass. "You'd better be off to bed before I forget that this engagement has no advantages. You're rather beautifully provoking and I'm only human. Go, before baser instincts overcome me."

Theresa thrilled to the husky tones and could not have cared less if his instincts were physical or spiritual. She wanted his arms around her. But the back turned to her was uncompromisingly straight and forbidding. A sigh of regret and frustration escaped her as she murmured a low "Good night" and left him.

She lay awake for a long time, her arms pillowing her head. Scott *was* attracted to a certain extent, even though he did not love her. He was hard, but presumably still capable of reactions to a woman, when that woman was enticingly close and alluring. Theresa knew, without being vain, that she was attractive, though probably not a patch on his ex-wife. If they could overcome the hurdle of meeting Elaine and Scott found that he really did not want her back, that his love was ashes after all, then perhaps he would soften towards her, Theresa. She could not expect love to blossom immediately on his side but she would hide her own feelings, offering him only calm, warm friendship. Melinda was a slender bond between them and that bond plus understanding companionship could strengthen, in time, to something deeper. Her love must kindle an answering spark eventually. But . . . that "but" loomed large and terrifying. Elaine Milward must be confronted first. She sighed deeply as she faced this.

On Saturday morning Scott ordered her to pack an overnight bag. "I'm taking you to Mary's. You're off duty until tomorrow night. About time too, you've been working too hard and you're looking pale and peaky."

"What about Melinda? Who will see to her?"

"I will. I've done so fairly often, and Cleo is here. I know what you're going to suggest and the answer is no, you're not taking her with you. A complete break is needed however much you're attached to my girl. I'll drop you at the Rourkes' after lunch. Mel and I are spending the night with friends in the village."

Theresa welcomed the idea of visiting Mary and Dan. The tension of being on her guard with Scott could be relaxed for a few blissful hours.

"Are we going to announce our engagement?" he asked, a humorous twist to his mouth.

"Is it necessary? The Rourke family will see through the farce quickly enough. Would you mind if we simply explained the position?"

"And let them know I'm hiding behind your brief little skirts?" he asked sarcastically.

"Don't forget I'm doing likewise behind your . . . er. . . ."

"Natty slacks?" Scott began to smile mischievously. "No, we will have to act madly in love to convince those two! So we'll forgo that torture and you can relax for the weekend. We shall suddenly announce the thrilling news before our trip to Salisbury. That will give respite from prying questions and exclamations of joy; the ladies out here give tea-parties and kitchen-teas at the drop of a hat!"

His grin was contagious, and Theresa found herself

chuckling. "Oh dear, I can foresee a lot of complications arising out of this unholy alliance!"

"Is it so unholy, after all? We're fairly companionable, there are no upsetting heights of emotion to contend with. All right, I'll shut up, knowing your views on Love (with a capital) but, Theresa," his voice suddenly low and urgent, "it need not be unholy. You and I could be happy and content. Melinda likes you and your presence here pleases me. . . ."

"Oh, it does, does it?" she retorted hotly, completely forgetting her vow to win him with friendship. "Comfy, very comfy, but I don't believe in milk-water, half measures, Scott Milward. We will stay engaged just as long as it remains convenient. After that. . . ." she faltered, could not continue.

"What then, Theresa Stanton? You look lovely when you're angry. Do you reckon hyacinths will grow here?"

Bewilderment replaced her anger. "Hyacinths? Y-yes, I think so. In the shade. . . , Why do you ask?" Theresa looked at him suspiciously. "Are you trying to change the subject?"

"Not at all. I want to compare the color of your eyes with the blooms, especially after a fall of rain."

"Oh, you're impossible!" She flushed and her hair swung out as she turned sharply away. Even so, a small sliver of joy entered her heart. He was taking notice of her, and if only Elaine could be consigned to the other end of the earth, she, Theresa Stanton, had a slender thread of hope.

So her presence pleased him, did it? A bone for a hungry dog. He sounded like a . . . a rajah, complimenting his dancing girl . . . "Dear Salome, your presence pleases me. I will clap my hands when I need you. Run along now and send in my first wife as you pass!'"

She found herself outside, grabbed a small fork and, through a haze of tears, weeded furiously. "Oh, darling beloved rajah, you can throw every bone you possess to this hungry dog-girl. I will hoard them like gold, precious beyond belief. You stupid, stupid fool, Theresa, why did you get yourself into this silly state. . . ."

A sedately composed young woman was safely deposited on Mary's doorstep and Theresa waved airily as Scott and Melinda drove away. She kept her inner feelings so superbly hidden that in the course of the day and evening, Mary Rourke wondered again if she had been wrong in her diagnosis. She did not notice that the girl often subsided into long faraway silences, that her volatile spirit was not at its best, while her blue eyes had strange new depths. All this could be attributed to the Derek affair, however.

On Sunday morning Theresa told her two friends of the letter she had received from Derek. Her manner was so noncommittal that they were assured that her only worry was that he would turn up and embarrass them by asking to be accommodated.

"There's a perfectly good little hotel in the village; I shall tell him so," Dan declared, but his wife hushed him. "We can't be so inhospitable, Dan. I have no liking for him especially now, but he's going to be a very disappointed man; we can afford to be generous for one night only."

"Thank you, Mary. I've written to him, stating in definite terms that I haven't the slightest wish to see him again, so his journey would be quite unnecessary. So chances are he won't even turn up unless he chooses to disregard my letter. Now, if you have no objection I'm going for a ride on my favorite horse. I have a secret cache of jewels to be inspected and gloated over." Theresa shook her head at their puzzled queries.

Stepping carefully across the stones in the river, she approached "her" rocky outcrop and scrambled up. Oh, glory be, they were still there! More blooms had opened and shone radiantly scarlet against the sun-drenched rocks. The recent rain had brought out clusters of sword and maidenhair ferns. Theresa sat down and leaned back carefully, not wanting to bruise the delicate fronds. An overhang of rock shaded the upper part of her body. Her hat was discarded, the ponytail of silky hair was loosened and spread in wild confusion by slim fingers. It had grown appeciably longer since her arrival in this land of the flame-lily.

She dug her fingers into the soft pockets of soil. Her land, where she had found affinity. Not only the land but love as well had fastened claws of velvet around her heart, and she was a willing prisoner. If only her stern jailer would cooperate by reciprocating that love.

Theresa gave dreamy thought to that mad, wild ride when Scott was still an unknown factor. He should have pointed the nose of his steed in the opposite direction. They would still be traveling, fast as the untrammeled wind. Free as the air—of course, detouring just long enough to gather up Melinda—who would have her own fast little steed. Theresa would stay where she was, firmly held in strong arms, her flying hair kissing his cheek—the girl closed her eyes, sleep claimed her, but fantasy still circled in dreams and there was an infinitely tender curve to her lips when Scott Milward walked up softly and looked down at her.

Very quietly he sat down and waited. Her dream became horror as she found herself tied to a stake in the blazing sun, Scott and Melinda were laughing madly as they rode away from her. She opened her eyes in a mist of tears and his face swam close to hers.

"Oh Scott, I'm so very glad you didn't leave me!" Theresa sat up, looked around her and reality returned with a jolt.

"What makes you think I would leave you?" Scott spoke softly, for she was still half in a dreamworld.

She stammered, "I had a . . . lovely dream, but it changed. What are you doing here?"

"Melinda and I thought you might be missing us, so we came back early. We were right, or you wouldn't be dreaming such silly things." He was teasingly gentle. "Things that bring raindrops into your eyes."

Theresa colored deeply with the thought; how right can you get? Aloud she wondered, "How late is it? Have we missed lunch? How did you find me?"

Scott raised three fingers and ticked off. "It's too late, I've brought lunch, and I found you by following my nose."

"Do I smell that strong? Why did you bring lunch? Are you going to have yours here as well?"

Up came three fingers. "The first I'll not answer, the third answers the second. The thought crossed my clever mind that it would be fun to lunch wherever I found you. Good lady Mary obliged by packing a basket and promising to mind Melinda. My turn for questions; why have you chosen this spot to sleep and dream, and what jewel cache are you hiding?"

Theresa promptly held up two fingers. "This is my special dream-spot, and here are the jewels." She indicated the flowers and ferns.

Scott held an imaginary eyeglass to inspect them. "You have perfect taste, nymph; they are indeed 100 percent." He looked around. "Isn't this the place where I rescued . . . er. . . ."

"Yes, and this is the place where you're going to feed me before I die of starvation."

They fed each other drumsticks and other morsels. Scott held his glass of iced lime to her lips and she did likewise with hers, spilling some on his shirt in the process. Her hand had trembled unaccountably.

"You're getting tipsy!" he accused her.

Theresa laughed. "This nectar is highly potent, sir."

Hunger satisfied, they both lay back and smoked contentedly. She thought, "he can be such fun. I could spend my life like this, like a rock rabbit. . . ."

"Like two stuffed pigs," Scott remarked out loud suddenly.

Now there was another memory jewel to hide. Theresa raised her hands, scooped the air and buried it beneath the fern fronds.

"What the devil are you doing, nymph?" Scott wanted enlightenment.

"Mind your own business, rajah." She experimented the word aloud.

"Hah, I've been promoted. For that, you may use my arm as headrest." He drew closer and slipped his arm under her neck. 'Relax, I'm not going to strangle you."

Very cautiously Theresa relaxed, while Scott put his other arm across his eyes.

"We should be walking, to work off all those calories."

"Should we, nymph? If you start I'll follow." His reply was muffled.

Her own eyelids started to droop and the last thing she heard was a muffled snore. Very much later, she woke up with the late sun in her eyes and sat up stiffly.

Scott opened his eyes. "Thank heavens you're awake, for the last ten minutes I've been tortured by pins and needles."

"Why didn't you wake me?"

"You were giggling in your sleep. At least I think it was a giggle." He yawned and sat up.

"And you snored," Theresa retorted, standing to dust her jeans.

He laughed. "Now that we've slept together and know each other's secrets we'd better be engaged, or else!"

"Scott! That sounds awfully . . . indecent."

"It sounds frightfully delicious, my sweet. Pity it only sounds so and not. . . ."

"That's enough, you wicked man!" Theresa interrupted hastily. "Lift your lazy bones; let's go. Mary will be thinking of police and search parties again."

Scott straightened sinuously. "Yeah, I guess so. Oh well, all idylls must end, more's the pity. Come, nymph, to our horses; I'll race you." He grabbed her hand and stepped out.

Slim legs stretched their utmost to keep up with him. If he had ordered her, just then, to jump off a cliff, she would have obliged blindly. She was happy because he looked happy; at least he had said it was idyllic, so he must feel that way too. Perhaps . . . perhaps. . . ?

The wind whistled through her hair as they raced across the veld. Scott graciously held back the speed of his mount to keep pace with her effort and they stopped neck to neck at the paddock gates. He slid easily off and held up his arms to help the girl, holding her for a moment longer than was strictly necessary. Abruptly he let go, the smile disappeared and he turned back to his horse, speaking curtly over his shoulder.

"Don't try racing so recklessly when you're on your own. Mishaps come very suddenly. I'll attend to the saddles, and tell Mary we'll be glad of a cup of tea before leaving for home."

Theresa walked quickly, a stinging behind her eyelids. Must be dust in her eyes. Why, oh, why did he treat her so wonderfully, teasing and friendly, then change suddenly into this . . . arrogant martinet? "I hate him!" she told herself furiously. "Scott Milward is just an irritating egotist, that's what he is, and I can't stand him!"

Scott's expression was blandly disengaged as he answered the Rourkes' teasing queries about the afternoon's outing. His glance flicked to Theresa sitting on the grass with Glynis and Melinda. She was intently examining the baby's tiny fingernails, but a flush on smooth cheeks gave evidence that she was listening.

Mary laughed softly. "Sleeping, hmmm? One way of passing a Sunday afternoon. Next time Terry visits, I shall lock him up. After all, she sees enough of you, so stop hogging all her time."

"So sorry, sweet. I'll keep away in future," he answered shortly, and turned to Dan to discuss ranch affairs.

Hugh Lessing and Georgia stopped by for a hasty greeting on their way to Chindi. The girl looked quite pale with excitement and extracted promises from all and sundry to come for a visit whenever expedient. The doctor grinned at them. "I'd swear that she's being kidnapped and taken to the East, judging by her manner. Do I look the sort, do you think? The sooner I deposit her with the aunts, the better for her virginal little heart . . . and my nerves!"

The ride back to Scott's house passed in silence. Melinda was tired and subdued; Scott kept his eyes on the road and Theresa gazed out of the window, her mind curiously blank, her eyes unseeing. Daniel had prepared a light supper and it was Cleo's day off, so Theresa welcomed the tasks that kept her busy when they arrived. She bathed and sat with her charge, coaxing her to eat and lingering in the bedroom when Melinda was sleeping peacefully. She decided to forgo supper, informing Daniel, when he came to call her, that she was not hungry.

Theresa fully expected him to come back with an imperious demand from Scott that she attend the evening meal. None was forthcoming, so she went to her room, had a bath and crawled into bed. She tried to read, but the book might as well have been blank; words and sentences did not penetrate her consciousness. Sleep came eventually, uneasy and troubled by vague, nebulous dreams.

The days passed in a cocoon of withdrawal on her part, made easier by Scott's apparent indifference to her presence. She seldom saw him other than at mealtimes and concluded that he was also deliberately avoiding her; perhaps he had sensed her feelings on that balmy Sunday afternoon and this was his way of taking steps to disillusion her of any serious participation on his part. Fun and flirting were all very well, but only when he was in the mood; it must be kept in bounds. He had not mentioned the engagement again and was probably regretting the hasty proposition!

Theresa dearly wished she could recall the letter to Derek, telling of her engagement to another man, in order to change the reason for not wishing to see him again. It was too late however, and anyway, it would not affect Scott if Derek took it at face value and consequently did not come. He was far away, there would be no contact unless he became awkward and appeared on the scene. She hoped not, for then Scott would have to acknowledge the engagement; she was sure he would not humiliate her to the extent of disclaiming the situation. He had proposed it, so if there were embarrassing repercussions, he would have to bear the brunt and stave them off to the best of his ability. In her heart she knew he would be courteous and circumspect; for all his autocratic ways, Scott was still gentlemanly and considerate.

A wail of pain sent Theresa flying out of the workroom to where Melinda lay sprawled on the graveled drive. She lifted her up, murmuring softly while inspecting grazed little knees. "All right, my love, Theresa will fix the hurt." She carried the sobbing child to the bathroom and sat her on the washing machine. "I'll sponge off the nasty dirt; don't cry, love, that's a good girl." Tears stopped and a small voice asked, "Will it hurt, Tresa?"

She was aware of Scott's presence in the doorway as she answered firmly, "No, sweetie, it will sting a bit and then it will be better."

The small girl met her steady gaze, and her trembling lips tightened, while threatening tears were defeated with quick blinking of her eyelids. Melinda spied her father and spoke bravely. "Tresa will fix it, Daddy; you can watch."

Scott's smile was full of loving compassion and his daughter responded with a watery grin. Theresa sponged the tiny knees, with quick, sensitive fingers as she picked out several pieces of grit. The dressing applied, she spoke cheerfully. "There you are; it's all over. Look, Daddy has brought Beth. She had a fall too, so let's attend to her as well."

She turned to take the doll and it was suddenly disconcerting to meet his bright gaze so close in the confined space. He came closer, his tone low and caressing, but he was addressing the child. "My, but you are a brave little soldier. Your knees look funny all painted pink. Do you reckon the nurse would paint mine too? Ah, here's Beth all nice and clean again. Thank you, Theresa."

Her heart turned over at the soft way he stressed her name. Dear heaven, how she loved him! It was unbearable to be so burningly aware, when she had, or thought she had mastered her feelings down to a slow dull ache. It was there all the time, just waiting to be sparked off again at the merest glance or sign of gentleness. Or the proximity of his lean, lithe body smelling of dust and horses. The physical magnetism and nearness were like an explosion on her senses, making her realize the dangerous capabilities of her unexplored but ardent nature.

Scott lifted Melinda and waited for Theresa to precede him. She did so, her heart thudding painfully. They went onto the porch; he lowered the child into a chair and straightened up.

"Theresa." He spoke to her back.

She turned slowly, emotions finally under control, to

meet his direct gaze. An inexplicable awareness of her thoughts and feelings must have touched him, for his smoky eyes glinted with a strange puzzlement of near-discovery.

"Yes, Scott?" Dark lashes fanned her cheeks as she dropped her eyes from his searching gaze.

"Do you consider it unconventional, living here in my house, without another European to allay suspicious minds?"

Her eyes flew to his. "Why, I—I've never given it a thought. Has . . . has someone. . . ?"

"Someone has," he remarked grimly. "Friend of mine warned me that it might damage your reputation, even though you are in my employ." He smiled cryptically at her outraged gasp. "You may well gasp. People are the same all over, even though this 'friend' implied he trusted me implicitly, especially after I almost blasted him off his horse. The thing is, how do you feel about it?"

Her eyes were a wide, angry blue. "I've never thought of it, I mean, what others would think. It's downright silly . . . old-fashioned!"

"Do you trust me, Theresa? Would I be the sort to . . . hmm, sully your nice reputation?"

"You don't have to be sarcastic, Scott Milward. If you're getting a dig at me concerning Derek's distrust, then I think it's rather demeaning . . ." She was not allowed to finish.

Scott stepped forward and took her wrist in a grip of steel, his face a tight mask of anger. "You dare to think that was my implication? I trust I can recognize honesty and integrity when faced with it. You're right off the beam, girl. Think again." He dropped her wrist as though it were redhot and stepped back. "Well?"

"Sorry. I'm still rather touchy on that subject. I should have known better. I trust you, Scott, with my life."

He smiled sardonically. "That's not what I meant either. Let it go. . . . I'm not allowing any talk about you, and to blast every gossiping biddy won't help any. I appreciate your trust in me, however. Nevertheless, I'm putting a call through to Salisbury, to a very dear old lady who used to do battle with me when I was very young.

She lives alone and would be delighted to play chaperon to the wicked, such as you and I. She disliked Elaine and left here soon after I brought my . . . wife . . . home."

"Oh, I see." Theresa still felt speechless from the blaze of anger he had displayed.

"Talkative lass, you are. Well, if Miss Matilda is willing, she can return with us. By the way, be ready to leave as early as possible tomorrow morning. It's a long ride."

"Tomorrow morning? But. . . ."

"Tomorrow morning!" Scott mimicked. "Oh, but, Mr. Milward, I haven't packed, I haven't a thing to wear! All the better, just toothbrushes and something for Poppet. A nice fat cheque is due anyway; you can have a delightful time in the shops." He patted her shoulder and started for the steps. "We can choose your engagement ring as well."

Dumbstruck, Theresa Stanton watched his receding back "But. . . ." came a belated, inane whisper.

"Can I walk now, Tresa? I'se better," Melinda implored.

She whirled. "Of course, honey. We'd better start packing pronto. Such short notice and I haven't a thing. . . ." She bit her lip sharply.

Some time later, Cleo came into her room with a pile of sorted clothes for Melinda, to find Theresa muttering to herself, "Early tomorrow—what does that mean, the crack o'dawn, before that or after breakfast? Oh, Cleo, what time is early?"

"Ask the master at dinner tonight, ma'am," Cleo sensibly advised. "I'll pack missy's clothes."

"Daddy 'n me usually go ver' early and the birdies are still asleep and then the sun looks like my red balloon," Melinda confided.

Daniel had rung the dinner bell when Theresa finally emerged from her room. A quick shower helped her look cool and fresh. Her dress was a pale yellow dacron, brown belted around the slim waist, and her hair hung loose and silken from a vigorous shampooing.

Scott kept glancing at her while they dined and she eventually became so self-conscious that she was forced to ask if something troubled him.

"Not troubled so much as disturbed. You're looking so

sweetly young and vulnerable, I'm beginning to think that tongues have a right to wag about the results of being solely in my charge, under my bachelor roof."

"But of course you know better," Theresa retorted, with sweet venom. "I'm not so young and vulnerable at all. Quite the contrary; and you're every inch the cultured gentleman, so why be disturbed?"

"Because by rights you should look the part—a prim tight bun of hair, stern-featured visage, corseted waist, black stockings and Mother's cameo locket. Slight difference, by jingo!"

Theresa sighed, despairing. "You're old-fashioned, Mr. Milward; *that* female went out, with corsets, years ago. The flightier, fluffier we are today, the better chances we have of landing a job. Witness mine. I bet if I'd looked like that, you wouldn't have glanced my way, so it stands to reason. . . ." She stopped, for Scott was laughing delightedly.

"My, my, the vainglorious female! So it was your looks that landed this job, Miss S.? Well, you have something there, but I actually succumbed to the defiant tilt of your stubborn chin, and it was your slight alarm, when I agreed, that clinched the deal."

Her reply was succinct. "Also the fact that you were in desperate need! I well remember the disparaging conversation on the station. Think of the effect on Melinda of such an individual as you've described, poor mite." She put an end to this leading interchange, and became businesslike. "What time are we leaving in the morning?"

He was amused at her abrupt change. "Early."

"What's early, crack o'dawn or after breakfast?"

"It's rather nice to be on the road when dawn breaks. The world is hushed and God's hand of peace is felt. To see the sun rise gives one a feeling of awe-inspiring humility. . . ." Scott came down to earth and asked matter-of-factly, "Can you make it?"

Theresa assimilated this new facet of his character as she, equally laconically, replied, "I'll make it."

"Let's take a stroll; it's stuffy in here," he invited.

His thumbs were hitched into trouser pockets as they strolled across the lawns. The night was still, there came only faint chirrupings from unseen birds nesting in the trees. The moon hid behind slivers of cloud and bright stars winked from their heavenly heights. An asbestos bench loomed white and Scott motioned her to sit down. Pipe in hand, an eyebrow was lifted for permission to smoke. The flame of his match burned briefly and he leaned back in contentment. Wafts of self-grown tobacco drifted to her nostrils and she savored the aroma.

Her imagination soared; it would be heavenly to be a contented married couple sitting here. She, nestled in the crook of a strong brown arm, not at least three feet away as now. Presently they would retire, first to peep in at Melinda while their eyes met in perfect harmony. Then . . . then she would change into a flimsy nightie and brush her teeth. He would be in bed, both arms under his head and smiling admiringly as she walked in. She would sit on the bed and he would hold out his arms invitingly. . . . Her mind balked at further flights of fancy and she stood up abruptly, then stooped to retrieve a forgotten toy of Milinda's that gleamed palely in the starlight.

The silence was suddenly painful. "I'm going in. I need sleep if we're leaving early."

Scott knocked the ash out of his pipe and did not speak. There was a closed look to his face, as if his thoughts too were deep and secretive. As they reached the steps he touched her arm. "Theresa?"

She stood at the soft inflection and waited.

"Theresa, I feel there's something . . . I want to ask. . . ." The proud voice was unaccountably hesitant and she waited, heart in her mouth. "I . . . I guess it can wait. Please don't be troubled about this fake engagement of ours. I won't make a fool of you under any circumstances. . . . Please believe me."

"I do believe you, thanks. I'm not troubled at all. Good night, Scott." Her head held high, Theresa walked steadily up the steps to her room. For a single moment her heart had beaten with tense hope. Would she ever learn, ever find out what he had been about to say? Or had second, cautious thoughts warned him against committing himself before the coming trip, before his meeting with Elaine? Well, she thought, time would tell whether her heart had hoped in vain.

The telephone rang and she stood inside her doorway to listen. Scott answered the summons.

"Yes? I'll hold on . . . hello, love, it's grand to hear your voice . . . of course I've missed you. Why? Well, I'll tell you. . . ." Theresa closed her door quickly and leaned against it. For all the grim insistence, that was a very intimate greeting. From her window she heard the soft knock on her door and hurriedly slipped into her gown as Scott's voice came.

She opened the door and faced him, a dull, thudding ache in her breast. "What do you want?"

"The call was from Miss Matilda. She's delighted at the prospect of coming back with us and is looking forward to meeting you."

"That's charming of her, thank you." The mist of apprehension cleared and left her eyes looking more like raindrenched hyacinths than ever.

"You do seem pleased. She's good company, bit of a tartar, but her mind is quite lucid and humorous, I . . . ah . . . took the liberty of declaring our engagement, to explain the position . . . predicament we're in."

"Oh?" Theresa looked at him woodenly.

Scott leaned laconically against the door frame. "She was thrilled and sends heartfelt congratulations. In her own words it's high time I settled down with a nice girl and she's glad that I've stopped pining for 'that witch'; there's no punches barred with Matilda!"

"There was no need to complicate things so soon by telling her. I wouldn't have minded if you had explained about the gossip."

"I do mind, so we'll say no more. She'll be ready and willing to come back with us."

The girl studied him curiously. "How is she to know I'm a 'nice' girl anyway? After all, your first . . . experience . . . was not a success, so how can she, not knowing me, conclude that I'm suitably nice for you?" Scepticism dripped.

A derisive quirk twisted the well-cut mouth. "Naturally, having chosen without success the first time, I'm not expected to do any better the second? You may have forgotten that this is only a temporary arrangement, so the implication of a second faulty choice doesn't arise."

"I haven't forgotten, but how do you intend breaking our fake alliance, if and when you discover that Elaine is not for you and Derek not for me?"

Woodsmoke eyes held captive devils. "I rather go for that 'fake alliance' stuff—it sounds devilishly medieval. We'll cross that hurdle when we come to it. I'll knock on your door if you're still asleep in the morning. 'Night, fiancée, pleasant dreams." Tall, lithe and brown, he turned and walked away.

It was quite wonderful to be out before daybreak. The only sound to be heard was the purr of the car's high-powered engine, in the soft hush of pre-dawn. Melinda had fallen asleep on the back seat with Theresa's promise to wake her when the 'red balloon' came up. Scott was quiet and preoccupied, his strong hands skilfully direct as they sped along the dusty ribbon of road that gleamed in the powerful headlamps. His passenger breathed deeply of the refreshingly cool air that breezed through her window.

Theresa had accepted this trip as the ultimate test. Either the culmination of her dreams or . . . relinquishing of all her heart's desires. She had forced down on her emotions a blanket of indifference, like an anaesthetic. *Que sera sera*. Nothing must mar her enjoyment of this trip; every moment would be savored, until the final showdown.

Melinda awoke of her own accord, and their awed wonder grew as a pearly-pink flush colored the horizon while the red gold rim of the morning sun grew ever larger, rising above its misty mountain nest. Pink candy clouds feathered teasingly above and you felt you could reach out quite easily to bounce this heavenly balloon along the blue hilltops. . . . All too soon the pink haze disappeared, turning to a yellow brightness that dazzled the naked eye.

Scott stopped the car under a spreading wild mimosa

tree. The breakfast hamper revealed individual bowls of pawpaw salad, hot crunchy rolls and steaming coffee in a flask. They tucked in with gusto and then Theresa took the small girl for an urgent walk behind a convenient jut of anthills. As far as the eye could see was wild, beautiful country; they were suspended in a world of their own, with the ribbon of road the only sign of civilization.

Back on the road Scott became more loquacious. His descriptive summaries of the far-reaching surroundings of his beloved country kept his companions entrancingly fascinated.

"You must visit the Zimbabwe ruins, they're quite fantastic. Then the Kariba Dam, one of the greatest man-made wonders of the present generation. Victoria Falls must be seen to be believed . . . the rain forest. . . ."

The powerful car ate up the miles and the sun was setting when they finally drew up alongside an imposing white-porticoed dwelling on the outskirts of Salisbury. Flamboyant shade-giving trees, covered with bright scarlet clusters, lined the driveway and lawns of the home of David and Valerie Martin, friends of Scott.

Val, a petite, vivacious brunette, was waiting on the steps to welcome her guests. Scott swung her up as she darted down wide steps and kissed her soundly on her mouth. Free of him, she hugged the little girl and then faced Theresa, a smile of welcome brightening her pixie face. A swift scrutiny circled the figure that stood so quietly to one side and Valerie Martin instantly liked what she saw and clasped the slender fingers as Scott introduced them.

"Come in, do, you must all be feeling hot, sticky and weary after that long trek. Dave will be with us in a jiffy; he's cleaning up." Val led the way into a large, airy lounge, then popped her head through the inner doorway to call someone to bring in the baggage. "I've been completely on edge all day waiting for you. Did you have a good trip? Oh, it's grand to see you again, and just look at our poppet—quite the young lady! Miss Stanton . . . Theresa, may I? I'm so excited and slightly dizzy. . . ."

"So excitedly dizzy that I was dashed off to the bath-room, ordered to clean and make myself respectable for our visitors. Mind you, I wasn't dirty, not even a speck!"

A deep voice interrupted her chatter and David Martin clasped Scott's outstretched hand warmly. One large hand on Melinda's head, the fair, rugged man surveyed Theresa. "Wow! It was worth the effort after all."

Scott walked across the room and seated himself on the arm of the chair on which Theresa was sitting rather primly, and rested his hand on her shoulder. The hand tightened slightly as he remarked laconically, "This 'wow' belongs to me, old chap. Be warned, she's engaged to me."

His action and words fell on a dumbstruck silence. Theresa stiffened involuntarily, to feel his hand, reassuringly, tighten still more. In the act of sitting down, Valerie became frozen and her husband's mouth went slack.

David recovered first. "Unwind, Val, you look awfully silly. Scott, you sly devil, you sure caught us by surprise. Congrats, and all that." He clamped a hand on his friend's shoulder and leaned over the girl. "A kiss is quite in order. Trust Scott to spring surprises; a passing thought for the joy of our bachelors has now promptly been nipped in the bud!" He kissed her soundly.

"You naughty man, you didn't even warn us in your letter, only saying you were bringing Melinda's nurse-companion. When did this happen? Come on, tell us." Val kissed Theresa and continued before either of them could form an answer, "Blissful heaven! This is going to rock a certain madam on her stiletto heels. You do know she's here, Scott?" Suddenly uncertain if she had made a *faux pas*, Val looked anxious.

Scott said blandly, "It's all right, Val, you don't have to sink out of sight. My Theresa knows all . . . and I'm perfectly aware that Elaine is in Salisbury. I shall contact her, concerning some personal belongings."

A thought stampeded unwillingly into Theresa's head. "Are you going to be added, thrown in with those personal belongings; are you, Scott Milward?"

"Oh." Val was relieved. "Well, come along to your rooms, girls. Sorry I'm such a bad hostess, but you sure shocked me into forgetting my manners. A fresh-up before drinks is indicated. Dave, you look after Scott."

The bedroom was tastefully cool in autumn shades, with Melinda's room leading off it. Theresa bathed the tired youngster and put her into shortie pyjamas. Val offered to feed Melinda while the other girl freshened herself up. Theresa showered and slipped into a slim dress patterned in pale blue paisley. She brushed her hair and rolled it into a chignon, low on the back of her neck. Her mind could not deny a certain phrase, repeating it endlessly, "My Theresa . . . my Theresa. . . ."

The two men stood up as she entered the lounge. Scott met her halfway and took her arm courteously. His back to the others, he flashed her a wicked conspiratorial wink. "You look lovely, darling. Who would ever guess that you've traveled so far!" He himself looked coolly suave in a cream silk shirt, blue cravat and tight-hipped tan trousers.

Theresa smiled sweetly back to him, and if there was a certain venom in the sweetness, no one but he noticed it.

David Martin raised his glass. "I drink to Theresa and Scott, to your future happiness. Have you set a date?"

"A date?" Scott looked blank.

"The wedding date, dear man." Val looked curiously at the tongue-tied girl by his side.

"The wedding date? Oh, that . . . good heavens, we haven't even bought the engagement ring. Don't rush us, dear friends!" Scott touched the fair head so close to his chest. "We must take time out tomorrow, to choose your ring, darling."

His touch, the nearness of him made her breathless and impeded vocal cords. Speech formulated with difficulty, making her answer rather short and submissive. "Yes, Scott."

David said, "You both sound in the clouds . . . to be expected, I reckon. Sit down, honey, here's your glass."

Theresa sat and Scott again settled on the arm of her chair, drink in hand.

David continued, "I contacted Mannering, in connection with the sales, and he's coming after dinner with the other agent chap. You'll be busy with them, so what shall we do with the ladies?" He raised an inquiring eyebrow at them. "Any plans?"

Val looked uncertainly at the other girl. Scott's free hand lightly fingered Theresa's neck, below her chignon.

She sat forward with an instinctive, reflex movement, out of reach of electrifying fingertips. "May I have an early night, please, Val. . . . That is, if you haven't made any specific plans? I'd rather . . . I'm rather tired."

Val smiled. "As you wish. We'll desert them after dinner, have a good natter in your room and you can boot me out when necessary. I'm simply eaten up with curiosity, so be warned, I shall worm out everything—how you met, how and why did you fall in love with that big lug, actually hook him. It's useless to frown so forbiddingly, David Martin, I shall be impossible to live with, if I'm not humored."

Theresa felt Scott's eyes on her. He asked whimsically, "Do you remember how we met, love? I'm dashed if I can."

Her cheeks went hot even as her eyes were drawn irresistibly to meet the impact of his deep-lashed gray eyes, so very close. She knew perfectly well he was remembering, not the brief encounter at the station, but their wild ride over the veld. With a heart beating uncomfortably fast, she replied serenely enough, emphasizing the adjective. "How dashing of you—I remember only too well. Do I have to divulge everything and expose your devious ways?"

The upward quirk of her mouth brought Scott to his feet suddenly, away from temptation. "Tell whatever you wish, just don't besmirch my character too much," he dared her.

"Only if you behave yourself, as you promised. No embarrassing display of emotions . . . in public. Our pact, remember?" Theresa mocked, unconscious of the extraordinary appeal of her upturned face.

A pulse started an irrational count in the hollow of his throat, but he spoke with sly solicitude. "I keep forgetting that you're shy of public demonstrations, honey, and promise to try and confine them within the bounds of . . . privacy."

David cleared his throat. He and his wife had watched this by-play in delighted silence. "Don't mind us, please. We're not 'public.' Val and I don't care a damn if other people notice that we love each other. Never be shy to show your love, Theresa. We revel in it, especially as it's directed at the one man we thought had forgotten he possesses a heart."

Scott looked at Theresa in silent derision. Sudden agitation at David's perception brought her upright and her hand shook as she helped herself to a cigarette out of the box on the table. Scott held his lighter, the tiny flame reflected in pools of gray as he looked at her.

"Dave is right, nymph, don't be shy. I appreciate that to you it's rather a fresh, new experience, something to get used to. I'll curb my impulses, however."

She knew he was mocking her and a thrill of freezing resentment flooded her body. Her voice was icy. 'They're rather exuberant at times, darling. Shall we change the subject lest we bore present company?"

Val was surprised at the man's sudden change of expression. Scott's eyes narrowed with some inexplicable anger. Then he chuckled softly, *"Touché!"*

The dinner gong sounded, and although Theresa still simmered with resentment, she found herself surprisingly hungry. She enjoyed the succulent pickled beef, new potatoes and avocado salad with peach melba as dessert. Scott's business associates arrived while they were drinking tiny cups of black coffee in the lounge. One was a large South African and the other a dapper Portuguese. Scott introduced Theresa, not adding that she was his fiancée. She thought: he's not going to let personal issues interfere with business, and that suited her just fine. The whole thing was already getting out of hand. The fewer who knew the better!

The men were eager to get down to business, so she and Val left them, to take a leisurely walk in the garden. Later, she sat at the dressing table in her room, brushing her hair while Val lounged on the bed asking eager questions about Scott's ranch and Melinda. The Martins had visited there some time back, had met and liked Mary and Dan. Theresa told her as much as she knew and then the questions became more personal.

She skirted the details and only outlined the fact that she had disagreed with her former fiancé, come on a visit to Mary Rourke, met Scott there and ended up by being employed to look after Melinda. She became silent, and Val exclaimed, "You've left out the most important part, your engagement to Scott. Come on, give, girl, give!"

Confusion threatened again and Theresa fiddled with her brush and comb while she sought composure.

"You don't have to tell me, Theresa. I was only joking when I said I would worm it out of you. It is your own personal affair, my dear. Please, I didn't mean to upset you." Val was distressed and apologetic, yet slightly puzzled at the girl's evident reluctance to disclose confidences.

Theresa turned to speak, then hesitated. It just was not fair to mislead these good people. She sensed their high regard for Scott Milward, and now he was deliberately deceiving them . . . with her connivance. She felt a quick sense of repulsion at the thought of their joint deceit. Far better to have explained, at the outset, the why and wherefore of the bogus arrangement. Val would have understood and aided them; she obviously did not care for Elaine.

Now it was too late. Scott had already chosen the way and she could only follow his lead, short of making fools of them both. Especially Scott; she suspected he would not take kindly to being exposed at this stage.

She said, "Val, there really is nothing more to add. We decided to become engaged, so . . . we did. . . ." her voice petered out, but she managed a bright smile.

Val snapped her fingers. "Just like that? What price romance! Yet Melinda adores you, Scott dotes on you and there's no doubt that you're very much in love with him."

Theresa stammered, aghast, "Isn't there, Val? Is it so evident?"

"But of course; don't look so astonished. It shines on

your face, any woman can recognize that look. Men are more obtuse. . . ."

"Thank goodness for that!" The exclamation came with great fervor, for the mere thought that Scott might read and interpret 'that' look sent a violent perturbation coursing through her entire body.

Val looked astonished at this outburst. "Whatever for? Oh, you are a little prude, why shouldn't the man see you're in love with him? It's a glorious feeling, and you should feel proud to show it, especially when it's reciprocated by the man of your choice."

Misery engulfed her at the utter untruth of Val's closing statement. Scott was an excellent actor if he could make his closest friends believe that he loved Theresa Stanton. She knew differently. . . .

Theresa made a gallent effort to curb the fast array of emotions, and partially succeeded. "I'm not a prude, and it *is* a glorious feeling, only . . . it's rather new. . . ."

"And you would rather hug it to yourself for a while longer?" Val laughed and stood up. "Very selfish, but quite illogically logical. I know how you feel and promise not to probe any deeper." She stretched sensuously. "I'm for bed. What's on the agenda for tomorrow?"

"Melinda and I want to explore, see all we can in the laziest possible manner."

"Good. I shall accompany you, as guide. Then I'll discreetly whisk the little one away while you and Scott choose the ring."

Theresa said cautiously, "Yes, the ring. It's very kind of you, offering to be our guide. So much easier to be with someone who knows the layout."

"I can't figure you out somehow, Theresa. . . . You're carefully polite, and I'm almost certain it's not your normal nature. You look as if you're hiding a vital, spontaneous joy under a matter-of-fact exterior. Cut it, girl, you can be natural with me. . . You can do handsprings and walk across the ceiling, and I wouldn't turn a hair. I want to be present when you crackle your chrysalis and take wing. Oh, yes indeed! Good night, angel, I'm glad Scott chose you." Val left, shutting the door gently behind her.

CHAPTER EIGHT

Theresa wished she could attend the auction sales of tobacco and cattle, having heard so much about them, but she did not have the courage to speak up and Scott did not invite her. After breakfast, as he and Dave were leaving, he turned at the doorway. "Theresa, I'll meet you at one o'clock on Jameson Avenue. Val knows the place; please be prompt as I won't have very much time to spare. My car is at your service, so use it for your shopping and sightseeing, as Dave is taking me. You can drive me back to the sales this afternoon after we've had lunch in town. 'Bye."

Val chuckled over her coffee cup. "Takes some getting used to, hmm, that lofty manner? But he is an absolute sweetie really, under that autocratic exterior. He took your threat seriously, I notice . . . didn't even kiss you goodbye, the so-and-so!" She chattered on while the other girl gathered together her wits and self-control (a battle which was becoming monotonously familiar). "Shall we visit the Gardens and Art Gallery this morning, or would you rather do the shops? Later you can dump Melinda and me back here, and still be on time for Scott and your lunch date. I'll point out the jewelers; they stock the most fabulous rings."

Theresa voted for the Parks, greatly to Melinda's satisfaction. Nervously dubious about driving Scott's big car, she found it pleasure once they started off. Val directing, they finally stopped under a magnificent avenue of trees and walked through imposing gates. The gardens were cleverly landscaped in a natural setting. An art and sculpture exhibition was in progress and they spent two happy hours wandering through the collection. Val was expertly knowledgeable about such things and Theresa came away happy and enlightened.

After an enjoyable tea at the restaurant they walked down to the lake and sat on incredibly green grass to feed the swans. Melinda was highly intrigued with one stately black swan who seemed to lord it over the others.

Theresa remarked, caustically, "He must be an Arabian swan—just look at all his wives and the way they bow meek, graceful necks when he sputters and pecks at them!" She studied him closely and said *sotto-voce*, "He reminds me of Scott."

Val heard and laughed delightedly. "That I'm going to repeat to the poor man! My imagination boggles at the spectacle of six or seven wives fluttering around Scott Milward!"

Theresa joined her laughter. "He would be quite capable of mounting his steed and dispersing them with flying hooves, trampling them into the dust and...."

"Theresa," Val interrupted softly. She was staring over her shoulder. "Elaine has just come out of the restaurant."

Theresa's eyes flew to where Melinda was sitting at the edge of the water, her back to them, still watching the swans. A shiver shot up her spine; she spoke quickly and quietly. "Turn your back so that she won't recognize you, Val. Is she coming this way?"

Val turned away, throwing a sidelong glance. "No-o, I don't think so.... She's wearing a large picture hat which may obscure her view of us."

"For goodness' sake make yourself inconspicuous, Val. Scott doesn't want her to see Melinda or upset her." She prayed that the swans would occupy the child's interest for just a while longer.

Val whipped the scarf she was holding over her hair and replaced her dark glasses, trying to appear as nonchalant as possible as she turned her head for another look. "They're coming down the cement walk, behind us, which leads to another exit gate. If they stick to it, we won't be noticed; there are quite a few people between them and us."

They waited in a tense silence.

"Those swans look ducky; let's feed them, Elaine." A woman's voice came clearly. A silence ensued that taxed their nerves to the utmost, and then the answer, with insolent languor. "Be your age, Madeline, there are enough trippers around to stop them from starving. It's so hot; all I crave for is a cool, cool shower, having been dragged for simply miles. . . ." The drawling voice died away as they walked on.

"Relax, Theresa." Val slumped her own tense body.

Theresa turned and watched as Elaine Milward walked away with her friends. All she saw was the back of a slim figure, clad in a gray sheath dress, smart gray shoes to match and a very fashionable wide-brimmed hat. Light laughter floated on the air.

Voices and laughter, which settled into her stream of consciousness, never to be forgotten. A woman had just, unknowingly, walked past her own daughter. Melinda ran to Theresa and she took the tiny hand in a trembling clasp. "I think we'd better get back, Val." She spoke huskily.

"Whew, yes!" They started to walk and Val continued urgently, "You're bound to run across her some time, Theresa. It's inevitable. What then?"

Her candid blue eyes held troubled depths, but she replied in a low, controlled way. "I know, but I'm not troubled about that. Scott is adamant about keeping . . ." she indicated the child, "away from her. Don't ask me if he's doing the right thing. Oh, lord, if she'd recognized you, seen Poppet, she would know. . . . She expects Scott and knows you and Dave are his friends." Appalled at the thought of Scott's anger at their close shave, her consternation almost overcame her.

"Don't panic now, honey, it didn't happen. Does she know about you? Not that it matters one scrap; she doesn't own him any more . . . but I have a queer feeling she would like to. Elaine treated Scott abominably and treacherously, maybe only Dave and I know how badly, for Scott is too reticent and chivalrous to talk about her. He was badly hurt and disillusioned. He became hard and cynical to cover the hurt, but I'm convinced that what hit him hardest was the way she ignored and abandoned the infant. Has he spoken to you?"

"Just the bare details; we haven't known each other very long. I don't really want to know, it's enough to judge by the way she simply left M., without a care. I don't even know if Scott has written or phoned her . . . about us."

"Well, I guess he knows what to do. I'm only glad that he has someone like you, to soften him, make him come alive again. He's a normal, vital person, not cut out to be an ascetic. The bitterness bit deeply, that's why Dave and I are so pleased. . . ."

Theresa cut in hurriedly, being deeply ashamed of the deceit. Scott's heart was still bitter, certainly not melting because of her. Face to face with his ex-wife, he might discover he loved her enough to forgive everything. She wished desperately that she could confide in this woman at her side. She would be kind, compassionate and understanding.

"Please, Val, let's not talk about it now, I have a nasty taste in my mouth. Must have been the fright I had, about Melinda." A shaky laugh followed her words.

Val studied her watch and thought, "There is something I can't quite put my finger on; all is not as it should be." The only certainty was that Theresa Stanton loved Scott Milward very deeply. Aloud she said, "You can take us home now and freshen up for your date with Scott. I can't picture him waiting very patiently if you happen to be late!" On the way home she pointed out the place where Theresa was to meet him.

Driving there later, pride began building up her resentment to a pitch of mutinous rebellion against her invidious position. She found a parking space right in front of the imposing building which housed the jewelers. Scott was not there, so she waited in the car. Five minutes later Dave stopped on the opposite side and Scott stepped out.

He came over and was about to open the door for her, but she stopped him. "I want to talk to you; it will only be a minute. Please, Scott."

He walked round and eased into the seat beside her, smiled and said, "Hello there. Fire away."

Theresa clenched hard on the wheel. "Scott, I really don't think it's necessary to go this far . . . to buy a ring.

Surely it's enough just to say we're engaged. Nowadays, couples aren't forced to show a ring to prove they're affianced, people take their word. And this is only fake, after all."

Scott offered her a cigarette. She refused and he took his time about lighting one for himself. "I intend to make this look genuine. We're going to choose a ring," he stated flatly.

She became angry. "It's unnecessary, I tell you. Apart from that, they cost a great deal of money. Think of that and the waste of it. Val and Dave accepted our, or rather, your declaration without looking for proof, so why shouldn't your Elaine?"

"My Elaine . . . you said it . . . needs visible proof. I'm not exactly penurious, so if I wish you to have a ring, you shall have a ring." His face remained inscrutable, but the gray eyes darkened and narrowed.

"What will I do with it afterward? You may decide to take her back . . . and even if you don't, it will still be redundant, for then the silly alliance becomes null and void. What then?" Theresa challenged, anger still bolstering a sinking sensation in the pit of her stomach.

"A diamond never loses its value, honey. You may keep it for a souvenir or throw it on the carpet, at my feet, in the good old traditional manner. It's immaterial. The point is, I don't want to be swayed by an alluring ex-wife to do something I might regret, and you promised protection against such a happening. Your Derek has evidently been put off by your letter, so you don't need my side of the bargain, but I would most certainly have kept it and I hold you to our bargain. We're wasting time, my beautiful fiancée; look happy and radiant." Scott stubbed out his cigarette, opened the door and stepped out.

Theresa sat woodenly for moments, then got out reluctantly while Scott patiently held her door open.

They were greeted ceremoniously at the door by a courteously suave gentleman. The next half-hour was passed somehow, with a rising desire in the girl to kick somebody, hard—Scott mostly, the salesman coming in a close second. She agreed to every ring that was held up for her inspection until Scott lost patience, finally selecting one to his own satisfaction.

She gave an involuntary gasp at the beauty of stone and setting, her heart wishing forlornly that everything could have been different, for real. That this lovely ring would join Scott and her in true love. . . .

The man attending them evidently mistook her manner for shyness. The price was not mentioned—that would be discreetly handled later—but she was certain it was fabulously high. Scott remained unconcerned. They were escorted to a private room where the proud man could slip the ring on to his sweetheart's precious finger and kiss her to their hearts' content, in complete privacy.

The door closed softly and Scott took the ring out of its velvet box. He lifted her hand and began to slide the gleaming circle gently onto her finger.

Theresa felt tears prickle under her eyelids and with sudden, frustrated, angry longing, snatched her hand away and jammed the ring into place. "Let's not be hypocritical about it. There, we're engaged; it's a beautiful ring and I'm duly impressed. Shall we go?"

"We shall not. I promised not to take advantage, but that man has charmed me into a kissing mood and you're very beautiful and my resistance is low. Now show me how impressed you are." Scott had his arms around her.

She pushed furiously against his chest. He waited, compelling her by his very magnetism, until she stopped at last and met his eyes in mute, desperate appeal. Only then did he bring his head down and claim her mouth.

The kiss started casually but seemed to get out of hand, and when he finally released her, it was with a savagely suppressed violence. He breathed heavily and flickers of flame danced in his eyes.

Theresa stood motionless, pale and powerless, afraid to lift her eyes lest he see the truth in them. Her heart was beating like the wings of an imprisoned bird, while an odd almost shamed wonder at the spontaneous response of her body prickled through her veins.

Scott regarded the bent head for a long while, then slowly put the back of one hand under her chin and brushed the hair from her cheek with the other. "I'm not going to insult you by apologizing for kissing you, only for losing my head and not stopping when I should have—and for shocking your sense of propriety so badly. You're very pale, Theresa. Can I bring you a glass of water? Come and sit down. I'm an insensitive brute."

"I'm perfectly all right, Scott, just slightly dizzy from your rib-cracking hold." Not for worlds would she let him know the truth—a million glasses of water could not help her sickness! He did not have to be in love with her to kiss like that; it did not mean as much to him as it did to her. For then surely he would declare his love in words, wouldn't he? She was convinced of that when she finally raised her head and looked at him. Scott was perfectly at ease, his mouth a trifle austere, showing only slight anxiety for her "dizzy spell."

A sudden image of water being forced down her throat by the gallon restored her natural sense of humor and helped her as nothing else could have at that moment. She looked for her bag, a whimsical curl to her lips. "Water won't help a cracked rib."

"Is that all it meant, for you?" His question hung in the air expectantly, sounding urgent, imperative.

Theresa lied, not wanting to embarrass him with any declarations of undying love at this stage. "Excepting the pain in my rib and a slight dizziness, it was fun . . . but I would be fearful of being the recipient when you become serious!"

Scott regarded her, his jaw stony. "Then try not looking so outrageously seductive in broad daylight. No wonder Derek was jealous and distrustful! Had I been in his place you'd be under lock and key. Did you respond to his kisses as you did to mine, and then laugh them off in the same way?"

Theresa said quietly, "Shall we leave now? They probably need this room for the next couple's blissful tryst. It's only your hurt pride hurling insults, so I forgive you." She walked to the door and waited politely for him to open it.

Her dignity was unassailable. Scott acknowledged it silently and they left, with the salesman's best wishes falling on deaf ears.

They walked toward the car and his hand on her arm held her back. "I've ordered a table at the hotel. It would be silly to forgo our lunch and their cuisine is good." A tantalizing smile played on his well-defined lips.

"Thank you, I'd like that," Theresa said steadily, determined to play it as coolly as he. The dining room was large and airy, one entire wall being sliding glass doors which were opened wide to a view of shady trees and smooth lawns.

While they ate she was very conscious of the ring on her finger. Its many facets sparkled every time she moved her hand. Scott's quick eyes noticed her interest and she was vexed at the sudden heat that flooded her face. His smile was without guile, sincere and charming.

"It looks fabulous, just right for your pretty hands, Theresa. I'm proud and honored to be the man who put it there, even though it's only temporary and done in such a clumsy way. Am I forgiven for my clumsy tongue?"

"Yes, Scott, I told you that I understood a man's pride." Theresa looked down as his hand covered hers.

"To be quite honest with you, it was not my pride, it was a streak of sheer jealousy that made me say what I did. Jealousy at the thought of another man having the right to kiss you and your possible response to his ardor."

"Jealousy?" The blue of her eyes deepened in disbelief.

"Oh hell, I know I had no right to feel that way, but there it was—a raging streak of jealousy. I know you're still feeling pretty raw about Derek and it was brutal of me. As for kissing you . . . well, I've told you before that I'm weak; you looked so irresistible, beating your little fists against my chest, some inner compulsion led me further than I intended. Will you be a dear and blot out that little episode and let's be friends again, with no hard feelings?" His hand tightened over hers, his voice deeply urgent.

Theresa gazed down at the brown hand while her heart,

which a moment ago had flared with hope, died down despairingly. It was just an episode, a flare of jealousy that was already gone . . . to him."

"Well, Theresa, are we friends?"

Turning her hand under the warm clasp, she laid her palm against his. Sweet torment came with the action, but she answered coolly, "My hand on our friendship, Scott."

"That's my girl!" Scott held her hand a moment longer and then removed his to look at his watch. "I must get back. You'll have to deliver me to my destination and then I suggest you go back to Val and have a good rest while it's so hot. Dave and I have plans for you girls; we're taking you to a posh new club tonight."

"It sounds great, but what about Melinda?"

"Pity we didn't bring Cleo, but with Miss Matilda coming back with us, it would have been rather a squash having the Cleo taking up air space. Dave said he would phone Val to ask their neighbor's teenage daughter to babysit. I'll be free tomorrow morning, so we can have tea with the old girl and you can make her acquaintance."

Theresa acquiesced, silently wondering when he would contact Elaine—or had he already done so? No, he would surely have shown some sign of the meeting or told her in his inimitable way. Hard on this thought came another; she had not told him of the almost disastrous encounter in the park, when Elaine had almost met up with Melinda. Well, nothing had come of it, so she would not arouse his anger by mentioning it, and Val would keep mum as well.

Aside from voicing directions Scott was silently preoccupied as she drove a few miles out of town to where the great auction sheds sprawled, dusty and hot in the shimmering afternoon sun. A salutory "thanks" and he strode off, indolent and long-legged, brown and tall.

She sat listening to the sounds of the droning auctioneers' tones with a background of unintelligible voices and, not being able to see or hear properly from where she sat, felt frustrated. She turned the car and headed for the Martin home.

That evening, she surveyed herself in the bedroom mirror. Dalene of Johannesburg had assured her that this was an exclusive model from their salon. The price had lowered her bank balance considerably, but it was worth the extravagance—purest white Thai silk, sheathed to fit her slender body with alluring perfection, the neckline high in front and slashed down daringly almost to her waist in the back. The cutaway sleeves emphasized smoothly moulded arms and shoulders that had acquired a delightful tan from the hot sun of Rhodesia. Her shoulder-length hair, brushed to a shining gloss, hung with the ends flicked slightly out and up. A soft pink on her lips, blue eye-shadow and the shimmer of her dress gave her an attractive, ethereal look.

Theresa slipped into silver sandals as Val put her head in at the doorway, to exclaim admiringly, "You look stunning, honey! Scott will have his time cut out tonight. The wolves are going to howl!"

Val was dressed in black chiffon, tight in the bodice and swirling from her waist. Shimmering pearls glowed round her neck. Theresa smiled and picked up her soft stole. "There'll be an awful din when they see you as well."

They walked to the lounge where the two men were having a leisurely drink. Theresa's eyes were drawn to Scott; he looked incredibly debonair and handsome in black trousers and a white tuxedo. David was equally distinguished in similar dress. A dead silence prevailed as the two women were critically studied.

David said softly, "I vote we stay right here tonight, old boy."

"I second that vote, old man." Scott followed instantly, his gray eyes resting on a vision in white. He put a glass in Theresa's hand, raised his own to touch rims. "I drink to a goddess."

Val and her husband exchanged glances and followed the action. "Drink to Love and lovely, romantic males!" Val sighed voluptuously. "And now, despite your vote, let's go!"

In the general exodus and laughter nobody seemed to

notice that Theresa had remained silent. Her love for Scott fired an ache in her breast that was almost unbearable, leaving her too tongue-tied to join in the gay badinage.

A wide, screened porch encircled the rambling building that was the Sporting Club. The dancing would take place on the outdoor floor, owing to the heat, and the diners could watch from their tables, which were set out on one side of the spacious porch. Lights were strung at intervals among the trees glowing invitingly.

The dinner was superb; music from the band floated in the air and gaiety was the keynote of the evening. Theresa relaxed and gave herself up to enjoyment of the good company. They settled in the lounge for liqueurs. David and Scott were well known and soon their party augmented alarmingly. Male eyes, drawn to the new and attractive girl in their midst, looked hard and their owners hovered expectantly. Brothers Victor and Gerry Belmont waited with polite impatience until David noticed and introduced them, then lost no time in drawing up chairs as close as possible, nearest Theresa. They vied for her attention.

Scott had excused himself in order to chat to an elderly couple who were seated in a far corner. He returned to find his chair occupied. Theresa felt his presence, looked up to see his gray eyes behind curling cigarette smoke watching her quizzically. His smile was cynically charming as he put the cigarette in the ashtray and spoke formally. "Shall we dance?"

She extricated herself from the boyish ardor of the two brothers and walked with Scott down the wide steps. The soft music and the encircling feel of hard, strong arms quietened her beating heart and she yielded to the languor of the rhythm. Oh, to be held thus, for ever, into infinity. . . . "Don't ever let me go, beloved," she pleaded silently. A soft touch on the top of her head as Scott rubbed his chin against her hair and she could almost believe that he had heard her plea . . . and answered.

The dance ended all too soon. The man's hand cupped her elbow and remained there when they had stepped aside onto the lawn. The next number started while they watched and Scott's eyes were drawn to the honeyed hair, so close to his shoulder, where stardust entangled to make a silvery sheen. Unconscious of darkening smoky eyes above her, Theresa watched the dancers. The sudden halt in midstep of one couple drew her attention and she looked straight into the startled eyes of her ex-fiancé!

Shock made her step closer to the man at her side, seeking protection instinctively. He sensed her sudden agitation and followed the direction of her eyes. They both watched as the couple left the floor and approached.

"Is it Dr. Mann, Theresa?"

Her "yes" was husky and muffled.

"Well, don't let it show. Your feelings, I mean . . . keep it covered, and straighten that backbone!" Peremptory and urgent came the order.

There was no time to protest that it was not love, but shock, that had shaken her. Derek Mann was standing in front of her.

"Terry, how nice to see you! I got the surprise of my life when I spotted you just now." He held out his hand.

A pressure on her arm forced her paralyzed hand into his. "Derek! I was surprised too. How are you?" The stilted phrases sounded formal.

Dr. Mann turned to the girl at his side. "Pardon me, Mary, for stopping so abruptly in the middle of that dance. Miss Stanton and I were . . . old friends . . . in Pretoria. Terry, meet Mary Bolton. Theresa Stanton. . . ." He hesitated, eyes on the man at her side.

"How do you do, Miss Bolton. Scott, this is Dr. Mann . . . Mr. Milward . . . Miss Bolton." Pride held her stiff and haughty.

Scott acknowledged the introductions in a level, casual way, his hand still firm on her arm.

Derek's eyes dropped to the sparkling gleam on Theresa's finger. He said, "In her letter, Terry didn't mention a name. May I presume you are the one she referred to?"

Scott replied evenly, although Theresa detected a hint of malice in his tones. "I lay claim to that privilege.

Theresa has honored me with her love , . . and trust." A deliberate emphasis on the final word.

The girl felt a thrust of pride at Scott's superb acting, more so when she observed its effect on Derek. The thrust had found its mark, for the doctor's austere features showed a certain amount of comprehensive embarrassment, before a cold smile replaced it.

"In that case, may I extend my congratulations? You're a very fortunate man, Mr. Milward. She deserves every happiness . . . and trust plays its own part toward that goal." This oblique apology for his own lack was not lost on either of them. "May I have the pleasure of one dance, Terry? That is, if your fiancé won't mind?"

Scott dropped his hand from her arm. "Not at all; it's good to see old friends, eh, Theresa? Miss Bolton, may I?" An arm was held politely and a slightly puzzled Mary Bolton smiled her consent.

"Well, Terry, although I'm somewhat shaken, I'm glad that your heart found solace so quickly and unexpectedly. I had hopes. . . ."

"Did you now? Still the complete egotist, dear Derek!" Theresa was cool and distant as they circled the floor.

The doctor's arm tightened. "After all, circumstances were against you, my dear. How could I guess that silly bitch had inveigled her brother to compromise you in order to play on my sympathies and honor? I found out quickly enough what her game was, one evening, when she visited my house. . . ."

"Spare me the sordid details, please. I haven't the remotest interest. I found out soon enough, as you remarked, that my heart was not affected at all, merely my pride. I hope, if your heart ever breaks, you'll find solace as quickly as I did." Theresa spoke lightly; she felt wholly free of this man. Mary Bolton was dancing with a complete stranger—the girl seemed destined not to finish a dance in one pair of arms—and she wondered what had happened to Scott.

Derek put her wise as his voice seeped into her consciousness. "And I was knocked for a loop when you introduced Scott Milward as your fiancé. I've heard of him; quite a big man in these parts. Strange to say, I've met his former wife. There he is, speaking to her, right now."

Theresa caught a glimpse of coppery hair under the lights before her vision was obscured by dancing couples. Derek was asking, "Have you met her? I'm rather bewildered, as I got the impression that she was looking forward to a reconciliation."

Theresa rejoined tartly, "That's the trouble with you, Derek Mann. You're too easily swayed by outward impressions. Granted, you're a good doctor, but in many other ways you're very obtuse."

The apprehension she felt was superbly concealed. They looked so intimate, another quick look told her; the tall man's interest was fully concentrated on the quite lovely woman facing him. Even as the band stopped she saw them walk toward the clubhouse.

Miss Bolton and her companion joined Derek and Theresa. "Mr. Milward apologized for not dancing with me. It seems the lady had urgent business to discuss. Anyway, I know her escort and he took over. Donald, meet Theresa and Derek. A drink is indicated; let's go, folks." Mary chattered on and Theresa dazedly allowed herself to accompany them up the steps of the club.

Following the contract of their engagement, was she now supposed to follow Scott and wrest him from the lure of the woman (he had gone with her willingly enough) or would he be angry if she interfered? After all, it was for this very purpose that their alliance had been concocted by Scott.

The dilemma was taken out of her hands the moment they entered the lounge. Dave, Val and the Belmont brothers were still there. Elaine Milward had joined them and was smiling up at Scott, who was in the act of lighting her cigarette. He slid the lighter into his pocket and stepped forward as they entered. "Enjoying yourself, honey?" He gave Theresa a secret smile, put his hand under her elbow and led her forward. She smiled back dazzlingly, acutely aware of the insolent scutiny of the woman lounging in the armchair.

Scott said casually, "I see you've met Donald; that's Elaine—"

"Don't tell me, dear man; she can be none other than the captivating Theresa Stanton," Elaine drawled nonchalantly, but Theresa caught the pure hatred that flared for an instant in amber eyes before they were hooded by white eyelids. "My dear, I can quite see why Scott waxed enthusiastic. Such fair charm must be so refreshing, after, . . ." She left the unfinished sentence to hang suggestively in the air, then continued roguishly, "I had high hopes of lighting smoldering fires, but it seems I prevaricated too long." A sorrowing sigh followed.

"How unfortunate for you and lucky for me, Mrs. Milward. Do I address you rightly, or have you reverted to your maiden name?" Theresa looked formally interested.

Obviously Elaine was not accustomed to, or did not expect such a direct thrust, and she stiffened perceptibly. Exhaling smoke through her nostrils, she snapped, "I have retained the title. After all, it's quite distinguished and observation has proved that the name carries power. To my benefit." She smiled sweetly at Scott.

"Admittedly it's very convenient for you, at present. But later . . . slightly confusing. . . ." Theresa put a bored hand to her lips, terminating the conversation, and turned to David Martin. "Lazybones, when are you going to dance with your wife? Come on, stop vegetating and breathe the glamor of the night. It's much fresher outside."

The whole party had listened to this interchange and various expressions now changed perceptibly. David gave a distinct "thumbs up" before taking his wife's hand to help her from her chair. Derek's party moved to the bar; Val smiled sweet venom at Elaine while Donald Somebody yanked that lady, from whom the sweetness had slipped somehow, unceremoniously to her feet and said, "Come, sweetie, your slip is showing."

Through it all, Scott had stood, still and unmoving, with his arm around Theresa's waist. She had felt him tense at her first words, but not by any movement had he indicated displeasure at her cool reception of Elaine's insolence.

Her legs weakened with a sudden reaction as she looked up at him. His expression was closed, enigmatic, but glinting depths in gray eyes denoted some unknown emotion. He waited until she was seated, then followed suit. The two Belmont boys had joined the general exodus, they were alone except for an unobtrusive, red-fezzed waiter in the background.

Scott watched Theresa while she leaned back against the high-backed chair and closed her eyes. "Quite some little protector you were." His voice came deep.

"Did I perhaps overdo it, then?" Eyes still closed, her question was lazily forced; she didn't dare lift her eyelids to read possible disapproval in his.

"You were superb, young woman. I didn't realize you had the spunk . . . but I think you have acquired an enemy. Elaine won't like being 'hoist with her own petard.' "

"Did you approve, Scott, or did I mess up any chances of reconciliation?" Theresa asked levelly.

"My fault if you did, nymph; you did exactly what I asked for when I proposed the protective arrangement." The oblique answer skirted her question; she still did not know if he cared or approved.

"It was rather hard on you, to have to play up like that with your ex-lover at your elbow." Blue eyes flew open to meet amused gray ones. "Or does he know all and is the romance palpably on, or still off?"

His cynical manner and her outraged senses decided Theresa to pay him back as obliquely as he had done. "Your malicious taunt about trust was equally superb. But they do say that love knows no barriers, least of all taunts and words. Shall we say we've each done our duty, as contracted? As for inspiring Elaine's enmity, I couldn't care less!"

Scott said with harsh finality, "I care, for it can quite easily boomerang back to my daughter. The whole object is to keep Elaine from Melinda. Whether I care for her or not is beside the point. I repeat, I do not want any contact between my former wife and my daughter."

Theresa's cool exterior disintegrated. She stammered "Wouldn't it be better, then, if I quietly disappeared from the scene? Then there would be no object in her becoming venomous toward Melinda, because of me. This business is becoming too complicated . . . I mean, she's never troubled about her daughter, so why now? Perhaps Elaine has learnt her lesson, will be a good mother . . . and wife . . . if you give her another chance?"

"I don't choose to do that. . . ."

"Don't be so hard, Scott!" Oh, why was she fighting Elaine's cause when her heart cried out for him to declare that he was no longer interested?

Scott looked at her with sudden, hard speculation. "Have you found your affections are still with the doctor, and this is your way out, to force Elaine back on me? Rest your busy mind; such lengths will not be necessary. We will, however, carry out our agreement until such time as it suits me to break it up. And it doesn't suit me as yet. Let your man dangle a while longer, before you crawl back to him. I'll safe-guard Melinda against any animosity." He sat back, lit a cigarette and studied her derisively as furious rage flooded her cheeks.

Val and Dave were coming back, so Theresa clenched her teeth and whispered sibilantly, "You're a wretched, arrogant monster and I hate your guts!"

Scott leaned forward, took her hands and said lovingly, "Language, your language, darling! Don't look so frustrated. . . ." As Val sat down he was smiling admiringly, "Don't you think my Theresa looks lovely when she blushes? Love makes her ravishing."

David bowed formally. "And now I'm going to take her away from your charm; it's time she sampled some of mine."

Reluctantly Scott released the trembling hand, and Theresa could have hugged David, for rescuing her from further indignities.

She stayed outside for a long time. Victor and Gerry

claimed their respective dances and then a succession of keen males vied for that pleasure. Scott never appeared and she realized that Elaine was not in evidence either.

Derek came to her to ask if she would have tea with him the following morning. Rather absently she informed him that her day was fully booked. He looked at her curiously as he said good night, adding, "I'm leaving for the Republic the day after tomorrow. Be happy, Terry, and know that for one man there will always be a regret that he didn't trust enough."

He leaned forward and kissed her cheek just as Scott halted a few feet away. Theresa met his eyes squarely as Derek left, and then she turned on her heel and walked up the steps in the direction of the cloakrooms.

Inside, she sat down and stared at her reflection, feeling somehow numb and exhausted. Let the man make what he could of that kiss of Derek's. She had known him a long time, bore him no animosity, and a farewell kiss on the cheek was nobody's affair but hers!

The door opened, a familiar voice drawled, "Ah, the fair charmer in person!" Elaine seated herself and also scrutinized her own reflection. "Heavens, some men can be masterful; just look at the disheveled state of my hair!" Deft movements tidied the copper red mass, and Theresa wondered in sudden misery if she referred to her escort, or Scott.

Elaine Milward's casual question came like a blow in her solar plexus. "How's my daughter Melinda? She must be quite a girl now. Does she look like me?"

Theresa managed woodenly, "She's the image of her father."

"Poor child." Elaine outlined her lips. "I do hope, for her sake, you have a chaperon. I believe you're living in the house with Scott." The innuendo was maliciously evil.

"That's my concern, I believe." Theresa went to the basin and started washing her hands.

"Your reputation is your concern, darling, but you see, I'm thinking of Melinda. Just think what such an immoral situation can do to her."

"Your own behavior doesn't warrant any sudden

concern for your daughter, Mrs. Milward. I'm referring to the desertion of a baby, not to any personal behavior on your part." The fair hair fell forward as she inspected her hands.

Venom dripped. "How sweetly pious! But it does warrant thought, dear, for if the Welfare were notified of any signs of—shall we be cosy and say lax morals?—on the part of a parent, well, they waste no time here in looking after the characters of dear little susceptible girls."

"Meaning Melinda? Your own morals separated you from your daughter."

Elain laughed. "Dear, righteous Scott may well find himself separated from his beloved child!"

The sheer spite in her declaration made Theresa quake inwardly with rage . . . and fear. She straightened up proudly and faced the hate in amber eyes.

"That will never happen. Miss Matilda has been a most correct chaperon!" She hoped desperately that Elaine had had no contact with that innocent lady, while the second lie fell from stiff lips. "Also, did Scott tell you, we're to be married while we're here."

Theresa knew then that it was not Scott who had mussed that lovely hair, for Elaine would have immediately called her a liar to her face, on that fantastic statement!

Instead, the older woman's face whitened, she looked suddenly tired . . . and older. "That old witch could chaperon the very devil into behaving. Spans of luck with Scott Milward, you'll need it!"

Theresa's heart was filled with sudden compassion for this one who had thrown away a mother's love, and the love of a man like Scott, so lightly. The smile she bestowed on Elaine was sweetly compassionate and left its mark on a stony heart. There was nothing more to say. Theresa quietly walked out.

Her fair head was held high, but she felt absolutely wretched inside, fearing the consequences of her lies. She would have to confess, sooner or later. Not too late either, for Scott must be given time to leash his anger and to warn Miss Matilda. If he decided to conspire in her lie. . . . What that unknown old lady would think of Theresa's devious ways, she dared not even think about.

As for her rash statement about getting married. . . ! Well, they could pretend to have one hell of a row, shattering that fallacy.

Theresa danced once more with Scott, her body and mind tensed against his attraction while the voice of conscience clamored in her head. She was also downright terrified that Elaine might join them again and mention the chaperon or their supposed marriage!

Scott sensed her withdrawal, wrongly attributing it to her encounter with Derek. Green fire smoldered in gray eyes as he envisaged again that picture of the doctor leaning over her so tenderly, kissing her. . . .

Theresa was immensely relieved when he suggested rather brusquely that they should leave and David agreed. Back at the house, sitting relaxed and sipping coffee, she decided to put off the moment of confession. Scott was taking her to meet Miss Matilda in the morning. She would tell him on their way.

A restless night followed and, at the breakfast table, Val remarked on her wan and hollow-eyed appearance. Scott's quick scrutiny made her flush and choke on her toast. Her throat was grittily dry and she felt headachey from the heat that could already be felt; also from the ordeal that lay before her.

The time came for the trip to the old lady. Theresa wore a cool blue dress with low-heeled tan sandals. Her hair was brushed up in a high pony-tail. As he drove off Scott thought she looked absurdly young and nervous. They approached an avenue of tall trees and she turned quickly to him before her courage ebbed completely.

"Scott, please stop here for a moment. I have something very important to tell you before we arrive."

His face grew grim and austere. He stopped the car and gazed straight ahead. "Go ahead, confess."

Confess? So he knew! She could have sworn he had not contacted Elaine before they left the club. Breathlessness impeded her speech. "Please believe me, Scott. I only said it to protect you and Melinda." She waited for the onslaught.

Scott turned his head and regarded her. "Go on."

"Well, she did say that the Welfare Officer wouldn't take kindly . . . wouldn't be kindly disposed . . . to you and me being in the same . . . house. So I made up those rash lies . . . on the spur of the moment. For Melinda's protection, so that they wouldn't take her from you." Theresa stopped, for the grim man at her side had drawn a deep, ragged breath and settled further down in his seat.

"Welfare Officer . . . lies . . . take Melinda from me? Kindly elaborate."

"But I thought you knew. You ordered me to confess!"

Scott's eyes darkened. "Just an expression, nymph. Your distressed manner told me you had something on your mind. Now start from the beginning."

Hesitantly, Theresa related her encounter with Elaine in the cloakroom. She did not tell of the hate and venom, sticking only to the bare facts. Her voice became silent.

The silence grew and she lifted her eyes, to see Scott studying his hands as they rested on the wheel. He spoke at last. "How vindictive can one get? A sullied mind will always find dirt where none is to be found. Miss Matilda will be glad to conspire, to nullify any mudslinging. Not that a Welfare Officer would take much notice of complaints from a . . . oh, never mind. Theresa, will you marry me? Within the next two days?"

She looked at him incredulously. "You must be mad!"

"Perfectly sane, I assure you," Scott answered levelly.

"You don't have to be chivalrous on my account, Scott."

"Chivalry was not intended. Will you, Theresa?"

Her blue eyes narrowed. "You're not so clever, after all. You should have asked me in front of witnesses, then my refusal would be noted and your conscience clear. My rash lie last night, to Elaine, would be. . . ."

Her arms were gripped in steel. "For that you will be held to our contract and little old Matilda will have the joy of being the first to hear of our marriage, to take place tomorrow!"

"Let me go, Scott Milward!" She struggled futilely.

Scott's voice continued inexorably. "Of course you're quite right. If we're married, there'll be no cause to feel that Melinda might possibly be removed from our care. You are now committed to honor your declaration."

"You're crazy, I tell you! There'll be no problem if I just walk out on you, disappear from your horizon." An avalanche of emotions threatened to choke her. She had longed for a proposal from him, and here she was, fighting it tooth and nail!

"And leave poor me in the nasty position of being the jilted one? Oh no, my ego won't stand for it; much too humiliating. Besides, who's going to look after Melinda?" The derisive note was back.

Theresa tilted her chin scornfully. "I'm not afraid of being jilted—again, I'm used to it. You need a housekeeper, not a wife. Let me go, please, Scott!"

He released her. "Good, it's settled. You'll stay on as Melinda's protector, and my salaried, married housekeeper. Married to me. Tongues won't wag. Great arrangement." His finger pressed the starter and they shot away.

Theresa stared straight ahead, her mutinous chin high. He need not think she would play along, she would refute every inch of the way. She was not preparing to argue now, for vague fires were dancing along her veins at the very thought of being married to Scott Milward. Fires of fury, she thought, that must be relentlessly controlled, and extinguished. This time his high-handed manner had gone too far, and would have to be grounded down to sane levels.

Matilda Todmore was typically "ye olde English," small, spirited, pink and white. One wondered how she could have survived her years under the tropical climate of the Rhodesias. Blue, beguiling eyes still sparkled with life as they frankly summed up "Scott's girl." She was delighted at their announcement and her eyes grew moist at the thought that she was needed. Scott should have sent for her long ago; she would have come now that that hussy was out of the way. Now her Scott could settle down sensibly and have sons and a wee sister for Melinda.

Thus the old lady chattered on while, under amused gray eyes, Theresa felt hot and uncomfortable. She waited tensely while Scott explained the necessity of her compliance with their deceiving Elaine by saying that she had been at Windimount during the past few weeks. Miss Matilda was suitably indignant, quite sure that her Scott would never be underhanded, and, although she did not connive with lies openly, to this one she would make her presence felt without opening her lips!

Scott did not carry out his threat to inform Miss Matilda of his marriage plans. Tea was served while the old lady reminisced about his childhood. Theresa became highly intrigued at anecdotes that emphasized Scott's young days and teenage pranks. An embarrassed man eventually put an end to it.

"Look, Matilda love, that's enough; your stories are getting too personal for this girl's tender ears. We've dallied long enough. By the way, we're not leaving tomorrow as planned, but the following day . . ." Theresa held her breath, steadied for a firm contradiction, " . . . as early as possible, so can you be ready? Walk to the gate with us."

Finally they were in the car, ready to leave. A relieved girl smiled at the little woman by the gate. Her companion's words penetrated too late.

"Matilda, I didn't tell you inside, for fear of too much dithering and . . . explosions. Be a dear and don your best rags tomorrow at three o'clock. Val will call for you," his grin was wicked. "Got that? You're being invited to a wedding, Theresa's and mine. 'Bye now!"

Scott shot forward, leaving a bewildered but joyous old lady behind him. At his side a young lady was shockingly aware of a paralysis that had attacked her vocal cords!

The monster smiled, captive devils in his eyes. "Thanks for not contradicting me. I may take your silence as consent?"

Paralysis passed swiftly. "I wasn't given much chance, was I? That poor deluded woman's illusions about your not being underhanded is sadly unfounded." Theresa turned her head, stared out of the window and spoke quitely. "You can't force me, Scott."

"Is the thought of marriage to me so odious to your fastidious mind?"

"A marriage of convenience is never very . . . palatable."

Scott's knuckles gleamed white on the steering wheel. "Need it be only that? We're always at each other's throats, but even you must admit there is a certain physical attraction apparent. We could be quite . . . compatible . . . if you weren't always so uppish, on the defensive. A good, full-blooded love affair might well clear the system of past illusions. Marriage makes it legal."

Her voice came whisperingly tight. "Getting married in order to obtain a housekeeper or nursemaid sounds quite logical, compared to the monstrous suggestion you've just made. Are you so desperate for . . . for sex . . . that you would forgo your freedom for such. . . ."

"I was thinking of you, nymph. Could you ever feel the way I . . . can't you see I . . . I. . . ."

Theresa interrupted with a fury that deepened her eyes to sparkling violet. "I could not and would not dream of satisfying your desires, however much you insist they're mine. How very thoughtful and conscientious of you to think only of my wellbeing, Scott Milward, even to the extent of making it legal! Look for your full-blooded affair elsewhere. I'm resigning my position and will leave as soon as we get back. I don't even need to go back, there's a hospital right here where I can offer my services." She stopped for breath.

The car came to a stop and Scott turned to her, a whimsical twist to his mouth. "I did put that rather badly. What an obstructionist you are, honey! Fury becomes you as much as blushes, and if you don't calm down quickly my wish to start a love-affair may well begin right now. Shall we make a bet that, given a moment's persuasion, you will be as passionately eager as I?"

The shock of his arrogant complacency held her

witlessly silent while she fought against the magnetism of his smoky eyes drawing hers, so compellingly. . . .

A muscle, or nerve, was visibly throbbing in a brown cheek when Scott turned away at last and dipped his hand in his pocket for his lighter. The keyed-up feeling became a sudden void under her ribs.

He said, "You're halfway to being in love already, Theresa Stanton. What I feel is not the most important thing at present, but we're still going to be married tomorrow afternoon, for the original protection of Melinda. Forget the love-affair suggestion. It can wait. I'll not provoke you again, and if you ever feel you . . . need me . . . well, it will be your move. No more nonsense about resignations. Our being engaged puts you under my care and marriage will ensure a comfortable future for you."

"You're determined on your course, to hold me to my silly statement to Elaine? Why?"

The muscle jerked again. "Need I explain. . . . Don't be so obtuse. Sorry, Theresa. Let's settle it as an eminently suitable arrangement. You may not think so now, but later, you will accept it."

Theresa knew that it would be easy to refute his words. He had no hold on her; she was a free agent; the engagement was phony and she could walk out when and where she pleased. For some obscure reason he wanted this marriage to take place and was banking on her natural integrity, to keep her word once it was given.

Melinda's pleas echoed back. "Please, Tresa, don't ever go away!" Love for this lean, hardboned man at her side had caused her passionate outburst, because he treated marriage as a convenience and his suggestion of an affair was proposed so lightly, so casually, as if it were a mere infection that needed a certain treatment, to clear the system. And yet her inner being yearned to accept because, even if he never touched her, she would be near to him. In little ways, he would rely on her, and their relationship would be cemented by mutual love for his daughter.

Theresa realized she had thought this way once before.

So far it hadn't helped, but with the added spur of matrimony, Elaine obviously out of his life, finer and deeper feelings could emerge from a closer, happier relationship. He had stated that what he felt was not important, but her physical attraction for him could be the start of a deeper, spiritual love. She would try very hard to make it so. . . .

"Are these second thoughts—don't deny that you *are* thinking mighty hard—more agreeable?" His voice quickened the slow excitement that had stirred her, as if he could almost read those thoughts.

"I believe they are. As you pointed out, romance is not so important. I'm very fond of Melinda and she of me, and if we keep out of each other's hair, I guess everything should work out and my future comfort be assured. That last item is a great worry to any single girl. . . ."

"Mercenary hussy! Did that decide you?" He was coolly amused.

". . . so I will accept your offer before you change that volatile mind again."

"Thanks. My state of wealth did the trick. I forgot that a woman can be more easily swayed by monetary gains than by passionate declarations." Scott started the car and took the highway.

Theresa said with sweet candor, "Your own words, sir, were that love is illusory, an explosion that fizzles out. I'm being as realistic as you."

He answered gruffly, "I'm pleased that we're agreeing at last. Church or register office?" His eyes flicked her startled face. "Church it will be . . . our denominations, fortunately, are the same." Stopping in the driveway, he leaned over to open the door and handed her an envelope. "This is all yours, to buy your wedding fripperies. I'll have to move, lots of things to see to, before I go back to the sales. Enjoy yourself, little bride-to-be!" The wheels sang as he pulled away.

Val came down the steps and draped an arm across Theresa's shoulders. "What's that dazed look for? What are you holding as if it's red-hot, and have you been kissed lately?"

"How . . . how is Melinda?" Bewildered blue eyes looked through her. "I'm going to be married . . . tomorrow . . , and I think this contains the . . . er . . . wedding outfit."

"You think? Married tomorrow? Hark at the girl! Come in, I personally think you have a touch of the sun."

In the cool of her room Theresa gathered her wits, and told Val of Scott's decision to marry while they were here now, as he could not consider another long trip for quite some time. (Surreptitiously cross fingers at one more untruth!)

Val laughed delightedly. "When Scott Milward makes up his mind about a thing, it's as good as done! No wonder you look dazed. Did you know about this last night?"

"No, he . . . we spoke about it on the way to Miss Matilda's."

"Ah, the spark of romance is still there, under that austere manner. . . . You haven't very much time; we'll have a hasty snack and then hare down to the salon. Are you going to wear a veil?"

"No!" The negative shot out, uncontrolled. Theresa lowered to her normal tone. "No, Val. I would prefer a simple dress and hat."

"How prosaic! Oh well it's your show," Val mourned.

A willing babysitter was once more called for, Theresa fearing an encounter with Elaine in town and feeling it wiser to leave the child safely at home.

They eventually settled on a slim, ivory sheath dress with a confection of a hat and shoes that were the exact color of hyacinth eyes. Scott's cheque was blank and Val persuaded Theresa to buy sheerest hose and underwear. "What about a going-away outfit? You never even told me where you're going to honeymoon."

"Back at Windimount, most probably, so I won't need a costume. Slacks are comfortable for the trip and I have those in my bags. Nothing more, thank you," Theresa said firmly to the hovering saleslady.

By mutual consent the two made for a nearby restaurant, where they sank down gratefully in the cool dimness, to quench their thirst. After that Val insisted that Theresa remain right there, while she popped over to the jeweler's to collect her watch, her real object being a wedding gift for Scott and Theresa.

Theresa was deep in thought, having a quiet cigarette, when Derek asked politely, "May I join you, Terry?"

She assented stiffly, for this man's hasty judgment of her still rankled.

"Unexpectedly nice to see you again, Terry. You were looking rather pensive just now. May I ask, as a friend, what you are doing here in Rhodesia? Are you on holiday or following your nursing career?"

"I told you in my letter I was staying with Mary and Dan."

"Was? Are you not with them any more?"

Theresa bit her lip and answered carefully, "I'm getting married tomorrow, so will return with Scott to his home. . . ."

"Tomorrow? You didn't tell me last night." Derek looked put out at her omission.

"I didn't know. . . ," she hastily repeated, "I didn't think it would interest you, Derek."

He looked at her intently. "Are you very sure this is the real thing, girl? Don't blunder into anything without deep thought, deep sureness that it is what you want, really want."

"Thank you for your concern. I *am* quite sure." Her answer came steadily.

Derek covered her hand with his slim, surgeon's fingers. "My blunder made me lose you, and regret will always be there. It has taught me one thing every doctor knows but seldom practises in his private life—not to jump to hasty conclusions."

"Diagnosis is cold and clinical while emotions are not so easily charted, Derek. I'm fair-minded and can see the unequivocal position you were in. The fact is quite clear and simple: you were not really in love with me."

"And now you've also found true love. It cuts both ways, my dear. You didn't love me enough to wait and forgive. Let's call it hurt pride, both ways."

"And they do say that pride comes before a fall, doctor," the cold voice of Scott Milward cut in.

Theresa drew her hand guiltily from Derek's clasp and he stood up to meet the cold gray eyes.

"So I found, to my cost and your good fortune, Milward. Terry tells me you're to be married tomorrow. Every happiness for yourself, Terry dear, and to you, sir; treat her gently." And Derek walked, erect and proper, out of her life.

"How touching!" Scott drawled.

"I didn't even offer him refreshment. . . ."

"Again, how touching. Too busy letting him down gently, or are there further meetings on the horizon?" he inquired caustically.

"Jealousy gets you nowhere, sir," Theresa retorted spiritedly, then lowered her voice timidly. "I didn't expect you to finish so early, nor did I expect to see you here. . . ."

"Hence the cosy tête-à-tête!"

"Forgive me Scott, it was irresistible." Lowered lashes fanned darkly on her cheeks and a dimple became alluringly elusive.

Scott watched her with hooded eyes. "I can't fathom you, Theresa Stanton. You're a sly witch and I don't believe you. . . ."

A breathless Val Martin plumped into the seat next to him. "Hello, Scott. Did I keep you waiting long, Theresa? So sorry. What are you doing here, groom-to-be?"

"Keeping tabs on my future."

"You're a secretive devil to spring surprises on us like this. One thing is puzzling me. Theresa informed me that you're going straight back to Windimount after the wedding. . . . Won't that be rather late? Fancy driving through the night with a new bride at your side and a child and elderly lady on the back seat! You simply can't—"

"Pipe down, nag-bag, all has been arranged. We're certainly not spending the night at your house. I've noticed the sad lack of door keys! With your dear husband's help, we tracked down a cosy little place in the hills, just right for . . . newlyweds. They even have trout fishing. I regret, though, that time is short and duty calls. We'll have to leave there very early in order to pick up our entourage and so on to home." Scott sat back languidly.

"Trout? You think of trout, while . . . oh!" Words were beyond Mrs. Martin.

Theresa sat up; she had not given a thought to that problem. So this was his discreet way of solving it, for if they stayed at David's house it would look distinctly odd not sharing a room on their wedding night. She returned his glance, an odd smile curving the corners of her lips. Trust this lean, arrogant man to think of everything!

No answer being forthcoming, Val put up her hands in mock despair. "Theresa, are you coming back with me, or this great fisherman?"

"With you, of course." Theresa hurriedly grabbed her purse.

"Methinks the lady hath great fear of being. . . ." Scott paused, and she interjected quickly, "Not ravished, but of being led along more devilish and devious paths." She smiled sweetly at him in passing, a slightly dazed Val in her wake.

Scott Milward sat, deep in thought, until David appeared. "You car is ready, Scott, serviced and cleaned, ready for the great event. I'll drop you at the garage."

"Thanks. Theresa and Val have just left."

"Didn't they offer you a lift home?"

"They never even guessed that I was stranded." Scott grinned boyishly at his friend.

That evening Val ordered her husband to take Scott out. "Have dinner or a splurge at the club, or any other place. Have you all forgotten tradition that it's bad luck for the groom to see his future bride on the night before the wedding?" Theresa started to protest, but was hushed determinedly. "None of you are worrying about anything; I've never seen such a dull lot! Why, Scott, I had to force that young woman to use your lovely blank cheque. Firstly, she reckoned she didn't need a wedding dress, one of her old dresses would do. Secondly, she had money of her own, to pay her way. My goodness, if I had free access to a blank cheque! But then my good spouse knows me; I'll never have that privilege. . . . Well, anyway, this tradition bit, I may be a square and superstitious, but that's how it's going to be."

Theresa was angry with her for bringing up the subject of Scott's cheque so blithely. As she saw anger in his face too, her chin came up a trifle and she stared back at him defiantly. He confounded her by suddenly dropping an eyelid in an unmistakable wink.

David reluctantly left his comfortable armchair. "We'd better obey my charming wife, Scott. Let's gather the boys and have a real blast, mourning your loss of freedom, in our cups."

"I'm with you, Dave. Lordy, I didn't realize there was so much entailed. Chasing after the minister beat me at the start."

"It was your idea, all this haste, darling." Theresa emphasized the endearment with tender venom and was instantly alarmed when Scott stepped nearer with a mocking smile.

"Shall I give you a taste now of the reason for my haste, sweetheart?" Mimicking her, he also put emphasis on the last word.

She hurriedly left the room, speaking over her shoulder, "I'm sure I heard Melinda call. . . ."

Later, while she was preparing for bed, Val gave a light tap on the door and entered, carrying a beribboned blue garter and dainty handkerchief. "Something borrowed, something blue. Theresa, you're all set now."

Theresa felt a lump in her throat and sudden moisture clouded her eyes. "Thank you, Val, you're very sweet . . . I only wish I could. . . ." she reached for a tissue and buried her face in it.

"Mop up, honey. We can't have you getting all red-eyed at this stage." Val's own eyes burned in sympathy and she also grabbed a tissue. "Bother it, my hay-fever is coming on again! Now, into bed with you, have a good sleep and there's no need to get up too early. I'm going to have the pleasure of bringing your breakfast to you and you're not to put your nose out of this door before that time." A strangely tender kiss was planted on Theresa's cheek and Val walked quickly out of the bedroom.

Midnight chimed as David's car returned and a wakeful girl listened to the hushed voices of the two men. Then the house settled into the silence of the night.

CHAPTER NINE

The wedding of Theresa Stanton and Scott Milward was suitably solemn, without noticeable incident, except for the bride's paleness when the ring was slipped onto her finger. Her husband kissed her tenderly while the Reverend Mr. Baker chaffed her on the forcefulness of her groom's behavior in practically shanghaiing him into marrying them, at such short notice. David and Val were best man and matron of honor respectively.

Miss Matilda Todmore had charge of Melinda, who sat big-eyed with suppressed excitement throughout the ceremony. A few selected friends of the Martins and Scott attended. Elaine, obviously cognizant of the facts through mutual acquaintances, showed good taste by her absence, for which both Scott and Theresa were extremely thankful.

The guests were invited to the house for a champagne toast and David Martin gravely did the honors. Scott stood, tall and proud, at his wife's side and took the ribbing of his friends with superb good humor.

It was over at last and Theresa, sitting next to her new husband, watched the passing scenery as the car purred over parallel strips of concrete. Finally, slowing down at a signboard, they turned off the highway onto a lesser, graveled road. The shadows were lengthening and the pink glow of a setting sun veiled deep, mountainous valleys through which they now traveled.

Scott sat relaxed behind the wheel and, apart from inquiries concerning her comfort, remained quietly preoccupied. Theresa was content to study the wonderful flora and terrain, almost afraid to shatter the peace by some remark that might start a sardonic comeback. Inevitably, her eyes turned to rest on the lean contours of his face. He had removed his jacket but not his tie and he looked incredibly handsome, distant, in sharp contrast to the man of Windimount, to the Scott who wore open-necked shirts and tight-hipped khaki trousers, with a hat that usually balanced precariously on the back of his head. Now the dark, unruly fall of hair was neatly brushed back and his long-sleeved shirt gleamed immaculately white against tanned neck and hands. The girl at his side sighed involuntarily and he turned immediately.

"Surely not bored, Mrs. Milward, on the most exciting day of any girl's life?"

"Not bored at all, Scott. The scenery is beautiful. I guess I'm a wee bit tired." An infinitesimal thrill shot through her at his use of her married title.

"Another five miles approximately and you can relax to a quiet dinner. After that . . ." he hesitated and she waited for the familiar mockery, ". . . a nice hot bath will set you up for a sound sleep and our early start back in the morning. What you need most of all is a few calories tucked under your belt, right now." His talk was light, with no evidence of mockery.

"Yes, I am starving. It's been quite a day." Relief made the words rush out.

Scott's eyes flicked her profile briefly as he answered gravely, "That's no lie. The gnawing against my backbone can only be hunger. . . . Look at that stream on your side; believe it or not, that shallow water is teeming with trout. We'll most likely have it on the menu tonight."

"Mmm, delicious. . . . Are you fond of fishing, Scott?"

"Fairly, but opportunities are few and far between. I've done some camping at Kariba, a trip on the Zambezi and sea fishing along the north coast of Natal. Once, a couple of my cronies and I flew over to Bazaruta."

"That must have been fabulous. I've heard of Paradise Island. Mary and Dan went there for their honeymoon."

Scott's lips quirked. "Sorry I couldn't arrange that for you. Maybe one day, when the chores are not so overwhelming, we can do a trip to see if it's all it's cracked up to be."

"Oh, I'm not that interested. Any place would be heavenly if you . . . when you're in. . . ."

"In love?" he caught her up swiftly. "But you're not, hence the disinterest? There's the chalet, ahead of us."

The hotel did indeed resemble a Swiss chalet, clinging to the side of the hill up which they were now curving. Pink-washed walls with facings of dark timber, a light already twinkling from an attic window that nestled under tilted eaves and a tiled roof. Scott stopped the car in the narrow driveway which sloped down again on the far side to a swimming pool and tennis courts. Incredibly green lawns, dotted with indigenous shrubs and trees, clung to gentle slopes.

A waiter ushered them into the foyer which served, jointly, as cocktail bar and lounge. The walls were lined with treated splitpoles, the rough bark showing and heavy, dark beams criss-crossing overhead. Native craft was displayed to advantage, light came from bulbs ingeniously attached to a huge wagon wheel suspended on brass chains and hanging from the central beam, the effect of Swiss architecture and African decoration being most intriguing and well balanced.

Scott and Theresa followed the waiter up the beamed staircase to a door on the split-level upper floor. They entered, and she felt herself flushing as she met Scott's whimsical gaze. He tipped the waiter and laconically surveyed the room.

"Ah, that's what I was looking for." Striding forward, he opened an inner door. "Come and see my monk's hole, it has only one bed. Very unfair! You can always move from one to the other, if they're lumpy, while I'll have to suffer in silence." He did not move and she had to duck under his outstretched arm resting across the open doorway. The color had cooled in her cheeks at his words.

Theresa studied the smaller room and walked to the curved window. "You have a gorgeous view from this angle."

Scott muttered an inaudible profanity. She raised an inquiring eyebrow and he spoke louder. "A lovely view is all I need to make everything 'luverly' in my private garden. Oh yes indeed!"

Ignoring his sarcasm, Theresa walked back into the other room. "I'm going in search of a bathroom."

He watched from the door, as she gathered soap and towels. "No need to change your dress, precious. Mustn't look too newly wed or someone will wonder why the two rooms . . . rather awkward explaining that my bride is awfully shy . . . much better to let 'em think my old spouse can't abide my snoring!"

"Much better, and you do snore," she retorted. Her ears felt hot as she walked down the passage to the bathroom.

Individual table candles lighted the dining room, lending it a softly intimate atmosphere. The tiny flame on their table reflected gold in blue pools as Theresa's eyes wandered from her table companion to the delicious food, her surroundings and then back to the lean, dark man. Sure enough, trout was served and was as delicious as they had anticipated. Muted radio music provided a soothing background.

The Swiss proprietor joined Scott and Theresa in the lounge for after-dinner liqueurs. Any friend of David Martin (who had not told him that the couple were newly married) was welcome and did not need recommendation, so he did not question the unusual arrangement of bedrooms. He kept them entertained with tales of Southwest Africa, when he had come to settle and start his little hotel, Cloud's End, in the hills of Rhodesia.

Theresa was startled out of a relaxed interlude when Scott glanced at his watch and commented on the late hour. "We have to make an early start, so let's catch some shut-eye. You go up, honey, while I settle with Mr. Jergens."

Clad in shortie pyjamas and blue gown, Theresa brushed her hair until it sparked with static. She decided on the bed nearest the window—farthest from that inner door. As she heard sounds on the other side, her gown was hastily discarded and she slipped between the pink sheets. Her heart started an irregular beat as a light tap came on the door and Scott said softly, "Theresa? I'm coming in." He waited a moment before suiting action to words. Two large, apprehensive blue eyes met his above a tightly held sheet.

Scott grinned as he approached. "Your eyes should be pink, you resemble a very scared rabbit." He sat down on the foot of her bed, took a pack of cigarettes from the pocket of his dark blue dressing gown and offered them. She shook her head and he lit one for himself. The smoke curled lazily upwards as he surveyed her dispassionately.

Tongue-tied, Theresa could only gaze back at him, hoping the pink cover did not reveal a betraying thud in her breast. Silence lengthened while Scott remained in the same position and finished his smoke at leisure. At last he stood up to press the stub into the ashtray on her side-table. Leaning over suddenly, he touched the soft curve of her lips with his own.

"Sleep without fear, little Rabbit Milward; the fox will not hunt tonight." At the door he turned. "Even though he has a license!"

Theresa battled with conflicting, chaotic emotions, afraid of any advances, yet betraying heart and body yearned for the embraces that were never offered. Shame at her longing buried burning eyes deep in her pillow. Her severe chastisement made not an iota of difference in stemming the flames coursing through her body. To think that she would welcome an embrace that had no spiritual loving, only physical attraction. . . . Where were her ideals, her self-control, that this man could turn them to nothing just by his very presence? What of his indifference to test the strength of her capitulation against his advances (what would have happened yesterday if he had carried out his threats to start a love affair, and how much persuasion would she have needed?) This love was bitter-sweet anguish. Just kiss your brand-new wife good night, Mr. Impartial Milward, and let her sleep the sleep of the innocent. Damn the innocent, damn you, Scott Milward! Long lashes were damp fans on her cheeks when at last white knuckles relaxed and Theresa slept.

Scarce had her eyes closed, or so it seemed, when a tap

at her door awakened her and she lifted heavy eyelids. The waiter murmured a polite good morning and deposited the tea-tray on a low table under the window. Scott, fully dressed, followed on his heels.

"Leave it there, Manuel, madam will pour, thank you." He waited for the door to close, then handed her dressing gown to the sleepy girl who had struggled to a sitting position.

"Morning, my wife; it's a crying shame to wake you so early, but duty calls." He took the gown out of her hands and held it up, perforce she had to slip out of bed to put her arms into the garment. Scott fumbled with the buttons and she pushed his hands away as awareness cleared her tired brain.

"I'll manage, thanks," she said in irritation.

"Hmm, not even a 'good morning' for me? I'm learning fast! You're not a cheerful waker-upper, evidently."

" 'Morning, Scott; I'm still drugged with sleep." Theresa excused her behavior. Fastening the last button, she pushed tumbled hair off her face and walked barefooted to the tea-tray.

Scott waited in patient amusement as she battled with cups and tea-pot while unruly hair obscured her vision. Aware of his tantalizing gaze, she straightened up. "My first chore, when we get back, will be to chop off this mop."

"Oh no, you don't! It's lovely, and I like my women with long tresses. Nothing doing!"

"Stop ordering and bossing so early, Scott Milward; I can't take it. Drink your tea." Theresa sank into a chair and sipped her tea. "I'm not one of your women," she added belatedly.

"I query that statement . . . as of yesterday you belong to me, lock, stock and barrel, hair and all. My chattel, in fact." Scott posed loftily.

"Movable property?" she defined, and yawned daintily. "If you don't vamoose very quickly, I shall dive back into that bed, and nothing on earth will move me then!"

Scott took indolent steps to the door. "As you're my

property, I'm at liberty to move wheresoever it moves, so take care, girl. Twenty minutes to pack!"

The Martin household were up and waiting when Scott stopped in their driveway. Miss Matilda had slept in Theresa's room. She sat primly on the porch with all the luggage stacked in readiness. Scott's daughter ran down the steps to greet them. "Where have you and Tresa been, Daddy? Have you been away all night?"

"Yes, Poppet."

"Did you take Theresa 'cos you got married?"

"Er . . . yes, Poppet." Tanned cheeks became slightly red.

Melinda stamped her foot and declared, "I'll marry Tresa too and then you must take me with you next time, Dad."

"What about me, Melinda?" Miss Matilda inquired mischievously.

"You can marry Daddy as well." Pleased at this solution, Melinda smiled importantly.

"One lovely marry-go-round!" Scott mispronounced.

"Lock, stock and chattels." Theresa's gibe reached only his ears.

He sent her a dark look. "Women!" and walked round the car to open the boot.

A quick breakfast, interposed with wicked innuendoes from David and Val's shining eyes on the flushed cheeks of the new Mrs. Milward, and then Scott and his entourage were on their way home. Midday brought them to Umtali where they stopped for lunch. Miss Matilda and Melinda dozed on the back seat as they continued their journey. Soon, with Scott's deft handling of the car, they left the highroad to traverse a lesser road under the shadowed Mtanda ranges. Again Scott kept her enthralled, this time on the great project, Kariba, one of the world's largest artificial lakes, and its power station, also one of man's greatest achievements.

He spoke of the fantastic fighting tiger-fish, a fisherman's ultimate, objective dream. Kariba could be reached by land, air and water, and his promise to take her there one day was stored in Theresa's memory, for did not all these promises mean that he was content to have her at Windimount indefinitely?

Theresa hugged the thought tenderly and vowed that she would make them come true, somehow. . . . Her heart leapt with a true homecoming feeling as she glimpsed the house through the avenue of trees. Everybody seemed to share that feeling. The elderly Matilda's eyes glistened with unshed tears, Melinda shouted to a beaming Cleo and Scott stretched his arms contentedly before taking a firm hold of the old lady's arm, to help her up the steps.

The servants' joy when they heard of their boss's marriage was high, somewhat mitigated by Cleo's disapproval, when she was told quite firmly by her new madam that she would not vacate her own bedroom to share the master's bedroom. Clucking in disgust at 'white ways and habits,' she took Melinda for her bath.

At dinner, Theresa suddenly suspended her fork halfway to her mouth and looked so dumbstruck that Scott lowered his own and leaned forward anxiously.

"Mary and Dan!" she gasped.

"Mary and Dan?" Scott repeated, looking around in a puzzled way.

"What are they going to say, about us . . . ? Oh, heavens, what am I going to do . . . to say? Mary is my best friend," Theresa stammered while her eyes, if possible, grew larger.

Scott relaxed, whistled through his teeth. "I thought, for a moment, you were on the verge of having a fit. Don't *do* that . . . look how pale our Matilda is. Mary and Dan . . . I presume you are aghast at their reactions when you disclose our hasty marriage?"

"Oh, Scott!" she wailed. "You're going to tell them, not me. Mary will flay me alive for not even sending a telegram, or letting her be the first to know . . . but I didn't even know myself. We didn't even let on about our temporary . . . I mean. . . ." flushing, she glanced at Miss Matilda, "our engagement. What am I going to do? Mary is almost family to me. . . ."

"Hush, girl, pull yourself together. We can't hide behind a phone call, so a nice little ride is in order, to face the lion in his den."

"Right now? No, Scott, I couldn't. . . ."

"You can. We'll finish our dinner first. Matilda won't mind, I'm sure . . . eat up now. You can stand behind my broad, manly back while I drop the bombshell."

Blue eyes looked at him, mutely appealing. Gray ones crinkled back in smiling assurance.

"You two run along, Melinda is perfectly safe with me. After all, Scott will grab every chance of being alone with his new bride and I will disappear as much as possible, so as not to spoil the new bliss. Just pretend I'm not here." Miss Matilda's appeal was uttered earnestly, but the twinkle of curiosity in her eyes belied the docile manner.

It was a very reluctant Theresa who preceded Scott into the Rourkes' sitting room. Mary jumped up, a smile of delighted welcome on her lips. Dan looked equally pleased.

Hugging Theresa, she exclaimed, "How very nice of you both to come over. I didn't expect to see you so soon. Did you enjoy the trip, honey?" Mary held the girl at arm's length, studying her. "You look a wee bit tired. It looks as if you need to recuperate—you must have had a high time, mmm, Scott?"

"Well, I thought it best to . . . er. . . ." Scott dithering!

Dan looked astonished at this phenomenon. "Well, you're here, and we're pleased indeed to see you. Sit you down, Terry. Would you like a sherry?"

Scott tried again. "We had a very good trip, thanks, so good, in fact, that we . . . er . . . we . . . that is, Theresa and I are. . . ." He stopped.

Astonishment turned to disbelief at the sight of cool, assured Scott Milward actually stammering!

Into the thick silence Theresa cut, clearly and calmly, "We're married, Scott and I." Instinctively she moved nearer to her husband and his arm came up in a protective gesture round her shoulders.

The Rourkes' gaze swiveled from one to the other, as one would look at normally sane friends who had suddenly gone crazily mad right under their noses. Hysteria was apparent as Mary turned to her Dan. "Not sherry, dear, I think there's a bottle of champagne in the back of the lower shelf." She trailed off in a whisper. "Joke is over?"

Scott regained control. "No joke, Mary. Look pleased and congratulate us, even if it is only out of politeness. Theresa was terrified of your reaction, and yet when it came to facing you, she was braver than I."

"They're not mad, Mary, they really mean it. For a moment my mind ran on 'mad dogs and Englishmen'—the sun is very hot, but both of them at once? No. Their embarrassment points to the truth." Dan took a lean brown hand in his and kissed Theresa. "May you both be very happy," he added, with a grave simplicity.

The dazed look cleared as Mary followed suit. "Forgive me, it was sprung so suddenly. I never dreamt . . . I couldn't have wished for anything better to happen to you both. Give me time to assimilate. . . . Ah, Terry, don't worry about Dan and me being hurt; I'll bet it was as sudden for you as well. Scott Milward can be a swift, menacing juggernaut, believe me!"

Scott dropped her at the front steps and drove off to garage the car. When he walked into the house, Theresa had already closed her bedroom door. He hesitated a moment, walked to his own room and stood at the open window for a long time smoking one cigarette after another.

The days fell into routine and Theresa found plenty to occupy herself with in the house and gardens. She unpacked shelves, took inventories, tidied and mended, so that when day was done she was exhausted and retired as early as possible. She dreaded the nights, for then, inevitably, her mind and heart dwelt on her love. Longing and yearning took possession, for the man who was so near and yet so far.

She took great care to avoid direct physical contact with him during the day, although certain inadvertent brushes were unavoidable, and then her senses would feel with the same sharp impact as before. Scott had a manner of appearing suddenly and flicking loose tendrils of her hair across her face with casual fingers. She hated it, for the simple reason that the gesture exploded the cocoon of withdrawal she was constantly weaving around her emotions.

Three weeks after their marriage, Scott announced, after dinner, that he would be going to Fort Victoria on the following day, and would the women want anything from the shops? They considered and declared "No, thanks, not a thing!" Later, however, when Miss Matilda had gone to bed Theresa took courage and joined him in the sitting room where he was reading a journal and smoking his pipe. He looked up as she stood hesitantly before him.

"Scott, will it be possible for you to buy new curtains for this room? These are impossibly heavy and suffocating."

Scott glanced from her to the offending drapes and drew deeply on his pipe.

Theresa rushed on before he could speak, "I know it's presumptuous of me, as it's your home. If you're satisfied with all this heavy stuff please don't think you have to. . . ." The spate of words came to a stop as he unwound from his chair and came closer.

"My dear girl, my house is your home, remember? If it looks lousy in your eyes by all means change it. Tell me roughly what you need and I'll supply it, if possible."

"It's not lousy, only I think a hot climate calls for lighter, cooler furnishings."

"You may be right at that. I'll see what can be done. Don't be nervous about asking for anything, Theresa. . . . As my wife you have every right, remember."

"I'm apt to forget, quite often. I feel more like an unpaid nurse and housekeeper," she rejoined lightly, but unconscious bitterness colored her tone.

Scott towered over her. "Are you in need? I never gave a thought to any requirements of your wardrobe or other things a woman may need." He took her arm in a rough grip. "Tell me, are you unhappy with our present arrangements?"

"Are you, Scott?" Theresa countered quietly, forcing down an irregularity in her breast.

"Don't prevaricate; answer me," he ordered, and as she stood, dumbly still, he took her in his arms and pressed her head against his shoulder. "What must I do to make you happy, make you feel like a wife? Buy new curtains or . . . perhaps this. . . ." A hand lifted her chin. Scott's eyes lit with flame as he pressed his mouth on hers with deep urgency.

The kiss had a fierce, sweet quality. Through drowning senses Theresa forced her mind to remember that this man did not love her, that this was his generous way of trying to make her happy. . . . Curtains or kisses?

Passion flowed from his mouth, his seeking hands, and the girl's head swam as she moaned an insistent "No, Scott, no!" against his lips.

"Yes, yes, darling, don't be so adorably obstinate. . . . You want me as much as I've wanted you . . . you're my wife and I need you." He kissed the quickening pulse in the hollow of her throat.

Through a mist of leaping responses, one sane thought hammered. No word of love from his questing lips, only want and need—just say it once, "Nymph darling, I love you" just once and nothing in this wide world will matter. Her heart pleaded while lips remained silent.

Scott did not say it. . . .

Coldness settled around her heart and chilled her spine. Her body lost its ardor, she stood limp, numbed and despairing. Scott became aware of the change in her and let her go, stepping back a pace. "Not satisfactory?"

"Not without love, Scott," Theresa whispered, and waited, giving him another chance to say what she most wanted to hear.

"That's rather unfortunate, isn't it?" Sarcasm was in the husky tones. "Maybe I could have that answer now. What do you want, need, to make you happy?"

"Curtains," Theresa voiced woodenly.

"One commodity being unobtainable, curtains it shall

be. Write down the measurements, etc." With that rather cryptic statement he turned away, dismissal in the uncompromising back.

"Good night, Scott." Small and slim, she walked out.

Theresa threw herself into furious activity the next morning after Scott had left, the cause being mainly the shock of his parting words—"I'll be at my solicitors, to finalize monetary affairs concerning Elaine. She'll most likely be there as well. Might take a day or two, so expect me back when you see me. Sam's got everything under control here; refer to him if any difficulties arise."

An urgent desire to get away, be on her own, motivated her actions, and in the late afternoon she left Miss Matilda to watch Melinda and set off in the utility jeep. A few miles of abstracted driving brought her to a huddle of blue-gum trees where she stopped the jeep and sat for a long while, smoking cigarette after cigarette. Impulsively she decided to carry on and visit Mary. Thoughts of Scott and his ex-wife were resolutely pushed aside.

Mary was tidying her bedroom cupboards. Theresa entreated her not to stop, Rina could serve the tea right there. The girls chattered for a while and Mary surveyed the pile of discarded clothing on the carpet. "One never knows what to do, discard or keep them for another wear or two." Innocently she queried, "What are you doing about your clothes? Have you kept your room on as a dressing room? I happen to know that Scott's bedroom is large, but his wardrobes are not big enough to hold . . . Terry love!"

For a welled-up heart had at last burst its tanks and Theresa put her head into Mary's pillow and sobbed heartbreakingly, unable to control herself or to hide her misery any longer from her friend. Mary sat beside her, stroked the fair head in silent compassion, until the racking shoulders gradually subsided.

Theresa could not, was not going to deceive any longer. In words that choked her at times, she told the whole story of her love for Scott, the phony engagement and subsequent events leading up to their marriage. " . . . and I love him so desperately . . . it hurts to be near him. I want to touch him, run my fingers through dusty hair when he comes in, trace the line of his mouth, help him to unlace his riding boots. . . . Dear heaven, Mary, will it be better or worse if I leave him, never to see the sun crinkles at the corners of proud gray eyes, not have the indescribable joy of mixing a drink for him and feel the warm touch of his hand when I hand it to him. . . . And that tender look he has for Melinda—turn to indifference when it settles on me?" Her shoulders shook again in an agony of remembering.

"Heavens, honey, you've fallen desperately hard. It's real, this time." A tender arm circled the girl's shoulders. "Have you considered why he's gone to the lengths of marrying you? Could it be that he loves you too? The question of protection or scandal wouldn't swerve Scott Milward to that extent. . . . He's a law unto himself and would treat all that with the contempt it deserves. Maybe he does love you, Terry, but can't show it through that hard crust of control he's built around himself, ever since Elaine disillusioned him so badly. If you could crash that obstacle, you would no doubt find a warm, generous, loving man . . . for he can be that, I know. . . ."

"He's a hateful, arrogantly conceited man who thinks a girl has only to be kissed by him for her to melt and succumb. . . ."

"Is he, Terry?" Mary interposed quietly.

"No . . . yes. He's all that, a wonderful devil, and I love him to distraction . . . and he doesn't love me. Now he's with Elaine. . . ." words failed her; misery darkened her eyes to a tear-drenched violet.

"I honestly believe that shouldn't worry you at all. Even if he did have some feelings for her, they were surely and certainly blotted out after Elaine's mucky dig about Melinda. You must do something drastic, to make Scott reveal himself, to show his true feelings soon; otherwise you'll be climbing the wall, with all this love and misery bottled up inside you!"

"I'll do no such thing, for if I do anything drastic and find he doesn't love me, what then? My own love isn't going to lessen."

"And if you find that he does love you?"

The stars that shone from glistening eyes almost blinded Mary, and then were gone again. "That would be the most lovely moment of my life. I shan't do anything drastic, though, I'm tired of deception. Thank you, Mary, for seeing me through all this. I . . . I feel much better now, partly relief and mostly because I hated deceiving you. So now you know, I'd better fly back before Miss Matilda starts panicking."

At home again, Theresa flew to answer the shrill ring of the telephone. Georgia's voice came. "Terry, we're engaged!"

"Engaged?"

"Yes, engaged, e-n-g-a-g-e-d."

"Oh, engaged. To whom are we engaged?"

"Not you, nitwit. Me, to Hugh. Hugh to me."

Theresa came alive. "How perfectly wonderful! I just knew a bit of manipulation. . . ."

"Just you wait, Mrs. Milward, just you wàit . . . ! That will be tomorrow. Hugh is bringing me out, in the afternoon."

"Lovely, Georgia dear!"

"And you're going to spill everything about your whirlwind romance as well. The whole town's agog. I suppose you've had visitors by the gallon?"

"A few, yes. Mostly calls from Scott's friends, with good wishes." Theresa spoke with sudden effort.

Georgia's tone was mysterious before she rang off. "See that you have on your prettiest dress. I have my reasons. 'Bye now!"

CHAPTER TEN

Breakfast finished, Theresa had the heavy curtains taken down in the sitting room, thus exposing the white terylene drop which she left hanging. The difference in light and air was amazing. She fitted the two cretonne slip-covers, that she had cut and stitched herself, over two armchairs and stepped back to survey her handiwork. Miss Matilda and Melinda gave their full approval; already the room appeared gayer and a low vase of yellow chrysanthemums on a corner table added a bright finishing touch.

In the afternoon Theresa showered and chose a cool blue linen dress. She combed her hair to a shining top-knot and slipped her feet into low-heeled sandals which matched her dress. While dressing, she wondered about Georgia's request that she wear her prettiest dress (a certain other call had been waited for, in vain).

Her wondering ceased when she went out to watch as Mary, Lily and Georgia piled out of Hugh Lessing's car and she saw the dust of other cars arriving. The ladies of the community had come to call on her!

Hugh waved self-consciously and disappeared in the direction of the paddocks, followed by other men drivers. The ladies, arms laden with goodies, bottles and parcels, crowded Theresa back into the room, delighted at the surprise on her face.

Mary looked anxiously at her friend and managed a quiet aside, "I didn't know a thing about this until they stopped by, Terry. Georgia pointedly omitted to tell me, fearing I would give you the tip. . . . It's a belated linen tea, for you. You're doing nicely, keep that chin up my brave one. . . ."

The traditional fun and jokes, at her expense, began then, and Theresa met new faces and acquaintances with superb aplomb, taking their ribbing in the spirit it was given. Cleo received a couple of mystery baskets, with orders to unpack them into the refrigerator.

Theresa was made to open the other parcels, some with notes which made for more hilarity, and the pile of linen disclosed grew at her feet. Tears almost overcame her at one stage, but Lily de Wet declared wickedly. "Too late for tears, woman, you've been an' gorn an' done it. Right under our noses too! Did you marry him after all to fix this sitting room—I notice those dark drapes have vanished?"

Theresa agreed solemnly, "Just for that did I snag the man."

"Ha! We'll wait a wee while, then make you eat those wild words, at your next party. Stork business thrives!"

The stricken girl blushed furiously and was saved further taunting by the entrance of Cleo and Daniel, laden with trays of tea and homemade cakes. Theresa made her little speech, thanking them all in a rather husky, small voice.

A setting sun was the cue for the men to make their appearance. They had been prepared to spend the earlier part of the day with Scott, unaware of his absence, so Sam had entertained them instead, in the barn. Besides Sam and Hugh were four others whom Theresa vaguely remembered seeing at the barbecue. They all paid respects, bemoaning the fact that Scott was away.

Hugh and Georgia now came in for their share of good wishes. Theresa suddenly found a brimming glass of champagne thrust into her hand and everybody drank to the couple's health. The glasses were refilled and they toasted the absent one and his wife, who had to drain her glass to shouts of "Down, down, down!"

Feeling slightly lightheaded, Theresa started down the passage toward the kitchen, but was headed back by Lily and Sam, both carrying trays loaded with savories and jugs of iced lemon drinks, quite evidently the contents of the mystery baskets. She managed to snatch a minute square of cheese and two olives.

The company were discussing the new craze for folk dancing and Sam boldly declared that he was an authority on same. At Theresa's nod of consent, the pile of linen was removed, the carpet rolled up and a blushing Sam was ordered to demonstrate. Someone had brought the appropriate records and the ensuing hour was earnestly passed with everyone following Sam's calls. Hugh changed the music to a deep, sensuous rumba, and Theresa found herself in his arms and they started to dance while the others watched.

Scott Milward stopped his car and gazed in alarm at the vehicles in the driveway. He shot out of the seat and took the steps on the double, came to a halt at the doorway and watched his wife and the doctor doing an exhibition dance. A cold rage filled him as he walked in, calmly maneuvered Hugh aside and took over. "Let me show you how it's done, old chap. Hello, darling."

Joy coursed through the girl's body, making her more lightheaded than ever. Surely she had drunk too much—this was a lovely hallucination? Scott was home again, she was dancing in his arms and he had called her 'darling'—what more could a girl want! She smiled dreamily up at him, "Hello, my love."

Oblivious of onlookers, he held her closer as he saw joyous welcome in the blue eyes. The champagne and his closeness gave her a heady moment and she missed a step. Righting her in an instant, Scott looked closer and discovered that his wife was slightly tipsy.

"Well, I'll be damned!" he exclaimed under his breath. The joy in her eyes was induced from a glass, not because of his unexpected presence. . . . As the music came to a stop he deliberately claimed her mouth.

Theresa closed her eyes, blissfully unaware of anyone but the man holding her. Dawning realization came, of mockery, when he let her go and bowed solemnly to the clapping of hands.

A glass was thrust into Scott's hand, another toast given and accepted. The object of the party was explained and he drew his wife to his side with an arm around her waist, while he smilingly thanked them all.

Only the girl at his side detected the grim line of mouth and the faint pulse in his cheek as he spoke and smiled.

He was not pleased with her, that was for sure, she could feel it. Well, they were his friends too. Why did he call her "darling" as if he meant it, and almost immediately become displeased with her? Still somewhat lightheaded, Theresa murmured inaudibly, "Damn your vacillating moods, rajah, see if I care!"

"I beg your pardon, Theresa?" Scott bent courteously.

She smiled sweetly. "How was your . . . business trip? Did things go satisfactorily?"

Scott stiffened, answered curtly, "Fair, thanks."

"Did you see the . . . fair lady?"

"I did. She sends venomous regards and tells me she has a doll which resembles you. She's got it stuck full of pins. Pardon me, please, I want to pass on some information to Sam, before it slips my mind."

His terse reply startled Theresa and her bemused mind speculated bitterly. There were several ways to accept this man's inconsistent behavior; consolation with Elaine had made it harder to tolerate his new wife; he might have had a difficult time with his solicitor and ex-wife and consequent bad temper covered her, Theresa, as well. . . .

Obligingly, their friends left early, under the impression that Scott was tired and wanted time to spend with his pretty wife after being away two whole days.

Miss Matilda and Scott sat down for a nightcap while Theresa busied herself emptying ashtrays and tidying the room. Laughter and chatter came from the kitchen where Cleo and Daniel were washing glasses and dishes.

"Do sit down and drink yours too." The old lady sighed. "That was a lovely surprise, Scott; you should see the lovely things they brought for Theresa and you."

"Linen stuff, I believe. Theresa can show it to me tomorrow."

Theresa stacked the records, switched off the radio, turned and tripped slightly on the edge of the carpet that had been rolled back. Scott eyed her warily.

"I wouldn't take another drink if I were you. Champagne and gin and tonic don't mix well."

"Well, you're not me, and I'm not under the influence," she retorted spiritedly. Sudden revolt at his manner, her own uncertainty of the outcome of his trip made her feel reckless, at the end of her tether. "A simple gin and tonic will not affect me any further, and being in my own home I'll drink gallons if I want to and still stagger on my own two feet to my bed. Don't be afraid your strength will be called upon to carry me. Save it for other trips . . . other things!"

"Theresa!" Miss Matilda looked shocked.

"Theresa!" Scott mimicked, amusement lurking in his eyes.

"Theresa, Theresa—I'm sick of that name. 'Theresa, I wouldn't do this, Theresa, don't do that, follow my orders, Theresa'!"

Scott watched in surprise as she actually stamped her foot. He said mildly, "Temper, love? I guess this isn't an appropriate moment to show you the new curtains."

Theresa stared at him in angry frustration and brought a clenched fist to her mouth. "You can keep them, Scott Milward!" she enunciated clearly, and walked out of the room.

Dead silence reigned. Miss Matilda clucked reprovingly and whispered a good night to the silent man. He did not answer, and she stopped at the doorway. "You've finally met your match, boy, so put that in your pipe and draw deeply."

"Traitor!" His husky whisper followed her down the passage.

A sleepless night had shown Theresa clearly what course she must take. She must leave Windimount.

She must give Scott an opportunity to assess facts, without her worrying presence to distract him. Being a full-blooded, virile male, he would naturally want and seek female contact sooner or later. She was not prepared to be that woman, not without his full love. If he wanted Elaine, or someone else for that matter, she would leave him free to choose. His quixotic gesture in marrying her need not make him feel bound to her. She would try hard to get over the loss of Melinda—and him.

Theresa did not dare allow herself to even dream that

Scott might seek her out, might discover that it was she he loved, fully and eternally. She would ride to her private dream-place and consider ways, means by which this heartbreak course she had decided on could be carried out. . . . Deliberately, she stayed in her room until she heard Scott leave in the utility jeep.

He must think she was suffering from a hangover, but she found it impossible to face him, after last night's inelegant outburst, of which she was much ashamed. Her invidious position was already creating a change in her nature. Any more of this and Theresa Milward would become a sharp-tongued, sour old nag-bag!

Melinda came looking for her and she reluctantly left the safety of her room to see and help open the box of curtains. The firm had made them up, ready to hang. Soft autumn colours matched the green in the cretonne chair covers and blended satisfyingly with the tan of the other chairs. Theresa forced down her enthusiasm. After all, soon she would not be here to enjoy relaxing with the family of an evening. Someone else, perhaps, would enjoy or change it again. What did it matter to her?

Miss Matilda was guiding Melinda's hand on her tiny sewing machine, Cleo and Daniel were cleaning the store-pantry; no one was about when Theresa saddled up and cantered off. Neither Sam or any of the stockmen were in evidence, for which she was thankful. She didn't want anyone tagging after her. The particular place she had in mind was much farther from Scott's homestead than Mary's. No matter, she didn't care if she stayed away all day. Melinda had Matilda, Scott was self-sufficient, in fact, she was beginning to feel miserably redundant. . . .

Theresa checked this dangerous self-pity and headed for the distant blue mountains. Noon found her in the foothills. She studied the sun-limned outlines while drinking from her water-bag. A bank of clouds was rising swiftly in the east. This seemed to be a roundabout way. She glimpsed a line of green—that would be the river—and the outcrops looked familiar. It was not too late to make for them; she could have a peaceful after-noon and be back by sunset. She came out on the ridge where she had seen Scott on that far-off day of their memorable ride, and there was her "treasure house."

The horse lapped thirstily at the river bank where the water ran cool and clear. Theresa walked him back, tethered the reins firmly under a shady mimosa, then started her walk up to the outcrop where she settled down, to think . . . to grieve awhile. Her lilies had died down, only the leaves and fern were still green. Her heart would lie buried here too, in the land she had come to love. But the flowers would bloom again next season while that heart would remain arid, unloved, with no spring rains to revive it, no all-powerful love to burst the chrysalis and let it take wing.

The girl closed her eyes and blank numbness enveloped her. Ways and means were forgotten while her tired brain succumbed to misery and heartbreak. A pregnant stillness in the air opened her eyes at last. The sun had disappeared behind a dark, heavy blanket of clouds. Theresa sat up slowly. So much for planning; the simplest course would be to pack her bags and tell Scott that she yearned for her home town. That she, like Elaine, did not care for this sort of life, or rather the lack of life and bright lights. Scott's arrogant nature would spurn any idea of holding her against her will; his contempt for a weak nature would show and hurt, but she could think of no other way.

She scrambled up the clefted rock to the top and stood straight while a wayward wind caressed her loosened hair. A measure of peace came then, she would always have this to remember. . . . Thunder clapped sharp and sudden, and forked lightning split the skies.

Theresa climbed down carefully under a jut of rock, back onto the clefted boulder. Her riding boot slipped on the smooth surface and she came down with a sharp bump, one foot imprisoned in the narrow cleft. In trying to free her foot she only forced it farther down to below her knee. A fierce struggle followed while she endeavored to get her hand in to unlace the boot. If that could be done, her foot could be slipped out of the confining space. She was in a sitting position under the overhang of rock. One leg remained free while the other, fortunately unhurt, was wedged firmly in the narrow clept and there was not room enough to admit her hand, to manipulate the bootlaces. If only she possessed a knife she could cut them loose; her boot had prevented scratches and possible damage to her leg; it was also a hindrance.

Theresa tried again, her panic rising as thunder rolled and zigzag lightning seemed to strike the very rocks of her prison. And then the rain came, hard and fast. It came from the rear and the rock at her back partly shielded her from the terrific onslaught. She cowered back as far as possible, but within seconds her clothing was soaking wet.

Not a soul knew where she had gone; the horse was securely fastened, and unless he reared hard enough to break the reins she could not even hope that his riderless appearance would set a search party out for her.

Another brilliant shaft of lightning split the heavens and mounting panic threatened menacingly.

In desperation she closed her eyes, willing her thoughts away from the frightening elements, to conjure up comforting pictures of Melinda in the safe, warm homestead: of Mary Rourke and little Theresa happily playing on the rug in the nursery. She had some denim remnants and simply must get down to making those cute little playsuits for her namesake . . . that is, when she was settled again, in Pretoria . . . or anywhere. . . .

Maybe, right now, Melinda would be lounging in her favorite stance, against the bathroom door, watching her precious daddy while he washed his hands . . . that was her favorite pastime too, watching her daddy. Theresa saw it quite clearly. . . . "Tresa gone 'way, Daddy." "Did she go for a walk, Poppet?" "I not know." Scott would be troubled enough to question the servants who would volunteer, "Missy don take the horse."

Her husband (what sweet heartbreak in one word) would look across the paddock, down the avenue, up at the darkening skies) most surely he would have some pretty grim thoughts on the uncaring, silly behavior of a certain female!

Brave resolutions dissolved as Theresa pictured the angular brown face, the sun wrinkles deepening at the corners of his smoky gray eyes. Her head drooped wearily and prickles started needling up her leg. She massaged it halfheartedly and wiggled her toes in an effort to keep up the circulation.

Scott would come to the conclusion that she would be taking shelter at Mary's and Miss Matilda would grumble that "the naughty lass" had been gone for ages, committing the unpardonable crime of not telling anyone where she was going.

Quite likely—please make it very likely—he would phone through to the Rourke household and Mary might remember that she, Theresa, was fond of going to the river.

Scott might not even be home yet. . . . Just when would someone finally become concerned?

She never knew if it was tears or rain on her face when the muffled whinny and drumming sound of a fast-moving horse reached her thunder-deafened ears. Seconds later Scott materialized and, to her blurred gaze, looked infinitely large, very dear and welcome in his streaming black slicker.

And very angry?

Theresa lifted rainwashed lashes and spoke through blue lips. "I'm glad you've come, Scott. I knew you would, sooner or later. I was beginning to feel awfully cold, wet, and lonely. P-please don't be angry!"

Relief roughened his voice. "Why didn't you come home? Or go to Mary, instead of sitting it out here, like a foolish child. . . ."

Theresa interrupted in a tone pitched higher than normal, "I do regret I was unable, Mr. Milward, to quote Miss Otis. . . ."

He caught sight of her imprisoned leg and came down instantly on to his knees beside her, asking quietly, "Does it hurt, Theresa?"

"No-o, not at a-all," she stuttered, near to tears again, now that help had arrived. The storm had seeped her will-power. She had cowered in absolute terror as shafts of lightning had danced around her semishelter to the accompaniment of clapping thunder.

Scott explored the crevice. His warm fingers touched her knee and she shivered as the pins-and-needles started again in her cramped foot. The man took another look at her bedraggled hair, blue lips and wet clothes. He vanished below the rock, appearing moments later with a flask, sweater and first-aid kit. The box was opened and he took out a small flask of brandy, tilted a stiff tot into the cup and filled it with hot black tea. He put an arm around her shoulders.

"Drink this."

Theresa spluttered at the strength of the mixture. He waited until she had drained the contents, then proceeded to unbutton her shirt. Peeling it off, Scott hesitated, raised on inquiring eyebrow as he surveyed wet, flimsy underthings. The water splattered from her hair as she shook her head, so he shrugged his shoulders and a whimsical smile turned his lips as he slipped the thick sweater over her head.

The rain stopped suddenly. Scott handed the girl a large handkerchief. "Rub your hair while I see what's to be done about this foot. Are you quite sure it's not hurting?"

"Quite sure. I'm sorry to cause you all this t-trouble."

He did not answer, but looked up for a moment. The flare in his gray eyes, inexplicable yet gentle, warmed her far more than the laced tea. He turned to the bag and extracted a long pointed pair of scissors, slipped it down until the points contacted her bootlaces. Grasping firmly, he managed to cut them almost to her instep. "Try now, nymph."

Theresa tugged, to no avail. "It's no use; my toes seemed to have become wedged in a small crevice at the bottom."

Scott studied the cleft intently. "Hold it, I have an idea," he smiled encouragingly. "Don't go away," planted a swift kiss on her warming lips and disappeared again.

Theresa's lips curved upwards at this order and she brought cold fingers to touch her mouth, to feel the comforting warmth.

He was back. "Thanks to a rancher's saddlebags. You'd be surprised what's in 'em, at all times. This hammer and chisel . . . it's only a wood chisel but will last out. I'm going to hammer bits of rock away until we can get that silly foot out." Suiting action to words, he continued casually, "Of course you must let me know if I happen to chisel through your leg, my darling, and . . . there, that's a small piece off. I mustn't let it fall in, otherwise . . . don't ever let me go mad with worry again. This could only happen to you . . . good, another sliver off. Whoops! Sorry, lass, that was very close, I'd not be much good as a sculptor. I've been such a blind fool, Theresa, fighting against my feelings. I was, quite possibly, sunk that very first time I saw you, a golden nymph on a wayside sation. I am ashamed to admit that I sneered at that feeling; it was only attraction, a trap. But the compulsion came later, to keep you, to bind you closer to me."

Theresa sat absolutely still and watched the strong brown hand falter for a moment. Scott carefully retrieved the sliver of stone that had slipped past his questing fingers.

"I can't begin to convey how uneasy I felt when Melinda told me that her Tresa had gone away. . . . More so when I observed the darkening sky and the stablehand said you'd taken a horse. I tried to get through to Mary, but the blasted line was down. That was when I got the wind up and sent the men in all directions while I grabbed the jeep to Dan's house . . . and you were not there."

Theresa sat, fascinated and bemused. Just so had she visualized his actions.

"I collected horse, sweater, tea and first-aid stuff. Mary told me about this, your favorite hideout. . . . I should have known, I found you here once before, remember? My one desperate hope was that you wouldn't take shelter under trees . . . they attract lightning like a magnet . . . that's a nice chunk out, hmmm? Do you also realize that I've lived in a private hell of my own, knowing that you didn't return the love I have for you?"

Theresa's lower lip trembled alarmingly. "Scott, I was going to . . . I mean, I'd . . . ."

"Save your breath, honey, scold me later. I've got it coming and will try not to chicken out. Right now I want to get things off my chest. I guess my conceited arrogance was a cover-up, to hide former disillusionments or to blind myself to what was happening to me. . . . I didn't want it to happen. . . . So, while I was searching for you, I thought of what Mary had told me. Oh yes, she told me, very succinctly, the truth about your heartbreak over Derek. And another interesting disclosure, which I'm struggling hard to believe. . . ." Scott stopped and looked up for the first time.

Theresa's eyes had widened considerably and now her cheeks raised banners of delicious color. "She told you . . . Mary Rourke went and told you. . . ." She was unable to continue and Scott gave a small smile as he dropped his eyes to the work in hand.

"Now I realize only too well what compelled me to force our engagement . . . and marriage. It was my heart, urging me, to hold onto something very precious. I was madly jealous of Derek Mann, that he could have the power to hurt you. Even jealous of Hugh when I watched you dancing so happily. Forgive me, I have to tell you all this, although it doesn't excuse my behavior. So, when Mary told me that you loved me, I could scarcely believe her. I love you, Theresa. If Mary is mistaken, and you don't love me, well then, my very dearest, I won't hold you, I won't add to the burdens you already have by forcing my will on you. You're free to choose your way, darling." Scott added, almost as an afterthought, "Melinda loves you too."

"Scott!" Theresa sat up and firmly straightened a back that had suddenly lost its ache.

"Yes, Theresa?"

She looked at the top of a dark head, bent as if in humility, almost as if he was afraid to look up, afraid to read the wrong answer in her hyacinth eyes. Theresa put out her hand and clutched a fistful of hair and gently forced his head back.

What he read in her face and eyes, so close to his own, was greatly enlightening. He put his tools down. Then Scott Milward took his wife in his arms, holding her head close to his fast-beating heart while one unbelieving hand stroked her damp, honeyed hair.

"Mary was right, bless her. Say it, darling, let me hear it from your lips and heart." He spoke deeply, urgently.

"I love you, my rajah." Theresa was breathlessly recovering from his casual chattering. Chatter that had made her whole world come singingly, vibrantly alive. Now she could keep her promise to Melinda. How close she had come to nearly losing everything!

"How and when did this wonderful phenomenon happen? I thought you hated my touch—you said so once, 'without love,' remember?"

"I did love you then . . . I meant without your love I couldn't . . . if only you'd said it, the way you wanted me to say it now."

"Darling, you mean we've wasted all this time because I was too stupid to utter a few vital words. . . . Darling nymph, come closer."

Their embrace was a miracle of awakening, seeking love between two people who had held emotions in check, long and unnecessarily.

Theresa drew back breathlessly. "My foot, Scott!"

Scott rubbed his chin along the soft skin under her ear and murmured thickly, "Yes, my love. It's a very pretty foot, I love it too."

"It's still stuck, you know," Theresa whispered conversationally.

Her husband reached reluctantly for the hammer and chisel. He sighed, but remarked with the wisdom of a sage, "Quite the cunningest, wisest little ole foot I've ever come across in all my born days!"